Ingathering

Ingathering

The Complete People Stories of Zenna Henderson

edited by Mark and Priscilla Olson

The NESFA Press
Post Office Box 809
Framingham, MA 01701-0203
1995

International Standard Book Number:
0-915368-58-7

Printed in the United States of America

Copyright Acknowledgments

The editors dedicate this book to

Anthony R. Lewis, F.N., Ph.D., F.B.I.S.
who created NESFA in his own image

and

George Flynn
Fan and Master Proofreader
who for years has sought to keep us—both fannishly
and typographically—on the straight and narrow.

Thank you.

Contents

Introduction by Priscilla Olson ix

Lea 1 1

Ararat 13

Lea 2 33

Gilead 39

Lea 3 65

Pottage 67

Lea 4 97

Wilderness 103

Lea 5 137

Captivity 141

Lea 6 181

Jordan 191

No Different Flesh 217

Mark & Meris 1 249

Deluge 253

Mark & Meris 2 283

Angels Unawares 287

Mark & Meris 3 319

Troubling of the Water 321

Mark & Meris 4 351

Return 353

Mark & Meris 5 385

Shadow on the Moon 387

Tell Us a Story 423

That Boy 461

Michal Without 497

The Indelible Kind 525

Katie-Mary's Trip 555

The People Series 569

Chronology of the People stories
  by Mark & Priscilla Olson 573

Introduction
Priscilla Olson

I'm a science fiction fan. Like many others, I started reading science fiction as an adolescent, and discovered Zenna Henderson then. Adolescence isn't easy, but the People helped some of us make it through....

Remember what those years were like? Like I said, adolescence isn't at all easy—how can it be? You're changing even faster than the world is, and that's pretty scary. You don't seem to fit in anywhere. You explore all of the nuances of loneliness, and *know* it's never (ever) going to get any better.

If you were a protofan, it was even worse. Some of us were lucky and eventually found science fiction fandom. It was (and is) a place where we could actually belong! Perhaps some of the things of our youth could be left behind then: things like the People stories—and need and hope....

The cynics among us might think it out of fashion to admit a liking for Zenna Henderson's unabashedly sentimental stories. To them, being separate-from-others—being an individual alone—is a sign of maturity. Perhaps they do not believe in redemption, of any kind. They feel no need to look through the eyes of the Outsider to see themselves.

But—*there's need!* (Feel it resonate.) The finer points of humanity—our aloneness—don't go away when we grow up.

And yet, those who are turned off by the "mawkishness" of Zenna Henderson's stories might be surprised by the excellence of the writing itself. She displays an impressive ability to evoke place, while her dialogue and descriptive prose are a match for the stripped-down language of any popular modern-day stylist. Regardless of whether you are a cynic or not, Valancy's calling up the storm ("Ararat") is a powerful image marking Zenna Henderson as a master of her craft. And that's just one of many.

Aside from that, "Gilead" will still make me cry, and "Wilderness" may convince me that (just maybe) hope was left in the box. For, above all else, these are the stories of people—of us. And they are the stories of us at our best, as we hope to be, and where (with work and with luck) we may be in some future....

These are the stories of the People. They are not *my* people, precisely—but like the children of Bendo, I remember the Home.

Ingathering

Interlude: Lea 1

The window of the bus was a dark square against the featureless night. Lea let her eyes focus slowly from their unthinking blur until her face materialized, faint and fragmentary, highlighted by the dim light of the bus interior. "Look," she thought, "I still have a face." She tilted her head and watched the wan light slide along the clean soft line of her cheek. There was no color except darkness for the wide eyes, the crisp turn of short curls above her ears, and the curve of her brows—all were an out-of-focus print against the outside darkness. "That's what I look like to people," she thought impersonally. "My outside is intact—an eggshell sucked of life."

The figure in the seat next to her stirred.

"Awake, deary?" The plump face beamed in the dusk. "Must have had a good nap. You've been so quiet ever since I got on. Here, let me turn on the reading light." She fumbled above her. "I think these lights are cunning. How'd they get them to point just in the right place?" The light came on and Lea winced away from it. "Bright, isn't it?" The elderly face creased into mirth. "Reminds me of when I was a youngster and we came in out of the dark and lighted a coal-oil lamp. It always made me squint like that. By the time I was your age, though, we had electricity. But I got my first two before we got electricity. I married at seventeen and the two of them came along about as quick as they could. You can't be much more than twenty-two or three. Lordee! I had four by then and buried another. Here, I've got pictures of my grandbabies. I'm just coming back from seeing the newest one. That's Jennie's latest. A little girl after three boys. You remind me of her a little, your eyes being dark and the color your hair is. She wears hers longer but it has that same kinda red tinge to it." She fumbled in her bag. Lea felt as though words were washing over her like a warm frothy flood. She automatically took the bulging billfold the woman tendered her and watched unseeingly as the glassine windows flipped. "...and this is Arthur and Jane. Ah, there's Jennie. Here, take a good look and see if she doesn't look like you."

Lea took a deep breath and came back from a long painful distance. She stared down at the billfold.

"Well?" The face beamed at her expectantly.

"She's—" Lea's voice didn't work. She swallowed dryly. "She's pretty."

"Yes, she is," the woman smiled. "Don't you think she looks a little like you, though?"

"A little—" Her repetition of the sentence died, but the woman took it for an answer.

"Go on, look through the others and see which one of her kids you think's the cutest."

Lea mechanically flipped the other windows, then sat staring down into her lap.

"Well, which one did you pick?" The woman leaned over. "Well!" She drew an indignant breath. "That's my driver's license! I didn't say snoop!" The billfold was snatched away and the reading light snapped off. There was a good deal of flouncing and muttering from the adjoining seat before quiet descended.

The hum of the bus was hypnotic and Lea sank back into her apathy, except for a tiny point of discomfort that kept jabbing her consciousness. The next stop she'd have to do something. Her ticket went no farther. Then what? Another decision to make. And all she wanted was nothing—nothing. And all she had was nothing—nothing. Why did she have to do anything? Why couldn't she just *not*—? She leaned her forehead against the glass, dissolving the nebulous reflection of herself, and stared into the darkness. Helpless against habit, she began to fit her aching thoughts back into the old ruts, the old footprints leading to complete futility—leading into the dark nothingness. She caught her breath and fought against the horrifying—threatening...

All the lights in the bus flicked on and there was a sleepy stirring murmur. The scattered lights of the outskirts of town slid past the slowing bus.

It was a small town. Lea couldn't even remember the name of it. She didn't know which way she turned when she went out the station door. She walked away from the bus depot, her feet swift and silent on the cracked sidewalk, her body appreciating the swinging rhythm of the walk after the long hours of inactivity. Her mind was still circling blindly, unnoticing, uncaring, unconcerned.

The business district died out thinly and Lea was walking up an incline. The walk leveled and after a while she wavered into a railing. She clutched at it, waiting for a faintness to go away. She looked out and down into darkness. "It's a bridge!" she thought. "Over a river." Gladness flared up in her. "It's the answer," she exulted. "This is it. After this—nothing!" She leaned her elbows on the railing, framing her chin and cheeks with her hands, her eyes on the darkness below, a darkness so complete that not even a ripple caught a glow from the bridge lights.

The familiar, so reasonable voice was speaking again. *Pain like this should be let go of. Just a momentary discomfort and it ends. No more breathing, no more thinking, no aching, no blind longing for anything.* Lea moved along the walk, her hand brushing the railing. "I can stand it now," she thought, "now that I know there is an end. I can stand to live a minute or so longer—to say good-by." Her shoulders shook and she felt the choke of laughter in her throat. Good-by? To whom? Who'd even notice she was gone? One ripple stilled in all a stormy sea. Let the quiet water take her breathing. Let its impersonal kindness hide her—dissolve her—so no one would ever be able to sigh and say, That was Lea. Oh, blessed water!

There was no reason not to. She found herself defending her action as though someone had questioned it. "Look," she thought, "I've told you so many times. There's no reason to go on. I could stand it when futility wrapped around me occasionally, but don't you remember? Remember the morning I sat there dressing, one shoe off and one shoe on, and couldn't think of one good valid reason why I should put the other shoe on? Not one reason! To finish dressing? Why? Because I had to work? Why? To earn a living? Why? To get something to eat? Why? To keep from starving to death? Why? Because you have to *live!* Why? *Why? Why!*

"And there were no answers. And I sat there until the grayness dissolved from around me as it did on lesser occasions. But then—" Lea's hands clutched each other and twisted painfully. "Remember what came then? The distorted sky wrenched open and gushed forth all the horror of a meaningless mindless universe—a reasonless existence that insisted on running on like a faceless clock—a menacing nothingness that snagged the little thread of reason I was hanging onto and unraveled it and unraveled it." Lea shuddered and her lips tightened with the effort to regain her composure. "That was only the beginning.

"So after that the depths of futility became a refuge instead of something to run from, its negativeness almost comfortable in contrast to the positive horror of what living has become. But I can't take either one any more." She sagged against the railing. "And I don't have to." She pushed herself upright and swallowed a sudden dry nausea. "The middle will be deeper," she thought. "Deep, swift, quiet, carrying me out of this intolerable—"

And as she walked she heard a small cry somewhere in the lostness inside her. "But I could have loved living so much! Why have I come to this pass?"

Shhh! the darkness said to the little voice. *Shhh! Don't bother to think. It hurts. Haven't you found it hurts? You need never think again or speak again or breathe again past this next inhalation....*

Lea's lungs filled slowly. *The last breath!* She started to slide across the concrete bridge railing into the darkness—into finishedness—into The End.

"You don't really want to." The laughing voice caught her like a splash of water across her face. "Besides, even if you did, you couldn't here. Maybe break a leg, but that's all."

"Break a leg?" Lea's voice was dazed and, inside, something broke and cried in disappointment, *"I've spoken again!"*

"Sure." Strong hands pulled her away from the railing and nudged her to a seat in a little concrete kiosk sort of thing. "You must be *very* new here, like on the nine-thirty bus tonight."

"Nine-thirty bus tonight," Lea echoed flatly.

" 'Cause if you'd been here by daylight you'd know this bridge is a snare and a delusion as far as water goes. You couldn't drown a gnat in the river here. It's dammed up above. Sand and tamarisks here, that's all. Besides you don't want to die, especially with a lovely coat like that—almost new!"

"Want to die," Lea echoed distantly. Then suddenly she jerked away from the gentle hands and twisted away from the encircling arm.

"I *do* want to die! Go *away!*" Her voice sharpened as she spoke and she almost spat the last word.

"But I *told* you!" The dim glow from the nearest light of the necklace of lights that pearled the bridge shone on a smiling girl-face, not much older than Lea's own. "You'd goof it up good if you tried to commit suicide here. Probably lie down there in the sand all night, maybe with a sharp stub of a tamarisk stuck through your shoulder and your broken leg hurting like mad. And tomorrow the ants would find you, and the flies—the big blowfly kind. Blood attracts them, you know. Your blood, spilling onto the sand."

Lea hid her face, her fingernails cutting into her hairline with the violence of the gesture. *This—this creature had no business peeling the bleeding scab off,* she thought. *It's so easy to think of jumping into darkness—into nothingness, but not to think of blowflies and blood—your own blood.*

"Besides—" the arm was around her again, gently leading her back to the bench, "you can't want to die and miss out on everything."

"Everything is nothing," Lea gasped, grabbing for the comfort of a well-worn groove. "It's nothing but gray chalk writing gray words on a gray sky in a high wind. There's nothing! There's nothing!"

"You must have used that carefully rounded sentence often and often to have driven yourself such a long way into darkness," the voice said, unsmiling now. "But you must come back, you know, back to wanting to live."

"No, no!" Lea moaned, twisting. "Let me go!"

"I can't." The voice was soft, the hands firm. "The Power sent me by on purpose. You can't return to the Presence with your life all unspent. But you're not hearing me, are you? Let me tell you.

"Your name is Lea Holmes. Mine, by the way, is Karen. You left your home in Clivedale two days ago. You bought a ticket for as far as your money would reach. You haven't eaten in two days. You're not even quite sure what state you're in, except the state of utter despair and exhaustion—right?"

"How—how did you know?" Lea felt a long-dead something stir inside her, but it died again under the flat monotone of her voice. "It doesn't matter. Nothing matters. You don't know anything about it!" A sick anger fluttered in her empty stomach. "You don't know what it's like to have your nose pressed to a blank wall and still have to walk and walk, day after day, with no way to get off the treadmill—no way to break through the wall—nothing, nothing, nothing! Not even an echo! Nothing!"

She snatched herself away from Karen's hands and, in a mad flurry of motion, scraped her way across the concrete railing and flung herself over into the darkness.

Endlessly tumbling—endlessly turning—slowly, slowly. Did it take so long to die? Softly the sand received her.

"You see," Karen said, shifting in the sand to cradle Lea's head on her lap. "I can't let you do it."

"But—I—I—jumped!" Lea's hands spatted sideways into the sand, and she looked up to where the lights of the passing cars ran like sticks along a picket fence.

"Yes, you did." Karen laughed a warm little laugh. "See, Lea, there *is* some wonder left in the world. Not everything is bogged down in hopelessness. What's that other quote you've been using for an anesthetic?"

Lea turned her head fretfully and sat up. "Leave me alone."

"What *was* that other quote?" Karen's voice was demanding now.

" 'There is for me no wonder more,' " Lea whispered into her hands, " 'Except to wonder where my wonder went, And why my wonder all is spent—' " Hot tears stung her eyes but could not fall. " '—no wonder more—' " The big emptiness that was always waiting, stretched and stretched, distorting—

"No wonder?" Karen broke the bubble with her tender laughter. "Oh, Lea, if only I had the time! No wonder, indeed! But I've *got* to go. The most incredibly wonderful—" There was a brief silence and the cars shh-ed by overhead, busily, busily. "Look!" Karen took Lea's hands. "You don't care what happens to you any more, do you?"

"No!" Lea said dully, but a faint voice murmured protest somewhere behind the dullness.

"You feel that life is unlivable, don't you?" Karen persisted. "That nothing could be worse?"

"Nothing," Lea said dully, squelching the murmur.

"Then listen." Karen hunched closer to her in the dark. "I'll take you with me. I really shouldn't, especially right now, but they'll understand. I'll take you along and then—*then*—if when it's all over you still feel there's no wonder left in the world, I'll take you to a much more efficient suicide-type place and *push* you over!"

"But where—" Lea's hands tugged to release themselves.

"Ah, ah!" Karen laughed. "Remember, you don't care! You don't care! Now I'll have to blindfold you for a minute. Stand up. Here, let me tie this scarf around your eyes. There, I guess that isn't too tight, but tight enough—" Her chatter poured on and Lea grabbed suddenly, feeling as though the world were dissolving around her. She clung to Karen's shoulder and stumbled from sand to solidness. "Oh, does being blindfolded make you dizzy?" Karen asked. "Well, okay. I'll take it off then." She whisked the scarf off. "Hurry, we have to catch the bus. It's almost due." She dragged Lea along the walk on the bridge, headed for the far bank, away from the town.

"But—" Lea staggered with weariness and hunger, "how did we get up on the bridge again? This is crazy! We were down—"

"Wondering, Lea?" Karen teased back over her shoulder. "If we hurry we'll have time for a hamburger for you before the bus gets here. My treat."

A hamburger and a glass of milk later, the InterUrban roared up to the curb, gulped Lea and Karen in, and roared away. Twenty minutes later the driver, expostulating, opened the door into blackness.

"But, lady, there's nothing out there! Not even a house for a mile!"

"I know," Karen smiled. "But this is the place. Someone's waiting for us." She tugged Lea down the steps. "Thanks!" she called. "Thanks a lot!"

"Thanks!" the driver muttered, slamming the doors. "This isn't even a *corner*! Screwballs!" And roared off down the road.

The two girls watched the glowworm retreat of the bus until it disappeared around a curve.

"Now!" Karen sighed happily. "Miriam is waiting for us somewhere around here. Then we'll go—"

"I won't." Lea's voice was flatly stubborn in the almost tangible darkness. "I won't go another inch. Who do you think you are, anyway? I'm going to stay here until a car comes along—"

"And jump in front of it?" Karen's voice was cold and hard. "You have no right to draft someone to be your executioner. Who do *you* think you are that you can splash your blood all over someone else?"

"Stop talking about blood!" Lea yelled, stung to have had her thoughts caught from her. "Let me die! Let me die!"

"It'd serve you right if I did," Karen said unsympathetically. "I'm not so sure you're worth saving. But as long as I've got you on my hands, shut up and come on. Cry babies bore me."

"But—you—don't—know!" Lea sobbed tearlessly, stumbling miserably along, towed at arm's length behind Karen, dodging cactus and greasewood, mourning the all-enfolding comfort of nothingness that could have been hers if Karen had only let her go.

"You might be surprised," Karen snapped. "But anyway *God* knows, and you haven't thought even once of Him this whole evening. If you're so all-fired eager to go busting into His house uninvited you'd better stop bawling and start thinking up a convincing excuse."

"You're mean!" Lea wailed, like a child.

"So I'm mean." Karen stopped so suddenly that Lea stumbled into her. "Maybe I *should* leave you alone. I don't want this most wonderful thing that's happening to be spoiled by such stupid goings on. Good-by!"

And she was gone before Lea could draw a breath. Gone completely. Not a sound of a footstep. Not a rustle of brush. Lea cowered in the darkness, panic swelling in her chest, fear catching her breath. The high arch of the sky glared at her starrily and the suddenly hostile night crept closer and closer. There was nowhere to go—nowhere to hide—no corner to back into. Nothing—nothing!

"Karen!" she shrieked, starting to run blindly. "Karen!"

"Watch it." Karen reached out of the dark and caught her. "There's cactus around here." Her voice went on in exasperated patience. "Scared to death of being alone in the dark for two minutes and fourteen seconds—and yet you think an eternity of it would be better than living—

"Well, I've checked with Miriam. She says she can help me manage you, so come along.

"Miriam, here she is. Think she's worth saving?"

Lea recoiled, startled, as Miriam materialized vaguely out of the darkness.

"Karen, stop sounding so mean," the shadow said. "You know wild horses couldn't pull you away from Lea now. She needs healing—not hollering at."

"She doesn't even *want* to be healed," Karen said.

"As though I'm not even here," Lea thought resentfully. "Not here. Not here." The looming wave of despair broke and swept over her. "Oh, let me go! Let me die!" She turned away from Karen, but the shadow of Miriam put warm arms around her.

"She didn't want to live either, but you wouldn't accept that—no more than you'll accept her not wanting to be healed."

"It's late," Karen said. "Chair-carry?"

"I suppose so," Miriam said. "It'll be shock enough, anyway. The more contact the better."

So the two made a chair, hand clasping wrist, wrist clasped by hand. They stooped down.

"Here, Lea," Karen said, "sit down. Arms around our necks."

"I can walk," Lea said coldly. "I'm not all that tired. Don't be silly."

"You can't walk where we're going. Don't argue. We're behind schedule now. Sit."

Lea folded her lips but awkwardly seated herself, clinging tightly as they stood up, lifting her from the ground.

"Okay?" Miriam asked.

"Okay," Karen and Lea said together.

"Well?" Lea said, waiting for steps to begin.

"Well," Karen laughed, "don't say I didn't warn you, but look down."

Lea looked down. And down! And *down!* Down to the scurrying sparks along a faded ribbon of a road. Down to the dew-jeweled cobweb of street lights stretching out flatly below. Down to the panoramic perfection of the whole valley, glowing magically in the night. Lea stared, unbelieving, at her two feet swinging free in the air—nothing beneath them but air—the same air that brushed her hair back and tangled her eyelashes as they picked up speed. Terror caught her by the throat. Her arms convulsed around the two girls' necks.

"Hey!" Karen strangled. "You're choking us! You're all right. Not so tight! Not so tight!"

"You'd better Still her," Miriam gasped. "She can't hear you."

"Relax," Karen said quietly. "Lea, relax."

Lea felt fear leave her like a tide going out. Her arms relaxed. Her uncomprehending eyes went up to the stars and down to the lights again. She gave a little sigh and her head drooped on Karen's shoulder.

"It did kill me," she said. "Jumping off the bridge. Only it's taken me a long time to die. This is just delirium before death. No wonder, with a stub of a tamarisk through my shoulder." And her eyes closed and she went limp.

Lea lay in the silvery darkness behind her closed eyes and savored the anonymous unfeeling between sleep and waking. Quietness sang through her, a humming stillness. She felt as anonymous as a transparent seaweed floating motionless between two layers of clear water. She breathed slowly, not wanting to disturb the mirror-stillness, the transparent peace. If you breathe quickly you think, and if you think— She stirred, her eyelids fluttering, trying to stay closed, but awareness and the growing light pried them open. She lay thin and flat on the bed, trying to be another white sheet between two muslin ones. But white sheets don't hear morning birds or smell breakfasts. She turned on her side and waited for the aching burden of life to fill her, to weigh her down, to beset her with its burning futility.

"Good morning." Karen was perched on the window sill, reaching out with one cupped hand. "Do you know how to get a bird to notice you, short of being a crumb? I wonder if they do notice anything except food and eggs. Do they ever take a deep breath for the sheer joy of breathing?" She dusted the crumbs from her hands out the window.

"I don't know much about birds." Lea's voice was thick and rusty. "Nor about joy either, I guess." She tensed, waiting for the heavy horror to descend.

"Relax," Karen said, turning from the window. "I've Stilled you."

"You mean I'm—I'm healed?" Lea asked, trying to sort out last night's memories.

"Oh, my, no! I've just switched you off onto a temporary siding. Healing is a slow thing. You have to do it yourself, you know. I can hold the spoon to your lips but you'll have to do the swallowing."

"What's in the spoon?" Lea asked idly, swimming still in the unbeset peace.

"What have you to be cured of?"

"Of life." Lea turned her face away. "Just cure me of living."

"*That* line again. We could bat words back and forth all day and arrive at nowhere—besides I haven't the time. I must leave now." Karen's face lighted and she spun around lightly. "Oh, Lea! Oh, Lea!" Then, hastily: "There's breakfast in the other room. I'm shutting you in. I'll be back later and then—well, by then I'll have figured out something. God bless!" She whisked through the door but Lea heard no lock click.

Lea wandered into the other room, a restlessness replacing the usual sick inertia. She crumbled a piece of bacon between her fingers and poured a cup of coffee. She left them both untasted and wandered back into the bedroom. She fingered the strange nightgown she was wearing and then, in a sudden breathless skirl of action, stripped it off and scrambled into her own clothes.

She yanked the doorknob. It wouldn't turn. She hammered softly with her fists on the unyielding door. She hurried to the open window and sitting on the sill started to swing her legs across it. Her feet thumped into an invisible something. Startled, she thrust out a hand and stubbed her fingers. She pressed both hands slowly outward and stared at them as they splayed against a something that stopped them.

She went back to the bed and stared at it. She made it up, quickly, meticulously, mitering the corners of the sheets precisely and plumping the pillow. She melted down to the edge of the bed and stared at her tightly clasped hands. Then she slid slowly down, turning and catching herself on her knees. She buried her face in her hands and whispered into the arid grief that burned her eyes, "Oh, God! Oh, God! Are You really there?"

For a long time she knelt there, feeling pressed against the barrier that confined her, the barrier that, probably because of Karen, was now an inert impersonal thing instead of the malicious agony-laden frustrating, deliberately evil creature it had been for so long.

Then suddenly, incongruously, she heard Karen's voice. "You haven't eaten." Her startled head lifted. No one was in the room with her. "You haven't eaten," she heard the voice again, Karen's matter-of-fact tone. "You haven't eaten."

She pulled herself up slowly from her knees, feeling the smart of returning circulation. Stiffly she limped to the other room. The coffee steamed gently at her although she had poured it out a lifetime ago. The bacon and eggs were still warm and uncongealed. She broke the warm crisp toast and began to eat.

"I'll figure it all out sometime soon," she murmured to her plate. "And then I'll probably scream for a while."

Karen came back early in the afternoon, bursting through the door that swung open before she reached it.

"Oh, Lea!" she cried, seizing her and whirling her in a mad dance. "You'd never guess—not in a million years! Oh, Lea! Oh, Lea!" She dumped the two of them onto the bed and laughed delightedly. Lea pulled away from her.

"Guess what?" Her voice sounded as dry and strained as her tearless eyes.

Karen sat up quickly. "Oh, Lea! I'm so sorry. In all the mad excitement I forgot.

"Listen, Jemmy says you're to come to the Gathering tonight. I can't tell you—I mean, you wouldn't be able to understand without a lengthy explanation, and even then—" She looked into Lea's haunted eyes. "It's bad, isn't it?" she asked softly. "Even Stilled, it comes through like a blunt knife hacking, doesn't it? Can't you cry, Lea? Not even a tear?"

"Tears—" Lea's hands were restless. " 'Nor all your tears wash out a word of it.' " She pressed her hands to the tight constriction in her chest. Her throat ached intolerably. "How can I bear it?" she whispered. "When you let it come back again how can I even bear it?"

"You don't have to bear it alone. You need never have borne it alone. And I won't release you until you have enough strength.

"Anyway—" Karen stood up briskly, "food again—then a nap. I'll give sleep to you. Then the Gathering. *There* will be your new beginning."

Lea shrank back into her corner, watching with dread as the Gathering grew. Laughter and cries and overtones and undercurrents swirled around the room.

"They won't bite!" Karen whispered. "They won't even notice you, if you don't want them to. Yes," she answered Lea's unasked question. "You must stay—like it or not, whether you can see any use in it or not. I'm not quite sure myself why Jemmy called this Gathering, but how appropriate can you get—having us meet in the schoolhouse? Believe it or not, this is where I got my education—and this is where— Well, teachers have been our undoing—or doing according to your viewpoint. You know, adults can fairly well keep themselves to themselves and not let anyone else in on their closely guarded secrets—but the kids—" She laughed. "Poor cherubs—or maybe they're wiser. They pour out the most personal things quite unsolicited to almost any adult who will listen—and who's more apt to listen than a teacher? Ask one sometime how much she learns of a child's background and everyday family activities from just what is let drop quite unconsciously. Kids are the key to any community—which fact has never been more true than among us. That's why teachers have been so involved in the affairs of the People. Remind me sometime when we have a minute to tell you about—well, Melodye, for instance. But now—"

The room suddenly arranged itself decorously and stilled itself expectantly and waited attentively.

Jemmy half sat on one corner of the teacher's desk in front of the Group, a piece of paper clutched in one hand. All heads bowed. "We are met together in Thy Name," Jemmy said. A settling rustle filled the room and subsided. "Out of consideration for some of us the proceedings here will be vocal. I know some of the Group have wondered that we included all of you in the summons. The reasons are twofold. One, to share this joy with us—" A soft musical trill of delight curled around the room, followed by faint laughter. "Francher!" Jemmy said. "The other is because of the project we want to begin tonight.

"In the last few days it has become increasingly evident that we all have an important decision to make. Whatever we decide there will be good-bys to say. There will be partings to endure. There will be changes."

Sorrow was tangible in the room, and a soft minor scale mourned over each note as it moved up and down, just short of tears. "The Old Ones have decided it would be wise to record our history to this point. That's why all of you are here. Each one of you holds an important part of our story within you. Each of you has influenced indelibly the course of events for our Groups. We want your stories. Not reinterpretations in the light of what you now know, but the original premise, the original groping, the original reaching—" There was a murmur through the room. "Yes," Jemmy answered. "Live it over, exactly the same—aching and all.

"Now," he smoothed out his piece of paper, "chronologically— Oh, first, where's Davey's recording gadget?"

"Gadget?" someone called. "What's wrong with our own memories?"

"Nothing," Jemmy said, "but we want this record independent of any of us, to go with whoever goes and stay with whoever stays. We share the general memories, of course, but all the little details—well, anyway. Davey's gadget." It had arrived on the table unobtrusively, small and undistinguished. "Now chronologically—Karen, you're first—"

"Who, me?" Karen straightened up, surprised. "Well, yes," she answered herself, settling back, "I guess I am."

"Come to the desk." Jemmy said. "Be comfortable."

Karen squeezed Lea's hand and whispered, "Make way for wonder!" and, after threading her way through the rows of desks, sat behind the table.

"I think I'll theme this beginning," she said. "We've remarked on the resemblance before, you know.

" 'And the Ark rested...upon the mountains of Ararat.' Ararat's more poetical than Baldy, anyway!

"And now," she smiled, "to establish Then again. Your help, please?"

Lea watched Karen, fascinated against her will. She saw her face alter and become younger. She saw her hair change its part and lengthen. She felt years peel back from Karen like thin tissue and she leaned forward, listening as Karen's voice, higher and younger, began...

Ararat

We've had trouble with teachers in Cougar Canyon. It's just an ac-
commodation school anyway, isolated and so unhandy to anything. There's
really nothing to hold a teacher. But the way the People bring forth their
young, in quantities and with regularity, even our small Group can usually muster the nine necessary for the county superintendent to arrange
for the schooling for the year.

Of course I'm past school age, Canyon school age, and have been
for years, but if the tally came up one short in the fall I'd go back for a
postgraduate course again. But now I'm working on a college level because Father finished me off for my high-school diploma two summers
ago. He's promised me that if I do well this year I'll get to go Outside next
year and get my training and degree so I can be the teacher and we won't
have to go Outside for one any more. Most of the kids would just as soon
skip school as not, but the Old Ones don't hold with ignorance and the
Old Ones have the last say around here.

Father is the head of the school board. That's how I get in on lots of
school things the other kids don't. This summer when he wrote to the
county seat that we'd have more than our nine again this fall and would
they find a teacher for us, he got back a letter saying they had exhausted
their supply of teachers who hadn't heard of Cougar Canyon and we'd
have to dig up our own teacher this year. That "dig up" sounded like a
dirty crack to me since we have the graves of four past teachers in the far
corner of our cemetery. They sent us such old teachers, the homeless, the
tottering, who were trying to piece out the end of their lives with a year
here and a year there in jobs no one else wanted because there's no adequate pension system in the state and most teachers seem to die in harness. And their oldness and their tottering were not sufficient in the Canyon, where there are apt to be shocks for Outsiders—unintentional as
most of them are.

We haven't done so badly the last few years, though. The Old Ones say we're getting adjusted, though some of the nonconformists say that the Crossing thinned our blood. It might be either or both or the teachers are just getting tougher. The last two managed to last until just before the year ended. Father took them in as far as Kerry Canyon and ambulances took them on in. But they were all right after a while in the sanatorium and they're doing okay now. Before them, though, we usually had four teachers a year.

Anyway Father wrote to a teachers' agency on the coast, and after several letters each way he finally found a teacher.

He told us about it at the supper table.

"She's rather young," he said, reaching for a toothpick and tipping his chair back on its hind legs.

Mother gave Jethro another helping of pie and picked up her own fork again. "Youth is no crime," she said, "and it'll be a pleasant change for the children."

"Yes, though it seems a shame." Father prodded at a back tooth and Mother frowned at him. I wasn't sure if it was for picking his teeth or for what he said. I knew he meant it seemed a shame to get a place like Cougar Canyon so early in a career. It isn't that we're mean or cruel, you understand. It's only that they're Outsiders and we sometimes forget—especially the kids.

"She doesn't *have* to come," Mother said. "She could say no."

"Well, now—" Father tipped his chair forward. "Jethro, no more pie. You go on out and help Kiah bring in the wood. Karen, you and Lizbeth get started on the dishes. Hop to it, kids."

And we hopped, too. Kids do to fathers in the Canyon, though I understand they don't always Outside. It annoyed me because I knew Father wanted us out of the way so he could talk adult talk to Mother, so I told Lizbeth I'd clear the table and then worked as slowly as I could, and as quietly, listening hard.

"She couldn't get any other job," Father said. "The agency told me they had placed her twice in the last two years and she didn't finish the year either place."

"Well," Mother said, pinching in her mouth and frowning. "If she's that bad why on earth did you hire her for the Canyon?"

"We have a choice?" Father laughed. Then he sobered. "No, it wasn't for incompetency. She was a good teacher. The way she tells it they just fired her out of a clear sky. She asked for recommendations and one place wrote, 'Miss Carmody is a very competent teacher but we dare not recommend her for a teaching position.'"

" 'Dare not'?" Mother asked.

" 'Dare not,' " Father said. "The agency assured me that they had investigated thoroughly and couldn't find any valid reasons for the dismissals, but she can't seem to find another job anywhere on the coast. She wrote me that she wanted to try another state."

"Do you suppose she's disfigured or deformed?" Mother suggested.

"Not from the neck up!" Father laughed. He took an envelope from his pocket. "Here's her application picture."

By this time I'd got the table cleared and I leaned over Father's shoulder.

"Gee!" I said. Father looked back at me, raising one eyebrow. I knew then that he had known all along that I was listening.

I flushed but stood my ground, knowing I was being granted admission to adult affairs, if only by the back door.

The girl in the picture was lovely. She couldn't have been many years older than I and she was twice as pretty. She had short dark hair curled all over her head and apparently that poreless creamy skin which seems to have an inner light of its own. She had a tentative look about her as though her dark eyebrows were horizontal question marks. There was a droop to the corners of her mouth—not much, just enough to make you wonder why, and want to comfort her.

"She'll stir the Canyon for sure," Father said.

"I don't know." Mother frowned thoughtfully. "What will the Old Ones say to a marriageable Outsider in the Canyon?"

"Adonday veeah!" Father muttered. "That never occurred to me. None of our other teachers was ever of an age to worry about."

"What *would* happen?" I asked. "I mean if one of the Group married an Outsider?"

"Impossible," Father said, so like the Old Ones that I could see why his name was approved in Meeting last spring.

"Why, there's even our Jemmy," Mother worried. "Already he's saying he'll have to start trying to find another Group. None of the girls here pleases him. Supposing this Outsider—how old is she?"

Father unfolded the application. "Twenty-three. Just three years out of college."

"Jemmy's twenty-four." Mother pinched her mouth together. "Father, I'm afraid you'll have to cancel the contract. If anything happened— well, you waited overlong to become an Old One to my way of thinking and it'd be a shame to have something go wrong your first year."

"I can't cancel the contract. She's on her way here. School starts next Monday." Father ruffled his hair forward as he does when he's disturbed. "We're probably making a something of a nothing," he said hopefully.

"Well, I only hope we don't have any trouble with this Outsider."

"Or she with us," Father grinned. "Where are my cigarettes?"

"On the bookcase," Mother said, getting up and folding the table-cloth together to hold the crumbs.

Father snapped his fingers and the cigarettes drifted in from the front room.

Mother went on out to the kitchen. The tablecloth shook itself over the wastebasket and then followed her.

Father drove to Kerry Canyon Sunday night to pick up our new teacher. She was supposed to have arrived Saturday afternoon but she didn't make bus connections at the county seat. The road ends at Kerry Canyon. I mean for Outsiders. There's not much of the look of a well-traveled road very far out our way from Kerry Canyon, which is just as well. Tourists leave us alone. Of course *we* don't have much trouble getting our cars to and fro, but that's why everything dead-ends at Kerry Canyon and we have to do all our own fetching and carrying—I mean the road being in the condition it is.

All the kids at our house wanted to stay up to see the new teacher, so Mother let them, but by seven-thirty the youngest ones began to drop off and by nine there was only Jethro and Kiah, Lizbeth and Jemmy and me. Father should have been home long before and Mother was restless and uneasy. But at nine-fifteen we heard the car coughing and sneezing up the draw. Mother's wide relieved smile was reflected on all our faces.

"Of course!" she cried. "I forgot. He has an Outsider in the car. He had to use the *road* and it's terrible across Jackass Flat."

I felt Miss Carmody before she came in the door. Already I was tingling all over from anticipation, but suddenly I felt her, so plainly that I knew with a feeling of fear and pride that I was of my grandmother, that soon I would be bearing the burden and blessing of her Gift—the Gift that develops into free access to any mind, one of the People or an Outsider, willing or not. And besides the access, the ability to counsel and help, to straighten tangled minds and snarled emotions.

And then Miss Carmody stood in the doorway, blinking a little against the light, muffled to the chin against the brisk fall air. A bright scarf hid her hair, but her skin *was* that luminous matte-cream it had looked. She was smiling a little but scared, too. I shut my eyes and—I went in, just like that. It was the first time I had ever sorted anybody. She was all fluttery with tiredness and strangeness, and there was a question deep inside her that had the wornness of repetition, but I couldn't catch what it was. And under the uncertainty there was a sweetness and dearness and such a bewildered sorrow that I felt my eyes dampen. Then I looked at her again (sorting takes such a little time) as Father introduced her. I heard a gasp beside me and suddenly I went into Jemmy's mind with a stunning rush.

Jemmy and I have been close all our lives and we don't always need words to talk with each other, but this was the first time I had ever gone in like this and I knew he didn't know what had happened. I felt embarrassed and ashamed to know his emotion so starkly. I closed him out as quickly as possible, but not before I knew that now Jemmy would never hunt for another Group; Old Ones or no Old Ones, he had found his love.

All this took less time than it takes to say how-do-you-do and shake hands. Mother descended with cries and drew Miss Carmody and Father out to the kitchen for coffee, and Jemmy swatted Jethro and made him carry the luggage instead of snapping it to Miss Carmody's room. After all, we didn't want to lose our teacher before she even saw the school-house.

I waited until everyone was bedded down. Miss Carmody in her cold cold bed, the rest of us of course with our sheets set for warmth—how I pity Outsiders! Then I went to Mother.

She met me in the dark hall and we clung together as she comforted me.

"Oh, Mother," I whispered, "I sorted Miss Carmody tonight. I'm afraid."

Mother held me tight again. "I wondered. It's a great responsibility. You have to be so wise and clear-thinking. Your grandmother carried the Gift with graciousness and honor. You are of her. You can do it."

"But, Mother! To be an Old One!"

Mother laughed. "You have years of training ahead of you before you'll be an Old One. Counselor to the soul is a weighty job."

"Do I have to tell?" I pleaded. "I don't want anyone to know yet. I don't want to be set apart."

"I'll tell the Oldest. No one else need know." She hugged me again and I went back, comforted, to bed.

I lay in the darkness and let my mind clear, not even knowing how I knew how to. Like the gentle reachings of quiet fingers I felt the family about me. I felt warm and comfortable as though I were cupped in the hollow palm of a loving hand. Someday I would belong to the Group as I now belonged to the family. Belong to others? With an odd feeling of panic I shut the family out. I wanted to be alone—to belong just to me and no one else. I didn't *want* the Gift.

I slept after a while.

Miss Carmody left for the schoolhouse an hour before we did. She wanted to get things started a little before schooltime, her late arrival making

it kind of rough on her. Kiah, Jethro, Lizbeth, and I walked down the lane
to the Armisters' to pick up their three kids. The sky was so blue you could
taste it, a winy fallish taste of harvest fields and falling leaves. We were all
feeling full of bubbly enthusiasm for the beginning of school. We were
lighthearted and light-footed, too, as we kicked along through the cottonwood leaves paving the lane with gold. In fact Jethro felt too light-footed,
and the third time I hauled him down and made him walk on the ground
I cuffed him good. He was still sniffling when we got to Armisters'.

"She's pretty!" Lizbeth called before the kids got out the gate, all
agog and eager for news of the new teacher.

"She's young," Kiah added, elbowing himself ahead of Lizbeth.

"She's littler'n me," Jethro sniffed, and we all laughed because he's
five six already even if he isn't twelve yet.

Debra and Rachel Armister linked arms with Lizbeth and scuffed
down the lane, heads together, absorbing the data of teacher's hair, dress,
nail polish, luggage, and night clothes, though goodness knows how
Lizbeth found out about all that.

Jethro and Kiah annexed Jeddy and they climbed up on the rail fence
that parallels the lane, and walked the top rail. Jethro took a tentative
step or two above the rail, caught my eye, and stepped back in a hurry.
He knows as well as any child in the Canyon that a kid his age has no
business lifting along a public road.

We detoured at the Mesa Road to pick up the Kroginold boys. More
than once Father has sighed over the Kroginolds.

You see, when the Crossing was made the People got separated in
that last wild moment when air was screaming past and the heat was building up so alarmingly. The members of our Group left their ship just seconds before it crashed so devastatingly into the box canyon behind Old
Baldy and literally splashed and drove itself into the canyon walls, starting a fire that stripped the hills bare for miles. After the People gathered
themselves together from the life slips and founded Cougar Canyon, they
discovered that the alloy the ship was made of was a metal much wanted
here. Our Group has lived on mining the box canyon ever since, though
there's something complicated about marketing the stuff. It has to be
shipped out of the country and shipped in again because everyone knows
that it isn't found in this region.

Anyway, our Group at Cougar Canyon is probably the largest of
the People, but we are reasonably sure that at least one Group and maybe
two survived along with us. Grandmother in her time sensed two Groups
but could never locate them exactly, and, since our object is to go unnoticed in this new life, no real effort has ever been made to find them.
Father can remember just a little of the Crossing, but some of the Old

Ones are blind and crippled from the heat and the terrible effort they put forth to save the others from burning up like falling stars.

But getting back, Father often mourned that of all the People who could have made up our Group we had to get the Kroginolds. They're rebels and were even before the Crossing. It's their kids who have been so rough on our teachers. The rest of us usually behave fairly decently and remember that we have to be careful around Outsiders.

Derek and Jake Kroginold were wrestling in a pile of leaves by the front gate when we got there. They didn't even hear us coming, so I leaned over and whacked the nearest rear end, and they turned in a flurry of leaves and grinned up at me for all the world like pictures of Pan in the mythology book at home.

"What kinda old bat we got this time?" Derek asked as he scrabbled in the leaves for his lunch box.

"She's not an old bat," I retorted, madder than need be because Derek annoys me so. "She's young and beautiful."

"Yeah, I'll bet!" Jake emptied the leaves from his cap onto the trio of squealing girls.

"She is so!" Kiah retorted. "The nicest teacher we ever had."

"She won't teach me nothing!" Derek yelled, lifting to the top of the cottonwood tree at the turnoff.

"Well, if she won't I will," I muttered, and reaching for a handful of sun I platted the twishers so quickly that Derek fell like a rock. He yelled like a catamount, thinking he'd get killed for sure, but I stopped him about a foot from the ground and then let go. Well, the stopping and the thump to the ground pretty well jarred the wind out of him, but he yelled:

"I'll tell the Old Ones! You ain't supposed to platt twishers!"

"Tell the Old Ones," I snapped, kicking on down the leafy road. "I'll be there and tell them why. And then, old smarty pants, what will be your excuse for lifting?"

And then I was ashamed. I was showing off as bad as a Kroginold, but they make me so mad!

Our last stop before school was at the Clarinades'. My heart always squeezed when I thought of the Clarinade twins. They just started school this year, two years behind the average Canyon kid. Mrs. Kroginold used to say that the two of them, Susie and Jerry, divided one brain between them before they were born. That's unkind and untrue—thoroughly a Kroginold remark—but it is true that by Canyon standards the twins were retarded. They lacked so many of the attributes of the People. Father said it might be a delayed effect of the Crossing that they would grow out of, or it might be advance notice of what our children will be like here— what is ahead for the People. It makes me shiver, wondering.

Susie and Jerry were waiting, clinging to each other's hands as they always were. They were shy and withdrawn, but both were radiant because of starting school. Jerry, who did almost all the talking for the two of them, answered our greetings with a shy hello.

Then Susie surprised us all by exclaiming, "We're going to school!"

"Isn't it wonderful?" I replied, gathering her cold little hand into mine. "And you're going to have the prettiest teacher we ever had."

But Susie had retired into blushing confusion and didn't say another word all the way to school.

I was worried about Jake and Derek. They were walking apart from us, whispering, looking over at us and laughing. They were cooking up some kind of mischief for Miss Carmody. And more than anything I wanted her to stay. I found right then that there *would* be years ahead of me before I became an Old One. I tried to go into Derek and Jake to find out what was cooking, but try as I might I couldn't get past the sibilance of their snickers and the hard flat brightness of their eyes.

We were turning off the road into the school yard when Jemmy, who should have been up at the mine long since, suddenly stepped out of the bushes in front of us, his hands behind him. He glared at Jake and Derek and then at the rest of the children.

"You kids mind your manners when you get to school," he snapped, scowling. "And you Kroginolds just try anything funny and I'll lift you to Old Baldy and platt the twishers on you. This is one teacher we're going to keep."

Susie and Jerry clung together in speechless terror. The Kroginolds turned red and pushed out belligerent jaws. The rest of us just stared at Jemmy, who never raised his voice and never pushed his weight around.

"I mean it, Jake and Derek. You try getting out of line and the Old Ones will find a few answers they've been looking for—especially about the bell in Kerry Canyon."

The Kroginolds exchanged looks of dismay and the girls sucked in breaths of astonishment. One of the most rigorously enforced rules of the Group concerns showing off outside the community. If Derek and Jake *had* been involved in ringing that bell all night last Fourth of July—*well!*

"Now you kids, scoot!" Jemmy jerked his head toward the schoolhouse, and the terrified twins scudded down the leaf-strewn path like a pair of bright leaves themselves, followed by the rest of the children, with the Kroginolds looking sullenly back over their shoulders and muttering.

Jemmy ducked his head and scowled. "It's time they got civilized anyway. There's no sense to our losing teachers all the time."

"No," I said noncommittally.

"There's no point in scaring her to death." Jemmy was intent on the leaves he was kicking with one foot.

"No," I agreed, suppressing my smile.

Then Jemmy smiled ruefully in amusement at himself. "I should waste words with you? Here." He took his hands from behind him and thrust a bouquet of burning-bright autumn leaves into my arms. "They're from you to her. Something pretty for the first day."

"Oh, Jemmy!" I cried through the scarlet and crimson and gold. "They're beautiful. You've been up on Baldy this morning."

"That's right. But she won't know where they came from." And he was gone.

I hurried to catch up with the children before they got to the door. Suddenly overcome with shyness, they were milling around the porch steps, each trying to hide behind the others.

"Oh, for goodness' sakes!" I whispered to our kids. "You ate breakfast with her this morning. She won't bite. Go on in."

But I found myself shouldered to the front and leading the subdued group into the schoolroom. While I was giving the bouquet of leaves to Miss Carmody, the others with the ease of established habit slid into their usual seats, leaving only the twins, stricken and white, standing alone.

Miss Carmody, dropping the leaves on her desk, knelt quickly beside them, pried a hand of each gently free from their frenzied clutching and held them in hers.

"I'm so glad you came to school," she said in her warm rich voice. "I need a first grade to make the school work out right and I have a seat that must have been built on purpose for twins."

And she led them over to the side of the room, close enough to the old potbellied stove for Outside comfort later and near enough to the window to see out. There, in dusted glory, stood one of the old double desks that the Group must have inherited from some ghost town out in the hills. There were two wooden boxes for footstools for small dangling feet and, spouting like a flame from the old inkwell hole, a spray of vivid red leaves—matchmates to those Jemmy had given me.

The twins slid into the desk, never loosening hands, and stared up at Miss Carmody, wide-eyed. She smiled back at them and, leaning forward, poked her fingertip into the deep dimple in each round chin.

"Buried smiles," she said, and the two scared faces lighted up briefly with wavery smiles. Then Miss Carmody turned to the rest of us.

I never did hear her introductory words. I was too busy mulling over the spray of leaves and how she came to know the identical routine, words and all, that the twins' mother used to make them smile, and how on earth she knew about the old desks in the shed. But by the time we rose to salute the flag and sing our morning song I had it figured out. Father must have briefed her on the way home last night. The twins were an ever-present concern of the whole Group, and we were all especially anxious to have their first year a successful one. Also, Father knew the smile routine and where the old desks were stored. As for the spray of leaves, well, some did grow this low on the mountain and frost is tricky at leaf-turning time.

So school was launched and went along smoothly. Miss Carmody was a good teacher and even the Kroginolds found their studies interesting.

They hadn't tried any tricks since Jemmy had threatened them. That is, except that silly deal with the chalk. Miss Carmody was explaining something on the board and was groping sideways for the chalk to add to the lesson. Jake deliberately lifted the chalk every time she almost had it. I was just ready to do something about it when Miss Carmody snapped her fingers with annoyance and grasped the chalk firmly. Jake caught my eye about then and shrank about six inches in girth and height. I didn't tell Jemmy, but Jake's fear that I might kept him straight for a long time.

The twins were really blossoming. They laughed and played with the rest of the kids, and Jerry even went off occasionally with the other boys at noontime, coming back as disheveled and wet as the others after a dam-building session in the creek.

Miss Carmody fitted so well into the community and was so well liked by us kids that it began to look like we'd finally keep a teacher all year. Already she had withstood some of the shocks that had sent our other teachers screaming. For instance...

The first time Susie got a robin-redbreast sticker on her bookmark for reading a whole page—six lines—perfectly, she lifted all the way back to her seat, literally walking about four inches in the air. I held my breath until she sat down and was caressing the glossy sticker with one finger, then I sneaked a cautious look at Miss Carmody. She was sitting very erect, her hands clutching both ends of her desk as though in the act of rising, a look of incredulous surprise on her face. Then she relaxed, shook her head and smiled, and busied herself with some papers.

I let my breath out cautiously. The last teacher but two went into hysterics when one of the girls absentmindedly lifted back to her seat because her sore foot hurt. I had hoped Miss Carmody was tougher, and apparently she was.

That same week, one noon hour, Jethro came pelting up to the schoolhouse where Valancy—that's her first name and I call her by it when we are alone; after all, she's only four years older than I—was helping me with that gruesome Tests and Measurements I was taking by extension from teachers' college.

"Hey, Karen!" he yelled through the window. "Can you come out a minute?"

"Why?" I yelled back, annoyed at the interruption just when I was trying to figure what was normal about a normal grade curve.

"There's need," Jethro yelled.

I put down my book. "I'm sorry, Valancy. I'll go see what's eating him."

"Should I come, too?" she asked. "If something's wrong—"

"It's probably just some silly thing," I said, edging out fast. When one of the People says, "There's need," that means Group business.

"Adonday Veeah!" I muttered at Jethro as we rattled down the steep rocky path to the creek. "What are you trying to do? Get us all in trouble? What's the matter?"

"Look," Jethro said, and there were the boys standing around an alarmed but proud Jerry, and above their heads, poised in the air over a half-built rock dam, was a huge boulder.

"Who lifted that?" I gasped.

"I did," Jerry volunteered, blushing crimson.

I turned on Jethro. "Well, why didn't you platt the twishers on it? You didn't have to come running—"

"On *that?*" Jethro squeaked. "You know very well we're not allowed to *lift* anything that big, let alone platt it. Besides," shamefaced, "I can't remember that dern girl stuff."

"Oh, Jethro! You're so stupid sometimes!" I turned to Jerry. "How on earth did you ever lift anything that big?"

He squirmed. "I watched Daddy at the mine once."

"Does he let you lift at home?" I asked severely.

"I don't know." Jerry squashed mud with one shoe, hanging his head. "I never lifted anything before."

"Well, you know better. You kids aren't allowed to lift anything an Outsider your age can't handle alone. And not even that if you can't platt it afterward."

"I know it." Jerry was still torn between embarrassment and pride.

"Well, remember it." And taking a handful of sun I platted the twishers and set the boulder back on the hillside where it belonged.

Platting does come easier to the girls—sunshine platting, that is. Of course only the Old Ones do the sun-and-rain one, and only the very Oldest of them all would dare the moonlight-and-dark, which can move mountains. But that was still no excuse for Jethro to forget and run the risk of having Valancy see what she mustn't see.

It wasn't until I was almost back to the schoolhouse that it dawned on me. Jerry had lifted! Kids his age usually lift play stuff almost from the time they walk. That doesn't need platting because it's just a matter of a few inches and a few seconds, so gravity manages the return. But Jerry and Susie never had. They were finally beginning to catch up. Maybe it *was* just the Crossing that slowed them down—and maybe only the Clarinades. In my delight *I* forgot and lifted to the school porch without benefit of the steps. But Valancy was putting up pictures on the high old-fashioned molding just below the ceiling, so no harm was done. She flushed from her efforts and asked me to bring the step stool so she could finish them. I brought it and steadied it for her—and then nearly let her fall as I stared. How had she hung those first four pictures before I got there?

The weather was unnaturally dry all fall. We didn't mind it much because rain with an Outsider around is awfully messy. We have to let ourselves get wet. But when November came and went and Christmas was almost upon us and there was practically no rain and no snow at all, we all began to get worried. The creek dropped to a trickle and then to scattered puddles and then went dry. Finally the Old Ones had to spend an evening at the Group reservoir doing something about our dwindling water supply. They wanted to get rid of Valancy for the evening, just in case, so Jemmy volunteered to take her to Kerry to the show. I was still awake when they got home long after midnight. Since I began to develop the Gift I have had long periods of restlessness when it seems I have no apartness but am of every person in the Group. The training I should start soon will help me shut out the others except when I want them. The only thing is that we don't know who is to train me. Since Grandmother died there has been no Sorter in our Group, and because of the Crossing we have no books or records to help.

Anyway, I was awake and leaning on my window sill in the darkness. They stopped on the porch—Jemmy is bunking at the mine during his stint there. I didn't have to guess or use a Gift to read the pantomime before me. I closed my eyes and my mind as their shadows merged. Under their strong emotion I could have had free access to their minds, but I had been watching them all fall. I knew in a special way what passed between them, and I knew that Valancy often went to bed in tears and that Jemmy spent too many lonely hours on the crag that juts out over the canyon from high on Old Baldy, as though he were trying to make his heart as inaccessible to Outsiders as the crag is. I knew what he felt, but oddly enough I had never been able to sort Valancy since that first night. There was something very un-Outsiderish and also very un-Groupish about her mind and I couldn't figure what.

I heard the front door open and close and Valancy's light steps fading down the hall and then I felt Jemmy calling me outside. I put my coat on over my robe and shivered down the hall. He was waiting by the porch steps, his face still and unhappy in the faint moonlight.

"She won't have me," he said flatly.

"Oh, Jemmy! You asked her—"

"Yes. She said no."

"I'm so sorry." I huddled down on the top step to cover my cold ankles. "But, Jemmy—"

"Yes, I know!" he retorted savagely. "She's an Outsider. I have no business even to want her. Well, if she'd have me I wouldn't hesitate a minute. This purity-of-the-Group deal is—"

"Is fine and right," I said softly, "as long as it doesn't touch you personally? But think for a minute, Jemmy. Would you be able to live a life as an Outsider? Just think of the million and one restraints that you would have to impose on yourself—and for the rest of your life, too, or lose her after all. Maybe it's better to accept 'no' now than to try to build something and ruin it completely later. And if there should be children—" I paused. "*Could* there be children, Jemmy?"

I heard him draw a sharp breath.

"We don't know," I went on. "We haven't had the occasion to find out. Do you want Valancy to be part of the first experiment?"

Jemmy slapped his hat viciously down on his thigh, then he laughed.

"You have the Gift," he said, though I had never told him. "Have you any idea, sister mine, how little you will be liked when you become an Old One?"

"Grandmother was well liked," I answered placidly. Then I cried, "Don't *you* set me apart, darn you, Jemmy. Isn't it enough to know that among a different people *I* am different? Don't *you* desert me now!" I was almost in tears.

Jemmy dropped to the step beside me and thumped my shoulder in his old way. "Pull up your socks, Karen. We have to do what we have to do. I was just taking my mad out on you. What a world!" He sighed heavily.

I huddled deeper in my coat, cold of soul.

"But the other one is gone," I whispered. "The Home."

And we sat there sharing the poignant sorrow that is a constant undercurrent among the People, even those of us who never actually saw the Home. Father says it's because of a sort of racial memory.

"But she didn't say no because she doesn't love me," Jemmy went on at last. "She does love me. She told me so."

"Then why not?" As his sister I couldn't imagine anyone turning Jemmy down.

Jemmy laughed—a short unhappy laugh. "Because she is different."

"*She's* different?"

"That's what she said, as though it was pulled out of her. 'I can't marry,' she said. 'I'm different!' That's pretty good, isn't it, coming from an Outsider!"

"She doesn't know we're the People. She must feel that she is different from everyone. I wonder why?"

"I don't know. There's something about her, though. A kind of shield or wall that keeps us apart. I've never met anything like it in an Outsider or in one of the People either. Sometimes it's like meshing with one of us and then *bang!* I smash the daylights out of me against that stone wall."

"Yes, I know. I've felt it, too."

We listened to the silent past-midnight world and then Jemmy stood. "Well, g'night, Karen. Be seeing you."

I stood up, too. "Good night, Jemmy." I watched him start off in the late moonlight. He turned at the gate, his face hidden in the shadows.

"But I'm not giving up," he said quietly. "Valancy is my love."

The next day was hushed and warm, unusually so for December in our hills. There was a kind of ominous stillness among the trees, and, threading thinly against the milky sky, the slender smokes of little brush fires pointed out the dryness of the whole country. If you looked closely you could see piling behind Old Baldy an odd bank of clouds, so nearly the color of the sky that it was hardly discernible, but puffy and summer-thunderheady.

All of us were restless in school, the kids reacting to the weather, Valancy pale and unhappy after last night. I was bruising my mind against the blank wall in hers, trying to find some way I could help her.

Finally the thousand and one little annoyances were climaxed by Jerry and Susie scuffling until Susie was pushed out of the desk onto an open box of wet water colors that Debra for heaven only knows what reason had left on the floor by her desk. Susie shrieked and Debra sputtered and Jerry started a high silly giggle of embarrassment and delight. Valancy, without looking, reached for something to rap for order with and knocked down the old cracked vase full of drooping wildflowers and three-day-old water. The vase broke and flooded her desk with the foul-smelling deluge, ruining the monthly report she had almost ready to send in to the county school superintendent.

For a stricken moment there wasn't a sound in the room, then Valancy burst into half-hysterical laughter and the whole room rocked with her. We all rallied around doing what we could to clean up Susie's and Valancy's desks, and then Valancy declared a holiday and decided that it would be the perfect time to go up-canyon to the slopes of Baldy and gather what greenery we could find to decorate our schoolroom for the holidays.

We all take our lunches to school, so we gathered them up and took along a square tarp the boys had brought to help build the dam in the creek. Now that the creek was dry they couldn't use it, and it'd come in handy to sit on at lunchtime and would serve to carry our greenery home in, too, stretcher fashion.

Released from the schoolroom, we were all loud and jubilant and I nearly kinked my neck trying to keep all the kids in sight at once to nip in the bud any thoughtless lifting or other Group activity. The kids were all so wild, they might forget.

We went on up-canyon past the kids' dam and climbed the bare dry waterfalls that stair-step up to the mesa. On the mesa we spread the tarp and pooled our lunches to make it more picnicky. A sudden hush from across the tarp caught my attention. Debra, Rachel, and Lizbeth were staring horrified at Susie's lunch. She was calmly dumping out a half dozen *koomatka* beside her sandwiches.

Koomatka are almost the only plants that lasted through the Crossing. I think four *koomatka* survived in someone's personal effects. They were planted and cared for as tenderly as babies, and now every household in the Group has a *koomatka* plant growing in some quiet spot out of casual sight. Their fruit is eaten not so much for nourishment as Earth knows nourishment but as a last remembrance of all other similar delights that died with the Home. We always save *koomatka* for special occasions. Susie must have sneaked some out when her mother wasn't looking. And there they were—across the table from an Outsider!

Before I could snap them to me or say anything, Valancy turned, too, and caught sight of the softly glowing bluey-green pile. Her eyes widened and one hand went out. She started to say something and then she dropped her eyes quickly and drew her hand back. She clasped her hands tightly together, and the girls, eyes intent on her, scrambled the *koomatka* back into the sack and Lizbeth silently comforted Susie, who had just realized what she had done. She was on the verge of tears at having betrayed the people to an Outsider.

Just then Kiah and Derek rolled across the picnic table fighting over a cupcake. By the time we salvaged our lunch from under them and they had scraped the last of the chocolate frosting off their T-shirts, the *koomatka* incident seemed closed. And yet as we lay back resting a little to settle our stomachs, staring up at the smothery low-hanging clouds that had grown from the milky morning sky, I suddenly found myself trying to decide about Valancy's look when she had seen the fruit. Surely it couldn't have been recognition!

At the end of our brief siesta we carefully buried the remains of our lunch—the hill was much too dry to think of burning it—and started on again. After a while the slope got steeper and the stubborn tangle of manzanita tore at our clothes and scratched our legs and grabbed at the rolled-up tarp until we all looked longingly at the free air above it. If Valancy hadn't been with us, we could have lifted over the worst and saved all this trouble. But we blew and panted for a while and then struggled on.

After an hour or so we worked out onto a rocky knoll that leaned against the slope of Baldy and made a tiny island in the sea of manzanita. We all stretched out gratefully on the crumbling granite outcropping, listening to our heart beats slowing.

Then Jethro sat up and sniffed. Valancy and I alerted. A sudden puff of wind from the little side canyon brought the acrid pungency of burning brush to us. Jethro scrambled along the narrow ridge to the slope of Baldy and worked his way around out of sight into the canyon. He came scrambling back, half lifting, half running.

"Awful!" he panted. "It's awful! The whole canyon ahead is on fire and it's coming this way fast!"

Valancy gathered us together with a glance.

"Why didn't we see the smoke?" she asked tensely. "There wasn't any smoke when we left the schoolhouse."

"Can't see this slope from school," he said. "Fire could burn over a dozen slopes and we'd hardly see the smoke. This side of Baldy is a rim fencing in an awful mess of canyons."

"What'll we do?" Lizbeth quavered, hugging Susie to her.

Another gust of wind and smoke set us all to coughing, and through my streaming tears I saw a long lapping tongue of fire reach around the canyon wall.

Valancy and I looked at each other. I couldn't sort her mind, but mine was a panic, beating itself against the fire and then against the terrible tangle of manzanita all around us. Bruising against the possibility of lifting out of danger, then against the fact that none of the kids was capable of sustained progressive self-lifting for more than a minute or so, and how could we leave Valancy? I hid my face in my hands to shut out the acres and acres of tinder-dry manzanita that would blaze like a torch at the first touch of fire. If only it would rain! You can't *set* fire to wet manzanita, but after these long months of drought—!

I heard the younger children scream and looked up to see Valancy staring at me with an intensity that frightened me even as I saw fire standing bright and terrible behind her at the mouth of the canyon.

Jake, yelling hoarsely, broke from the group and lifted a yard or two over the manzanita before he tangled his feet and fell helpless into the ugly angled branches.

"Get under the tarp!" Valancy's voice was a whiplash. "All of you get under the tarp!"

"It won't do any good," Kiah bellowed. "It'll burn like paper!"

"Get—under—the—tarp!" Valancy's spaced icy words drove us to unfolding the tarp and spreading it to creep under. Hoping even at this awful moment that Valancy wouldn't see me, I lifted over to Jake and yanked him back to his feet. I couldn't lift with him, so I pushed and prodded and half carried him back through the heavy surge of black smoke to the tarp and shoved him under. Valancy was standing, back to the fire, so changed and alien that I shut my eyes against her and started to crawl in with the other kids.

And then she began to speak. The rolling terrible thunder of her voice shook my bones and I swallowed a scream. A surge of fear swept through our huddled group and shoved me back out from under the tarp.

Till I die I'll never forget Valancy standing there tense and taller than life against the rolling convulsive clouds of smoke, both her hands outstretched, fingers wide apart as the measured terror of her voice went on and on in words that plagued me because I should have known them and didn't. As I watched I felt an icy cold gather, a paralyzing unearthly cold that froze the tears on my tensely upturned face.

And then lightning leaped from finger to finger of her lifted hands. And lightning answered in the clouds above her. With a toss of her hands she threw the cold, the lightning, the sullen shifting smoke upward, and the roar of the racing fire was drowned in a hissing roar of down-drenching rain.

I knelt there in the deluge, looking for an eternal second into her drained despairing hopeless eyes before I caught her just in time to keep her head from banging on the granite as she pitched forward, inert.

Then as I sat there cradling her head in my lap, shaking with cold and fear, with the terrified wailing of the kids behind me, I heard Father shout and saw him and Jemmy and Darcy Clarinade in the old pickup, lifting over the steaming streaming manzanita, over the trackless mountainside through the rain to us. Father lowered the truck until one of the wheels brushed a branch and spun lazily; then the three of them lifted all of us up to the dear familiarity of that beat-up old jalopy.

Jemmy received Valancy's limp body into his arms and crouched in back, huddling her in his arms, for the moment hostile to the whole world that had brought his love to such a pass.

We kids clung to Father in an ecstasy of relief. He hugged us all tight to him; then he raised my face.

"Why did it rain?" he asked sternly, every inch an Old One while the cold downpour dripped off the ends of my hair and he stood dry inside his shield.

"I don't know," I sobbed, blinking my streaming eyes against his sternness. "Valancy did it—with lightning—it was cold—she talked—" Then I broke down completely, plumping down on the rough floor boards and, in spite of my age, howling right along with the other kids.

It was a silent solemn group that gathered in the schoolhouse that evening. I sat at my desk with my hands folded stiffly in front of me, half scared of my own People. This was the first official meeting of the Old Ones I'd ever attended. They all sat in desks, too, except the Oldest, who sat in Valancy's chair. Valancy sat stony-faced in the twins' desk, but her nervous fingers shredded one Kleenex after another as she waited.

The Oldest rapped the side of the desk with his cane and turned his sightless eyes from one to another of us.

"We're all here," he said, "to inquire—"

"Oh, stop it!" Valancy jumped up from her seat. "Can't you fire me without all this rigmarole? I'm used to it. Just say go and I'll go!" She stood trembling.

"Sit down, Miss Carmody," said the Oldest. And Valancy sat down meekly.

"Where were you born?" the Oldest asked quietly.

"What does it matter?" Valancy flared. Then resignedly, "It's in my application. Vista Mar, California."

"And your parents?"

"I don't know."

There was a stir in the room.

"Why not?"

"Oh, this is so unnecessary!" Valancy cried. "But if you *have* to know, both my parents were foundlings. They were found wandering in the streets after a big explosion and fire in Vista Mar. An old couple who lost everything in the fire took them in. When they grew up, they married. I was born. They died. Can I go now?"

A murmur swept the room.

"Why did you leave your other jobs?" Father asked.

Before Valancy could answer the door was flung open and Jemmy stalked defiantly in.

"Go!" the Oldest said.

"Please," Jemmy said, deflating suddenly. "Let me stay. It concerns me, too."

The Oldest fingered his cane and then nodded. Jemmy half smiled with relief and sat down in a back seat.

"Go on," the Oldest One said to Valancy.

"All right then," Valancy said. "I lost my first job because I—well—I guess you'd call it levitated—to fix a broken blind in my room. It was stuck and I just—went up—in the air until I unstuck it. The principal saw me. He couldn't believe it and it scared him so he fired me." She paused expectantly.

The Old Ones looked at one another, and my silly confused mind began to add up columns that only my lack of common sense had kept me from giving totals to long ago.

"And the other one?" The Oldest leaned his cheek on his doubled-up hand as he bent forward.

Valancy was taken aback and she flushed in confusion.

"Well," she said hesitantly, "I called my books to me—I mean they were on my desk—"

"We know what you mean," the Oldest said.

"You know!" Valancy looked dazed.

The Oldest stood up.

"Valancy Carmody, open your mind!"

Valancy stared at him and then burst into tears.

"I can't, I can't," she sobbed. "It's been too long. I can't let anyone in. I'm different. I'm alone. Can't you understand? They all died. I'm alien!"

"You are alien no longer," the Oldest said. "You are home now, Valancy." He motioned to me. "Karen, go in to her."

So I did. At first the wall was still there; then with a soundless cry, half anguish and half joy, the wall went down and I was with Valancy. I saw all the secrets that had cankered in her since her parents died—the parents who were of the People.

They had been reared by the old couple who were not only of the People but had been the Oldest of the whole Crossing.

I tasted with her the hidden frightening things—the need for living as an Outsider, the terrible need for concealing all her differences and suppressing all the extra Gifts of the People, the ever-present fear of betraying herself, and the awful lostness that came when she thought she was the last of the People.

And then suddenly *she* came in to *me* and my mind was flooded with a far greater presence than I had ever before experienced.

My eyes flew open and I saw all of the Old Ones staring at Valancy. Even the Oldest had his face turned to her, wonder written as widely on his scarred face as on the others.

He bowed his head and made the Sign. "The lost Persuasions and Designs," he murmured. "She has them all."

And then I knew that Valancy, Valancy who had wrapped herself so tightly against the world to which any thoughtless act might betray her that she had lived with us all this time without our knowing about her or her knowing about us, was one of us. Not only one of us but such a one as had not been since Grandmother died, and even beyond that. My incoherent thoughts cleared to one.

Now I would have someone to train me. Now I could become a Sorter, but only second to her.

I turned to share my wonder with Jemmy. He was looking at Valancy as the People must have looked at the Home in the last hour. Then he turned to the door.

Before I could draw a breath Valancy was gone from me and from the Old Ones and Jemmy was turning to her outstretched hands.

Then I bolted for the outdoors and rushed like one possessed down the lane, lifting and running until I staggered up our porch steps and collapsed against Mother, who had heard me coming.

"Oh, Mother! She's one of us! She's Jemmy's love! She's wonderful!" And I burst into noisy sobs in the warm comfort of Mother's arms.

So now I don't have to go Outside to become a teacher. We have a permanent one. But I'm going anyway. I want to be as much like Valancy as I can and she has her degree. Besides I can use the discipline of living Outside for a year.

I have so much to learn and so much training to go through, but Valancy will always be there with me. I won't be set apart alone because of the Gift.

Maybe I shouldn't mention it, but one reason I want to hurry my training is that we're going to try to locate the other People. None of the boys here please me.

Interlude: Lea 2

It was as though silver curtains were shimmering back across some magic picture, warm with remembered delight. Lea took a deep breath and, with a realization as sudden as the bursting of a bubble, became aware that she had completely forgotten herself and her troubles for the first time in months and months. And it felt good—oh, so good—so smooth, so smilingly relaxing. "If only," she thought wistfully. *"If only!"* And then shivered under the bare echoless *thunk* as things-as-they-are thudded against the blessed shelter Karen had loaned her. Her hands tightened bitterly.

Someone laughed softly into the silence. "Have you found him yet, Karen? You started looking long enough ago—"

"Not so long," Karen smiled, still entangled in the memories she had relived. "And I *have* got my degree now. Oh, I had forgotten so much—the wonder—the terror—" She dreamed a moment longer, then shook her head and laughed.

"There, Jemmy, I seen my duty and I done it. Whose hot little hands hold the next installment?"

Jemmy smoothed out his crumpled paper. "Well, Peter's next, I guess. Unless Bethie wants to—"

"Oh no, oh no!" Bethie's soft voice protested. "Peter, Peter can do it better—he was the one—I mean—Peter!"

Everyone laughed. "Okay, Bethie, okay!" Jemmy said. "Cool down. Peter it will be. Well, Peter, you have until tomorrow evening to get organized. I think after the excitement of the day, one—well—installment will be enough."

The crowd stood up and swirled and moved. The soft murmur of their voices and laughter washed over Lea like a warm ocean.

"Lea." It was Karen. "Here's Jemmy and Valancy. They want to meet you."

Lea struggled to her feet, feeling impaled by their interested eyes. She felt welcome enwrapping her—a welcome far beyond any words. She felt a pang catch painfully somewhere in her chest, and to her bewilderment tears began to wash down her cheeks. She turned her head aside and groped for a handkerchief. Someone tucked a huge white one into her hands and someone's shoulder was strong and steady for a moment and someone's arms were deft and sure as they lifted her and bore her, blind with sobless weeping, away from the schoolhouse.

Later—oh, much later—she suddenly sat up in her bed. Karen was there instantly, noiselessly.

"Karen, was that supposed to be real?"

"Was what supposed to be real?"

"That story you told. It wasn't true, was it?"

"But of course. Every word of it."

"But it can't be!" Lea cried. "People from space! Magic people! It can't be true."

"Why don't you want it to be true?"

"Because—because! It doesn't fit. There's nothing outside of what is— I mean, you go around the world and come back to where you started from. Everything ends back where it started from. There are boundaries beyond which—" Lea groped for words. "Anything outside the bounds isn't true!"

"Who defines the boundaries?"

"Why, they're just there. You get trapped in them when you're born. You have to bear them till you die."

"Who sold *you* into slavery?" Karen asked wonderingly. "Or did you volunteer? I agree with you that everything comes back to where it started, but where did everything start?"

"No!" Lea shrieked, clenching her fists over her eyes and writhing back on her pillow. "Not back to that muck and chaos and mindless seething!"

The blackness rolled and flared and roared its insidious whimper— the crowded emptiness, the incinerating cold—the impossibility of all possibilities...

"Lea, Lea." Karen's voice cut softly but authoritatively through the tangled horror. "Lea, sleep now. Sleep now, knowing that everything started with the Presence and all things can return joyfully to their beginning."

Lea ate breakfast with Karen the next morning. The wind was blowing the short ruffled curtains in and out of the room.

"No screens?" Lea asked, carrying the armed truce with darkness as carefully as a cup of water, not to brim it over.

"No, no screens," Karen said. "We keep the bugs out another way."

"A way that works for keeping bugs in, too." Lea smiled. "I tried to leave yesterday."

"I know." Karen held a slice of bread in her hand and watched it brown slowly and fragrantly. "That's why I blocked the windows a little more than usual. They aren't that way today."

"You trust me?" Lea asked, feeling the secret slop of terror in the balanced cup.

"This isn't jail! Yesterday you were still clinging to the skirts of death. Today you can smile. Yesterday I put the lye up on the top shelf. Today you can read the label for yourself."

"Maybe I'm illiterate," Lea said somberly. Then she pushed her cup back. "I'd like to go outside today, if it's okay. It's been a long time since I looked at the world."

"Don't go too far. Most of the going around here is climbing—or lifting. We haven't many Outside-type trails. Only don't go beyond the schoolhouse. Right now we'd rather you didn't—the flat beyond—" She smiled softly. "Anyway there's lots of other places to go."

"Maybe I'll see some of the children," Lea said. "Davy or Lizbeth or Kiah."

Karen laughed. "It isn't very likely—not under the circumstances, and 'the children' would be vastly insulted if they heard you. They've grown up—at least they think they have. My story was years ago, Lea."

"Years ago! I thought it just happened!"

"Oh, my golly, no! What made you think—?"

"You remembered so completely! Such little things. And the way Jemmy looked at Valancy and Valancy at him—"

"The People have their special memory. And Jemmy was only looking love at Valancy. Love doesn't die—"

"Love doesn't—" Lea's mouth twisted. "Come, then, let us define love—" She stood up briskly. "I do want to walk a little—" She hesitated. "And maybe wade a little? In real wet water, free-running—"

"Why, sure," Karen said. "The creek is running. Wade to your heart's content. Lunch will be here for you and I'll be back by supper. We'll go to the school together for Peter's installment."

Lea came upon the pool, her bare feet bruised, her skirt hem dabbled with creek water, and her stomach empty of the lunch she had forgotten.

The pool was wide and quiet. Water murmured into it at one end and chuckled out at the other. In between the surface was like a mirror. A yellow leaf fell slowly from a cottonwood tree and touched so gently down on the water that the resultant rings ran as fine as wire out to the sandy edge. Lea sighed, gathered up her skirts, and stepped cautiously into the pool. The clean cold bite of the water caught her breath, but she waded deeper. The water crept up to her knees and over them. She stood under the cottonwood tree, waiting, waiting so quietly that the water closed smoothly around her legs and she could feel its flow only in the tiny crumblings of sand under her feet. She stood there until another leaf fell, brushed her cheek, slipped down her shoulder, and curved over her crumpled blouse, catching briefly in the gathered-up folds of her skirt before it turned a leisurely circle on the surface of the shining water.

Lea stared down at the leaf and the silver shadow behind it that was herself, then lifted her face to the towering canyon walls around her. She hugged her elbows tightly to her sides and thought, "I am becoming an entity again. I have form and proportion. I have boundaries and limits. I should be able to learn how to manage a finite being. The burden of being a nothing in infinite nothingness was too much—too much—"

A restless stirring that could turn to panic swung Lea around and she started for shore. As she clambered up the bank, hands encumbered by her skirt, she slipped and, flailing wildly for balance, fell backward into the pool with a resounding splat. Dripping and gasping, she scrambled wetly to a sitting position, her shoulders barely out of the water. She blinked the water out of her eyes and saw the man.

He had one foot in the water, poised in the act of starting toward her. He was laughing. She spluttered indignantly, and the water sloshed up almost to her chin.

"I might have drowned!" she cried, feeling very silly and very wet.

"If you go on sitting there you can drown yet!" he called. "High water comes in October."

"At the rate you're helping me out," she answered, "I'll make it! I can't get up without getting my head all wet."

"But you're already wet all over," he laughed, wading toward her.

"That was accidental," she spluttered. "It's different, doing it on purpose!"

"Female logic!" He grabbed her hands and hoisted her to her feet, pushed her to shore and shoved her up the bank.

Lea looked up into his smiling face and, smiling back, started to thank him. Suddenly his face twisted all out of focus—and retreated a thousand miles away. Faintly, faintly from afar, she heard his voice and her own gasping breath. Woodenly she turned away and started to grope away from him. She felt him catch her hand, and as she tugged away from him she felt all her being waver and dissolve and nothingness roll in, darker and darker.

"Karen!" she cried. "Karen! Karen!" And she lost herself.

"I won't go." She turned fretfully away from Karen's proffered hand. The bed was soft.

"Oh, yes, you will," Karen said. "You'll love Peter's installment. And Bethie! You *must* hear about Bethie."

"Oh, Karen, please don't make me try any more," Lea pleaded. "I can't bear the slipping back after—after—" She shook her head mutely.

"You haven't even started to try yet," Karen said, coolly. "You've got to go tonight. It's lesson two for you, so you'll be ready to go on."

"My clothes," Lea groped for an excuse. "They must be a mess."

"They are," Karen said, undisturbed. "You're about Lizbeth's size. I brought you plenty. Choose."

"No." Lea turned away.

"Get up." Karen's voice was still cool but Lea got up. She fumbled wordlessly into the proffered clothes.

"Hmm!" Karen said. "You're taller than I thought. You slump around so since you gave up."

Lea felt a stir of indignation but stood still as Karen knelt and tugged at the hem of the dress. The material stretched and stayed stretched, making the skirt a more seemly length for Lea.

"There," Karen said, standing and settling the dress smoothly around Lea's waist by pinching a fullness into a pleat. Then, with a stroke of her hand, she deepened the color of the material. "Not bad. It's your color. Come on now or we'll be late."

Lea stubbornly refused to be interested in anything. She sat in her corner and concentrated on her clasped hands, letting the ebb and flow of talk and movement lap around her, not even looking. Suddenly, after the quiet invocation, she felt a pang of pure homesickness—homesickness for strong hands holding hers with the coolness of water moving between them. She threw back her head, startled, just as Jemmy said, "I yield the desk to you, Peter. It's yours, every decrepit splinter of it."

"Thanks," Peter said. "I hope the chair's comfortable. This'll take a while. I've decided to follow Karen's lead and have a theme, too. It could well have been my question at almost any time in those long years.

" 'Is there no balm in Gilead; is there no physician there? Why then is not the health of the daughter of my people recovered?' "

In the brief pause Lea snatched at a thought that streaked through her mind. "I forgot all about the pond! Who was it? Who was it?" But she found no answer as Peter began...

Gilead

I don't know when it was that I found out that our family was different from other families. There was nothing to point it out. We lived in a house very like the other houses in Socorro. Our pasture lot sloped down just like the rest through arrowweed and mesquite trees to the sometime Rio Gordo that looped around town. And on occasion our cow bawled just as loudly across the river at the Jacobses' bull as all the other cows in all the other pasture lots. And I spent as many lazy days as any other boy in Socorro lying on my back in the thin shade of the mesquites, chewing on the beans when work was waiting somewhere. It never occurred to me to wonder if we were different.

I suppose my first realization came soon after I started to school and fell in love—with the girl with the longest pigtails and the widest gap in her front teeth of all the girls in my room. I think she was seven to my six.

My girl and I had wandered down behind the school woodshed, under the cottonwoods, to eat our lunch together, ignoring the chanted "Peter's got a gir-ul! Peter's got a gir-ul!" and the whittling fingers that shamed me for showing my love. We ate our sandwiches and pickles and then lay back, arms doubled under our heads, and blinked at the bright sky while we tried to keep the crumbs from our cupcakes from falling into our ears. I was so full of lunch, contentment, and love that I suddenly felt I just had to do something spectacular for my lady love. I sat up, electrified by a great idea and by the knowledge that I could carry it out.

"Hey! Did you know that I can fly?" I scrambled to my feet, leaving my love sitting gape-mouthed in the grass.

"You can't neither fly! Don't be crazy!"

"I can too fly!"

"You can not neither!"

"I can so! You just watch!" And lifting my arms, I swooped up to the roof of the shed. I leaned over the edge and said, "See there? I can, too!"

"I'll tell teacher on you!" she gasped, wide-eyed, staring up at me. "You ain't supposed to climb up on the shed."

"Oh, poof," I said. "I didn't climb. Come on, you fly up, too. Here, I'll help you."

And I slid down the air to the ground. I put my arms around my love and lifted. She screamed and wrenched away from me and fled shrieking back to the schoolhouse. Somewhat taken aback by her desertion, I gathered up the remains of my cake and hers and was perched comfortably on the ridgepole of the shed, enjoying the last crumbs, when teacher arrived with half the school trailing behind her.

"Peter Merrill! How many times have you been told not to climb things at school?"

I peered down at her, noting with interest that the spit curls on her cheeks had been jarred loose by her hurry and agitation and one of them was straightening out, contrasting oddly with the rest of her shingled bob.

"Hang on tight until Stanley gets the ladder!"

"I can get down," I said, scrambling off the ridgepole. "It's easy."

"Peter!" teacher shrieked. "Stay where you are!"

So I did, wondering at all the fuss.

By the time they got me down and teacher yanked me by one arm back up to the schoolhouse, I was bawling at the top of my voice, outraged and indignant because no one would believe me, even my girl denying obstinately the evidence of her own eyes. Teacher, annoyed at my persistence, said over and over, "Don't be silly, Peter. You can't fly. Nobody can fly. Where are your wings?"

"I don't need wings," I bellowed. "People don't need wings. I ain't a bird!"

"Then you can't fly. Only things with wings can fly."

So I alternately cried and kicked the schoolhouse steps for the rest of the noon hour, and then I began to worry for fear teacher would tattle to Dad. After all, I had been on forbidden territory, no matter how I got there.

As it turned out she didn't tell Dad, but that night after I was put to bed I suddenly felt an all-gone feeling inside me. Maybe I *couldn't* fly. Maybe teacher was right. I sneaked out of bed and cautiously flew up to the top of the dresser and back. Then I pulled the covers up tight under my chin and whispered to myself, "I can so fly," and sighed heavily. Just another fun stuff that grownups didn't allow, like having cake for breakfast or driving the tractor or borrowing the cow for an Indian-pony-on-a-warpath.

And that was all of that incident except that when teacher met Mother and me at the store that Saturday she ruffled my hair and said, "How's my little bird?" Then she laughed and said to Mother, "He thinks he can fly!"

I saw Mother's fingers tighten whitely on her purse, and she looked down at me with all the laughter gone from her eyes. I was overflooded with incredulous surprise mixed with fear and dread that made me want to cry, even though I knew it was Mother's emotions and not my own that I was feeling.

Mostly Mother had laughing eyes. She was the laughingest mother in Socorro. She carried happiness inside her as if it were a bouquet of flowers, and she gave part of it to everyone she met. Most of the other mothers seemed to have hardly enough to go around to their own families. And yet there were other times, like at the store, when laughter fled and fear showed through—and an odd wariness. Other times she made me think of a caged bird, pressing against the bars. Like one night I remember vividly.

Mother stood at the window in her ankle-length flannel nightgown, her long dark hair lifting softly in the draft from the rattling window frames. A high wind was blowing in from a spectacular thunderstorm in the Huachucas. I had been awakened by the rising crescendo and was huddled on the sofa wondering if I was scared or excited as the house shook with the constant thunder. Dad was sitting with the newspaper in his lap.

Mother spoke softly, but her voice came clearly through the tumult. "Have you ever wondered what it would be like to be up there in the middle of the storm with clouds under your feet and over your head and lightning lacing around you like hot golden rivers?"

Dad rattled his paper. "Sounds uncomfortable," he said.

But I sat there and hugged the words to me in wonder. I knew! *I remembered!* " 'And the rain like icy silver hair lashing across your lifted face,' " I recited as though it were a loved lesson.

Mother whirled from the window and stared at me. Dad's eyes were on me, dark and troubled.

"How do you know?" he asked.

I ducked my head in confusion. "I don't know," I muttered.

Mother pressed her hands together, hard, her bowed head swinging the curtains of her hair forward over her shadowy face. "He knows because I know. I know because my mother knew. She knew because our People used to—" Her voice broke. "Those were her words—"

She stopped and turned back to the window, leaning her arm against the frame, her face pressed to it, like a child in tears.

"Oh, Bruce, I'm sorry!"

I stared, round-eyed in amazement, trying to keep tears from coming to my eyes as I fought against Mother's desolation and sorrow.

Dad went to Mother and turned her gently into his arms. He looked over her head at me. "Better run on back to bed, Peter. The worst is over."

I trailed off reluctantly, my mind filled with wonder. Just before I shut my door I stopped and listened.

"I've never said a word to him, honest." Mother's voice quivered. "Oh, Bruce, I try so hard, but sometimes—oh sometimes!"

"I know, Eve. And you've done a wonderful job of it. I know it's hard on you, but we've talked it out so many times. It's the only way, honey."

"Yes," Mother said. "It's the only way, but—oh, be my strength, Bruce! Bless the Power for giving me you!"

I shut my door softly and huddled in the dark in the middle of my bed until I felt Mother's anguish smooth out to loving warmness again. Then for no good reason I flew solemnly to the top of the dresser and back, crawled into bed, and relaxed. And remembered. Remembered the hot golden rivers, the clouds over and under, and the wild winds that buffeted like foam-frosted waves. But with all the sweet remembering was the reminder, *You can't because you're only eight. You're only eight. You'll have to wait.*

And then Bethie was born, almost in time for my ninth birthday. I remember peeking over the edge of the bassinet at the miracle of tiny fingers and spun-sugar hair. Bethie, my little sister. Bethie, who was whispered about and stared at when Mother let her go to school, though mostly she kept her home even after she was old enough. Because Bethie was different—too.

When Bethie was a month old I smashed my finger in the bedroom door. I cried for a quarter of an hour, but Bethie sobbed on and on until the last pain left my finger.

When Bethie was six months old our little terrier, Glib, got caught in a gopher trap. He dragged himself, yelping, back to the house dangling the trap. Bethie screamed until Glib fell asleep over his bandaged paw.

Dad had acute appendicitis when Bethie was two, but it was Bethie who had to be given a sedative until we could get Dad to the hospital.

One night Dad and Mother stood over Bethie as she slept restlessly under sedatives. Mr. Tyree-next-door had been cutting wood and his ax slipped. He lost a big toe and a pint or so of blood, but as Doctor Dueff skidded to a stop on our street it was into our house that he rushed first and then to Mr. Tyree-next-door, who lay with his foot swathed and propped up on a chair, his hands pressed to his ears to shut out Bethie's screams.

"What can we do, Eve?" Dad asked. "What does the doctor say?"

"Nothing. They can do nothing for her. He hopes she will outgrow it. He doesn't understand it. He doesn't know that she—"

"What's the matter? What makes her like this?" Dad asked despairingly.

Mother winced. "She's a Sensitive. Among my People there were such—but not so young. Their perception made it possible for them to help sufferers. Bethie has only half the Gift. She has no control."

"Because of me?" Dad's voice was ragged.

Mother looked at him with steady loving eyes. "Because of us, Bruce. It was the chance we took. We pushed our luck after Peter."

So there we were, the two of us—different—but different in our differences. For me it was mostly fun, but not for Bethie.

We had to be careful for Bethie. She tried school at first, but skinned knees and rough rassling and aching teeth and bumped heads and the janitor's Monday hangover sent her home exhausted and shaking the first day, with hysteria hanging on the flick of an eyelash. So Bethie read for Mother and learned her numbers and leaned wistfully over the gate as the other children went by.

It wasn't long after Bethie's first day in school that I found a practical use for my difference. Dad sent me out to the woodshed to stack a cord of mesquite that Delfino dumped into our back yard from his old wood wagon. I had a date to explore an old fluorspar mine with some other guys and bitterly resented being sidetracked. I slouched out to the woodpile and stood, hands in pockets, kicking the heavy rough stove lengths. Finally I carried in one armload, grunting under the weight, and afterward sucking the round of my thumb where the sliding wood had peeled me. I hunkered down on my heels and stared as I sucked. Suddenly something prickled inside my brain. If I could fly why couldn't I make the wood fly? *And I knew I could!* I leaned forward and flipped a finger under half a dozen sticks, concentrating as I did so. They lifted into the air and hovered. I pushed them into the shed, guided them to where I wanted them, and distributed them like dealing a pack of cards. It didn't take me long to figure out the maximum load, and I had all the wood stacked in a wonderfully short time.

I whistled into the house for my flashlight. The mine was spooky and dark, and I was the only one of the gang with a flashlight.

"I told you to stack the wood." Dad looked up from his milk records.

"I did," I said, grinning.

"Cut the kidding," Dad grunted. "You couldn't be done already."

"I am, though," I said triumphantly. "I found a new way to do it. You see—" I stopped, frozen by Dad's look.

"We don't need any new ways around here," he said evenly. "Go back out there until you've had time to stack the wood right!"

"It *is* stacked," I protested. "And the kids are waiting for me!"

"I'm not arguing, son," said Dad, white-faced. "Go back out to the shed."

I went back out to the shed—past Mother, who had come in from the kitchen and whose hand half went out to me. I sat in the shed fuming for a long time, stubbornly set that I wouldn't leave till Dad told me to.

Then I got to thinking. Dad wasn't usually unreasonable like this. Maybe I'd done something wrong. Maybe it was bad to stack wood like that. Maybe—my thoughts wavered as I remembered whispers I'd overheard about Bethie. Maybe it—it was a crazy thing to do—an insane thing.

I huddled close upon myself as I considered it. *Crazy* means not doing like other people. *Crazy* means doing things ordinary people don't do. Maybe that's why Dad made such a fuss. Maybe I'd done an insane thing! I stared at the ground, lost in bewilderment. What *was* different about our family? And for the first time I was able to isolate and recognize the feeling I must have had for a long time—the feeling of being on the outside looking in—the feeling of apartness. With this recognition came a wariness, a need for concealment. If something were wrong, no one else must know—I must not betray...

Then Mother was standing beside me. "Dad says you may go now," she said, sitting down on my log.

"Peter—" She looked at me unhappily. "Dad's doing what is best. All I can say is: remember that whatever you do, wherever you live, different is dead. You have to conform or—or die. But Peter, don't be ashamed. Don't ever be ashamed!" Then swiftly her hands were on my shoulders and her lips brushed my ear. "Be different!" she whispered. "Be as different as you can. But don't let anyone see—don't let anyone know!" And she was gone up the back steps, into the kitchen.

As I grew further into adolescence I seemed to grow further and further away from kids my age. I couldn't seem to get much of a kick out of what they considered fun. So it was that with increasing frequency in the years that followed I took Mother's whispered advice, never asking for explanations I knew she wouldn't give. The wood incident had opened up a whole vista of possibilities—no telling what I might be able to do—so I got in the habit of going down to the foot of our pasture lot. There, screened by the brush and greasewood, I tried all sorts of experiments, never knowing whether they would work or not. I sweated plenty over some that didn't work—and some that did.

I found that I could snap my fingers and bring things to me, or send them short distances from me without bothering to touch them as I had the wood. I roosted regularly in the tops of the tall cottonwoods, swan-diving ecstatically down to the ground, warily, after I got too ecstatic once and crash-landed on my nose and chin. By headaching concentration that left me dizzy, I even set a small campfire ablaze. Then blistered and charred both hands unmercifully by confidently scooping up the crackling fire.

Then I guess I got careless about checking for onlookers because some nasty talk got started. Bub Jacobs whispered around that I was "doing things" all alone down in the brush. His sly grimace as he whispered made the "doing things" any nasty perversion the listeners' imaginations could conjure up, and the "alone" damned me on the spot. I learned bitterly then what Mother had told me. Different is dead—and one death is never enough. You die and die and die.

Then one day I caught Bub cutting across the foot of our wood lot. He saw me coming and hit for tall timber, already smarting under what he knew he'd get if I caught him. I started full speed after him, then plowed to a stop. Why waste effort? If I could do it to the wood, I could do it to a blockhead like Bub.

He let out a scream of pure terror as the ground dropped out from under him. His scream flatted and strangled into silence as he struggled in midair, convulsed with fear of falling and the terrible thing that was happening to him. And I stood and laughed at him, feeling myself a giant towering above stupid dopes like Bub.

Sharply, before he passed out, I felt his terror, and an echo of his scream rose in my throat. I slumped down in the dirt, sick with sudden realization, knowing with a knowledge that went beyond ordinary experience that I had done something terribly wrong, that I had prostituted whatever powers I possessed by using them to terrorize unjustly.

I knelt and looked up at Bub, crumpled in the air, higher than my head, higher than my reach, and swallowed painfully as I realized that I had no idea how to get him down. He wasn't a stick of wood to be snapped to the ground. He wasn't me, to dive down through the air. I hadn't the remotest idea how to get a human down.

Half dazed, I crawled over to a shaft of sunlight that slit the cotton-wood branches overhead and felt it rush through my fingers like something to be lifted—and twisted—and fashioned and *used! Used on Bub!* But how? *How?* I clenched my fist in the flood of light, my mind beating against another door that needed only a word or look or gesture to open, but I couldn't say it, or look it, or make it.

I stood up and took a deep breath. I jumped, batting at Bub's heels that dangled a little lower than the rest of him. I missed. Again I jumped and the tip of one finger flicked his heel and he moved sluggishly in the air. Then I swiped the back of my hand across my sweaty forehead and laughed—laughed at my stupid self.

Cautiously, because I hadn't done much hovering, mostly just up and down, I lifted myself up level with Bub. I put my hands on him and pushed down hard. He didn't move.

I tugged him up and he rose with me. I drifted slowly and deliberately away from him and pondered. Then I got on the other side of him and pushed him toward the branches of the cottonwood. His head was beginning to toss and his lips moved with returning consciousness. He drifted through the air like a waterlogged stump, but he moved and I draped him carefully over a big limb near the top of the tree, anchoring his arms and legs as securely as I could. By the time his eyes opened and he clutched frenziedly for support, I was standing down at the foot of the tree, yelling up at him.

"Hang on, Bub! I'll go get someone to help you down!"

So for the next week or so people forgot me, and Bub squirmed under "Who treed you, feller?" and "How's the weather up there?" and "Get a ladder, Bub, get a ladder!"

Even with worries like that it was mostly fun for me. Why couldn't it be like that for Bethie? Why couldn't I give her part of my fun and take part of her pain?

Then Dad died, swept out of life by our Rio Gordo as he tried to rescue a fool Easterner who had camped on the bone-dry white sands of the river bottom in cloudburst weather. Somehow it seemed impossible to think of Mother by herself. It had always been Mother and Dad. Not just two parents but Mother-and-Dad, a single entity. And now our thoughts must limp to Mother-and, Mother-and. And Mother—well, half of her was gone.

After the funeral Mother and Bethie and I sat in our front room, looking at the floor. Bethie was clenching her teeth against the stabbing pain of Mother's fingernails gouging Mother's palms.

I unfolded the clenched hands gently and Bethie relaxed.

"Mother," I said softly, "I can take care of us. I have my part-time job at the plant. Don't worry. I'll take care of us."

I knew what a trivial thing I was offering to her anguish, but I had to do something to break through to her.

"Thank you, Peter," Mother said, rousing a little. "I know you will—" She bowed her head and pressed both hands to her dry eyes with restrained desperation. "Oh, Peter, Peter! I'm enough of this world now to find death a despair and desolation instead of the solemnly sweet calling it is. Help me, help me!" Her breath labored in her throat and she groped blindly for my hand.

"If I can, Mother," I said, taking one hand as Bethie took the other. "Then help me remember. Remember with me."

And behind my closed eyes I remembered. Unhampered flight through a starry night, a flight of a thousand happy people like birds in the sky, rushing to meet the dawn—the dawn of the Festival. I could smell the flowers that garlanded the women and feel the quiet exultation that went with the Festival dawn. Then the leader sounded the magnificent opening notes of the Festival song as he caught the first glimpse of the rising sun over the heavily wooded hills. A thousand voices took up the song. A thousand hands lifted in the Sign....

I opened my eyes to find my own fingers lifted to trace a sign I did not know. My own throat throbbed to a note I had never sung. I took a deep breath and glanced over at Bethie. She met my eyes and shook her head sadly. She hadn't seen. Mother sat quietly, eyes closed, her face cleared and calmed.

"What was it, Mother?" I whispered.

"The Festival," she said softly. "For all those who had been called during the year. For your father, Peter and Bethie. We remembered it for your father."

"Where was it?" I asked. "Where in the world—?"

"Not in this—" Mother's eyes flicked open. "It doesn't matter, Peter. You are of this world. There is no other for you."

"Mother," Bethie's voice was a hesitant murmur, "what do you mean, 'remember'?"

Mother looked at her and tears swelled into her dry burned-out eyes.

"Oh, Bethie, Bethie, all the burdens and none of the blessings! I'm sorry, Bethie, I'm sorry." And she fled down the hall to her room.

Bethie stood close against my side as we looked after Mother.

"Peter," she murmured, "what did Mother mean, 'none of the blessings'?"

"I don't know," I said.

"I'll bet it's because I can't fly like you."

"Fly!" My startled eyes went to hers. "How do you know?"

"I know lots of things," she whispered. "But mostly I know we're different. Other people aren't like us. Peter, what made us different?"

"Mother?" I whispered. "Mother?"

"I guess so," Bethie murmured. "But how come?"

We fell silent and then Bethie went to the window, where the late sun haloed her silvery blond hair in fire.

"I can do things, too," she whispered. "Look."

She reached out and took a handful of sun, the same sort of golden sun-slant that had flowed so heavily through my fingers under the cottonwoods while Bub dangled above me. With flashing fingers she fashioned the sun into an intricate glowing pattern. "But what's it for?" she murmured, "except for pretty?"

"I know," I said, looking at my answer for lowering Bub. "I know, Bethie." And I took the pattern from her. It strained between my fingers and flowed into darkness.

The years that followed were casual uneventful years. I finished high school, but college was out of the question. I went to work in the plant that provided work for most of the employables in Socorro.

Mother built up quite a reputation as a midwife—a very necessary calling in a community which took literally the injunction to multiply and replenish the earth and which lay exactly seventy-five miles from a hospital, no matter which way you turned when you got to the highway.

Bethie was in her teens and with Mother's help was learning to control her visible reactions to the pain of others, but I knew she still suffered as much as, if not more than, she had when she was smaller. But she was able to go to school most of the time now and was becoming fairly popular in spite of her quietness.

So all in all we were getting along quite comfortably and quite ordinarily except—well, I always felt as though I were waiting for something to happen or for someone to come. And Bethie must have, too, because she actually watched and listened—especially after a particularly bad spell. And even Mother. Sometimes as we sat on the porch in the long evenings she would cock her head and listen intently, her rocking chair still. But when we asked what she heard, she'd sigh and say, "Nothing. Just the night." And her chair would rock again.

Of course I still indulged my differences. Not with the white fire of possible discovery that they had kindled when I first began, but more like the feeding of a small flame just "for pretty." I went farther afield now for my "holidays," but Bethie went with me. She got a big kick out of our excursions, especially after I found that I could carry her when I flew, and most especially after we found, by means of a heart-stopping accident, that though she couldn't go up she could control her going down. After that it was her pleasure to have me carry her up as far as I could and she would come down, sometimes taking an hour to make the descent, often weaving about her the intricate splendor of her sunshine patterns.

It was a rustling russet day in October when our world ended—again. We talked and laughed over the breakfast table, teasing Bethie about her date the night before. Color was high in her usually pale cheeks, and, with all the laughter and brightness, the tingle of fall, everything just felt good.

But between one joke and another the laughter drained out of Bethie's face and the pinched set look came to her lips.

"Mother!" she whispered, and then she relaxed.

"Already?" asked Mother, rising and finishing her coffee as I went to get her coat. "I had a hunch today would be the day. Reena would ride that jeep up Peppersauce Canyon this close to her time."

I helped her on with her coat and hugged her tight.

"Bless-a-mama," I said, "when are you going to retire and let someone else snatch the fall and spring crops of kids?"

"When I snatch a grandchild or so for myself," she said, joking, but I felt her sadness. "Besides she's going to name this one Peter—or Bethie, as the case may be." She reached for her little black bag and looked at Bethie. "No more yet?"

Bethie smiled. "No," she murmured.

"Then I've got plenty of time. Peter, you'd better take Bethie for a holiday. Reena takes her own sweet time and being just across the road makes it bad on Bethie."

"Okay, Mother," I said. "We planned one anyway, but we hoped this time you'd go with us."

Mother looked at me, hesitated, and turned aside. "I—I might sometime."

"Mother! Really?" This was the first hesitation from Mother in all the times we'd asked her.

"Well, you've asked me so many times and I've been wondering. Wondering if it's fair to deny our birthright. After all, there's nothing wrong in being of the People."

"What people, Mother?" I pressed. "*Where* are you from? Why *can* we—?"

"Some other time, son," Mother said. "Maybe soon. These last few months I've begun to sense—yes, it wouldn't hurt you to know even if nothing could ever come of it; and perhaps soon something *can* come, and you will have to know. But no," she chided as we clung to her. "There's no time now. Reena might fool us after all and produce before I get there. You kids scoot, now!"

We looked back as the pickup roared across the highway and headed for Mendigo's Peak. Mother answered our wave and went in the gate of Reena's yard, where Dalt, in spite of this being their sixth, was running like an anxious puppy dog from Mother to the porch and back again.

It was a day of perfection for us. The relaxation of flight for me, the delight of hovering for Bethie, the frosted glory of the burning-blue sky, the russet and gold of grasslands stretching for endless miles down from the snow-flecked blue and gold Mendigo.

At lunchtime we lolled in the pleasant warmth of our favorite baby box canyon that held the sun and shut out the wind. After we ate we played our favorite game, Remembering. It began with my clearing my mind so that it lay as quiet as a hidden pool of water, as receptive as the pool to every pattern the slightest breeze might start quivering across its surface.

Then the memories would come—strange un-Earthlike memories that were like those Mother and I had had when Dad died. Bethie could not remember with me, but she seemed to catch the memories from me almost before the words could form in my mouth.

So this last lovely "holiday" we remembered again our favorite. We walked the darkly gleaming waters of a mountain lake, curling our toes in the liquid coolness, loving the tilt and sway of the waves beneath our feet, feeling around us from shore and sky a dear familiarity that was stronger than any Earth ties we had yet formed.

Before we knew it the long lazy afternoon had fled and we shivered in the sudden chill as the sun dropped westward, nearing the peaks of the Huachucas. We packed the remains of our picnic in the basket, and I turned to Bethie, to lift her and carry her back to the pickup.

She was smiling her soft little secret smile.

"Look, Peter," she murmured. And flicking her fingers over her head, she shook out a cloud of snowflakes, gigantic whirling tumbling snow-flakes that clung feather-soft to her pale hair and melted, glistening, across her warm cheeks and mischievous smile.

"Early winter, Peter!" she said.

"Early winter, punkin!" I cried, and snatching her up, boosted her out of the little canyon and jumped over her, clearing the boulders she had to scramble over. "For that you walk, young lady!"

But she almost beat me to the car anyway. For one who couldn't fly she was learning to run awfully light.

Twilight had fallen before we got back to the highway. We could see the headlights of the scurrying cars that seldom even slowed down for Socorro. "So this is Socorro, wasn't it?" was the way most traffic went through.

We had topped the last rise before the highway when Bethie screamed. I almost lost control of the car on the rutty road. She screamed again, a wild tortured cry as she folded in on herself.

"Bethie!" I called, trying to get through to her. "What is it? Where is it? Where can I take you?"

But her third scream broke off short and she slid limply to the floor. I was terrified. She hadn't reacted like this in years. She had never fainted like this before. Could it be that Reena hadn't had her child yet? That she was in such agony—but even when Mrs. Allbeg had died in childbirth Bethie hadn't— I lifted Bethie to the seat and drove wildly homeward, praying that Mother would be...

And then I saw it. In front of our house. The big car skewed across the road. The kneeling cluster of people on the pavement.

The next thing I knew I was kneeling, too, beside Dr. Dueff, clutching the edge of the blanket that mercifully covered Mother from chin to toes. I lifted a trembling hand to the dark trickle of blood that threaded crookedly down from her forehead.

"Mother," I whispered. "Mother!"

Her eyelids fluttered and she looked up blindly. "Peter." I could hardly hear her. "Peter, where's Bethie?"

"She fainted. She's in the car," I faltered. "Oh, Mother!"

"Tell the doctor to go to Bethie."

"But, Mother!" I cried. "You—"

"I am not called yet. Go to Bethie."

We knelt by her bedside, Bethie and I. The doctor was gone. There was no use trying to get Mother to a hospital. Just moving her indoors had started a dark oozing from the corner of her mouth. The neighbors were all gone except Gramma Reuther, who always came to troubled homes and had folded the hands of the dead in Socorro from the founding of the town. She sat now in the front room holding her worn Bible in quiet hands, after all these years no longer needing to look up the passages of comfort and assurance.

The doctor had quieted the pain for Mother and had urged sleep upon Bethie, not knowing how long the easing would last, but Bethie wouldn't take it.

Suddenly Mother's eyes were open.

"I married your father," she said clearly, as though continuing a conversation. "We loved each other so, and they were all dead—all my People. Of course I told him first, and oh, Peter! He believed me! After all that time of having to guard every word and every move I had someone to talk to—someone to believe me. I told him all about the People and lifted myself and then I lifted the car and turned it in mid-air above the highway—just for fun. It pleased him a lot but it made him thoughtful and later he said, 'You know, honey, your world and ours took different turns way back there. We turned to gadgets. You turned to the Power.' "

Her eyes smiled. "He got so he knew when I was lonesome for the Home. Once he said, 'Homesick, honey? So am I. For what this world could have been. Or maybe—God willing—what it may become.'

"Your father was the other half of me." Her eyes closed, and in the silence her breath became audible, a harsh straining sound. Bethie crouched with both hands pressed to her chest, her face dead white in the shadows.

"We discussed it and discussed it," Mother cried. "But we had to decide as we did. We thought I was the last of the People. I had to forget the Home and be of Earth. You children had to be of Earth, too, even if— That's why he was so stern with you, Peter. Why he didn't want you to—experiment. He was afraid you'd do too much around other people if you found out—" She stopped and lay panting. "Different is dead," she whispered, and lay scarcely breathing for a moment.

"I knew the Home." Her voice was heavy with sorrow. "I remember the Home. Not just because my People remembered it but because I saw it. I was born there. It's gone now. Gone forever. There is no Home. Only a band of dust between the stars!" Her face twisted with grief and Bethie echoed her cry of pain.

Then Mother's face cleared and her eyes opened. She half propped herself up in her bed.

"You have the Home, too. You and Bethie. You will have it always. And your children after you. Remember, Peter? Remember?"

Then her head tilted attentively and she gave a laughing sob. "Oh, Peter! Oh, Bethie! Did you hear it? I've been called! I've been called!" Her hand lifted in the Sign and her lips moved tenderly.

"Mother!" I cried fearfully. "What do you mean? Lie down. Please lie down!" I pressed her back against the pillows.

"I've been called back to the Presence. My years are finished. My days are totaled."

"But, Mother," I blubbered like a child, "what will we do without you?"

"Listen!" Mother whispered rapidly, one hand pressed to my hair. "You must find the rest. You must go right away. They can help Bethie. They can help you, Peter. As long as you are separated from them you are not complete. I have felt them calling the last year or so, and now that I am on the way to the Presence I can hear them clearer, and clearer." She paused and held her breath. "There is a canyon—north. The ship crashed there, after our life slips—here, Peter, give me your hand." She reached urgently toward me and I cradled her hand in mine.

And I saw half the state spread out below me like a giant map. I saw the wrinkled folds of the mountains, the deceptively smooth roll of the desert up to the jagged slopes. I saw the blur of timber blunting the hills and I saw the angular writhing of the narrow road through the passes. Then I felt a sharp pleasurable twinge, like the one you feel when seeing home after being away a long time.

"There!" Mother whispered as the panorama faded. "I wish I could have known before. It's been lonely—

"But you, Peter," she said strongly. "You and Bethie must go to them."

"Why should we, Mother?" I cried in desperation. "What are they to us or we to them that we should leave Socorro and go among strangers?"

Mother pulled herself up in bed, her eyes intent on my face. She wavered a moment and then Bethie was crouched behind her, steadying her back.

"They are not strangers," she said clearly and slowly. "They are the People. We shared the ship with them during the Crossing. They were with us when we were out in the middle of emptiness with only the fading of stars behind and the brightening before to tell us we were moving. They, with us, looked at all the bright frosting of stars across the blackness, wondering if on one of them we would find a welcome.

"You are woven of their fabric. Even though your father was not of the People—"

Her voice died, her face changed. Bethie moved from in back of her and lowered her gently. Mother clasped her hands and sighed.

"It's a lonely business," she whispered. "No one can go with you. Even with them waiting it's lonely."

In the silence that followed we heard Gramma Reuther rocking quietly in the front room. Bethie sat on the floor beside me, her cheeks flushed, her eyes wide with a strange dark awe.

"Peter, it didn't hurt. It didn't hurt at all. It—healed!"

But we didn't go. How could we leave my job and our home and go off to—where? Looking for—whom? Because—why? It was mostly me, I guess, but I couldn't quite believe what Mother had told us. After all, she hadn't said anything definite. We were probably reading meaning where it didn't exist. Bethie returned again and again to the puzzle of Mother and what she had meant, but we didn't go.

And Bethie got paler and thinner, and it was nearly a year later that I came home to find her curled into an impossibly tight ball on her bed, her eyes tight shut, snatching at breath that came out again in sharp moans.

I nearly went crazy before I at last got through to her and uncurled her enough to get hold of one of her hands. Finally, though, she opened dull dazed eyes and looked past me.

"Like a dam, Peter," she gasped. "It all comes in. It should—it should! I was born to—" I wiped the cold sweat from her forehead. "But it just piles up and piles up. It's supposed to go somewhere. I'm supposed to do something! Peter Peter Peter!" She twisted on the bed, her distorted face pushing into the pillow.

"What does, Bethie?" I asked, turning her face to mine. "What does?"

"Glib's foot and Dad's side and Mr. Tyree-next-door's toe—" and her voice faded down through the litany of years of agony.

"I'll go get Dr. Dueff," I said hopelessly.

"No." She turned her face away. "Why build the dam higher? Let it break. Oh, soon soon!"

"Bethie, don't talk like that," I said, feeling inside me my terrible aloneness that only Bethie could fend off now that Mother was gone. "We'll find something—some way—"

"Mother could help," she gasped. "A little. But she's gone. And now I'm picking up mental pain, too! Reena's afraid she's got cancer. Oh, Peter Peter!" Her voice strained to a whisper. "Let me die! Help me die!"

Both of us were shocked to silence by her words. Help her die? I leaned against her hand. Go back into the Presence with the weight of unfinished years dragging at our feet? For if she went I went, too.

Then my eyes flew open and I stared at Bethie's hand. What Presence? Whose ethics and mores were talking in my mind?

And so I had to decide. I talked Bethie into a sleeping pill and sat by her even after she was asleep. And as I sat there all the past years wound through my head. The way it must have been for Bethie all this time and I hadn't let myself know.

Just before dawn I woke Bethie. We packed and went. I left a note on the kitchen table for Dr. Dueff saying only that we were going to look for help for Bethie and would he ask Reena to see to the house. And thanks.

I slowed the pickup over to the side of the junction and slammed the brakes on.

"Okay," I said hopelessly. "You choose which way this time. Or shall we toss for it? Heads straight up, tails straight down! I can't tell where to go, Bethie. I had only that one little glimpse that Mother gave me of this country. There's a million canyons and a million side roads. We were fools to leave Socorro. After all, we have nothing to go on but what Mother said. It might have been delirium."

"No," Bethie murmured. "It can't be. It's got to be real."

"But, Bethie," I said, leaning my weary head on the steering wheel, "you know how much I want it to be true, not only for you but for myself, too. But look. What do we have to assume if Mother was right? First, that space travel is possible—was possible nearly fifty years ago. Second, that Mother and her People came here from another planet. Third, that we are, bluntly speaking, half-breeds, a cross between Earth and heaven knows what world. Fourth, that there's a chance in ten million of our finding the other People who came at the same time Mother did, presupposing that any of them survived the Crossing.

"Why, any one of these premises would brand us as crazy crackpots to any normal person. No, we're building too much on a dream and a hope. Let's go back, Bethie. We've got just enough gas money along to make it. Let's give it up."

"And go back to what?" Bethie asked, her face pinched. "No, Peter. Here."

I looked up as she handed me one of her sunlight patterns, a handful of brilliance that twisted briefly in my fingers before it flickered out.

"Is that Earth?" she asked quietly. "How many of our friends can fly? How many—" she hesitated, "how many can Remember?"

"Remember!" I said slowly, and then I whacked the steering wheel with my fist. "Oh, Bethie, of all the stupid—! Why, it's Bub all over again!"

I kicked the pickup into life and turned on the first faint desert trail beyond the junction. I pulled off even that suggestion of a trail and headed across the nearly naked desert toward a clump of ironwood, mesquite, and catclaw that marked a sand wash against the foothills. With the westering sun making shadow lace through the thin foliage, we made camp.

I lay on my back in the wash and looked deep into the arch of the desert sky. The trees made a typical desert pattern of warmth and coolness on me, warm in the sun, cool in the shadow, as I let my mind clear smoother, smoother, until the soft intake of Bethie's breath as she sat beside me sent a bright ripple across it.

And I remembered. But only Mother-and-Dad and the little campfire I had gathered up, and Glib with the trap on his foot and Bethie curled, face to knees on the bed, and the thin crying sound of her labored breath.

I blinked at the sky. I *had* to Remember. I just had to. I shut my eyes and concentrated and concentrated, until I was exhausted. Nothing came now, not even a hint of memory. In despair I relaxed, limp against the chilling sand. And all at once unaccustomed gears shifted and slipped into place in my mind and there I was, just as I had been, hovering over the life-sized map.

Slowly and painfully I located Socorro and the thin thread that marked the Rio Gordo. I followed it and lost it and followed it again, the finger of my attention pressing close. Then I located Vulcan Springs Valley and traced its broad rolling to the upsweep of the desert, to the Sierra Cobreña Mountains. It was an eerie sensation to look down on the infinitesimal groove that must be where I was lying now. Then I handspanned my thinking around our camp spot. Nothing. I probed farther north, and east, and north again. I drew a deep breath and exhaled it shakily. There it was. The Home twinge. The call of familiarity.

I read it off to Bethie. The high thrust of a mountain that pushed up baldly past its timber, the huge tailings dump across the range from the mountain. The casual wreathing of smoke from what must be a logging town, all forming sides of a slender triangle. Somewhere in this area was the place.

I opened my eyes to find Bethie in tears.

"Why, Bethie!" I said. "What's wrong? Aren't you glad—?"

Bethie tried to smile but her lips quivered. She hid her face in the crook of her elbow and whispered, "I saw, too! Oh, Peter, this time I saw, too!"

We got out the road map and by the fading afternoon light we tried to translate our rememberings. As nearly as we could figure out, we should head for a place way off the highway called Kerry Canyon. It was apparently the only inhabited spot anywhere near the big bald mountain. I looked at the little black dot in the kink in the third-rate road and wondered if it would turn out to be a period to all our hopes or the point for the beginning of new lives for the two of us. Life and sanity for Bethie, and for me... In a sudden spasm of emotion I crumpled the map in my hand. I felt blindly that in all my life I had never known anyone but Mother and Dad and Bethie. That I was a ghost walking the world. If only I could see even one other person that felt like our kind! Just to know that Bethie and I weren't all alone with our unearthly heritage!

I smoothed out the map and folded it again. Night was on us and the wind was cold. We shivered as we scurried around looking for wood for our campfire.

Kerry Canyon was one business street, two service stations, two saloons, two stores, two churches, and a handful of houses flung at random over the hillsides that sloped down to an area that looked too small to accommodate the road. A creek, which was now thinned to an intermittent trickle that loitered along, waited for the fall rains to begin. A sudden speckling across our windshield suggested it hadn't long to wait.

We rattled over the old bridge and half through the town. The road swung up sharply over a rusty single-line railroad and turned left, shying away from the bluff that was hollowed just enough to accommodate one of the service stations.

We pulled into the station. The uniformed attendant came alongside.

"We just want some information," I said, conscious of the thinness of my billfold. We had picked up our last tankful of gas before plunging into the maze of canyons between the main highway and here. Our stopping place would have to be soon whether we found the People or not.

"Sure! Sure! Glad to oblige." The attendant pushed his cap back from his forehead. "How can I help you?"

I hesitated, trying to gather my thoughts and words—and some of the hope that had jolted out of me since we had left the junction. "We're trying to locate some—friends—of ours. We were told they lived out the other side of here, out by Baldy. Is there anyone—?"

"Friends of *them* people?" he asked in astonishment. "Well, say now, that's interesting! You're the first I ever had come asking after them."

I felt Bethie's arm trembling against mine. Then there *was* something beyond Kerry Canyon!

"How come? What's wrong with them?"

"Why, nothing, Mac, nothing. Matter of fact they're dern nice people. Trade here a lot. Come in to church and the dances."

"Dances?" I glanced around the steep sloping hills.

"Sure. We ain't as dead as we look," the attendant grinned. "Come Saturday night we're quite a town. Lots of ranches around these hills. Course, not much out Cougar Canyon way. That's where your friends live, didn't you say?"

"Yeah. Out by Baldy."

"Well, nobody else lives out that way." He hesitated. "Hey, there's something I'd like to ask."

"Sure. Like what?"

"Well, them people pretty much keep themselves to themselves. I don't mean they're stuck-up or anything, but—well, I've always wondered. Where they from? One of them overrun countries in Europe? They're foreigners, ain't they? And seems like most of what Europe exports any more is DP's. Are them people some?"

"Well, yes, you might call them that. Why?"

"Well, they talk just as good as anybody and it must have been a war a long time ago because they've been around since my Dad's time, but they just—feel different." He caught his upper lip between his teeth reflectively. "Good different. Real nice different." He grinned again. "Wouldn't mind shining up some of them gals myself. Don't get no encouragement, though.

"Anyway, keep on this road. It's easy. No other road going that way. Jackass Flat will beat the tar outa your tires, but you'll probably make it, less'n comes up a heavy rain. Then you'll skate over half the county and most likely end up in a ditch. Slickest mud in the world. Colder'n hell—beg pardon, lady—out there on the flat when the wind starts blowing. Better bundle up."

"Thanks, fella," I said. "Thanks a lot. Think we'll make it before dark?"

"Oh, sure. 'Tain't so awful far but the road's lousy. Oughta make it in two-three hours, less'n like I said, comes up a heavy rain."

We knew when we hit Jackass Flat. It was like dropping off the edge. If we had thought the road to Kerry Canyon was bad, we revised our opinions, but fast. In the first place it was choose your own ruts. Then the tracks were deep sunk in heavy clay generously mixed with sharp splintery shale and rocks as big as your two fists that were like a gigantic gravel as far as we could see across the lifeless expanse of the flat.

But to make it worse, the ruts I chose kept ending abruptly as though the cars that had made them had either backed away from the job or jumped over. Jumped over! I drove, in and out of ruts, so wrapped up in surmises that I hardly noticed the rough going until a cry from Bethie aroused me.

"Stop the car!" she cried. "Oh, Peter! Stop the car!"

I braked so fast that the pickup swerved wildly, mounted the side of a rut, lurched and settled sickeningly down on the back tire, which sighed itself flatly into the rising wind.

"What on earth!" I yelped, as near to being mad at Bethie as I'd ever been in my life. "What was that for?"

Bethie, white-faced, was emerging from the army blanket she had huddled in against the cold. "It just came to me. Peter, supposing they don't want us?"

"Don't want us? What do you mean?" I growled, wondering if that lace doily I called my spare tire would be worth the trouble of putting it on.

"We never thought. It didn't even occur to us. Peter, we—we don't belong. We won't be like them. We're partly of Earth—as much as we are of wherever else. Supposing they reject us? Supposing they think we're undesirable—?" Bethie turned her face away. "Maybe we don't belong anywhere, Peter, not anywhere at all."

I felt a chill sweep over me that was not of the weather. We had assumed so blithely that we would be welcome. But how did we know? Maybe they *wouldn't* want us. We weren't of the People. We weren't of Earth. Maybe we didn't belong—not anywhere.

"Sure they'll want us," I forced out heartily. Then my eyes wavered away from Bethie's and I said defensively, "Mother said they would help us. She said we were woven of the same fabric—"

"But maybe the warp will only accept genuine woof. Mother couldn't know. There weren't any—half-breeds—when she was separated from them. Maybe our Earth blood will mark us—"

"There's nothing wrong with Earth blood," I said defiantly. "Besides, like you said, what would there be for you if we went back?"

She pressed her clenched fists against her cheeks, her eyes wide and vacant. "Maybe," she muttered, "maybe if I'd just go on and go completely insane it wouldn't hurt so terribly much. It might even feel good."

"Bethie!" My voice jerked her physically. "Cut out that talk right now! We're going on. The only way we can judge the People is by Mother. She would never reject us or any others like us. And that fellow back there said they were good people."

I opened the door. "You better try to get some kinks out of your legs while I change the tire. By the looks of the sky we'll be doing some skating before we get to Cougar Canyon."

But for all my brave words it wasn't just for the tire that I knelt beside the car, and it wasn't only the sound of the lug wrench that the wind carried up into the darkening sky.

I squinted through the streaming windshield, trying to make out the road through the downpour that fought our windshield wiper to a standstill. What few glimpses I caught of the road showed a deceptively smooth-looking chocolate river, but we alternately shook like a giant maraca, pushed out sheets of water like a speedboat, or slithered aimlessly and terrifyingly across sudden mud flats that often left us yards off the road. Then we'd creep cautiously back until the soggy squelch of our tires told us we were in the flooded ruts again.

Then all at once it wasn't there. The road, I mean. It stretched a few yards ahead of us and then just flowed over the edge, into the rain, into nothingness.

"It couldn't go there," Bethie murmured incredulously. "It can't just drop off like that."

"Well, I'm certainly not dropping off with it, sight unseen," I said, huddling deeper into my army blanket. My jacket was packed in back and I hadn't bothered to dig it out. I hunched my shoulders to bring the blanket up over my head. "I'm going to take a look first."

I slid out into the solid wall of rain that hissed and splashed around me on the flooded flat. I was soaked to the knees and mud-coated to the shins before I slithered to the drop-off. The trail—call that a road?—tipped over the edge of the canyon and turned abruptly to the right, then lost itself along a shrub-grown ledge that sloped downward even as it paralleled the rim of the canyon. If I could get the pickup over the rim and onto the trail, it wouldn't be so bad. But—I peered over the drop-off at the turn. The bottom was lost in shadows and rain. I shuddered.

Then quickly, before I could lose my nerve, I squelched back to the car.

"Pray, Bethie. Here we go."

There was the suck and slosh of our turning tires, the awful moment when we hung on the brink. Then the turn. And there we were, poised over nothing, with our rear end slewing outward.

The sudden tongue-biting jolt as we finally landed, right side up, pointing the right way on the narrow trail, jarred the cold sweat on my face so it rolled down with the rain.

I pulled over at the first wide spot in the road and stopped the car. We sat in the silence, listening to the rain. I felt as though something infinitely precious were lying just before me. Bethie's hand crept into mine and I knew she was feeling it, too. But suddenly Bethie's hand was snatched from mine and she was pounding with both fists against my shoulder in most un-Bethie-like violence.

"I can't stand it, Peter!" she cried hoarsely, emotion choking her voice. "Let's go back before we find out any more. If they should send us away! Oh, Peter! Let's go before they find us! Then we'll still have our dream. We can pretend that someday we'll come back. We can never dream again, never hope again!" She hid her face in her hands. "I'll manage somehow. I'd rather go away, hoping, than run the risk of being rejected by them."

"Not me," I said, starting the motor. "We have as much chance of a welcome as we do of being kicked out. And if they can help you—say, what's the matter with you today? I'm supposed to be the doubting one, remember? You're the mustard seed of this outfit!" I grinned at her, but my heart sank at the drawn white misery of her face. She almost managed a smile.

The trail led steadily downward, lapping back on itself as it worked back and forth along the canyon wall, sometimes steep, sometimes almost level. The farther we went the more rested I felt, as though I were shutting doors behind or opening them before me.

Then came one of the casual miracles of mountain country. The clouds suddenly opened and the late sun broke through. There, almost frighteningly, a huge mountain pushed out of the featureless gray distance. In the flooding light the towering slopes seemed to move, stepping closer to us as we watched. The rain still fell, but now in glittering silver-beaded curtains; and one vivid end of a rainbow splashed color recklessly over trees and rocks and a corner of the sky.

I didn't watch the road. I watched the splendor and glory spread out around us. So when, at Bethie's scream, I snatched back to my driving, all I took down into the roaring splintering darkness was the thought of Bethie and the sight of the other car, slanting down from the bobbing top branches of a tree, seconds before it plowed into us broadside, a yard above the road.

I thought I was dead. I was afraid to open my eyes because I could feel the rain making little puddles over my closed lids. And then I breathed.

I was alive, all right. A knife jabbed itself up and down the left side of my chest and twisted itself viciously with each reluctant breath I drew.

Then I heard a voice.

"Thank the Power they aren't hurt too badly. But, oh, Valancy! What will Father say?" The voice was young and scared.

"You've known him longer than I have," another girl-voice answered. "You should have some idea."

"I never had a wreck before, not even when I was driving instead of lifting."

"I have a hunch that you'll be grounded for quite a spell," the second voice replied. "But that isn't what's worrying me, Karen. Why didn't we know they were coming? We always can sense Outsiders. We should have known—"

"Q.E.D. then," said the Karen-voice.

" 'Q.E.D.'?"

"Yes. If we didn't sense them, then they're not Outsiders—" There was the sound of a caught breath and then, "Oh, what I said, Valancy! You don't suppose!" I felt a movement close to me and heard the soft sound of breathing. "Can it really be two more of us? Oh, Valancy, they must be second generation—they're about our age. How did they find us? Which of our Lost Ones were their parents?"

Valancy sounded amused. "Those are questions they're certainly in no condition to answer right now, Karen. We'd better figure out what to do. Look, the girl is coming to."

I was snapped out of my detached eavesdropping by a moan beside me. I started to sit up. "Bethie—" I began, and all the knives twisted through my lungs. Bethie's scream followed my gasp.

My eyes were open now, but good, and my leg was an agonized burning ache down at the far end of my consciousness. I gritted my teeth but Bethie moaned again.

"Help her, help her!" I pleaded to the two fuzzy figures leaning over us as I tried to hold my breath to stop the jabbing.

"But she's hardly hurt," Karen cried. "A bump on her head. Some cuts."

With an effort I focused on a luminous clear face—Valancy's—whose deep eyes bent close above me. I licked the rain from my lips and blurted foolishly, "You're not even wet in all this rain!" A look of consternation swept over her face. There was a pause as she looked at me intently and then said, "Their shields aren't activated, Karen. We'd better extend ours."

"Okay, Valancy." And the annoying sibilant wetness of rain stopped. "How's the girl?"

"It must be shock or maybe internal—"

I started to turn to see, but Bethie's sobbing cry pushed me flat again.

"Help her," I gasped, grabbing wildly in my memory for Mother's words. "She's a—a Sensitive!"

"A Sensitive?" The two exchanged looks. "Then why doesn't she—?" Valancy started to say something, then turned swiftly. I crooked my arm over my eyes as I listened.

"Honey—Bethie—hear me!" The voice was warm but authoritative. "I'm going to help you. I'll show you how, Bethie."

There was a silence. A warm hand clasped mine and Karen squatted close beside me.

"She's sorting her," she whispered. "Going into her mind. To teach her control. It's so simple. How could it happen that she doesn't know—?"

I heard a soft wondering "Oh!" from Bethie, followed by a breathless "Oh, thank you, Valancy, thank you!"

I heaved myself up onto my elbow, fire streaking me from head to foot, and peered over at Bethie. She was looking at me, and her quiet face was happier than smiles could ever make it. We stared for the space of two relieved tears, then she said softly, "Tell them now, Peter. We can't go any farther until you tell them."

I lay back again, blinking at the sky where the scattered raindrops were still falling, though none of them reached us. Karen's hand was warm on mine and I felt a shiver of reluctance. If they sent us away...! But then they couldn't take back what they had given to Bethie, even if—I shut my eyes and blurted it out as bluntly as possible.

"We aren't of the People—not entirely. Father was not of the People. We're half-breeds."

There was a startled silence.

"You mean your mother married an Outsider?" Valancy's voice was filled with astonishment. "That you and Bethie are—?"

"Yes she did and yes we are!" I retorted. "And Dad was the best—" My belligerence ran thinly out across the sharp edge of my pain. "They're both dead now. Mother sent us to you."

"But Bethie is a Sensitive—" Valancy's voice was thoughtful.

"Yes, and I can fly and make things travel in the air and I've even made fire. But Dad—" I hid my face and let it twist with the increasing agony.

"Then we *can!*" I couldn't read the emotion in Valancy's voice. "Then the People and Outsiders—but it's unbelievable that you—" Her voice died.

In the silence that followed, Bethie's voice came fearful and tremulous, "Are you going to send us away?" My heart twisted to the ache in her voice.

"Send you away! Oh, my people, my people! Of course not! As if there were any question!" Valancy's arms went tightly around Bethie, and Karen's hand closed warmly on mine. The tension that had been a hard twisted knot inside me dissolved, and Bethie and I were home.

Then Valancy became very brisk.

"Bethie, what's wrong with Peter?"

Bethie was astonished. "How did you know his name?" Then she smiled. "Of course. When you were sorting me!" She touched me lightly along my sides, along my legs. "Four of his ribs are hurt. His left leg is broken. That's about all. Shall I control him?"

"Yes," Valancy said. "I'll help."

And the pain was gone, put to sleep under the persuasive warmth that came to me as Bethie and Valancy came softly into my mind.

"Good," Valancy said. "We're pleased to welcome a Sensitive. Karen and I know a little of their function because we are Sorters. But we have no full-fledged Sensitive in our Group now."

She turned to me. "You said you know the inanimate lift?"

"I don't know," I said. "I don't know the words for lots of things."

"You'll have to relax completely. We don't usually use it on people. But if you let go all over, we can manage."

They wrapped me warmly in our blankets and lightly, a hand under my shoulders and under my heels, lifted me carrying-high and sped with me through the trees, Bethie trailing from Valancy's free hand.

Before we reached the yard, the door flew open and warm yellow light spilled out into the dusk. The girls paused on the porch and shifted me to the waiting touch of two men. In the wordless pause before the babble of question and explanation, I felt Bethie beside me draw a deep wondering breath and merge like a raindrop in a river into the People around us.

But even as the lights went out for me again, and I felt myself slide down into comfort and hunger-fed belongingness, somewhere deep inside of me was a core of something that couldn't quite—no, *wouldn't* quite dissolve—wouldn't yet yield itself completely to the People.

Interlude: Lea 3

Lea stepped soundlessly toward the door almost before Peter's last words were said. She was halfway up the steep road that led up the canyon before she heard the sound of Karen coming behind her. Lifting and running, Karen caught up with her.

"Lea!" she called, reaching for her arm.

With a twist of her shoulder Lea evaded Karen and wordlessly, breathlessly ran on up the road.

"Lea!" Karen grabbed both her shoulders and stopped her bodily. "Where on earth are you going!"

"Let me go!" Lea shouted. "Sneak! Peeping Tom! Let me go!" She tried to wrench out of Karen's hands.

"Lea, whatever you're thinking it isn't so."

"Whatever I'm thinking!" Lea's eyes blazed. "Don't you *know* what I'm thinking? Haven't you done enough scrabbling around in all the muck and mess—?" Her fingernails dented Karen's hands. "Let me go!"

"Why do you *care,* Lea?" Karen's cold voice jabbed mercilessly. "Why should you care? What difference does it make to you? You left life a long time ago."

"Death—" Lea choked, feeling the dusty bitterness of the word she had thought so often and seldom said. "Death is at least private—no one nosing around—"

"Can you be so sure?" It was Karen's quiet voice. "Anyway, believe me, Lea, I haven't gone in to you even once. Of course I could if I wanted to and I will if I have to, but I never would without your knowledge—if not your consent. All I've learned of you has been from the most open outer part of your mind. Your inner mind is sacredly your own. The People are taught reverence for individual privacy. Whatever powers we have are for healing, not for hurting. We have health and life for you if you'll accept it. You see, there *is* balm in Gilead! Don't refuse it, Lea."

Lea's hands drooped heavily. The tension went out of her body slowly.

"I heard you last night," she said, puzzled. "I heard your story and it didn't even occur to me that you could—I mean, it just wasn't real and I had no idea—" She let Karen turn her back down the road. "But then when I heard Peter—I don't know—he seemed more true. You don't expect men to go in for fairy tales—" She clutched suddenly at Karen. "Oh, Karen, what shall I do? I'm so mixed up that I can't—"

"Well, the simplest and most immediate thing is to come on back. We have time to hear another report and they're waiting for us. Melodye is next. She saw the People from quite another angle."

Back in the schoolroom Lea fitted herself self-consciously into her corner again, though no one seemed to notice her. Everyone was busy reliving or commenting on the days of Peter and Bethie. The talking died as Melodye Amerson took her place at the desk.

"Valancy's helping me," she smiled. "We chose the theme together, too. Remember—?

" 'Behold, I am at a point to die and what profit shall this birthright do to me? And he sold his birthright for bread and pottage.'

"I couldn't do the recalling alone, either. So now, if you don't mind, there'll be a slight pause while we construct our network."

She relaxed visibly and Lea could feel the receptive quietness spread as though the whole room were becoming mirror-placid like the pool in the creek, and then Melodye began to speak...

Pottage

You get tired of teaching after a while. Well, maybe not of teaching itself, because it's insidious and remains a tug in the blood for all of your life, but there comes a day when you look down at the paper you're grading or listen to an answer you're giving a child and you get a *boinnng!* feeling. And each reverberation of the *boing* is a year in your life, another set of children through your hands, another beat in monotony, and it's frightening. The value of the work you're doing doesn't enter into it at that moment and the monotony is bitter on your tongue.

Sometimes you can assuage that feeling by consciously savoring those precious days of pseudofreedom between the time you receive your contract for the next year and the moment you sign it. Because you *can* escape at that moment, but somehow—you don't.

But I did, one spring. I quit teaching. I didn't sign up again. I went chasing after—after what? Maybe excitement—maybe a dream of wonder—maybe a new bright wonderful world that just *must* be somewhere else because it isn't here-and-now. Maybe a place to begin again so I'd never end up at the same frightening emotional dead end. So I quit.

But by late August the emptiness inside me was bigger than boredom, bigger than monotony, bigger than lusting after freedom. It was almost terror to be next door to September and not care that in a few weeks school starts—tomorrow school starts—first day of school. So, almost at the last minute, I went to the placement bureau. Of course it was too late to try to return to my other school, and besides, the mold of the years there still chafed in too many places.

"Well," the placement director said as he shuffled his end-of-the-season cards, past Algebra and Home Ec and PE and High School English, "there's always Bendo." He thumbed out a battered-looking three-by-five. "There's *always* Bendo."

And I took his emphasis and look for what they were intended as and sighed.

"Bendo?"

"Small school. One room. Mining town, or used to be. Ghost town now." He sighed wearily and let down his professional hair. "Ghost people, too. Can't keep a teacher there more than a year. Low pay—fair housing—at someone's home. No community activities—no social life. No city within fifty or so miles. No movies. No nothing but children to be taught. Ten of them this year. All grades."

"Sounds like the town I grew up in," I said. "Except we had two rooms and lots of community activities."

"I've been to Bendo." The director leaned back in his chair, hands behind his head. "Sick community. Unhappy people. No interest in anything. Only reason they have a school is because it's the law. Law-abiding anyway. Not enough interest in anything to break a law, I guess."

"I'll take it," I said quickly before I could think beyond the feeling that this sounded about as far back as I could go to get a good running start at things again.

He glanced at me quizzically. "If you're thinking of lighting a torch of high reform to set Bendo afire with enthusiasm, forget it. I've seen plenty of king-sized torches fizzle out there."

"I have no torch," I said. "Frankly I'm fed to the teeth with bouncing bright enthusiasm and huge PTA's and activities until they come out your ears. They usually turn out to be the most monotonous kind of monotony. Bendo will be a rest."

"It will that," the director said, leaning over his cards again. "Saul Diemus is the president of the board. If you don't have a car, the only way to get to Bendo is by bus—it runs once a week."

I stepped out into the August sunshine after the interview and sagged a little under its savage pressure, almost hearing a hiss as the refrigerated coolness of the placement bureau evaporated from my skin.

I walked over to the quad and sat down on one of the stone benches I'd never had time to use, those years ago when I had been a student here. I looked up at my old dorm window and, for a moment, felt a wild homesickness—not only for years that were gone and hopes that had died and dreams that had had grim awakenings, but for a special magic I had found in that room. It was a magic—a true magic—that opened such vistas to me that for a while anything seemed possible, anything feasible—if not for me right now, then for others, someday. Even now, after the dilution of time, I couldn't quite believe that magic, and even now, as then, I wanted fiercely to believe it. If only it could be so! If only it could be so!

I sighed and stood up. I suppose everyone has a magic moment somewhere in his life and, like me, can't believe that anyone else could have the same—but mine *was* different! No one else *could* have had the same experience! I laughed at myself. Enough of the past and of dreaming. Bendo waited. I had things to do.

I watched the rolling clouds of red-yellow dust billow away from the jolting bus, and cupped my hands over my face to get a breath of clean air. The grit between my teeth and the smothering sift of dust across my clothes was familiar enough to me, but I hoped by the time we reached Bendo we would have left this dust plain behind and come into a little more vegetation. I shifted wearily on the angular seat, wondering if it had ever been designed for anyone's comfort, and caught myself as a sudden braking of the bus flung me forward.

We sat and waited for the dust of our going to catch up with us, while the last-but-me passenger, a withered old Indian, slowly gathered up his gunny-sack bundles and his battered saddle and edged his Levied velveteen-bloused self up the aisle and out to the bleak roadside.

We roared away, leaving him a desolate figure in a wide desolation. I wondered where he was headed. How many weary miles to his hogan in what hidden wash or miniature greenness in all this wilderness.

Then we headed straight as a die for the towering redness of the bare mountains that lined the horizon. Peering ahead I could see the road, ruler straight, disappearing into the distance. I sighed and shifted again and let the roar of the motor and the weariness of my bones lull me into a stupor on the border between sleep and waking.

A change in the motor roar brought me back to the jouncing bus. We jerked to a stop again. I looked out the window through the settling clouds of dust and wondered who we could be picking up out here in the middle of nowhere. Then a clot of dust dissolved and I saw

BENDO POST OFFICE
GENERAL STORE
Garage & Service Station
Dry Goods & Hardware
Magazines

in descending size on the front of the leaning, weather-beaten building propped between two crumbling smoke-blackened stone ruins. After so much flatness it was almost a shock to see the bare tumbled boulders crowding down to the roadside and humping their lichen-stained shoulders against the sky.

"Bendo," the bus driver said, unfolding his lanky legs and hunching out of the bus. "End of the line—end of civilization—end of everything!" He grinned and the dusty mask of his face broke into engaging smile patterns.

"Small, isn't it?" I grinned back.

"Usta be bigger. Not that it helps now. Roaring mining town years ago." As he spoke I could pick out disintegrating buildings dotting the rocky hillsides and tumbling into the steep washes. "My dad can remember it when he was a kid. That was long enough ago that there was still a river for the town to be in the bend o'."

"Is *that* where it got its name?"

"Some say yes, some say no. Might have been a feller named Bendo." The driver grunted as he unlashed my luggage from the bus roof and swung it to the ground.

"Oh, hi!" said the driver.

I swung around to see who was there. The man was tall, well built, good-looking—and old. Older than his face—older than years could have made him because he was really young, not much older than I. His face was a stern unhappy stillness, his hands stiff on the brim of his Stetson as he held it waist high.

In that brief pause before his "Miss Amerson?" I felt the same feeling coming from him that you can feel around some highly religious person who knows God only as a stern implacable vengeful deity, impatient of worthless man, waiting only for an unguarded moment to strike him down in his sin. I wondered who or what his God was that prisoned him so cruelly. Then I was answering, "Yes, how do you do?" And he touched my hand briefly with a "Saul Diemus" and turned to the problem of my two large suitcases and my record player.

I followed Mr. Diemus' shuffling feet silently, since he seemed to have slight inclination for talk. I hadn't expected a reception committee, but kids must have changed a lot since I was one, otherwise curiosity about teacher would have lured out at least a couple of them for a preview look. But the silent two of us walked on for a half block or so from the highway and the post office and rounded the rocky corner of a hill. I looked across the dry creek bed and up the one winding street that was residential Bendo. I paused on the splintery old bridge and took a good look. I'd never see Bendo like this again. Familiarity would blur some outlines and sharpen others, and I'd never again see it, free from the knowledge of who lived behind which blank front door.

The houses were scattered haphazardly over the hillsides, and erratic flights of rough stone steps led down from each to the road that paralleled the bone-dry creek bed. The houses were not shacks but they were unpainted and weathered until they blended into the background almost perfectly. Each front yard had things growing in it, but such subdued blossoming and unobtrusive planting that they could easily have been only accidental massings of natural vegetation.

Such a passion for anonymity...

"The school—" I had missed the swift thrust of his hand.

"Where?" Nothing I could see spoke school to me.

"Around the bend." This time I followed his indication and suddenly, out of the featurelessness of the place, I saw a bell tower barely topping the hill beyond the town, with the fine pencil stroke of a flagpole to one side. Mr. Diemus pulled himself together to make the effort.

"The school's in the prettiest place around here. There's a spring and trees, and—" He ran out of words and looked at me as though trying to conjure up something else I'd like to hear. "I'm board president," he said abruptly. "You'll have ten children from first grade to second-year high school. You're the boss in your school. Whatever you do is your business. Any discipline you find desirable—use. We don't pamper our children. Teach them what you have to. Don't bother the parents with reasons and explanations. The school is yours."

"And you'd just as soon do away with it and me, too." I smiled at him.

He looked startled. "The law says school them." He started across the bridge. "So school them."

I followed meekly, wondering wryly what would happen if I asked Mr. Diemus why he hated himself and the world he was in and even— oh, breathe it softly—the children I was to "school."

"You'll stay at my place," he said. "We have an extra room,"

I was uneasily conscious of the wide gap of silence that followed his pronouncement, but couldn't think of a thing to fill it. I shifted my small case from one hand to the other and kept my eyes on the rocky path that protested with shifting stones and vocal gravel every step we took. It seemed to me that Mr. Diemus was trying to make all the noise he could with his shuffling feet. But, in spite of the amplified echo from the hills around us, no door opened, no face pressed to a window. It was a distinct relief to hear suddenly the happy unthinking rusty singing of hens as they scratched in the coarse dust.

I hunched up in the darkness of my narrow bed trying to comfort my uneasy stomach. It wasn't that the food had been bad—it had been quite adequate—but such a dingy meal! Gloom seemed to festoon itself from the ceiling and unhappiness sat almost visibly at the table.

I tried to tell myself that it was my own travel weariness that slanted my thoughts, but I looked around the table and saw the hopeless endurance furrowed into the adult faces and beginning faintly but unmistakably on those of the children. There were two children there. A girl, Sarah (fourth grade, at a guess), and an adolescent boy, Matt (seventh?)—too silent, too well mannered, too controlled, avoiding much too pointedly looking at the empty chair between them.

My food went down in lumps and quarreled fiercely with the coffee that arrived in square-feeling gulps. Even yet—long difficult hours after the meal—the food still wouldn't lie down to be digested.

Tomorrow I could slip into the pattern of school, familiar no matter where school was, since teaching kids is teaching kids no matter where. Maybe then I could convince my stomach that all was well, and then maybe even start to thaw those frozen unnatural children. Of course they well might be little demons away from home—which is very often the case. Anyway I felt, thankfully, the familiar September thrill of new beginnings.

I shifted in bed again, then, stiffening my neck, lifted my ears clear of my pillow.

It was a whisper, the intermittent hissing I had been hearing. Someone was whispering in the next room to mine. I sat up and listened unashamedly. I knew Sarah's room was next to mine, but who was talking with her? At first I could get only half words and then either my ears sharpened or the voices became louder.

"...and did you hear her laugh? Right out loud at the table!" The quick whisper became a low voice. "Her eyes crinkled in the corners and she laughed."

"Our other teachers laughed, too." The uncertainly deep voice must be Matt.

"Yes," Sarah whispered. "But not for long. Oh, Matt! What's wrong with us? People in our books have fun. They laugh and run and jump and do all kinds of fun stuff and nobody—" Sarah faltered, "no one calls it evil."

"Those are only stories," Matt said. "Not real life."

"I don't believe it!" Sarah cried. "When I get big I'm going away from Bendo. I'm going to see—"

"Away from Bendo!" Matt's voice broke in roughly. "Away from the Group?"

I lost Sarah's reply. I felt as though I had missed an expected step. As I wrestled with my breath, the sights and sounds and smells of my old dorm room crowded back upon me. Then I caught myself. It was probably only a turn of phrase. This futile desolate unhappiness couldn't possibly be related in any way to *that* magic...

"Where *is* Dorcas?" Sarah asked, as though she knew the answer already.

"Punished." Matt's voice was hard and unchildlike. "She jumped."

"Jumped!" Sarah was shocked.

"Over the edge of the porch. Clear down to the path. Father saw her. I think she let him see her on purpose." His voice was defiant. "Someday when I get older I'm going to jump, too—all I want to—even over the house. Right in front of Father."

"Oh, Matt!" The cry was horrified and admiring. "You wouldn't! You couldn't. Not so far, not right in front of Father!"

"I would so," Matt retorted. "I could so, because I—" His words cut off sharply. "Sarah," he went on, "can you figure any way, *any* way, that jumping could be evil? It doesn't hurt anyone. It isn't ugly. There isn't any law—"

"Where is Dorcas?" Sarah's voice was almost inaudible. "In the hidey hole again?" She was almost answering Matt's question instead of asking one of her own.

"Yes," Matt said. "In the dark with only bread to eat. So she can learn what a hunted animal feels like. An animal that is different, that other animals hate and hunt." His bitter voice put quotes around the words.

"You see," Sarah whispered. "You see?"

In the silence following I heard the quiet closing of a door and the slight vibration of the floor as Matt passed my room. I eased back onto my pillow. I lay back, staring toward the ceiling. What dark thing was here in this house? In this community? Frightened children whispering in the dark. Rebellious children in hidey holes learning how hunted animals feel. And a Group...? No, it couldn't be. It was just the recent reminder of being on campus again that made me even consider that this darkness might in some way be the reverse of the golden coin Karen had shown me.

My heart almost failed me when I saw the school. It was one of those monstrosities that went up around the turn of the century. This one had been built for a boom town, but now all the upper windows were boarded up and obviously long out of use. The lower floor was blank, too, except for two rooms—though with the handful of children quietly standing around the door it was apparent that only one room was needed. And not only was the building deserted, the yard was swept clean from side to side, innocent of grass or trees—or playground equipment. There *was* a deep grove just beyond the school, though, and the glint of water down canyon.

"No swings?" I asked the three children who were escorting me. "No slides? No seesaws?"

"No!" Sarah's voice was unhappily surprised. Matt scowled at her warningly.

"No," he said, "we don't swing or slide—nor see a saw!" He grinned up at me faintly.

"What a shame!" I said. "Did they all wear out? Can't the school afford new ones?"

"We don't swing or slide or seesaw." The grin was dead. "We don't believe in it."

There's nothing quite so flat and incontestable as that last statement. I've heard it as an excuse for practically every type of omission, but, so help me, never applied to playground equipment. I couldn't think of a reply any more intelligent than "Oh," so I didn't say anything.

All week long I felt as if I were wading through knee-deep jello or trying to lift a king-sized feather bed up over my head. I used up every device I ever thought of to rouse the class to enthusiasm—about anything, *anything!* They were polite and submissive and did what was asked of them, but joylessly, apathetically, enduringly.

Finally, just before dismissal time on Friday, I leaned in desperation across my desk.

"Don't you like *anything?*" I pleaded. "Isn't *anything* fun?"

Dorcas Diemus' mouth opened into the tense silence. I saw Matt kick quickly, warningly, against the leg of the desk. Her mouth closed.

"I think school is fun," I said. "I think we can enjoy all kinds of things. I want to enjoy teaching but I can't unless you enjoy learning."

"We learn," Dorcas said quickly. "We aren't stupid."

"You learn," I acknowledged. "You aren't stupid. But don't any of you *like* school?"

"I like school," Martha piped up, my first grade. "I think it's fun!"

"Thank you, Martha," I said. "And the rest of you—" I glared at them in mock anger, "you're going to have fun if I have to beat it into you!"

To my dismay they shrank down apprehensively in their seats and exchanged troubled glances. But before I could hastily explain myself, Matt laughed and Dorcas joined him. And I beamed fatuously to hear the hesitant rusty laughter spread across the room, but I saw ten-year-old Esther's hands shake as she wiped tears from her eyes. Tears—of laughter?

That night I twisted in the darkness of my room, almost too tired to sleep, worrying and wondering. What had blighted these people? They had health, they had beauty—the curve of Martha's cheek against the window was a song, the lift of Dorcas' eyebrows was breathless grace. They were fed—adequately, clothed—adequately, housed—adequately, but nothing like they could have been. I'd seen more joy and delight and enthusiasm from little campground kids who slept in cardboard shacks and washed—if they ever did—in canals and ate whatever edible came their way, but grinned, even when impetigo or cold sores bled across their grins.

But these lifeless kids! My prayers were troubled and I slept restlessly.

A month or so later things had improved a little bit, but not much. At least there was more relaxation in the classroom. And I found that they had no deep-rooted convictions against plants, so we had things growing on the deep window sills—stuff we transplanted from the spring and from among the trees. And we had jars of minnows from the creek and one drowsy horned toad that roused in his box of dirt only to flick up the ants brought for his dinner. And we sang, loudly and enthusiastically, but, miracle of miracles, without even one monotone in the whole room. But we *didn't* sing "Up, Up in the Sky" or "How Do You Like to Go Up in a Swing?" My solos of such songs were received with embarrassed blushes and lowered eyes!

There had been one dust-up between us, though—this matter of shuffling everywhere they walked.

"Pick up your feet, for goodness' sake," I said irritably one morning when the *shoosh, shoosh, shoosh* of their coming and going finally got my skin off. "Surely they're not so heavy you can't lift them."

Timmy, who happened to be the trigger this time, nibbled unhappily at one finger. "I can't," he whispered. "Not supposed to."

"Not supposed to?" I forgot momentarily how warily I'd been going with these frightened mice of children. "Why not? Surely there's no reason in the world why you can't walk quietly."

Matt looked unhappily over at Miriam, the sophomore who was our entire high school. She looked aside, biting her lower lip, troubled. Then she turned back and said, "It is customary in Bendo."

"To shuffle along?" I was forgetting any manners I had. "Whatever for?"

"That's the way we do in Bendo." There was no anger in her defense, only resignation.

"Perhaps that's the way you do at home. But here at school let's pick our feet up. It makes too much disturbance otherwise."

"But it's bad—" Esther began.

Matt's hand shushed her in a hurry.

"Mr. Diemus said what we did at school was my business," I told them. "He said not to bother your parents with our problems. One of our problems is too much noise when others are trying to work. At least in our schoolroom let's lift our feet and walk quietly."

The children considered the suggestion solemnly and turned to Matt and Miriam for guidance. They both nodded and we went back to work.

For the next few minutes, from the corner of my eyes, I saw with amazement all the unnecessary trips back and forth across the room, with high-lifted feet, with grins and side glances that marked such trips as high adventure—as a delightfully daring thing to do! The whole deal had me bewildered. Thinking back, I realized that not only the children of Bendo scuffled but all the adults did, too—as though they were afraid to lose contact with the earth, as though... I shook my head and went on with the lesson.

Before noon, though, the endless *shoosh, shoosh, shoosh* of feet began again. Habit was too much for the children. So I silently filed the sound under "Uncurable, Endurable," and let the matter drop.

I sighed as I watched the children leave at lunchtime. It seemed to me that with the unprecedented luxury of a whole hour for lunch they'd all go home. The bell tower was visible from nearly every house in town. But instead they all brought tight little paper sacks with dull crumbly sandwiches and unimaginative apples in them. And silently with their dull scuffly steps they disappeared into the thicket of trees around the spring.

"Everything is dulled around here," I thought. "Even the sunlight is blunted as it floods the hills and canyons. There is no mirth, no laughter. No high jinks or cutting up. No preadolescent silliness. No adolescent foolishness. Just quiet children, enduring."

I don't usually snoop but I began wondering if perhaps the kids were different when they were away from me—and from their parents. So when I got back at twelve thirty from an adequate but uninspired lunch at Diemuses' house I kept on walking past the schoolhouse and quietly down into the grove, moving cautiously through the scanty undergrowth until I could lean over a lichened boulder and look down on the children.

Some were lying around on the short still grass, hands under their heads, blinking up at the brightness of the sky between the leaves. Esther and little Martha were hunting out fillaree seed pods and counting the tines of the pitchforks and rakes and harrows they resembled. I smiled, remembering how I used to do the same thing.

"I dreamed last night." Dorcas thrust the statement defiantly into the drowsy silence. "I dreamed about the Home."

My sudden astonished movement was covered by Martha's horrified "Oh, Dorcas!"

"What's wrong with the Home?" Dorcas cried, her cheeks scarlet. "There *was* a Home! There was! There was! Why shouldn't we talk about it?"

I listened avidly. This couldn't be just coincidence—a Group and now the Home. There must be some connection.... I pressed closer against the rough rock.

"But it's bad!" Esther cried. "You'll be punished! We can't talk about the Home!"

"Why not?" Joel asked as though it had just occurred to him, as things do just occur to you when you're thirteen. He sat up slowly. "Why can't we?"

There was a short tense silence.

"I've dreamed, too," Matt said. "I've dreamed of the Home—and it's *good*, it's good!"

"Who hasn't dreamed?" Miriam asked. "We all have, haven't we? Even our parents. I can tell by Mother's eyes when she has."

"Did you ever ask how come we aren't supposed to talk about it?" Joel asked. "I mean and ever get any answer except that it's bad."

"I think it has something to do with a long time ago," Matt said. "Something about when the Group first came—"

"I don't think it's just dreams," Miriam declared, "because I don't have to be asleep. I think it's remembering."

"Remembering?" asked Dorcas. "How can we remember something we never knew?"

"I don't know," Miriam admitted, "but I'll bet it is."

"I remember," volunteered Talitha, who never volunteered anything.

"Hush!" whispered Abie, the second-grade next-to-youngest who always whispered.

"I remember," Talitha went on stubbornly. "I remember a dress that was too little so the mother just stretched the skirt till it was long enough and it stayed stretched. 'Nen she pulled the waist out big enough and the little girl put it on and flew away."

"Hoh!" Timmy scoffed. "I remember better than that." His face stilled and his eyes widened. "The ship was so tall it was like a mountain and the people went in the high high door and they didn't have a ladder. 'Nen there were stars, big burning ones—not squinchy little ones like ours."

"It went too fast!" That was Abie! Talking eagerly! "When the air came it made the ship hot and the little baby died before all the little boats left the ship." He scrunched down suddenly, leaning against Talitha and whimpering.

"You see!" Miriam lifted her chin triumphantly. "We've all dreamed— I mean remembered!"

"I guess so," said Matt. "I remember. It's *lifting*, Talitha, not flying. You go and go as high as you like, as far as you want to and don't *ever* have to touch the ground—at all! At all!" He pounded his fist into the gravelly red soil beside him.

"And you can dance in the air, too," Miriam sighed. "Freer than a bird, lighter than—"

Esther scrambled to her feet, white-faced and panic-stricken. "Stop! Stop! It's evil! It's bad! I'll tell Father! We can't dream—or lift—or dance! It's bad, it's bad! You'll die for it! You'll die for it!"

Joel jumped to his feet and grabbed Esther's arm.

"Can we die any deader?" he cried, shaking her brutally. "You call *this* being alive?" He hunched down apprehensively and shambled a few scuffling steps across the clearing.

I fled blindly back to school, trying to wink away my tears without admitting I was crying, crying for these poor kids who were groping so hopelessly for something they knew they should have. Why was it so rigorously denied them? Surely, if they were what I thought them... And they could be! They could be!

I grabbed the bell rope and pulled hard. Reluctantly the bell moved and rolled.

One o'clock, it clanged. *One o'clock!*

I watched the children returning with slow uneager shuffling steps.

That night I started a letter:

"Dear Karen,

"Yep, 'sme after all these years. And, oh, Karen! I've found some more! Some more of the People! Remember how much you wished you knew if any other Groups besides yours had survived the Crossing? How you worried about them and wanted to find them if they had? Well, *I've* found a whole Group! But it's a sick unhappy group. Your heart would break to see them. If you could come and start them on the right path again..."

I put my pen down. I looked at the lines I had written and then crumpled the paper slowly. This was *my* Group. *I* had found them. Sure, I'd tell Karen—but later. Later, after—well, after *I* had tried to start them on the right path—at least the children.

After all, I knew a little of their potentialities. Hadn't Karen briefed me in those unguarded magical hours in the old dorm, drawn to me as I was to her by some mutual sympathy that seemed stronger than the usual roommate attachment, telling me things no Outsider had a right to hear? And if, when I finally told her and turned the Group over to her, if it could be a joyous gift, then I could feel that I had repaid her a little for the wonder world she had opened for me.

"Yes," I thought ruefully, "and there's nothing like a large portion of ignorance to give one a large portion of confidence." But I did want to try—desperately. Maybe if I could break prison for someone else, then perhaps my own bars... I dropped the paper in the wastebasket.

But it was several weeks before I could bring myself to do anything to let the children know I knew about them. It was such an impossible situation, even if it was true—and if it wasn't, what kind of lunacy would they suspect me of?

When I finally set my teeth and swore a swear to myself that I'd do something definite, my hands shook and my breath was a flutter in my dry throat.

"Today—" I said with an effort, "today is Friday." Which gem of wisdom the children received with charitable silence. "We've been working hard all week, so let's have fun today." This stirred the children—half with pleasure, half with apprehension. They, poor kids, found my "fun" much harder than any kind of work I could give them. But some of them were acquiring a taste for it. Martha had even learned to skip!

"First, monitors pass the composition paper." Esther and Abie scuffled hurriedly around with the paper, and the pencil sharpener got a thorough workout. At least these kids didn't differ from others in their pleasure in grinding their pencils away at the slightest excuse.

"Now," I gulped, "we're going to write." Which obvious asininity was passed over with forbearance, though Miriam looked at me wonderingly before she bent her head and let her hair shadow her face. "Today I want you all to write about the same thing. Here is our subject."

Gratefully I turned my back on the children's waiting eyes and printed slowly:

I REMEMBER THE HOME

I heard the sudden intake of breath that worked itself downward from Miriam to Talitha and then the rapid whisper that informed Abie and Martha. I heard Esther's muffled cry and I turned slowly around and leaned against the desk.

"There are so many beautiful things to remember about the Home," I said into the strained silence. "So many wonderful things. And even the sad memories are better than forgetting, because the Home was *good*. Tell me what you remember about the Home."

"We can't!" Joel and Matt were on their feet simultaneously.

"Why can't we?" Dorcas cried. "Why can't we?"

"It's bad!" Esther cried. "It's evil!"

"It ain't either!" Abie shrilled, astonishingly. "It ain't either!"

"We shouldn't." Miriam's trembling hands brushed her heavy hair upward. "It's forbidden."

"Sit down," I said gently. "The day I arrived at Bendo, Mr. Diemus told me to teach you what I had to teach you. I have to teach you that remembering the Home is good."

"Then why don't the grownups think so?" Matt asked slowly. "They tell us not to talk about it. We shouldn't disobey our parents."

"I know," I admitted. "And I would never ask you children to go against your parents' wishes, unless I felt that it is very important. If you'd rather they didn't know about it at first, keep it as our secret. Mr. Diemus told me not to bother them with explanations or reasons. I'll make it right with your parents when the time comes." I paused to swallow and blink away a vision of me leaving town in a cloud of dust, barely ahead of a posse of irate parents. "Now, everyone, busy," I said briskly. " 'I Remember the Home.' "

There was a moment heavy with decision and I held my breath, wondering which way the balance would dip. And then—surely it must have been because they wanted so to speak and affirm the wonder of what had been that they capitulated so easily. Heads bent and pencils scurried. And Martha sat, her head bowed on her desk with sorrow.

"I don't know enough words," she mourned. "How do you write *'toolas'*?"

And Abie laboriously erased a hole through his paper and licked his pencil again.

"Why don't you and Abie make some pictures?" I suggested. "Make a little story with pictures and we can staple them together like a real book."

I looked over the silent busy group and let myself relax, feeling weakness flood into my knees. I scrubbed the dampness from my palms with Kleenex and sat back in my chair. Slowly I became conscious of a new atmosphere in my classroom. An intolerable strain was gone, an unconscious holding back of the children, a wariness, a watchfulness, a guilty feeling of desiring what was forbidden.

A prayer of thanksgiving began to well up inside me. It changed hastily to a plea for mercy as I began to visualize what might happen to me when the parents found out what I was doing. How long must this containment and denial have gone on? This concealment and this carefully nourished fear? From what Karen had told me it must be well over fifty years—long enough to mark indelibly three generations.

And here I was with my fine little hatchet trying to set a little world afire! On which very mixed metaphor I stiffened my weak knees and got up from my chair. I walked unnoticed up and down the aisles, stepping aside as Joel went blindly to the shelf for more paper, leaning over Miriam to marvel that she had taken out her Crayolas and part of her writing was with colors, part with pencil—and the colors spoke to something in me that the pencil couldn't reach, though I'd never seen the forms the colors took.

The children had gone home, happy and excited, chattering and laughing, until they reached the edge of the school grounds. There, smiles died and laughter stopped and faces and feet grew heavy again. All but Esther's. Hers had never been light. I sighed and turned to the papers. Here was Abie's little book. I thumbed through it and drew a deep breath and went back through it slowly again.

A second grader drawing this? Six pages—six finished adult-looking pages. Crayolas achieving effects I'd never seen before—pictures that told a story loudly and clearly.

Stars blazing in a black sky, with the slender needle of a ship, like a mote in the darkness.

The vasty green cloud-shrouded arc of Earth against the blackness. A pink tinge of beginning friction along the ship's belly. I put my finger to the glow. I could almost feel the heat.

Inside the ship, suffering and pain, heroic striving, crumpled bodies and seared faces. A baby dead in its mother's arms. Then a swarm of tinier needles erupting from the womb of the ship. And the last shriek of incandescence as the ship volatilized against the thickening drag of the air.

I leaned my head on my hands and closed my eyes. All this, all *this* in the memory of an eight-year-old? All *this* in the feelings of an eight-year-old? Because Abie knew—he *knew* how this felt. He knew the heat and strivings and the dying and fleeing. No wonder Abie whispered and leaned. Racial memory was truly a two-sided coin.

I felt a pang of misgivings. Maybe I was wrong to let him remember so vividly. Maybe I shouldn't have let him...

I turned to Martha's papers. They were delicate, almost spidery drawings of some fuzzy little animal *(toolas?)* that apparently built a hanging hammocky nest and gathered fruit in a huge leaf basket and had a bird for a friend. A truly out-of-this-world bird. Much of her story escaped me because first graders—if anyone at all—produce symbolic art and, since her frame of reference and mine were so different, there was much that I couldn't interpret. But her whole booklet was joyous and light.

And now, the stories...

I lifted my head and blinked into the twilight. I had finished all the papers except Esther's. It was her cramped writing, swimming in darkness, that made me realize that the day was gone and that I was shivering in a shadowy room with the fire in the old-fashioned heater gone out.

Slowly I shuffled the papers into my desk drawer, hesitated and took out Esther's. I would finish at home. I shrugged into my coat and wandered home, my thoughts intent on the papers I had read. And suddenly I wanted to cry—to cry for the wonders that had been and were no more. For the heritage of attainment and achievement these children had but couldn't use. For the dream-come-true of what they were capable of doing but weren't permitted to do. For the homesick yearning that filled every line they had written—these unhappy exiles, three generations removed from any physical knowledge of the Home.

I stopped on the bridge and leaned against the railing in the half dark. Suddenly *I* felt a welling homesickness. *That* was what the world should be like—what it *could* be like if only—if only...

But my tears for the Home were as hidden as the emotions of Mrs. Diemus when she looked up uncuriously as I came through the kitchen door.

"Good evening," she said. "I've kept your supper warm."

"Thank you." I shivered convulsively. "It *is* getting cold."

I sat on the edge of my bed that night, letting the memory of the kids' papers wash over me, trying to fill in around the bits and snippets that they had told of the Home. And then I began to wonder. All of them who wrote about the actual Home had been so happy with their memories. From Timmy and his *Shinny ship as high as a montin and faster than two jets,* and Dorcas' wandering tenses as though yesterday and today were one: *The flowers were like lights. At night it isn't dark becas they shine so bright and when the moon came up the breeos sing and the music was so you can see it like rain falling around only happyer;* up to Miriam's wistful *On Gathering Day there was a big party. Everybody came dressed in beautiful clothes with* flahmen *in the girls' hair.* Flahmen *are flowers but they're good to eat. And if a girl felt her heart sing for a boy they ate a* flahmen *together and started two-ing.*

Then, if all these memories were so happy, why the rigid suppression of them by grownups? Why the pall of unhappiness over everyone? You can't mourn forever for a wrecked ship. Why a hidey hole for disobedient children? Why the misery and frustration when, if they could do half of what I didn't fully understand from Joel and Matt's highly technical papers, they could make Bendo an Eden?

I reached for Esther's paper. I had put it on the bottom on purpose. I dreaded reading it. She had sat with her head buried on her arms on her desk most of the time the others were writing busily. At widely separated intervals she had scribbled a line or two as though she were doing something shameful. She, of all the children, had seemed to find no relief in her remembering.

I smoothed the paper on my lap.

I remember, she had written. *We were thursty. There was water in the creek we were hiding in the grass. We could not drink. They would shoot us. Three days the sun was hot. She screamed for water and ran to the creek. They shot. The water got red.*

Blistered spots marked the tears on the paper.

They found a baby under a bush. The man hit it with the wood part of his gun. He hit it and hit it and hit it. I hit scorpins like that.

They caught us and put us in a pen. They built a fire all around us. Fly "they said," fly and save yourselfs. We flew because it hurt. They shot us.

Monster "they yelled" evil monsters. People can't fly. People can't move things. People are the same. You aren't people, Die die die.

Then blackly, traced and retraced until the paper split:

If anyone finds out we are not of earth we will die.

Keep your feet on the ground.

Bleakly I laid the paper aside. So there was the answer, putting Karen's bits and snippets together with these. The shipwrecked ones finding savages on the desert island. A remnant surviving by learning caution, suppression, and denial. Another generation that pinned the *evil* label on the Home to insure continued immunity for their children, and now, a generation that questioned and wondered—and rebelled.

I turned off the light and slowly got into bed. I lay there staring into the darkness, holding the picture Esther had evoked. Finally I relaxed. "God help her," I sighed. "God help us all."

Another week was nearly over. We cleaned the room up quickly, for once anticipating the fun time instead of dreading it. I smiled to hear the happy racket all around me, and felt my own spirits surge upward in response to the lightheartedness of the children. The difference that one afternoon had made in them! Now they were beginning to feel like children to me. They were beginning to accept me. I swallowed with an effort. How soon would they ask, "How come? How come you knew?" There they sat, all nine of them—nine, because Esther was my first absence in the year—bright-eyed and expectant.

"Can we write again?" Sarah asked. "I can remember lots more."

"No," I said. "Not today." Smiles died and there was a protesting wiggle through the room. "Today we are going to *do*. Joel." I looked at him and tightened my jaws. "Joel, give me the dictionary." He began to get up. *"Without leaving your seat!"*

"But I—!" Joel broke the shocked silence. "I can't!"

"Yes, you can," I prayed. "Yes, you can. Give me the dictionary. Here, on my desk."

Joel turned and stared at the big old dictionary that spilled pages 1965 to 1998 out of its cracked old binding. Then he said, "Miriam?" in a high tight voice. But she shook her head and shrank back in her seat, her eyes big and dark in her white face.

"You can." Miriam's voice was hardly more than a breath. "It's just bigger—"

Joel clutched the edge of his desk and sweat started out on his forehead. There was a stir of movement on the bookshelf. Then, as though shot from a gun, pages 1965 to 1998 whisked to my desk and fell fluttering. Our laughter cut through the blank amazement and we laughed till tears came.

"That's a-doing it, Joel!" Matt shouted. "That's showing them your muscles!"

"Well, it's a beginning." Joel grinned weakly. "You do it, brother, if you think it's so easy."

So Matt sweated and strained and Joel joined with him, but they only managed to scrape the book to the edge of the shelf, where it teetered dangerously.

Then Abie waved his hand timidly. "I can, teacher."

I beamed that my silent one had spoken and at the same time frowned at the loving laughter of the big kids.

"Okay, Abie," I encouraged. "You show them how to do it."

And the dictionary swung off the shelf, and glided unhastily to my desk, where it came silently to rest.

Everyone stared at Abie and he squirmed. "The little ships," he defended. "That's the way they moved them out of the big ship. Just like that."

Joel and Matt turned their eyes to some inner concentration and then exchanged exasperated looks.

"Why, sure," Matt said. "Why, sure." And the dictionary swung back to the shelf.

"Hey!" Timmy protested. "It's my turn!"'

"That poor dictionary," I said. "It's too old for all this bouncing around. Just put the loose pages back on the shelf."

And he did.

Everyone sighed and looked at me expectantly.

"Miriam?" She clasped her hands convulsively. "*You* come to me," I said, feeling a chill creep across my stiff shoulders. "*Lift* to me, Miriam."

Without taking her eyes from me she slipped out of her seat and stood in the aisle. Her skirts swayed a little as her feet lifted from the floor. Slowly at first and then more quickly she came to me, soundlessly, through the air, until in a little flurried rush her arms went around me and she gasped into my shoulder. I put her aside, trembling. I groped for my handkerchief. I said shakily, "Miriam, help the rest. I'll be back in a minute."

And I stumbled into the room next door. Huddled down in the dust and debris of the catchall storeroom it had become, I screamed soundlessly into my muffling hands. And screamed and screamed! Because after all—*after all!*

And then suddenly, with a surge of pure panic, I heard a sound—the sound of footsteps, many footsteps, approaching the schoolhouse. I jumped for the door and wrenched it open just in time to see the outside door open. There was Mr. Diemus and Esther and Esther's father, Mr. Jonso.

In one of those flashes of clarity that engrave your mind in a split second, I saw my whole classroom.

Joel and Matt were chinning themselves on nonexistent bars, their heads brushing the high ceiling as they grunted upward. Abie was swinging in a swing that wasn't there, arcing across the corner of the room, just missing the stovepipe from the old stove, as he chanted, "Up in a swing, up in a swing!" This wasn't the first time *they* had tried their wings! Miriam was kneeling in a circle with the other girls and they were all coaxing their books up to hover unsupported above the door, while Jimmy *vroomm-vroomed* two paper jet planes through intricate maneuvers in and out the rows of desks.

My soul curdled in me as I met Mr. Diemus' eyes. Esther gave a choked cry as she saw what the children were doing, and the girls' stricken faces turned to the intruders. Matt and Joel crumpled to the floor and scrambled to their feet. But Abie, absorbed in his wonderful new accomplishment, swung on, all unconscious of what was happening until Talitha frantically screamed, "Abie!"

Startled, he jerked around and saw the forbidding group at the door. With a disappointed cry, as though a loved toy had been snatched from him, he stopped there in midair, his fists clenched. And then, realizing, he screamed, a terrified panic-stricken cry, and slanted sharply upward, trying to escape, and ran full tilt into the corner of the high old map case, sideswiping it with his head, and, reeling backward, fell!

I tried to catch him. I did! I did! But I caught only one small hand as he plunged down onto the old wood-burning heater beneath him. And the crack of his skull against the ornate edge of the cast-iron lid was loud in the silence.

I straightened the crumpled little body carefully, not daring to touch the quiet little head. Mr. Diemus and I looked at each other as we knelt on opposite sides of the child. His lips opened, but I plunged before he could get started.

"If he dies," I bit my words off viciously, "you killed him!"

His mouth opened again, mainly from astonishment. "I—" he began.

"Barging in on my classroom!" I raged. "Interrupting classwork! Frightening my children! It's all your fault, your fault!" I couldn't bear the burden of guilt alone. I just had to have someone share it with me. But the fire died and I smoothed Abie's hand, trembling.

"Please call a doctor. He might be dying."

"Nearest one is in Tortura Pass," Mr. Diemus said. "Sixty miles by road."

"Cross country?" I asked.

"Two mountain ranges and an alkali plateau."

"Then—then—" Abie's hand was so still in mine.

"There's a doctor at the Tumble A Ranch," Joel said faintly. "He's taking a vacation."

"Go get him." I held Joel with my eyes. *Go as fast as you know how!*"

Joel gulped miserably. "Okay."

"They'll probably have horses to come back on," I said. "Don't be too obvious."

"Okay," and he ran out the door. We heard the thud of his running feet until he was halfway across the schoolyard, then silence. Faintly, seconds later, creek gravel crunched below the hill. I could only guess at what he was doing—that he couldn't lift all the way and was going in jumps whose length was beyond all reasonable measuring.

The children had gone home, quietly, anxiously. And after the doctor arrived we had improvised a stretcher and carried Abie to the Peterses' home. I walked along close beside him watching his pinched little face, my hand touching his chest occasionally just to be sure he was still breathing.

And now—the waiting...

I looked at my watch again. A minute past the last time I looked. Sixty seconds by the hands, but hours and hours by anxiety.

"He'll be all right," I whispered, mostly to comfort myself. "The doctor will know what to do."

Mr. Diemus turned his dark empty eyes to me. "Why did you do it?" he asked. "We almost had it stamped out. We were almost free."

"Free of what?" I took a deep breath. "Why did *you* do it? Why did you deny your children their inheritance?"

"It isn't your concern—"

"Anything that hampers my children is my concern. Anything that turns children into creeping frightened mice is wrong. Maybe I went at the whole deal the wrong way, but you told me to teach them what I had to—and I did."

"Disobedience, rebellion, flouting authority—"

"They obeyed *me*," I retorted. "They accepted *my* authority!" Then I softened. "I can't blame them," I confessed. "They were troubled. They told me it was wrong—that they had been *taught* it was wrong. I argued them into it. But oh, Mr. Diemus! It took so little argument, such a tiny breach in the dam to loose the flood. They never even questioned my knowledge—any more than you have, Mr. Diemus! All this—this *wonder* was beating against their minds, fighting to be set free. The rebellion was there long before I came. I didn't incite them to something new. I'll bet there's not one, except maybe Esther, who hasn't practiced and practiced, furtively and ashamed, the things I permitted—demanded that they do for me.

"It wasn't fair—not fair at all—to hold them back."

"You don't understand." Mr. Diemus' face was stony. "You haven't all the facts—"

"I have enough," I replied. "So you have a frightened memory of an unfortunate period in your history. But what people *doesn't* have such a memory in larger or lesser degree? That you and your children have it more vividly should have helped, not hindered. You should have been able to figure out ways of adjusting. But leave that for the moment. Take the other side of the picture. What possible thing could all this suppression and denial yield you more precious than what you gave up?"

"It's the only way," Mr. Diemus said. "We are unacceptable to Earth but we have to stay. We have to conform—"

"Of course you had to conform," I cried. "Anyone has to when they change societies. At least enough to get them by until others can adjust to them. But to crawl in a hole and pull it in after you! Why, the other Group—"

"Other Group!" Mr. Diemus whitened, his eyes widening. "Other Group? There are others? There are others?" He leaned tensely forward in his chair. "Where? Where?" And his voice broke shrilly on the last word. He closed his eyes and his mouth trembled as he fought for control. The bedroom door opened. Dr. Curtis came out, his shoulders weary.

He looked from Mr. Diemus to me and back. "He should be in a hospital. There's a depressed fracture and I don't know what all else. Probably extensive brain involvement. We need X rays and—and—" He rubbed his hand slowly over his weary young face. "Frankly, I'm not experienced to handle cases like this. We need specialists. If you can scare up some kind of transportation that won't jostle—" He shook his head, seeing the kind of country that lay between us and anyplace, and went back into the bedroom.

"He's dying," Mr. Diemus said. "Whether you're right or we're right, he's dying."

"Wait! Wait!" I said, catching at the tag end of a sudden idea. "Let me think." Urgently I willed myself back through the years to the old dorm room. Intently I listened and listened and remembered.

"Have you a—a—*Sorter* in this Group?" I asked, fumbling for unfamiliar terms.

"No," said Mr. Diemus. "One who could have been, but isn't."

"Or *any* Communicator? Anyone who can send or receive?"

"No," Mr. Diemus said, sweat starting on his forehead. "One who could have been, but—"

"See?" I accused. "See what you've traded for—for what? Who are the could-but-can'ts? Who are they?"

"I am," Mr. Diemus said, the words a bitterness in his mouth. "And my wife."

I stared at him, wondering confusedly. How far did training decide? What could we do with what we had?

"Look," I said quickly. "There *is* another Group. And they—they have all the persuasions and designs. Karen's been trying to find you—to find any of the People. She told me—oh, Lord, it's been years ago, I hope it's still so—every evening they send out calls for the People. If we can catch it—if *you* can catch the call and answer it, they can help. I know they can. Faster than cars, faster than planes, more surely than specialists—"

"But if the doctor finds out—" Mr. Diemus wavered fearfully.

I stood up abruptly. "Good night, Mr. Diemus," I said, turning to the door. "Let me know when Abie dies."

His cold hand shook on my arm.

"Can't you see!" he cried. "I've been taught, too—longer and stronger than the children! We never even dared *think* of rebellion! Help me, help me!"

"Get your wife," I said. "Get her and Abie's mother and father. Bring them down to the grove. We can't do anything here in the house. It's too heavy with denial."

I hurried on ahead and sank on my knees in the evening shadows among the trees.

"I don't know what I'm doing," I cried into the bend of my arm. "I have an idea but I don't know! Help us! Guide us!"

I opened my eyes to the arrival of the four.

"We told him we were going out to pray," said Mr. Diemus.

And we all did.

Then Mr. Diemus began the call I worded for him, silently, but with such intensity that sweat started again on his face. *Karen, Karen. Come to the People, Come to the People.* And the other three sat around him, bolstering his effort, supporting his cry. I watched their tense faces, my own twisting in sympathy, and time was lost as we labored.

Then slowly his breathing calmed and his face relaxed and I felt a stirring as though something brushed past my mind. Mrs. Diemus whispered, "He remembers now. He's found the way."

And as the last spark of sun caught mica highlights on the hilltop above us, Mr. Diemus stretched his hands out slowly and said with infinite relief, "There they are."

I looked around startled, half expecting to see Karen coming through the trees. But Mr. Diemus spoke again.

"Karen, we need help. One of our Group is dying. We have a doctor, an Outsider, but he hasn't the equipment or the know-how to help. What shall we do?"

In the pause that followed I became slowly conscious of a new feeling. I couldn't tell you exactly what it was—a kind of unfolding—an opening—a relaxation. The ugly tight defensiveness that was so characteristic of the grownups of Bendo was slipping away.

"Yes, Valancy," said Mr. Diemus. "He's in a bad way. We can't help because—" His voice faltered and his words died. I felt a resurgence of fear and unhappiness as his communication went beyond words and then ebbed back to speech again.

"We'll expect you then. You know the way."

I could see the pale blur of his face in the dusk under the trees as he turned back to us.

"They're coming," he said, wonderingly. "Karen and Valancy. They're so pleased to find us—" His voice broke. "We're *not* alone—"

And I turned away as the two couples merged in the darkness. I had pushed them somewhere way beyond me.

It was a lonely lonely walk back to the house for me—alone.

They dropped down through the half darkness—four of them. For a fleeting second I wondered at myself that I could stand there matter-of-factly watching four adults slant calmly down out of the sky. Not a hair ruffled, not a stain of travel on them, knowing that only a short time before they had been hundreds of miles away—not even aware that Bendo existed.

But all strangeness was swept away as Karen hugged me delightedly.

"Oh, Melodye," she cried, "it *is* you! He said it was, but I wasn't sure! Oh, it's so *good* to see you again! Who owes who a letter?"

She laughed and turned to the smiling three. "Valancy, the Old One of our Group." Valancy's radiant face proved the Old One didn't mean age. "Bethie, our Sensitive." The slender fair-haired young girl ducked her head shyly. "And my brother Jemmy. Valancy's his wife."

"This is Mr. and Mrs. Diemus," I said. "And Mr. and Mrs. Peters, Abie's parents. It's Abie, you know. My second grade." I was suddenly overwhelmed by how long ago and far away school felt. How far I'd gone from my accustomed pattern!

"What shall we do about the doctor?" I asked. "Will he have to know?"

"Yes," said Valancy. "We can help him but we can't do the actual work. Can we trust him?"

I hesitated, remembering the few scanty glimpses I'd had of him. "I—" I began.

"Pardon me," Karen said. "I wanted to save time. I went in to you. We know now what you know of him. We'll trust Dr. Curtis."

I felt an eerie creeping up my spine. To have my thoughts taken so casually! Even to the doctor's name!

Bethie stirred restlessly and looked at Valancy. "He'll be in convulsions soon. We'd better hurry."

"You're sure you have the knowledge?" Valancy asked.

"Yes," Bethie murmured. "If I can make the doctor see—if he's willing to follow."

"Follow what?"

The heavy tones of the doctor's voice startled us all as he stepped out on the porch.

I stood aghast at the impossibility of the task ahead of us and looked at Karen and Valancy to see how they would make the doctor understand. They said nothing. They just looked at him. There was a breathless pause. The doctor's startled face caught the glint of light from the open door as he turned to Valancy. He rubbed his hand across his face in bewilderment and, after a moment, turned to me.

"Do *you* hear her?"

"No," I admitted. "She isn't talking to me."

"Do you *know* these people?"

"Oh, yes!" I cried, wishing passionately it were true. "Oh, yes!"

"And believe them?"

"Implicitly."

"But she says that Bethie—who's Bethie?" He glanced around.

"She is," Karen said, nodding at Bethie.

"*She* is?" Dr. Curtis looked intently at the shy lovely face. He shook his head wonderingly and turned back to me.

"Anyway this one, Valancy, says Bethie can sense every condition in the child's body and that she will be able to tell all the injuries, their location and extent without X rays! Without equipment!"

"Yes," I said. "If they say so."

"You would be willing to risk a child's life—?"

"Yes. They know. They really do." And I swallowed hard to keep down the fist of doubt that clenched in my chest.

"You believe they can *see* through flesh and bone?"

"Maybe not see," I said, wondering at my own words. "But *know* with a knowledge that is sure and complete." I glanced, startled, at Karen. Her nod was very small but it told me where my words came from.

"Are *you* willing to trust these people?" The doctor turned to Abie's parents.

"They're *our* People," Mr. Peters said with quiet pride. "I'd operate on him myself with a pickax if they said so."

"Of all the screwball deals—!" The doctor's hand rubbed across his face again. "I know I needed this vacation, but this is ridiculous!"

We all listened to the silence of the night and—at least I—to the drumming of anxious pulses until Dr. Curtis sighed heavily.

"Okay, Valancy. I don't believe a word of it. At least I wouldn't if I were in my right mind, but you've got the terminology down pat as if you knew *something*— Well, I'll do it. It's either that or let him die. And God have mercy on our souls!"

I couldn't bear the thought of shutting myself in with my own dark fears, so I walked back toward the school, hugging myself in my inadequate coat against the sudden sharp chill of the night. I wandered down to the grove, praying wordlessly, and on up to the school. But I couldn't go in. I shuddered away from the blank glint of the windows and turned back to the grove. There wasn't any more time or direction or light or anything familiar, only a confused cloud of anxiety and a final icy weariness that drove me back to Abie's house.

I stumbled into the kitchen, my stiff hands fumbling at the doorknob. I huddled in a chair, gratefully leaning over the hot wood stove that flicked the semidarkness of the big homey room with warm red light, trying to coax some feeling back into my fingers.

I drowsed as the warmth began to penetrate, and then the door was flung open and slammed shut. The doctor leaned back against it, his hand still clutching the knob.

"Do you know what they did?" he cried, not so much to me as to himself. "What they made *me* do? Oh, Lord!" He staggered over to the stove, stumbling over my feet. He collapsed by my chair, rocking his head between his hands. "They made me operate on his brain! *Repair* it. Trace circuits and rebuild them. *You can't do that!* It can't be done! Brain cells damaged can't be repaired. No one can restore circuits that are destroyed! It can't be done. But I did it! *I did it!*"

I knelt beside him and tried to comfort him in the circle of my arms. "There, there, there," I soothed.

He clung like a terrified child. "No anesthetics!" he cried. "*She* kept him asleep. And no bleeding when I went through the scalp! *They* stopped it. And the impossible things I did with the few instruments I have with me! And the brain starting to mend right before my eyes! Nothing was right!"

"But nothing was wrong," I murmured. "Abie will be all right, won't he?"

"How do I know?" he shouted suddenly, pushing away from me. "I don't know anything about a thing like this. I put his brain back together and he's still breathing, but how do I know!"

"There, there," I soothed. "It's over now."

"It'll never be over!" With an effort he calmed himself, and we helped each other up from the floor. "You can't forget a thing like this in a lifetime."

"We can give you forgetting," Valancy said softly from the door. "If you *want* to forget. We can send you back to the Tumble A with no memory of tonight except a pleasant visit to Bendo."

"You can?" He turned speculative eyes toward her. "You can," he amended his words to a statement.

"Do you want to forget?" Valancy asked.

"Of course not," he snapped. Then, "I'm sorry. It's just that I don't often work miracles in the wilderness. But if I did it once, maybe—"

"Then you understand what you did?" Valancy asked, smiling.

"Well, no, but if I could—if you would— There must be some way—"

"Yes," Valancy said, "but you'd have to have a Sensitive working with you, and Bethie is it as far as Sensitives go right now."

"You mean it's true what I saw—what you told me about the—the Home? You're extraterrestrials?"

"Yes," Valancy sighed. "At least our grandparents were." Then she smiled. "But we're learning where we can fit into this world. Someday—someday we'll be able—" She changed the subject abruptly.

"You realize, of course, Dr. Curtis, that we'd rather you wouldn't discuss Bendo or us with anyone else. We would rather be just people to Outsiders."

He laughed shortly, "Would I be believed if I did?"

"Maybe no, maybe so," Valancy said. "Maybe only enough to start people nosing around. And that would be too much. We have a bad situation here and it will take a long time to erase—" Her voice slipped into silence, and I knew she had dropped into thoughts to brief him on the local problem. How long is a thought? How fast can you think of hell—and heaven? It was that long before the doctor blinked and drew a shaky breath.

"Yes," he said. "A long time."

"If you like," Valancy said, "I can block your ability to talk of us."

"Nothing doing!" the doctor snapped. "I can manage my own censorship, thanks."

Valancy flushed. "I'm sorry. I didn't mean to be condescending."

"You weren't," the doctor said. "I'm just on the prod tonight. It has been *a day*, and that's for sure!"

"Hasn't it, though?" I smiled and then, astonished, rubbed my cheeks because tears had begun to spill down my face. I laughed, embarrassed, and couldn't stop. My laughter turned suddenly to sobs and I was bitterly ashamed to hear myself wailing like a child. I clung to Valancy's strong hands until I suddenly slid into a warm welcome darkness that had no thinking or fearing or need for believing in anything outrageous, but only in sleep.

It was a magic year and it fled on impossibly fast wings, the holidays flicking past like telephone poles by a railroad. Christmas was especially magical because my angels actually flew and the glory actually shone round about because their robes had hems woven of sunlight—I watched the girls weave them. And Rudolph the red-nosed reindeer, complete with cardboard antlers that wouldn't stay straight, really took off and circled the room. And as our Mary and Joseph leaned raptly over the manger, their faces solemn and intent on the miracle, I felt suddenly that they were really seeing, really kneeling beside the manger in Bethlehem.

Anyway the months fled, and the blossoming of Bendo was beautiful to see. There was laughter and frolicking and even the houses grew subtly into color. Green things crept out where only rocks had been before, and a tiny tentative stream of water had begun to flow down the creek again. They explained to me that they had to take it slow because people might wonder if the creek filled overnight! Even the rough steps up to the houses were being overgrown because they were so seldom used, and I was becoming accustomed to seeing my pupils coming to school like a bevy of bright birds, playing tag in the treetops. I was surprised at myself for adjusting so easily to all the incredible things done around me by the People, and I was pleased that they accepted me so completely. But

I always felt a pang when the children escorted me home—with me, they had to walk

But all things have to end, and one May afternoon I sat staring into my top desk drawer, the last to be cleaned out, wondering what to do with the accumulation of useless things in it. But I wasn't really seeing the contents of the drawer, I was concentrating on the great weary emptiness that pressed my shoulders down and weighted my mind. "It's not fair," I muttered aloud and illogically, "to show me heaven and then snatch it away."

"That's about what happened to Moses, too, you know."

My surprised start spilled an assortment of paper clips and thumb-tacks from the battered box I had just picked up.

"Well, forevermore!" I said, righting the box. "Dr. Curtis! What are you doing here?"

"Returning to the scene of my crime," he smiled, coming through the open door. "Can't keep my mind off Abie. Can't believe he recovered from all that—shall we call it repair work? I have to check him every time I'm anywhere near this part of the country—and I still can't believe it."

"But he has."

"He has for sure! I had to fish him down from a treetop to look him over—" The doctor shuddered dramatically and laughed. "To see him hurtling down from the top of that tree curdled my blood! But there's hardly even a visible scar left."

"I know," I said, jabbing my finger as I started to gather up the tacks. "I looked last night. I'm leaving tomorrow, you know." I kept my eyes resolutely down to the job at hand. "I have this last straightening up to do."

"It's hard, isn't it?" he said, and we both knew he wasn't talking about straightening up.

"Yes," I said soberly. "Awfully hard. Earth gets heavier every day."

"I find it so lately, too. But at least you have the satisfaction of knowing that you—"

I moved uncomfortably and laughed.

"Well, they do say: those as can, do; those as can't, teach."

"Umm," the doctor said noncommittally, but I could feel his eyes on my averted face and I swiveled away from him, groping for a better box to put the clips in.

"Going to summer school?" His voice came from near the windows.

"No," I sniffed cautiously. "No, I swore when I got my Master's that I was through with education—at least the kind that's come-every-day-and-learn-something."

"Hmm!" There was amusement in the doctor's voice. "Too bad. I'm going to school this summer. Thought you might like to go there, too."

"Where?" I asked bewildered, finally looking at him.

"Cougar Canyon summer school," he smiled. "Most exclusive."

"Cougar Canyon! Why, that's where Karen—"

"Exactly," he said. "That's where the other Group is established. I just came from there. Karen and Valancy want us both to come. Do you object to being an experiment?"

"Why, no—" I cried, and then, cautiously, "What kind of an experiment?" Visions of brains being carved up swam through my mind.

The doctor laughed. "Nothing as gruesome as you're imagining, probably." Then he sobered and sat on the edge of my desk. "I've been to Cougar Canyon a couple of times, trying to figure out some way to get Bethie to help me when I come up against a case that's a puzzler. Valancy and Karen want to try a period of training with Outsiders—" he grimaced wryly, "—that's us—to see how much of what *they* are can be transmitted by training. You know Bethie is half Outsider. Only her mother was of the People."

He was watching me intently.

"Yes," I said absently, my mind whirling. "Karen told me."

"Well, do you want to try it? Do you want to go?"

"Do I want to go!" I cried, scrambling the clips into a rubber-band box. "How soon do we leave? Half an hour? Ten minutes? Did you leave the motor running?"

"Woops, woops!" The doctor took me by both arms and looked soberly into my eyes.

"We can't set our hopes too high," he said quietly. "It may be that for such knowledge we aren't teachable—"

I looked soberly back at him, my heart crying in fear that it might be so.

"Look," I said slowly. "If you had a hunger, a great big gnawing-inside hunger and no money and you saw a bakery shop window, which would you do? Turn your back on it? Or would you press your nose as close as you could against the glass and let at least your eyes feast? I know what *I'd* do." I reached for my sweater.

"And, you know, you never can tell. The shop door might open a crack, maybe—someday—"

Interlude: Lea 4

"I'd like to talk with her a minute," Lea said to Karen as the chattering group broke up. "May I?"

"Why, sure," Karen said. "Melodye, have you a minute?"

"Oh, Karen!" Melodye threaded the rows back to Lea's corner. "That was wonderful! It was just like living it for the first time again, only underneath I knew what was coming next. But even so my blood ran cold when Abie——" She shuddered. "Bro——ther! Was that ever a day!"

"Melodye," Karen said, "this is Lea. She wants to talk with you."

"Hi, fellow alien," Melodye smiled. "I've been wanting to meet you."

"Do you believe——" Lea hesitated. "Was that really true?"

"Of course it was," Melodye said. "I can show you my scars——mental, that is——from trying to learn to lift." Then she laughed. "Don't feel funny about doubting it. I still have my 3 A.M.-ses when I can't believe it myself." She sobered. "But it is true. The People *are* the People."

"And even if you're not of the People," Lea faltered, "could they—— could they help anyway? I don't mean anything broken. I mean, nothing visible——" She was suddenly covered with a sense of shame and betrayal as though caught hanging out a black line of sins in the morning sun. She turned her face away.

"They can help." Melodye touched Lea's shoulder gently. "And, Lea, they never judge. They mend where mending is needed and leave the judgment to God." And she was gone.

"Maybe," Lea mourned, "if I *had* sinned some enormous sins I could have something big to forgive myself so I could start over, but all these niggling nibbling little nothingnesses——"

"All these niggling little, nibbling little nothingnesses that compounded themselves into such a great despair," Karen said. "And what is despair but a separation from the Presence——"

"Then the People do believe that there is——?"

"Our Home may be gone," Karen said firmly, "and all of us exiles if you want to look at it that way, but there's no galaxy wide enough to separate us from the Presence."

Later that night Lea sat up in bed. "Karen?"

"Yes?" Karen's voice came instantly from the darkness though Lea knew she was down the hall.

"Are you still shielding me from—from whatever it was?"

"No," Karen said. "I released you this morning."

"That's what I thought." Lea drew a quavering breath. "Right now it's all gone away, as though it had never been, but I'm still nowhere and going nowhere. Just waiting. And if I wait long enough it'll come back again, that I know. Karen, what can I do to—not to be where I am now when it comes back?"

"You're beginning to work at it now," Karen said. "And if it does come back we're here to help. It will never be so impenetrable again."

"How could it be?" Lea murmured. "How could I have gone through anything as black as that and survived—or ever do it again?"

Lea lay back with a sigh. Then, sleepily, "Karen?"

"Yes?"

"Who was that down at the pool?"

"Don't you know?" Karen's voice smiled. "Have you looked around at all?"

"What good would it do? I can't remember what he looked like. It's been so long since I've noticed anything—and then the blackness—But he brought me back to the house, didn't he? You must have seen him—"

"Must I?" Karen teased. "Maybe we could arrange to have him carry you again. 'Arms remember when eyes forget.' "

"There's something wrong with that quotation," Lea said drowsily. "But I'll skip it for now."

It seemed to Lea that she had just slipped under the edge of sleep when she heard Karen.

"What!" Karen cried. "Right now? Not tomorrow?"

"Karen!" Lea called, groping in the darkness for the light switch. "What's the matter?"

"The matter!" Karen laughed and shot through the window, turning and tumbling ecstatically in midair.

"Nothing's the matter! Oh, Lea, come and be joyful!" She grabbed Lea's hands and pulled her up from the bed.

"No! Karen! No!" Lea cried as her bare feet curled themselves away from the empty air that seemed to lick at them. "Put me down!" Terror sharpened her voice.

"Oh, I'm sorry!" Karen said, releasing her to plump gently down on her bed. She herself flashed again across the room and back in a froth of nightgowny ruffles. "Oh, be joyful! Be joyful unto the Lord!"

"What *is* it!" Lea cried, suddenly afraid, afraid of anything that might change things as they were. The vast emptiness began to cave away inside her. The blackness was a cloud the size of a man's hand on the far horizon.

"It's Valancy!" Karen cried, shooting away back through the window. "I have to get dressed! The baby's here!"

"The baby!" Lea was bewildered. "What baby?"

"Is there any other baby?" Karen's voice floated back, muffled. "Valancy and Jemmy's. It's here! I'm an aunt! Oh, dear, now I'm well on the way to becoming an ancestress. I thought they would never get around to it. It's a girl! At least Jemmy says he thinks it's a girl. He's so excited that it could be both, or even triplets! Well, as soon as Valancy gets back—" She walked back through the door, brushing her hair briskly.

"What hospital did she go to?" Lea asked. "Isn't this pretty isolated—"

"Hospital? Oh, none, of course. She's at home."

"But you said when she gets back—"

"Yes. It's a far solemn journey to bring back a new life from the Presence. It takes a while."

"But I didn't even notice!" Lea cried. "Valancy was there tonight and I don't remember—"

"But then you haven't been noticing much of anything for a long time," Karen said gently.

"But anything as obvious as that!" Lea protested.

"Fact remains, the baby's here and it's Valancy's—with a little cooperation from Jemmy—and she *didn't* carry it around in a knitting bag!"

"Okay, Jemmy, I'm coming. Hold the fort!" She flashed, feet free of the floor, out the door, her hairbrush hovering forlornly, forgotten, in midair, until it finally drifted slowly out the door to the hall.

Lea huddled on the tumbled bed. A baby. A new life. "I had forgotten," she thought. "Birth and death have still been going on. The world is still out there, wagging along as usual. I thought it had stopped. It *had* stopped for me. I lost winter. I lost spring. It must be summer now. Just think! Just think! There are people who found all my black days full of joyful anticipation—bright jewels slipping off the thread of time! And I've been going around and around like a donkey dragging a weight around a stake, winding myself tighter and tighter—" She straightened suddenly on the bed, spread-eagling out of her tight huddle. The darkness poured like a heavy flood in through the door—down from the ceiling—up from the floor.

"Karen!" she cried, feeling herself caught up to be crammed back into the boundaryless nothingness of herself again.

"No!" she gritted through her teeth. "Not this time!" She turned face down on the bed, clutching the pillow tightly with both hands. "Give me strength! Give me strength!" With an effort, almost physical, she turned her thoughts. "The baby—a new baby—crying. Do babies of the People cry? They must, having to leave the Presence for Earth. The baby—tiny fists clenched tightly, eyes clenched tightly shut. All powder and flannel and tiny curling feet. I can hold her. Tomorrow I can hold her. And feel the continuity of life—the eternal coming of God into the world. Rockabye baby. Sleep, baby, sleep. Thy father watches His sheep. A new baby—tiny red fingers to curl around my finger. A baby—Valancy's baby—"

And by the time dawn arrived Lea was sleeping, her face smoothing out from the agony of the black night. There was almost triumph upon it.

That evening Karen and Lea walked through the gathering twilight to the schoolhouse. The softly crisp evening air was so clear and quiet that voices and far laughter echoed around them.

"Wait, Lea." Karen was waving to someone. "Here comes Santhy. She's just learning to lift. Bet her mother doesn't know she's still out." She laughed softly.

Lea watched with wonder as the tiny five-year-old approached them in short abrupt little arcs, her brief skirts flattening and flaring as she lifted and landed.

"She's using more energy lifting than if she walked," Karen said softly, "but she's so proud of herself. Let's wait for her. She wants us."

By now Lea could see the grave intent look on Santhy's face and could almost hear the little grunts as she took off until she finally landed, staggering, against Lea. Lea steadied her, dropping down beside her, holding her gently in the circle of her arms.

"You're Lea," Santhy said, smiling shyly.

"Yes," Lea said. "How did you know?"

"Oh, we all know you. You're our new God-bless every night."

"Oh." Lea was taken aback.

"I brought you something," Santhy said, her hand clenched in a bulging little pocket. "I saved it from our 'joicing party for the new baby. *I* don't care if you're an Outsider. I saw you wading in the creek and you're pretty." She pulled her hand out of her pocket and deposited on Lea's palm a softly glowing bluey-green object. "It's a *koomatka*," she whispered. "Don't let Mama see it. I was s'posed to eat it but I had two—" She spread her arms and lifted up right past Lea's nose.

"A *koomatka*," Lea said, getting up and holding out her hand wonderingly, the glow from it deepening in the dusk.

"Yes," Karen said. "She really shouldn't have. It's forbidden to show to Outsiders, you know."

"Must I give it back?" Lea asked wistfully. "Can't I keep it even if I don't belong?"

Karen looked at her soberly for a moment, then she smiled. "You can keep it, or eat it, though you probably won't like it. It tastes like music sounds, you know. But you may have it—even if you don't belong."

Lea's hand closed softly around the *koomatka* as the two turned toward the schoolhouse. "Speaking of belonging—" Karen said, "it's Dita's turn tonight. She knows plenty about belonging and not belonging."

"I wondered about tonight. I mean not waiting for Valancy—" Lea shielded her eyes against the bright open door as they mounted the steps.

"Oh, she wouldn't miss it," Karen said. "She'll listen in from home."

They were the last to arrive. Invocation over, Dita was already in the chair behind the desk, her hands folded primly in front of her. "Valancy," she said, "we're all here now. Are you ready?"

"Oh, yes." Lea could feel Valancy's answer. "Our Baby's asleep now." The group laughed at the capitals in Valancy's voice.

"You didn't *invent* babies," Dita laughed.

"Hah!" Jemmy's voice answered triumphantly. "*This* one we did!"

Lea looked around the laughing group. "They're happy!" she thought. "In a world like this they're happy anyway! What do they have as a touchstone?" She studied the group as Dita began, and under the first flow of Dita's words she thought, "Maybe this is the answer. Maybe this is the touchstone. When any one of them cries out the others hear— and *listen*. Not just with their ears but with their hearts. No matter who cries out—*someone* listens—"

"My theme," Dita said soberly, "is very brief—but oh, the heartbreak in it. It's 'And your children shall wander in the wilderness.' " Her clasped hands tightened on each other. "I was wandering that day..."

Wilderness

"Well, how do you expect Bruce to concentrate on spelling when he's so worried about his daddy?" I thumbed through my second graders' art papers, hoping to find one lift out of the prosaic.

" 'Worried about his daddy'?" Mrs. Kanz looked up from her spelling tests. "What makes you think he's worried about him?"

"Why, he's practically sick for fear he won't come home this time." I turned the paper upside down and looked again. "I thought you knew everything about everyone," I teased. "You've briefed me real good in these last three weeks. I feel like a resident instead of a newcomer." I sighed and righted the paper. It was still a tree with six apples on it.

"But I certainly didn't know Stell and Mark were having trouble." Mrs. Kanz was chagrined.

"They had an awful fight the night before he left," I said. "Nearly scared the waddin' out of Bruce."

"How do you know?" Mrs. Kanz's eyes were suddenly sharp. "You haven't met Stell yet and Bruce hasn't said a word all week except yes and no."

I let my breath out slowly. "Oh, no!" I thought. "Not already! Not already!"

"Oh, a little bird told me," I said lightly, busying myself with my papers to hide the small tremble of my hands.

"Little bird, toosh! You probably heard it from Marie, though how she—"

"Could be," I said, "could be." I bundled up my papers hurriedly. "Oops! Recess is almost over. Gotta get downstairs before the thundering herd arrives."

The sound of the old worn steps was hollow under my hurried feet, but not nearly so hollow as the feeling in my stomach.

Only three weeks and I had almost betrayed myself already. Why couldn't I *remember!* Besides, the child wasn't even in my room. I had no business knowing anything about him. Just because he had leaned so quietly, so long, over his literature book last Monday—and I had only looked a little...

At the foot of the stairs I was engulfed waist-deep in children sweeping in from the playground. Gratefully I let myself be swept with them into the classroom.

That afternoon I leaned with my back against the window sill and looked over my quiet class. Well, quiet insofar as moving around the room was concerned, but each child humming audibly or inaudibly with the untiring dynamos of the young—the mostly inarticulate thought patterns of happy children. All but Lucine, my twelve-year-old first grader, who hummed briefly to a stimulus and then clicked off, hummed again and clicked off. There was a short somewhere, and her flat empty eyes showed it.

I sighed and turned my back on the room, wandering my eyes up the steepness of Black Mesa as it towered above the school, trying to lose myself from apprehension, trying to forget why I had run away—nearly five hundred miles—trying to forget those things that tugged at my sanity, things that could tear me loose from reality and set me adrift... Adrift? Oh, glory! Set me free! Set me free! I hooked my pointer fingers through the old wire grating that protected the bottom of the window and tugged sharply. Old nails grated and old wire gave, and I sneezed through the dry acid bite of ancient dust.

I sat down at my desk and rummaged for a Kleenex and sneezed again, trying to ignore, but knowing too well, the heavy nudge and tug inside me. That tiny near betrayal had cracked my tight protective shell. All that I had packed away so resolutely was shouldering and elbowing its way...

I swept my children out of spelling into numbers so fast that Lucine poised precariously on the edge of tears until she clicked on again and murkily perceived where we had gone.

"Now, look, Petie," I said, trying again to find a way through his stubborn block against number words, "this is the picture of two, but this is the name of two..."

After the school buses were gone I scrambled and slid down the steep slope of the hill below the gaunt old schoolhouse and walked the railroad ties back toward the hotel–boarding house where I stayed. Eyes intent on my feet but brightly conscious of the rails on either side, I counted my way through the clot of old buildings that was town, and out the other side. If I could keep something on my mind I could keep ghosts out of my thoughts.

I stopped briefly at the hotel to leave my things and then pursued the single rail line on down the little valley, over the shaky old trestle that was never used any more, and left it at the tailings dump and started up the hill, enjoying fiercely the necessary lunge and pull, tug and climb, that stretched my muscles, quickened my heartbeat, and pumped my breath up hard against the top of my throat.

Panting, I grabbed a manzanita bush and pulled myself up the last steep slope. I perched myself, knees to chest, on the crumbly outcropping of shale at the base of the huge brick chimney, arms embracing my legs, my cheek pressed to my knees. I sat with closed eyes, letting the late-afternoon sun soak into me. "If only this could be all," I thought wistfully. "If only there were nothing but sitting in the sun, soaking up warmth. Just being, without questions." And for a long blissful time I let that be all.

But I couldn't put it off any longer. I felt the first slow trickling through the crack in my armor. I counted trees, I counted telephone poles, I said timestables until I found myself thinking six times nine is ninety-six, and then I gave up and let the floodgates open wide.

"It's always like this," one of me cried to the rest of me. "You promised! You promised and now you're giving in again—after all this time!"

"I could promise not to breathe, too," I retorted.

"But this is insanity—you know it is! Anyone knows it is!"

"Insane or not, it's me!" I screamed silently. "It's me! *It's me!*"

"Stop your arguing," another of me said. "This is too serious for bickering. We've got problems."

I took a dry manzanita twig and cleared a tiny space on the gravelly ground, scratching up an old square nail and a tiny bit of sun-purpled glass as I did so. Shifting the twig to my other hand, I picked up the nail and rubbed the dirt off with my thumb. It was pitted with rust but still strong and heavy. I wondered what it had held together back in those days, and if the hand that last held it was dust now, and if whoever it was had had burdens...

I cast the twig from me with controlled violence and, rocking myself forward, I made a straight mark on the cleared ground with the nail. This was a drearily familiar inventory, and I had taken it so many times before, trying to simplify this complicated problem of mine, that I fell automatically into the same old pattern.

Item one. Was I really insane—or going insane—or on the way to going insane? It must be so. Other people didn't see sounds. Nor taste colors. Nor feel the pulsing of other people's emotions like living things. Nor find the weight of flesh so like a galling straitjacket. Nor more than half believe that the burden was lay-downable short of death.

"But then," I defended, "I'm still functioning in society and I don't drool or foam at the mouth. I don't act very crazy, and as long as I guard my tongue I don't sound crazy."

I pondered the item awhile, then scribbled out the mark. "I guess I'm still sane—so far."

Item two. "Then what's wrong with me? Do I just let my imagination run away with me?" I jabbed holes all around my second heavy mark. No, it was something more, something beyond just imagination, something beyond—what?

I crossed that marking with another to make an X.

"What shall I do about it then? Shall I fight it out like I did before? Shall I deny and deny and deny until—" I felt a cold grue, remembering the blind panic that had finally sent me running until I had ended up at Kruper, and all the laughter went out of me, clear to the bottom of my soul.

I crosshatched the two marks out of existence and hid my eyes against my knees again and waited for the sick up-gushing of apprehension to foam into despair over my head. Always it came to this. Did I *want* to do anything about it? Should I stop it all with an act of will? *Could* I stop it all by an act of will? Did I *want* to stop it?

I scrambled to my feet and scurried around the huge stack, looking for the entrance. My feet cried, No *no!* on the sliding gravel. Every panting breath cried, No *no!* as I slipped and slithered around the steep hill. I ducked into the shadowy interior of the huge chimney and pressed myself against the blackened crumbling bricks, every tense muscle shouting, No *no!* And in the wind-shuddery silence I cried, "No!" and heard it echo up through the blackness above me. I could almost see the word shoot up through the pale elliptical disk of the sky at the top of the stack.

"Because I could!" I shrieked defiantly inside me. "If I weren't afraid I could follow that word right on up and erupt into the sky like a Roman candle and never, never, never feel the weight of the world again!"

But the heavy drag of reason grabbed my knees and elbows and rubbed my nose forcibly into things-as-they-really-are, and I sobbed impotently against the roughness of the curving wall. The sting of salty wetness across my cheek shocked me out of rebellion.

Crying? Wailing against a dirty old smelter wall because of a dream? Fine goings on for a responsible pedagogue!

I scrubbed at my cheeks with a Kleenex and smiled at the grime that came off. I'd best get back to the hotel and get my face washed before eating the inevitable garlicky supper I'd smelled on my way out.

I stumbled out into the red flood of sunset and down the thread of a path I had ignored when coming up. I hurried down into the duskiness of the cottonwood thicket along the creek at the bottom of the hill. Here, where no eyes could see, no tongues could clack at such undignified behavior, I broke into a run, a blind headlong run, pretending that I could run away—just away! Maybe with salty enough tears and fast enough running I could buy a dreamless night.

I rounded the turn where the pinky-gray granite boulder indented the path—and reeled under a sudden blow. I had run full tilt into someone. Quicker than I could focus my eyes, I was grabbed and set on my feet. Before I could see past a blur of tears from my smarting nose, I was alone in the dusk.

I mopped my nose tenderly. "Well," I said aloud, "that's one way to knock the nonsense out of me." Then immediately began to wonder if it was a sign of unbalance to talk aloud to yourself.

I looked back uphill when I came out of the shadow of the trees. The smelter stack was dark against the sky, massive above the remnants of the works. It was beautiful in a stark way, and I paused to enjoy it briefly. Suddenly there was another darkness up there. Someone had rounded the stack and stood silhouetted against the lighter horizon.

I wondered if the sound of my sorrow was still echoing up the stack, and then I turned shamefaced away. Whoever it was up there had more sense than to listen for the sounds of old sorrows.

That night, in spite of my outburst of the afternoon, I barely slipped under the thin skin of sleep and, for endless ages, clutched hopelessly for something to pull me down into complete forgetfulness. Then despairingly I felt the familiar tug and pull and, hopelessly, eagerly, slipped headlong into my dream that I had managed to suppress for so long.

There are no words—there are no words anywhere for my dream. Only the welling of delight, the stretching of my soul, the boundless freedom, the warm belongingness. And I held the dearness close to me—oh, so close to me!—knowing that awakening must come...

And it did, smashing me down, forcing me into flesh, binding me leadenly to the earth, squeezing out the delight, cramping my soul back into finiteness, snapping bars across my sky and stranding me in the thin watery glow of morning so alone again that the effort of opening my eyes was almost too much to be borne.

Lying rigidly under the press of the covers, I gathered up all the tatters of my dream and packed them tightly into a hard little knot way back of my consciousness. "Stay there. Stay there," I pleaded. "Oh, stay there!"

Forcing myself to breakfast, I came warily into the dining room at the hotel. As the only female-type woman guest in the hotel, I was somewhat disconcerted to walk into the place when it was full and to have every hand pause and every jaw still itself until I found my way to the only empty seat, and then to hear the concerted return to eating, as though on cue. But I was later this morning, and the place was nearly empty.

"How was the old stack?" Half of Marie's mouth grinned as she pushed a plate of hotcakes under my nose and let go of it six inches above the table. I controlled my wince as it crashed to the table, but I couldn't completely ignore the sooty thumbprint etched in the grease on the rim. Marie took the stiffly filthy rag she had hanging as usual from her apron pocket, and smeared the print around until I at least couldn't see the whorls and ridges any more.

"It was interesting," I said, not bothering to wonder how she knew I'd been there. "Kruper must have been quite a town when the smelter was going full blast."

"Long's I've been here it's been dyin'," Marie said. "Been here thirty-five years next February and *I* ain't never been up to the stack. I ain't lost nothing up there!"

She laughed soundlessly but gustily. I held my breath until the garlic went by. "But I hear there's some girls that's gone up there and lost—"

"Marie!" Old Charlie bellowed from across the table. "Cut out the chatter and bring me some grub. If teacher wants to climb *up* that da-dang stack leave her be. Maybe she likes it!"

"Crazy way to waste time," Marie muttered, teetering out to the kitchen, balancing her gross body on impossibly spindly legs.

"Don't mind her," Old Charlie bellowed. "Only thing she thinks is fun is beer. Why, lots of people like to go look at worthless stuff like that. Take—well—take Lowmanigh here. He was up there only yesterday—"

"Yesterday?" My lifted brows underlined my question as I looked across the table. It was one of the fellows I hadn't noticed before. His name had probably been thrown at me with the rest of them by Old Charlie on my first night there, but I had lost all the names except Old Charlie and Severeid Swanson, which was the name attached to a wavery fragile-looking Mexicano, with no English at all, who seemed to subsist mostly on garlic and *vino* and who always blinked four times when I smiled at him.

"Yes." Lowmanigh looked across the table at me, no smile softening his single word. My heart caught as I saw across his cheek the familiar pale quietness of chill-of-soul. I knew the look well. It had been on my own face that morning before I had made my truce with the day.

He must have read something in my eyes, because his face shuttered itself quickly into a noncommittal expression and, with a visible effort, he added, "I watched the sunset from there."

"Oh?" My hand went thoughtfully to my nose.

"Sunsets!" Marie was back with the semiliquid she called coffee. "More crazy stuff. Why waste good time?"

"What do you spend your time on?" Lowmanigh's voice was very soft.

Marie's mind leaped like a startled bird. "Waiting to die!" it cried.

"Beer," she said aloud, half of her face smiling. "Four beers equal one sunset." She dropped the coffeepot on the table and went back to the kitchen, leaving a clean, sharp, almost visible pain behind her as she went.

"You two oughta get together," Old Charlie boomed. "Liking the same things like you do. Low here knows more junk heaps and rubbish dumps than anybody else in the county. He collects ghost towns."

"I like ghost towns," I said to Charlie, trying to fill a vast conversational vacancy. "I have quite a collection of them myself."

"See, Low!" he boomed. "Here's your chance to squire a pretty schoolmarm around. Together you two oughta be able to collect up a storm!" He choked on his pleasantry and his last gulp of coffee and left the room, whooping loudly into a blue bandanna.

We were all alone in the big dining room. The early-morning sun skidded across the polished hardwood floor, stumbled against the battered kitchen chairs, careened into the huge ornate mirror above the buffet, and sprayed brightly from it over the cracked oilcloth covering on the enormous oak table.

The silence grew and grew until I put my fork down, afraid to click it against my plate any more. I sat for half a minute, suspended in astonishment, feeling the deep throbbing of a pulse that slowly welled up into almost audibility, questioning, "Together? Together? Together?" The beat broke on the sharp edge of a wave of desolation, and I stumbled blindly out of the room.

"No!" I breathed as I leaned against the newel post at the bottom of the stairs. "Not involuntarily! Not so early in the day!"

With an effort I pulled myself together. "Cut out this cotton-pickin' nonsense!" I told myself. "You're enough to drive anybody crazy!"

Resolutely I started up the steps, only to pause, foot suspended, halfway up. "That wasn't my desolation," I cried silently. "It was his!"

"How odd," I thought when I wakened at two o'clock in the morning, remembering the desolation.

"How odd!" I thought when I wakened at three, remembering the pulsing "Together?"

"How very odd," I thought when I wakened at seven and slid heavy-eyed out of bed—having forgotten completely what Lowmanigh looked like, but holding wonderingly in my consciousness a better-than-three-dimensional memory of him.

School kept me busy all the next week, busy enough that the old familiar ache was buried almost deep enough to be forgotten. The smoothness of the week was unruffled until Friday, when the week's restlessness erupted on the playground twice. The first time I had to go out and peel Esperanza off Joseph and pry her fingers out of his hair so he could get his snub nose up out of the gravel. Esperanza had none of her Uncle Severeid's fragility and waveriness as she defiantly slapped the dust from her heavy dark braid.

"He calls me Mexican!" she cried. "So what? I'm Mexican. I'm proud to be Mexican. I hit him some more if he calls me Mexican like a bad word again. I'm proud to be—"

"Of course you're proud," I said, helping her dust herself off. "God made us all. What do different names matter?"

"Joseph!" I startled him by swinging around to him suddenly. "Are you a girl?"

"Huh?" He blinked blankly with dusty lashes, then, indignantly: " 'Course not! I'm a boy!"

"Joseph's a boy! Joseph's a boy!" I taunted. Then I laughed. "See how silly that sounds? We are what we are. How silly to tease about something like that. Both of you go wash the dirt off." I spatted both of them off toward the schoolhouse and sighed as I watched them go.

The second time the calm was interrupted when the ancient malicious chanting sound of teasing pulled me out on the playground again.

"Lu-cine is crazy! Lu-cine is crazy! Lu-cine is crazy!"

The dancing taunting group circled twelve-year-old Lucine where she stood backed against the one drooping tree that still survived on our playground. Her eyes were flat and shallow above her gaping mouth, but smoky flames were beginning to flicker in the shallowness and her muscles were tightening.

"Lucine!" I cried, fear winging my feet. "Lucine!"

I sent me ahead of myself and caught at the ponderous murderous massiveness of her mind. Barely I slowed her until I could get to her.

"Stop it!" I shrieked at the children. "Get away, quick!"

My voice pierced through the mob-mind, and the group dissolved into frightened individuals. I caught both of Lucine's hands and for a tense moment had them secure. Then she bellowed, a peculiarly animallike bellow, and with one flip of her arm sent me flying.

In a wild flurry I was swept up almost bodily, it seemed, into the irrational delirium of her anger and bewilderment. I was lost in the mazes of unreasoning thoughts and frightening dead ends, and to this day I can't remember what happened physically.

When the red tide ebbed and the bleak gray click-off period came, I was hunched against the old tree with Lucine's head on my lap, her mouth lax and wet against my hand, her flooding quiet tears staining my skirt, the length of her body very young and very tired.

Her lips moved.

"Ain't crazy."

"No," I said, smoothing her ruffled hair, wondering at the angry oozing scratch on the back of my hand. "No, Lucine. I know."

"He does, too," Lucine muttered. "He makes it almost straight but it bends again."

"Oh?" I said soothingly, hunching my shoulder to cover its bareness with my torn blouse sleeve. "Who does?"

Her head tensed under my hand, and her withdrawal was as tangible as the throb of a rabbit trying to escape restricting hands. "He said don't tell."

I let the pressure of my hand soothe her and I looked down at her ravaged face. "Me," I thought. "Me with the outside peeled off. I'm crippled inside in my way as surely as she is in hers, only my crippling passes for normal. I wish I could click off sometimes and not dream of living without a limp—sweet impossible dream."

There was a long moist intake of breath, and Lucine sat up. She looked at me with her flat incurious eyes.

"Your face is dirty," she said. "Teachers don't got dirty faces."

"That's right." I got up stiffly, shifting the zipper of my skirt around to the side where it belonged. "I'd better go wash. Here comes Mrs. Kanz."

Across the play field the classes were lined up to go back inside. The usual scuffling horseplay was going on, but no one even bothered to glance our way. If they only knew, I thought, how close some of them had been to death...

"I been bad," Lucine whimpered. "I got in a fight again."

"Lucine, you bad girl!" Mrs. Kanz cried as soon as she got within earshot. "You've been fighting again. You go right in the office and sit there the rest of the day. Shame on you!"

And Lucine blubbered off toward the school building.

Mrs. Kanz looked me over. "Well," she laughed apologetically, "I should have warned you about her. Just leave her alone when she gets in a rage. Don't try to stop her."

"But she was going to *kill* someone!" I cried, tasting again the blood lust, feeling the grate of broken bones.

"She's too slow. The kids always keep out of her way."

"But someday—"

Mrs. Kanz shrugged. "If she gets dangerous she'll have to be put away."

"But why do you let the children tease her?" I protested, feeling a spasmodic gush of anger.

She looked at me sharply. "I don't 'let.' Kids are always cruel to anyone who's different. Haven't you discovered that yet?"

"Yes, I have," I whispered. "Oh, yes, yes!" And huddled into myself against the creeping cold of memory.

"It isn't good but it happens," she said. "You can't make everything right. You have to get calluses sometimes."

I brushed some of the dust off my clothes. "Yes," I sighed. "Calluses come in handy. But I still think something should be done for her."

"Don't say so out loud," Mrs. Kanz warned. "Her mother has almost beat her own brains out trying to find some way to help her. These things happen in the best of families. There's no help for them."

"Then who is—?" I choked on my suppressed words, belatedly remembering Lucine's withdrawal.

"Who is who?" asked Mrs. Kanz over her shoulder as we went back to the schoolhouse.

"Who is going to take care of her all her life?" I asked lamely.

"Well! Talk about borrowing trouble!" Mrs. Kanz laughed. "Just forget about the whole thing. It's all in a day's work. It's a shame your pretty blouse had to get ruined, though."

I was thinking of Lucine while I was taking off my torn blouse at home after school. I squinted tightly sideways, trying to glimpse the point of my shoulder to see if it looked as bruised as it felt, when my door was flung open and slammed shut and Lowmanigh was leaning against it, breathing heavily.

"Well!" I slid quickly into my clean shirt and buttoned it up briskly. "I didn't hear you knock. Would you like to go out and try it over again?"

"Did Lucine get hurt?" He pushed his hair back from his damp forehead. "Was it a bad spell? I thought I had it controlled—"

"If you want to talk about Lucine," I said out of my surprise, "I'll be out on the porch in a minute. Do you mind waiting out there? My ears are still burning from Marie's lecture to me on 'proper decorum for a female in this here hotel.' "

"Oh." He looked around blankly. "Oh, sure—sure."

My door was easing shut before I knew he was gone. I tucked my shirttail in and ran my comb through my hair.

"Lowmanigh and Lucine?" I thought blankly. "What gives? Mrs. Kanz *must* be slipping. This she hasn't mentioned." I put the comb down slowly. "Oh. 'He makes it almost straight but it bends again.' But how can that be?"

Low was perched on the railing of the sagging balcony porch that ran around two sides of the second story of the hotel. He didn't turn around as I creaked across the floor toward the dusty dilapidated wicker settle and chair that constituted the porch furniture.

"Who are you?" His voice was choked. "What are you doing here?"

Foreboding ran a thin cold finger across the back of my neck. "We were introduced," I said thinly. "I'm Perdita Verist, the new teacher, remember?"

He swung around abruptly. "Stop talking on top," he said. "I'm listening underneath. You know as well as I do that you can't run away— But how *do* you know? Who are you?"

"You stop it!" I cried. "You have no business listening underneath. Who are *you?*"

We stood there stiffly glaring at each other until with a simultaneous sigh we relaxed and sat down on the shaky wickerware. I clasped my hands loosely on my lap and felt the tight hard knot inside me begin to melt and untie until finally I was turning to Low and holding out my hand, only to meet his as he reached for mine. Some one of me cried, "My kind? My kind?" But another of me pushed the panic button.

"No," I cried, taking my hand back abruptly and standing up. "No!"

"No." Low's voice was soft and gentle. "It's no betrayal."

I swallowed hard and concentrated on watching Severeid Swanson tacking from one side of the road to the other on his way home to the hotel for his garlic, his two *vino* bottles doing very little to maintain his balance.

"Lucine," I said. "Lucine and you."

"Was it bad?" His voice was all on top now, and my bones stopped throbbing to that other wave length.

"About par for the course according to Mrs. Kanz," I said shallowly. "I just tried to stop a buzz saw."

"Was it bad!" His voice spread clear across the band.

"Stay out!" I cried. "Stay out!"

But he was in there with me and I was Lucine and he was I and we held the red-and-black horror in our naked hands and stared it down. Together we ebbed back through the empty grayness until he was Lucine and I was I and I saw me inside Lucine and blushed for her passionately grateful love of me. Embarrassed, I suddenly found a way to shut him out and blinked at the drafty loneliness.

"...and stay out!" I cried.

"That's right!" I jumped at Marie's indignant wheeze. "I seen him go in your room without knocking and Shut the Door!" Her voice was capitalized horror. "You done right chasing him out and giving him What For!"

My inner laughter slid the barrier open a crack to meet his amusement.

"Yes, Marie," I said soberly. "You warned me and I remembered."

"Well, now, good!" Half of Marie's face smirked, gratified. "I knew you was a good girl. And, Low, I'm plumb ashamed of you. I thought you was a cut above these gaw-danged muckers around here and here you go wolfing around in broad daylight!" She tripped off down the creaky hall, her voice floating back up the lovely curved stairway. "In broad daylight! Supper'll be ready in two jerks of a dead lamb's tail. Git washed."

Low and I laughed together and went to "git washed."

I paused over a double handful of cold water I had scooped up from my huge china washbowl, and watched it all trickle back as I glowed warmly with the realization that this was the first time in uncountable ages that I had laughed underneath. I looked long on my wavery reflection in the water. "And not alone," one of me cried, erupting into astonishment, "not alone!"

The next morning I fled twenty-five miles into town and stayed at a hotel that had running water, right in the house, and even a private bath! And reveled in the unaccustomed luxury, soaking Kruper out of me—at least all of it except the glitter bits of loveliness or funniness or niceness that remained on the riffles of my soul after the dust, dirt, inconvenience, and ugliness sluiced away.

I was lying there drowsing Sunday afternoon, postponing until the last possible moment the gathering of myself together for the bus trip back to Kruper. Then suddenly, subtly, between one breath and the next, I was back into full wary armor, my attention twanged taut like a tightened wire, and I sat up stiffly. Someone was here in the hotel. Had Low come into town? Was he here? I got up and finished dressing hastily. I sat quietly on the edge of the bed, conscious of the deep ebb and flow of *something*. Finally I went down to the lobby. I stopped on the last step. Whatever it had been, it was gone. The lobby was just an ordinary lobby. Low was nowhere among the self-consciously ranch-style furnishings. But as I started toward the window to see again the lovely drop of the wooded canyon beyond the patio, he walked in.

"Were you here a minute ago?" I asked him without preliminaries.

"No. Why?"

"I thought—" I broke off. Then gears shifted subtly back to the commonplace and I said, "Well! What are you doing here?"

"Old Charlie said you were in town and that I might as well pick you up and save you the bus trip back." He smiled faintly. "Marie wasn't quite sure I could be trusted after showing my true colors Friday, but she finally told me you were here at this hotel."

"But I didn't know myself where I was going to stay when I left Kruper!"

Low grinned engagingly. "My! You *are* new around here, aren't you? Are you ready to go?"

"I hope you're not in a hurry to get back to Kruper." Low shifted gears deftly as we nosed down to Lynx Hill bridge and then abruptly headed on up Lynx Hill at a perilous angle. "I have a stop to make."

I could feel his wary attention on me in spite of his absorption in the road.

"No," I said, sighing inwardly, visualizing long hours waiting while he leaned over the top fence rail exchanging long silences and succinct remarks with some mining acquaintance. "I'm in no hurry, just so I'm at school by nine in the morning."

"Fine." His voice was amused, and, embarrassed, I tested again the barrier in my mind. It was still intact. "Matter of fact," he went on, "this will be one for your collection, too."

"My collection?" I echoed blankly.

"Your ghost-town collection. I'm driving over to Macron, or where it used to be. It's up in a little box canyon above Bear Flat. It might be that it—" An intricate spot in the road—one small stone and a tiny pine branch—broke his sentence.

"Might be what?" I asked, deliberately holding onto the words he was trying to drop.

"Might be interesting to explore." Aware amusement curved his mouth slightly.

"I'd like to find an unbroken piece of sun glass," I said. "I have one old beautiful purple tumbler. It's in pretty good condition except that it has a piece out of the rim."

"I'll show you my collection sometime," Low said. "You'll drool for sure."

"How come you like ghost towns? What draws you to them? History? Treasure? Morbid curiosity?"

"Treasure—history—morbid curiosity—" He tasted the words slowly and approved each with a nod of his head. "I guess all three. I'm questing."

"Questing?"

"Questing." The tone of his voice ended the conversation. With an effort I detached myself from my completely illogical up-gush of anger at being shut out, and lost myself in the wooded wonder of the hillsides that finally narrowed the road until it was barely wide enough for the car to scrape through.

Finally Low spun the wheel and, fanning sand out from our tires, came to a stop under a huge black-walnut tree.

"Got your walking shoes on? This far and no farther for wheels."

Half an hour later we topped out on a small plateau above the rocky pass where our feet had slid and slithered on boulders grooved by high-wheeled ore wagons of half a century ago. The town had spread itself in its busiest days, up the slopes of the hills and along the dry creeks that spread fingerlike up from the small plateau. Concrete steps led abortively up to crumbled foundations, and sagging gates stood fenceless before shrub-shattered concrete walks.

There were a few buildings that were nearly intact, just stubbornly resisting dissolution. I had wandered up one faint street and down another before I realized that Low wasn't wandering with me. Knowing the solitary ways of ghost-town devotees, I made no effort to locate him, but only wondered idly what he was questing for—carefully refraining from wondering again who he was and why he and I spoke together underneath as we did. But even unspoken, the wonder was burning deep under my superficial scratching among the junk heaps of this vanished town.

I found a white button with only three holes in it and the top of a doll's head with one eye still meltingly blue, and scrabbled, bare-handed, with delight when I thought I'd found a whole sun-purpled sugar bowl—only to find it was just a handle and half a curve held in the silt.

I was muttering over a broken fingernail when a sudden soundless cry crushed into me and left me gasping with the unexpected force. I stumbled down the bank and ran clattering down the rock-strewn road. I found Low down by the old town dump, cradling something preciously in the bend of his arm.

He lifted his eyes blindly to me.

"Maybe—!" he cried. "This might be some of it. It was never a part of this town's life. Look! Look at the shaping of it! Look at the flow of lines!" His hands drank in the smooth beauty of the metal fragment. "And if this is part of it, it might not be far from here that—" He broke off abruptly, his thumb stilling on the underside of the object. He turned it over and looked closely. Something died tragically as he looked. " 'General Electric,' " he said tonelessly. " 'Made in the USA.' " The piece of metal dropped from his stricken hands as he sagged to the ground. His fist pounded on the gravelly silt. "Dead end! Dead end! Dead—"

I caught his hands in mine and brushed the gravel off, pressing Kleenex to the ooze of blood below his little finger.

"What have you lost?" I asked softly.

"Myself," he whispered. "I'm lost and I can't find my way back."

He took no notice of our getting up and my leading him to the fragment of a wall that kept a stunted elderberry from falling into the canyon. We sat down and for a while tossed on the ocean of his desolation as I thought dimly, "Too. Lost, too. Both of us." Then I helped him channel into speech, though I don't know whether it was vocal or not.

"I was so little then," he said. "I was only three, I guess. How long can you live on a three-year-old's memories? Mom told me all they knew, but I could remember more. There was a wreck—a head-on collision the other side of Chuckawalla. My people were killed. The car tried to fly just before they hit. I remember Father lifted it up, trying to clear the other car, and Mother grabbed a handful of sun and platted me out of danger, but the crash came and I could only hear Mother's cry 'Don't forget! Go back to the Canyon,' and Father's 'Remember! Remember the Home!' and they were gone, even their bodies, in the fire that followed. Their bodies and every identification. Mom and Dad took me in and raised me like their own, but I've got to go back. I've got to go back to the Canyon. I belong there."

"What Canyon?" I asked.

"What Canyon?" he asked dully. "The Canyon where the People live now—my People. The Canyon where they located after the starship crashed. The starship I've been questing for, praying I might find some little piece of it to point me the way to the Canyon. At least to the part of the state it's in. The Canyon I went to sleep in before I woke at the crash. The Canyon I can't find because I have no memory of the road there.

"But *you* know!" he went on. "You surely must know! You aren't like the others. You're one of us. You must be!"

I shrank down into myself.

"I'm nobody," I said. "I'm not one of anybody. My mom and dad can tell me my grandparents and great-grandparents and great-great-grandparents, and they used to all the time, trying to figure out why they were burdened with such a child, until I got smart enough to get 'normal.'

"You think *you're* lost! At least you know what you're lost from. You could get un-lost. But I can't. I haven't *ever* been un-lost!"

"But you can talk underneath." He blinked before my violence. "You showed me Lucine—"

"Yes," I said recklessly. "And look at this!"

A rock up on the hillside suddenly spurted to life. It plowed down the slope, sending gravel flying, and smashed itself to powder against a boulder at the base.

"And I never tried this before, but look!"

I stepped up onto the crumbling wall and walked away from Low, straight on out over the canyon, feeling Earth fall away beneath my feet, feeling the soft cradling sweep of the wind, the upness and outness and unrestrainedness. I cried out, lifting my arms, reaching ecstatically for the hem of my dream of freedom. One minute, one minute more and I could slide out of myself and never, never, *never*...

And then...

Low caught me just before I speared myself on the gaunt stubby pines below us in the canyon. He lifted me, struggling and protesting, back up through the fragile emptiness of air, back to the stunted elderberry tree.

"But I did! I did!" I sobbed against him. "I didn't just fall. For a while I really *did!*"

"For a while you really did, Dita," he murmured as to a child. "As good as I could do myself. So you do have some of the Persuasions. Where did you get them if you aren't one of us?"

My sobs cut off without an after-echo, though my tears continued. I looked deep into Low's eyes, fighting against the anger that burned at this persistent returning to the wary hurting place inside me. He looked steadily back until my tears stopped and I finally managed a ghost of a smile. "I don't know what a Persuasion is, but I probably got it the same place you got that tilt to your eyebrows."

He reddened and stepped back from me.

"We'd better start back. It's not smart to get night-caught on these back roads."

We started back along the trail.

"Of course you'll fill in the vacancies for me as we go back," I said, barely catching myself as my feet slithered on a slick hump of granite. I felt his immediate protest. "You've got to," I said, pausing to shake the gravel out of one shoe. "You can't expect me to ignore today, especially since I've found someone as crazy as I am."

"You won't believe—" He dodged a huge buckbrush that crowded the narrow road.

"I've had to believe things about myself all these years that I couldn't believe," I said, "and it's easier to believe things about other people."

So we drove through the magic of an early twilight that deepened into a star-brilliant night, and I watched the flick of the stars through the overarching trees along the road and listened to Low's story. He stripped it down to its bare bones, but underneath, the bones burned like fire in the telling.

"We came from some other world," he said, wistful pride at belonging showing in his "we." "The Home was destroyed. We looked for a refuge and found this Earth. Our ships crashed or burned before they could land. But some of us escaped in life slips. My grandparents were with the original Group that gathered at the Canyon. But we were all there, too, because our memories are joined continuously back into the Bright Beginning. That's why I know about my People. Only I can't remember where the Canyon is, because I was asleep the one time we left it, and Mother and Father couldn't tell me in that split second before the crash.

"I've got to find the Canyon again. I can't go on living forever limping." He didn't notice my start at his echoing of that thought of mine when I was with Lucine. "I can't achieve any stature at all until I am with my People.

"I don't even know the name of the Canyon, but I do remember that our ship crashed in the hills and I'm always hoping that someday I'll find some evidence of it in one of these old ghost towns. It was before the turn of the century that we came, and somewhere, somewhere, there must be some evidence of the ship still in existence."

His was a well-grooved story, too, worn into commonplace by repetition as mine had been—lonely aching repetition to himself. I wondered for a moment, in the face of his unhappiness, why I should feel a stirring of pleased comfort, but then I realized that it was because between us there was no need for murmurs of sympathy or trite little social sayings or even explanations. The surface words were the least of our communication.

"You aren't surprised?" He sounded almost disappointed.

"That you are an out-worlder?" I asked. I smiled. "Well, I've never met one before and I find it interesting. I only wish I could have dreamed up a fantasy like that to explain me to me. It's quite a switch on the old 'I *must* be adopted because I'm so different.' But—"

I stiffened as Low's surge of rage caught me offguard.

"Fantasy! I *am* adopted. I remember! I thought you'd know. I thought since you surely must be one of us that you'd be—"

"I'm not one of you!" I flared. "Whatever 'you' are. I'm of Earth—so much so that it's a wonder the dust doesn't puff out of my mouth when I speak—but at least I don't try to kid myself that I'm normal by *any* standard, Earth-type or otherwise."

For a hostile minute we were braced stonily against each other. My teeth ached as the muscles on my jaws knotted. Then Low sighed and, reaching out a finger, he traced the line of my face from brow to chin to brow again.

"Think your way," he said. "You've probably been through enough bad times to make anyone want to forget. Maybe someday you'll remember that you *are* one of us and then—"

"Maybe, maybe, maybe!" I slid through my weary shaken breath. "But I can't any more. It's too much for one day." I slammed all the doors I could reach and shoved my everyday self up to the front. As we started off I reopened one door far enough to ask, "What's this between you and Lucine? Are you a friend of the family or something that you're working with her?"

"I know the family casually," Low said. "They don't know about Lucine and me. She caught my imagination once last year when I was passing the school. The kids were pestering her. I never felt such heart-broken bewilderment in all my life. Poor little Earth kid. She's a three-year-old in a twelve-year-old body—"

"Four-year-old," I murmured. "Or almost five. She's learning a little."

"Four or five," Low said. "It must be awful to be trapped in a body—"

"Yes," I sighed. "To be shut in the prison of yourself."

Tangibly I felt again the warm running of his finger around my face, softly, comfortingly, though he made no move toward me. I turned away from him in the dusk to hide the sudden tears that came.

It was late when we got home. There were still lights in the bars and a house or two when we pulled into Kruper, but the hotel was dark, and in the pause after the car stopped I could hear the faint creaking of the sagging front gate as it swung in the wind. We got out of the car quietly, whispering under the spell of the silence, and tiptoed up to the gate. As usual the scraggly rosebush that drooped from the fence snagged my hair as I went through, and as Low helped free me we got started giggling. I suppose neither of us had felt young and foolish for so long, and we had both unburdened ourselves of bitter tensions, and found tacit approval of us as the world refused to accept us and as we most wanted to be; and, each having at least glimpsed a kindred soul, well, we suddenly bubbled over. We stood beneath the upstairs porch and tried to muffle our giggles.

"People *will* think we're crazy if they hear us carrying on like this," I choked.

"I've got news for you," said Low, close to my ear. "We *are* crazy. And I dare you to prove it."

"Hoh! As though it needed any proof!"

"I dare you." His laughter tickled my cheek.

"How?" I breathed defiantly.

"Let's not go up the stairs," he hissed. "Let's lift through the air. Why waste the energy when we can—?"

He held out his hand to me. Suddenly sober, I took it and we stepped back to the gate and stood hand in hand, looking up.

"Ready?" he whispered, and I felt him tug me upward.

I lifted into the air after him, holding all my possible fear clenched in my other hand.

And the rosebush reached up and snagged my hair.

"Wait!" I whispered, laughter trembling again. "I'm caught."

"Earth-bound!" he chuckled as he tugged at the clinging strands.

"Smile when you say that, podner," I returned, feeling my heart melt with pleasure that I had arrived at a point where I could joke about such a bitterness—and trying to ignore the fact that my feet were treading nothing but air. My hair freed, he lifted me up to him. I think our lips only brushed, but we overshot the porch and had to come back down to land on it. Low steadied me as we stepped across the railing.

"We did it," he whispered.

"Yes," I breathed. "We did."

Then we both froze. Someone was coming into the yard. Someone who stumbled and wavered and smashed glassily against the gatepost.

"Ay! Ay! Madre mía!" Severeid Swanson fell to his knees beside the smashed bottle. *"Ay, virgen purísima!"*

"Did he see us?" I whispered on an indrawn breath.

"I doubt it." His words were warm along my cheek. "He hasn't seen anything outside himself for years."

"Watch out for the chair." We groped through the darkness into the upper hall. A feeble fifteen-watt bulb glimmered on the steady drip of water splashing down into the sagging sink from the worn faucets that blinked yellow through the worn chrome. By virtue of these two leaky outlets we had bathing facilities on the second floor.

Our good nights were subvocal and quick.

I was in my nightgown and robe, sitting on the edge of my bed, brushing my hair, when I heard a shuffle and a mutter outside my door. I checked the latch to be sure it was fastened, and brushed on. There was a thud and a muffled rapping and my doorknob turned.

"Teesher!" It was a cautious voice. "Teesher!"

"Who on earth!" I thought, and went to the door. "Yes?" I leaned against the peeling panel.

"Lat—me—een." The words were labored and spaced.

"What do you want?"

"To talk weeth you, teesher."

Filled with astonished wonder, I opened the door. There was Severeid Swanson swaying in the hall! But they had told me he had no English... He leaned precariously forward, his face glowing in the light, years younger than I'd ever seen him.

"My bottle is broken. You have done eet. It is not good to fly without the wings. *Los ángeles santos, sí, pero* not the lovers to fly to kiss. It makes me drop my bottle. On the ground is spilled all the dreams."

He swayed backward and wiped the earnest sweat from his forehead. "It is not good. I tell you this because you have light in the face. You are good to my Esperanza. You have dreams that are not in the bottle. You have smiles and not laughing for the lost ones. But you must not fly. It is not good. My bottle is broken."

"I'm sorry," I said through my astonishment. "I'll buy you another."

"No," Severeid said. "Last time they tell me this, too, but I cannot drink it because of the wondering. Last time, like birds, all, all in the sky—over the hills—the kind ones. The ones who also have no laughter for the lost."

"Last time?" I grabbed his swaying arm and pulled him into the room, shutting the door, excitement tingling along the insides of my elbows. "Where? When? Who was flying?"

He blinked owlishly at me, the tip of his tongue moistening his dry lips.

"It is not good to fly without wings," he repeated.

"Yes, yes, I know. Where did you see the others fly without wings? I must find them—I must!"

"Like birds," he said, swaying. "Over the hills."

"Please," I said, groping wildly for what little Spanish I possessed.

"I work there a long time. I don't see them no more. I drink some more. Chinee Joe give me new bottle."

"*Por favor, señor,*" I cried, "*dónde—dónde—?*"

All the light went out of his face. His mouth slackened. Dead eyes peered from under lowered lids.

"*No comprendo.*" He looked around, dazed. "*Buenas noches, señorita.*" He backed out of the door and closed it softly behind him.

"But—!" I cried to the door. "But please!"

Then I huddled on my bed and hugged this incredible piece of information to me.

"Others!" I thought. "Flying over the hills! All, all in the sky! Maybe, oh maybe one of them was at the hotel in town. Maybe they're not too far away. If only we knew...!"

Then I felt the sudden yawning of a terrifying chasm. If it was true, if Severeid had really seen others lifting like birds over the hills, then Low was right—there *were* others! There *must* be a Canyon, a starship, a Home. But where did that leave me? I shrank away from the possibilities. I turned and buried my face in my pillow. But Mother and Dad! And Granpa Josh and Gramma Malvina and Great-granpa Benedaly and— I clutched at the memories of all the family stories I'd heard. Crossing the ocean in steerage. Starting a new land. Why, my ancestors were as solid as a rock wall back of me as far back as—as *Adam,* almost. I leaned against the certainty and cried out to feel the stone wall waver and become a curtain stirring in the winds of doubt.

"No, *no!*" I sobbed, and for the first time in my life I cried for my mother, feeling as bereft as though she had died.

Then I suddenly sat up in bed. "It might not be *so!*" I cried. "He's just a drunken wino. No telling what he might conjure out of his bottle. It might not be *so!*"

"But it might," one of me whispered maliciously. "It might!"

The days that followed were mostly uneventful. I had topped out onto a placid plateau in my battle with myself, perhaps because I had something new to occupy my mind or perhaps it was just a slack place since any emotion has to rest sometime.

However, the wonder of finding Low was slow to ebb. I could sense his "Good morning" with my first step down the stairs each day, and occasionally roused in the darkness to his silent "Good night."

Once after supper Marie planted herself solidly in front of me as I rose to leave. Silently she pointed at my plate, where I had apparently made mud pies of my food. I flushed.

"No good?" she asked, crossing her wrists over the grossness of her stomach and teetering perilously backward.

"It's fine, Marie," I managed. "I'm just not hungry." And I escaped through the garlicky cloud of her indignant exhalation and the underneath amusement of Low. How could I tell her that Low had been showing me a double rainbow he had seen that afternoon and that I had been so engrossed in the taste of the colors and the miracle of being able to receive them from him that I had forgotten to eat?

Low and I spent much time together, getting acquainted, but during most of it we were ostensibly sitting with the others on the porch in the twilight, listening to the old mining and cattle stories that were the well-worn coins that slipped from hand to hand wherever the citizens of Kruper gathered together. A good story never wore out, so after a while it was an easy matter to follow the familiar repetitions and still be alone together in the group.

"Don't you think you need a little more practice in lifting?" Low's silent question was a clarity behind the rumble of voices.

"Lifting?" I stirred in my chair, not quite so adept as he at carrying two threads simultaneously.

"Flying," he said with exaggerated patience. "Like you did over the canyon and up to the porch."

"Oh." Ecstasy and terror puddled together inside me. Then I felt myself relaxing in the strong warmth of Low's arms instead of fighting them as I had when he had caught me over the canyon.

"Oh, I don't know," I answered, quickly shutting him out as much as I could. "I think I can do it okay."

"A little more practice won't hurt." There was laughter in his reply. "But you'd better wait until I'm around—just in case."

"Oh?" I asked. "Look." I lifted in the darkness until I sat gently about six inches above my chair. "So!"

Something prodded me gently and I started to drift across the porch. Hastily I dropped back, just barely landing on the forward edge of my chair, my heels thudding audibly on the floor. The current story broke off in mid-episode and everyone looked at me.

"Mosquitoes," I improvised. "I'm allergic to them."

"That's not fair!" I sputtered silently to Low. "You cheat!"

"All's fair—" he answered, then shut hastily as he remembered the rest of the quotation.

"Hmm!" I thought. "Hmm! And this is war?" And felt pleased all out of proportion the rest of the evening.

Then there was the Saturday when the sky was so tangily blue and the clouds so puffily light that I just couldn't stay indoors scrubbing clothes and sewing on buttons and trying to decide whether to repair my nail polish or take it all off and start from scratch again. I scrambled into my saddle shoes and denim skirt, turned back the sleeves of my plaid shirt, tied the sleeves of my sweater around my waist, and headed for the hills. This was the day to follow the town water pipe up to the spring that fed it and see if all the gruesome stories I'd heard about its condition were true.

I paused, panting, atop the last steep ledge above the town and looked back at the tumbled group of weathered houses that made up this side of Kruper. Beyond the railroad track there was enough flatland to make room for the four new houses that had been built when the Golden Turkey Mine reopened. They sat in a neat row, bright as toy blocks against the tawny red of the hillside.

I brushed my hair back from my hot forehead and turned my back on Kruper. I could see sections of the town water pipe scattered at haphazard intervals up among the hills—in some places stilted up on timbers to cross from one rise to another, in other places following the jagged contour of the slopes. A few minutes and sections later I was amusing myself trying to stop with my hands the spray of water from one of the numerous holes in one section of the rusty old pipe and counting the hand-whittled wooden plugs that stopped up others. It looked a miracle that any water at all got down to town. I was so engrossed that I unconsciously put my hand up to my face when a warm finger began to trace...

"Low!" I whirled on him. "What are you doing up here?"

He slid down from a boulder above the line.

"Johnny's feeling poorely today. He wanted me to check to see if any of the plugs had fallen out."

We both laughed as we looked up-line and traced the pipe by the white gush of spray and the vigorous greenness that utilized the spilling water.

"I'll bet he has at least a thousand plugs hammered in," Low said.

"Why on earth doesn't he get some new pipe?"

"Family heirlooms," Low said, whittling vigorously. "It's only because he's feeling so porely that he even entertains the thought of letting me plug his line. All the rest of the plugs are family affairs. About three generations' worth."

He hammered the plug into the largest of the holes and stepped back, reaming the water from his face where it had squirted him.

"Come on up. I'll show you the spring."

We sat in the damp coolness of the thicket of trees that screened the cave where the spring churned and gurgled, blue and white and pale green before it lost itself in the battered old pipes. We were sitting on opposite sides of the pipe, resting ourselves in the consciousness of each other, when all at once, for a precious minute, we flowed together like coalescing streams of water, so completely one that the following rebound to separateness came as a shock. Such sweetness without even touching one another...?

Anyway we both turned hastily away from this frightening new emotion, and, finding no words handy, Low brought me down a flower from the ledge above us, nipping a drooping leaf off it as it passed him.

"Thanks," I said, smelling of it and sneezing vigorously. "I wish I could do that."

"Well, you can! You lifted that rock at Macron and you can lift yourself."

"Yes, myself." I shivered at the recollection. "But not the rock. I could only move it."

"Try that one over there." Low lobbed a pebble toward a small slaty blue rock lying on the damp sand. Obligingly it plowed a small furrow up to Low's feet.

"*Lift* it," he said.

"I can't. I told you I can't lift anything clear off the ground. I can just move it." I slid one of Low's feet to one side.

Startled, he pulled it back.

"But you *have* to be able to lift, Dita. You're one of—"

"I am not!" I threw the flower I'd been twiddling with down violently into the spring and saw it sucked into the pipe. Someone downstream was going to be surprised at the sink or else one of the thousands of fountains between here and town was going to blossom.

"But all you have to do is—is—" Low groped for words.

"Yes?" I leaned forward eagerly. Maybe I could learn...

"Well, just *lift!*"

"Twirtle!" I said, disappointed. "Anyway, can you do *this*? Look." I reached in my pocket and pulled out two bobby pins and three fingernails full of pocket fluff. "Have you got a dime?"

"Sure." He fished it out and brought it to me. I handed it back. "Glow it," I said.

"Glow it? You mean blow it?" He turned it over in his hand.

"No, *glow* it. Go on. It's easy. All you have to do is glow it. Any metal will do but silver works better."

"Never heard of it," he said, frowning suspiciously.

"You must have," I cried, "if you are part of me. If we're linked back to the Bright Beginning, you must remember!"

Low turned the dime slowly. "It's a joke to you. Something to laugh at."

"A joke!" I moved closer to him and looked up into his face. "Haven't I been looking for an answer long enough? Wouldn't I belong if I could? Would my heart break and bleed every time I have to say no if I could mend it by saying yes? If I could only hold out my hands and say, 'I belong...' " I turned away from him, blinking. "Here," I sniffed. "Give me the dime."

I took it from his quiet fingers and, sitting down again, spun it quickly in the palm of my hand. It caught light immediately, glowing stronger until I slitted my eyes to look at it and finally had to close my fingers around its cool pulsing.

"Here." I held my hand out to Low, my bones shining pinkly through. "It's glowed."

"Light," he breathed, taking the dime wonderingly. "Cold light! How long can you hold it?"

"I don't have to hold it. It'll glow until I damp it."

"How long?"

"How long does it take metal to turn to dust?" I shrugged. "I don't know. Do your People know how to glow?"

"No." His eyes stilled on my face. "I have no memory of it."

"So I *don't* belong." I tried to say it lightly above the wrenching of my heart. "It almost looks like we're simultaneous, but we aren't. You came one way. I came t'other." "Not even to him!" I cried inside. "I can't even belong to him!" I drew a deep breath and put emotion to one side.

"Look," I said. "Neither of us fits a pattern. You deviate and I deviate and you're satisfied with your explanation of why you are what you are. I haven't found my explanation yet. Can't we let it go at that?"

Low grabbed my shoulders, the dime arching down into the spring. He shook me with a tight controlled shaking that was hardly larger than a trembling of his tensed hands. "I tell you, Dita, I'm not making up stories! I belong and you belong and all your denying won't change it. We are the same—"

We stared stubbornly at each other for a long moment, then the tenseness ran out of his fingers and he let them slide down my arms to my hands. We turned away from the spring and started silently, hand in hand, down the trail. I looked back and saw the glow of the dime and damped it.

"No," I said to myself. "It isn't so. I'd know it if it were true. We aren't the same. But what am I then? What am I?" And I stumbled a little wearily on the narrow path.

During this time everything at school was placid, and Pete had finally decided that "two" could have a name *and* a picture, and learned his number words to ten in one day.

And Lucine—symbol to Low and me of our own imprisonment— with our help was blossoming under the delight of reading her second pre-primer.

But I remember the last quiet day. I sat at my desk checking the tenth letter I'd received in answer to my inquiries concerning a possible Chinee Joe and sadly chalking up another "no." So far I had been able to conceal from Low the amazing episode of Severeid Swanson. I wanted to give him back his Canyon myself, if it existed. I wanted it to be my gift to him—and to my own shaken self. Most of all I wanted to be able to know at least one thing for sure, even if that one thing proved me wrong or even parted Low and me. Just one solid surety in the whole business would be a comfort and a starting place for us truly to get together.

I wished frequently that I could take hold of Severeid bodily and shake more information out of him, but he had disappeared—walked off from his job without even drawing his last check. No one knew where he had gone. The last Kruper had seen of him was early the next morning after he had spoken with me. He had been standing, slack-kneed and wavering, a bottle in each hand, at the crossroads—not even bothering to thumb a ride, just waiting blankly for someone to stop for him—and apparently someone had.

I asked Esperanza about him, and she twisted her thick shining braid around her hand twice and tugged at it.

"He's a wino," she said dispassionately. "They ain't smart. Maybe he got losted." Her eyes brightened. "Last year he got losted and the cops picked him up in El Paso. He brang me some perfume when he came back. Maybe he went to El Paso again. It was pretty perfume." She started down the stairs. "He'll be back," she called, "unless he's dead in a ditch somewhere."

I shook my head and smiled ruefully. And she'd fight like a wildcat if anyone else talked about Severeid like that...

I sighed at the recollection and went back to my disappointing letter. Suddenly I frowned and moved uneasily in my chair. What was wrong?

I felt acutely uncomfortable. Quickly I checked me over physically. Then my eyes scanned the room. Petie was being jet planes while he drew pictures of them, and the soft *skoosh! skoosh! skoosh!* of the take-offs was about the only on-top sound in the room. I checked underneath and the placid droning hum was as usual. I had gone back on top when I suddenly dived back again. There was a sharp stinging buzz like an angry bee—a malicious angry buzz! Who was it? I met Lucine's smoldering eyes and I knew.

I almost gasped under the sudden flood of hate-filled anger. And when I tried to reach her, down under, I was rebuffed—not knowingly but as though there had never been a contact between us. I wiped my trembling hands against my skirt, trying to clean them of what I had read.

The recess bell came so shatteringly that I jumped convulsively and shared the children's laughter over it. As soon as I could I hurried to Mrs. Kanz's room.

"Lucine's going to have another spell," I said without preface.

"What makes you think so?" Mrs. Kanz marked "46 1/2%" on the top of a literature paper.

"I don't think so, I know so. And this time she won't be too slow. Someone will get hurt if we don't do something."

Mrs. Kanz laid down her pencil and folded her arms on the desk top, her lips tightening. "You've been brooding too much over Lucine," she said, none too pleased. "If you're getting to the point where you think you can predict her behavior, you're pretty far gone. People are going to be talking about *your* being queer pretty soon. Why don't you just forget about her and concentrate on—on—well, on Low? He's more fun than she is anyway, I'll bet."

"He'd know," I cried. "He'd tell you, too! He knows more about Lucine than anyone thinks."

"So I've heard." There was a nasty purr to her voice that I didn't know it possessed. "They've been seen together out in the hills. Well, it's only her mind that's retarded. Remember, she's over twelve now, and some men—"

I slapped the flat of my hand down on the desk top with a sharp crack. I could feel my eyes blazing, and she dodged back as though from a blow. She pressed the back of one hand defensively against her cheek.

"I—" she gasped, "I was only kidding!"

I breathed deeply to hold my rage down. "*Are* you going to do anything about Lucine?" My voice was very soft.

"What can I do? What is there to do?"

"Skip it," I said bitterly. "Just skip it."

I tried all afternoon to reach Lucine, but she sat lumpish and unheeding—on top. Underneath violence and hatred were seething like lava, and once, without apparent provocation, she leaned across the aisle and pinched Petie's arm until he cried.

She was sitting in isolation with her face to the wall when the last bell rang.

"You may go now, Lucine," I said to the sullen stranger who had replaced the child I knew. I put my hand on her shoulder. She slipped out of my touch with one fluid quick motion. I caught a glimpse of her profile as she left. The jaw muscles were knotted and the cords in her neck were tensed.

I hurried home and waited, almost wild from worry, for Low to get off shift. I paced the worn Oriental rug in the living room, circling the potbellied cast-iron heater. I peered a dozen times through the lace curtains, squinting through the dirty cracked window panes. I beat my fist softly into my palm as I paced, and I felt physical pain when the phone on the wall suddenly shrilled.

I snatched down the receiver.

"Yes!" I cried. "Hello!"

"Marie. I want Marie." The voice was far and crackling. "You tell Marie I gotta talk to her."

I called Marie and left her to her conversation and went out on the porch. Back and forth, back and forth I paced, Marie's voice swelling and fading as I passed.

"...well, I expected it a long time ago. A crazy girl like that—"

"Lucine!" I shouted and rushed indoors. "What happened?"

"Lucine?" Marie frowned from the telephone. "What's Lucine gotta do with it? Marson's daughter ran off last night with the hoistman at the Golden Turkey. He's fifty if he's a day and she's just turned sixteen." She turned back to the phone. "Yah, yah, yah?" Her eyes gleamed avidly.

I just got back to the door in time to see the car stop at the gate. I grabbed my coat and was down the steps as the car door swung open.

"Lucine?" I gasped.

"Yes." The sheriff opened the back door for me, his deputy goggle-eyed with the swiftness of events. "Where is she?"

"I don't know," I said. "What happened?"

"She got mad on the way home." The car spurted away from the hotel. "She picked Petie up by the heels and bashed him against a boulder. She chased the other kids away with rocks and went back and started to work on Petie. He's still alive, but Doc lost count of the stitches and they're transfusing like crazy. Mrs. Kanz says you likely know where she is."

"No." I shut my eyes and swallowed. "But we'll find her. Get Low first."

The shift bus was just pulling in at the service station. Low was out of it and into the sheriff's car before a word could be spoken. I saw my anxiety mirrored on his face before we clasped hands.

For the next two hours we drove the roads around Kruper. We went to all the places we thought Lucine might have run to, but nowhere, nowhere in all the scrub-covered foothills or the pine-pointed mountains, could I sense Lucine.

"We'll take one more sweep—through Poland Canyon. Then if it's no dice we'll hafta get a posse and Claude's hounds." The sheriff gunned for the steep rise at the canyon entrance. "Beats me how a kid could get so gone so fast."

"You haven't seen her really run," Low said. "She never can when she's around other people. She's just a little lower than a plane and she can run me into the ground any time. She just shifts her breathing into overdrive and takes off. She could beat Claude's hounds without trying, if it ever came to a run-down."

"Stop!" I grabbed the back of the seat. "Stop the car!"

The car had brakes. We untangled ourselves and got out.

"Over there," I said. "She's over there somewhere." We stared at the brush-matted hillside across the canyon.

"Gaw-dang!" the sheriff moaned. "Not in Cleo II! That there hell hole's been nothing but a jinx since they sunk the first shaft. Water and gas and cave-in sand, every gaw-dang thing in the calendar. I've lugged my share of dead men out of there—me and my dad before me. What makes you think she's in there, Teacher? Yuh see something?"

"I know she's somewhere over there," I evaded. "Maybe not in the mine but she's there."

"Let's get looking," the sheriff sighed. "I'd give a pretty to know how you saw her clear from the other side of the car." He edged out of the car and lifted a shotgun after him.

"A gun?" I gasped. "For Lucine?"

"You didn't see Petie, did you?" he said. "I did. I go animal hunting with guns."

"No!" I cried. "She'll come for us."

"Might be," he spat reflectively. "Or maybe not."

We crossed the road and plunged into the canyon before the climb.

"Are you sure, Dita?" Low whispered. "I don't reach her at all. Only some predator—"

"That's Lucine," I choked. "That's Lucine."

I felt Low's recoil. "That—that *animal?*"

"That animal. Did we do it? Maybe we should have left her alone."

"I don't know." I ached with his distress. "God help me, I don't know."

She *was* in Cleo II.

Over our tense silence we could hear the rattling of rocks inside as she moved. I was almost physically sick.

"Lucine," I called into the darkness of the drift. "Lucine, come on out. It's time to go home."

A fist-sized rock sent me reeling, and I nursed my bruised shoulder with my hand.

"Lucine!" Low's voice was commanding and spread all over the band. An inarticulate snarl answered him.

"Well?" The sheriff looked at us.

"She's completely crazy," Low said. "We can't reach her at all."

"Gaw-dang," the sheriff said. "How we gonna get her out?"

No one had an answer, and we stood around awkwardly while the late-afternoon sun hummed against our backs and puddled softly in the mine entrance. There was a sudden flurry of rocks that rattled all about us, thudding on the bare ground and crackling in the brush—then a low guttural wail that hurt my bones and whitened the sheriff's face.

"I'm gonna shoot," he said, thinly. "I'm gonna shoot it daid." He hefted the shotgun and shuffled his feet.

"No!" I cried. "A child! A little girl!"

His eyes turned to me and his mouth twisted.

"That?" he asked and spat.

His deputy tugged at his sleeve and took him to one side and muttered rapidly. I looked uneasily at Low. He was groping for Lucine, his eyes closed, his face tense.

The two men set about gathering up a supply of small-sized rocks. They stacked them ready-to-hand near the mine entrance. Then, taking simultaneous deep breaths, they started a steady bombardment into the drift. For a while there was an answering shower from the mine, then an outraged squall that faded as Lucine retreated farther into the darkness.

"Gotter!" The two men redoubled their efforts, stepping closer to the entrance, and Low's hand on my arm stopped me from following.

"There's a drop-off in there," he said. "They're trying to drive her into it. I dropped a rock in it once and never heard it land."

"It's murder!" I cried, jerking away, grabbing the sheriff's arm. "Stop it!"

"You can't get her any other way," the sheriff grunted, his muscles rippling under my restraining hand. "Better her dead than Petie and all the rest of us. She's fixing to kill."

"I'll get her," I cried, dropping to my knees and hiding my face in my hands. "I'll get her. Give me a minute." I concentrated as I had never concentrated before. I sent myself stumbling out of me into the darkness of the mine, into a heavier deeper uglier darkness, and I struggled with the darkness in Lucine until I felt it surging uncontrollably into my own mind. Stubbornly I persisted, trying to flick a fingernail of reason under the edge of this angry unreason to let a little sanity in. Low reached me just before the flood engulfed me. He reached me and held me until I could shudder myself back from hell.

Suddenly there was a rumble from inside the hill—a cracking crash and a yellow billow of dust from the entrance.

There was an animal howl that cut off sharply and then a scream of pure pain and terror—a child's terrified cry, a horrified awakening in the darkness, a cry for help—for light!

"It's Lucine!" I half sobbed. "She's back. What happened?"

"Cave-in!" the sheriff said, his jaws working. "Shoring gone—rotted out years ago. Gotter for sure now, I guess."

"But it's Lucine again," Low said. "We've got to get her out."

"If that cave-in's where I think it is," the sheriff said, "she's a goner. There's a stretch in there that's just silt. Finest slitheriest stuff you ever felt. Comes like a flood of water. Drowns a feller in dirt." His lips tightened. "First dead man I ever saw I dragged out of a silt-down in here. I was sixteen, I guess—skinniest feller in the batch, so they sent me in after they located the body and shored up a makeshift drift. Dragged him out feet first. Stubborn feller—sucked out of that silt like outa mud. Drownded in dirt. We'll sweat getting this body out, too.

"Well," he hitched up his Levi's, "might as well git on back to town and git a crew out here."

"She's not dead," Low said. "She's still breathing. She's caught under something and can't get loose."

The sheriff looked at him through narrowed eyes. "I've heard you're kinda tetched," he said. "Sounds to me like you're having a spell yourself, talking like that.

"Wanta go back to town, ma'am?" His voice gentled. "Nothing you can do around here any more. She's a goner."

"No, she isn't," I said. "She's still alive. I can hear her."

"Gaw-dang!" the sheriff muttered. "Two of them. Well, all right then. You two are deppytized to watch the mine so it don't run away while I'm gone." Grinning sourly at his own wit, he left, taking the deputy with him.

We listened to the echoes of the engine until they died away in the quiet, quiet upsurging of the forested hills all around us. We heard the small wind in the brush and the far cry of some flying bird. We heard the pounding of our own pulses and the frightened bewilderedness that was Lucine. And we heard the pain that began to beat its brassy hammers through her body, and the sharp piercing stab of sheer agony screaming up to the bright twanging climax that snapped down into unconsciousness. And then both of us were groping in the darkness of the tunnel. I stumbled and fell and felt a heavy flowing something spread across my lap, weighting me down. Low was floundering ahead of me. "Go back," he warned. "Go back or we'll both be caught!"

"No!" I cried, trying to scramble forward. "I can't leave you!"

"Go back," he said. "I'll find her and hold her until the men come. You've got to help me hold the silt back."

"I can't," I whimpered. "I don't know how!" I scooped at the heaviness in my lap.

"Yes, you do," he said down under. "Just look and see."

I scrambled back the interminable distance I hadn't even been conscious of when going in, and crouched just outside the mine entrance, my dirty hands pressed to my wet face. I looked deep, deep inside me, down into a depth that suddenly became a height. I lifted me, mind and soul, up, up, until I found a new Persuasion, a new ability, and slowly, slowly, stemmed the creeping dry tide inside the mine—slowly began to part the black flood that had overswept Lucine so that only the arch of her arm kept her mouth and nose free of the invading silt.

Low burrowed his way into the mass, straining to reach Lucine before all the air was gone.

We were together, working such a work that we weren't two people any more. We were one, but that one was a multitude, all bound together in this tremendous outpouring of effort. Since we were each other, we had no need for words as we worked in toward Lucine. We found a bent knee, a tattered hem, a twisted ankle—and the splintery edge of timber that pinned her down. I held the silt back while Low burrowed to find her head. Carefully we cleared a larger space for her face. Carefully we worked to free her body. Low finally held her limp shoulders in his arms— *and was gone! Gone completely, between one breath and another.*

"Low!" I screamed, scrambling to my feet at the tunnel's mouth, but the sound of my cry was drowned in the smashing crash that shook the ground. I watched horrified as the hillside dimpled and subsided and sank into silence after a handful of pebbles, almost hidden in a puff of dust, rattled to rest at my feet.

I screamed again and the sky spun in a dizzy spiral rimmed with sharp pine tops, and suddenly unaccountably Severeid Swanson was there joining the treetops and the sky and spinning with them as he said, "Teesher! Teesher!"

The world steadied as though a hand had been put upon it. I scrambled to my feet.

"Severeid!" I cried. "They're in there! Help me get them out! Help me!"

"Teesher," Severeid shrugged helplessly, "*no comprendo*. I bring a flying one. I go get him. You say you gotta find. I find him. What you do out here with tears?"

Before I was conscious of another person standing beside Severeid, I felt another person in my mind. Before I could bring my gasping into articulation, the words were taken from me. Before I could move, I heard the rending of rocks, and turning I sank to my knees and watched, in terrified wonder, the whole of the hillside lift itself and arch away like a furrow of turned earth before a plowshare. I saw silt rise like a yellow-red fountain above the furrow. I saw Low and Lucine rise with the silt. I saw the hillside flow back upon itself. I saw Low and Lucine lowered to the ground before me and saw all the light fading as I fell forward, my fingertips grazing the curve of Low's cheek just before I drank deeply of blackness.

The sun was all. Through the thin blanket I could feel the cushioning of the fine sand under my cheek. I could hear the cold wind blowing overhead through the sighing trees, but where we were the warmth of the late-fall sun was gathered between granite palms and poured down into our tiny pocket against the mountain. Without moving I could reach Low and Valancy and Jemmy. Without opening my eyes I could see them around me, strengthening me. The moment grew too dear to hold. I rolled over and sat up.

"Tell me again," I said. "How did Severeid ever find you the second time?"

I didn't mind the indulgent smile Valancy and Jemmy exchanged. I didn't mind feeling like a child—if they were the measure of adults.

"The first time he ever saw us," Jemmy said, "was when he chose to sleep off his *vino* around a boulder from where we chose to picnic. He was so drunk, or so childlike, or both, that he wasn't amazed or outraged by our lifting and tumbling all over the sky. He was intrigued and delighted. He thought he had died and by-passed purgatory, and we had to restrain him to keep him from taking off after us. Of course, before we let him go we blocked his memory of us so he couldn't talk of us to anyone except others of the People." He smiled at me. "That's why we got real shook when we found that he'd told you and that you're not of the People. At least not of the Home. You're the third blow to our provincialism. Peter and Bethie were the first, but at least they were half of the People, but you—" he waggled his head mournfully, "you just didn't track."

"Yes," I shivered, remembering the long years I hadn't tracked with anyone. "I just didn't track—" And I relaxed under the triple reassurance that flooded in from Low and Jemmy and his wife Valancy.

"Well, when you told Severeid you wanted to find us, he stumbled as straight as a wino string back to our old picnic grounds. He must have huddled over that tiny fire of his for several days before we found him—parched with thirst and far past his last memory of food." Jemmy drew a long breath.

"Well, when we found out that Severeid knew of what we thought were two more of us—we've been in-gathering ever since the ships first arrived—*well!* We slept him all the way back. He would have been most unhappy with the speed and altitude of that return trip, especially without a car or plane.

"I caught your struggle to save Lucine when we were still miles away, and, praise the Power, I got there in time."

"Yes," I breathed, taking warmth from Low's hand to thaw my memory of that moment.

"That's the quickest I ever platted anything," Jemmy said. "And the first time I ever did it on a scale like that. I wasn't sure that the late sunlight, without the moonlight, was strong enough, so I was openmouthed myself at the way the mountain ripped open." He smiled weakly. "Maybe it's just as well that we curb our practice of some of our Persuasions. It was really shake-making!"

"That's for sure!" I shivered. "I wonder what Severeid thought of the deal?"

"We gave Severeid forgetfulness of the whole mine episode," Valancy said. "But, as Jemmy would say, the sheriff was considerably shook when he got back with the crew. His only articulate pronouncement was, 'Gawdang! Cleo II's finally gone!' "

"And Lucine?" I asked, savoring the answer I already knew.

"And Lucine is learning," Valancy said. "Bethie, our Sensitive, found what was wrong and it is mended now. She'll be normal very shortly."

"And—me?" I breathed, hoping I knew.

"One of us!" the three cried to me down under. "Earth born or not—one of us!"

"But what a problem!" Jemmy said. "We thought we had us all catalogued. There were those of us completely of the People and those who were half of the People and half of Earth like Bethie and Peter. And then *you* came along. Not one bit of the People!"

"No," I said, comfortably leaning against my ancestral stone wall again. "Not one bit of the People."

"You look like confirmation of something we've been wondering about, though," Valancy said. "Perhaps after all this long time of detour the people of Earth are beginning to reach the Persuasions, too. We've had hints of such developments but in such little bits and snippets in these research deals. We had no idea that anyone was so far along the way. No telling how many others there are all over the world waiting to be found."

"Hiding, you mean," I said. "You don't go around asking to be found. Not after the first few reactions you get. Oh, maybe in the first fine flush of discovery you hurry to share the wonder, but you learn quickly enough to hide."

"But so like us!" Valancy cried. "Two worlds and yet you're so like us!"

"But she can't inanimate-lift," Low teased.

"And you can't glow," I retorted.

"And you can't sun-and-moonlight-platt," Jemmy said.

"Nor you cloud-herd," I said. "And if you don't stop picking on me I'll do just that right now and snatch that shower away from—from Morenci and drench you all!"

"And she could do it!" Valancy laughed. "And we can't, so let's leave her alone."

We all fell silent, relaxing on the sun-warmed sand until Jemmy rolled over and opened one eye.

"You know, Valancy, Dita and Low can communicate more freely than you and I. With them it's sometimes almost involuntary."

Valancy rolled over, too. "Yes," she said. "And Dita can block me out, too. Only a Sorter is supposed to be able to block a Sorter and she's not a Sorter."

Jemmy waggled his head. "Just like Earthlings! Always out of step. What a problem this gal is going to be!"

"Yep," Low cut in underneath. "A problem and a half, but I think I'll keep her anyway." I could feel his tender laughter.

I closed my eyes against the sun, feeling it golden across my lids.

"I'm un-lost," I thought incredulously, aching with the sudden joy of it. "I'm really un-lost!"

I took tight hold of the hem of my dream, knowing finally and surely that someday I would be able to wrap the whole fabric of it not just around me but around others who were lost and bewildered, too. Someday we would all *be* what was only a dream now.

Softly I drowsed, Low's hand warm upon my cheek—drowsed finally, without dreading an awakening.

Interlude: Lea 5

"Oh, but! Oh, but!" Lea thought excitedly. "Maybe, maybe—!" She turned at the pressure of a hand on her shoulder and met Melodye's understanding eyes.

"No," she said, "we're still Outsiders. It's like the color of your eyes. You're either brown-eyed or you're not. We're not the People. Welcome to my bakery window."

"Seems to me you're fattening on just the sight and smell then." It was Dr. Curtis.

"Fattening!" Melodye wailed. "Oh, no! Not after all my efforts—"

"Well, perhaps being nourished would be a more tactful way of saying it, as well as being more nearly exact. You don't seem to be wasting away."

"Maybe," Melodye said, sobering, "maybe it's because knowing there can be this kind of communication between the People, and trying to reach it for myself, I have made myself more receptive to communication from a source that knows no Outsiders—no East or West—no bond or free—"

"Hmm," Dr. Curtis said. "There you have a point for pondering."

Karen and Lea separated from the happily chattering groups as they passed the house. The two girls lingered, huddling in their jackets, until the sound of the other voices died in shadowy echoes down-canyon. Lea lifted her chin to a sudden cool breeze.

"Karen, do you think I'll ever get straightened out?" she asked.

"If you're not too enamored of your difficulties," Karen said, her hand on the doorknob. "If you're not too firmly set on remodeling 'nearer to *your* heart's desire.' We may think this is a 'sorry scheme of things' but we have to learn that our own judgment is neither completely valid nor the polestar for charting our voyage. Too often we operate on the premise that what *we* think just *has* to be the norm for all things. Really, you'd

find it most comforting to admit that you aren't running the universe—
that you can't be responsible for everything, that there are lots of things
you can and must relinquish into other hands—"

"To let go—" Lea looked down at her clenched hands. "I've held
them like this so much it's a wonder my nails haven't grown through my
palms."

"Sneaky way to keep from having to use nail polish!" Karen laughed.
"But come—to bed, to bed. Oh, I'll be so glad when I can take you over
the hill!" She opened the door and went in, tugging at her jacket. "I just
ache to talk it over with you, good old Outsider-type talking. I acquired
quite a taste for it that year I spent Outside—" Her voice faded down the
hall. Lea looked up at the brilliant stars that punctuated the near horizon.

"The stars come down," she thought, "down to the hills and the
darkness. The darkness lifts up to the hills and the stars. And here on the
porch is a me-sized empty place trying to Become. It's so hard to reconcile darkness and the stars—but what else are we but an attempt at recon-
ciliation?"

Night came again. It seemed to Lea that time was like a fan. The
evenings were the carefully carved, tangible bones of the fan that held
their identity firmly. The days folded themselves meekly away between
the nights—days containing patterns only in that they were bounded on
each side by evenings—folded days scribbled on unintelligibly. She held
herself carefully away from any attempt to read the scrawling scribbles. If
they meant anything she didn't want to know it. Only so long as she could
keep from reading meanings into anything or trying to relate one thing
to another—only that long could she maintain the precarious peace of
the folded days and active evenings.

She settled down almost gladly into the desk that had become pleas-
antly familiar. "It's rather like drugging myself on movies or books or TV,"
she thought. "I bring my mind empty to the Gatherings, let the stories
flow through and take my mind empty home again." Home? Home? She
felt the fist clench in her chest and twist sharply, but she stubbornly concentrated on the lights that swung from the ceiling. Her attention sharpened on them. "Those aren't electric lights," she whispered to Karen. "Nor
Coleman lanterns. What are they?"

"Lights," Karen smiled. "They cost a dime apiece. A dime and Dita.
She glowed them for us. I've been practicing like mad and I almost glowed
one the other day." She laughed ruefully. "And she an Outsider! Oh, I tell
you, Lea, you never know how much you use pride to keep yourself warm in
this cold world until someone tears a hole in it and you shiver in the draft.
Dita was a much-needed rip to a lot of us, bless her pointed little ears!"

"Greetings." Dr. Curtis slid into his seat next to Lea. "You'll like the story tonight," he nodded at Lea. "You share a great deal with Miss Carolle. I find it very interesting—the story, that is—well, and your similarity, too. Well, anyway, I find the story interesting because my own fine Italian hand—" He subsided as Miss Carolle came down the aisle.

"Why, she's crippled!" Lea thought in amazement. "Or has been," she amended. Then wondered what there was about Miss Carolle that made her think of handicaps.

"Handicaps?" Lea flushed. "I share a great deal with her?" She twisted the corner of her Kleenex. "Of course," she admitted humbly, ducking her head. "Handicapped—crippled—" She caught her breath as the darkness swelled—ripping to get in—or out—or just ripping. Before the tiny beads of cold sweat had time to finish forming on her upper lip and at her hairline, she felt Karen touch her with a healing strength. "Thank you, my soothing syrup," she thought wryly. "Don't be silly!" she heard Karen think sharply. "Laugh at your Band-Aids after the scabs are off!"

Miss Carolle murmured into the sudden silence, "We are met together in Thy Name."

Lea let the world flow away from her.

"I have a theme song instead of just a theme," Miss Carolle said. "Ready?"

Music strummed softly, coming from nowhere and from everywhere. Lea felt wrapped about by its soft fullness. Then a clear voice took up the melody, so softly, so untrespassingly, that it seemed to Lea that the music itself had modulated to words, voicing some cry of her own that had never found words before.

"By the rivers of Babylon,
There we sat down and wept,
When we remembered Zion.
We hanged our harps
Upon the willows in the midst thereof.
For there they that carried us away captive
Required of us a song
And they that wasted us
Required of us mirth
Saying, 'Sing us one of the songs of Zion.'
How shall we sing the Lord's song
In a strange land?"

Lea closed her eyes and felt weak tears slip from under the lids. She put her head down on her arms on the desk top to hide her face. Her heart, torn by the anguish of the music, was sore for all the captives who had ever been, of whatever captivity, but most especially for those who drove themselves into exile, who locked themselves into themselves and lost the key.

The crowd had become a listening person as Miss Carolle twisted her palms together, fingers spread and tense for a moment, and then began...

Captivity

I suppose many lonely souls have sat at their windows many nights looking out into the flood of moonlight, sad with a sadness that knows no comfort, a sadness underlined by a beauty that is in itself a pleasant kind of sorrow—but very few ever have seen what I saw that night.

I leaned against the window frame, close enough to the inflooding light so that it washed across my bare feet and the hem of my gown and splashed whitely against the foot of my bed, but picked up none of my features to identify me as a person, separate from the night. I was enjoying hastily, briefly, the magic of the loveliness before the moon would lose itself behind the heavy grove of cottonwoods that lined the creek below the curve of the back-yard garden. The first cluster of leaves had patterned itself against the edge of the moon when I saw him—the Francher kid. I felt a momentary surge of disappointment and annoyance that this perfect beauty should be marred by any person at all, let alone the Francher kid, but my annoyance passed as my interest sharpened.

What was he doing—half black and half white in the edge of the moonlight? In the higgledy-piggledy haphazardness of the town Groman's Grocery sidled in at an angle to the back yard of the Somansons' house, where I boarded—not farther than twenty feet away. The tiny high-up windows under the eaves of the store blinked in the full light. The Francher kid was standing, back to the moon, staring up at the windows. I leaned closer to watch. There was a waitingness about his shoulders, a prelude to movement, a beginning of something. Then there he was—up at the windows, pushing softly against the panes, opening a dark rectangle against the white side of the store. And then he was gone. I blinked and looked again. Store. Windows. One opened blankly. No Francher kid. Little windows. High up under the eaves. One opened blankly. No Francher kid.

Then the blank opening had movement inside it, and the Francher kid emerged with both hands full of something and slid down the moonlight to the ground outside.

"Now looky here!" I said to myself. "Hey! Lookit now!"

The Francher kid sat down on one end of a twelve-by-twelve that lay half in our garden and half behind the store. Carefully and neatly he arranged his booty along the timber. Three Cokes, a box of candy bars, and a huge harmonica that had been in the store for years. He sat and studied the items, touching each one with a fingertip. Then he picked up a Coke and studied the cap on it. He opened the box of candy and closed it again. He ran a finger down the harmonica and then lifted it between the pointer fingers of his two hands. Holding it away from him in the moonlight, he looked at it, his head swinging slowly down its length. And, as his head swung, faintly, faintly, I heard a musical scale run up, then down. Careful note by careful note singing softly but clearly in the quiet night.

The moon was burning holes through the cottonwood tops by now and the yard was slipping into shadow. I heard notes riff rapidly up and cascade back down, gleefully, happily, and I saw the glint and chromium glitter of the harmonica, dancing from shadow to light and back again, singing untouched in the air. Then the moon reached an opening in the trees and spotlighted the Francher kid almost violently. He was sitting on the plank, looking up at the harmonica, a small smile on his usually sullen face. And the harmonica sang its quiet song to him as he watched it. His face shadowed suddenly as he looked down at the things laid out on the plank. He gathered them up abruptly and walked up the moonlight to the little window and slid through, head first. Behind him, alone, unattended, the harmonica danced and played, hovering and darting like a dragonfly. Then the kid reappeared, sliding head first out of the window. He sat crosslegged in the air beside the harmonica and watched and listened. The gay dance slowed and changed. The harmonica cried softly in the moonlight, an aching asking cry as it spiraled up and around until it slid through the open window and lost its voice in the darkness. The window clicked shut and the Francher kid thudded to the ground. He slouched off through the shadows, his elbows winging sharply backward as he jammed his fists in his pockets.

I let go of the curtain where my clenched fingers had cut four nail-sized holes through the age-fragile lace, and released a breath I couldn't remember holding. I stared at the empty plank and wet my lips. I took a deep breath of the mountain air that was supposed to do me so much good, and turned away from the window. For the thousandth time I muttered "I won't," and groped for the bed. For the thousandth time I finally reached for my crutches and swung myself over to the edge of the bed. I dragged the unresponsive half of me up onto the bed, arranging myself for sleep. I leaned against the pillow and put my hands in back of my head, my elbows fanning out on either side. I stared at the light square that was the window until it wavered and rippled before my sleepy eyes.

Still my mind was only nibbling at what had happened and showed no inclination to set its teeth into any sort of explanation. I awakened with a start to find the moonlight gone, my arms asleep, and my prayers unsaid.

Tucked in bed and ringed about with the familiar comfort of my prayers, I slid away from awareness into sleep, following the dance and gleam of a harmonica that cried in the moonlight.

Morning sunlight slid across the boardinghouse breakfast table, casting alpine shadows behind the spilled corn flakes that lay beyond the sugar bowl. I squinted against the brightness and felt aggrieved that anything should be alive and active and so—so—hopeful so early in the morning. I leaned on my elbows over my coffee cup and contemplated a mood as black as the coffee.

"…Francher kid."

I rotated my head upward on the axis of my two supporting hands, my interest caught. "Last night," I half remembered, "last night—"

"I give up." Anna Semper put a third spoonful of sugar in her coffee and stirred morosely. "Every child has a something—I mean there's *some* way to reach every child—all but the Francher kid. I can't reach him at all. If he'd even be aggressive or actively mean or actively *anything,* maybe I could do something, but he just sits there being a vegetable. And then I get so spittin' mad when he finally *does* do something, just enough to keep him from flunking, that I could bust a gusset. I can't abide a child who can and won't." She frowned darkly and added two more spoonfuls of sugar to her coffee. "I'd rather have an eager moron than a won't-do genius!" She tasted the coffee and grimaced. "Can't even get a decent cup of coffee to arm me for my struggle with the little monster."

I laughed. "Five spoonfuls of sugar would spoil almost anything. And don't give up hope. Have you tried music? Remember, 'Music hath charms—' "

Anna reddened to the tips of her ears. I couldn't tell if it was anger or embarrassment. "Music!" Her spoon clished against her saucer sharply. She groped for words. "This is ridiculous, but I have had to send that Francher kid out of the room during music appreciation."

"Out of the room? Why ever for? I thought he was a vegetable."

Anna reddened still further. "He is," she said stubbornly, "but—" She fumbled with her spoon, then burst forth, "But sometimes the record player won't work when he's in the room."

I put my cup down slowly. "Oh, come now! This coffee is awfully strong, I'll admit, but it's not *that* strong."

"No, really!" Anna twisted her spoon between her two hands. "When he's in the room that darned player goes too fast or too slow or even backwards. I swear it. And one time—" Anna looked around furtively and lowered her voice, "one time it played a whole record and it wasn't even plugged in!"

"You ought to patent that! That'd be a real money-maker."

"Go on, laugh!" Anna gulped coffee again and grimaced. "I'm beginning to believe in poltergeists—you know, the kind that are supposed to work through or because of adolescent kids. If you had that kid to deal with in class—"

"Yes." I fingered my cold toast. "If only I did."

And for a minute I hated Anna fiercely for the sympathy on her open face and for the studied not-looking at my leaning crutches. She opened her mouth, closed it, then leaned across the table.

"Polio?" she blurted, reddening.

"No," I said. "Car wreck."

"Oh." She hesitated. "Well, maybe someday—"

"No," I said. "No." Denying the faint possibility that was just enough to keep me nagged out of resignation.

"Oh," she said. "How long ago?"

"How long?" For a minute I was suspended in wonder at the distortion of time. How long? Recent enough to be a shock each time of immobility when I expected motion. Long enough ago that eternity was between me and the last time I moved unthinkingly.

"Almost a year," I said, my memory aching to *this time last year I could...*

"You were a teacher?" Anna gave her watch a quick appraising look.

"Yes." I didn't automatically verify the time. The immediacy of watches had died for me. Then I smiled. "That's why I can sympathize with you about the Francher kid. I've had them before."

"There's always one," Anna sighed, getting up. "Well, it's time for my pilgrimage up the hill. I'll see you." And the swinging door to the hall repeated her departure again and again with diminishing enthusiasm. I struggled to my feet and swung myself to the window.

"Hey!" I shouted. She turned at the gate, peering back as she rested her load of workbooks on the gatepost.

"Yes?"

"If he gives you too much trouble send him over here with a note for me. It'll take him off your hands for a while at least."

"Hey, that's an idea. Thanks. That's swell! Straighten your halo!" And she waved an elbow at me as she disappeared beyond the box elder outside the gate.

I didn't think she would, but she did.

It was only a couple of days later that I looked up from my book at the creak of the old gate. The heavy old gear that served as a weight to pull it shut thudded dully behind the Francher kid. He walked up the porch steps under my close scrutiny with none of the hesitant embarrassment that most people would feel. He mounted the three steps and wordlessly handed me an envelope. I opened it. It said:

"Dust off your halo! I've reached the !! stage. Wouldn't you like to keep him permanent-like?"

"Won't you sit down?" I gestured to the porch swing, wondering how I was going to handle this deal.

He looked at the swing and sank down on the top porch step.

"What's your name?"

He looked at me incuriously. "Francher." His voice was husky and unused-sounding.

"Is that your first name?"

"That's my name."

"What's your other name?" I asked patiently, falling into a first-grade dialogue in spite of his age.

"They put down Clement."

"Clement Francher. A good-sounding name, but what do they call you?"

His eyebrows slanted subtly upward, and a tiny bitter smile lifted the corners of his mouth.

"With their eyes—juvenile delinquent, lazy trash, no-good off-scouring, potential criminal, burden—"

I winced away from the icy malice of his voice.

"But mostly they call me a whole sentence, like— 'Well, what can you expect from a background like that?' "

His knuckles were white against his faded Levi's. Then as I watched them the color crept back and, without visible relaxation, the tension was gone. But his eyes were the eyes of a boy too big to cry and too young for any other comfort.

"What *is* your background?" I asked quietly, as though I had the right to ask. He answered as simply as though he owed me an answer.

"We were with the carnival. We went to all the fairs around the country. Mother—" his words nearly died, "Mother had a mind-reading act. She was good. She was better than anyone knew—better than she wanted to be. It hurt and scared her sometimes to walk through people's minds. Sometimes she would come back to the trailer and cry and cry and take a long long shower and wash herself until her hands were all water-soaked and her hair hung in dripping strings. They curled at the end. She couldn't get all the fear and hate and—and tired dirt off even that way. Only if she could find a Good to read, or a dark church with tall candles."

"And where is she now?" I asked, holding a small warm picture in my mind of narrow fragile shoulders, thin and defenseless under a flimsy moist robe, with one wet strand of hair dampening one shoulder of it.

"Gone." His eyes were over my head but empty of the vision of the weatherworn siding of the house. "She died. Three years ago. This is a foster home. To try to make a decent citizen of me."

There was no inflection in his words. They lay as flat as paper between us in our silence.

"You like music," I said, curling Anna's note around my forefinger, remembering what I had seen the other night.

"Yes." His eyes were on the note. "Miss Semper doesn't think so, though. I hate that scratchy wrapped-up music."

"You sing?"

"No. I make music."

"You mean you play an instrument?"

He frowned a little impatiently. "No. I make music with instruments."

"Oh," I said. "There's a difference?"

"Yes." He turned his head away. I had disappointed him or failed him in some way.

"Wait," I said. "I want to show you something." I struggled to my feet. Oh, deftly and quickly enough under the circumstances, I suppose, but it seemed an endless aching effort in front of the Francher kid's eyes. But finally I was up and swinging in through the front door. When I got back with my key chain, the kid was still staring at my empty chair, and I had to struggle back into it under his unwavering eyes.

"Can't you stand alone?" he asked, as though he had a right to.

"Very little, very briefly," I answered, as though I owed him an answer.

"You don't walk without those braces."

"I can't walk without those braces. Here." I held out my key chain. There was a charm on it: a harmonica with four notes, so small that I had never managed to blow one by itself. The four together made a tiny breathy chord, like a small hesitant wind.

He took the chain between his fingers and swung the charm back and forth, his head bent so that the sunlight flickered across its tousledness. The chain stilled. For a long moment there wasn't a sound. Then clearly, sharply, came the musical notes, one after another. There was a slight pause and then four notes poured their separateness together to make a clear sweet chord.

"You make music," I said, barely audible.

"Yes." He gave me back my key chain and stood up. "I guess she's cooled down now. I'll go on back."

"To work?"

"To work." He smiled wryly. "For a while anyway." He started down the walk.

"What if I tell?" I called after him.

"I told once," he called back over his shoulder. "Try it if you want to."

I sat for a long time on the porch after he left. My fingers were closed over the harmonica as I watched the sun creep up my skirts and into my lap. Finally I turned Anna's envelope over. The seal was still secure. The end was jagged where I had torn it. The paper was opaque. I blew a tiny breathy chord on the harmonica. Then I shivered as cold crept across my shoulders. The chill was chased away by a tiny hot wave of excitement. So his mother could walk through the minds of others. So he knew what was in a sealed letter—or had he got his knowledge from Anna before the letter? So he could make music with harmonicas. So the Francher kid was... My hurried thoughts caught and came to a full stop. What *was* the Francher kid?

After school that day Anna toiled up the four front steps and rested against the railing, half sitting and half leaning. "I'm too tired to sit down," she said. "I'm wound up like a clock and I'm going to strike something pretty darned quick." She half laughed and grimaced a little. "Probably my laundry. I'm fresh out of clothes." She caught a long ragged breath. "You must have built a fire under that Francher kid. He came back and piled into his math book and did the whole week's assignments that he hadn't bothered with before. Did them in less than an hour, too. Makes me mad, though—" She grimaced again and pressed her hand to her chest. "Darn that chalk dust anyway. Thanks a million for your assist. I wish I were optimistic enough to believe it would last." She leaned and breathed, her eyes closing with the effort. "Awful shortage of air around here." Her hands fretted with her collar. "Anyway the Francher kid said you'd substitute for me until my pneumonia is over." She laughed, a little soundless laugh. "He doesn't know that it's just chalk dust and that I'm never sick." She buried her face in her two hands and burst into tears. "I'm not sick, am I? It's only that darn Francher kid!"

She was still blaming him when Mrs. Somanson came out and led her into her bedroom and when the doctor arrived to shake his head over her chest.

So that's how it was that the first-floor first grade was hastily moved upstairs and the junior high was hastily moved downstairs and I once more found myself facing the challenge of a class, telling myself that the Francher kid needed no special knowledge to say that I'd substitute. After all, I like Anna, I was the only substitute available, and besides, any slight—substitute's pay!—addition to the exchequer was most welcome. You *can* live on those monthly checks, but it's pleasant to have a couple of extra coins to clink together.

By midmorning I knew a little of what Anna was sweating over. The Francher kid's absolutely dead-weight presence in the room was a drag on everything we did. Recitations paused, limped, and halted when they came to him. Activities swirled around his inactivity, creating distracting eddies. It wasn't only a negative sort of nonparticipation on his part but an aggressively positive not-doingness. It wasn't just a hindrance but an active opposition, without any overt action for any sort of proof of his attitude. This, along with my disappointment in not having the same comfortable rapport with him that I'd had before, and the bone-weariness of having to be vertical all day instead of collapsing horizontally at intervals, and the strain of getting back into harness, cold, with a roomful of teeners and subteeners, had me worn down to a nubbin by early afternoon.

So I fell back on the perennial refuge of harried teachers and opened a discussion of "what I want to be when I grow up." We had gone through the usual nurses and airplane hostesses and pilots and bridge builders and the usual unexpected ballet dancer and CPA (and he still can't add six and nine!) until the discussion frothed like a breaking wave against the Francher kid and stilled there.

He was lounging down in his seat, his weight supported by the back of his neck and the remote end of his spine. The class sighed collectively though inaudibly and waited for his contribution.

"And you, Clement?" I prompted, shifting vainly, trying to ease the taut cry of aching muscles.

"An outlaw," he said huskily, not bothering to straighten up. "I'm going to keep a list and break every law there is—and get away with it, too."

"Whatever for?" I asked, trying to reassure the sick pang inside me. "An outlaw is no use at all to society."

"Who wants to be of use?" he asked. "I'll use society—and I can do it."

"Perhaps," I said, knowing full well it was so. "But that's not the way to happiness."

"Who's happy? The bad are unhappy because they are bad. The good are unhappy because they're afraid to be bad—"

"Clement," I said gently, "I think you are—"

"I think he's crazy," said Rigo, his black eyes flashing. "Don't pay him no never mind, Miss Carolle. He's a screwball. He's all the time saying crazy things."

I saw the heavy world globe on the top shelf of the bookcase behind Rigo shift and slide toward the edge. I saw it lift clear of the shelf and I cried out, "Clement!" The whole class started at the loud urgency of my voice, the Francher kid included, and Rigo moved just far enough out of line that the falling globe missed him and cracked itself apart at his feet.

Someone screamed and several gasped and a babble of voices broke out. I caught the Francher kid's eyes, and he flushed hotly and ducked his head. Then he straightened up proudly and defiantly returned my look. He wet his forefinger in his mouth and drew an invisible tally mark in the air before him. I shook my head at him, slowly, regretfully. What could I do with a child like this?

Well, I had to do something, so I told him to stay in after school, though the kids wondered why. He slouched against the door, defiance in every awkward angle of his body and in the hooking of his thumbs into his front pockets. I let the parting noises fade and die, the last hurried clang of lunch pail, the last flurry of feet, the last reverberant slam of the outside door. The Francher kid shifted several times, easing the tension of his shoulders as he waited. Finally I said, "Sit down."

"No." His word was flat and uncompromising. I looked at him, the gaunt young planes of his face, the unhappy mouth thinned to stubbornness, the eyes that blinded themselves with dogged defiance. I leaned across the desk, my hands clasped, and wondered what I could say. Argument would do no good. A kid of that age has an answer for everything.

"We all have violences," I said, tightening my hands, "but we can't always let them out. Think what a mess things would be if we did." I smiled wryly into his unresponsive face. "If we gave in to every violent impulse, I'd probably have slapped you with an encyclopedia before now." His eyelids flicked, startled, and he looked straight at me for the first time.

"Sometimes we can just hold our breath until the violence swirls away from us. Other times it's too big and it swells inside us like a balloon until it chokes our lungs and aches our jaw hinges." His lids flickered down over his watching eyes. "But it can be put to use. Then's when we stir up a cake by hand or chop wood or kick cans across the back yard or—" I faltered, "or run until our knees bend both ways from tiredness."

There was a small silence while I held my breath until my violent rebellion against unresponsive knees swirled away from me.

"There are bigger violences, I guess," I went on. "From them come assault and murder, vandalism and war, but even those can be used. If you want to smash things there are worthless things that need to be smashed and things that ought to be destroyed, ripped apart and ruined. But you have no way of knowing what those things are, yet. You must keep your violences small until you learn how to tell the difference."

"I can smash." His voice was thick.

"Yes," I said. "But smash to build. You have no right to hurt other people with your own hurt."

"People!" The word was profanity.

I drew a long breath. If he were younger... You can melt stiff rebellious arms and legs with warm hugs or a hand across a wind-ruffled head or a long look that flickers into a smile, but what can you do with a creature that's neither adult nor child but puzzlingly both? I leaned forward.

"Francher," I said softly, "if your mother could walk through your mind now—"

He reddened, then paled. His mouth opened. He swallowed tightly. Then he jerked himself upright in the doorway.

"Leave my mother alone." His voice was shaken and muffled. "You leave her alone. She's dead."

I listened to his footsteps and the crashing slam of the outside door. For some sudden reason I felt my heart follow him down the hill to town. I sighed, almost with exasperation. So this was to be a My Child. We teacher-types sometimes find them. They aren't our pets; often they aren't even in our classes. But they are the children who move unasked into our hearts and make claims upon them over and above the call of duty. And this My Child I had to reach. Somehow I had to keep him from sliding on over the borderline to lawlessness as he so surely was doing—this My Child who, even more than the usual My Child, was different.

I put my head down on the desk and let weariness ripple up over me. After a minute I began to straighten up my papers. I made the desk top tidy and took my purse out of the bottom drawer. I struggled to my feet and glared at my crutches. Then I grinned weakly.

"Come, friends," I said. "Leave us help one another depart."

Anna was out for a week. After she returned I was surprised at my reluctance to let go of the class. The sniff of chalk dust was in my nostrils and I ached to be busy again. So I started helping out with the school programs and teen-age dances, which led naturally to the day my committee and I stood in the town recreation hall and looked about us despairingly.

"How long have those decorations been up?" I craned my neck to get a better view of the wilderness of sooty cobwebby crepe paper that clotted the whole of the high ceiling and the upper reaches of the walls of the ramshackle old hall that leaned wearily against the back of the saloon. Twyla stopped chewing the end of one of her heavy braids. "About four years, I guess. At least the newest. Pea-Green put it all up."

"Pea-Green?"

"Yeah. He was a screwball. He used up every piece of crepe paper in town and used nails to put the stuff up—big nails. He's gone now. He got silicosis and went down to Hot Springs."

"Well, nails or no nails, we can't have a Hallowe'en dance with that stuff up."

"Going to miss the old junk. How we going to get it down?" Janniset asked.

"Pea-Green used an extension ladder he borrowed from a power crew that was stringing some wires up to the Bluebell Mine," Rigo said. "But we'll have to find some other way to get it down, now."

I felt a flick of something at my elbow. It might have been the Francher kid shifting from one foot to the other, or it might have been just a thought slipping by. I glanced sideways but caught only the lean line of his cheek and the shaggy back of his neck.

"I think I can get a ladder." Rigo snapped his thumbnail loudly with his white front teeth. "It won't reach clear up but it'll help."

"We could take rakes and just drag it down," Twyla suggested.

We all laughed until I sobered us all with, "It might come to that yet, bless the buttons of whoever thought up twenty-foot ceilings. Well, tomorrow's Saturday. Everybody be here about nine and we'll get with it."

"Can't." The Francher kid cast anchor unequivocally, snapping all our willingness up short.

"Oh?" I shifted my crutches, and, as usual, his eyes fastened on them, almost hypnotically. "That's too bad."

"How come?" Rigo was belligerent. "If the rest of us can, you oughta be able to. Ever'body's s'posed to do this together. Ever'body does the dirty work and ever'body has the fun. You're nobody special. You're on this committee, aren't you?"

I restrained myself from a sudden impulse to clap my hand over Rigo's mouth midway in his protest. I didn't like the quietness of the Francher kid's hands, but he only looked slantwise up at Rigo and said, "I got volunteered on this committee. I didn't ask to. And to fix this joint up today. I gotta work tomorrow."

"Work? Where?" Rigo frankly disbelieved.

"Sorting ore at the Absalom."

Rigo snapped his thumbnail again derisively. "That penny-picking stuff? They pay peanuts."

"Yes." And the Francher kid slouched off around the corner of the building without a glance or a good-by.

"Well, he's working!" Twyla thoughtfully spit out a stray hair and pointed the wet end of her braid with her fingers. "The Francher kid's doing something. I wonder how come?"

"Trying to figure that dopey dilldock out?" Janniset asked. "Don't waste your time. I bet he's just goofing off."

"You kids run on," I said. "We can't do anything tonight. I'll lock up. See you in the morning."

I waited inside the dusty echoing hall until the sound of their going died down the rocky alley that edged around the rim of the railroad cut and dissolved into the street of the town. I still couldn't reconcile myself to slowing their steps to match my uncertain feet. Maybe someday I would be able to accept my braces as others accept glasses; but not yet—oh, not yet!

I left the hall and snapped the dime-store padlock shut. I struggled precariously along through the sliding shale and loose rocks until suddenly one piece of shale shattered under the pressure of one of my crutches and I stumbled off balance. I saw with shake-making clarity in the accelerated speed of the moment that the only place my groping crutch could reach was the smooth curving of a small boulder, and, in that same instant, I visualized myself sprawling helplessly, hopelessly, in the clutter of the alley, a useless nonfunctioning piece of humanity, a drag and a hindrance on everyone again. And then, at the last possible instant, the smooth boulder slid aside and my crutch caught and steadied on the solid damp hollow beneath it. I caught my breath with relief and unclenched my spasmed hands a little. Lucky!

Then all at once there was the Francher kid at my elbow again, quietly waiting.

"Oh!" I hoped he hadn't seen me floundering in my awkwardness. "Hi! I thought you'd gone."

"I really will be working." His voice had lost its flatness. "I'm not making much but I'm saving to buy me a musical instrument."

"Well, good!" I said, smiling into the unusualness of his straightforward look. "What kind of instrument?"

"I don't know. Something that will sing like this—"

And there on the rocky trail with the long light slanting through the trees for late afternoon, I heard soft tentative notes that stumbled at first and then began to sing: "Oh, Danny Boy, the pipes, the pipes are calling—" Each note of this, my favorite, was like a white flower opening inside me in ascending order like steps—steps that I could climb freely, lightly....

"What kind of instrument am I saving for?" The Francher kid's voice pulled me back down to earth.

"You'll have to settle for less." My voice shook a little. "There isn't one like that."

"But I've heard it—" He was bewildered.

"Maybe you have. But was anyone playing it?"

"Why yes—no. I used to hear it from Mom. She thought it to me."

"Where did your mom come from?" I asked impulsively.

"From terror and from panic places. From hunger and from hiding—to live midway between madness and the dream—" He looked at me, his mouth drooping a little. "She promised me I'd understand someday, but this is someday and she's gone."

"Yes," I sighed, remembering how once I had dreamed that someday I'd run again. "But there are other somedays ahead—for you."

"Yes," he said. "And time hasn't stopped for you either." And he was gone.

I looked after him. "Doggone!" I thought. "There I go again, talking to him as though he made sense!" I poked the end of my crutch in the damp earth three times, making interlacing circles. Then with quickened interest I poked the boulder that had rolled *up* out of the slight hollow before the crutch tip had landed there.

"Son-a-gun!" I cried aloud. "Well, son-a-gun!"

Next morning at five of nine the kids were waiting for me at the door to the hall, huddled against the October chill that the milky sun hadn't yet had time to disperse. Rigo had a shaky old ladder with two broken rungs and splashes of old paint gumming it liberally.

"That looks awfully rickety," I said. "We don't want any blood spilled on our dance floor. It's bad for the wax."

Rigo grinned. "It'll hold me up," he said. "I used it last night to pick apples. You just have to be kinda careful."

"Well, be so then," I smiled, unlocking the door. "Better safe than—" My words faltered and died as I gaped in at the open door. The others pushed in around me, round-eyed and momentarily silenced. My first wild impression was that the ceiling had fallen in.

"My gorsh!" Janniset gasped. "What hit this place?"

"Just look at it!" Twyla shrilled. "Hey! Just look at it!"

We looked as we scuffled forward. Every single piece of paper was gone from the ceiling and walls. Every scrap of paper was on the floor, in tiny twisted confetti-sized pieces like a tattered faded snowfall, all over the floor. There must have been an incredible amount of paper tangled in the decorations, because we waded wonderingly almost ankle-deep through it.

"Looky here!" Rigo was staring at the front of the bandstand. Lined up neatly across the front stood all the nails that had been pulled out of the decorations, each balanced precisely on its head.

Twyla frowned and bit her lip. "It scares me," she said. "It doesn't feel right. It looks like somebody was mad or crazy—like they tore up the paper wishing they was killing something. And then to put all those nails so—so even and careful, like they had been put down gently—that looks madder than the paper." She reached over and swept her finger sideways, wincing as though she expected a shock. A section of the nails toppled with faint pings on the bare boards of the stand. In a sudden flurry Twyla swept all the nails over. "There!" she said, wiping her finger on her dress. "Now it's all crazy."

"Well," I said, "crazy or not, somebody's saved us a lot of trouble. Rigo, we won't need your ladder. Get the brooms and let's get this mess swept out."

While they were gone for the brooms I picked up two nails and clicked them together in a metrical cadence: "Oh, Danny Boy, the pipes, the pipes are calling—"

By noon we had the place scrubbed out and fairly glistening through its shabby paint. By evening we had the crisp new orange-and-black decorations up, low down and with thumbtacks, and all sighed with tired satisfaction at how good the place looked. As we locked up, Twyla suddenly said in a small voice, "What if it happens again before the dance Friday? All our work—"

"It won't," I promised. "It won't."

In spite of my hanging back and trying the lock a couple of times, Twyla was still waiting when I turned away from the door. She was examining the end of her braid carefully as she said, "It was him, wasn't it?"

"Yes, I suppose so."

"How did he do it?"

"You've known him longer than I have. How did he do it?"

"Nobody knows the Francher kid," she said. Then softly, "He looked at me once, really looked at me. He's funny—but not to laugh," she hastened. "When he looks at me it—" her hand tightened on her braid until her head tilted and she glanced up slantingly at me, "it makes music in me.

"You know," she said quickly into the echo of her unorthodox words, "you're kinda like him. He makes me think things and believe things I wouldn't ever by myself. You make me say things I wouldn't ever by myself—no, that's not quite right. You *let* me say things I wouldn't dare to say to anyone else."

"Thank you," I said. "Thank you, Twyla."

I had forgotten the trembling glamor of a teen-age dance. I had forgotten the cautious stilted gait of high heels on loafer-type feet. I had forgotten how the look of maturity could be put on with a tie and sport jacket and how—how *peoplelike* teen-agers could look when divorced for a while from Levi's and flannel shirts. Janniset could hardly contain himself for his own splendor and turned not a hair of his incredibly polished head when I smiled my "Good evening, Mr. Janniset." But in his pleased satisfaction at my formality he forgot himself as he turned away and hoisted up his sharply creased trousers as though they were his old Levi's.

Rigo was stunning in his Latin handsomeness, and he and Angie so drowned in each other's dark eyes that I could see why our Mexican youngsters usually marry so young. And Angie! Well, she didn't look like any eighth grader—her strapless gown, her dangly earrings, her laughing flirtatious eyes—but taken out of the context and custom and tradition she was breath-takingly lovely. Of course it was on her "unsuitable for her age" dress and jewelry and make-up that the long line of mothers and aunts and grandmothers fixed disapproving eyes, but I'd be willing to bet that there were plenty who wished their own children could look as lovely.

In this small community the girls always dressed up to the hilt at the least provocation, and the Hallowe'en dance was usually the first event of the fall that could serve as an excuse. Crinolined skirts belled like blossoms across the floor above the glitter of high heels, but it was only a matter of a few minutes before the shoes were kicked off, to toe in together forlornly under a chair or dangle from some motherly forefinger while unprotected toes braved the brogans of the boys.

Twyla was bright-cheeked and laughing, dance after dance, until the first intermission. She and Janniset brought me punch where I sat among the other spectators; then Janniset skidded off across the floor, balancing his paper cup precariously as he went to take another look at Marty, who at school was only a girl but here, all dressed up, was dawn of woman-wonder for him. Twyla gulped her punch hastily and then licked the corners of her mouth.

"He isn't here," she said huskily.

"I'm sorry," I said. "I wanted him to have fun with the rest of you. Maybe he'll come yet."

"Maybe." She twisted her cup slowly, then hastily shoved it under the chair as it threatened to drip on her dress.

"That's a beautiful dress," I said. "I love the way your petticoat shows red against the blue when you whirl."

"Thank you." She smoothed the billowing of her skirt. "I feel funny with sleeves. None of the others have them. That's why he didn't come, I bet. Not having any dress-up clothes like the others, I mean. Nothing but Levi's."

"Oh, that's a shame. If I had known—"

"No. Mrs. McVey is supposed to buy his clothes. She gets money for them. All she does is sit around and talk about how much she sacrifices to take care of the Francher kid, and she doesn't take care of him at all. It's her fault—"

"Let's not be too critical of others. There may be circumstances we know nothing of—and besides—" I nodded my head, "he's here now."

I could almost see the leap of her heart under the close-fitting blue as she turned to look.

The Francher kid was lounging against the door, his face closed and impassive. I noted with a flame of anger at Mrs. McVey that he was dressed in his Levi's, faded almost white from many washings, and a flannel shirt, the plaid of which was nearly indistinguishable except along the seams. It wasn't fair to keep him from being like the other kids even in this minor way—or maybe especially in this way, because clothes can't be hidden the way a mind or soul can.

I tried to catch his eye and beckon him in, but he looked only at the bandstand, where the band members were preparing to resume playing. It was tragic that the Francher kid had only this handful of inexpertly played instruments to feed his hunger on. He winced back into the darkness at their first blare, and I felt Twyla's tenseness as she turned to me.

"He won't come in," she half shouted against the take-a-melody-tear-it-to-pieces-stick-it-back-together-bleeding type of music that was going on.

I shook my head regretfully. "I guess not," I mouthed and then was drawn into a half-audible, completely incomprehensible conversation with Mrs. Frisney. It wasn't until the next dance started and she was towed away by Grampa Griggs that I could turn back to Twyla. She was gone. I glanced around the room. Nowhere the swirl of blue echoing the heavy brown-gold swing of her ponytail.

There was no reason for me to feel apprehensive. There were any number of places she might have gone and quite legitimately, but I suddenly felt an overwhelming need for fresh air and swung myself past the romping dancers and out into the gasping chill of the night. I huddled closer inside my jacket, wishing it were on right instead of merely flung around my shoulders. But the air tasted clean and fresh. I don't know what we'd been breathing in the dance hall, but it wasn't air. By the time I'd got the whatever-it-was out of my lungs and filled them with the freshness of the night, I found myself halfway down the path over the edge of the railroad cut. There hadn't been a train over the single track since nineteen-aught-something, and just beyond it was a thicket of willows and cottonwoods and a few scraggly piñon trees. As I moved into the shadow of the trees I glanced up at the sky, ablaze with a skrillion stars that dissolved into light near the lopsided moon and perforated the darker horizon with brilliance. I was startled out of my absorption by the sound of movement and music. I took an uncertain step into the dark. A few yards away I saw the flick of skirts and started to call out to Twyla. But instead I rounded the brush in front of me and saw what she was intent upon.

The Francher kid was dancing—dancing all alone in the quiet night. No, not alone, because a column of yellow leaves had swirled up from the ground around him and danced with him to a melody so exactly like their movement that I couldn't be sure there was music. Fascinated, I watched the drift and sway, the swirl and turn, the treetop-high rise and the hesitant drifting fall of the Francher kid and the autumn leaves. But somehow I couldn't see the kid as a separate Levied flannel-shirted entity. He and the leaves so blended together that the sudden sharp definition of a hand or a turning head was startling. The kid was just a larger leaf borne along with the smaller in the chilly winds of fall. On a final minor glissade of the music the Francher kid slid to the ground.

He stood for a moment, head bent, crumbling a crisp leaf in his fingers; then he turned swiftly defensive to the rustle of movement. Twyla stepped out into the clearing. For a moment they stood looking at each other without a word. Then Twyla's voice came so softly I could barely hear it.

"I would have danced with you."

"With me like this?" He gestured at his clothes.

"Sure. It doesn't matter."

"In front of everyone?"

"If you wanted to. I wouldn't mind."

"Not there," he said. "It's too tight and hard."

"Then here," she said, holding out her hands.

"The music—" But his hands were reaching for hers.

"Your music," she said.

"My mother's music," he corrected.

And the music began, a haunting lilting waltz-time melody. As lightly as the leaves that stirred at their feet the two circled the clearing.

I have the picture yet, but when I return to it my heart is emptied of adjectives because there are none for such enchantment. The music quickened and swelled, softly, richly full—the lost music that a mother bequeathed to her child.

Twyla was so completely engrossed in the magic of the moment that I'm sure she didn't even know when their feet no longer rustled in the fallen leaves. She couldn't have known when the treetops brushed their shoes—when the long turning of the tune brought them back, spiraling down into the clearing. Her scarlet petticoat caught on a branch as they passed, and left a bright shred to trail the wind, but even that did not distract her.

Before my heart completely broke with wonder, the music faded softly away and left the two standing on the ragged grass. After a breathless pause Twyla's hand went softly, wonderingly, to Francher's cheek. The kid turned his face slowly and pressed his mouth to her palm. Then they turned and left each other, without a word.

Twyla passed so close to me that her skirts brushed mine. I let her cross the tracks back to the dance before I followed. I got there just in time to catch the whisper on apparently the second round, "...alone out there with the Francher kid!" and the gleefully malicious shock of "...and her petticoat is torn..."

It was like pigsty muck clotting an Easter dress.

Anna said, "Hi!" and flung herself into my one armchair. As the front leg collapsed she caught herself with the dexterity of long practice, tilted the chair, reinserted the leg, and then eased herself back into its dusty depths.

"From the vagaries of the small town, good Lord deliver me!" she moaned.

"What now?" I asked, shifting gears on my crochet hook as I finished another row of my rug.

"You mean you haven't heard the latest scandal?" Her eyes widened in mock horror and her voice sank conspiratorially. "They were out there in the dark—alone—doing *nobody knows what.* Imagine!" Her voice shook with avid outrage. "With the Francher kid!

"Honestly!" Her voice returned to normal. "You'd think the Francher kid was leprosy or something. What a to-do about a little nocturnal smooching. I'd give you odds that most of the other kids are being shocked to ease their own consciences of the same kind of carryings-on. But just because it's the Francher kid—"

"They weren't alone," I said casually, holding a tight rein on my indignation. "I was there."

"You were?" Anna's eyebrows bumped her crisp bangs. "Well, well. This complexions things different. What did happen? Not," she hastened, "that I credit these wild tales about, my golly, Twyla, but what did happen?"

"They danced," I said. "The Francher kid was ashamed of his clothes and wouldn't come in the hall. So they danced down in the clearing."

"Without music?"

"The Francher kid—hummed," I said, my eyes intent on my work.

There was a brief silence. "Well," Anna said, "that's interesting, especially that vacant spot I feel in there. But you *were* there?"

"Yes."

"And they just danced?"

"Yes." I apologized mentally for making so pedestrian the magic I had seen. "And Twyla caught her petticoat on a branch and it tore before she knew it."

"Hmmm." Anna was suddenly sober. "You ought to take your rug up to the Sew-Sew Club."

"But I—" I was bewildered.

"They're serving nice heaping portions of Twyla's reputation for refreshments, and Mrs. McVey is contributing the dessert—the unplumbed depravity of foster children."

I stuffed my rug back into its bag. "Is my face on?" I asked.

Well, I got back to the Somansons' that evening considerably wider of eye than I had left it. Anna took my things from me at the door.

"How did it go?"

"My gorsh!" I said, easing myself into a chair. "If they ever got started on me, what would I have left?"

"Bare bones," Anna said promptly. "With plenty of tooth marks on them. Well, did you get them told?"

"Yes, but they didn't want to believe me. It was too tame. And of course Mrs. McVey didn't like being pushed out on a limb about the Francher kid's clothes. Her delicate hint about the high cost of clothes didn't impress Mrs. Holmes much, not with her six boys. I guess I've got me an enemy for life. She got a good-sized look at herself through my eyes and she didn't like it at all, but I'll bet the Francher kid won't turn up Levied for a dance again."

"Heaven send he'll never do anything worse," Anna intoned piously.

That's what I hoped fervently for a while, but lightning hit Willow Creek anyway, a subtle slow lightning—a calculated, coldly angry lightning. I held my breath as report after report came in. The Turbows' old shed exploded without a sound on the stroke of nine o'clock Tuesday night and scattered itself like kindling wood over the whole barnyard. Of course the Turbows had talked for years of tearing the shaky old thing down but— I began to wonder how you went about bailing a juvenile out of the clink.

Then the last sound timber on the old railroad bridge below the Thurmans' house shuddered and dissolved loudly into sawdust at eleven o'clock Tuesday night. The rails, deprived of their support, trembled briefly, then curled tightly *up* into two absurd rosettes. The bridge being gone meant an hour's brisk walk to town for the Thurmans instead of a fifteen-minute stroll. It also meant safety for the toddlers too young to understand why the rotting timbers weren't a wonderful kind of jungle gym.

Wednesday evening at five all the water in the Holmeses' pond geysered up and crashed down again, pureeing what few catfish were still left in it and breaking a spillway over into the creek, thereby draining the stagnant old mosquito-bearing spot with a conclusive slurp. As the neighbors had nagged at the Holmeses to do for years—but...

I was awestruck at this simple literal translation of my words and searched my memory with wary apprehensiveness. I could almost have relaxed by now if I could have drawn a line through the last two names on my mental roll of the club.

But Thursday night there was a crash and a roar and I huddled in my bed praying a wordless prayer against I didn't know what, and Friday morning I listened to the shrill wide-eyed recitals at the breakfast table.

"...since the devil was an imp and now there it is..."

"...right in the middle, big as life and twice as natural..."

"What is?" I asked, braving the battery of eyes that pinned me like a moth in a covey of searchlights.

There was a stir around the table. Everyone was aching to speak, but there's always a certain rough protocol to be observed, even in a boardinghouse.

Ol' Hank cleared his throat, took a huge mouthful of coffee, and sloshed it thoughtfully and noisily around his teeth before swallowing it.

"Balance Rock," he choked, spraying his vicinity finely, "came plumb unbalanced last night. Came a-crashing down, bouncing like a dang ping-pong ball an'nen it hopped over half a dozen fences an'nen *whammo!* it lit on a couple of the Scudders' pigs an'nen tore out a section of the Lelands' stone fence and now it's settin there in the middle of their alfalfa field as big as a house. He'll have a helk of a time mowing that field now." He slurped largely of his coffee.

"Strange things going on around here." Blue Nor's porchy eyebrows rose and fell portentously. "Never heard of a balance rock falling before. And all them other funny things. The devil's walking our land sure enough!"

I left on the wave of violent argument between proponents of the devil theory and the atom-bomb testing theory as the prime cause. Now I could draw another line through the list. But what of the last name? What of it?

That afternoon the Francher kid materialized on the bottom step at the boardinghouse, his eyes intent on my braces. We sat there in silence for a while, mostly I suppose because I could think of nothing rational to say. Finally I decided to be irrational.

"What about Mrs. McVey?"

He shrugged. "She feeds me."

"And what's with the Scudders' pigs?"

Color rose blotchily to his cheeks. "I goofed. I was aiming for the fence and let it go too soon."

"I told all those ladies the truth Monday. They knew they had been wrong about you and Twyla. There was no need—"

"No need!" His eyes flashed, and I blinked away from the impact of his straight indignant glare. "They're dern lucky I didn't smash them all flat."

"I know," I said hastily. "I know how you feel, but I can't congratulate you on your restraint, because however little you did compared to what you might have done, it was still more than you had a right to do. Especially the pigs and the wall."

"I didn't mean the pigs," he muttered as he fingered a patch on his knee. "Old man Scudder's a pretty right guy."

"Yes," I said. "So what are you going to do about it?"

"I don't know. I could swipe some pigs from somewhere else for him, but I suppose that wouldn't fix things."

"No, it wouldn't. You should buy—do you have any money?"

"Not for pigs!" he flared. "All I have is what I'm saving for my musical instrument, and not one penny of that'll ever go for pigs!"

"All right, all right," I said. "You figure out something."

He ducked his head again, fingering the patch, and I watched the late sun run across the curve of his cheek, thinking what an odd conversation this was.

"Francher," I said, leaning forward impulsively, "do you ever wonder how come you can do the things you do?"

His eyes were quick on my face. "Do you ever wonder why you *can't* do what you can't do?"

I flushed and shifted my crutches. "I *know* why."

"No, you don't. You only know when your 'can't' began. You don't know the real why. Even your doctors don't know all of it. Well, I don't know the why of my 'cans.' I don't even know the beginning of them, only that sometimes I feel a wave of something inside me that hollers to get out of all the 'can'ts' that are around me like you-can't-do-this, you-can't-do-that, and then I *remember* that I can."

He flicked his fingers and my crutches stirred. They lifted and thudded softly down the steps and then up again to lean back in their accustomed place.

"Crutches *can't* walk," the Francher kid said. "But you—something besides your body musta got smashed in that wreck."

"Everything got smashed," I said bitterly, the cold horror of that night and all that followed choking my chest. "Everything ended—everything."

"There aren't any endings," the Francher kid said. "Only new beginnings. When you going to get started?" Then he slouched away, his hands in his pockets, his head bent as he kicked a rock along the path. Bleakly I watched him go, trying to keep alive my flame of anger at him.

Well, the Lelands' wall had to be rebuilt and it was the Francher kid who got the job. He toiled mightily, lifting the heavy stones and cracking his hands with the dehydrating effect of the mortar he used. Maybe the fence wasn't as straight as it had been but it was repaired, and perhaps, I hoped, a stone had been set strongly somewhere in the Francher kid by this act of atonement. That he received pay for it didn't detract too much from the act itself, especially considering the amount of pay and the fact that it all went in on the other reparation.

The appearance of two strange pigs in the Scudders' east field created quite a stir, but the wonder of it was dulled by all the odd events preceding it. Mr. Scudder made inquiries but nothing ever came of them so he kept the pigs, and I made no inquiries but relaxed for a while about the Francher kid.

It was along about this time that a Dr. Curtis came to town briefly. Well, "came to town" is a euphemism. His car broke down on his way up into the hills, and he had to accept our hospitality until Bill Thurman could get around to finding a necessary part. He stayed at Somansons' in a room opposite mine after Mrs. Somanson had frantically cleared it out, mostly by the simple expedient of shoving all the boxes and crates and odds and ends to the end of the hall and draping a tarp over them. Then she splashed water across the barely settled dust and mopped out the resultant mud, put a brick under one corner of the bed, made it up with two army-surplus mattresses, one sheet edged with crocheted lace and one of heavy unbleached muslin. She unearthed a pillow that fluffed beautifully but sighed itself to a wafer-thin odor of damp feathers at a touch, and topped the splendid whole with two hand-pieced hand-quilted quilts and a chenille spread with a Technicolor peacock flamboyantly dominating it.

"There," she sighed, using her apron to dust the edge of the dresser where it showed along the edge of the dresser scarf, "I guess that'll hold him."

"I should hope so," I smiled. "It's probably the quickest room he's ever had."

"He's lucky to have this at such short notice," she said, turning the ragrug over so the burned place wouldn't show. "If it wasn't that I had my eye on that new winter coat—"

Dr. Curtis was a very relaxing comfortable sort of fellow, and it seemed so good to have someone to talk to who cared to use words of more than two syllables. It wasn't that the people in Willow Creek were ignorant, they just didn't usually care to discuss three-syllable matters. I guess, besides the conversation, I was drawn to Dr. Curtis because he neither looked at my crutches nor not looked at them. It was pleasant except for the twinge of here's-someone-who-has-never-known-me-without-them.

After supper that night we all sat around the massive oil burner in the front room and talked against the monotone background of the radio turned low. Of course the late shake-making events in the area were brought up. Dr. Curtis was most interested, especially in the rails that curled up into rosettes. Because he was a doctor and a stranger, the group expected an explanation of these goings-on from him, or at least an educated guess.

"What do I think?" He leaned forward in the old rocker and rested his arms on his knees. "I think a lot of things happen that can't be explained by our usual thought patterns, and once we get accustomed to certain patterns we find it very uncomfortable to break over into others. So maybe it's just as well not to want an explanation."

"Hmmm." Ol' Hank knocked the ashes out of his pipe into his hand and looked around for the wastebasket. "Neat way of saying you don't know either. Think I'll remember that. It might come in handy sometime. Well, g'night all." He glanced around hastily, dumped the ashes in the geranium pot, and left, sucking on his empty pipe.

His departure was a signal for the others to drift off to bed at the wise hour of ten, but I was in no mood for wisdom, not of the early-to-bed type anyway.

"Then there *is* room in this life for inexplicables." I pleated my skirt between my fingers and straightened it out again.

"It would be a poor lackluster sort of world if there weren't," the doctor said. "I used to rule out anything that I couldn't explain, but I got cured of that good one time." He smiled reminiscently. "Sometimes I wish I hadn't. As I said, it can be mighty uncomfortable."

"Yes," I said impulsively. "Like hearing impossible music and sliding down moonbeams—" I felt my heart sink at the sudden blankness of his face. Oh, gee! Goofed again. He could talk glibly of inexplicables but he didn't really believe in them. "And crutches that walk by themselves," I rushed on rashly, "and autumn leaves that dance in the windless clearing—" I grasped my crutches and started blindly for the door. "And maybe someday if I'm a good girl and disbelieve enough I'll walk again—"

" 'And disbelieve enough'?" His words followed me. "Don't you mean 'believe enough'?"

"Don't strain your pattern," I called back. "It's 'disbelieve.' "

Of course I felt silly the next morning at the breakfast table, but Dr. Curtis didn't refer to the conversation so I didn't either. He was discussing renting a jeep for his hunting trip and leaving his car to be fixed.

"Tell Bill you'll be back a week before you plan to," said Ol' Hank. "Then your car will be ready when you do get back."

The Francher kid was in the group of people who gathered to watch Bill transfer Dr. Curtis' gear from the car to the jeep. As usual he was a little removed from the rest, lounging against a tree. Dr. Curtis finally came out, his .30-06 under one arm and his heavy hunting jacket under the other. Anna and I leaned over our side fence watching the whole procedure.

I saw the Francher kid straighten slowly, his hands leaving his pockets as he stared at Dr. Curtis. One hand went out tentatively and then faltered. Dr. Curtis inserted himself in the seat of the jeep and fumbled at the knobs on the dashboard. "Which one's the radio?" he asked Bill.

"Radio? In this jeep?" Bill laughed.

"But the music—" Dr. Curtis paused for a split second, then turned on the ignition. "Have to make my own, I guess," he laughed.

The jeep roared into life, and the small group scattered as he wheeled it in reverse across the yard. In the pause as he shifted gears, he glanced sideways at me and our eyes met. It was a very brief encounter, but he asked questions and I answered with my unknowing and he exploded in a kind of wonderment—all in the moment between reverse and low.

We watched the dust boil up behind the jeep as it growled its way down to the highway.

"Well," Anna said, "a-hunting we do go indeed!"

"Who's he?" The Francher kid's hands were tight on the top of the fence, a blind sort of look on his face.

"I don't know," I said. "His name is Dr. Curtis."

"He's heard music before."

"I should hope so," Anna said.

"*That* music?" I asked the Francher kid.

"Yes," he nearly sobbed. "Yes!"

"He'll be back," I said. "He has to get his car."

"Well," Anna sighed. "The words are the words of English but the sense is the sense of confusion. Coffee, anybody?"

That afternoon the Francher kid joined me, wordlessly, as I struggled up the rise above the boardinghouse for a little wideness of horizon to counteract the day's shut-in-ness. I would rather have walked alone, partly because of a need for silence and partly because he just couldn't ever keep his—accusing?—eyes off my crutches. But he didn't trespass upon my attention as so many people would have, so I didn't mind too much. I leaned, panting, against a gray granite boulder and let the fresh-from-distant-snow breeze lift my hair as I caught my breath. Then I huddled down into my coat, warming my ears. The Francher kid had a handful of pebbles and was lobbing them at the scattered rusty tin cans that dotted the hillside. After one pebble turned a square corner to hit a can, he spoke.

"If he knows the name of the instrument, then—" He lost his words.

"What is the name?" I asked, rubbing my nose where my coat collar had tickled it.

"It really isn't a word. It's just two sounds it makes."

"Well, then, make me a word. 'Musical instrument' is mighty unmusical and unhandy."

The Francher kid listened, his head tilted, his lips moving. "I suppose you could call it a *'rappoor,'*" he said, softening the *a*. "But it isn't that."

"*'Rappoor,'*" I said. "Of course you know by now we don't have any such instrument." I was intrigued at having been drawn into another Francher-type conversation. I was developing quite a taste for them. "It's probably just something your mother dreamed up for you."

"And for that doctor?"

"Ummm." My mental wheels spun, tractionless. "What do you think?"

"I almost know that there are some more like Mother. Some who know 'the madness and the dream,' too."

"Dr. Curtis?" I asked.

"No," he said slowly, rubbing his hand along the boulder. "No, I could feel a faraway, strange-to-me feeling with him. He's like you. He—he knows someone who knows, but he doesn't know."

"Well, thanks. He's a nice bird to be a feather of. Then it's all very simple. When he comes back you ask him who he knows."

"Yes—" The Francher kid drew a tremulous breath. "Yes!"

We eased down the hillside, talking money and music. The Francher kid had enough saved up to buy a good instrument of some kind—but what kind? He was immersed in tones and timbres and ranges and keys and the possibility of sometime finding a something that would sound like a *rappoor*.

We paused at the foot of the hill. Impulsively I spoke.

"Francher, why do you talk with me?" I wished the words back before I finished them. Words have a ghastly way of shattering delicate situations and snapping tenuous bonds.

He lobbed a couple more stones against the bank and turned away, hands in his pockets. His words came back to me after I had given them up.

"You don't hate me—yet."

I was jarred. I suppose I had imagined all the people around the Francher kid were getting acquainted with him as I was, but his words made me realize differently. After that I caught at every conversation that included the Francher kid, and alerted at every mention of his name. It shook me to find that to practically everyone he was still juvenile delinquent, lazy trash, no-good off-scouring, potential criminal, burden. By some devious means it had been decided that he was responsible for all the odd happenings in town. I asked a number of people how the kid could possibly have done it. The only answer I got was, "The Francher kid can do anything—bad."

Even Anna still found him an unwelcome burden in her classroom despite the fact that he was finally functioning on a fairly acceptable level academically.

Here I'd been thinking—heaven knows why!—that he was establishing himself in the community. Instead he was doing well to hold his own. I reviewed to myself all that had happened since first I met him, and found hardly a thing that would be positive in the eyes of the general public.

"Why," I thought to myself, "I'm darned lucky he's kept out of the hands of the law!" And my stomach knotted coldly at what might happen if the Francher kid ever did step over into out-and-out lawlessness. There's something insidiously sweet to the adolescent in flouting authority, and I wanted no such appetite for any My Child of mine.

Well, the next few days after Dr. Curtis left were typical hunting-weather days. Minutes of sunshine and shouting autumn colors—hours of cloud and rain and near snow and raw aching winds. Reports came of heavy snow across Mingus Mountain, and Dogietown was snowed in for the winter, a trifle earlier than usual. We watched our own first flakes idle down, then whip themselves to tears against the huddled houses. It looked as though all excitement and activity were about to be squeezed out of Willow Springs by the drab grayness of winter.

Then the unexpected, which sometimes splashes our grayness with scarlet, happened. The big dude-ranch school, the Half Circle Star, that occupied the choicest of the range land in our area, invited all the school kids out to a musical splurge. They had imported an orchestra that played concerts as well as being a very good dance band, and they planned a gala weekend with a concert Friday evening followed by a dance for the teeners Saturday night. The ranch students were usually kept aloof from the town kids, poor little tikes. They were mostly unwanted or maladjusted children whose parents could afford to get rid of them with a flourish under the guise of giving them the advantage of growing up in healthful surroundings.

Of course the whole town was flung into a tizzy. There were the children of millionaires out there and famous people's kids, too, but about the only glimpse we ever got of them was as they swept grandly through the town in the ranch station wagons. On such occasions we collectively blinked our eyes at the chromium glitter, and sighed—though perhaps for different reasons. I sighed for thin unhappy faces pressed to windows and sad eyes yearning back at houses where families lived who wanted *their* kids.

Anyway the consensus of opinion was that it would be worth suffering through a "music concert" to get to go to a dance with a real orchestra, because only those who attended the concert were eligible for the dance.

There was much discussion and much heartburning over what to wear to the two so divergent affairs. The boys were complacent after they found out that their one good outfit was right for both. The girls discussed endlessly, and embarked upon a wild lend-borrow spree when they found that fathers positively refused to spend largely even for this so special occasion.

I was very pleased for the Francher kid. Now he'd have a chance to hear live music—a considerable cut above what snarled in our staticky wave lengths from the available radio stations. Now maybe he'd hear a faint echo of his *rappoor* and in style, too, because Mrs. McVey had finally broken down and bought him a new suit, a really nice one by the local standards. I was as anxious as Twyla to see how the Francher kid would look in such splendor.

So it was with a distinct shock that I saw the kid at the concert, lounging, thumbs in pockets, against the door of the room where the crowd gathered. His face was shut and dark, and his patched faded Levi's made a blotch in the dimness of the room.

"Look!" Twyla whispered. "He's in Levi's!"

"How come?" I breathed. "Where's his new suit?"

"I don't know. And those Levi's aren't even clean!" She hunched down in her seat, feeling the accusing eyes of the whole world searing her through the Francher kid.

The concert was splendid. Even our rockin'est rollers were caught up in the wonderful web of music. Even I lost myself for long lovely moments in the bright melodic trails that led me out of the gray lanes of

familiarity. But I also felt the bite of tears behind my eyes. Music is made
to be moved to, and my unresponsive feet wouldn't even tap a tempo. I
let the brasses and drums smash my rebellion into bearable-sized pieces
again and joined joyfully in the enthusiastic applause.

"Hey!" Rigo said behind me as the departing stir of the crowd began. "I didn't know anything could sound like that. Man! Did you hear
that horn! I'd like to get me one of them things and blow it!"

"You'd sound like a sick cow," Janniset said. "Them's hard to play."
Their discussion moved on down the aisle.

"He's gone." Twyla's voice was a breath in my ear.

"Yes," I said. "But we'll probably see him out at the bus."

But we didn't. He wasn't at the bus. He hadn't come out on the bus.
No one knew how he got out to the ranch or where he had gone.

Anna and Twyla and I piled into Anna's car and headed back for
Willow Creek, my heart thudding with apprehension, my thoughts busy.
When we pulled up at Somansons' there was a car parked in front.

"The McVey!" Anna sizzled in my ear. "Ah ha! Methinks I smell
trouble."

I didn't even have time to take my coat off in the smothery warmth
of the front room before I was confronted by the monumental violence
of Mrs. McVey's wrath.

"Dress him!" she hissed, her chin thrust out as she lunged forward
in the chair. "Dress him so's he'll feel equal to the others!" Her hands flashed
out, and I dodged instinctively and blinked as a bunch of white rags fluttered to my feet. "His new shirt!" she half screamed. Another shower of
tatters, dark ones this time. "His new suit! Not a piece in it as big as your
hand!" There was a spatter like muffled hail. "His shoes!" Her voice caught
on the edge of her violence, and she repeated raggedly, "His *shoes!*" Fear
was battling with anger now. "Look at those pieces—as big as stamps—
shoes!" Her voice broke. "Anybody who can tear up *shoes!*"

She sank back in her chair, spent and breathless, fishing for a
crumpled Kleenex to wipe the spittle from her chin. I eased into a chair
after Anna helped me shrug out of my coat. Twyla huddled, frightened,
near the door, her eyes big with fascinated terror.

"Let him be like the others," McVey half whispered. "That limb of
Satan ever be like anyone decent?"

"But why?" My voice sounded thin and high in the calm after the
hurricane.

"For no reason at all," she gasped, pressing her hand to her panting
ribs. "I gave all them brand-new clothes to him to try on, thinking he'd be
pleased. Thinking—" her voice slipped to a whining tremolo, "thinking he'd
see how I had his best interest at heart." She paused and sniffed lugubriously.

No ready sympathy for her poured into the hiatus, so she went on, angrily aggrieved. "And he took them and went into his room and came out with them like that!" Her finger jabbed at the pile of rags. "He—he *threw* them at me! You and your big ideas about him wanting to be like other kids!" Her lips curled away from the venomous spate of words. "He don't want to be like nobody 'cepting hisself. And he's a devil!" Her voice sank to a whisper and her breath drew in on the last word, her eyes wide.

"But why did he do it?" I asked. "He must have said *something*."

Mrs. McVey folded her hands across her ample middle and pinched her lips together. "There are some things a lady don't repeat," she said prissily, tossing her head.

"Oh, cut it out!" I was suddenly dreadfully weary of trying to be polite to the McVeys of this world. "Stop tying on that kind of an act. You could teach a stevedore—" I bit my lips and swallowed hard. "I'm sorry, Mrs. McVey, but this is no time to hold back. What did he say? What excuse did he give?"

"He didn't give any excuse," she snapped. "He just—just—" Her heavy cheeks mottled with color. "He called names."

"Oh." Anna and I exchanged glances.

"But what on earth got into him?" I asked. "There must be some reason—"

"Well." Anna squirmed a little. "After all, what can you expect—?"

"From a background like that?" I snapped. "Well, Anna, I certainly expected something different from a background like yours!"

Anna's face hardened and she gathered up her things. "I've known him longer than you have," she said quietly.

"Longer," I admitted, "but not better. Anna," I pleaded, leaning toward her, "don't condemn him unheard."

"Condemn?" She looked up brightly. "I didn't know he was on trial."

"Oh, Anna." I sank back in my chair. "The poor kid's been on trial, presumed guilty of anything and everything, ever since he arrived in town, and you know it."

"I don't want to quarrel with you," Anna said. "I'd better say good night."

The door clicked behind her. Mrs. McVey and I measured each other with our eyes. I had opened my mouth to say something when I felt a whisper of a motion at my elbow. Twyla stood under the naked flood of the overhead light, her hands clasped in front of her, her eyes shadowed by the droop of her lashes as she narrowed her glance against the glare.

"What did you buy his clothes with?" Her voice was very quiet.

"None of your business, young lady," Mrs. McVey snapped, reddening.

"This is almost the end of the month," Twyla said. "Your check doesn't come till the first. Where did you get the money?"

"*Well!*" Mrs. McVey began to hoist her bulk out of the chair. "I don't have to stay here and have a sassy snip like this—"

Twyla swept in closer—so close that Mrs. McVey shrank back, her hands gripping the dusty overstuffed arms of the chair.

"You never have any of the check left after the first week," Twyla said. "And you bought a purple nylon nightgown this month. It took a week's pay—"

Mrs. McVey lunged forward again, her mouth agape with horrified outrage.

"You took *his* money," Twyla said, her eyes steely in her tight young face. "You stole the money he was saving!" She whirled away from the chair, her skirts and hair flaring. "Someday—" she said with clenched teeth, "someday I'll probably be old and fat and ugly, but heaven save me from being old and fat and ugly and a *thief!*"

"Twyla!" I warned, truly afraid that Mrs. McVey would have a stroke then and there.

"Well, she *is* a thief!" Twyla cried. "The Francher kid has been working and saving almost a year to buy—" she faltered, palpably feeling the thin ice of betraying a confidence, "to buy something. And he had almost enough! And she must have gone snooping around—"

"Twyla!" I had to stop her.

"It's true! It's true!" Her hands clenched rebelliously.

"Twyla." My voice was quiet but it silenced her.

"Good-by, Mrs. McVey," I said. "I'm sorry this happened."

"Sorry!" she snorted, rearing up out of her chair. "Sour old maids with never a chick or child of their own sticking their noses into decent people's affairs—" She waddled hastily to the door. She reached for the doorknob, her eyes narrow and venomous over her shoulder. "I got connections. I'll get even with you." The door shuddered as it emphasized her departure.

I let the McVey sweep out of my mind.

"Twyla," I took her cold hands in mine, "you'd better go on home. I've got to figure out how to find the Francher kid."

The swift movement of her hands protested. "But *I* want—"

"I'm sorry, Twyla. I think it'd be better."

"Okay." Her shoulders relaxed in acquiescence.

Just as she left, Mrs. Somanson bustled in. "Y' better come on out to the table and have a cup of coffee," she said. I straightened wearily.

"That McVey! She'd drive the devil to drink," she said cheerfully. "Well, I guess people are like that. I've had more teachers over the years say that it wasn't the kids they minded but the parents." She shooed me through the door and went to the kitchen for the percolator. "Now I was always one to believe that the teacher was right—right or wrong—" Her voice faded out in a long familiar story that proved just the opposite of what she'd said, as I stared into my cup of coffee, wondering despairingly where in all this world I could find the Francher kid. After the episode of the gossip I had my fears. Still, oftentimes people who react violently to comparatively minor troubles were seemingly unshaken by really serious ones—a sort of being at a loss for a proportionate emotional reaction.

But what would he do? Music—music—he'd planned to buy the means for music and had lost the wherewithal. Now he had nothing to make music with. What would he do first? Revenge—or find his music elsewhere? Run away? To where? Steal the money? Steal the music? *Steal!*

I snapped to awareness, my abrupt movement slopping my cold coffee over into the saucer. Mrs. Somanson was gone. The house was quiet with the twilight pause, the indefinable transitional phase from day to night.

This time it wouldn't be only a harmonica! I groped for my crutches, my mind scrabbling for some means of transportation. I was reaching for the doorknob when the door flew open and nearly bowled me over.

"Coffee! Coffee!" Dr. Curtis croaked, to my complete bewilderment. He staggered over, all bundled in his hunting outfit, his face ragged with whiskers, his clothes odorous of campfires and all out-of-doors, to the table and clutched the coffeepot. It was very obviously cold.

"Oh, well," he said in a conversational tone. "I guess I can survive without coffee."

"Survive what?" I asked.

He looked at me a moment, smiling, then he said, "Well, if I'm going to say anything about it to anyone it might as well be you, though I hope that I've got sense enough not to go around babbling indiscriminately. Of course it might be a slight visual hangover from this hunting trip— you should hunt with these friends of mine sometime—but it kinda shook me."

"Shook you?" I repeated stupidly, my mind racing around the idea of asking him for help in finding the Francher kid.

"A somewhatly," he admitted. "After all there I was, riding along, minding my own business, singing, lustily if not musically, 'A Life on the Ocean Waves,' when there they were, marching sedately across the road."

"They?" This story dragged in my impatient ears.

"The trombone and the big bass drum," he explained.

"The what!" I had the sensation of running unexpectedly into a mad tangle of briars.

"The trombone and the big bass drum," Dr. Curtis repeated. "Keeping perfect time and no doubt in perfect step, though you couldn't thump your feet convincingly six feet off the ground. Supposing, of course, you were a trombone with feet, which this wasn't."

"Dr. Curtis." I grabbed a corner of his hunting coat. "Please, *please!* What happened? Tell me! I've got to know."

He looked at me and sobered. "You are taking this seriously, aren't you?" he said wonderingly.

I gulped and nodded.

"Well, it was about five miles above the Half Circle Star Ranch, where the heavy pine growth begins. And so help me, a trombone and a bass drum marched in the air across the road, the bass drum marking the time—though come to think of it, the drumsticks just lay on top. I stopped the jeep and ran over to where they had disappeared. I couldn't see anything in the heavy growth there, but I swear I heard a faint Bronx cheer from the trombone. I have no doubt that the two of them were hiding behind a tree, snickering at me." He rubbed his hand across his fuzzy chin. "Maybe I'd better drink that coffee, cold or not."

"Dr. Curtis," I said urgently, "can you help me? Without waiting for questions? Can you take me out there? Right now?" I reached for my coat. Wordlessly he helped me on with it and opened the door for me. The day was gone and the sky was a clear aqua around the horizon, shading into rose where the sun had dropped behind the hills. It was only a matter of minutes before we were roaring up the hill to the junction. I shouted over the jolting rattle.

"It's the Francher kid," I yelled. "I've got to find him and make him put them back before they find out."

"Put who back where?" Dr. Curtis shouted into the sudden diminution of noise as we topped the rise, much to the astonishment of Mrs. Frisney, who was pattering across the intersection with her black umbrella protecting her from the early starshine.

"It's too long to explain," I screamed as we accelerated down the highway. "But he must be stealing the whole orchestra because Mrs. McVey bought him a new suit, and I've got to make him take them back or they'll arrest him, then heaven help us all."

"You mean the Francher kid had that bass drum and trombone?" he yelled.

"Yes!" My chest was aching from the tension of speech. "And probably all the rest."

I caught myself with barked knuckles as Dr. Curtis braked to a sudden stop.

"Now look," he said, "let's get this straight. You're talking wilder than I am. Do you mean to say that that kid is swiping a whole orchestra?"

"Yes, don't ask me how. I don't know how, but he can do it—" I grabbed his sleeve. "But he said you knew! The day you left on your trip, I mean, he said you knew someone who would know. We were waiting for you!"

"Well, I'll be blowed!" he said in slow wonder. "Well, dang me!" He ran his hand over his face. "So now it's *my* turn!" He reached for the ignition key. "Gangway, Jemmy!" he shouted. "Here I come with another! Yours or mine, Jemmy? Yours or mine?"

It was as though his outlandish words had tripped a trigger. Suddenly all this strangeness, this out-of-stepness became a mad foolishness. Despairingly I wished I'd never seen Willow Creek or the Francher kid or a harmonica that danced alone or Twyla's tilted side glance, or Dr. Curtis or the white road dimming in the rapid coming of night. I huddled down in my coat, my eyes stinging with weary hopeless tears, and the only comfort I could find was in visualizing myself twisting my hated braces into rigid confetti and spattering the road with it.

I roused as Dr. Curtis braked the jeep to a stop.

"It was about there," he said, peering through the dusk. "It's mighty deserted up here—the raw end of isolation. The kid's probably scared by now and plenty willing to come home."

"Not the Francher kid," I said. "He's not the run-of-the-mill type kid."

"Oh, so!" Dr. Curtis said. "I'd forgotten."

Then there it was. At first I thought it the evening wind in the pines, but it deepened and swelled and grew into a thunderous magnificent shaking chord—a whole orchestra giving tongue. Then, one by one, the instruments soloed, running their scales, displaying their intervals, parading their possibilities. Somewhere between the strings and woodwinds I eased out of the jeep.

"You stay here," I half whispered. "I'll go find him. You wait."

It was like walking through a rainstorm, the notes spattering all around me, the shrill lightning of the piccolos and the muttering thunder of the drums. There was no melody, only a child running gleefully through a candy store, snatching greedily at everything, gathering delight by the handful and throwing it away for the sheer pleasure of having enough to be able to throw it.

I struggled up the rise above the road, forgetting in my preoccupation to be wary of unfamiliar territory in the half-dark. There they were, in the sand hollow beyond the rise—all the instruments ranged in orderly precise rows as though at a recital, each one wrapped in a sudden shadowy silence, broken only by the shivery giggle of the cymbals, which hastily stilled themselves against the sand.

"Who's there?" He was a rigid figure, poised atop a boulder, arms half lifted.

"Francher," I said.

"Oh." He slid through the air to me. "I'm not hiding any more," he said. "I'm going to be me all the time now."

"Francher," I said bluntly, "you're a thief."

He jerked in protest. "I'm not either—"

"If this is being you, you're a thief. You stole these instruments."

He groped for words, then burst out: "They stole my money! They stole all my music."

" 'They'?" I asked. "Francher, you can't lump people together and call them 'they.' Did I steal your money? Or Twyla—or Mrs. Frisney—or Rigo?"

"Maybe you didn't put your hands on it," the Francher kid said. "But you stood around and let McVey take it."

"That's a guilt humanity has shared since the beginning. Standing around and letting wrong things happen. But even Mrs. McVey felt she was helping you. She didn't sit down and decide to rob you. Some people have the idea that children don't have any exclusive possessions, but what they have belongs to the adults who care for them. Mrs. McVey thinks that way. Which is quite a different thing from deliberately stealing from strangers. What about the owners of all these instruments? What have they done to deserve your ill will?"

"They're people," he said stubbornly. "And I'm not going to be people any more." Slowly he lifted himself into the air and turned himself upside down. "See," he said, hanging above the hillside. "People can't do things like this."

"No," I said. "But apparently whatever kind of creature you have decided to be can't keep his shirttails in either."

Hastily he scrabbled his shirt back over his bare midriff and righted himself. There was an awkward silence in the shadowy hollow, then I asked:

"What are you going to do about the instruments?"

"Oh, they can have them back when I'm through with them—if they can find them," he said contemptuously. "I'm going to play them to pieces tonight." The trumpet jabbed brightly through the dusk and the violins shimmered a silver obbligato.

"And every downbeat will say 'thief,' " I said. "And every roll of the drums will growl 'stolen.' "

"I don't care, I don't care!" he almost yelled. " 'Thief' and 'stolen' are words for people and I'm not going to be people any more, I told you!"

"What are you going to be?" I asked, leaning wearily against a tree trunk. "An animal?"

"No, sir." He was having trouble deciding what to do with his hands. "I'm going to be *more* than just a human."

"Well, for a more-than-human this kind of behavior doesn't show very many smarts. If you're going to be more than human, you have to be thoroughly a human first. If you're going to be better than a human, you have to be the best a human can be, first—then go on from there. Being entirely different is no way to make a big impression on people. You have to be able to outdo them at their own game first and then go beyond them. It won't matter to them that you can fly like a bird unless you can walk straight like a man, first. To most people different is wrong. Oh, they'd probably say, 'My goodness! How wonderful!' when you first pulled some fancy trick, but—" I hesitated, wondering if I were being wise, "but they'd forget you pretty quick, just as they would any cheap carnival attraction."

He jerked at my words, his fists clenched.

"You're as bad as the rest." His words were tight and bitter. "You think I'm just a freak—"

"I think you're an unhappy person, because you're not sure who you are or what you are, but you'll have a much worse time trying to make an identity for yourself if you tangle with the law."

"The law doesn't apply to me," he said coldly. "Because I know who I am—"

"Do you, Francher?" I asked softly. "Where did your mother come from? Why could she walk through the minds of others? Who are you, Francher? Are you going to cut yourself off from people before you even try to find out just what wonders you are capable of? Not these little side-show deals, but maybe miracles that really count." I swallowed hard as I looked at his averted face, shadowy in the dusk. My own face was congealing from the cold wind that had risen, but he didn't even shiver in its iciness, though he had no jacket on. My lips moved stiffly. "Both of us know you could get away with this lawlessness, but you know as well as I do that if you take this first step you won't ever be able to untake it. And, how do we know, it might make it impossible for you to be accepted by your own kind—if you're right in saying there are others. Surely they're above common theft. And Dr. Curtis is due back from his hunting trip. So close to knowing—maybe—

"I didn't know your mother, Francher, but I do know this is not the dream she had for you. This is not why she endured hunger and hiding, terror and panic places—"

I turned and stumbled away from him, making my way back to the road. It was dark, horribly dark, around me and in me as I wailed soundlessly for this My Child. Somewhere before I got back, Dr. Curtis was helping me. He got me back into the jeep and pried my frozen fingers from my crutches and warmed my hands between his broad-gloved palms.

"He *isn't* of this world, you know," he said. "At least his parents or grandparents weren't. There are others like him. I've been hunting with some of them. He doesn't know, evidently, nor did his mother, but he *can* find his People. I wanted to tell you to help you persuade him—"

I started to reach for my crutches, peering through the dark, then I relaxed. "No," I said with tingling lips. "It wouldn't be any good if he only responded to bribes. He has to decide now, with the scales weighted against him. He's got to *push* into his new world. He can't just slide in limply. You kill a chick if you help it hatch."

I dabbled all the way home at tears for a My Child, lost in a wilderness I couldn't chart, bound in a captivity from which I couldn't free him.

Dr. Curtis saw me to the door of my room. He lifted my averted face and wiped it.

"Don't worry," he said. "I promise you the Francher kid will be taken care of."

"Yes," I said, closing my eyes against the nearness of his. "By the sheriff if they catch him. They'll discover the loss of the orchestra any minute now, if they haven't already."

"You made him think," he said. "He wouldn't have stood still for all that if you hadn't."

"Too late," I said. "A thought too late."

Alone in my room I huddled on my bed, trying not to think of anything. I lay there until I was stiff with the cold, then I crept into my warm woolly robe up to my chin. I sat in the darkness there by the window, looking out at the lacy ghosts of the cottonwood trees, in the dim moonlight. How long would it be before some kindly soul would come blundering in to regale me with the latest about the Francher kid?

I put my elbows on the window sill and leaned my face on my hands, the heels of my palms pressing against my eyes. "Oh, Francher, My Child, My lonely lost Child—"

"I'm not lost."

I lifted a startled face. The voice was so soft. Maybe I had imagined...

"No, I'm here." The Francher kid stepped out into the milky glow of the moon, moving with a strange new strength and assurance, quite divorced from his usual teen-age gangling.

"Oh, Francher—" I couldn't let myself sob, but my voice caught on the last of his name.

"It's okay," he said. "I took them all back."

My shoulders ached as the tension ran out of them.

"I didn't have time to get them all back in the hall, but I stacked them carefully on the front porch." A glimmer of a smile crossed his face. "I guess they'll wonder how they got out there."

"I'm so sorry about your money," I said awkwardly.

He looked at me soberly. "I can save again. I'll get it yet. Someday I'll have my music. It doesn't *have* to be now."

Suddenly a warm bubble seemed to be pressing up against my lungs. I felt excitement tingle clear out to my fingertips. I leaned across the sill. "Francher," I cried softly, "you *have* your music. Now. Remember the harmonica? Remember when you danced with Twyla? Oh, Francher. All sound is is vibration. You can vibrate the air without an instrument. Remember the chord you played with the orchestra? Play it again, Francher!"

He looked at me blankly, and then it was as if a candle had been lighted behind his face. "Yes!" he cried. "Yes!"

Softly—oh, softly—because miracles come that way, I heard the chord begin. It swelled richly, fully, softly, until the whole back yard vibrated to it—a whole orchestra crying out in a whisper in the pale moonlight.

"But the tunes!" he cried, taking this miracle at one stride and leaping beyond it. "I don't know any of the tunes for an orchestra!"

"There are books," I said. "Whole books of scores for symphonies and operas and—"

"And when I know the instruments better!" Here was the eager alive voice of the-Francher-kid-who-should-be. "Anything I hear—" The back yard ripped raucously to a couple of bars of the latest rock 'n' roll, then blossomed softly to an *"Adoramus te"* and skipped to "The Farmer in the Dell." "Then someday I'll make my own—" Tremulously a *rappoor* threaded through a melodic phrase and stilled itself.

In the silence that followed, the Francher kid looked at me, not at my face but deep inside me somewhere.

"Miss Carolle!" I felt my eyes tingle to tears at his voice. "You've given me my music!" I could hear him swallow. "I want to give you something." My hand moved in protest, but he went on quickly, "Please come outside."

"Like this? I'm in my robe and slippers."

"They're warm enough. Here, I'll help you through the window."

And before I knew it I was over the low sill and clinging dizzily to it from the outside.

"My braces," I said, loathing the words with a horrible loathing. "My crutches."

"No," the Francher kid said. "You don't need them. Walk across the yard, Miss Carolle, all alone."

"I can't!" I cried through my shock. "Oh, Francher, don't tease me!"

"Yes, you can. That's what I'm giving you. I can't mend you but I can give you that much. Walk."

I clung frantically to the sill. Then I saw again Francher and Twyla spiraling down from the treetops, Francher upside down in the air with his midriff showing, Francher bouncing Balance Rock from field to field.

I let go of the sill. I took a step. And another, and another. I held my hands far out from my sides. Glorious freedom from clenched hands and aching elbows! Across the yard I went, every step in the milky moonlight a paean of praise. I turned at the fence and looked back. The Francher kid was crouched by the window in a tight huddle of concentration. I lifted onto tiptoe and half skipped, half ran back to the window, feeling the wind of my going lift my hair back from my cheeks. Oh, it was like a drink after thirst! Like food after famine! Like gates swinging open!

I fell forward and caught at the window sill. And cried out inarticulately as I felt the old bonds clamp down again, the old half-death seize hold of me. I crumpled to the ground beside the Francher kid. His tormented eyes looked into mine, his face pale and haggard. His forearm went up to wipe his sweat-drenched face. "I'm sorry," he panted. "That's all I can do now."

My hands reached for him. There was a sudden movement, so quick and so close that I drew my foot back out of the way. I looked up, startled. Dr. Curtis and a shadowy someone else were standing over us. But the surprise of their being there was drowned in the sudden upsurge of wonderment.

"It moved!" I cried. "My foot moved. Look! Look! It moved!" And I concentrated on it again—hard, hard! After laborious seconds my left big toe wiggled.

My hysterical laugh was half a shout. "One toe is better than none!" I sobbed. "Isn't it, Dr. Curtis? Doesn't that mean that someday—that maybe—?"

He had dropped to his knees and he gathered my frantic hands into his two big quiet ones.

"It might well be," he said. "Jemmy will help us find out."

The other figure knelt beside Dr. Curtis. There was a curious waiting kind of silence, but it wasn't me he was looking at. It wasn't my hands he reached for. It wasn't my voice that cried out softly.

But it was the Francher kid who suddenly launched himself into the arms of the stranger and began to wail, the wild noisy crying of a child—a child who could be brave as long as he was completely lost but who had to dissolve into tears when rescue came.

The stranger looked over the Francher kid's head at Dr. Curtis. "He's mine," he said. "But she's almost one of yours."

It could all have been a dream, or a mad explosion of imagination of some sort; but they don't come any less imaginative than Mrs. McVey, and I know she will never forget the Francher kid. She has another foster child now, a placid plump little girl who loves to sit and listen to woman-talk—but the Francher kid is indelible in the McVey memory. Unborn generations will probably hear of him and his shoes.

And Twyla—she will carry his magic to her grave, unless (and I know she sometimes hopes prayerfully) Francher someday goes back for her.

Jemmy brought him to Cougar Canyon, and here they are helping him sort out all his many gifts and capabilities—some of which are unique to him—so that he will be able, finally, to fit into his most effective slot in their scheme of things. They tell me that there are those of this world who are developing even now in the footsteps of the People. That's what Jemmy meant when he told Dr. Curtis I was almost one of his.

And I am walking. Dr. Curtis brought Bethie. She only touched me softly with her hands and read me to Dr. Curtis. And I *had* to accept it then—that it was mostly myself that stood in my own way. That my doctor had been right: that time, patience, and believing could make me whole again.

The more I think about it, the more I think that those three words are the key to almost everything.

Time, patience, and believing—and the greatest of these is believing.

Interlude: Lea 6

Lea sat in the dark of the bedroom and swung her feet over the edge of the bed. She groped for and shrugged into a robe and huddled it around her. She went softly to the window and sat down on the broad sill. A lopsided moon rolled in the clouds above the hills, and all the Canyon lay ebony and ivory under its lights. Lea could see the haphazard dotting of houses that made up the community. All were dark except for one far window near the creek cliff.

Suddenly the whole scene seemed to take a sharp turn, completely out of focus. The hills and canyons became as strange as though she were looking at a moonscape or the hidden hills of Venus. Nothing looked familiar; even the moon suddenly became a leering frightening thing that could come closer and closer and closer. Lea hid her face in the bend of her elbow and drew her knees up sharply to support her shaking arms.

"What am I doing here?" she whispered. "What on earth am I doing here? I don't belong here. I've got to get away. What have I to do with all these—these—creatures? I don't believe them! I don't believe anything. It's madness. I've gone mad somewhere along the way. This must be an asylum. All these evenings—just pooling madnesses to see if a sanity will come out of it!"

She shuddered and lifted her head slowly, reluctantly opening her eyes. Determinedly she stared at the moon and the hills and the billowing clouds until they came back to familiarity. "A madness," she whispered. "But such a comforting madness. If only I could stay here forever—" Wistful tears blurred the moon. "If only, if only!"

"Fool!" Lea buried her face fiercely on her knees again. "Make up your mind. Is this or isn't this insanity? You can't have it both ways—not at one time." Then the wistful one whispered, "If this is insanity—I'll take it anyway. Whatever it is it makes a wonderful kind of sense that I've never been able to find before. I'm so tired of suspecting everything. Miss Carolle said the greatest was believing. I've got to believe, whether I'm mistaken or not." She leaned her forehead against the cold glass of the window, her eyes intent on the far light. "I wonder what their wakefulness is," she sighed.

She shivered away from the chill of the glass and rested her cheek on her knees again.

"But it's time," she thought. "Time for me to take a hand in my drifting. That's all it is, my staying here. Drifting in the warm waters of prebirth. Oh, it's lovely here. No worries about earning a living. No worries about what to do. No wondering which branch of the Y in the road to take. But it can't last." She turned her face and looked up at the moon. "Nothing is forever," she smiled wryly, "though unhappiness comes pretty close to it.

"How long can I expect Karen to take care of me? I'm no help to anyone. I have nothing to contribute. I'm a drag on her whatever she does. And I can't—how can I ever get cured of anything in such a protected environment? I've got to go out and learn to look the world full in the face." Her mouth twisted. "And even spit in its eye if necessary."

"Oh, I can't, I can't," one of her wailed. "Pull the ground up over me and let me be quit of everything."

"Shut up!" Lea answered sternly. "I'm running things now. Get dressed. We're leaving."

She dressed hastily in the darkness beyond the reach of the moonlight, tears flooding down her face. As she bent over to slip her shoes on, she crumpled against the bed and sobbed deep wrenching sobs for a moment, then finished dressing. She put on her own freshly laundered clothes. She shrugged into her coat—"nearly new"—and gathered up her purse.

"Money—" she thought. "I have no money—"

She dumped the purse on the bed. The few articles clinked on the bedspread. "I threw everything else away before I left—" able at last to remember leaving without darkness descending upon her, "and spent my last dollar—" She opened her billfold and spread it wide. "Not a cent."

She tugged out the miscellany of cards in the card compartment—little rectangles out of the past. "Why didn't I throw these out, too? Useless—" She started to cram them back blindly into the compartment, but her fingers hesitated on a projecting corner. She pulled out a thin navy-blue folder.

"Well! I did forget! My traveler's checks—if there's anything left." She unsnapped the folder and fingered the thin crisp sheaf. "Enough," she whispered. "Enough for running again—" She dumped everything back into her purse, then she opened the top dresser drawer. A faint blue light touched the outline of her face. She picked up the *koomatka* and turned it in her hand. She closed her fingers softly over it as she tore the margin from a magazine on the dresser top. She scrawled on it, "Thank you," and weighted the scrap of paper with the *koomatka*.

The shadows were so black, but she was afraid to walk in the light. She stumbled down from the house toward the road, not letting herself think of the miles and miles to be covered before reaching Kerry Canyon or anywhere. She had just reached the road when she started convulsively and muffled a cry against her clenched fists. Something was moving in the moonlight. She stood paralyzed in the shadow.

"Oh, hi!" came a cheerful voice, and the figure turned to her. "Just getting ready to leave. Didn't know anyone was going in, this trip. You just about got left. Climb in—"

Wordlessly Lea climbed into the battered old pickup.

"Some old jalopy, isn't it?" The fellow went on blithely, slamming the door and hooking it shut with a piece of baling wire. "I guess if you keep anything long enough it'll turn into an antique. This turned long ago! That's the only reason I can think of for their keeping it."

Lea made a vague noise and clutched the side of the car grimly as it took off and raced down the road a yard above the white gravelly surface.

"I haven't noticed you around," the driver said, "but then there's more people here than ever in the history of the Canyon with all this excitement going on. It's my first visit. It's comforting somehow, knowing there are so many of us, isn't it?"

"Yes, it is." Lea's voice was a little rusty. "It's a wonderful feeling."

"Nuisance, though, having to make all our trips in and out by night. They say that they used to be able to lift at least across Jackass Flat even in the daytime and then wheel in the rest of the way. But it's getting mighty close to dude season and we have to be more careful than during the winter. Travel at night. Wheel in from Widow's Peak. Lousy road, too. Takes twice as long. Have you decided yet?"

"Decided?" Lea glanced at him in the moonlight.

"Oh, I know I have no business asking," he smiled, "but it's what everyone is wondering." He sobered, leaning his arms on the steering wheel. "I've decided. Six times. Thought I'd finally decided for sure. Then comes a moonlight night like this—" He looked out over the vast panorama of hills and plains and far reaches—and sighed.

The rest of the trip was made in silence. Lea laughed shakily at her own clutching terror as the wheels touched down with a thud on the road near Widow's Peak. After that, conversation was impossible over the jolting bumping bouncing progress of the truck.

They arrived at Kerry Canyon just as the sunlight washed across the moon. The driver unhooked the door for her and let her out into the shivery dawn.

"We're in and out almost every morning and evening," he said. "You coming back tonight?"

"No." Lea shivered and huddled into her coat. "Not tonight."

"Don't be too long," the driver smiled. "It can't be much longer, you know. If you get back when no truck's in, just call. Mmm. Karen's Receptor this week. Bethie next. Someone'll come in to get you."

"Thank you," Lea said. "Thanks a lot." And she turned blindly away from his good-by.

The diner next to the bus stop was small and stuffy, clumsy still with the weight of the night, not quite awake in the bare drafty dawn. The cup of coffee was hot but hurried, and a little weak. Lea sipped and set it down, staring into its dark shaken depths.

"Even if this is all," she thought. "If I'm never to have any more of order and peace and sense of direction—why, I've at least had a glimpse, and some people never get even that much. I think I have the key now— the almost impossible key to my locked door. Time, patience, and believing—and the greatest of these is believing."

After a while she sipped again, not looking up, and found that the coffee had cooled.

"Hot it up for you?" A new waitress was behind the counter, briskly tying her apron strings. "Bus'll be along in just a little while."

"Thank you." Lea held out her cup, firmly putting away the vision of a cup of coffee that had steamed gently far into the morning, waiting, patient.

Time is a word—a shadow of an idea; but always, always, out of the whirlwind of events, the multiplicity of human activities or the endless boredom of disinterest, there is the sky—the sky with all its unchanging changeableness showing the variations of Now and the stability of Forever. There are the stars, the square-set corners of our eternities that wheel and turn and always find their way back. There are the transient tumbled clouds, the windy wisps of mares' tails, the crackling mackerel skies, and the romping delightful tumult of the thunderstorms. And the moon— the moon that dreams and sets to dreaming—that mends the world with its compassionate light and makes everything look as though newness is forever.

On such a night as this...

Lea leaned on the railing and sighed into the moonlight. Was it two such moons ago or only one that she had been on the bridge or fainting in the skies or receiving in the crisp mountain twilight love's gift of light from a child? She had shattered the rigidness of her old time-pattern and had not yet confined herself in a new one. Time had not yet paced itself into any sort of uniformity for her.

Tomorrow Grace would be back from her appendectomy, back to her job at the Lodge, the job Lea had been fortunate enough to step right into. But now this lame little temporary refuge would be gone. It meant another step into uncertainty. Lea would be free again, free from the clatter of the kitchen and dining room, free to go into the bondage of aimlessness again.

"Except that I have come a little way out of my darkness into a twilight zone. And if I take this next step patiently and believingly—"

"It will lead you right back to the Canyon—" The laughing voice came softly.

Lea whirled with an inarticulate cry. Then she was clutching Karen and crying, "Oh, Karen! Karen!"

"Watch it! Watch it!" Karen laughed, her arms tender around Lea's shaken shoulders. "Don't bruise the body! Oh, Lea! It's good to see you again! This is a better suicide-type place than that bridge." Her voice ran on, covering Lea's struggle for self-possession. "Want me to push you over here? Must be half a mile straight down. And into a river, yet—a river with water."

"Wet water," Lea quavered, releasing Karen and rubbing her arm across her wet cheeks. "And much too cold for comfortable dying. Oh, Karen! I was such a fool! Just because my eyes were shut I thought the sun had been turned off. Such a f-fool!" She gulped.

"Always last year a fool," Karen said. "Which isn't too bad if this year we know it and aren't the same kind of fool. When can you come back with me?"

"Back with you?" Lea stared. "You mean back to the Canyon?"

"Where else?" Karen asked. "For one thing you didn't finish all the installments—"

"But surely by now—"

"Not quite yet," Karen said. "You haven't even missed one. The last one should be ready by the time we get back. You see; just after you left— Well, you'll hear it all later. But I'm so sorry you left when you did. I didn't get to take you over the hill—"

"But the hill's still there, isn't it?" Lea smiled. "The eternal hills—?"

"Yes," Karen sighed. "The hill's still there but I could take anyone there now. Well, it can't be helped. When can you leave?"

"Tomorrow Grace will be back," Lea said. "I was lucky to get this job when I did. It helped tide me over—"

"As tiding-over goes it's pretty good," Karen agreed. "But it isn't a belonging-type thing for you."

Lea shivered, suddenly cold in the soul, fearing a change of pattern. "It'll do."

"Nothing will *do*," Karen said sharply, "if it's just a make-do, a time-filler, a drifting. If you won't fill the slot you were meant to, you might as well just sit and count your fingers. Otherwise you just interfere with everything."

"Oh, I'm willing to try to fill my slot. It's just that I'm still in the uncomfortable process of trying to find out what rating I am in whose category, and, even if I don't like it much, I'm beginning to feel that I belong to something and that I'm heading somewhere."

"Well, your most immediate somewhere is the Canyon," Karen said. "I'll be by for you tomorrow evening. You're not so far from us as the People fly! Your luggage?"

Lea laughed. "I have a toothbrush now, and a nightgown."

"Materialist!" Karen put out her forefinger and touched Lea's cheek softly. "The light is coming back. The candle is alight again."

"Praised be the Power." The words came unlearned to Lea's lips.

"The Presence be with you." Karen lifted to the porch railing, her back to the moon, her face in shadow. Her hands were silvered with moonlight as she reached out to touch Lea's two shoulders in farewell.

Before moonrise the next night Lea stood on the dark porch hugging her small bundle to her, shivering from excitement and the wind that strained icily through the piñon trees on the canyon's rim. The featureless bank of gray clouds had spread and spread over the sky since sundown. Moonrise would be a private thing for the upper side of the growing grayness. She started as the shadows above her stirred and coagulated and became a figure.

"Oh, Karen," she cried softly, "I'm afraid. Can't I wait and go by bus? It's going to rain. Look—look!" She held her hand out and felt the sting of the first few random drops.

"Karen sent *me*." The deep amused voice shook Lea back against the railing. "She said she was afraid your toothbrush and nightgown might have compounded themselves. For some reason or other she seems to have suddenly developed a Charley horse in her lifting muscles. Will I do?"

"But—but—" Lea clutched her bundle tighter. "I can't lift! I'm afraid! I nearly died when Karen transported me last time. Please let me wait and go by bus. It won't take much longer. Only overnight. I wasn't even thinking when Karen told me last night." She squeezed her eyes shut.

"I'm going to cry," she choked, "or cuss, and I don't do either gracefully, so please go. I'm just too darn scared to go with you."

She felt him pry her bundle gently out of her spasmed fingers. "It's not all that bad," he said matter-of-factly.

"Darn you People!" Lea wanted to yell. "Don't you ever understand? Don't you ever sympathize?"

"Sure we understand." The voice held laughter. "And we sympathize when sympathy is indicated, but we don't slop all over everyone who has a qualm. Ever see a little kid fall down? He always looks around to see whether or not he should cry. Well, you looked around. You found out and you're not crying, are you?"

"No, darn you!" Lea half laughed. "But honestly I really am too scared—"

"Well—say, my name is Deon in case you'd like to personalize your cussing. Anyway we have ways of managing. I can sleep you or opaque my personal shield so you can't see out—only you'd miss so much either way. I should have brought the jalopy after all."

"The jalopy?" Lea clutched the railing.

"Sure, you know the jalopy. They weren't planning to use it tonight."

"If you were thinking I'd feel more secure in that bucket of bolts—" Lea hugged her arms above the elbows. "I'd still be afraid."

"Look." Deon lifted Lea's bundle briskly. "It's going to rain in about half a minute. We're a long way from home. Karen's expecting you tonight and I promised her. So let's make a start of some kind, and if you find it unbearable we'll try some other way. It's dark and you won't be able to see—"

A jab of lightning plunged from the top of the sky to the depth of the canyon below them, and thunder shook the projecting porch like an explosion. Lea gasped and clutched Deon. His arms closed around her as she buried her face against his shoulder, and she felt his face pressed against her hair.

"I'm sorry," she shuddered, still clinging. "I'm scared of so many things."

Wind whipped her skirts about her and stilled. The tumultuous threshing of the trees quieted, and Lea felt the tension drain out. She laughed a little and started to lift her head. Deon pressed it back to his shoulder.

"Take it easy," he said. "We're on our way."

"Oh!" Lea gasped, clutching again. "Oh, no!"

"Oh, yes," Deon said. "Don't bother to look. Right now you couldn't see anything anyway. We're in the clouds. But start getting used to the idea. We'll be above them soon and the moon is full. *That* you must see."

Lea fought her terror, and slowly, slowly, it withdrew before a faint dawning wonder. "Oh!" she thought. "Oh!" as Karen's forgotten words welled softly up out of memory—"arms remember when eyes forget." "Oh, my goodness!" And her eyes flew open only to wince shut again against the outpouring of the full moon.

"Wasn't it—didn't you—?" she faltered, peering narrowly up into Deon's moon-whitened face.

"That's just what I was going to ask you," Deon smiled. "Seems to me I should have recognized you before this, but remember, the first time I ever saw you you were neck-deep in water and stringy in the hair—one piece of it was plastered across your nose—and Karen didn't even clue me!"

"But look now! Just look now!"

They had broken out of the shadows, and Lea looked below her at the serene tumble of clouds—the beyond-words wonder of a field of clouds under the moon. It was a beauty that not only fed the eyes but made all the senses yearn to encompass it and comprehend it. It sorrowed her not to be able to fill her arms with it and hold it so tight that it would melt right into her own self.

Silently the two moved over acres and acres of the purity of curves, the ineffable delight of depth and height and changing shadows—a world, whole and complete in itself, totally unrelated to the earth below in the darkness.

Finally Lea whispered, "Could I touch one? Could I actually put my hands into one of those clouds?"

"Why, sure," Deon said. "But, baby, it's cold out there. We have considerable altitude to get over the storm. But if you like—"

"Oh, yes!" Lea breathed. "It would be like touching the hem of heaven!"

Not even feeling the bite of cold when Deon opened the shield, Lea reached out gently to touch the welling flank of the cloud. It closed over her hands, bodiless, beautiful, as intangible as light, as insubstantial as a dream, and, like a dream, it dissolved through her fingers. As Deon closed the shield again, Lea found herself gasping and shivering. She looked at her hands and saw them glisten moistly in the moonlight. She looked up at Deon, turning in his arms. "Share my cloud," she said, and touched his cheek softly.

It was hard to gauge time, moving above a wonderland of clouds like that below them, but it didn't seem very long before Deon's voice vibrated against Lea's cheek where it rested against his shoulder. "We're going down now. Stand by for turbulence. We'll probably get tossed around a little."

Lea stirred and smiled. "I must have slept. I'm only dreaming all this."

"Pleasant dreams?"

"Pleasant dreams."

"Here we go! Hang on!"

Lea gasped as they plunged down toward the whiteness. All the serenity and beauty was gone with the snuffing out of the moon. Darkness and tumult were all around them. Wind grabbed them roughly and tossed them raggedly through the clouds, up, impossibly fast, down, incredibly far, twisting and tumbling, laced about by lightning, shaken by the blare of thunder, deafened—even though protected—by the myriad shrieking voices of the wind.

"It's death!" Lea thought frantically. "Nothing can live! It's madness! It's chaos!"

And then, in the middle of the terrifying tumult, she became conscious of warmth and shelter and, more personally, the awareness of someone—the nearness of another's breathing, the strength of arms.

"This," she thought wistfully, "must be like that love Karen mentioned. Out there all the storms of the world. In here, strength, warmth, and someone else."

A sudden down-draft flung them bodily out of the storm cloud, spinning them down to a staggering landing in the depth of Cougar Canyon, finally scraping them to a halt roughly against a yellow pine.

"Hoosh!" Deon leaned against the trunk and sagged. "Now I'm glad I *didn't* take the jalopy. That would have unscrewed every bolt in it. Thunderstorms are violent!"

"I should say so." Lea stirred in the circle of his arms. "But I wouldn't have missed it for the world. It'd be better than cussing or crying any time! Such wonderful slam-banging!" She stepped away from him and looked around.

"Where are we?" She prodded with her foot at the edge of a long indentation that ran darkly in the bright flush of lightning across the flat.

"Just over the hill from the schoolhouse."

"Over the hill?" Lea looked around her in startled interest, "But there's nothing here."

"How true." Deon kicked a small clod into the darkness. "Nothing here but me. And this time last week I'd have sworn—Oh, well—"

"You had me worried." The two jumped, startled at the sudden voice from the darkness above. "I thought maybe you might have been dumped miles away or maybe that Lea's toothbrush had slowed you down. Everyone's waiting." Karen touched down on the flat beside them.

"Then it came?" Deon surged forward eagerly. "Did it work? What was—?"

Karen laughed. "Simmer down, Deon. It arrived. It works. The Old Ones have called the Gathering and it's all ready to go except for three empty seats we're not filling. Alley-ooop!"

And Lea found herself snatched into the air and over the hill beyond the flat before she could gasp or let fear catch up with her. And she was red-cheeked and laughing, her hair sparkling with the first of a sudden shower, when they landed on the school porch and let the sudden snarl of thunder and shout of wind push them through the door. They threaded their way through the chattering groups and found seats. Lea looked over at the corner where she usually sat—almost afraid she might see herself still sitting there, hunched over the miserly counting of the coins of her misery.

She felt wonder and delight flood out into her arms and legs, and could hardly contain a wordless cry of joy. She spread her fingers on both hands, reaching, reaching openhanded, for what might be ahead.

"Darkness will come again," she admitted to herself. "This is just a chink in my prison—a promise of what is on the other side of me. But, oh! how wonderful—how wonderful!" She curled her fingers softly to hold a handful of the happiness and found it not strange that another hand closed warmly over hers. "These are people who will listen when I cry. They will help me find my answers. They will sustain me in the long long way that I must grope back to find myself again. But I'm not alone! Never alone again!"

She let everything but the present moment shudder away on a happy shaken sigh as she murmured with the Group, "We are met together in Thy Name."

No one was at the desk. In the middle of it was the same small gadget, or one very like it, that had always been there. Valancy, tenderly burdened on one arm with the flannelly bundle of Our Baby, leaned over and touched the gadget.

"I told you it would arrive okay." The voice came so lifelike that Lea involuntarily searched the front of the room for the absent speaker.

"And I'm to have the last say, after all.

"Well, I suppose you'd like a theme, just to round out things for you—so here it is.

" 'For ye shall pass over Jordan to go in to possess the land which the Lord your God giveth you and ye shall possess it and dwell therein....' "

❧

Jordan

I guess I was the first to see it—the bright form among the clouds above Baldy. There seemed to be no interval of wondering or questioning in my mind. I knew the moment I caught the metallic gleam—the instant the curl-back of the clouds gave a brief glimpse of a long sleek curve. I knew and I gave a shout of delight. Here it was! What more direct answer to a prayer could any fellow want? Just like that! My release from rebellion, the long-awaited answer to my protests against restrictions! There above me was release! I emptied my two hands of the gravel I had made of two small rocks during the time I had brooded on my boulder, dusted my palms against my Levi's, and lifted myself above the brush. I turned toward home, the tops of the underbrush ticking off the distance against my trailing toes. But oddly I felt a brief remote pang—almost of—regret?

As I neared the Canyon I heard the cry and saw one after another of the Group shoot upward toward Baldy. I forgot that momentary pang and shot upward with the rest of them. And my hands were among the first to feel the tingly hot-and-cold sleekness of the ship that was cooling yet from the heat of entry into the atmosphere. It was only a matter of minutes before the hands of the whole Group from the Canyon bore the ship downward from the clouds to the haven of the pine flats beyond Cougar—bore it rejoicing, singing an almost forgotten welcome song of the People.

Still tingling to the song, I rushed to Obla's house, bringing, as always, any new event to her, since she could come to none.

"Obla! Obla!" I cried as I slammed in through her door. "They've come! They've come! They're here! Someone from the New Home—" Then I remembered, and I went in to her mind. The excitement so filled my own mind that I didn't even have to verbalize for her before she caught the sight. Through my wordlessly sputtering delight I caught her faint chuckle. "Bram, the ship couldn't have rainbows around it and be diamond-studded from end to end!"

I laughed, too, a little abashed. "No, I guess not," I thought back at her. "But it should have a halo on it!"

Then for the next while I sat in the quiet room and relived every second of the event for Obla: the sights, the sounds, the smells, the feel of everything, including a detailed description of the—haloless—ship. And Obla, deaf, blind, voiceless, armless, legless, Obla who would horrify most any Outsider, lived the whole event with me, questioned me minutely, and finally lifted her unheard voice with the rest of us in the song of welcome.

"Obla." I moved closer to her and looked down at the quiet scarred face, framed in the abundance of dark vigorous hair. "Obla, it means the Home, the real Home. And for you—"

"And for me—" Her lips tightened and her eyelids flattened. Then the curtain of her hair swirled across her face as she hid herself from my eyes. "Perhaps a kinder world to hide this hideous—"

"Not hideous!" I cried indignantly.

Her soft chuckle tickled my mind. "Well, *not*, anyway," she said. "You'll have to admit that the explosion didn't leave much of me—" Her hair flowed back from her face and spread across the pillow.

"The part of you that counts!" I exclaimed.

"On Earth you need a physical container. One that functions. And just once I wish that—" Her mind blanked before I could catch her wish. The glass of water lifted from the bedside stand and hovered at her mouth. She drank briefly. The glass slid back to its place.

"So you're all afire to blast off?" her thought teased. "Back to civilization! Farewell to the rugged frontier!"

"Yes, I am," I said defiantly. "You know how I feel. It's criminal to waste lives like ours. If we can't live to capacity here, let's go Home!"

"To which Home?" she questioned. "The one we knew is gone. What is the new one like?"

"Well—" I hesitated, "I don't know. We haven't communicated yet. But it must be almost like the old Home. At least it's probably inhabited by the People, our People."

"Are you so sure we're still the same People?" Obla persisted. "Or that they are? Time and distance can change—"

"Of course we're the same," I cried. "That's like asking if a dog is a dog in the Canyon just because he was born in Socorro."

"I had a dog once," Obla said. "A long time ago. He thought he was people because he'd never been around other dogs. It took him six months to learn to bark. It came as quite a blow to him when he found out he was a dog."

"If you mean we've deteriorated since we came—"

"You chose the dog, not I. Let's not quarrel. Besides I didn't say that *we* were the dog."

"Yeah, but—"

"Yeah, but—" she echoed, amused, and I laughed.

"Darn you, Obla, that's the way most of my arguments with you end—yeah-but, yeah-but!"

"Why don't they come out?" I rapped impatiently against the vast seamless bulk, shadowy above me in the night. "What's the delay?"

"You're being a child, Bram," Jemmy said. "They have their reasons for waiting. Remember this is a strange world to them. They must be sure—"

"Sure!" I gestured impatiently. "We've *told* them the air's okay and there's no viruses waiting to snap them off. Besides they have their personal shields. They don't even have to *touch* this earth if they don't want to. Why don't they come out?"

"Bram." I recognized the tone of Jemmy's voice.

"Oh, I know, I know," I said. "Impatience, impatience. Everything in its own good time. But now, Jemmy, now that they're here, you and Valancy will have to give in. They'll make you see that the thing for us People to do is to get out completely or else get in there with the Outsiders and clean up this mess of a world. With this new help we could do it easily. We could take over key positions—"

"No matter how many have come—and we don't know yet how many there are," Jemmy said, "this 'taking over' isn't the way of the People. Things must grow. You only graft in extreme cases. And destroy practically never. But let's not get involved in all that again now. Valancy—"

Valancy slanted down, the stars behind her, from above the ship. "Jemmy." Their hands brushed as her feet reached the ground. There it was again. That wordless flame of joy, that completeness as they met, after a long ten minutes' separation. *That* made me impatient, too. I never felt that kind of oneness with anyone.

I heard Valancy's little laugh. "Oh, Bram," she said, "do you have to have your whole dinner in one gulp? Can't you be content to wait for anything?"

"It might be a good idea for you to do a little concentrated thinking," Jemmy said. "They won't be coming out until morning. You stay here on guard tonight—"

"On guard against what?" I asked.

"Against impatience," Jemmy said, his voice taking on the Old One tone that expected obedience without having to demand it. Amusement had crept back into his voice before his next sentence. "For the good of your soul, Bram, and the contemplation of your sins, keep watch this whole night. I have a couple of blankets in the pickup." He gestured, and the blankets drifted through the scrub oak. "There, that'll hold you till morning."

I watched the two of them meet with the pickup truck above the thin trickle of the creek. Valancy called back, "Thinking *might* help, Bram. You should try it."

A startled night bird flapped dismally ahead of them for a while, and then the darkness took them all.

I spread the blankets on the sand by the ship, leaning against the smooth coolness of its outer skin, marveling anew at its seamlessness, the unbroken flow along its full length. Somewhere there had to be an exit, but right now the evening light ran uninterrupted from glowing end to glowing end.

Who was in there? How many were in there? A ship of this size could carry hundreds. Their communicator and ours had spoken briefly together, ours stumbling a little with words we remembered of the Home tongue that seemed to have changed or fallen out of use, but no mention of numbers was made before the final thought: "We are tired. It's a long journey. Thanks be to the Power, the Presence, and the Name that we have found you. We will rest until morning."

The drone of a high-flying turbo-jet above the Canyon caught my ear. I glanced quickly up. Our un-light still humped itself up over the betraying shine of the ship. I relaxed on the blankets, wondering—wondering...

It was so long ago—back in my grandparents' day—that it all happened. The Home, smashed to a handful of glittering confetti—the People scattered to every compass point, looking for refuge. It was all in my memory, the stream of remembrance that ties the People so strongly together. If I let myself I could suffer the loss, the wandering, the tedium and terror of the search for a new world. I could live again the shrieking incandescent entry into Earth's atmosphere, the heat, the vibration, the wrenching and shattering. And I could share the bereavement, the tears, the blinding maiming agony of some of the survivors who made it to Earth. And I could hide and dodge and run and die with all who suffered the settlement period—trying to find the best way to fit in unnoticed among the people of Earth and yet not lose our identity as the People.

But this was all the past—though sometimes I wonder if anything is ever past. It is the future I'm impatient for. Why, look at the area of international relations alone. Valancy could sit at the table at the next summit conference and read the truth behind all the closed wary sparring faces—truth naked and blinding as the glint of the moon on the edge of a metal door—opening—opening...

I snatched myself to awareness. Someone was leaving the ship. I lifted a couple of inches off the sand and slid along quietly in the shadow. The figure came out, carefully, fearfully. The door swung shut and the figure straightened. Cautious step followed cautious step; then, in a sudden flurry of movement, the figure was running down the creek bed—fast! Fast! For about a hundred feet, and then it collapsed, face down into the sand.

I streaked over and hovered. "Hi!" I said.

Convulsively the figure turned over and I was looking down into her face. I caught her name—Salla.

"Are you hurt?" I asked audibly.

"No," she thought. "No," she articulated with an effort. "I'm not used to—" she groped, "running." She sounded apologetic, not for being unused to running but for running. She sat up and I sat down. We acquainted each other with our faces, and I liked very much what I saw. It was a sort of restatement of Valancy's luminously pale skin and dark eyes and warm lovely mouth. She turned away and I caught the faint glimmer of her personal shield.

"You don't need it," I said. "It's warm and pleasant tonight."

"But—" Again I caught the embarrassed apology.

"Oh, surely not always!" I protested. "What a grim deal! Shields are only for emergencies!"

She hesitated a moment and then the glimmer died. I caught the faint fragrance of her and thought ruefully that if I had a—fragrance?— it was probably compounded of barnyard, lumber mill, and supper hamburgers.

She drew a deep cautious breath. "Oh! Growing things! Life everywhere! We've been so long on the way. Smell it!"

Obligingly I did, but was conscious only of a crushed manzanita smell from beneath the ship.

This is a kind of an aside, because I can't stop in my story at every turn and try to explain. Outsiders, I suppose, have no parallel for the way Salla and I got acquainted. Under all the talk, under all the activity and busy-ness in the times that followed, was a deep underflow of communication between us. I had felt this same type of awareness before when our in-gathering brought new members of the Group to the Canyon, but never quite so strongly as with Salla. It must have been more noticeable because we lacked many of the common experiences that are shared by those who have occupied the same earth together since birth. That must have been it.

"I remember," Salla said as she sifted sand through slender unused-looking hands, "when I was very small I went out in the rain." She paused, as though for a reaction. "Without my shield," she amplified. Again the pause. "I got *wet!*" she cried, determined, apparently, to shock me.

"Last week," I said, "I walked in the rain and got so wet that my shoes squelched at every step and the clean taste of rain was in my mouth. It's one of my favorite pastimes. There's something so quiet about rain. Even when there's wind and thunder there's a stillness about it. I like it."

Then, shaken by hearing myself say such things aloud, I sifted sand, too, a little violently at first.

She reached over with a slender milky finger and touched my hand. "Brown," she said. Then, "Tan," as she caught my thought.

"The sun," I said. "We're out in the sun so much, unshielded, that it browns our skins or freckles them, or burns the living daylight out of us if we're not careful."

"Then you still live in touch of Earth. At Home we seldom ever—" Her words faded and I caught a capsuled feeling that might have been real cozy if you were born to it, but...

"How come?" I asked. "What's with your world that you have to shield all the time?" I felt a pang for my pictured Eden....

"We don't *have* to. At least not any more. When we arrived at the new Home we had to do a pretty thorough renovating job. We—of course this was my grandparents—wanted it as nearly like the old Home as possible. We've done wonderfully well copying the vegetation and hills and valleys and streams, but—" guilt tinged her words, "it's still a copy—nothing casual and—and thoughtless. By the time the new Home was livable, we'd got into the habit of shielding. It was just what one did automatically. I don't believe Mother has gone unshielded outside her own sleep-room in all her life. You just—don't—"

I sprawled my arm across the sand, feeling it grit against my skin. Real cozy, but...

She sighed. "One time—I was old enough to know better, they told me—one time I walked in the sun unshielded. I got muddy and got my hands dirty and tore my dress." She brought out the untidy words with an effort, as though using extreme slang at a very prim gathering. "And I tangled my hair so completely in a tree that I had to pull some of it out to get free." There was no bravado in her voice now. Now she was sharing with me one of the most precious of her memories—one not quite socially acceptable among her own.

I touched her hand lightly, since I do not communicate too freely without contact, and saw her.

She was stealing out of the house before dawn—strange house, strange landscape, strange world—easing the door shut, lifting quickly out into the grove below the house. Her flame of rebellion wasn't strange to me, though. I knew it too well myself. Then she dropped her shield. I gasped with her because I was feeling, as newly as though I were the First in a brand-new Home, the movement of wind on my face, on my arms. I was even conscious of it streaming like tiny rivers between my fingers. I felt the soil beneath my hesitant feet, the soft packed clay, the outline of a leaf, the harsh stab of gravel, the granular sandiness of the water's edge. The splash of water against my legs was as sharp as a bite into lemon. And wetness! I had no idea that wetness was such an individual feeling. I can't remember when first I waded in water, or whether I ever felt wetness to know consciously, "This is wetness." The newness! It was like nothing I'd felt before.

Then suddenly there was the smell of crushed manzanita again, and Salla's hand had moved from beneath mine.

"Mother's questing for me," she whispered. "She has no idea I'm here. She'd have a *quanic* if she knew. I must go before she gets no answer from my room."

"When are you all coming out?"

"Tomorrow, I think. Laam will have to rest longer. He's our Motiver, you know. It was exhausting bringing the ship into the atmosphere. More so than the whole rest of the trip. But the rest of us—"

"How many?" I whispered as she glided away from me and up the curve of the ship.

"Oh," she whispered back, "there's—" The door opened and she slid inside and it closed.

"Dream sweetly," I heard soundlessly, then astonishingly, the touch of a soft cheek against one of my cheeks, and the warm movement of lips against the other. I was startled and confused, though pleased, until with a laugh I realized that I had been caught between the mother's questing and Salla's reply.

"Dream sweetly," I thought, and rolled myself in my blankets.

Something wakened me in the empty hours before dawn. I lay there feeling snatched out of sleep like a fish out of water, shivering in the interval between putting off sleep and putting on awakeness.

"I'm supposed to think," I thought dully. "Concentrated thinking."

So I thought. I thought of my People, biding their time, biding their time, waiting, waiting, walking when they could be flying. Think, *think*, what we could do if we stopped waiting and really got going. Think of Bethie, our Sensitive, in a medical center, reading the illnesses and ailments to the doctors. No more chance for patients to hide behind imaginary illnesses. No wrong diagnoses, no delay in identification of conditions. Of course there are only one Bethie and the few Sorters we have who could serve a little less effectively, but it would be a beginning.

Think of our Sorters, helping to straighten people out, able to search their deepest beings and pry the scabs off ancient cankers and wounds and let healing into the suffering intricacies of the mind.

Think of our ability to lift, to transport, to communicate, to *use* Earth instead of submitting to it. Hadn't Man been given dominion over Earth? Hadn't he forfeited it somewhere along the way? Couldn't we help point him back to the path again?

I twisted with this concentrated restatement of all my questions. Why couldn't this all be so now, *now!*

But, "No," say the Old Ones. "Wait," says Jemmy. "Not now," says Valancy.

"But look!" I wanted to yell. "They're headed for space! Trying to get there on a Pogo stick. Look at Laam! He brought that ship to us from some far Homeland without lifting his hand, without gadgets in his comfortable motive-room. Take any of us. I myself could lift our pickup high enough to need my shield to keep me breathing. I'll bet even I in one of those sealed high-flying planes could take it to the verge of space, just this side of the escape rim. And any Motiver could take it over the rim and the hard part is over. Of course, though all of us can lift we have only two Motivers, but it would be a start!"

But, "No," say the Old Ones. "Wait," says Jemmy. "Not now," says Valancy.

All right, so it would be doing violence to the scheme of things, grafting a third arm onto an organism designed for two. So the Earth ones will develop along our line someday—look at Peter and Dita and that Francher kid and Bethie. So someday when it is earned they will have it. So—let's go, then! Let's find another Home. Let's take to space and leave them their Earth. Let's let them have their time—if they don't die of it first. Let's leave. Let's get out of this crummy joint. Let's go somewhere where we can be ourselves all the time, openly, unashamed!

I pounded my fists on the blanket, then ruefully wiped the flecks of sand from my lips and tongue and grunted a laugh at myself. I caught my breath, then relaxed.

"Okay, Davy," I said, "what are you doing out so early?"

"I haven't been to bed," Davy said, drifting out of the shadows. "Dad said I could try my scriber tonight. I just got it finished."

"That thing?" I laughed up at him. "What could you scribe at night?"

"Well—" Davy sat down in the air above my blanket, rubbing his thumbs on the tiny box he was holding. "I thought it might be able to scribe dreams, but it won't. Not enough verbalizing in them. I checked my whole family and used up half my scribe tape. Gotta make some more today!"

"Nasty break," I said. "Back to the drawing boards, boy."

"Oh, I don't know," Davy said. "I tried it on your dreams—" He flipped up out of my casual swipe at him. "But I couldn't get anything. So I ran a chill down your spine—"

"You rat," I said, too lazy to resent it very much. "That's why I woke up so hard and quick."

"Yup," he said, drifting back over me. "So I tried it on you awake. More concentrated thought patterns."

"Hey!" I sat up slowly. "Concentrated thought?"

"Take this last part." Davy drifted up again. There was a quacking gabble. "Ope!" he said. "Forgot the slowdown. Thoughts are fast. Now—"

And clearly and minutely, the way a voice sometimes sounds from a telephone receiver, I heard myself yelling, "Let's leave, let's get out of this crummy joint—"

"Davy!" I yelled, launching myself upward, encumbered as I was with blankets.

"Watch it! Watch it!" he cried, holding the scriber away from me as we tumbled in the air. "Group interest! I claim Group interest! With the ship here now—"

"Group interest, nothing!" I said as I finally got my hands on the scriber. "You're forgetting privacy of thought—and the penalty for violation thereof." I caught his flying thought and pushed the right area on the box to erase the record.

"Dagnab!" said Davy, disgruntled. "My first invention and you erase my first recording on it."

"Nasty break!" I said. Then I tossed the box to him. "But say!" I reached up and pulled him down to me. "Obla! Think about Obla and this screwy gadget!"

"Yeah!" His face lighted up, then blanked as he was snatched along by the train of thought. "Yeah! Obla—no audible voice—" He had already forgotten me before the trees received him.

It wasn't that I had been ashamed of my thoughts. It was only that they sounded so—so naked, made audible. I stood there, my hands flattened against the beautiful ship, and felt my conviction solidify. "Let's go. Let's leave. If there isn't room for us on this ship, we can build others. Let's find a real Home somewhere. Either find one or build one."

I think it was at that moment that I began to say good-by to Earth, almost subconsciously beginning to sever the ties that bound me to it. Like the slow out-fanning of a lifting wing, the direction of my thoughts turned skyward. I lifted my eyes. "This time next year," I thought, "I won't be watching morning lighting up Old Baldy."

By midmorning the whole of the Group, including the whole Group from Bendo, which had been notified, was waiting on the hillside near the ship. There was very little audible speech and not much gaiety. The ship brought back too much of the past, and the dark streams of memory were coursing through the Group. I latched onto one stream and found only the shadows of the Crossing in it. "But the Home," I interjected, "the Home before!"

Just then a glitter against the bulk of the ship drew our attention. The door was opening. There was a pause, and then there were the four of them, Salla and her parents and another older fellow. The slight glintings of their personal shields were securely about them, and, as they winced against the downpouring sun, their shields thickened above their heads and took on a deep blue tint.

The Oldest, his blind face turned to the ship, spoke on a Group stream.

"Welcome to the Group." His thought was organ-toned and cordial. "Thrice welcome among us. You are the first from the Home to follow us to Earth. We are eager for the news of our friends."

There was a sudden babble of thoughts. "Is Anna with you? Is Mark? Is Santhy? Is Bediah?"

"Wait, wait—" The Father lifted his arms imploringly. "I cannot answer all of you at once except by saying—there are only the four of us in the ship."

"Four!" The astonished thought almost lifted an echo from Baldy.

"Why, yes," answered—he gave us his name—Shua. "My family and I and our Motiver here, Laam."

"Then all the rest—?" Several of us slipped to our knees with the Sign trembling on our fingers.

"Oh, no! No!" Shua was shocked. "No, we fared very well in our new Home. Almost all your friends await you eagerly. As you remember, ours was the group living adjacent to yours on the Home. Our Group and two others reached our new Home. Why, we brought this ship empty so we could take you all Home!"

"Home?" For a stunned moment the word hung almost visibly in the air above us.

Then, "Home!" The cry rose and swelled and broke to audibility as the whole Group took to the sky as one. It was such a jubilant ecstatic cry that it shook an echo sufficient to frighten a pair of blue jays from a clump of pines on the flat.

"Why, they must all think the way I do!" I thought, astonished, as I joined in the upsurge and the jubilant chorus of the wordless Homeward song. Then I flatted a little as I wondered if any of them shared with me the sudden pang I had felt before. I tucked it quickly away, deep enough so that only a Sorter would be able to find it, and quickly cradled the Francher kid in my lifting—he hadn't learned to go much beyond the treetops yet, and the Group was leaving him behind....

"There's four of them," I thought breathlessly at Obla. "Only four. They brought the ship to take us Home."

Obla turned her blind face to me. "To take us all? Just like that?"

"Well, yes," I replied, frowning a little. "I guess just like that—whatever *that* means."

"After all, I suppose castaways are always eager for rescue," Obla said. Then, gently mocking, "I suppose you're all packed?"

"I've been packed almost since I was born. Haven't I always been talking about getting out of this bind that holds us back?"

"You have," Obla thought. "Exhaustively talked about it. Put your hand out the window, Bram. Take a handful of sun." I did, filling my palm with the tingling brightness. "Pour it out." I tilted my hand and felt the warm flow of escaping light. "No more Earth sun ever again," she said. "Not ever!"

"Darn you, Obla, cut it out!" I cried.

"You weren't so entirely sure yourself, were you? Even after all your protestations. Even in spite of that big warm wonder growing inside you."

"Warm wonder?" Then I felt my face heat up. "Oh," I said awkwardly. "That's only natural interest in a stranger—a stranger from Home!" I felt excitement mounting. "Just think, Obla! From Home!"

"A stranger from Home." Obla's thought was a little sad. "Listen to your words, Bram. A *stranger* from Home. Whenever have People been strangers to one another?"

"You're playing with words now. Let me tell you the whole thing—"

I have used Obla for a sounding board ever since I can remember. I have no memory of her physically complete. I became conscious of her only after her disaster and mine. The same explosion that maimed her took my parents. They were trying to get some Outsiders out of a crashed plane and didn't quite make it. Some of my most grandiose schemes have echoed hollow and empty against the listening receptiveness of Obla. And some of my shyest thoughts have grown to monumental strength with her uncritical acceptance of them. Somehow, when you hear your own ideas, crisply cut for transmission, they are stripped of anything extraneous and stand naked of pretensions, and *then* you can get a decent perspective on them.

"Poor child," she cut in when I told her of Salla's hair being caught. "Poor child, to feel that pain is a privilege—"

"Better that than having pain a way of life!" I flashed. "Who should know better than you?"

"Perhaps, perhaps. Who is to say which is better—to hunger and be fed, or to be fed so continuously that you never know hunger? Sometimes a little fasting is good for the soul. Think of a cold drink of water after an afternoon in the hayfield."

I shivered at the delicious recollection. "Well, *anyway...*" and I finished the account for her. I was almost out of the door before I suddenly realized that I hadn't mentioned Davy at all! I went back and told her. Before I was half through, her face twisted and her hair swirled protectively over it. When I finished I stood there awkwardly, not knowing exactly what to do. Then I caught a faint echo of her thought. "A voice again..." I think a little of my contempt for gadgets died at that moment. Anything that could pleasure Obla...

I thought I was troubled about whether we should go or stay, until the afternoon I found all the Blends and In-gathereds sitting together on the boulders above Cougar Creek. Dita was trailing the water from her bare toes, and all the rest were concentrating on the falling of the drops as though there were some answer in them. The Francher kid was making a sharp crystal scale out of their falling. I came openly so there was no thought of eavesdropping, but I don't think they were fully aware that I was there.

"But for me—" Dita drew her knees up to her chest and clasped her wet feet in her hands, "for me it's different. You're Blends, or all of the People. But I'm all of Earth. My roots are anchored in this old rock. Think what it would mean to me to say good-by to my world. Think back to the Crossing—" A ripple of discomfort moved through the Group. "You see? And yet, to stay—to watch the People go, to know them gone—" She laid her cheek against her knees.

The quick comfort of the others enveloped her, and Low moved to the boulder beside her.

"It'd be as bad for us to leave," he said. "Sure, we're of the People, but this is the only Home we've known. I didn't grow up in a Group. None of us did. All of our roots are firmly set here, too. To leave—"

"What has the New Home to offer that we don't have here?" Peter started a little whirlpool in the shallow stream below.

"Well—" Low stilled the whirlpool and spoke into a lengthening silence, "ask Bram. He's all afire to blast off." He grinned over his shoulder at me.

"The new Home is *our* world," I said, drifting over to them, gathering my scattered thoughts. "We would be among our own. No more concealment. No more trying to fit in where we don't fit. No more holding back, holding back, when we could be doing so much."

I could feel the surge and swirl of thoughts around me—each person aligning himself to the vision of the Home. Without any further word they all left the creek, absorbed in the problem. As they slowly scattered there was not an echo of a thought. Everyone was shutting himself up with his own reactions.

All the peace and tranquillity of Cougar Canyon was gone. Oh, sure, the light still slanted brightly through the trees at dawn, the wind still stirred the branches in the hot quiet afternoons and occasionally whipped up little whirlwinds to dance the dried leaves in a brief flurry of action, and the slender new moon was cleanly bright in the evening sky—but it was all overlaid with a big question mark.

I couldn't settle to anything. Halfway through ripping a plank at the mill I'd think, "Why bother? We'll be gone soon." And then the spasm of acute pleasure and anticipation would somehow turn to the pain of bereavement and I'd feel like clutching a handful of sawdust and—well— sobbing into it.

And late at night, changing the headgates to irrigate another alfalfa field, I'd kick the moss-slick wet boards and think exultantly, "When we get *there* we won't have to go through this mumbo-jumbo. We'll rain the water where and when we want it!"

Then again, I'd lie in the edge of the hot sun, my head in the shade of the cottonwoods, and feel the deep soaking warmth to my very bone, smell the waiting dusty smell of the afternoon, feel sleep wrapping itself around my thoughts, and hear the sudden creaking cries of the red-winged blackbirds in the far fields, and suddenly *know* that I couldn't leave it. Couldn't give up Earth for any thing or any place.

But there was Salla. Showing her Earth was like nothing you could ever imagine. For instance, it never occurred to her that things could hurt her. Like the day I found her halfway across Furnace Flat, huddled under a piñon pine, cradling her bare feet in her hands and rocking with pain.

"Where are your shoes?" It was the first thing I could think of as I hunched beside her.

"Shoes?" She caught the picture from me. "Oh, shoes. My—san-dals—are at the ship. I wanted to *feel* this world. We shield so much at home that I couldn't tell you a thing about textures there. But the sand was so good the first night, and water is wonderful, I thought this black glowing smoothness and splinteredness would be a different sort of tex-ture." She smiled ruefully. "It is. It's hot and—and—"

I supplied a word, "Hurty. I should think so. This shale flat heats up like a furnace this time of day. That's why it's called Furnace Flat."

"I landed in the middle of it, running. I was so surprised that I didn't have sense enough to lift or shield."

"Let me see." I loosened her fingers and took one of her slender white feet in my hand. *"Adonday Veeah!"* I whistled. Carefully I picked off a few loose flakes of bloodstained shale. "You've practically blistered your feet, too. Don't you know the sun can be vicious this time of day?"

"I know now." She took her feet back and peered at the sole. "Look! There's blood!"

"Yep. That's usual when you puncture your skin. Better come on back to the house and get those feet taken care of."

"Taken care of?"

"Sure. Antiseptic for the germs, salve for the burns. You won't go hunting for a day or two. Not with your feet, anyway."

"Can't we just no-bi and transgraph? It's so much simpler."

"Indubitably," I said, lifting sitting as she did and straightening up in the air above the path. "If I knew what you were talking about." We headed for the house.

"Well, at Home the Healers—"

"This is Earth," I said. "We have no Healers as yet. Only in so far as our Sensitive can help out those who know about healing. It's mostly a do-it-yourself deal with us. And who knows, you might be allergic to us and sprout day lilies at every puncture. It'll probably worry your mother—"

"Mother—" There was a curious pause. "Mother is annoyed with me already. She feels that I'm definitely *undene.* She wishes she'd left me Home. She's afraid I'll never be the same again."

"Undene?" I asked, because Salla had sent out no clarification with the term.

"Yes," she said, and I caught at visualization until light finally be-gan to dawn.

"Well! We don't exactly eat peas with our knives or wipe our noses on our sleeves! We can be pretty couth when we set our minds to it."

"I know, I know," she hastened to say, "but Mother—well, you know some mothers."

"Yes, I know. But if you never walk or climb or swim or anything like that, what do you do for fun?"

"It's not that we never do them. But seldom casually and unthinkingly. We're supposed to outgrow the need for childish activities like that. We're supposed to be capable of more intellectual pleasures."

"Like what?" I held the branches aside for her to descend to the kitchen door, and nearly kinked my shoulder trying to do that and open the door for her simultaneously. After several false starts and stops and a feeling of utter foolishness, like the one you get when you try to dodge past a person who tries to dodge past you, we ended up at the kitchen table with Salla gasping at the smart of the Merthiolate. "Like what?" I repeated.

"Hoosh! That's quite a sensation." She loosened her clutch on her ankles and relaxed under the soothing salve I spread on her reddened feet. "Well, Mother's favorite—and she does it very well—is Anticipating. She likes roses."

"So do I," I said, bewildered, "but I seldom Anticipate in connection with them."

Salla laughed. I liked to hear her laugh. It was more nearly a musical phrase than a laugh. The Francher kid, the first time he heard it, made a composition of it. Of course neither he nor I liked it very much when the other kids in the Canyon revved it up and used it for a dance tune, but I must admit it had quite a beat....Well, anyway, Salla laughed.

"You know, for two people using the same words we certainly come out at different comprehensions. No—what Mother likes is Anticipating a rose. She chooses a bud that looks interesting—she knows all the finer distinctions—then she *makes* a rose, synthetic, as nearly like the real bud as she can. Then, for two or three days, she sees if she can anticipate every movement of the opening of the real rose by opening her synthetic simultaneously, or, if she's very adept, just barely ahead of the other." She laughed again. "It's one of our family stories—the time she chose a bud that did nothing for two days, then shivered to dust. Somehow it had been sprayed with *destro*. Mother's never quite got over the humiliation."

"Maybe I'm being *undene*," I said, "but I can't see spending two days watching a rose bud."

"And yet you spent a whole hour just looking at the sky last evening. And four of you spent hours last night receiving and displaying cards. You got quite emotional over it several times."

"Umm—well, yes. But that's different. A sunset like that, and the way Jemmy plays—" I caught the teasing in her eyes and we laughed together. Laughter needs no interpreter, at least not our laughter.

Salla took so much pleasure in sampling our world that, as is usual, I discovered things about our neighborhood I hadn't known before. It was she who found the cave, because she was curious about the tiny trickle of water high on the slope of Baldy.

"Just a spring," I told her as we looked up at the dark streak that marked a fold in the massive cliff.

"Just a spring," she mocked. "In this land of little water is there such a thing as *just* a spring?"

"It's not worth anything," I protested, following her up into the air. "You can't even drink from it."

"It could ease a heart hunger, though. The sight of wetness in an arid land."

"It can't even splash," I said as we neared the streak.

"No," Salla said, holding her forefinger to the end of the moisture. "But it can grow things." Lightly she touched the minute green plants that clung to the rock wall and the dampness.

"Pretty," I said perfunctorily. "But look at the view from here."

We turned around, pressing our backs to the sheer cliff, and looked out over the vast stretches of red-to-purple-to-blue ranges of mountains, jutting fiercely naked or solidly forested or speckled with growth as far as we could see. And lazily, far away, a shaft of smelter smoke rose and bent almost at right angles as an upper current caught it and thinned it to haze. Below, fold after fold of the hills hugged protectively to themselves the tiny comings and goings and dwelling places of those who had lost themselves in the vastness.

"And yet," Salla almost whispered, "if you're lost in vast enough vastness you find yourself—a different self, a self that has only Being and the Presence to contemplate."

"True," I said, breathing deeply of sun and pine and hot granite. "But not many reach that vastness. Most of us size our little worlds to hold enough distractions to keep us from having to contemplate Being and God."

There was a moment's deep silence as we let our own thoughts close the subject. Then Salla lifted and I started down.

"Hey!" I called. "That's up!"

"I know it," she called. "And that's down! I still haven't found the spring!"

So I lifted, too, grumbling at the stubbornness of women, and arrived even with Salla just as she perched tentatively on a sharp spur of rock on the edge of the vegetation-covered gash that was the beginning of the oozing wetness. She looked straight down the dizzy thousands of feet below us.

"What beautiful downness!" she said, pleasured.

"If you were afraid of heights—"

She looked at me quickly. "*Are* some people? Really?"

"Some are. I read one, one time. Would you care to try the texture of *that?*" And I created for her the horrified frantic dying terror of an Outsider friend of mine who hardly dares look out of a second-story window.

"Oh, no!" She paled and clung to the scanty draping of vines and branches of the cleft. "No more! No more!"

"I'm sorry. But it *is* a different sort of emotion. I think of every time I read—'neither height nor depth nor any other creature.' Height to my friend is a creature—a horrible hovering destroyer waiting to pounce on him."

"It's too bad," Salla said, "that he doesn't remember to go on to the next phrase, and learn to lose his fear—"

By quick common consent we switched subjects in midair.

"This is the source," I said. "Satisfied?"

"No." She groped among the vines. "I want to see a trickle trickle, and a drop drop from the beginning." She burrowed deeper.

Rolling my eyes to heaven for patience, I helped her hold back the vines. She reached for the next layer—and suddenly wasn't there.

"Salla!" I scrabbled at the vines. "Salla!"

"H-h-here," I caught her subvocal answer.

"Talk!" I said as I felt her thought melt out of my consciousness.

"I *am* talking!" Her reply broke to audibility on the last word. "And I'm sitting in some awfully cold wet water. Do come in." I squirmed cautiously through the narrow cleft into the darkness and stumbled to my knees in icy water almost waist-deep.

"It's dark," Salla whispered, and her voice ran huskily around the place.

"Wait for your eyes to change," I whispered back, and, groping through the water, caught her hand and clung to it. But even after a breathless sort of pause our eyes could not pick up enough light to see by—only faint green shimmer where the cleft was.

"Had enough?" I asked. "Is this trickly and drippy enough?" I lifted our hands and the water sluiced off our elbows.

"I want to see," she protested.

"Matches are inoperative when they're wet. Flashlight have I none. Suggestions?"

"Well, no. You don't have any Glowers living here, do you?"

"Since the word rings no bell, I guess not. But, say!" I dropped her hand and, rising to my knees, fumbled for my pocket. "Dita taught me—

or tried to after Valancy told her how come—" I broke off, immersed in the problem of trying to get a hand into and out of the pocket of skin-tight wet Levi's.

"I know I'm an Outlander," Salla said plaintively, "but I thought I had a fairly comprehensive knowledge of your language."

"Dita's the Outsider that we found with Low. She's got some Designs and Persuasions none of us have. There!" I grunted, and settled back in the water. "Now if I can remember."

I held the thin dime between my fingers and shifted all those multiples of mental gears that are so complicated until you work your way through their complexity to the underlying simplicity. I concentrated my whole self on that little disc of metal. There was a sudden blinding spurt of light. Salla cried out, and I damped the light quickly to a more practical level.

"I did it!" I cried. "I glowed it first thing, this time! It took me half an hour last time to get a spark!"

Salla was looking in wonder at the tiny globe of brilliance in my hand. "And an Outsider can do *that?*"

"Can do!" I said, suddenly very proud of our Outsiders. "And so can I, now! There you are, ma'am," I twanged. "Yore light, yore cave—look to yore little heart's content."

I don't suppose it was much as caves go. The floor was sand, pale, granular, almost sugarlike. The pool—out of which we both dripped as soon as we sighted dry land—had no apparent source, but stayed always at the same level in spite of the slender flow that streaked the cliff. The roof was about twice my height and the pool was no farther than that across. The walls curved protectively close around the water. At first glance there was nothing special about the cave. There weren't even any stalactites or stalagmites—just the sand and the quiet pool shimmering a little in the light of the glowed coin.

"Well!" Salla sighed happily as she pushed back her heavy hair with wet hands. "This is where it begins."

"Yes." I closed my hand around the dime and watched the light spray between my fingers. "Wetly, I might point out."

Salla was scrambling across the sand on all fours.

"It's high enough to stand," I said, following her.

"I'm being a cave creature," she smiled back over her shoulder. "Not a human surveying a kingdom. It looks different from down here."

"Okay, troglodyte. How does it look down there?"

"Marvelous!" Salla's voice was very soft. "Bring the light and look!"

We lay on our stomachs and peered into the tiny tunnel, hardly a foot across, that Salla had found. I focused the light down the narrow passageway. The whole thing was a lacy network of delicate crystals, white, clear, rosy and pale green, so fragile that I held my breath lest they break. The longer I looked the more wonder I saw—miniature forests and snowflakelike laciness, flights of fairy steps, castles and spires, flowers terraced up gentle hillsides, and branches of blossoms almost alive enough to sway. An arm's length down the tunnel a quietly bright pool reflected the perfection around it to double the enchantment.

Salla and I looked at each other, our faces so close together that we were mirrored in each other's eyes—eyes that stated and reaffirmed: *Ours— no one else in all the universe shares this spot with us.*

Wordlessly we sat back on the sand. I don't know about Salla, but I was having a little difficulty with my breathing, because, for some odd reason, it seemed necessary to hold my breath to shield from being as easily read as a child.

"Let's leave the light," Salla whispered. "It'll stay lighted without you, won't it?"

"Yeah. Indefinitely."

"Leave it by the little cave. Then we'll know it's always lighted and lovely."

We edged our way out of the cleft in the cliff and hovered there for a minute, laughing at our bedraggled appearance. Then we headed for home and dry clothes.

"I wish Obla could see the cave," I said impulsively. Then wished I hadn't because I caught Salla's immediate displeased protest.

"I mean," I said awkwardly, "she never gets to see—" I broke off. After all, she wouldn't be able to see any better if she were there. I would have to be her eyes.

"Obla." Salla wasn't vocalizing now. "She's very near to you."

"She's almost my second self."

"A relative?"

"No. Only as souls are related."

"I can feel her in your thoughts so often. And yet—have I ever met her?"

"No. She doesn't meet people." I was holding in my mind the clean uncluttered strength of Obla; then again I caught Salla's distressed protest and her feeling of being excluded, before she shielded. Still I hesitated. I didn't want to share. Obla was more an expression of myself than a separate person. An expression that was hidden and precious. I was afraid to share—afraid that it might be like touching a finger to a fragile chemi-

cal fern in the little tunnel, that there wouldn't even be a *ping* before the
perfection shivered to a shapeless powder.

Two weeks after the ship arrived, a general Group meeting was called.
We all gathered on the flat around the ship. It looked like a field day at
first, with the flat filled with laughing lifting children playing tag above
the heads of the more sedate elders. The kids my age clustered at one side,
tugged toward playing tag, too, but restrained because after all you do
outgrow some things—when people are looking. I sat there with them,
feeling an emptiness beside me. Salla was with her parents.

The Oldest was not there. He was at home struggling to contain his
being in the broken body that was becoming more and more a dissolving
prison. So Jemmy called us to attention.

"Long-drawn periods of indecision are not good," he said without preliminary. "The ship has been here two weeks. We have all faced
our problem—to go or to stay. There are many of us who have not yet
come to a decision. This we must do soon. The ship will up a week
from today. To help us decide we are now open to *brief* statements pro
or con."

There was an odd tightening feeling as the whole Group flowed into
a common thought stream and became a single unit instead of a mass of
individuals.

"I will go." It was the thought of the Oldest from his bed back in
the Canyon. "The new Home has the means to help me, so that the years
yet allotted to me may be nearly painless. Since the Crossing—" He broke
off, flashing an amused " 'Brief'!"

"I will stay." It was the voice of one of the young girls from Bendo.
"We have only started to make Bendo a place fit to live in. I like beginnings. The new Home sounds finished, to me."

"I don't want to go away," a very young voice piped. "My radishes
are just coming up and I hafta water them all the time. They'd die if I
left." Amusement rippled through the Group and relaxed us.

"I'll go." It was Matt, called back from Tech by the ship's arrival. "In
the Home my field of specialization has developed far beyond what we
have at Tech or anywhere else. But I'm coming back."

"There can be no free and easy passage back and forth between the
Home and Earth," Jemmy warned, "for a number of very valid reasons."

"I'll chance it," ·Matt said. "I'll make it back."

"I'm staying," the Francher kid said. "Here on Earth we're different
with a plus. There we'd be different with a minus. What we can do and
do well won't be special there. I don't want to go where I'd be making
ABC songs. I want my music to go on being big."

"I'm going," Jake said, his voice mocking as usual. "I'm through horsing around. I'm going to become a solid citizen. But I want to go in for—" His verbalization stopped, and all I could comprehend was an angular sort of concept wound with time and space as with serpentine. I saw my own blankness on the faces around me and felt a little less stupid. "See," Jake said. "That's what I've been having on the tip of my mind for a long time. Shua tells me they've got a fair beginning on it there. I'll be willing to ABC it for a while for a chance at something like that."

I cleared my throat. Here was my chance to broadcast to the whole Group what I intended to do! Apparently I was the only one seeing the situation clearly enough. "I—"

It was as though I'd stepped into a dense fog bank. I felt as though I'd gone blind and dumb at one stroke. I had a feeling of being torn like a piece of paper. I lost all my breath as I became vividly conscious of my actual thoughts. *I didn't want to go!* I was snatched into a mad whirlpool of thoughts at this realization. How could I stay after all I'd said? How could I go and know Earth no more? How could I stay and let Salla go? How could I go and leave Obla behind? Dimly I heard someone else's voice finishing:

"...because Home or no Home, *this* is Home to me!"

I closed my gaping wordless mouth and wet my dry lips. I could see again—see the Group slowly dissolving—the Bendo Group gathering together under the trees, the rest drifting away from the flat. Low leaned across the rock. "S'matter, feller?" he laughed. "Cat got your tongue? I expected a blast of eloquence from you that'd push the whole Group up the gangplank."

"Bram's bashful!" Dita teased. "He doesn't like to make his convictions known!"

I tried a sort of smile. "Pity me, people," I said. "Before you stands a creature shorn of convictions, nekkid as a jay bird in the cold winds of indecision."

"Fresh out of long-johns," Peter said, sobering. "But there's plenty of sympathy available."

"Thanks," I said. "Noted and appreciated."

I couldn't take my new doubt and indecision, the new tumult and pain to Obla—not when she was so much a part of it, so I took them up into the hills. I perched like a brooding buzzard on the stone spur outside the little cave, high above the Canyon. Wildly, until my throat ached and my voice croaked, I railed against this world and its limitations. Hoarsely I whispered over all the lets and hindrances that plagued us—that plagued me. And, infuriatingly, the world and all its echoes placidly paced my every argument with solid rebuttal. I was hearing with both ears now, one for my own voice, one for the world's reply. And my voice got fainter and fainter, and Earth's voice wasn't a whisper any more.

"Nothing is the way it should be!" I hoarsely yelled my last weary assault at the evening sky.

"And never will be, short of eternity," replied the streak of sunset crimson.

"But we could do so much more—"

"Whoever heard of bread made only of leaven?" replied the first evening star.

"We're being wasted," I whispered.

"So is the wheat when it's broadcast in the field," answered the fringe of pines on the crest of a far hill.

"But Salla will go. She'll be gone—"

And nothing answered—only the wind cried and a single piece of dislodged gravel rattled down into the darkness.

"Salla!" I cried. "Salla will be gone! Answer *that* one if you can!" But the world was through with answers. The wind became very busy humming through the dusk.

"Answer me!" I had only a whisper left.

"I will." The voice was very soft but it shook me like a blast of lightning. "I can answer." Salla eased lightly down on the spur beside me. "Salla is staying."

"Salla!" I could only clutch the rock and stare.

"Mother had a *quanic* when I told her." Salla smiled, easing the tight uncomfortable emotion. "I told her I needed a research paper to finish my Level requirements and that this would be just perfect for it.

"She said I was too young to know my own mind. I said finishing high in my Level would be quite a feather in her cap—if you'll pardon the provincialism. And she said she didn't even know your parents." Salla colored, her eyes wavering. "I told her there had been no word between us. That we were not Two-ing. Yet. Much."

"It doesn't have to be now!" I cried, grabbing both her hands. "Oh, Salla! Now we can afford to wait!" And I yanked her off the spur into the maddest wildest flight of my life. Like a couple of crazy things we split and resplit the air above Baldy, soaring and diving like drunken lightning. But all the time part of us was moving so far, so fast, another part of us was talking quietly together, planning, wondering, rejoicing, as serenely as if we were back in the cave again, seeing each other in quiet reflective eyes. Finally darkness closed in entirely and we leaned exhausted against each other, drifting slowly toward the canyon floor.

"Obla—" I said, "let's go tell Obla." There was no need to shield any part of my life from Salla any more. In fact there was a need to make it a cohesive whole, complete with both Obla and Salla.

Obla's windows were dark. That meant no one was visiting her. She would be alone. I rapped lightly on the door—my own particular rap.

"Bram? Come in!" I caught welcome from Obla.

"I brought Salla," I said. "Let me turn the light on." I stepped in. "Wait—"

But simultaneously with her cry I flipped the light switch.

"Salla," I started, "this is—"

Salla screamed and threw her arm across her eyes; a sudden over-flooding of horrified revulsion choked the room, and Obla was fluttering in the far upper corner of the room—hiding—hiding herself behind the agonized swirl of her hair, her broken body in the twisting of her white gown, pressing itself to the walls, struggling for escape, her startled physical and mental anguish moaning almost audibly around us.

I grabbed Salla and yanked her out of the room, snapping the light off as we went. I dragged her out to the edge of the yard where the canyon walls shot upward. I flung her against the sandstone wall. She turned and hid her face against the rock, sobbing. I grabbed her shoulders and shook her.

"How could you!" I gritted between my teeth, outraged anger thickening my words. "Is *that* the kind of people the Home is turning out now? Counting arms and legs and eyes more than the person?" Her tumbling hair whipped across my chin. "Permitting rejection and disgust for any living soul? Aren't you taught even common kindness and compassion?" I wanted to hit her—to hit anything solid to protest this unthinkable thing that had been done to Obla, this unhealable wounding.

Salla snatched herself out of my grasp and hovered just out of reach, wet eyes glaring angrily down at me.

"It's your fault, too!" she snapped, tears flowing. "I'd have died rather than do a thing like that to Obla or anyone else—if I had known! You didn't tell me. You never visualized her that way—only strength and beauty and wholeness!"

"Why not!" I shot back angrily, lifting level with her. "That's the only way I ever see her any more. And trying to shift the blame—"

"It *is* your fault! Oh, Bram!" And she was crying in my arms. When she could speak again between sniffs and hiccoughs, she said, "We don't have people like that at Home. I mean, I never saw a—an incomplete person. I never saw scars and mutilation. Don't you see, Bram? I was holding myself ready to receive her, completely—because she was part of you.

And then to find myself embracing—" She choked. "Look—look, Bram, we have transgraph and—and regeneration—and *no* one ever stays unfinished."

I let go of her slowly, lost in wonder. "Regeneration? Transgraph?"

"Yes, yes!" Salla cried. "She can have back her legs. She can have arms again. She can have her beautiful face again. She may even get back her eyes and her voice, though I don't know for sure about that. She can be Obla again, instead of a dark prison for Obla."

"No one told us."

"No one asked."

"Common concern."

"I'll ask then. Have you any *dobic* children? Any cases of *cazerinea*? Any *trimorph semia*? It's not that we don't want to ask. How are we to know *what* to ask? We've never even heard of a—a basket case." She took the word from me. "It just didn't occur to us to ask."

"I'm sorry," I said, drying her eyes with the palms of my hands, lacking anything better. "I should have told you." My words were but scant surface indications of my deep abject apology.

"Come," she said, pulling away from me. "We must go to Obla—now—right now."

It was Salla who finally coaxed Obla back down to her bed. It was Salla who held the broken weeping face against her slight young shoulder and poured the healing balms of her sorrow and understanding over Obla's wounds. And it was Salla who told Obla of what the Home held for her. Told her and told her and told her, until Obla finally believed.

All three of us were limp and weary by then, and all three content just to sit for a minute, so the explosion of Davy into the room was twice the shock it ordinarily would have been.

"Hi, Bram! Hi, Salla! Hey, Obla! I got it fixed now. It won't hiss on the *s*'s any more and you can trip the playback yourself. Here." He plopped onto her pillow the little cube I recognized as his scriber. "Try it out. Go on. Try it out on Bram."

Obla turned her face until her cheek felt the cube. Salla looked at me in wonderment and then at Obla. There was a brief pause and then a slight click and I heard, tiny but distinct, the first audible word I'd ever heard from Obla.

"Bram! Oh, Bram! Now I can go with you. I won't be left behind. And when we get to the Home I'll be whole again! Whole again!"

Through my shock I heard Davy say, "You didn't even use one *s*, Obla! Say something essy, so's I can check it."

Obla thought I was going to the Home! She expected me to go with her! She didn't know I'd decided to stay. That *we* were going to stay. I met

Salla's eyes. Our communication was quick and complete before the small voice said, "Salla, my sweet sister! I trust that's sufficiently 'essy'!" And I heard Obla's laugh for the first time.

So, somewhere way back there, there is a tiny cave with a dime glowing in it, keeping in trust a preciousness between Salla and me—a candle in the window of memory. Somewhere way back there are the sights and sounds, the smells and tastes, the homeness of Earth. For a while I have turned my back on the Promised Land. For our Jordan was crossed those long years ago. My trouble was that I thought that wherever I looked, just because *I* did the looking, was the goal ahead. But all the time, the Crossing, shimmering in the light of memory, had been something completed, not something yet to reach. My yearning for the Home must have been a little of the old hunger for the fleshpots that haunts any pioneering effort.

And Salla...Well, sometimes when I'm not looking she looks at me and then at Obla. And sometimes when she isn't looking I look at her and then at Obla. Obla has no eyes, but sometimes when we aren't looking she looks at me and then at Salla.

Things will happen to all three of us before Earth swells again in the portholes, but whatever happens, Earth *will* swell in the portholes again— at least for me. And *then* I will truly be coming Home.

No Different Flesh

Meris watched the darkness rip open and mend itself again in the same blinding flash that closed her eyes. Behind her eyelids the dark reversals flicked and faded. Thunder jarred the cabin window where she leaned and troubled her bones. The storm had been gathering all afternoon, billowing up in blue and white thunderheads over the hills, spreading darkly, somberly to snuff the sunset. The wind was not the straight-blowing, tree-lashing, branch-breaker of the usual summer storm. Instead, it blew simultaneously from several directions. It mourned like a snow wind around the eaves of the cabin. It ripped the length of the canyon through the treetops while the brush below hardly stirred a twig. Lightning was so continuous now that glimpses of the outdoors came through the windows like vast shouts and sudden blows.

Lights in the cabin gasped, recovered, and died. Meris heard Mark's sigh and the ruffle of his pushed-back papers.

"I'll get the lantern," he said. "It's out in the storeroom, isn't it?"

"Yes." Lightning flushed the whole room, now that the light no longer defended it. "But it needs filling. Why don't we wait to see if the lights come back on. We could watch the storm—"

"I'm sorry." Mark's arm was gentle across her shoulders. "I'd like to, but I can't spare the time. Every minute—"

Meris pressed her face to the glass, peering out into the chaotic darkness of the canyon wall. She still wasn't quite used to being interested in anything outside her own grief and misery—all those long months of painful numbness that at the same time had been a protesting hammering at the Golden Gates and a wild shrieking at God. What a blessed relief it was finally to be able to let go of the baby—to feel grief begin to drain away as though a boil had been lanced. Not that sorrow would be gone, but now there could be healing for the blow that had been too heavy to be mortal.

"Take good care of her," she whispered to the bright slash of the lightning. "Keep her safe and happy until I come."

She winced away from the window, startled at the sudden audible splat of rain against the glass. The splat became a rattle and the rattle a gushing roar and the fade-and-flare of the outdoors dissolved into streaming rain.

Mark came back into the cabin, the light in his hands flooding blue-white across the room. He hung the lantern on the beam above the table and joined Meris at the window.

"The storm is about over," said Meris, turning in the curve of his arm. "It's only rain now."

"It'll be back," he said. "It's just taking a deep breath before smacking us amidships again."

"Mark." The tone of Meris's voice caught his attention. "Mark, my baby—our baby—is dead." She held out the statement to him as if offering a gift—her first controlled reference to what had happened.

"Yes," said Mark, "our baby is dead." He accepted the gift.

"We waited for her so long," said Meris softly, "and had her for so short a time."

"But long enough that you are a mother and I am a father," said Mark. "We still have that."

"Now that I can finally talk about her," said Meris, "I won't have to talk about her any more. I can let her be gone now. Oh, Mark!" Meris held his hand to her cheek. "Having you to anchor me is all that's kept me from—"

"I'm set in my ways," smiled Mark. "But of late you've been lifting such a weight off me that I don't think I could anchor a butterfly now!"

"*Love* you, Mark!"

"*Love* you, Meris!" Mark hugged her tightly a moment and then let her go. "Back to work again. No flexibility left in the deadline any more. It has to be done on time this time or—"

Lightning splashed brightness against the wall. Meris moved back to the window again, the floorboards under her feet vibrating to the thunder. "Here it comes again!" But Mark was busy, his scurrying fingers trying to catch up with the hours and days and months lost to Meris's grief and wild mourning.

Meris cupped her hands around her temples and leaned her forehead to the windowpane. The storm was truly back again, whipping the brush and trees in a fury that ripped off leaves and small branches. A couple of raindrops cracked with the force of hail against the glass. Lightning and a huge explosion arrived at the same moment, jarring the whole cabin.

"Hit something close?" asked Mark with no pause in the staccato of his typing.

"Close," said Meris. "The big pine by the gate. I saw the bark fly."

"Hope it didn't kill it," said Mark. "We lost those two in back like that last summer, you know."

Meris tried to see the tree through the darkness, but the lightning had withdrawn for the moment.

"What was that?" she cried, puzzled.

"What?" asked Mark.

"I heard something fall," she said. "Through the trees."

"Probably the top of our pine," said Mark. "I guess the lightning made more than bark fly. Well, there goes another of our trees."

"That's the one the jays liked particularly, too," said Meris.

Rain drenched again in a vertical obscurity down the glass and the flashes of lightning flushed heavily through the watery waver.

Later the lights came on and Meris, blinking against the brightness, went to bed, drawing the curtain across the bunk corner, leaving Mark at work at his desk. She lay awake briefly, hearing the drum of the rain and the mutter of the thunder, hardly noticing the clatter of the typewriter. She touched cautiously with her thoughts the aching emptiness where the intolerable burden of her unresolved grief had been. Almost, she felt without purpose—aimless—since that painful focusing of her whole life was going. She sighed into her pillow. New purpose and new aim would come—would have to come—to fill the emptinesses.

Somewhere in the timeless darkness of the night she was suddenly awake, sitting bolt upright in bed. She pulled the bedclothes up to her chin, shivering a little in the raw, damp air of the cabin. What had wakened her? The sound came again. She gasped and Mark stirred uneasily, then was immediately wide awake and sitting up beside her.

"Meris?"

"I heard something," she said. "Oh, Mark! Honestly, I heard something."

"What was it?" Mark pulled the blanket up across her back.

"I heard a baby crying," said Meris.

She felt Mark's resigned recoil and the patience in his long indrawn breath.

"Honest, Mark!" In the semi-obscurity her eyes pleaded with him. "I really heard a baby crying. Not a tiny baby—like—like ours. A very young child, though. Out there in the cold and wet."

"Meris—" he began, and she knew the sorrow that must be marking his face.

"There!" she cried. "Hear it?"

The two were poised motionless for a moment, then Mark was out of bed and at the door. He flung it open to the night and they listened again, tensely.

They heard a night bird cry and, somewhere up-canyon, the brief barking of a dog, but nothing else.

Mark came back to bed, diving under the covers with a shiver.

"Come warm me, woman!" he cried, hugging Meris tightly to him.

"It did sound like a baby crying," she said with a half question in her voice.

"It sure did," said Mark. "I thought for a minute— Must have been some beast or bird or denizen of the wild—" His voice trailed away sleepily, his arms relaxing. Meris lay awake listening—to Mark's breathing, to the night, to the cry that didn't come again. Refusing to listen for the cry that would never come again, she slept.

Next morning was so green and gold and sunny and wet and fresh that Meris felt a-tiptoe before she even got out of bed. She dragged Mark, protesting, from the warm nest of the bedclothes and presented him with a huge breakfast. They laughed at each other across the table, their hands clasped over the dirty dishes. Meris felt a surge of gratitude. The return of laughter is a priceless gift.

While she did the dishes and put the cabin to rights, Mark, shrugging into his Levi jacket against the chill, went out to check the storm damage.

Meris heard a shout and the dozen echoes that returned diminishingly from the heavily wooded mountainsides. She pushed the window curtain aside and peered out as she finished drying a plate.

Mark was chasing a fluttering something, out across the creek. The boisterous waters were slapping against the bottom of the plank bridge and Mark was splashing more than ankle-deep on the flat beyond as he plunged about trying to catch whatever it was that evaded him.

"A bird," guessed Meris. "A huge bird waterlogged by the storm. Or knocked down by the wind—maybe hurt—" She hurried to put the plate away and dropped the dish towel on the table. She peered out again. Mark was half hidden behind the clumps of small willows along the bend of the creek. She heard his cry of triumph and then of astonishment. The fluttering thing shot up, out of reach above Mark, and seemed to be trying to disappear into the ceaseless shiver of the tender green and white aspens. Whatever it was, a whitish blob against the green foliage, dropped down again and Mark grabbed it firmly.

Meris ran to the door and flung it open, stepping out with a shiver into the cold air. Mark saw her as he rounded the curve in the path.

"Look what I found!" he cried. "Look what I caught for you!"

Meris put a hand on the wet, muddy bundle Mark was carrying and thought quickly, "Where are the feathers?"

"I caught a baby for you!" cried Mark. Then his smile died and he thrust the bundle at her. "Good Lord, Meris!" he choked, "I'm not fooling! It *is* a baby!"

Meris turned back a sodden fold and gasped. A face! A child face, mud-smudged, with huge dark eyes and tangled dark curls. A quiet, watchful face—not crying. Maybe too frightened to cry?

"Mark!" Meris clutched the bundle to her and hurried into the cabin. "Build up the fire in the stove," she said, laying her burden on the table. She peeled the outer layer off quickly and let it fall soggily to the floor. Another damp layer and then another. "Oh, poor messy child!" she crooned. "Poor wet, messy, little girl!"

"Where did she come from?" Mark wondered. "There must be some clue—" He changed quickly from his soaked sneakers into his hiking boots. "I'll go check. There must be something out there." His hands paused on the knotting of the last bootlace. "Or someone." He stood up, settling himself into his jeans and boots. "Take it easy, Meris." He kissed her cheek as she bent over the child and left.

Meris's fingers recalled more and more of their deftness as she washed the small girl-body, improvised a diaper of a dish towel, converted a tee shirt into a gown, all the time being watched silently by the big dark eyes that now seemed more wary than frightened, watched as though the child were trying to read her lips that were moving so readily in the old remembered endearments and croonings. Finally, swathing the small form in her chenille robe in lieu of a blanket, she sat on the edge of the bed, rocking and crooning to the child. She held a cup of warm milk to the small mouth. There was a firming of lips against it at first and then the small mouth opened and two small hands grasped the cup and the milk was gulped down greedily. Meris wiped the milky crescent from the child's upper lip and felt the tenseness going out of the small body as the warmth of the milk penetrated it. The huge dark eyes in the small face closed, jerked open, closed slowly, and stayed closed.

Meris sat cradling the heavy warmth of the sleeping child. She felt healing flow through her own body and closed her eyes in silent thanksgiving before she put her down, well back from the edge of the bed. The she gathered up the armful of wet muddy clothes and reached for the box of detergent.

When Mark returned some time later, Meris gestured quickly. "She's sleeping," she said. "Oh, Mark! Just think! A baby!" Tears came to her eyes and she bent her head.

"Meris," Mark's gentle voice lifted her face. "Meris, just don't forget that the baby is not ours to keep."

"I know—!" She began to protest and then she smoothed the hair back from her forehead, knowing what Mark wanted to save her from. "The baby is not ours—to keep," she relinquished. "Not ours to keep. Did you find anything, or anyone," she hesitated.

"Nothing," said Mark. "Except the top of our pine is still there, if you've bothered to check it. And," his face tightened and his voice was grim, "those vandals have been at it again. Since I was at the picnic area at Beaver Bend, they've been there and sawed every table in two and smashed them all to the ground in the middle!"

"Oh, Mark!" Meris was distressed. "Are you sure it's the same bunch?"

"Who else around here would do anything so senseless?" asked Mark. "It's those kids. If I ever catch them—"

"You did once," said Meris with a half smile, "and they didn't like what you and the ranger said to them."

"Understatement of the week," said Mark. "They'll like even less what's going to happen to them the next time they get caught."

"They're mad enough at you already," suggested Meris.

"Well," said Mark, "I'm proud to count that type among my enemies!"

"The Winstel boy doesn't seem the type," said Meris.

"He was a good kid," acknowledged Mark, "until he started running with those three from the Valley. They've got him hypnotized with that car and all their wild stories and crazy pranks. I guess he thinks their big-town fooling around has a glamor that can't be duplicated here in the mountains. Thank heaven it can't, but I wish he'd wise up to what's happening to him."

"The child!" Meris started toward the bed, her heart throbbing suddenly to the realization that there was a baby to be considered again. They looked down at the flushed, sleeping face and then turned back to the table. "She must be about three or four," said Meris over the coffee cups. "And healthy and well cared for. Her clothes—" she glanced out at the clothes line where the laundry billowed and swung "—they're well-made, but—"

"But what?" Mark stirred his coffee absently, then gulped a huge swallow.

"Well, look," said Meris, reaching to the chair. "This outer thing she had on. It's like a trundle bundle—arms but no legs—just a sleeping-bag thing. That's not too surprising, but look. I was going to rinse off the mud before I washed it, but just one slosh in the water and it came out clean—and dry! I didn't even have to hang it out. And Mark, it isn't material. I mean fabric. At least it isn't like any that I've ever seen."

Mark lifted the garment, flexing a fold in his fingers. "Odd," he said.

"And look at the fasteners," said Meris.

"There aren't any," he said, surprised.

"And yet it fastens," said Meris, smoothing the two sections of the front together, edge to edge. She tugged mightily at it. It stayed shut. "You can't rip it apart. But look here." And she laid the two sides back gently with no effort at all. "It seems to be which direction you pull. There's a rip here in the back," she went on. "Or I'll bet she'd never have got wet at all—at least not from the outside," she smiled. "Look, the rip *was* from here to here." Her fingers traced six inches across the garment. "But look—" She carefully lapped the edges of the remaining rip and drew her thumb nail along it. The material seemed to melt into itself and the rip was gone.

"How did you find out all this so soon?" asked Mark. "Your own research lab?"

"Maybe so," smiled Meris. "I was just looking at it—women look at fabrics and clothing with their fingers, you know. I could never choose a piece of material for a dress without touching it. And I was wondering how much the seam would show if I mended it." She shook the garment. "But how she ever managed to run in it."

"She didn't," said Mark. "She sort of fluttered around like a chicken. I thought she was a feathered thing at first. Every time I thought I had her, she got away, flopping and fluttering, above my head half the time. I don't see how she ever— Oh! I found a place that might be where she spent the night. Looks like she crawled back among the roots of the deadfall at the bend of the creek. There's a pressed down, grassy hollow, soggy wet, of course, just inches above the water."

"I don't understand this fluttering bit," said Meris. "You mean she jumped so high you—"

"Not exactly jumped—" began Mark.

A sudden movement caught them both. The child had wakened, starting up with a terrified cry, "Muhlala! Muhlala!"

Before Meris could reach her, she was fluttering up from the bed, trailing the chenille robe beneath her. She hovered against the upper windowpane, like a moth, pushing her small hands against it, sobbing, "Muhlala! Muhlala!"

Meris gaped up at her. "Mark! Mark!"

"Not exactly—jump!" grunted Mark, reaching up for the child. He caught one of the flailing bare feet and pulled the child down into his arms, hushing her against him.

"There, there, muhlala, muhlala," he comforted awkwardly.

"Muhlala?" asked Meris, taking the struggling child from him.

"Well, she said it first," he said. "Maybe the familiarity will help."

"Well, maybe," said Meris. "There, there, muhlala, muhlala."

The child quieted and looked up at Meris.

"Muhlala?" she asked hopefully.

"Muhlala," said Meris as positively as she could.

The big wet eyes looked at her accusingly and the little head said no, unmistakably, but she leaned against Meris, her weight suddenly doubling as she relaxed.

"Well now," said Mark. "Back to work."

"Work? Oh, Mark!" Meris was contrite. "I've broken into your workday again!"

"Well, it's not every day I catch a child flying in the forest. I'll make it up—somehow."

Meris helped Mark get settled to his work and, dressing the child—"What's your name, honey? What's your name?"—in her own freshly dried clothes, she took her outside to leave Mark in peace.

"Muhlala," said Meris, smiling down at the upturned wondering face. The child smiled and swung their linked hands.

"Muhlala!" she laughed.

"Okay," said Meris, "we'll call you Lala." She skoonched down to child height. "Lala," she said, prodding the small chest with her finger. "Lala!"

Lala looked solemnly down at her own chest, tucking her chin in tightly in order to see. "Lala," she said, and giggled. "Lala!"

The two walked toward the creek, Lala in the lead, firmly leashed by Meris's hand. "No flying," she warned. "I can't interrupt Mark to have him fish you out of the treetops."

Lala walked along the creek bank, peering down into the romping water and keeping up a running commentary of unintelligible words. Meris kept up a conversation of her own, fitting it into the brief pauses of Lala's. Suddenly Lala cried out triumphantly and pointed. Meris peered down into the water.

"Well!" she cried indignantly. "Those darn boys! Dropping trash in our creek just because they're mad at Mark. Tin cans—"

Lala was tugging at her hand, pulling her toward the creek.

"Wait a bit, Lala," laughed Meris. "You'll fall us both into the water."

Then she gasped and clutched Lala's hand more firmly. Lala was standing on the water, the speed of the current ruffling it whitely against the sides of her tiny shoes. She was trying to tug Meris after her, across the water toward the metallic gleam by the other bank of the creek.

"No, baby," said Meris firmly, pulling Lala back to the bank. "We'll use the bridge." So they did and Lala, impatient of delay, tried to free her hand so she could run along the creek bed, but Meris clung firmly. "Not without me!" she said.

When they arrived at the place where the metallic whatever lay under the water, Meris put Lala down firmly on a big gray granite boulder, back from the creek. "Stay there," she said, pushing firmly down on the small shoulders. "*Stay* there." Then she turned to the creek. Starting to wade, sneakers and all, into the stream, she looked back at Lala. The child was standing on the boulder visibly wanting to come. Meris shook her head. "Stay *there*," she repeated.

Lala's face puckered but she sat down again. "Stay *there*," she repeated unhappily.

Meris tugged and pulled at the metal, the icy bite of the creek water numbing her feet. "Must be an old hot water tank," she grunted as she worked to drag it ashore. "When could they have dumped it here? We've been home—"

The current caught the thing as it let go of the mud at the bottom of the creek. It rolled and almost tore loose from Meris's hands, but she clung, feeling a fingernail break, and, putting her back to the task, towed the thing out of the current into the shallows. She turned its gleaming length over to drain the water out through the rip down its side.

"Water tank?" she puzzled. "Not like any I ever—"

"Stay there?" cried Lala excitedly. "Stay there?" She was jumping up and down on the boulder.

Meris laughed. "Come here," she said, holding out her muddy hands. "Come here!" Lala came. Meris nearly dropped her as she staggered under the weight of the child. Lala hadn't bothered to slide down the boulder and run to her. She had launched herself like a little rocket, airborne the whole distance.

She wiggled out of Meris's astonished arms and rummaging, head hidden in the metal capsule, came out with a triumphant cry, "Deeko! Deeko!" And she showed Meris her sodden treasure. It was a doll, a wet, muddy, battered doll, but a doll nevertheless, dressed in miniature duplication of Lala's outer garment which they had left in the cabin.

Lala plucked at the wet folds of the doll's clothes and made unhappy noises as she wiped the mud from the tiny face. She held the doll up to Meris, her voice asking and coaxing. So Meris squatted down by the child and together they undressed Deeko and washed her and her tiny clothes in the creek, then spread the clothes on the boulder in the sun. Lala gave Deeko a couple of soggy hugs, then put her on the rock also.

Just before supper, Mark came out to the creek-side to see the metallic object. He was still shaking his head in wonderment over the things Meris had told him of Lala. He would have discounted them about ninety percent except that Lala did them all over again for him. When he saw the ripped cylinder, he stopped shaking his head and just stared for a moment. Then he was turning it, and exploring in it, head hidden, hefting the weight of it, flexing a piece of its ripped metal. Then he lounged against the gray boulder and lipped thoughtfully at a dry cluster of pine needles.

"Let's live dangerously," he said, "and assert that this is the How that Lala arrived in our vicinity last night. Let us further assert that it has no earthly origin. Therefore, let us, madly but positively, assert that this is a Space capsule of some sort and Lala is an extra-terrestrial."

"You mean," gasped Meris, "that Lala is a little green man! And that this is a flying saucer?"

"Well, yes," said Mark. "Inexact, but it conveys the general idea."

"But, Mark! She's just a baby. She couldn't possibly have traveled all that distance alone—"

"I'd say also that she couldn't have traveled all that distance in this vehicle, either," said Mark. "Point one, I don't see anything resembling a motor or a fuel container or even a steering device. Point two, there are no provisions of any kind—water or food—or even any evidence of an air supply."

"Then?" said Meris, deftly fielding Lala from the edge of the creek.

"I'd say—only as a guess—that this is a sort of lifeboat in case of a wreck. I'd say something happened in the storm last night and here's Lala, Castaway."

"Where did you come from, baby dear?" chanted Meris to the wiggly Lala. "The heavens opened and you were here?"

"They'll be looking for her," said Mark, "whoever her people are. Which means they'll be looking for us." He looked at Meris and smiled. "How does it feel, Mrs. Edwards, to be Looked For by denizens of Outer Space?"

"Should we try to find them?" asked Meris. "Should we call the sheriff?"

"I don't think so," said Mark. "Let's wait a day or so. They'll find her. I'm sure of it. Anyone who had a Lala would comb the whole state, inch by inch, until they found her."

He caught up Lala and tossed her, squealing, into the air. For the next ten minutes Mark and Meris were led a merry chase trying to get Lala down out of the trees! Out of the sky! She finally fluttered down into Meris's arms and patted her cheek with a puzzled remark of some kind.

"I suppose," said Mark, taking a relieved breath, "that she's wondering how come we didn't chase her up there. Well, small one, you're our duckling. Don't laugh at our unwebbed feet."

That evening Meris sat rocking a drowsy-eyed Lala to sleep. She reached to tuck the blanket closer about the small bare feet, but instead cradled one foot in her hand. "You know what, Mark?" she said softly. "It's just dawned on me what you were saying about Lala. You were saying that this foot might have walked on another world! It just doesn't seem possible!"

"Well, try this thought, then." Mark pushed back from his desk, stretching widely and yawning. "If that world was very far away or their speed not too fast, that foot may never have touched a world anywhere. She may have been born en route."

"Oh, I don't think so," said Meris, "she knows too much about—about—*things* for that to be so. She knew to look *in* water for that—that vehicle of hers and she knew to wash her doll in running water and to spread clothes in the sun to dry. If she'd lived her life in Space—"

"Hmm!" Mark tapped his mouth with his pencil. "You could be right, but there might be other explanations for her knowledge. But then, maybe the real explanation of Lala is a very pedestrian one." He smiled at her unbelieving smile and went back to work.

Meris was awake again in the dark. She stretched comfortably and smiled. How wonderful to be able to awaken in the dark and smile—instead of slipping inevitably into the aching endless grief and despair. How pleasant to be able to listen to Mark's deep breathing and Lala's little murmur as she turned on the camp cot beside the bed. How warm and relaxing the flicker of firelight from the cast-iron stove patterning ceiling and walls dimly. She yawned and stopped in mid-stretch. What was that? Was that what had wakened her?

There was a guarded thump on the porch, a fumbling at the door, an audible breath, and then, "Mr. Edwards! Are you there?" The voice was a forced whisper.

Meris's hand closed on Mark's shoulder. He shrugged away in his sleep, but as her fingers tightened, he came wide awake, listening.

"Mr. Edwards!"

"Someone for Lala!" Meris gasped and reached toward the sleeping child.

"No," said Mark. "It's Tad Winstel." He lifted his voice. "Just a minute, Tad!" There was a muffled cry at the door and then silence. Mark padded barefoot to the door, blinking as he snapped the lights on, and, unlatching the door, swung it open. "Come on in, fellow, and close the door. It's cold." He shivered back for his jacket and sneakers.

Tad slipped in and stood awkwardly thin and lanky by the door, hugging his arms to himself convulsively. Mark opened the stove and added a solid chunk of oak.

"What brings you here at this hour?" he asked calmly.

Tad shivered. "It isn't you, then," he said, "but it's bad trouble. You told me that gang was no good to mess around with. Now I know it. Can they hang me for just being there?" His voice was very young and shaken.

"Come over here and get warm," said Mark. "For being where?"

"In the car when it killed the guy."

"Killed!" Mark fumbled the black lid-lifter. "What happened?"

"We were out in that Porsche of Rick's, just tearing around seeing how fast it could take that winding road on the other side of Sheep's Bluff." Tad gulped. "They called me chicken because I got scared. And I am! I saw Mr. Stegemeir after his pickup went off the road by the fish hatchery last year and I—I can't help remembering it. Well, anyway—" His voice broke off and he gulped. "Well, they made such good time that they got to feeling pretty wild and decided to come over on this road and—" His eyes dropped away from Mark's and his feet moved apologetically. "They wanted to find some way to get back at you again."

Then his words tumbled out in a wild spurt of terror. "All at once there was this man. Out of nowhere! Right in the road! And we hit him! And knocked him clear off the road. And they weren't even going to stop, but I grabbed the key and made them! I made them back up and I got out to look for the man. I found him. All bloody. Lying in the bushes. I tried to find out where he was bleeding—they—they went off and left me there with him!" His voice was outraged. "They didn't give a dern about that poor guy! They went off and left him lying there and me with not even a flashlight!"

Mark had been dressing rapidly. "He may not be dead," he said, reaching for his cap. "How far is he?"

"The other side of the creek bridge," said Tad. "We came the Rim way. Do you think he might—"

"We'll see," said Mark. "Meris, give me one of those army blankets and get Lala off the cot. We'll use that for a stretcher. Build the fire up and check the first aid kit." He got the Coleman lantern from the storeroom, then he and Tad gathered up the canvas cot and went out into the chilly darkness.

Lala fretted a little, then, curled in the warmth Mark had left, she slept again through all the bustling about as Meris prepared for Mark's return.

Meris ran to the door when she heard their feet in the yard. She flung the outer door wide and held the screen as they edged the laden cot through the door. "Is he—?"

"Don't think so." Mark grunted as they lowered the cot to the floor. "Still bleeding from the cut on his head and I don't think dead men bleed. Not this long, anyway. Get a gauze pad, Meris, and put pressure on the cut. Tad, get his boots off while I get his shirt—"

Meris glanced up from her bandage as Mark's voice broke off abruptly. He was staring at the shirt. His eyes caught Meris's and he ran a finger down the front of the shirt. No buttons. Meris's mouth opened, but Mark shook his head warningly. Then, taking hold of the muddied shirt, he gently turned both sides back away from the chest that was visibly laboring now.

Meris's hands followed the roll of the man's head, keeping the bandage in place, but her eyes were on the bed, where Lala had turned away from the light and was burrowed nearly out of sight under the edge of Mark's pillow.

Tad spoke from where he was struggling with the man's boots. "I thought it was you, Mr. Edwards," he said. "I nearly passed out when you answered the door. Who else could it have been? No one else lives way out here and I couldn't see his face. I knew he was bleeding because my hands—" He broke off as one boot thumped to the floor. "And we knocked him so far! So high! And I thought it was you!" He shuddered and huddled over the other boot. "I'm cured, honest, Mr. Edwards. I'm cured. Only don't let him die. Don't let him die!" He was crying now, unashamed.

"I'm no doctor," said Mark, "but I don't think he's badly hurt. Lots of scratches, but that cut on his head seems to be the worst."

"The bleeding's nearly stopped," said Meris. "And his eyes are fluttering."

Even as she spoke, the eyes opened, dark and dazed, the head turning restlessly. Mark leaned over the man. "Hello," he said, trying to get the eyes to focus on him. "You're okay. You're okay. Only a cut—"

The man's head stilled. He blinked and spoke, his eyes closing before his words were finished.

"What did he say?" asked Tad. "What did he say?"

"I don't know," said Mark. "And he's gone again. To sleep, this time, I hope. I'm quite sure he isn't dying."

Later, when Mark was satisfied that the man was sleeping, in the warm pajamas he and Tad had managed to wrestle him into, he got dressed in clean clothes and had Tad wash up, and put on a clean flannel shirt in place of his blood-stained one.

"We're going to the sheriff, after we find the doctor," he told Tad. "We're going to have to take care of those kids before they do kill someone or themselves. And you, Tad, are going to have to put the finger on them whether you like it or not. You're the only witness—"

"But if I do, then I'll get in trouble, too—" began Tad.

"Look, Tad," said Mark patiently, "if you walk in mud, you get your feet muddy. You knew when you got involved with these fellows that you were wading in mud. Maybe you thought it didn't matter much. Mud is easy to wash off. That might be true of mud, but what about blood?"

"But Rick's not a juvenile any more—" Tad broke off before the grim tightening of Mark's face.

"So that's what they've been trading on. So he's legally accountable now? Nasty break!"

After they were gone, Meris checked the sleeping man again. Then, crawling into bed, shoving Lala gently toward the back of the bunk, she cuddled, shivering under the bedclothes. She became conscious of the steady outflow of warmth from Lala and smiled as she fanned her cold hands out under the cover toward the small body. "Bless the little heater!" she said. Her eyes were sleepy and closed in spite of her, but her mind still raced with excitement and wonder. What if Mark was right? What if Lala had come from a spaceship! What if this man, sleeping under their own blankets on their own cot, patched by their own gauze and adhesive, was really a Man from Outer Space! Wouldn't that be something? "But," she sighed, "no bug-eyed monsters? No set, staring eyes and slavering teeth?" She smiled at herself. She had been pretty bug-eyed herself, when she had seen his un-unbuttonable shirt.

Dr. Hilf arrived, large, loud, and lively, before Meris got back to sleep—in fact, while she was in the middle of her *Bless Mark, bless Tad, bless Lala, bless the bandaged man, bless*— He examined the silently cooperative man thoroughly, rebandaged his head and a few of the deeper scratches, grabbed a cup of coffee, and boomed, "Doesn't look to me as if he's been hit by a car! Aspirin if his head aches. No use wasting stitches where they aren't needed!" His voice woke Lala and she sat up, blinking silently at him. "He's not much worried himself! Asleep already! That's an art!" The doctor gave Meris a practiced glance. "Looking half alive again yourself, young lady. Good idea having a child around. Your niece?" He didn't wait for an answer. "Good to help hold the place until you get another of your own!" Meris winced away from the idea. The doctor's eyes softened, but not his voice. "There'll be others," he boomed. "We need offspring from good stock like yours and Mark's. Leaven for a lot of the makeweights popping up all over." He gathered up his things and flung the door open. "Mark says the fellow's a foreigner. No English. Understood though. Let me know his name when you get it. Just curious. Mark'll be along pretty quick. Waiting for the sheriff to get the juvenile officers from county seat." The house door slammed. A car door slammed. A car roared away. Meris automatically smoothed her hair as she always did after a conversation with Dr. Hilf.

She turned wearily back toward the bunk. And gasping, stumbled forward. Lala was hovering in the air over the strange man like a flanneled angel over a tombstoned crusader. She was peering down, her bare feet flipping up as she lowered her head toward him. Meris clenched her hands and made herself keep back out of the way.

"Muhlala!" whispered Lala softly. Then louder, "Muhlala!" Then she wailed, "Muhlala!" and thumped herself down on the quiet, sleeping chest.

"Well," said Meris aloud to herself as she collapsed on the edge of the bunk. "There seems to be no doubt about it!" She watched—a little enviously—the rapturous reunion, and listened—more than a little curiously—to the flood of strange-sounding double conversation going on without perceptible pauses. Smiling, she brought tissues for the man to mop his face after Lala's multitude of very moist kisses. The man was sitting up now, holding Lala closely to him. He smiled at Meris and then down at Lala. Lala looked at Meris and then patted the man's chest.

"Muhlala," she said happily, "muhlala!" and burrowed her head against him.

Meris laughed. "No wonder you thought it funny when I called you muhlala," she said. "I wonder what Lala means."

"It means 'daddy,' " said the man. "She is quite excited about being called daddy."

Meris swallowed her surprise. "Then you do have English," she said.

"A little," said the man. "As you give it to me. Oh, I am Johannan." He sagged then, and said something un-English to Lala. She protested, but even protesting, lifted herself out of his arms and back to the bunk, after planting a last smacking kiss on his right ear. The man wiped the kiss away and held his drooping head between his hands.

"I don't wonder," said Meris, going to the medicine shelf. "Aspirin for your headache." She shook two tablets into his hand and gave him a glass of water. He looked bewilderedly from one hand to the other.

"Oh, dear," said Meris. "Oh, well, I can use one myself," and she took an aspirin and a glass of water and showed him how to dispose of them. The man smiled and gulped the tablets down. He let Meris take the glass, slid flat on the cot, and was breathing asleep before Meris could put the glass in the sink.

"Well!" she said to Lala and stood her, curly-toed, on the cold floor and straightened the bedclothes. "Imagine a grown-up not knowing what to do with an aspirin! And now," she plumped Lala into the freshly made bed, "now, my Daddy-girl, shall we try that instant sleep bit?"

The next afternoon, Meris and Lala lounged in the thin warm sunshine near the creek with Johannan. In the piny, water-loud clearing, empty of unnecessary conversation, Johannan drowsed and Lala alternately bandaged her doll and unbandaged it until all the stickum was off the tape. Meris watched her with that sharp awareness that comes so often before an unwished-for parting from one you love. Then, with an almost audible click, afternoon became evening and the shadows were suddenly long. Mark came out of the cabin, stretching his desk-kinked self widely, then walking his own long shadow down to the creek bank.

"Almost through," he said to Meris as he folded himself to the ground beside her. "By the end of the week, barring fire, flood, and the cussedness of man, I'll be able to send it off."

"I'm so glad," said Meris, her happiness welling strongly up inside her. "I was afraid my foolishness—"

"The foolishness is all past now," said Mark. "It is remembered against us no more."

Johannan had sat up at Mark's approach. He smiled now and said carefully, "I'm glad my child and I haven't interrupted your work too much. It would be a shame if our coming messed up things for you."

"You have a surprising command of the vernacular if English is not your native tongue," said Mark, his interest in Johannan suddenly sharpening.

"We have a knack for languages," smiled Johannan, not really answering anything.

"How on earth did you come to lose Lala?" Meris asked, amazed at herself for asking such a direct question.

Johannan's face sobered. "That was quite a deal—losing a child in a thunderstorm over a quarter of a continent." He touched Lala's cheek softly with his finger as she patiently tried to make the worn-out tape stick again on Deeko. "It was partly her fault," said Johannan, smiling ruefully. "If she weren't precocious— You see, we do not come into the atmosphere with the large ship—too many complications about explanations and misinterpretations and a very real danger from trigger-happy—or unhappy—military, so we use our life-slips for landings."

"We?" murmured Meris.

"Our People," said Johannan simply. "Of course there's no Grand Central Station of the Sky. We are very sparing of our comings and goings. Lala and I were returning because Lala's mother has been Called and it is best to bring Lala to Earth to her grandparents."

"Her mother was called?" asked Mark.

"Back to the Presence," said Johannan. "Our years together were very brief." His face closed smoothly over his sorrow. "We move our life-slips," he went on after a brief pause, "without engines. It is an adult ability, to bring the life-slips through the atmosphere to land at the Canyon.

But Lala is precocious in many Gifts and Persuasions and she managed to jerk her life-slip out of my control on the way down. I followed her into the storm—" He gestured and smiled. He had finished.

"But where were you headed?" asked Mark. "Where on earth—?"

"On Earth," Johannan smiled, "there is a Group of the People. More than one Group, they say. They have been here, we know, since the end of the last century. My wife was of Earth. She returned to the New Home on the ship we sent to Earth for the refugees. She and I met on the New Home. I am not familiar with Earth—that's why, though I was oriented to locate the Canyon from the air, I am fairly thoroughly lost to it from the ground."

"Mark." Meris leaned over and tapped Mark's knee. "He thinks he has explained everything."

Mark laughed. "Maybe he has. Maybe we just need a few years for absorption and amplification. Questions, Mrs. Edwards?"

"Yes," said Meris, her hand softly on Lala's shoulder. "When are you leaving, Johannan?"

"I must first find the Group," said Johannan. "So, if Lala could stay—" Meris's hands betrayed her. "For a *little* while longer," he emphasized. "It would help."

"Of course," said Meris. "Not ours to keep."

"The boys," said Johannan suddenly. "Those in the car. There was a most unhealthy atmosphere. It was an accident, of course. I tried to lift out of the way, but I was taken unawares. But there was little concern—"

"There will be," said Mark grimly. "Their hearing is Friday."

"There was one," said Johannan slowly, "who felt pain and compassion—"

"Tad," said Meris. "He doesn't really belong—"

"But he associated—"

"Yes," said Mark, "consent by silence."

The narrow, pine-lined road swept behind the car, the sunlight flicking across the hood like pale, liquid pickets. Lala bounced on Meris's lap, making excited, unintelligible remarks about the method of transportation and the scenery going by the windows. Johannan sat in the back seat being silently absorbed in his new world. The trip to town was a threefold expedition—to attend the hearing for the boys involved in the accident, to start Johannan on his search for the Group, and to celebrate the completion of Mark's manuscript.

They had left it blockily beautiful on the desk, awaiting the triumphant moment when it would be wrapped and sent on its way and when Mark would suddenly have large quantities of uncommitted time on his hands for the first time in years.

"What is it?" Johannan had asked.

"His book," said Meris. "A reference textbook for one of those frightening new fields that are in the process of developing. I can't even remember its name, let alone understand what it's about."

Mark laughed. "I've explained a dozen times. I don't think she wants to remember. The book's to be used by a number of universities for their textbook in the field *if*, if it can be ready for next year's classes. If it can't be available in time, another one will be used and all the concentration of years—" He was picking up Johannan's gesture.

"So complicated—" said Meris.

"Oh, yes," said Johannan. "Earth's in the complication stage."

"Complication stage?" asked Meris.

"Yes," said Johannan. "See that tree out there? Simplicity says—a tree. Then wonder sets in and you begin to analyze it—cells, growth, structure, leaves, photosynthesis, roots, bark, rings—on and on until the tree is a mass of complications. Then, finally, with reservations not quite to be removed, you can put it back together again and sigh in simplicity once more—a tree. You're in the complication period in the world now."

"Is true!" laughed Mark. "Is true!"

"Just put the world back together again, someday," said Meris, soberly.

"Amen," said the two men.

But now the book was at the cabin and they were in town for a day that was remarkable for its widely scattered, completely unorganized, confusion. It started off with Lala, in spite of her father's warning words, leaving the car through the open window, headlong, without waiting for the door to be opened. A half a block of pedestrians—five to be exact—rushed to congregate in expectation of blood and death, to be angered in their relief by Lala's laughter, which lit her eyes and bounced her dark curls. Johannan snatched her back into the car—forgetting to take hold of her in the process—and un-Englished at her severely, his brief gestures making clear what would happen to her if she disobeyed again.

The hearing for the boys crinkled Meris's shoulders unpleasantly. Rick appeared with the minors in the course of the questioning and glanced at Mark the whole time, his eyes flicking hatefully back and forth across Mark's face. The gathered parents were an unhappy, uncomfortable bunch, each overreacting according to his own personal pattern and the boys either echoing or contradicting the reactions of their own parents. Meris wished herself out of the whole unhappy mess.

Midway in the proceedings, the door was flung open and Johannan, who had left with a wiggly Lala as soon as his small part was over, gestured at Mark and Meris and un-Englished at them across the whole room.

The two left, practically running, under the astonished eyes of the judge and, leaning against the securely closed outside door, looked at Johannan. After he understood their agitation and had apologized in the best way he could pluck from their thoughts, he said, "I had a thought." He shifted Lala, squirming, to his other arm. "He—the doctor who came to look at my head—he—he—" He gulped and started again. "All the doctors have ties to each other, don't they?"

"Why, I guess so," said Meris, rescuing Lala and untangling her brief skirts from under her armpits. "There's a medical society—"

"That is too big," said Johannan after a hesitation. "I mean, Dr.—Dr.—Hilf would know other doctors in this part of the country?" His voice was a question.

"Sure he would," said Mark. "He's been around here since Territorial days. He knows everyone and his dog—including a lot of the summer people."

"Well," said Johannan, "there is a doctor who knows my People. At least there was. Surely he must still be alive. He knows the Canyon. He could tell me."

"Was he from around here?" asked Mark.

"I'm not sure where here is," Johannan reminded, "but a hundred miles or so one way or the other."

"A hundred miles isn't much out here," confirmed Meris. "Lots of times you have to drive that far to get anywhere."

"What was the doctor's name?" asked Mark, snatching for Lala as she shot up out of Meris's arms in pursuit of a helicopter that clacked overhead. He grasped one ankle and pulled her down. Grim-faced, Johannan took Lala from him.

"Excuse me," he said, and, facing Lala squarely to him on one arm, he held her face still and looked at her firmly. In the brief silence that followed, Lala's mischievous smile faded and her face crumpled into sadness and then to tears. She flung herself upon her father, clasping him around his neck and wailing heartbrokenly, her face pushed hard against his shoulder. He un-Englished at her tenderly for a moment, then said, "You see why it is necessary for Lala to come to her grandparents? They are Old Ones and know how to handle such precocity. For her own protection she should be among the People."

"Well, cherub," said Mark, retrieving her from Johannan, "let's go salve your wounded feelings with an ice cream cone."

They sat at one of the tables in the back of one of the general stores and laughed at Lala's reaction to ice cream; then, with her securely involved with two straws and a glass full of crushed ice, they returned to the topic under discussion.

"The only way they ever referred to the doctor was just Doctor—"

He was interrupted by the front door slapping open. Shelves rattled. A can of corn dropped from a pyramid and rolled across the floor. "Dern fool summer people!" trumpeted Dr. Hilf. "Sit around all year long at sea-level getting exercise with a knife and fork, then come roaring up here and try to climb Devil's Slide eleven thousand feet up in one morning!"

Then he saw the group at the table. "Well! How'd the hearing go?" he roared, making his way rapidly and massively toward them as he spoke. The three exchanged looks of surprise, then Mark said, "We weren't in at the verdict." He started to get up. "I'll phone—"

"Never mind," boomed Dr. Hilf. "Here comes Tad." They made room at the table for Tad and Dr. Hilf.

"We're on probation," confessed Tad. "I felt about an inch high when the judge got through with us. I've had it with that outfit!" He brooded briefly. "Back to my bike, I guess, until I can afford my own car. Chee!" He gazed miserably at the interminable years ahead of him. Maybe even five!

"What about Rick?" asked Mark.

"Lost his license," said Tad uncomfortably. "For six months, anyway. Gee, Mr. Edwards, he's sure mad at you now. I guess he's decided to blame you for everything."

"He should have learned long ago to blame himself for his own misdoings," said Meris. "Rick was a spoiled-rotten kid long before he ever came up here."

"Mark's probably the first one ever to make him realize that he was a brat," said Dr. Hilf. "That's plenty to build a hate on."

"Walking again!" muttered Tad. "So okay! So t'heck with wheels!"

"Well, since you've renounced the world, the flesh, and Porsches," smiled Mark, "maybe you could beguile the moments with learning about vintage cars. There's plenty of them still functioning around here."

"Vintage cars?" said Tad. "Never heard of them. Imports?"

Mark laughed, "Wait. I'll get you a magazine." He made a selection from the magazine rack in back of them and plopped it down in front of Tad. "There. Read up. There might be a glimmer of light to brighten your dreary midnight."

"Dr. Hilf," said Johannan, "I wonder if you would help me."

"English?" bellowed Dr. Hilf. "Thought you were a foreigner! You don't look as if you need help! Where's your head wound? No right to be healed already!"

"It's not medical," said Johannan. "I'm trying to find a doctor friend of mine. Only I don't know his name or where he lives."

"Know what *state* he lives in?" Laughter rumbled from Dr. Hilf.

"No," confessed Johannan, "but I do know he is from this general area and I thought you might know of him. He has helped my People in the past."

"And your people are—" asked Dr. Hilf.

"Excuse me, folks," said Tad, unwinding his long legs and folding the magazine back on itself. "There's my dad, ready to go. I'm grounded. Gotta tag along like a kid. Thanks for everything—and the magazine." And he dejectedly trudged away.

Dr. Hilf was waiting on Johannan, who was examining his own hands intently. "I know so little," said Johannan. "The doctor cared for a small boy with a depressed fracture of the skull. He operated in the wilderness with only the instruments he had with him." Dr. Hilf's eyes flicked to Johannan's face and then away again. "But that was a long way from where he found one of Ours who could make music and was going wrong because he didn't know who he was."

Dr. Hilf waited for Johannan to continue. When he didn't, the doctor pursed his lips and hummed massively.

"I can't help much," said Johannan, finally, "but are there so many doctors who live in the wilds of this area?"

"None," boomed Dr. Hilf. "I'm the farthest out—if I may use that loaded expression. Out in these parts, a sick person has three choices— die, get well on his own, or call me. Your doctor must have come from some town."

It was a disconsolate group that headed back up-canyon. Their mood even impressed itself on Lala and she lay silent and sleepy-eyed in Meris's arms, drowsing to the hum of the motor.

Suddenly Johannan leaned forward and put his hand on Mark's shoulder. "Would you stop, please?" he asked. Mark pulled off the road onto the nearest available flat place, threading expertly between scrub oak and small pines. "Let me take Lala." And Lala lifted over the back of the seat without benefit of hands upon her. Johannan sat her up on his lap. "Our People have a highly developed racial memory," he said. "For instance, I have access to the knowledge any of our People have known since the Bright Beginning, and, in lesser measure, to the events that have happened to any of them. Of course, unless you have studied the technique of recall—it is difficult to take knowledge from the past, but it's there, available. I am going to see if I can get Lala to recall for me. Maybe her precocity will include recollection also." He looked down at his nestling child and smiled. "It won't be spectacular," he said. "No eyeballs will light up. I'm afraid it'll be tedious for you, especially since it will be subvocal.

Lala's spoken vocabulary lags behind her other Gifts. You can drive on, if you like." And he leaned back with Lala in his arms. The two to all appearances were asleep.

Meris looked at Mark and Mark looked at Meris, and Meris felt an irrepressible bubble of laughter start up her throat. She spoke hastily to circumvent it.

"Your manuscript," she said.

"I got a box for it," said Mark, easing out onto the road again. "Chip found one for me when you took Lala to the rest room. Couldn't have done better if I'd had it made to measure. What a weight—" he yawned in sudden release— "What a weight off my mind. I'll be glad when it's off my hands, too. Thank God! Thank God it's finished!"

The car was topping the Rim when Johannan stirred, and a faint twitter of release came from Lala. Meris turned sideways to look at them inquiringly.

"May I get out?" asked Johannan. "Lala has recalled enough that I think my search won't be too long."

"I'll drive you back," said Mark, pulling up by the road.

"Thanks, but it won't be necessary." Johannan opened the door and, after a tight embrace for Lala and an un-English word or two, stepped out. "I have ways of going. If you will care for Lala until I return."

"Of course!" said Meris, reaching for the child, who flowed over the back of the seat into her arms in one complete motion. "God bless, and return soon."

"Thank you," said Johannan and walked into the roadside bushes. They saw a ripple in the branches, the turn of a shoulder, the flick of a foot, one sharp startling glimpse of Johannan rising against the blue and white of the afternoon sky, and then he was hidden in the top branches of the trees.

"Shoosh!" Meris slumped under Lala's entire weight. "Mark, is this a case of *folie à deux,* or is it really happening?"

"Well," said Mark, starting the car again, "I doubt if we two could achieve the same hallucinations simultaneously, so let's assume it's really happening."

When they finally reached the cabin and stopped the motor, they sat for a moment in the restful, active silence of the hills. Meris, feeling the soft warmth of Lala against her and the precious return of things outside herself, shivered a little, remembering her dead self who had stared so blankly so many hours out of the small windows, tearlessly crying, soundlessly wailing, wrapped in misery. She laughed and hugged Lala. "Maybe we should get a leash for this small person," she said to Mark. "I don't think I could follow in Johannan's footsteps."

"Supper first," said Mark as he fumbled with the padlock on the cabin door. He glanced, startled, back over his shoulder at Meris. "It's broken," he said. "Wrenched open—" He flung the door open hastily, and froze on the doorstep. Meris pushed forward to look beyond him.

Snow had fallen in the room—snow covered everything—a smudged, crumpled snow of paper, flour, sugar, and detergent. Every inch of the cabin was covered by the tattered, soaked, torn, crumpled snow of Mark's manuscript! Mark stooped slowly, like an old man, and took up one page. Mingled detergent and maple syrup clung, clotted, and slithered off the edge of one of the diagrams that had taken two days to complete. He let the page fall and shuffled forward, ankle-deep in the obscene, incredible chaos. Meris hardly recognized the face he turned to her.

"I've lost our child again," he said tightly. "This—" he gestured at the mess about them, "—this was my weeping and my substitute for despair. My creation to answer death." He backhanded a clutter of papers off the bunk and slumped down until he lay, face to the wall, motionless.

Mark said not a word nor turned around in the hours that followed. Meris thought perhaps he slept at times, but she said nothing to him as she cautiously scrabbled through the mess in the cabin. She found, miraculously undamaged, a chapter and a half of pages under the cupboard. With careful hands she salvaged another sheaf of papers from where they had sprayed across the top of the cupboard. All the time she searched and sorted through the mess in the cabin, Lala sat, unnaturally well behaved and solemn, and watched her, getting down only once to salvage Deeko from a mound of sugar and detergent, clucking unhappily as she dusted the doll off.

It was late and cold when Meris put the last ruined sheet in the big cardboard box they had carried groceries home in, and the last salvageable sheet on the desk. She looked silently the clutter in the box and the slender sheaf on the desk, shivered, and turned to build up the dying fire in the stove. Her mouth tightened and the sullen flicker of charring, wadded paper in the stove painted age and pain upon her face. She stirred the embers with the lid-lifter and rebuilt the fire. She prepared supper, fed Lala, and put her to bed. Then she sat on the edge of the lower bunk by Mark's rigid back and touched him gently.

"Supper's ready," she said. "Then I'll need some help in scrubbing up—the floor, the walls, the furniture." She choked a sound that was half laughter and half sob. "There's plenty of detergent around already. We may bubble ourselves out of house and home."

For a sick moment she was afraid he wouldn't respond. *Just like I was,* she thought achingly. *Just like I was!* Then he sat up slowly, brushed his arm back across his expressionless face and his rumpled hair, and stood up.

When they finally threw out the last bucket of scrub water and hung out the last scrub rag, Meris rubbed her water-wrinkled hands down her weary sides and said, "Tomorrow we'll start on the manuscript again."

"No," said Mark. "That's all finished. The boys got carbon-copy and all. It would take weeks for me to do a rewrite if I could ever do it. We don't have weeks. My leave of absence is over, and the deadline for the manuscript is this next week. We'll just have to chalk this up as lost. Let the dead past bury the dead."

He went to bed, his face turned again from the light. Meris, through the blur of her slow tears, gathered up the crumpled pages that had pulled out with the blankets from the back of the bunk, smoothed them onto the salvage pile, and went to bed, too.

For the next couple of days Mark was like an old man. He sat against the cabin wall in the sun, his arms resting on his thighs, his hands dangling from limp wrists, looking at the nothing that the senile and finished find on the ground. He moved slowly and reluctantly to the table to push his food around, to bed to lie, hardly breathing, but wide-eyed in the dark, to whatever task Meris set him, forgetting in the middle of it what he was doing.

Lala followed him at first, chattering un-English at her usual great rate, leaning against him when he sat, peering into his indifferent face. Then she stopped talking to him and followed him only with her eyes. Then the third day she came crying into Meris's arms and wept heartbrokenly against her shoulder.

Then her tears stopped, glistened on her cheeks a moment, and were gone. She squirmed out of Meris's embrace and trotted to the window. She pushed a chair up close to the wall, climbed up on it, pressed her forehead to the chilly glass, and stared out into the late afternoon.

Tad came over on his bike, bubbling over with the new idea of old cars.

"Why, there's parts of a whole bunch of these cars all over around here—" he cried, fluttering the tattered magazine at Mark. "And have you seen how much they're asking for some of them! Why, I could put myself through college on used parts out of our old dumps! And some of these vintage jobs are still running around here! Kiltie has a model A—you've seen it! He shines it like a new shoe every week! And there's an old Overland touring car out in back of our barn, just sitting there, falling apart—"

Mark's silence got through to him then, and he asked, troubled, "What's wrong? Are you mad at me for something?"

Meris spoke into Mark's silence. "No, Tad, it's nothing you've done—" She took him outside, ostensibly to help bring in wood to fill the woodbox, and filled him in on the events. When they returned, loaded down with firewood, he dumped his armload into the box and looked at Mark.

"Gee, whiz, Mr. Edwards. Uh—uh—gee whiz!" He gathered up his magazine and his hat and, shuffling his feet for a moment, said, "Well, 'bye now," and left, grimacing back at Meris, wordless.

Lala was still staring out the window. She hadn't moved or made a sound while Tad was there. Meris was frightened.

"Mark!" She shook his arm gently. "Look at Lala. She's been like that for almost an hour. She pays no attention to me at all. Mark!"

Mark's attention came slowly back to the cabin and to Meris.

"Thank goodness!" she cried. "I was beginning to feel that I was the one that was missing!"

At that moment, Lala plopped down from the chair and trotted off to the bathroom, a round red spot marking her forehead where she had leaned so long.

"Well!" Meris was pleased. "It must be suppertime. Everyone's gathering around again." And she began the bustle of supper-getting. Lala trotted around with her, getting in the way, hindering with her help.

"No, Lala!" said Meris. "I told you once already. Only three plates. Here, put the other one over there." Lala took the plate, waited patiently until Meris turned to the stove, then, lifting both feet from the floor, put the plate back on the table. The soft click of the flatware as she patterned it around the plate caught Meris's attention. "Oh, Lala!" she cried, half-laughing, half-exasperated. "Well, all right. If you can't count, okay. Four it will be." She started convulsively and dropped a fork as a knock at the door roused even Mark. "Hungry guest coming," she laughed nervously as she picked up the fork. "Well, stew stretches."

She started for the door, fear, bred of senseless violence, crisping along her spine, but Lala was ahead of her, fluttering like a bird, with excited bird cries against the door panels, her hands fumbling at the knob and the night chain Meris had insisted on installing. Meris unfastened and unlocked and opened the door.

It was Johannan, anxious-eyed and worried, who slipped in and gathered up a shrieking Lala. When he had finally un-Englished her to a quiet, contented clinging, he turned to Meris. "Lala called me back," he said. "I've found my Group. She told me Mark was sick—that bad things had happened."

"Yes," said Meris, stirring the stew and moving it to the back of the stove. "The boys came while we were gone and ruined Mark's manuscript beyond salvage. And Mark—Mark is crushed. He lost all those months of labor through senseless, vindictive—" She turned away from Johannan's questioning face and stirred the stew again, blindly.

"But," protested Johannan, "if once it was written, he has it still. He can do it again."

"Time is the factor." Mark's voice, rusty and harsh, broke in on Johannan. "And to rewrite from my notes—" He shook his head and sagged again.

"But—but—!" cried Johannan, still puzzled, putting Lala to one side, where she hovered, sitting on air, crooning to Deeko, until she drifted slowly down to the floor. "It's all there! It's been written! It's a whole thing! All you have to do is put it again on paper. Your word scriber—"

"I don't have total recall," said Mark. "Even if I did, just to put it on paper again—come see our 'word scriber.'" He smiled a small bent smile as Johannan poked fingers into the mechanism of the typewriter and clucked unhappily, sounding so like Lala that Meris almost laughed. "Such slowness! Such complications!"

Johannan looked at Mark. "If you want, my People can help you get your manuscript back again."

"It's finished," said Mark. "Why agonize over it any more?" He turned to the blank darkness of the window.

"Was it worth the effort of writing?" asked Johannan.

"I thought so," said Mark. "And others did, too."

"Would it have served a useful purpose?" asked Johannan.

"Of course it would have!" Mark swung angrily from the window. "It covered an area that needs to be covered. It was new—the first book in the field!" He turned again to the window.

"Then," said Johannan simply, "we will make it again. Have you paper enough?"

Mark swung back, his eyes glittering. Meris stepped between his glare and Johannan. "This summer I have come back from the dead," she reminded. "And you caught a baby for me, pulling her down from the sky by one ankle. Johannan went looking for his people through the tree-tops. And a three-year-old called him back by leaning against the window. If all these things could happen, why can't Johannan bring your manuscript back?"

"But if he tries and can't—" Mark began.

"*Then* we can let the dead past bury the dead," said Meris sharply, "which little item you have not been letting happen so far!"

Mark stared at her, then flushed a deep, painful flush. "Okay, then," he said. "Stir the bones again! Let him put meat back on them if he can!"

The next few hours were busy with patterned confusion. Mark roared off through the gathering darkness to persuade Chip to open the store for typing paper. And people arrived. Just arrived, smiling, at the door, familiar friends before they spoke, and Meris, glancing out to see if the heavens themselves had split open from astonishment, saw, hovering tree-top high, a truly vintage car, an old pickup that clanked softly to itself, spinning a wheel against a branch as it waited. "If Tad could see that!" she thought, with a bubble of laughter nudging her throat.

She hurried back indoors further to make welcome the newcomers—Valancy, Karen, Davy, Jemmy. The women gathered Lala in with soft cries and shining eyes and she wept briefly upon them in response to their emotions, then leaped upon the fellows and nearly strangled them with her hugs.

Johannan briefed the four in what had happened and what was needed. They discussed the situation, glanced at the few salvaged pages on the desk, and sent, eyes closed briefly, for someone else. His name was Remy and he had a special "Gift" for plans and diagrams. He arrived just before Mark got back, so the whole group of them confronted him when he flung the door open and stood there with his bundle of paper.

He blinked, glanced at Meris, then, shifting his burden to one arm, held out a welcoming hand. "I hadn't expected an invasion," he smiled. "To tell the truth, I didn't know what to expect." He thumped the package down on the table and grinned at Meris. "Chip's sure now that writers are psychos," he said. "Any normal person could wait till morning for paper or use flattened grocery bags!" He shrugged out of his jacket. "Now."

Jemmy said, "It's really quite simple. Since you wrote your book and have read it through several times, the thing exists as a whole in your memory, just as it was on paper. So all we have to do is put it on paper again." He gestured.

"That's all?" Mark's hands went back through his hair. "That's all? Man, that's all I had to do after my notes were organized, months ago! Maybe I should have settled for flattened grocery bags! Why, the sheer physical—" The light was draining out of his face.

"Wait—wait!" Jemmy's hand closed warmly over his sagging shoulder. "Let me finish."

"Davy, here, is our gadgeteer. He dreams up all kinds of knick-knacks and, among other things, he has come forth with a word scriber. Even better"—he glanced at Johannan—"than the ones brought from the New Home. All you have to do is think and the scriber writes down your thoughts. Here— try it—" he said into Mark's very evident skepticism.

Davy put a piece of paper on the table in front of Mark and, on it, a small gadget that looked vaguely like a small sanding block in that it was curved across the top and flat on the bottom. "Go on," urged Davy, "think something. You don't even have to vocalize. I've keyed it to you. Karen sorted your setting for me."

Mark looked around at the interested, watching faces, at Meris's eyes, blurred with hesitant hope, and then down at the scriber. The scriber stirred, then slid swiftly across the paper, snapping back to the beginning of a line again, as quick as thought. Davy picked up the paper and handed it to Mark. Meris crowded to peer over his shoulder.

Of all the dern-fool things! As if it were possible— Look at the son-a-gun go!

All neatly typed, neatly spaced, appropriately punctuated. Hope flamed up in Mark's eyes. "Maybe so," he said, turning to Jemmy. "What do I do, now?"

"Well," said Jemmy, "you have your whole book in your mind, but a mass of other things, too. It'd be almost impossible for you to think through your book without any digressions or side thoughts, so Karen will blanket your mind for you except for your book—"

"Hypnotism—" Mark's withdrawal was visible.

"No," said Karen. "Just screening out interference. Think how much time was taken up in your original draft by distractions—"

Meris clenched her hands and gulped, remembering all the hours Mark had had to—to *baby-sit* her while she was still rocking her grief like a rag doll with all the stuffings pulled out. She felt an arm across her shoulders and turned to Valancy's comforting smile. "All over," said her eyes, kindly, "all past."

"How about all the diagrams—" suggested Mark. "I can't vocalize—"

"That's where Remy comes in," said Jemmy. "All you have to do is visualize each one. He'll have his own scriber right here and he'll take it from there."

The cot was pulled up near the table and Mark disposed himself comfortably on it. The paper was unwrapped and stacked all ready. Remy and Davy arranged themselves strategically. Surrounded by briefly bowed heads, Jemmy said, "We are met together in Thy name." Then Karen touched Mark gently on the forehead with one fingertip.

Mark suddenly lifted himself on one elbow. "Wait," he said, "things are going too fast. Why—why are you doing this for us, anyway? We're strangers. No concern of yours. Is it to pay us for taking care of Lala? In that case—"

Karen smiled. "Why *did* you take care of Lala? You could have turned her over to the authorities. A strange child, no relation, no concern of yours."

"That's a foolish question," said Mark. "She needed help. She was cold and wet and lost. Anyone—"

"You did it for the same reason we are doing this for you," said Karen. "Just because we had our roots on a different world doesn't make us of different flesh. There are no strangers in God's universe. You found an unhappy situation that you could do something about, so you did it. Without stopping to figure out the whys and wherefores. You did it just because that's what love does."

Mark lay back on the narrow pillow. "Thank you," he said. Then he turned his face to Meris. "Okay?"

"Okay." Her voice jerked a little past her emotion. "*Love* you, Mark!"

"*Love* you, Meris!"

Karen's fingertip went to Mark's forehead again. "I need contact," she said a little apologetically, "especially with an Outsider."

Meris fell asleep, propped up on the bunk, eyes lulled by the silent *sli-i-i-ide, flip! sli-i-i-ide, flip!* of the scriber, and the brisk flutter of finished pages from the tall pile of paper to the short one. She opened drowsy eyes to a murmur of voices and saw that the two piles of paper were almost balanced. She sat up to ease her neck where it had been bent against the cabin wall.

"But it's wrong, I tell you!" Remy was waving the paper. "Look, this line, here, where it goes—"

"Remy," said Jemmy, "are you sure it's wrong or is it just another earlier version of what we know now?"

"No!" said Remy. "This time it's not that. This is a real mistake. He couldn't possibly have meant it to be like that—"

"Okay." Jemmy nodded to Karen and she touched Mark's forehead. He opened his eyes and half sat up. The scriber flipped across the paper and Karen stilled it with a touch. "What is it?" he asked. "Something go wrong?"

"No, it's this diagram." Remy brought it to him. "I think you have an error here. Look where this goes—"

The two bent over the paper. Meris looked around the cabin. Valancy was rocking a sleeping Lala in her arms. Davy was sound asleep in the upper bunk. At least his dangling leg looked very asleep. Johannan was absorbed in two books simultaneously. He seemed to be making a comparison of some sort. Meris lay back again, sliding down to a more comfortable position. For the first time in months and months the cabin was lapped from side to side with peace and relaxation. Even the animated discussion going on was no ruffling of the comfortable calmness. She heard, on the edge of her ebbing consciousness,

"Why, no! That's not right at all!" Mark was astonished. "Hoo boy! If I'd sent that in with an error like that! Thanks, fella—" And sleep flowed over Meris.

She awoke later to the light chatter of Lala's voice and opened drowsy eyes to see her trailing back from the bathroom, her feet tucked up under her gown away from the chilly floor as she drifted back to Valancy's arms. The leg above Meris's head swung violently and withdrew, to be replaced by Davy's dangling head. He said something to Lala. She laughed and lifted herself up to his outstretched arms. There was a stirring around above Meris's head before sleeping silence returned.

Valancy stood and stretched widely. She moved over to the table and thumbed the stack of paper.

"Going well," she said softly.

"Yes," said Jemmy. "I feel a little like a midwife, snatching something new-born in the middle of the night."

"Dern shame to stop here, though," said Remy. "With such a good beginning—oh, barring a few excursions down dead ends—if we could only tack on a few more chapters."

"Uh-uh!" Jemmy stood and stretched, letting his arms fall around Valancy's shoulders. "You know better than that—"

"Not even one little hint?"

"Not even." Jemmy was firm.

Sleep flowed over Meris again until pushed back by Davy's sliding over the edge of the upper bunk.

"Right in the stomach!" he moaned as he dropped to the floor. "Such a kicking kid I never met. How'd *you* survive?" he asked Valancy.

"Nary a kick," she laughed. "Technique—that's what it takes."

"I was just wondering," said Davy, opening the stove and probing the coals before he put in another chunk of oak. "That kid Johannan was talking about—the one that's got interested in vintage cars. What about that place up on Bearcat Flat? You know, that little box canyon where we put all our old jalopies when we discarded them. Engines practically unused. Lifting's cheaper and faster. Of course the seats and the truck beds are kinda beat up, and the paint. Trees scratch the daylights out of paint. How many are there? Let's see. The first one was about 19-ought-something—"

Johannan looked up from his books. "He said something about selling parts or cars to get money for college—"

"Or restoring them!" Davy cried. "Hey, that could be fun! If he's the kind that would—"

"He is," said Johannan and went back to his reading.

"It's almost daylight." Davy went to the window and parted the curtains. "Wonder how early a riser he is?"

Meris turned her back to the light and slid back under sleep again.

Noise and bustle filled the cabin.

Coffee was perking fragrantly, eggs cracking, bacon spitting itself to crispness. Remy was cheerfully mashing slices of bread down on the hot stove lid and prying up the resultant toast. Lala was flicking around the table, putting two forks at half the places and two knives at the others, then giggling her way back around with redistribution after Johannan pointed out her error.

Meris, reaching for a jar of peach marmalade on the top shelf of the cupboard, wondered how a day could feel so new and so wonderful. Mark sat at his desk opening and closing the box wherein lay the finished manuscript. He opened it again and fingered the top edge of the stack. He caught Jemmy's sympathetic grin and grinned back.

"Just making sure it's really there," he explained. "Magic put it in there. Magic might take it out again."

"Not this magic. I'll even ride shotgun for you into town and see that it gets sent off okay," said Jemmy.

"Magic or no," said Mark, sobering, "once more I can say Thank God! Thank God it's done!"

"Amen!" said a hovering Lala, and, laughing, Jemmy scooped her out of the air as they all found places at the table.

Tad was an early riser. He was standing under the hovering pickup, gaping upward in admiring astonishment.

"Oops!" said Davy, with a sidewise glance at Jemmy. Tad was swept up in a round of introductions during which the pickup lowered slowly to the ground.

Tad turned from the group back to the pickup. "Look at it!" he said. "It must be at least forty years old!" His voice pushed its genesis back beyond the pyramids.

"At least that," said Davy. "Wanta see the motor?"

"Do I!" He stood by impatiently as Davy wrestled with the hood. Then he blinked. "Hey! How did it get way up there? I mean, how'd it get down—"

"Look," said Davy hastily, "see this goes to the spark—"

The others, laughing, piled into Mark's car and drove away from the two absorbed autophiles-in-embryo.

The car pulled over onto a pine flat halfway back from town and the triumphal mailing of the manuscript. This was the parting place. Davy would follow later with the pickup.

"It's over," said Meris, her shoulders sagging a little as she put Lala's small bundle of belongings into Valancy's hands. "All over." Her voice was desolate.

"Only this little episode," comforted Valancy. "It's really only begun." She put Lala into Meris's arms. "Tell her good-by, Lala."

Lala hugged Meris stranglingly tight saying, "*Love* you, Meris!"

"*Love* you, Lala!" Meris's voice was shaken with laughter and sorrow.

"It's just that she filled up the empty places so wonderfully well," she explained to Valancy.

"Yes," said Valancy softly, her eyes tender and compassionate. "But, you know," she went on, "you *are* pregnant again!"

Before Meris could produce an intelligible thought, good-bys were finished and the whole group was losing itself in the tangle of creek-side vegetation. Lala's vigorous waving of Deeko was the last sign of them before the leaves closed behind them.

Meris and Mark stood there, Meris's head pressed to Mark's shoulder, both too drained for any emotion. Then Meris stirred and moved toward the car, her eyes suddenly shining. "I don't think I can wait," she said. "I don't think—"

"Wait for what?" asked Mark, following her.

"To tell Dr. Hilf—" She covered her mouth, dismayed. "Oh, Mark! We never did find out that doctor's name!"

"Not that Hilf is drooling to know," said Mark, starting the car, "but next time— "

"Oh, yes," Meris sat back, her mouth curving happily, "next time, next time!"

Interlude: Mark & Meris 1

The next time wasn't so long by the calendar, but measured by the anticipation and the marking time, it seemed an endless eternity. Then one night Meris, looking down into the warm, moistly fragrant blanket-bundle in the crook of her elbow, felt time snap back into focus. It snapped back so completely and satisfyingly that the long, empty time of grief dwindled to a memory-ache tucked back in the fading past.

"And the next one," she said drowsily to Mark, "will be a brother for her."

The nurse laughed. "Most new mothers feel, at this point, that they are through with childbearing. But I guess they soon forget because we certainly get a lot of repeaters!"

The Saturday before the baby's christening, Meris felt a stir of pleasure as she waited for her guests to arrive. So much of magic was interwoven with her encounters with them, the magic of being freed from grief, of bringing forth a new life, and the magic of the final successful production of Mark's book. She was wondering, with a pleasurable apprehension, what means of transportation the guests would use, *treetop high, one wheel spinning lazily!* when a clanging clatter drew her to the front window.

There in all its glory, shining with love, new paint, and dignity, sailed the Overland that had been moldering behind Tad's barn. Flushed with excitement and pride, Tad, with an equally proud Johannan seated beside him, steered the vehicle ponderously over to the curb. There it hiccoughed, jumped, and expired with a shudder.

In the split second of silence after the noise cut off, there was a clinking rattle and a nut fell down from somewhere underneath and rolled out into the street.

There was a shout of relieved and amused laughter and the car erupted people apparently through and over every door. Meris shrank back a little, still tender in her social contact area. Then calling, "Mark, they're here," she opened the door to the babble of happy voices.

All the voices turned out to be female-type voices and she looked around and asked, "But where—?"

"The others?" Karen asked. "Behold!" And she gestured toward the old car, where the only signs of life were three sets of feet protruding from under it, with a patient Jemmy leaning on a brightly black fender above them. "May I present, the feet, Tad, Davy, and Johannan?" Karen laughed. "Johannan is worse than either of the boys. You see, he'd never ever *seen* a car before he rode in yours!"

Finally everyone was met and greeted and all the faces swam up to familiarity again out of the remoteness of the time Before the Baby.

Lala—forever Lala in spite of translations!—peered at the bundle on Valancy's lap. "It's little," she said.

Meris was startled. Valancy smiled at her. "Did you expect her to un-English forever?" she teased. "Yes, Lala, it's a girl baby, very new and very little."

"I'm not little," said Lala, straightening from where she leaned against Meris and tightening to attention, her tummy rounding out in her effort to assume proportions. "I'm big!" She moved closer to Meris. "I had a birthday."

"Oh, how nice!" said Meris.

"We don't know what year to put on it, though," said Lala solemnly. "I want to put six, but they want to put five."

"Oh, six, of course!" exclaimed Meris.

Lala launched herself onto Meris and hugged her hair all askew. "*Love* you, Meris!" she cried. "Six, of course!"

"There has been a little discussion about the matter," said Valancy. "The time element differs between here and the New Home. And since she *is* precocious—"

"The *New* Home," said Meris thoughtfully. "The New Home. You know, I suspended all my disbelief right at the beginning of this Lala business, but now I feel questions bubbling and frothing—"

"I thought I saw question marks arising in both your eyes," laughed Valancy. "After church tomorrow, after this cherub receives her name before God and the congregation, we'll tackle a few of those questions. But now—" she hugged the wide-eyed, moist-mouthed child gently "—now this is the center of our interest."

The warm Sunday afternoon was slipping into evening. Davy, Tad, and Johannan were—again—three pairs of feet protruding from under the Overland. The three had managed to nurse it along all the way to the

University City, but now it stubbornly sat in the driveway and merely rocked, voiceless, no matter how long they cranked it.

The three of them had been having the time of their lives. They had visited the Group's auto boneyard up-canyon and then, through avid reading of everything relevant that they could put their hands on, had slowly and bedazzledly come to a realization of what a wealth of material they had to work with.

Tad, after a few severe jolts from working with members of the People, such as seeing cars and parts thereof clattering massively unsupported through the air and watching Johannan weld a rip in a fender by tracing it with a fingertip, then concentrating on the task, had managed to compartmentalize the whole car business and shut it off securely from any need to make the methods of the People square with Outsiders' methods. And his college fund was building beautifully.

So there the three of them were under the Overland that was the current enthusiasm, ostensibly to diagnose the trouble, but also to delight in breathing deeply of sun-warmed metal and to taste the oily fragrance of cup grease and dust.

Mark and Jemmy were perched on the patio wall, immersed in some point from Mark's book. Lala was wrapped up in the wonder of Alicia's tiny, flailing fist, that if intercepted, would curl so tightly around a finger or thumb.

Meris smiled at Valancy and shifted the burden of 'Licia to her other arm. "I think I'd better park this bundle somewhere. She's gained ten pounds in the last five minutes, so I think that a nap is indicated." With the help of Valancy, Karen, and Bethie, Meris gathered up various odds and ends of equipment and carried the already sleeping 'Licia into the house.

Later, in the patio, the women gathered again, Lala a warm weight in Valancy's lap.

"Now," said Meris, comfortably. "Now's the time to erase a few of my question marks. What is the Home? Where is the Home? Why is it the *New* Home?"

"Not so fast—not so fast!" laughed Valancy. "This is Bethie's little red wagon. Let her drag it!"

"Oh, but—!" Bethie blushed and shook her head. "Why mine? I'd rather—"

"But you have been wanting to Assemble for Shadow, anyway, so that she'd have a verbalized memory of the Crossing. It's closer through your line." Her smile softened as she turned to Meris. "My parents were in the Crossing, but they were Called during the landing. Bethie's mother was *in* the Crossing and survived. Karen's grandparents did, too, but that's a step farther back. And, Bethie, haven't you already—"

"Yes," said Bethie softly, "from the Home to the beginning of the Crossing. Oh, how strange! How strange and wonderful! Oh, Valancy! To have lost the Home!"

"Now you're question-marking *my* eyes," laughed Valancy. "I've never gone by chapter and verse through that life myself. Jemmy—Mark—we're ready!"

"It'll be better, subvocal," said Bethie shyly. "Karen, you could touch Meris's hand so she can see, too. And Jemmy, you and Mark." The group settled comfortably.

"I went back through my mother's remembrances," Bethie's soft voice came through a comfortable dimming and fading of the patio. "Her grandmother before her verbalized a great deal. It was a big help. We can take it from her. We will begin on one happy morning—"

Deluge

...and bare up the ark, and it was lift up above the earth.

GEN. 7:17

"The children are up already, Eva-lee?" asked David, lounging back in his chair after his first long, satisfying swallow from his morning cup.

"Foolish question, David, on Gathering Day," I laughed. "They've been up since before it was light. Have you forgotten how you used to feel?"

"Of course not." My son cradled his cup in his two hands to warm it and watched idly until steam plumed up fragrantly. "I just forgot—oh, momentarily, I assure you—that it was Gathering Day. So far it hasn't felt much like *failova* weather."

"No, it hasn't," I answered, puckering my forehead thoughtfully. "It has felt—odd—this year. The green isn't as— Oh, good morning, 'Chell," to my daughter-of-love, "I suppose the little imps waked you first thing?"

"At least half an hour before that," yawned 'Chell. "I suppose I used to do it myself. But just wait—they'll have their yawning time when they're parents."

"Mother! Mother! Father! Gramma!"

The door slapped open and the children avalanched in, all talking shrilly at once until David waved his cup at them and lifted one eyebrow. 'Chell laughed at the sudden silence.

"That's better," she said. "What's all the uproar?"

The children looked at one another and the five-year-old Eve was nudged to the fore, but, as usual, David started talking. "We were out gathering *panthus* leaves to make our Gathering baskets, and all at once—" He paused and nudged Eve again. "You tell, Eve. After all, it's you—"

"Oh, no!" cried 'Chell. "Not my last baby! Not already!"

"Look," said Eve solemnly. "Look at me."

She stood tiptoe and wavered a little, her arms outstretched for balance, and then she lifted slowly and carefully up into her mother's arms.

We all laughed and applauded and even 'Chell, after blotting her surprised tears on Eve's dark curls, laughed with us.

"Bless-a-baby!" she said, hugging her tight. "Lifting all alone already—and on Gathering Day, too! It's not everyone who can have Gathering Day for her Happy Day!" Then she sobered and pressed the solemn ceremonial kiss on each cheek. "Lift in delight all your life, Eve!" she said.

Eve matched her parents' solemnity as her father softly completed the ritual. "By the Presence and the Name and the Power, lift to good and the Glory until your Calling." And we all joined in making the Sign.

"I speak for her next," I said, holding out my arms. "Think you can lift to Gramma, Eve?"

"Well..." Eve considered the gap between her and me—the chair, the breakfast table—all the obstacles before my waiting arms. And then she smiled. "Look at me," she said. "Here I come, Gramma."

She lifted carefully above the table, overarching so high that the crisp girl-frill around the waist of her close-fitting briefs brushed the ceiling. Then she was safe in my arms.

"That's better than I did," called Simon through the laughter that followed. "I landed right in the *flahmen* jam!"

"So you did, son," laughed David, ruffling Simon's coppery-red hair. "A full dish of it."

"Now that that's taken care of, let's get organized. Are you all Gathering together—"

"No." Lytha, our teener, flushed faintly. "I—we—our party will be mostly—well—" She paused and checked her blush, shaking her dark hair back from her face. "Timmy and I are going with Beckie and Andy. We're going to the Mountain."

"Well!" David's brow lifted in mock consternation. "Mother, did you know our daughter was two-ing?"

"Not really, Father!" cried Lytha hastily, unable to resist the bait though she knew he was teasing. "Four-ing, it is, really."

"*Adonday veeah!*" he sighed in gigantic relief. "Only half the worry it might be!" He smiled at her. "Enjoy," he said, "but it ages me so much so fast that a daughter of mine is two—oh, pardon, four-ing already."

"The rest of us are going together," said Davie. "We're going to the Tangle-meadows. The *failova* were thick there last year. Bet we three get more than Lytha and her two-ing foursome! They'll be looking mostly for *flahmen* anyway!" with the enormous scorn of the almost-teen for the activities of the teens.

"Could be," said David. "But after all, your sole purpose this Gathering Day is merely to Gather."

"I notice you don't turn up your nose at the *flahmen* after they're made into jam," said Lytha. "And you just wait, smarty, until the time comes—and it will," her cheeks pinked up a little, "when you find yourself wanting to share a *flahmen* with some gaggly giggle of a girl!"

"*Flahmen!*" muttered Davie. "Girls!"

"They're both mighty sweet, Son," laughed David. "You wait and see."

Ten minutes later, 'Chell and David and I stood at the window watching the children leave. Lytha, after nervously putting on and taking off, arranging and rearranging her Gathering Day garlands at least a dozen times, was swept up by a giggling group that zoomed in a trio and went out a quartet and disappeared in long, low lifts across the pastureland toward the heavily wooded Mountain.

Davie tried to gather Eve up as in the past, but she stubbornly refused to be trailed, and kept insisting, "I can lift now! Let me do it. I'm big!"

Davie rolled exasperated eyes and then grinned and the three started off for Tangle-meadows in short hopping little lifts, with Eve always just beginning to lift as they landed or just landing as they lifted, her small Gathering basket bobbing along with her. Before they disappeared, however, she was trailing from Davie's free hand and the lifts were smoothing out long and longer. My thoughts went with them as I remembered the years I had Gathered the lovely luminous flowers that popped into existence in a single night, leafless, almost stemless, as though formed like dew, or falling like concentrated moonlight. No one knows now how the custom of loves sharing a *flahmen* came into being, but it's firmly entrenched in the traditions of the People. To share that luminous loveliness, petal by petal, one for me and one for you and all for us—

"How pleasant that Gathering Day brings back our loves," I sighed dreamily as I stood in the kitchen and snapped my fingers for the breakfast dishes to come to me. "People that might otherwise be completely forgotten come back so vividly every year—"

"Yes," said 'Chell, watching the tablecloth swish out the window, huddling the crumbs together to dump them in the feather-pen in back of the house. "And it's a good anniversary-marker. Most of us meet our loves at the Gathering Festival—or discover them there." She took the returning cloth and folded it away. "I never dreamed when I used to fuss with David over mud pies and playhouses that one Gathering Day he'd blossom into my love."

"*Me* blossom?" David peered around the doorjamb. "Have you forgotten how you looked, preblossom? Knobby knees, straggly hair, toothless grin—!"

"David, put me down!" 'Chell struggled as she felt herself being lifted to press against the ceiling. "We're too old for such nonsense!"

"Get yourself down, then, Old One," he said from the other room. "If I'm too old for nonsense, I'm too old to *platt* you."

"Never mind, funny fellow," she said, "I'll do it myself." Her down-reaching hand strained toward the window and she managed to gather a handful of the early morning sun. Quickly she platted herself to the floor and tiptoed off into the other room, eyes aglint with mischief, finger hushing to her lips.

I smiled as I heard David's outcry and 'Chell's delighted laugh, but I felt my smile slant down into sadness. I leaned my arms on the window-sill and looked lovingly at all the dear familiarity around me. Before Thann's Calling, we had known so many happy hours in the meadows and skies and waters of this loved part of the Home.

"And he is still here," I thought comfortably. "The grass still bends to his feet, the leaves still part to his passing, the waters still ripple to his touch, and my heart still cradles his name.

"Oh, Thann, Thann!" I wouldn't let tears form in my eyes. I smiled. "I wonder what kind of a grampa you'd have made!" I leaned my fore-head on my folded arms briefly, then turned to busy myself with straightening the rooms for the day. I was somewhat diverted from routine by finding six mismated sandals stacked, for some unfathomable reason, above the middle of Simon's bed, the top one, inches above the rest, bobbing in the breeze from the open window.

The oddness we had felt about the day turned out to be more than a passing uneasiness, and we adults were hardly surprised when the children came straggling back hours before they usually did.

We hailed them from afar, lifting out to them expecting to help with their burdens of brightness, but the children didn't answer our hails. They plodded on toward the house, dragging slow feet in the abundant grass.

"What do you suppose has happened?" breathed 'Chell. "Surely not Eve—"

"*Adonday veeah!*" murmured David, his eyes intent on the children. "Something's wrong, but I see Eve."

"Hi, young ones," he called cheerfully. "How's the crop this year?"

The children stopped, huddled together, almost fearfully.

"Look." Davie pushed his basket at them. Four misshapen *failova* glowed dully in the basket. No flickering, glittering brightness. No flushing and paling of petals. No crisp, edible sweetness of blossom. Only a dull glow, a sullen winking, an unappetizing crumbling.

"That's all," said Davie, his voice choking. "That's all we could find!" He was scared and outraged—outraged that his world dared to be different from what he had expected—had counted on.

Eve cried, "No, no! I have one. Look!" Her single flower was a hard-clenched *flahmen* bud with only a smudge of light at the tip.

"No *failova?*" Chell took Davie's proffered basket. "No *flahmen?* But they always bloom on Gathering Day. Maybe the buds—"

"No buds," said Simon, his face painfully white under the brightness of his hair. I glanced at him quickly. He seldom ever got upset over anything. What was there about this puzzling development that was stirring him?

"David!" 'Chell's face turned worriedly to him. "What's wrong? There have always been *failova!*"

"I know," said David, fingering Eve's bud and watching it crumble in his fingers. "Maybe it's only in the meadows. Maybe there's plenty in the hills."

"No," I said. "Look."

Far off toward the hills we could see the teeners coming, slowly, clustered together; *panthus* baskets trailing.

"No *failova*," said Lytha as they neared us. She turned her basket up, her face troubled. "No *failova* and no *flahmen*. Not a flicker on all the hills where they were so thick last year. Oh, Father, why not? It's as if the sun hadn't come up! Something's wrong."

"Nothing catastrophic, Lytha." David comforted her with a smile. "We'll bring up the matter at the next meeting of the Old Ones. Someone will have the answer. It is unusual, you know." (Unheard of, he should have said.) "We'll find out then." He boosted Eve to his shoulder. "Come on, young ones, the world hasn't ended. It's still Gathering Day! I'll race you to the house. First one there gets six *koomatka* to eat all by himself! One, two, three—"

Off shot the shrieking, shouting children, Eve's little heels pummeling David's chest in her excitement. The teeners followed for a short way and then slanted off on some project of their own, waving good-by to 'Chell and me. We women followed slowly to the house, neither speaking.

I wasn't surprised to find Simon waiting for me in my room. He sat huddled on my bed, his hands clasping and unclasping and trembling, a fine, quick trembling deeper than muscles and tendons. His face was so white it was almost luminous and the skiff of golden freckles across the bridge of his nose looked metallic.

"Simon?" I touched him briefly on his hair that was so like Thann's had been.

"Gramma." His breath caught in a half hiccough. He cleared his throat carefully as though any sudden movement would break something fragile. "Gramma," he whispered. "I can See!"

"See!" I sat down beside him because my knees suddenly evaporated. "Oh, Simon! You don't mean—"

"Yes, I do, Gramma." He rubbed his hands across his eyes. "We had just found the first *failova* and were wondering what was wrong with it when everything kinda went away and I was—somewhere—Seeing!" He looked up, terrified. "It's my Gift!"

I gathered the suddenly wildly sobbing child into my arms and held him tightly until his terror spent itself and I felt his withdrawal. I let him go and watched his wet, flushed face dry and pale back to normal.

"Oh, Gramma," he said, "I don't want a Gift yet. I'm only ten. David hasn't found his Gift and he's twelve already. I don't *want* a Gift—especially this one—" He closed his eyes and shuddered. "Oh, Gramma, what I've seen already! Even the Happy scares me because it's still in the Presence!"

"It's not given to many," I said, at a loss how to comfort him. "Why, Simon, it would take a long journey back to our Befores to find one in our family who was permitted to See. It is an honor—to be able to put aside the curtain of time—"

"I don't *want* to!" Simon's eyes brimmed again. "I don't think it's a bit of fun. Do I have to?"

"Do you have to breathe?" I asked him. "You could stop if you wanted to, but your body would die. You can refuse your Gift, but part of you would die—the part of you the Power honors—your place in the Presence—your syllable of the Name." All this he knew from first consciousness, but I could feel him taking comfort from my words. "Do you realize the People have had no one to See for them since—since—why, clear back to the Peace! And now you are it! Oh, Simon, I am so proud of you!" I laughed at my own upsurge of emotion. "Oh, Simon! May I touch my thrice-honored grandson?"

With a wordless cry, he flung himself into my arms and we clung tightly, tightly, before his deep renouncing withdrawal. He looked at me then and slowly dropped his arms from around my neck, separation in every movement. I could see growing, in the topaz tawniness of his eyes, his new set-apartness. It made me realize anew how close the Presence is to us always and how much nearer Simon was than any of us. Also, naked and trembling in my heart was the recollection that never did the People have one to See for them unless there lay ahead portentous things to See.

Both of us shuttered our eyes and looked away, Simon to veil the eyes that so nearly looked on the Presence, I, lest I be blinded by the Glory reflected in his face.

"Which reminds me," I said in a resolutely everyday voice, "I will now listen to explanations as to why those six sandals were left on, over, and among your bed this morning."

"Well," he said with a tremulous grin, "the red ones are too short—" He turned stricken, realizing eyes to me. "I won't ever be able to tell anyone anything any more unless the Power wills it!" he cried. Then he grinned again. "And the green ones need the latchets renewed—"

A week later the usual meeting was called and David and I—we were among the Old Ones of our Group—slid into our robes. I felt a pang as I smoothed the shimmering fabric over my hips, pressing pleats in with my thumb and finger to adjust for lost weight. The last time I had worn it was the Festival the year Thann was Called. Since then I hadn't wanted to attend the routine Group meetings—not without Thann. I hadn't realized that I was losing weight.

'Chell clung to David. "I wish now that I were an Old One too," she said. "I've got a nameless worry in the pit of my stomach heavy enough to anchor me for life. Hurry home, you two!"

I looked back as we lifted just before the turnoff. I smiled to see the warm lights begin to well up in the windows. Then my smile died. I felt, too, across my heart the shadow that made 'Chell feel it was Lighting Time before the stars had broken through the last of the day.

The blow—when it came—was almost physical, so much so that I pressed my hands to my chest, my breath coming hard, trying too late to brace against the shock. David's sustaining hand was on my arm but I felt the tremor in it, too. Around me I felt my incredulity and disbelief shared by the other Old Ones of the Group.

The Oldest spread his hands as he was deluged by a flood of half-formed questions. "It has been Seen. Already our Home has been altered so far that the *failova* and *flahmen* can't come to blossom. As we accepted the fact that there were no *failova* and *flahmen* this year, so we must accept the fact that there will be no more Home for us."

In the silence that quivered after his words, I could feel the further stricken sag of heartbeats around me, and suddenly my own heart slowed until I wondered if the Power was stilling it now—now—in the midst of this confused fear and bewilderment.

"Then we are all Called?" I couldn't recognize the choked voice that put the question. "How long before the Power summons us?"

"*We* are not Called," said the Oldest. "Only the Home is Called. We—go."

"Go!" The thought careened from one to another.

"Yes," said the Oldest. "Away from the Home. Out."

Life apart from the Home? I slumped. It was too much to be taken in all at once. Then I remembered. Simon! Oh, poor Simon! If he were Seeing clearly already—but of course he was. He was the one who had told the Oldest! No wonder he was terrified! *Simon*, I said to the Oldest subvocally. *Yes,* answered the Oldest. *Do not communicate to the others. He scarcely can bear the burden now. To have it known would multiply it past his bearing. Keep his secret—completely.*

I came back to the awkward whirlpool of thoughts around me.

"But," stammered someone, speaking what everyone was thinking, "can the People *live* away from the Home? Wouldn't we die like uprooted plants?"

"We can live," said the Oldest. "This we know, as we know that the Home can no longer be our biding place."

"What's wrong? What's happening?" It was Neil—Timmy's father.

"We don't know." The Oldest was shamed. "We have forgotten too much since the Peace to be able to state the mechanics of what is happening, but one of us Sees us go and the Home destroyed, so soon that we have no time to go back to the reasons."

Since we were all joined in our conference mind, which is partially subvocal, all our protests and arguments and cries were quickly emitted and resolved, leaving us awkwardly trying to plan something of which we had no knowledge of our own.

"If we are to go," I said, feeling a small spurt of excitement inside my shock, "we'll have to make again. Make a tool. No, that's not the word. We have tools still. Man does with tools. No, it's a—a machine we'll have to make. Machines do to man. We haven't been possessed by machines—"

"For generations," said David. "Not since—" He paused to let our family's stream of history pour through his mind. "Since Eva-lee's thrice great-grandfather's time."

"Nevertheless," said the Oldest, "we must make ships." His tongue was hesitant on the long unused word. "I have been in communication with the other Oldest Ones around the Home. Our Group must make six of them."

"How can we?" asked Neil. "We have no plans. We don't know such things any more. We have forgotten almost all of it. But I do know that to break free from the Home would take a pushing something that all of us together couldn't supply."

"We will have the—the fuel," said the Oldest. "When the time comes. My Befores knew the fuel. We would not need it if only our motivers had developed their Gift fully, but as they did not—

"We must each of us search the Before stream of our lives and find the details that we require in this hour of need. By the Presence, the Name, and the Power, let us remember."

The evening sped away almost in silence as each mind opened and became receptive to the flow of racial memory that lay within. All of us partook in a general way of that stream that stemmed almost from the dawn of the Home. In particular, each family had some specialized area of the memory in greater degree than the others. From time to time came a sigh or a cry prefacing, "My Befores knew of the metals," or "Mine of the instruments"—the words were unfamiliar—"the instruments of pressure and temperature."

"Mine"—I discovered with a glow—and a sigh—"the final putting together of the shells of ships."

"Yes," nodded David, "and also, from my father's Befores, the settings of the—the—the settings that guide the ship."

"Navigation," said Neil's deep voice. "My Befores knew of the making of the navigation machine yours knew how to set."

"And all," I said, "all of this going back to nursery school would have been unnecessary if we hadn't rested so comfortably so long on the achievements of our Befores!" I felt the indignant withdrawal of some of those about me, but the acquiescence of most of them.

When the evening ended, each of us Old Ones carried not only the burden of the doom of the Home but a part of the past that, in the Quiet Place of each home, must, with the help of the Power, be probed and probed again, until—

"Until—" The Oldest stood suddenly, clutching the table as though he had just realized the enormity of what he was saying. "Until we have the means of leaving the Home—before it becomes a band of dust between the stars—"

Simon and Lytha were waiting up with 'Chell when David and I returned. At the sight of our faces, Simon slipped into the bedroom and woke Davie and the two crept quietly back into the room. Simon's thought reached out ahead of him. *Did he tell?* And mine went out reassuringly. *No. And he won't.*

In spite of—or perhaps because of—the excitement that had been building up in me all evening, I felt suddenly drained and weak. I sat down, gropingly, in a chair and pressed my hands to my face. "You tell them, David," I said, fighting an odd vertigo.

David shivered and swallowed hard. "There were no *failova* because the Home is being broken up. By next Gathering Day there will be no Home. It is being destroyed. We can't even say why. We have forgotten too much and there isn't time to seek out the information now, but long before next Gathering Day, we will be gone—out."

'Chell's breath caught audibly. "No Home!" she said, her eyes widening and darkening. "No Home? Oh, David, don't joke. Don't try to scare—"

"It's true." My voice had steadied now. "It has been Seen. We must build ships and seek asylum among the stars." My heart gave a perverse jump of excitement. "The Home will no longer exist. We will be homeless exiles."

"But the People away from the Home!" 'Chell's face puckered, close to tears. "How can we live anywhere else? We are a part of the Home as much as the Home is a part of us. We can't just amputate—"

"Father!" Lytha's voice was a little too loud. She said again, "Father, are all of us going together in the same ship?"

"No," said David. "Each Group by itself." Lytha relaxed visibly. "Our Group is to have six ships," he added.

Lytha's hands tightened. "Who is to go in which ship?"

"It hasn't been decided yet," said David, provoked. "How can you worry about a detail like that when the Home, *the Home* will soon be gone!"

"It's important," said Lytha, flushing. "Timmy and I—"

"Oh," said David. "I'm sorry, Lytha. I didn't know. The matter will have to be decided when the time comes."

It didn't take long for the resiliency of childhood to overcome the shock of the knowledge born on Gathering Day. Young laughter rang as brightly through the hills and meadows as always. But David and 'Chell clung closer to one another, sharing the heavy burden of leave-taking, as did all the adults of the Home. At times I, too, felt wildly, hopefully, that this was all a bad dream to be awakened from. But other times I had the feeling that this *was* an awakening. This was the dawn after a long twilight—a long twilight of slanting sun and relaxing shadows. Other times I felt so detached from the whole situation that wonder welled up in me to see the sudden tears, the sudden clutching of familiar things, that had become a sort of pattern among us as realization came and went. And then, there were frightening times when I felt weakness flowing into me like a river—a river that washed all the Home away on a voiceless wave. I was almost becoming more engrossed in the puzzle of me than in the puzzle of the dying Home—and I didn't like it.

David and I went often to Meeting, working with the rest of the Group on the preliminary plans for the ships. One night he leaned across the table to the Oldest and asked, "How do we know how much food will be needed to sustain us until we find asylum?"

The Oldest looked steadily back at him. "We *don't* know," he said. "We don't know that we will ever find asylum."

"Don't know?" David's eyes were blank with astonishment.

"No," said the Oldest. "We found no other habitable worlds before the Peace. We have no idea how far we will have to go or if we shall any of us live to see another Home. Each Group is to be assigned to a different sector of the sky. On Crossing Day, we say good-by—possibly forever— to all the other Groups. It may be that only one Ship will plant the seeds of the People upon a new world. It may be that we will all be Called before a new Home is found."

"Then," said David, "why don't we stay here and take our Calling with the Home?"

"Because the Power has said to go. We are given time to go back to the machines. The Power is swinging the gateway to the stars open to us. We must take the gift and do what we can with it. We have no right to deprive our children of any of the years they might have left to them."

After David relayed the message to 'Chell, she clenched both her fists tight up against her anguished heart and cried, "We can't! Oh, David! We can't! We can't leave the Home for—for—nowhere! Oh, David!" And she clung to him, wetting his shoulder with her tears.

"We can do what we must do," he said. "All of the People are sharing this sorrow, so none of us must make the burden any heavier for the others. The children learn their courage from us, 'Chell. Be a good teacher." He rocked her close-pressed head, his hand patting her tumbled hair, his troubled eyes seeking mine.

"Mother—" David began—Eva-lee was for every day.

"Mother, it seems to me that the Presence is pushing us out of the Home deliberately and crumpling it like an empty eggshell so we can't creep back into it. We have sprouted too few feathers on our wings since the Peace. I think we're being pushed off the branch to make us fly. This egg has been too comfortable." He laughed a little as he held 'Chell away from him and dried her cheeks with the palms of his hands. "I'm afraid I've made quite an omelet of my egg analogy, but can you think of anything really new that we have learned about Creation in our time?"

"Well," I said, searching my mind, pleased immeasurably to hear my own thoughts on the lips of my son. "No, I can honestly say I can't think of one new thing."

"So if you were Called to the Presence right now and were asked, 'What do you know of My Creation?' all you could say would be 'I know all that my Befores knew—my immediate Befores, that is—I mean, my father—' " David opened his hands and poured out emptiness. "Oh, Mother! What we have forgotten! And how content we have been with so little!"

"But some other way," 'Chell cried. "This is so—so drastic and cruel!"

"All baby birds shiver," said David, clasping her cold hands. "Sprout a pin feather, 'Chell!"

And then the planning arrived at the point where work could begin. The sandal shops were empty. The doors were closed in the fabric centers and the ceramic workrooms. The sunlight crept unshadowed again and again across the other workshops, and weeds began tentative invasions of the garden plots.

Far out in the surrounding hills, those of the People who knew how hovered in the sky, rolling back slowly the heavy green cover of the mountainsides, to lay bare the metal-rich underearth. Then the Old Ones, making solemn mass visits from Group to Group, quietly concentrated above the bared hills and drew forth from the very bones of the Home the bright, bubbling streams of metal, drew them forth until they flowed liquidly down the slopes to the workplaces—the launching sites. And the rush and the clamor and the noise of the hurried multitudes broke the silence of the hills of the Home and sent tremors through all our windows—and through our shaken souls.

I often stood at the windows of our house, watching the sky-pointing monsters of metal slowly coming to form. From afar they had a severe sort of beauty that eased my heart of the hurt their having-to-be caused. But it was exciting! Oh, it was beautifully exciting! Sometimes I wondered what we thought about and what we did before we started all this surge out into space. On the days that I put in my helping hours on the lifting into place of the strange different parts that had been fashioned by other Old Ones from memories of the Befores, the upsurge of power and the feeling of being one part of such a gigantic undertaking, made me realize that we had forgotten without even being conscious of it, the warmth and strength of working together. Oh, the People are together even more than the leaves on a tree or the scales on a *dolfeo,* but *working* together? I knew this was my first experience with its pleasant strength. My lungs seemed to breathe deeper. My reach was longer, my grasp stronger. Odd, unfinished feelings welled up inside me and I wanted to *do.* Perhaps this was the itching of my new pin feathers. And then, sometimes when I reached an exultation that almost lifted me off my feet, would come the weakness, the sagging, the sudden desire for tears and withdrawal. I worried, a little, that there might come a time when I wouldn't be able to conceal it.

The Crossing had become a new, engrossing game for the children. At night, shivering in the unseasonable weather, cool, but not cold enough to shield, they would sit looking up at the glory-frosted sky and pick out the star they wanted for a new Home, though they knew that none they could see would actually be it. Eve always chose the brightest pulsating one in the heavens and claimed it as hers. Davie chose one that burned steadily but faintly straight up above them. But when Lytha was asked, she turned the question aside and I knew that any star with Timmy would be Home to Lytha.

Simon usually sat by himself, a little withdrawn from the rest, his eyes quiet on the brightness overhead.

"What star is yours, Simon?" I asked one evening, feeling intrusive but knowing the guard he had for any words he should not speak.

"None," he said, his voice heavy with maturity. "No star for me."

"You mean you'll wait and see?" I asked.

"No," said Simon. "There won't be one for me."

My heart sank. "Simon, you haven't been Called, have you?"

"No," said Simon. "Not yet. I will see a new Home, but I will be Called from its sky."

"Oh, Simon," I cried softly, trying to find a comfort for him. "How wonderful to be able to See a new Home!"

"Not much else left to See," said Simon. "Not that has words." And I saw a flare of Otherside touch his eyes. "But, Gramma, you should see the Home when the last moment comes! That's one of the things I have no words for."

"But we will have a new Home, then," I said, going dizzily back to a subject I hoped I could comprehend. "You said—"

"I can't See beyond my Calling," said Simon. "I will see a new Home. I will be Called from its strange sky. I can't See what is for the People there. Maybe they'll all be Called with me. For me there's flame and brightness and pain—then the Presence. That's all I know.

"But, Gramma"—his voice had returned to that of a normal ten-year-old—"Lytha's feeling awful bad. Help her."

The children were laughing and frolicking in the thin blanket of snow that whitened the hills and meadows, their clear, untroubled laughter echoing through the windows to me and 'Chell, who, with close-pressed lips, were opening the winter chests that had been closed so short a time ago. 'Chell fingered the bead stitching on the toes of one little ankle-high boot.

"What will we need in the new Home, Eva-lee?" she asked despairingly.

"We have no way of knowing," I said. "We have no idea of what kind of Home we'll find." *If any, if any, if any,* our unspoken thoughts throbbed together.

"I've been thinking about that," said 'Chell. "What will it be like? Will we be able to live as we do now or will we have to go back to machines and the kind of times that went with our machines? Will we still be one People or be separated mind and soul?" Her hands clenched on a bright sweater and a tear slid down her cheek. "Oh, Eva-lee, maybe we won't even be able to feel the Presence there!'"

"You know better than that!" I chided. "The Presence is with us always, even if we have to go to the ends of the Universe. Since we can't know now what.the new Home will be like, let's not waste our tears on it." I shook out a gaily patterned quilted skirt. "Who knows?" I laughed. "Maybe it will be a water world and we'll become fish. Or a fire world and we the flames!"

"We can't adjust quite that much!" protested 'Chell, smiling moistly as she dried her face on the sweater. "But it is a comfort to know we can change some to match our environment."

I reached for another skirt and paused, hand outstretched

" 'Chell," I said, taken by a sudden idea, "what if the new Home is already inhabited? What if life is already there?"

"Why then, so much the better," said 'Chell. "Friends, help, places to live—"

"They might not accept us," I said.

"But refugees—homeless!" protested 'Chell. "If any in need came to the Home—"

"Even if they were different?"

"In the Presence, all are the same," said 'Chell.

"But remember." My knuckles whitened on the skirt. "Only remember far enough back and you will find the Days of Difference before the Peace."

And 'Chell remembered. She turned her stricken face to me. "You mean there might be no welcome for us if we do find a new Home?"

"If we could treat our own that way, how might others treat strangers?" I asked, shaking out the scarlet skirt. "But, please the Power, it will not be so. We can only pray."

It turned out that we had little need to worry about what kind of clothing or anything else to take with us. We would have to go practically possessionless—there was room for only the irreducible minimum of personal effects. There was considerable of an uproar and many loud lamentations when Eve found out that she could not take all of her play-People with her, and, when confronted by the necessity of making a choice—one single one of her play-People—she threw them all in a tumbled heap in the corner of her room, shrieking that she would take none at all. A sharp smack of David's hand on her bare thighs for her tantrum, and a couple of enveloping hugs for her comfort, and she sniffed up her tears and straightened out her play-People into a staggering, tumbling row across the floor. It took her three days to make her final selection. She chose the one she had named the Listener.

"She's not a him and he's not a her," she had explained. "This play-People is to listen."

"To what?" teased Davie.

"To anything I have to tell and can't tell anyone," said Eve with great dignity. "You don't even have to verb'lize to Listener. All you have to do is to touch and Listener knows what you feel and it tells you why it doesn't feel good and the bad goes away."

"Well, ask the Listener how to make the bad grammar go away," laughed Davie. "You've got your sentences all mixed up."

"Listener knows what I mean and so do you!" retorted Eve.

So when Eve made her choice and stood hugging Listener and looking with big solemn eyes at the rest of her play-People, Davie suggested casually, "Why don't you go bury the rest of them? They're the same as Called now and we don't leave cast-asides around."

And from then until the last day, Eve was happy burying and digging up her play-People, always finding better, more advantageous, or prettier places to make her miniature casting-place.

Lytha sought me out one evening as I leaned over the stone wall around the feather-pen, listening to the go-to-bed contented cluckings and cooings. She leaned with me on the rough gray stones and, snapping an iridescent feather to her hand, smoothed her fingers back and forth along it wordlessly. We both listened idly to Eve and Davie. We could hear them talking together somewhere in the depths of the *koomatka* bushes beyond the feather-pen.

"What's going to happen to the Home after we're gone?" asked Eve idly.

"Oh, it's going to shake and crack wide open and fire and lava will come out and everything will fall apart and burn up," said Davie, no more emotionally than Eve.

"Ooo!" said Eve, caught in the imagination. "Then what will happen to my play-People? Won't they be all right under here? No one can see them."

"Oh, they'll be set on fire and go up in a blaze of glory," said Davie.

"A blaze of glory!" Eve drew a long happy sigh. "In a blaze of glory! Inna blaza glory! Oh, Davie! I'd like to see it. Can I, Davie? Can I?"

"Silly *toola!*" said Davie. "If you were here to see it, *you'd* go up in a blaze of glory, too!" And he lifted up from the *koomatka* bushes, the time for his chores with the animals hot on his heels.

"Inna blaza glory! Inna blaza glory!" sang Eve happily. "All the play-People inna blaza glory!" Her voice faded to a tuneless hum as she left, too.

"Gramma," said Lytha, "is it really true?"

"Is what really true?" I asked.

"That the Home won't be any more and that we will be gone."

"Why, yes, Lytha, why do you doubt it?"

"Because—because—" She gestured with the feather at the wall. "Look, it's all so solid—the stones set each to the other so solidly—so—so *always-looking*. How can it all come apart?"

"You know from your first consciousness that nothing This-side is forever," I said. "Nothing at all except Love. And even that gets so tangled up in the things of This-side that when your love is Called—"the memory of Thann was a heavy burning inside me—"Oh, Lytha! To look into the face of your love and know that Something has come apart and that never again This-side will you find him whole!"

And then I knew I had said the wrong thing. I saw Lytha's too young eyes looking in dilated horror at the sight of her love—her not-quite-yet love, being pulled apart by this same whatever that was pulling the Home apart. I turned the subject.

"I want to go to the Lake for a good-by," I said. "Would you like to go with me?"

"No, thank you, Gramma." Hers was a docile, little-girl voice—surely much too young to be troubled about loves as yet! "We teeners are going to watch the new metal-melting across the hills. It's fascinating. I'd like to be able to do things like that."

"You can—you could have—" I said, "—if we had trained our youth as we should have."

"Maybe I'll learn," said Lytha, her eyes intent on the feather. She sighed deeply and dissolved the feather into a faint puff of blue smoke. "Maybe I'll learn." And I knew her mind was not on metal-melting.

She turned away and then back again. "Gramma, The Love—" She stopped. I could feel her groping for words. "The Love is forever, isn't it?"

"Yes," I said.

"Love This-side is part of The Love, isn't it?"

"A candle lighted from the sun," I said.

"But the candle will go out!" she cried. "Oh, Gramma! The candle will go out in the winds of the Crossing!" She turned her face from me and whispered, "Especially if it never quite got lighted."

"There are other candles," I murmured, knowing how like a lie it must sound to her.

"But never the same!" She snatched herself away from my side. "It isn't fair! It isn't fair!" and she streaked away across the frost-scorched meadow.

And as she left, I caught a delightful, laughing picture of two youngsters racing across a little lake, reeling and spinning as the waves under their feet lifted and swirled, wrapping white lace around their slender brown ankles. Everything was blue and silver and laughter and fun. I was caught up in the wonder and pleasure until I suddenly realized that it wasn't my memory at all. Thann and I had another little lake we loved more. I had seen someone else's Happy Place that would dissolve like mine with the Home. Poor Lytha.

The crooked sun was melting the latest snow the day all of us Old Ones met beside the towering shells of the ships. Each Old One was wrapped against the chilly wind. No personal shields today. The need for power was greater for the task ahead than for comfort. Above us, the huge bright curved squares of metal, clasped each to each with the old joinings, composed the shining length of each ship. Almost I could have cried to see the scarred earth beneath them—the trampledness that would never green again, the scars that would never heal. I blinked up the brightness of the nearest ship, up to the milky sky, and blinked away from its strangeness.

"The time is short," said the Oldest. "A week."

"A week." The sigh went through the Group.

"Tonight the ship loads must be decided upon. Tomorrow the inside machines must be finished. The next day, the fuel." The Oldest shivered and wrapped himself in his scarlet mantle. "The fuel that we put so completely out of our minds after the Peace. Its potential for evil was more than its service to us. But it is there. It is still there." He shivered again and turned to me.

"Tell us again," he said. "We must complete the shells." And I told them again, without words, only with the shaping of thought to thought. Then the company of Old Ones lifted slowly above the first ship, clasping hands in a circle like a group of dancing children and, leaning forward into the circle, thought the thought I had shaped for them.

For a long time there was only the thin fluting of the cold wind past the point of the ship and then the whole shell of metal quivered and dulled and became fluid. For the span of three heartbeats it remained so and then it hardened again, complete, smooth, seamless, one cohesive whole from tip to base, broken only by the round ports at intervals along its length.

In succession the other five ships were made whole, but the intervals between the ships grew longer and grayer as the strength drained from us, and, before we were finished, the sun had gone behind a cloud and we were all shadows leaning above shadows, fluttering like shadows.

The weakness caught me as we finished the last one. David received me as I drifted down, helpless, and folded on myself. He laid me on the brittle grass and sat panting beside me, his head drooping. I lay as though I had become fluid and knew that something more than the fatigue of the task we had just finished had drained me. "But I *have* to be strong!" I said desperately, knowing weakness had no destiny among the stars. I stared up at the gray sky while a tear drew a cold finger from the corner of my eye to my ear.

"We're just not used to using the Power," said David softly.

"I know, I know," I said, knowing that he did not know. I closed my eyes and felt the whisper of falling snow upon my face, each palm-sized flake melting into a tear.

Lytha stared from me to David, her eyes wide and incredulous. "But you *knew*, Father! I told you! I told you Gathering Night!"

"I'm sorry, Lytha," said David. "There was no other way to do it. Ships fell by lot and Timmy's family and ours will be in different ships."

"Then let me go to his ship or let him come to mine!" she cried, her cheeks flushing and paling.

"Families must remain together," I said, my heart breaking for her. "Each ship leaves the Home with the assumption that it is alone. If you went in the other ship, we might never all be together again."

"But Timmy and I—we might someday be a family! We might—" Lytha's voice broke. She pressed the backs of her hands against her cheeks and paused. Then she went on quietly. "I would go with Timmy, even so."

'Chell and David exchanged distressed glances. "There's not room for even one of you to change your place. The loads are computed, the arrangements finished," I said, feeling as though I were slapping Lytha.

"And besides," said 'Chell, taking Lytha's hands, "it isn't as though you and Timmy were loves. You have only started two-ing. Oh, Lytha, it was such a short time ago that you had your Happy Day. Don't rush so into growing up!"

"And if I told you Timmy is my love?" cried Lytha.

"Can you tell us so in truth, Lytha?" said 'Chell, "and say that Timmy feels that you are his love?"

Lytha's eyes dropped. "Not for sure," she whispered. "But in time—" She threw back her head impetuously, light swirling across her dark hair. "It isn't fair! We haven't had time!" she cried. "Why did all this have to happen now? Why not later? Or sooner?" she faltered, "before we started two-ing! If we have to part now, we might never know—or live our lives without a love because he is really—I am—" She turned and ran from the room, her face hidden.

I sighed and eased myself up from the chair. "I'm old, David," I said. "I ache with age. Things like this weary me beyond any resting."

It was something after midnight the next night that I felt Neil call to me. The urgency of his call hurried me into my robe and out of the door, quietly, not to rouse the house.

"Eva-lee." His greeting hands on my shoulders were cold through my robe, and the unfamiliar chilly wind whipped my hems around my bare ankles. "Is Lytha home?"

"Lytha?" The unexpectedness of the question snatched the last web of sleepiness out of my mind. "Of course. Why?"

"I don't think she is," said Neil. "Timmy's gone with all our camping gear and I think she's gone with him."

My mind flashed back into the house, Questing. Before my hurried feet could get there, I knew Lytha was gone. But I had to touch the undented pillow and lift the smooth spread before I could convince myself. Back in the garden that flickered black and gold as swollen clouds raced across the distorted full moon, Neil and I exchanged concerned looks.

"Where could they have gone?" he asked. "Poor kids. I've already Quested the whole neighborhood and I sent Rosh up to the hillplace to get something—he thought. He brought it back but said nothing about the kids."

I could see the tightening of the muscles in his jaws as he tilted his chin in the old familiar way, peering at me in the moonlight.

"Did Timmy say anything to you about—about anything?" I stumbled.

"Nothing—the only thing that could remotely—well, you know both of them were upset about being in different ships and Timmy— well, he got all worked up and said he didn't believe anything was going to happen to the Home, that it was only a late spring and he thought we were silly to go rushing off into Space—"

"Lytha's words Timmyized," I said. "We've got to find them."

"Carla's frantic." Neil shuffled his feet and put his hands into his pockets, hunching his shoulders as the wind freshened. "If only we had *some* idea. If we don't find them tonight we'll have to alert the Group tomorrow. Timmy'd never live down the humiliation—"

"I know—'Touch a teener—touch a tender spot,' " I quoted absently, my mind chewing on something long forgotten or hardly noticed.

"Clearance," I murmured. And Neil closed his mouth on whatever he was going to say as I waited patiently for the vague drifting and isolated flashes in my mind to reproduce the thought I sought.

—Like white lace around their bare brown ankles—

"I have it," I said. "At least I have an idea. Go tell Carla I've gone for them. Tell her not to worry."

"Blessings," said Neil, his hands quick and heavy on my shoulders. "You and Thann have always been our cloak against the wind, our hand up the hill—" And he was gone toward Tangle-meadows and Carla.

You and Thann—you and Thann. I was lifting through the darkness, my personal shield activated against the acceleration of my going. Even Neil forgets sometimes that Thann is gone on ahead, I thought, my heart lifting to the memory of Thann's aliveness. And suddenly the night was full of Thann—of Thann and me—laughing in the skies, climbing the hills, dreaming in the moonlight. Four-ing with Carla and Neil. Two-ing after Gathering Day. The bittersweet memories came so fast that I almost crashed into the piney sighings of a hillside. I lifted above it barely in time. One treetop drew its uppermost twig across the curling of the bare sole of my foot.

Maybe Timmy's right! I thought suddenly. Maybe Simon and the Oldest are all wrong. How can I possibly leave the Home with Thann still here—waiting. Then I shook myself, quite literally, somersaulting briskly in mid-air. Foolish thoughts, trying to cram Thann back into the limitations of an existence he had outgrown!

I slanted down into the cup of the hills toward the tiny lake I had recognized from Lytha's thought. This troubled night it had no glitter or gleam. Its waves were much too turbulent for walking or dancing or even for daring. I landed on a pale strip of sand at its edge and shivered as a wave dissolved the sand under my feet into a shaken quiver and then withdrew to let it solidify again.

"Lytha!" I called softly, Questing ahead of my words. "Lytha!" There was no response in the wind-filled darkness. I lifted to the next pale crescent of sand, feeling like a driven cloud myself. "Lytha! Lytha!" Calling on the family band so it would be perceptible to her alone and Timmy wouldn't have to know until she told him. "Lytha!"

"Gramma!" Astonishment had squeezed out the answer. "Gramma!" The indignation was twice as heavy to make up for the first involuntary response.

"May I come to you?" I asked, taking refuge from my own emotion in ritual questions that would leave Lytha at least the shreds of her pride. There was no immediate reply. "May I come to you?" I repeated.

"You may come." Her thoughts were remote and cold as she guided me in to the curve of hillside and beach.

She and Timmy were snug and secure and very unhappily restless in the small camp cubicle. They had even found some Glowers somewhere. Most of them had died of the lack of summer, but this small cluster clung with their fragile-looking legs to the roof of the cubicle and shed a warm golden light over the small area. My heart contracted with pity and my eyes stung a little as I saw how like a child's playhouse they had set up the cubicle, complete with the two sleeping mats carefully the cubicle's small width apart with a curtain hiding them from each other.

They had risen ceremoniously as I entered, their faces carefully respectful to an Old One—no Gramma-look in the face of either. I folded up on the floor and they sat again, their hands clasping each other for comfort.

"There is scarcely time left for an outing," I said casually, holding up one finger to the Glowers. One loosed itself and glided down to clasp its wiry feet around my finger. Its glowing paled and flared and hid any of our betraying expressions. Under my idle talk I could feel the cry of the two youngsters—wanting some way in honor to get out of this impasse. Could I find the way or would they stubbornly have to—

"We have our lives before us." Timmy's voice was carefully expressionless.

"A brief span if it's to be on the Home," I said. "We must be out before the week ends."

"We do not choose to believe that." Lytha's voice trembled a little.

"I respect your belief," I said formally, "but fear you have insufficient evidence to support it."

"Even so," her voice was just short of a sob. "Even so, however short, we will have it together—"

"Yes, without your mothers or fathers or any of us," I said placidly. "And then finally, soon, without the Home. Still it has its points. It isn't given to everyone to be—in—at the death of a world. It's a shame that you'll have no one to tell it to. That's the best part of anything, you know, telling it—sharing it."

Lytha's face crumpled and she turned it away from me.

"And if the Home doesn't die," I went on, "that will truly be a joke on us. We won't even get to laugh about it because we won't be able to come back, being so many days gone, not knowing. So you will have the whole Home to yourself. Just think! A whole Home! A new world to begin all over again—alone—" I saw the two kids' hands convulse together and Timmy's throat worked painfully. So did mine. I knew the aching of having to start a new world over—alone. After Thann was Called. "But such space! An emptiness from horizon to horizon—from pole to pole—for you two! Nobody else anywhere—anywhere. If the Home doesn't die—"

Lytha's slender shoulders were shaking now, and they both turned their so-young faces to me. I nearly staggered under the avalanche of their crying out—all without a word. They poured out all their longing and uncertainty and protest and rebellion. Only the young could build up such a burden and have the strength to bear it. Finally Timmy came to words.

"We only want a chance. Is that too much to ask? Why should this happen, now, to us?"

"Who are we," I asked sternly, "to presume to ask *why* of the Power? For all our lives we have been taking happiness and comfort and delight and never asking *why,* but now that sorrow and separation, pain and discomfort are coming to us from the same Power, we are crying *why.* We have taken unthinkingly all that has been given to us unasked, but now that we must take sorrow for a while, you want to refuse to take, like silly babies whose milk is cold!"

I caught a wave of desolation and lostness from the two and hurried on. "But don't think the Power has forgotten you. You are as completely enwrapped now as you ever were. Can't you trust your love—or your possible love—to the Power that suggested love to you in the first place? I promise you, I *promise* you, that no matter where you go, together or apart if the Power leaves you life, you will find love. And even if it turns out that you do not find it together, you'll never forget these first magical steps you have taken together towards your own true loves."

I let laughter into my voice. "Things change! Remember, Lytha, it wasn't so long ago that Timmy was a—if you'll pardon the expression—'gangle-legged, clumsy *poodah* that I'd rather be caught dead than ganging with, let alone two-ing.' "

"And he was, too!" Lytha's voice had a hiccough in it, but a half smile, too.

"You were no vision of delight, yourself," said Timmy. "I never saw such stringy hair—"

"I was *supposed* to look like that—"

Their wrangling was a breath of fresh air after the unnatural, uncomfortable emotional binge they had been on.

"It's quite possible that you two might change—" I stopped abruptly. "Wait!" I said. "Listen!"

"To what?" Lytha's face was puzzled. How could I tell her I heard Simon crying "Gramma! Gramma!" Simon at home, in bed miles and miles—

"Out, quick!" I scrambled up from the floor. "Oh, hurry!" Panic was welling up inside me. The two snatched up their small personal bundles as I pushed them, bewildered and protesting, ahead of me out into the inky blackness of the violent night. For a long terrified moment I stood peering up into the darkness, trying to interpret! Then I screamed, "Lift! Lift!" and, snatching at them both, I launched us upward, away from the edge of the lake. The clouds snatched back from the moon and its light poured down onto the convulsed lake. There was a crack like the loudest of thunder—a grinding, twisting sound—the roar and surge of mighty waters, and the lake bed below us broke cleanly from one hill to another, pulling itself apart and tilting to pour all its moon-bright waters down into the darkness of the gigantic split in the earth. And the moon was glittering only on the shining mud left behind in the lake bottom. With a frantic speed that seemed so slow I enveloped the children and shot with them as far up and away as I could before the earsplitting roar of returning steam threw us even farther. We reeled drunkenly away, and away, until we stumbled across the top of a hill. We clung to each other in terror as the mighty plume of steam rose and rose and split the clouds and still rose, rolling white and awesome. Then, as casually as a shutting door, the lake bed tilted back and closed itself. In the silence that followed, I fancied I could hear the hot rain beginning to fall to fill the emptiness of the lake again, a pool of rain no larger than my hand in a lake bottom.

"Oh, poor Home," whispered Lytha, "poor hurting Home! It's dying!" And then, on the family band, Lytha whispered to me, *Timmy's my love, for sure, Gramma, and I am his, but we're willing to let the Power hold our love for us, until your promise is kept.*

I gathered the two to me and I guess we all wept a little, but we had no words to exchange, no platitudes, only the promise, the acquiescence, the trust—and the sorrow.

We went home. Neil met us just beyond our feather-pen and received Timmy with a quiet thankfulness and they went home together. Lytha and I went first into our household's Quiet Place and then to our patient beds.

I stood with the other Old Ones high on the cliff above the narrow valley, staring down with them at the raw heap of stones and earth that scarred the smooth valley floor. All eyes were intent on the excavation and every mind so much with the Oldest as he toiled out of sight, that our concentrations were almost visible flames above each head.

I heard myself gasp with the others as the Oldest slowly emerged, his clumsy heavy shielding hampering his lifting. The brisk mountain breeze whined as it whipped past suddenly activated personal shields as we reacted automatically to possible danger even though our shields were tissue paper to tornadoes against this unseen death should it be loosed.

The Oldest stepped back from the hole until the sheer rock face stopped him. Slowly a stirring began in the shadowy depths and then the heavy square that shielded the thumb-sized block within lifted into the light. It trembled and turned and set itself into the heavy metal box prepared for it. The lid clicked shut. By the time six boxes were filled, I felt the old—or rather, the painfully new—weariness seize me and I clung to David's arm. He patted my hand, but his eyes were wide with dreaming and I forced myself upright. "I don't like me any more," I thought. "Why do I do things like this? Where has *my* enthusiasm and wonder gone? I am truly old and yet—" I wiped the cold beads of sweat from my upper lip and, lifting with the others, hovered over the canyon, preparatory to conveying the six boxes to the six shells of ships that they were to sting into life.

It was the last day. The sun was shining with a brilliance it hadn't known in weeks. The winds that wandered down from the hills were warm and sweet. The earth beneath us that had so recently learned to tremble and shift was quietly solid for a small while. Everything about the Home was suddenly so dear that it seemed a delirious dream that death was less than a week away for it. Maybe it was only some pre-adolescent, unpatterned behavior—But one look at Simon convinced me. His eyes were aching with things he had had to See. His face was hard under the soft contours of childhood and his hands trembled as he clasped them. I hugged him with my heart and he smiled a thank you and relaxed a little.

'Chell and I set the house to rights and filled the vases with fresh water and scarlet leaves because there were no flowers. David opened the corral gate and watched the beasts walk slowly out into the tarnished meadows. He threw wide the door of the feather-pen and watched the ruffle of feathers, the inquiring peering, the hesitant walk into freedom. He smiled as the master of the pen strutted vocally before the flock. Then Eve gathered up the four eggs that lay rosy and new in the nests and carried them into the house to put them in the green egg dish.

The family stood quietly together. "Go say good-by," said David. "Each of you say good-by to the Home."

And everyone went, each by himself, to his favorite spot. Even Eve burrowed herself out of sight in the *koomatka* bush where the leaves locked above her head and made a tiny Eve-sized green twilight. I could hear her soft croon, "Inna blaza glory, play-People! Inna blaza glory!"

I sighed to see Lytha's straight-as-an-arrow flight toward Timmy's home. Already Timmy was coming. I turned away with a pang. Supposing even after the lake they— No, I comforted myself. They trust the Power—

How could I go to any one place, I wondered, standing by the windows of my room. All of the Home was too dear to leave. When I went I would truly be leaving Thann—all the paths he walked with me, the grass that bent to his step, the trees that shaded him in summer, the very ground that held his cast-aside. I slid to my knees and pressed my cheek against the side of the window frame. "Thann, Thann!" I whispered. "Be with me. Go with me since I must go. Be my strength!" And clasping my hands tight, I pressed my thumbs hard against my crying mouth.

We all gathered again, solemn and tear-stained. Lytha was still frowning and swallowing to hold back her sobs. Simon looked at her, his eyes big and golden, but he said nothing and turned away. 'Chell left the room quietly and, before she returned, the soft sound of music swelled from the walls. We all made the Sign and prayed the Parting prayers, for truly we were dying to this world. The whole house, the whole of the Home was a Quiet Place today, and each of us without words laid the anguishing of this day of parting before the Presence and received comfort and strength.

Then each of us took up his share of personal belongings and was ready to go. We left the house, the music reaching after us as we went. I felt a part of me die when we could no longer hear the melody.

We joined the neighboring families on the path to the ships and there were murmurs and gestures and even an occasional excited laugh. No one seemed to want to lift. Our feet savored every step of this last walk on the Home. No one lifted, that is, except Eve, who was still intrigued by her new accomplishment. Her short little hops amused everyone and, by the time she had picked herself out of the dust three times and had been disentangled from the branches of overhanging trees twice and finally firmly set in place on David's shoulder, there were smiles and tender laughter and the road lightened even though clouds were banking again.

I stood at the foot of the long lift to the door of the ship and stared upward. People brushing past me were only whisperings and passing shadows.

"How can they?" I thought despairingly out of the surge of weakness that left me clinging to the wall. "How can they do it? Leaving the Home so casually!" Then a warm hand crept into mine and I looked down into Simon's eyes. "Come on, Gramma," he said. "It'll be all right."

"I—I—" I looked around me helplessly, then, kneeling swiftly, I took up a handful of dirt—a handful of the Home—and, holding it tightly, I lifted up the long slant with Simon.

Inside the ship we put our things away in their allotted spaces and Simon tugged me out into the corridor and into a room banked with dials and switches and all the vast array of incomprehensibles that we had all called into being for this terrible moment. No one was in the room except the two of us. Simon walked briskly to a chair in front of a panel and sat down.

"It's all set," he said, "for the sector of the sky they gave us, but it's wrong." Before I could stop him, his hands moved over the panels, shifting, adjusting, changing.

"Oh, Simon!" I whispered, "you mustn't!"

"I must," said Simon. "Now it's set for the sky I See."

"But they'll notice and change them all back," I trembled.

"No," said Simon. "It's such a small change that they won't notice it. And we will be where we have to be when we have to be."

It was as I stood there in the control room that I left the Home. I felt it fade away and become as faint as a dream. I said good-by to it so completely that it startled me to catch a glimpse of a mountaintop through one of the ports as we hurried back to our spaces. Suddenly my heart was light and lifting, so much so that my feet didn't even touch the floor. Oh, how wonderful! What adventures ahead! I felt as though I were spiraling up into a bright Glory that outshone the sun—

Then, suddenly, came the weakness. My very bones dissolved in me and collapsed me down on my couch. Darkness rolled across me and breathing was a task that took all my weakness to keep going. I felt vaguely the tightening of the restraining straps around me and the clasp of Simon's hand around my clenched fist.

"Half an hour," the Oldest murmured.

"Half an hour," the People echoed, amplifying the murmur. I felt myself slipping into the corporate band of communication, feeling with the rest of the Group the incredible length and heartbreaking shortness of the time.

Then I lost the world again. I was encased in blackness. I was suspended, waiting, hardly even wondering.

And then it came—the Call.

How unmistakable! I was Called back into the Presence! My hours were totaled. It was all finished. This-side was a preoccupation that concerned me no longer. My face must have lighted as Thann's had. All the struggle, all the sorrow, all the separation—finished. Now would come the three or four days during which I must prepare, dispose of my possessions, say my good-bys— Good-bys? I struggled up against the restraining straps. But we were leaving! In less than half an hour I would have no quiet, cool bed to lay me down upon when I left my body, no fragrant grass to have pulled up over my cast-aside, no solemn sweet remembrance by my family in the next Festival for those Called during the year.

Simon, I called subvocally. *You know!* I cried. *What shall I do?*

I See you staying. His answer came placidly.

Staying? Oh, how quickly I caught the picture. How quickly my own words came back to me, coldly white against the darkness of my confusion. *Such space and emptiness from horizon to horizon, from pole to pole, from skytop to ground. And only me. Nobody else anywhere, anywhere!*

Stay here all alone? I asked Simon. But he wasn't Seeing me any more. Already I was alone. I felt the frightened tears start and then I heard Lytha's trusting voice—*until your promise is kept.* All my fear dissolved. All my panic and fright blazed up suddenly in a repeat of the Call.

"Listen!" I cried, my voice high and excited, my heart surging joyously. "Listen!

"Oh, David! Oh, 'Chell! I've been Called! Don't you hear it? Don't you hear it!"

"Oh, Mother, no! No! You must be mistaken!" David loosed himself and bent over me.

"No," whispered 'Chell. "I feel it. She is Called."

"Now I can stay," I said, fumbling at the straps. "Help me, David, help me."

"But you're not summoned right now!" cried David. "Father knew four days before he was received into the Presence. We can't leave you alone in a doomed, empty world!"

"An empty world!" I stood up quickly, holding to David to steady myself. "Oh, David! A world full of all dearness and nearness and remembering! And doomed? It will be a week yet. I will be received before then. Let me out! Oh, let me out!"

"Stay with us, Mother!" cried David, taking both my hands in his. "We need you. We can't let you go. All the tumult and upheaval that's to start so soon for the Home—"

"How do we know what tumult and upheaval you will be going through in the Crossing?" I asked. "But beyond whatever comes there's a chance of a new life waiting for you. But for me— What of four days from now? What would you do with my cast-aside? What could you do but push it out into the black nothingness. Let it be with the Home. Let it at least become dust among familiar dust!" I felt as excited as a teener. "Oh, David! To be with Thann again!"

I turned to Lytha and quickly unfastened her belt. "There'll be room for one more in this ship," I said.

For a long moment, we looked into each other's eyes and then, almost swifter than thought, Lytha was up and running for the big door. My thoughts went ahead of her and before Lytha's feet lifted out into the open air, all the Old Ones in the ship knew what had happened and their thoughts went out. Before Lytha was halfway up the little hills that separated ship from ship, Timmy surged into sight and gathered her close as they swung around toward our ship.

Minutes ran out of the half hour like icy beads from a broken string, but finally I was slanting down from the ship, my cheeks wet with my own tears and those of my family. Clearly above the clang of the closing door I heard Simon's call. *Good-by, Gramma! I told you it'd be all right. See—you—soon!*

Hurry hurry hurry whispered my feet as I ran. *Hurry hurry hurry* whispered the wind as I lifted away from the towering ships. *Now now now* whispered my heart as I turned back from a safe distance, my skirts whipped by the rising wind, my hair lashing across my face.

The six slender ships pointing at the sky were like silver needles against the rolling black clouds. Suddenly there were only five—then four—then three. Before I could blink the tears from my eyes, the rest were gone, and the ground where they had stood flowed back on itself and crackled with cooling.

The fingers of the music drew me back into the house. I breathed deeply of the dear familiar odors. I straightened a branch of the scarlet leaves that had slipped awry in the blue vase. I steadied myself against a sudden shifting under my feet and my shield activated as hail spattered briefly through the window. I looked out, filled with a great peace, to the swell of browning hills, to the upward reach of snow-whitened mountains, to the brilliant huddled clumps of trees sowing their leaves on the icy wind. "My Home!" I whispered, folding my heart around it all, knowing what my terror and lostness would have been had I stayed behind without the Call.

With a sigh, I went out to the kitchen and counted the four rosy eggs in the green dish. I fingered the stove into flame and, lifting one of the eggs, cracked it briskly against the pan.

That night there were no stars, but the heavy rolls of clouds were lighted with fitful lightnings and somewhere far over the horizon the molten heart of a mountain range was crimson and orange against the night. I lay on my bed letting the weakness wash over me, a tide that would soon bear me away. The soul is a lonely voyager at any time, but the knowledge that I was the last person in a dying world was like a weight crushing me. I was struggling against the feeling when I caught a clear, distinct call—

"Gramma!"

"Simon!" My lips moved to his name.

"We're all fine, Gramma, and I just Saw Eve with two children of her own, so they *will* make it to a new Home."

"Oh, Simon! I'm so glad you told me!" I clutched my bed as it rocked and twisted. I heard stones falling from the garden wall, then one wall of my room dissolved into dust that glowed redly before it settled.

"Things are a little untidy here," I said. "I must get out another blanket. It's a little drafty, too."

"You'll be all right, Gramma," Simon's thought came warmly. "Will you wait for me when you get Otherside?"

"If I can," I promised.

"Good night, Gramma," said Simon.

"Good night, Simon." I cradled my face on my dusty pillow. "Good night."

Interlude: Mark & Meris 2

"Oh!" breathed Meris, out of her absorption. "All alone like that! The last, *last* anyone, anywhere—"

"But she had the Home longer than anyone else," said Valancy. "She had that dear familiarity to close her eyes upon before opening them in the Presence—"

"But how could Bethie possibly remember—" began Meris.

"It's something we can't quite explain," said Jemmy. "It's a Group consciousness that unites us across time and distance. I guess Simon's communicating with Eva-lee before he was Called brought her Assembling more directly to us. Eve, you know, was Bethie's mother."

"It's overwhelming," said Karen soberly. "We know, of course, about the Home and how it was lost, but until you're actually inside an emotion, you can't really comprehend it. Just imagine, to know that the solidness of earth beneath your feet is to become dust scattered across the sky so soon—so soon!"

The group was silent for a while, listening to memories and to a Past that was so Present.

The silence was suddenly shattered by a crashing roar that startled everyone into an awareness of Now.

"Good heavens!" cried Meris. "What's that!"

"*Adonday veeah!*" muttered Jemmy. "They've got that old clunker going again. Johannan must have done something drastic to it."

"Well, he started it just in time to stop it," said Valancy. "We've got a journey to go and we'd better eat and run. Karen, is it all ready?"

"Yes," said Karen, heading for the shadowy house. "Meris has a lovely kitchen. I move that we move in there to eat. It's chilling a little out here now. Jemmy, will you get the boys?"

"I'll set the table!" cried Lala, launching herself airborne toward the kitchen door.

"Lala." Valancy's voice was quiet, but Lala checked in mid-flight and tumbled down to her feet.

"Oh!" she said, her hands over her mouth. "I *did* forget, after I promised!"

"Yes, you did forget," said Valancy, her voice disappointed, "and after you promised."

"I guess I need some more discipline," said Lala solemnly. "A promise is not lightly broken."

"What would you suggest?" asked Karen from the kitchen door, as solemnly as Lala.

"Not set the table?" suggested Lala, with a visible reluctance. "Not tonight," she went on, gauging carefully the adult reaction. "Not for a week?" She sighed and capitulated. "Not set the table for a whole month. And every meal remember a promise is not lightly broken. Control is necessary. Never be un-Earth away from the Group unless I'm told to." And she trudged, conscientiously heavy-footed, into the house with Karen.

"Isn't that a little harsh?" asked Meris. "She does so love to set the table."

"She chose the discipline," said Valancy. "She must learn not to act thoughtlessly. Maybe she has a little more to remember in the way of rules and regulations than the usual small child, but it must become an automatic part of her behavior."

"But at six—" protested Meris, then laughed "—or is it five!"

"Five or six, she understands," said Valancy. "An undisciplined child is an abomination under any circumstances. And doubly so when it's possible to show off as spectacularly as Lala could. Debbie had quite a problem concerning control when she returned from the New Home, and she was no child."

"Returned from the New Home?" said Meris, pausing in the door. "Someone else? Oh, Valancy, do you *have* to go home tonight? Couldn't you stay for a while and tell me some more? You want to Assemble anyway, don't you? Couldn't you now? You can't leave me hanging like this!"

"Well." Valancy smiled and followed Meris into the kitchen. "That's an idea. We'll take it up after supper."

Jemmy sipped his after-supper coffee and leaned back in his chair. "I've been thinking," he said. "This business of Assembling. We have already Assembled our history from when Valancy joined our Group up to the time Lala and the ship came. We did it while we were all trying to make up our minds whether to leave Earth or stay. Davy's recording gadget has preserved it for us. I think it would be an excellent idea for us to get Eva-lee's story recorded, too, and whatever other ones are available to us or can be made available."

"Mother Assembled a lot because she was separated from the People when she was so young," said Bethie softly. "Assembling was almost her only comfort, especially before and after Father. She didn't know anything about the rest of her family—" Bethie whitened. "Oh, *must* we remember the bad times? The aching, hurting, cruel times?"

"There was kindness and love and sacrifice for us interwoven with the cruel times, too, you know," said Jemmy. "If we refuse to remember those times, we automatically refuse to remember the goodness that we found along with the evil."

"Yes," admitted Bethie. "Yes, of course."

"Well, if I can't persuade all of you to stay, why can't Bethie stay a while longer and Assemble?" asked Meris. "Then she'll have a lot of material ready for Davy's gadget when she gets home."

And so it was that Meris, Mark, and Bethie stood in the driveway and watched the rest of the party depart prosaically by car for the canyon—if you can call prosaic the shuddering, slam-bang departing of the Overland, now making up clamorously for its long afternoon of silence.

Assembling is not a matter of turning a faucet on and dodging the gushing of memories. For several days Bethie drifted, speechless and perhaps quite literally millions of miles away, through the house, around the patio, up and down the quiet street, and back into the patio. She came to the table at mealtimes and sometimes ate. Other times her eyes were too intent on far away and long ago to notice food. At times tears streaked her face, and once she woke Mark and Meris with a sharp cry in the night. Meris was worried by her pallor and the shadows on her face as the days passed.

Then finally came the day when Bethie's eyes were suddenly back in focus and, relaxing with a sigh onto the couch, she smiled at Meris.

"Hi!" she said shyly. "I'm back."

"And all in one piece again," said Meris. "And about time, too! 'Licia has a drake-tail in her hair now—all both of them. And she smiled once when it couldn't possibly have been a gas pain!"

So, after supper that night, Mark and Meris sat in the deepening dusk of the patio, each holding lightly one of Bethie's hands.

"This one," said Bethie, her smile fading, "is one I didn't enjoy. Not all of it. But, as Jemmy said, it had good things mixed in."

Hands tightened on hands, then relaxed as the two listened to Bethie Assembling, subvocally.

Angels Unawares

"Be not forgetful to entertain strangers: for thereby some
have entertained angels unawares."

Hebrews 13:2

I still have it, the odd, flower-shaped piece of metal, showing the
flow marks on top and the pocking of sand and gravel on its bottom. It
fits my palm comfortably with my fingers clasped around it, and has fitted it so often that the edges are smooth and burnished now, smooth
against the fine white line of the scar where the sharp, shining, still-hot
edge gashed me when I snatched it up, unbelievingly, from where it had
dripped, molten, from the sloping wall to the sandy floor of the canyon
beyond Margin. It is a Remembrance thing and, as I handled it just now,
looking unseeingly out across the multiple roofs of Margin Today, it recalled to me vividly Margin Yesterday—and even before Margin.

We had been on the road only an hour when we came upon the
scene. For fifteen minutes or so before, however, there had been an odd
smell on the wind, one that crinkled my nose and made old Nig snort
and toss his head, shaking the harness and disturbing Prince, who lifted
his patient head, looked around briefly, then returned to the task.

We were the task, Nils and I and our wagonload of personal belongings, trailing behind us Molly, our young Jersey cow. We were on our
way to Margin to establish a home. Nils was to start his shining new mining engineering career, beginning as superintendent of the mine that had
given birth to Margin. This was to be a first step only, of course, leading
to more accomplished, more rewarding positions culminating in all the
vague, bright, but most wonderful of futures that could blossom from
this rather unprepossessing present seed. We were as yet three days' jour-

ney from Margin when we rounded the sharp twist of the trail, our iron tires grating in the sand of the wash, and discovered the flat.

Nils pulled the horses up to a stop. A little below us and near the protective bulge of the gray granite hillside were the ruins of a house and the crumpled remains of sheds at one end of a staggering corral. A plume of smoke lifted finger-straight in the early morning air. There was not a sign of life anywhere.

Nils flapped the reins and clucked to the horses. We crossed the flat, lurching a little when the left wheels dipped down into one of the cuts that, after scoring the flat, disappeared into the creek.

"Must have burned down last night," said Nils, securing the reins and jumping down. He lifted his arms to help me from the high seat and held me in a tight, brief hug as he always does. Then he released me and we walked over to the crumple of the corral.

"All the sheds went," he said, "and apparently the animals, too." He twisted his face at the smell that rose from the smoldering mass.

"They surely would have saved the animals," I said, frowning. "They wouldn't have left them locked in a burning shed."

"If they were here when the fire hit," said Nils

I looked over at the house. "Not much of a house. It doesn't look lived in at all. Maybe this is an abandoned homestead. In that case, though, what about the animals?"

Nils said nothing. He had picked up a length of stick and was prodding in the ashes.

"I'm going to look at the house," I said, glad of an excuse to turn away from the heavy odor of charred flesh.

The house was falling in on itself. The door wouldn't open and the drunken windows spilled a few shards of splintered glass out onto the sagging front porch. I went around to the back. It had been built so close to the rock that there was only a narrow roofed-over passage between the rock and the house. The back door sagged on one hinge and I could see the splintered floor behind. It must have been quite a nice place at one time—glass in the windows—a board floor—when most of us in the Territory made do with a hard trampled dirt floor and butter muslin in the windows.

I edged through the door and cautiously picked my way across the creaking, groaning floor. I looked up to see if there was a loft of any kind and felt my whole body throb one huge throb of terror and surprise! Up against the sharp splintering of daylight, through a shattered roof, was a face—looking down at me! It was a wild, smudged, dirty face, surrounded by a frizz of dark hair that tangled and wisped across the filthy cheeks. It stared down at me from up among the tatters of what had been a muslin ceiling, then the mouth opened soundlessly, and the eyes rolled and went shut. I lunged forward, almost instinctively, and caught the falling body full in my arms, crumpling under it to the floor. Beneath me the splintered planks gave way and sagged down into the shallow air space under the floor.

I screamed, "Nils!" and heard an answering "Gail!" and the pounding of his running feet.

We carried the creature outside the ruined house and laid it on the scanty six-weeks grass that followed over the sand like a small green river the folds in the earth that held moisture the longest. We straightened the crumpled arms and legs and it was a creature no longer but a girl-child. I tried to pull down the tattered skirt to cover more seemly, but the bottom edge gave way without tearing and I had the soft smudge of burned fabric and soot between my fingers. I lifted the head to smooth the sand under it and stopped, my attention caught.

"Look, Nils, the hair. Half of it's burned away. This poor child must have been in the fire. She must have tried to free the animals—"

"It's not animals," said Nils, his voice tight and angered. "They're people."

"People!" I gasped. "Oh, no!"

"At least four," nodded Nils.

"Oh, how awful!" I said, smoothing the stub of hair away from the quiet face. "The fire must have struck in the night."

"They were tied," said Nils shortly. "Hand and foot."

"Tied? But, Nils—"

"Tied. Deliberately burned—"

"Indians!" I gasped, scrambling to my feet through the confusion of my skirts. "Oh, Nils!"

"There have been no Indian raids in the Territory for almost five years. And the last one was on the other side of the Territory. They told me at Margin that there had never been any raids around here. There are no Indians in this area."

"Then who—what—" I dropped down beside the still figure. "Oh, Nils," I whispered. "What kind of a country have we come to?"

"No matter what kind it is," said Nils, "we have a problem here. Is the child dead?"

"No." My hand on the thin chest felt the slight rise and fall of breathing. Quickly I flexed arms and legs and probed lightly. "I can't find any big hurt. But so dirty and ragged!"

We found the spring under a granite overhang halfway between the house and the corral. Nils rummaged among our things in the wagon and found me the hand basin, some rags, and soap. We lighted a small fire and heated water in a battered bucket Nils dredged out of the sand below the spring. While the water was heating, I stripped away the ragged clothing. The child had on some sort of a one-piece undergarment that fitted as closely as her skin and as flexible. It covered her from shoulder to upper thigh, and the rounding of her body under it made me revise my estimate of her age upward a little. The garment was undamaged by the fire but I couldn't find any way to unfasten it to remove it so I finally left it and wrapped the still unconscious girl in a quilt. Then carefully I bathed her, except for her hair, wiping the undergarment, which came clean and bright without any effort at all. I put her into one of my nightgowns, which came close enough to fitting her since I am of no great size myself.

"What shall I do about her hair?" I asked Nils, looking at the snarled, singed tousle of it. "Half of it is burned off clear up to her ear."

"Cut the rest of it to match," said Nils. "Is she burned anywhere?"

"No," I replied, puzzled. "Not a sign of a burn, and yet her clothing was almost burned away and her hair—" I felt a shiver across my shoulders and looked around the flat apprehensively, though nothing could be more flatly commonplace than the scene. Except—except for the occasional sullen wisp of smoke from the shed ruins.

"Here are the scissors." Nils brought them from the wagon. Reluctantly, because of the heavy flow of the tresses across my wrist, I cut away the long dark hair until both sides of her head matched, more or less. Then, scooping out the sand to lower the basin beneath her head, I wet and lathered and rinsed until the water came clear, then carefully dried the hair, which, released from length and dirt, sprang into profuse curls all over her head.

"What a shame to have cut it," I said to Nils, holding the damp head in the curve of my elbow. "How lovely it must have been." Then I nearly dropped my burden. The eyes were open and looking at me blankly. I managed a smile and said, "Hello! Nils, hand me a cup of water."

At first she looked at the water as though at a cup of poison, then, with a shuddering little sigh, drank it down in large hasty gulps.

"That's better now, isn't it?" I said, hugging her a little. There was no answering word or smile, but only a slow tightening of the muscles under my hands until, still in my arms, the girl had withdrawn from me completely. I ran my hand over her curls. "I'm sorry we had to cut it, but it was—" I bit back my words. I felt muscles lifting, so I helped the girl sit up. She looked around in a daze and then her eyes were caught by a sullen up-puff of smoke. Seeing what she was seeing, I swung my shoulder between her and the ashes of the shed. Her mouth opened, but no sound came out. Her fingers bit into my arm as she dragged herself to see past me.

"Let her look," Nils said. "She knows what happened. Let her see the end of it. Otherwise she'll wonder all her life." He took her from me and carried her over to the corral. I couldn't go. I busied myself with emptying the basin and burying the charred clothing. I spread the quilt out to receive the child when they returned.

Nils finally brought her back and put her down on the quilt. She lay, eyes shut, as still as if breath had left her, too. Then two tears worked themselves out of her closed lids, coursed down the sides of her cheeks, and lost themselves in the tumble of curls around her ears. Nils took the shovel and grimly tackled the task of burying the bodies.

I built up the fire again and began to fix dinner. The day was spending itself rapidly but, late or not, when Nils finished, we would leave. Eating a large meal now, we could piece for supper and travel, if necessary, into the hours of darkness until this place was left far behind.

Nils finally came back, pausing at the spring to snort and blow through double handful after double handful of water. I met him with a towel.

"Dinner's ready," I said. "We can leave as soon as we're finished."

"Look what I found." He handed me a smudged tatter of paper. "It was nailed to the door of the shed. The door didn't burn."

I held the paper gingerly and puzzled over it. The writing was almost illegible— "Ex. 22:18."

"What is it?" I asked. "It doesn't say anything."

"Quotation," said Nils. "That's a quotation from the Bible."

"Oh," I said. "Yes. Let's see. Exodus, Chapter 22, verse 18. Do you know it?"

"I'm not sure, but I have an idea. Can you get at the Bible? I'll verify it."

"It's packed in one of my boxes at the bottom of the load. Shall we—"

"Not now," said Nils. "Tonight when we make camp."

"What do you think it is?" I asked.

"I'd rather wait," said Nils. "I hope I'm wrong."

We ate. I tried to rouse the girl, but she turned away from me. I put half a slice of bread in her hand and closed her fingers over it and tucked it close to her mouth. Halfway through our silent meal, a movement caught my eye. The girl had turned to hunch herself over her two hands that now clasped the bread, tremblingly. She was chewing cautiously. She swallowed with an effort and stuffed her mouth again with bread, tears streaking down her face. She ate as one starved, and, when she had finished the bread, I brought her a cup of milk. I lifted her shoulders and held her as she drank. I took the empty cup and lowered her head to the quilt. For a moment my hand was caught under her head and I felt a brief deliberate pressure of her cheek against my wrist. Then she turned away.

Before we left the flat, we prayed over the single mound Nils had raised over the multiple grave. We had brought the girl over with us and she lay quietly, watching us. When we turned from our prayers, she held out in a shaking hand a white flower, so white that it almost seemed to cast a light across her face. I took it from her and put it gently on the mound. Then Nils lifted her and carried her to the wagon. I stayed a moment, not wanting to leave the grave lonely so soon. I shifted the white flower. In the sunlight its petals seemed to glow with an inner light, the golden center almost fluid. I wondered what kind of flower it could be. I lifted it and saw that it was just a daisy-looking flower after all, withering already in the heat of the day. I put it down again, gave a last pat to the mound, a last tag of prayer, and went back to the wagon.

By the time we made camp that night, we were too exhausted from the forced miles and the heat and the events of the day to do anything but care for the animals and fall onto our pallets spread on the ground near the wagon. We had not made the next water hole because of the delay, but we carried enough water to tide us over. I was too tired to eat, but I roused enough to feed Nils on leftovers from dinner and to strain Molly's milk into the milk crock. I gave the girl a cup of the fresh, warm milk and some more bread. She downed them both with a contained eagerness as though still starved. Looking at her slender shaking wrists and the dark hollows of her face, I wondered how long she had been so hungry.

We all slept heavily under the star-clustered sky, but I was awakened somewhere in the shivery coolness of the night and reached to be sure the girl was covered. She was sitting up on the pallet, legs crossed tailor-fashion, looking up at the sky. I could see the turning of her head as she scanned the whole sky, back and forth, around and around, from zenith to horizon. Then she straightened slowly back down onto the quilt with an audible sigh.

I looked at the sky, too. It was spectacular with the stars of a moonless night here in the region of mountains and plains, but what had she been looking for? Perhaps she had just been enjoying being alive and able, still, to see the stars.

We started on again, very early, and made the next watering place while the shadows were still long with dawn.

"The wagons were here," said Nils, "night before last, I guess."

"What wagons?" I asked, pausing in my dipping of water.

"We've been in their tracks ever since the flat back there," said Nils. "Two light wagons and several riders."

"Probably old tracks—" I started. "Oh, but you said they were here night before last. Do you suppose they had anything to do with the fire back there?"

"No signs of them before we got to the flat," said Nils. "Two recent campfires here—as if they stayed the night here and made a special trip to the flat and back here again for the next night."

"A special trip." I shivered. "Surely you can't think that civilized people in this nineteenth century could be so violent—so—so—I mean people just don't—" My words died before the awful image in my mind.

"Don't tie up other people and burn them?" Nils started shifting the water keg back toward the wagon. "Gail, our next camp is supposed to be at Grafton's Vow. I think we'd better take time to dig out the Bible before we go on."

So we did. And we looked at each other over Nils's pointing finger and the flattened paper he had taken from the shed door.

"Oh, surely not!" I cried horrified. "It can't be! Not in this day and age!"

"It can be," said Nils. "In any age when people pervert goodness, love, and obedience and set up a god small enough to fit their shrunken souls." And his finger traced again the brief lines: *Thou shalt not suffer a witch to live.*

"Why did you want to check that quotation before we got to Grafton's Vow?" I asked.

"Because it's that kind of place," said Nils. "They warned me at the county seat. In fact, some thought it might be wise to take the other trail— a day longer—one dry camp—but avoid Grafton's Vow. There have been tales of stonings and—"

"What kind of place is it, anyway?" I asked.

"I'm not sure," said Nils. "I've heard some very odd stories about it though. It was founded about twenty years ago by Arnold Grafton. He brought his little flock of followers out here to establish the new Jerusalem. They're very strict and narrow. Don't argue with them and no levity or lewdness. No breaking of God's laws, of which they say they have all. When they ran out of Biblical ones, they received a lot more from Grafton to fill in where God forgot."

"But," I was troubled, "aren't they Christians?"

"They say so." I helped Nils lift the keg. "Except they believe they have to conform to all the Old Testament laws, supplemented by all those that Grafton has dictated. Then, if they obey enough of them well enough after a lifetime of struggle, Christ welcomes them into a heaven of no laws. Every law they succeed in keeping on earth, they will be exempted from keeping for all of eternity. So the stricter observance here, the greater freedom there. Imagine what their heaven must be—teetotaler here—rigidly chaste here—never kill here—never steal here—just save up for the promised Grand Release!"

"And Mr. Grafton had enough followers of *that* doctrine to found a town?" I asked, a little stunned.

"A whole town," said Nils, "into which we will not be admitted. There is a campground outside the place where we will be tolerated for the night if they decide we won't contaminate the area."

At noon we stopped just after topping out at Millman's Pass. The horses, lathered and breathing heavily, and poor dragged-along Molly drooped grateful heads in the shadows of the aspen and pines.

I busied myself with the chuck box and was startled to see the girl sliding out of the wagon where we had bedded her down for the trip. She clung to the side of the wagon and winced as her feet landed on the gravelly hillside. She looked very young and slender and lost in the fullness of my nightgown, but her eyes weren't quite so sunken and her mouth was tinged with color.

I smiled at her. "That gown is sort of long for mountain climbing. Tonight I'll try to get to my other clothes and see if I can find something. I think my old blue skirt—" I stopped because she very obviously wasn't understanding a word I was saying. I took a fold of the gown she wore and said, "Gown."

She looked down at the crumpled white muslin and then at me but said nothing.

I put a piece of bread into her hands and said, "Bread." She put the bread down carefully on the plate where I had stacked the other slices for dinner and said nothing. Then she glanced around, looked at me, and, turning, walked briskly into the thick underbrush, her elbows high to hold the extra length of gown up above her bare feet.

"Nils!" I called in sudden panic. "She's leaving!"

Nils laughed at me across the tarp he was spreading. "Even the best of us," he said, "have to duck into the bushes once in a while!"

"Oh, Nils!" I protested and felt my face redden as I carried the bread plate to the tarp. "Anyway, she shouldn't be running around in a nightgown like that. What would Mr. Grafton say! And have you noticed? She hasn't made a sound since we found her." I brought the eating things to the tarp. "Not one word. Not one sound."

"Hmm," said Nils, "you're right. Maybe she's a deaf mute."

"She hears," I said. "I'm sure she hears."

"Maybe she doesn't speak English," he suggested. "Her hair is dark. Maybe she's Mexican. Or even Italian. We get all kinds out here on the frontier. No telling where she might be from."

"But you'd think she'd make some sound. Or try to say something," I insisted.

"Might be the shock," said Nils soberly. "That was an awful thing to live through."

"That's probably it, poor child." I looked over to where she had disappeared. "An awful thing. Let's call her Marnie, Nils," I suggested. "We need some sort of name to call her by."

Nils laughed. "Would having the name close to you reconcile you a little to being separated from your little sister?"

I smiled back. "It does sound homey—Marnie, Marnie."

As if I had called her, the girl, Marnie, came back from the bushes, the long gown not quite trailing the slope, completely covering her bare feet. Both her hands were occupied with the long stem of red bells she was examining closely. *How graceful she is,* I thought. *How smoothly—* Then my breath went out and I clutched the plate I held. That gown was a good foot too long for Marnie! She couldn't possibly be walking with it not quite trailing the ground without holding it up! And where was the pausing that came between steps? I hissed at Nils. "Look!" I whispered hoarsely, "she's—she's floating! She's not even touching the ground!"

Just at that moment Marnie looked up and saw us and read our faces. Her face crumpled into terror and she dropped down to the ground. Not only down to her feet, but on down into a huddle on the ground with the spray of flowers crushed under her.

I ran to her and tried to lift her, but she suddenly convulsed into a mad struggle to escape me. Nils came to help. We fought to hold the child, who was so violent that I was afraid she'd hurt herself.

"She's—she's afraid!" I gasped. "Maybe she thinks—we'll—kill her!"

"Here!" Nils finally caught a last flailing arm and pinioned it. "*Talk* to her! Do something! I can't hold her much longer!"

"Marnie, Marnie!" I smoothed the tangled curls back from her blank, tense face, trying to catch her attention. "Marnie, don't be afraid!" I tried a smile. "Relax, honey, don't be scared." I wiped her sweat- and tear-streaked face with the corner of my apron. "There, there, it doesn't matter—we won't hurt you—" I murmured on and on, wondering if she was taking in any of it, but finally the tightness began to go out of her body and at last she drooped, exhausted, in Nils's arms. I gathered her to me and comforted her against my shoulder.

"Get her a cup of milk," I said to Nils, "and bring me one, too." My smile wavered. "This is hard work!"

In the struggle I had almost forgotten what had started it, but it came back to me as I led Marnie to the spring and demonstrated that she should wash her face and hands. She did so, following my example, and dried herself on the flour-sack towel I handed her. Then, when I started to turn away, she sat down on a rock by the flowing water, lifted the sadly bedraggled gown, and slipped her feet into the stream. When she lifted each to dry it, I saw the reddened, bruised soles and said, "No wonder you didn't want to walk. Wait a minute." I went back to the wagon and got my old slippers, and, as an afterthought, several pins. Marnie was still sitting by the stream, leaning over the water, letting it flow between her fingers. She put on the slippers—woefully large for her—and stood watching with interest as I turned up the bottom of the gown and pinned it at intervals.

"Now," I said, "now at least you can walk. But this gown will be ruined if we don't get you into some other clothes."

We ate dinner and Marnie ate some of everything we did, after a cautious tasting and a waiting to see how we handled it. She helped me gather up and put away the leftovers and clear the tarp. She even helped with the dishes—all with an absorbed interest as if learning a whole new set of skills.

As our wagon rolled on down the road, Nils and I talked quietly, not to disturb Marnie as she slept in the back of the wagon.

"She's an odd child," I said. "Nils, do you think she really was floating? How could she have? It's impossible."

"Well, it looked as if she was floating," he said. "And she acted as if she had done something wrong—something—" Nils's words stopped and he frowned intently as he flicked at a roadside branch with the whip "—something we would hurt her for. Gail, maybe that's why—I mean, we found that witch quotation. Maybe those other people were like Marnie. Maybe someone thought they were witches and burned them—"

"But witches are evil" I cried. "What's evil about floating—"

"Anything is evil," said Nils, "if it lies on the other side of the line you draw around what you will accept as good. Some people's lines are awfully narrow."

"But that's murder!" I said, "to kill—"

"Murder or execution—again, a matter of interpretation," said Nils. "*We* call it murder, but it could never be proved—"

"Marnie," I suggested. "She saw—"

"Can't talk—or won't," said Nils.

I hated the shallow valley of Grafton's Vow at first glance. For me it was shadowed from one side to the other in spite of the down-flooding sun that made us so grateful for the shade of the overhanging branches. The road was running between rail fences now as we approached the town. Even the horses seemed jumpy and uneasy as we rattled along.

"Look," I said, "there's a notice or something on that fence post."

Nils pulled up alongside the post and I leaned over to read: " 'Ex. 20:16.' That's all it says!"

"Another reference," said Nils. " 'Thou shalt not bear false witness.' This must be a habit with them, putting up memorials on the spot where a law is broken."

"I wonder what happened here." I shivered as we went on.

We were met at a gate by a man with a shotgun in his hands who said, "God have mercy," and directed us to the campgrounds safely separated from town by a palisade kind of log wall. There we were questioned severely by an anxious-faced man, also clutching a shotgun, who peered up at the sky at intervals as though expecting the wrath of heaven at any moment.

"Only one wagon?" he asked.

"Yes," said Nils. "My wife and I and—"

"You have your marriage lines?" came the sharp question.

"Yes," said Nils patiently, "they're packed in the trunk."

"And your Bible is probably packed away, too!" the man accused.

"No," said Nils, "here it is." He took it from under the seat. The man sniffed and shifted.

"Who's that?" He nodded at the back of Marnie's dark head where she lay silently, sleeping or not, I don't know.

"My niece," Nils said steadily, and I clamped my mouth shut. "She's sick."

"Sick!" The man backed away from the wagon. "What sin did she commit?"

"Nothing catching," said Nils, shortly.

"Which way you come?" asked the man.

"Through Millman's Pass," Nils answered, his eyes unwavering on the anxious questioning face. The man paled and clutched his gun tighter, the skin of his face seeming to stretch down tight and then flush loose and sweaty again.

"What—" he began, then he licked dry lips and tried again. "Did you—was there—"

"Was there what?" asked Nils shortly. "Did we what?"

"Nothing," stammered the man, backing away. "Nothing.

"Gotta see her," he said, coming reluctantly back to the wagon. "Too easy to bear false witness—" Roughly he grabbed the quilt and pulled it back, rolling Marnie's head toward him. I thought he was going to collapse. "That's—that's the one!" he whimpered hoarsely. "How did she get— Where did you—" Then his lips clamped shut. "If you say it's your niece, it's your niece."

"You can stay the night," he said with an effort. "Spring just outside the wall. Otherwise keep to the compound. Remember your prayers. Comport yourself in the fear of God." Then he scuttled away.

"Niece!" I breathed. "Oh, Nils! Shall I write out an 'Ex. 20:16' for you to nail on the wagon?"

"She'll have to be someone," said Nils. "When we get to Margin, we'll have to explain her somehow. She's named for your sister, so she's our niece. Simple, isn't it?"

"Sounds so," I said. "But, Nils, *who* is she? How did that man know—? If those were her people that died back there, where are their wagons? Their belongings? People don't just drop out of the sky—"

"Maybe these Graftonites took the people there to execute them," he suggested, "and confiscated their goods."

"Be more characteristic if they burned the people in the town square," I said shivering. "And their wagons, too."

We made camp. Marnie followed me to the spring. I glanced around, embarrassed for her in the nightgown, but no one else was around and darkness was falling. We went through the wall by a little gate and were able for the first time to see the houses of the village. They were very ordinary looking except for the pale flutter of papers posted profusely on everything a nail could hold to. How could they think of anything *but* sinning, with all these ghosty reminders?

While we were dipping the water, a small girl, enveloped in gray calico from slender neck to thin wrists and down to clumsy shoes, came pattering down to the spring, eyeing us as though she expected us to leap upon her with a roar.

"Hello," I said and smiled.

"God have mercy," she answered in a breathless whisper. "Are you right with God?"

"I trust so," I answered, not knowing if the question required an answer.

"She's wearing white," said the child, nodding at Marnie. "Is she dying?"

"No," I said, "but she's been ill. That is her nightgown."

"Oh!" The child's eyes widened and her hand covered her mouth. "How wicked! To use such a bad word! To be in her—her—to be like that outside the house! In the daytime!" She plopped her heavy bucket into the spring and, dragging it out, staggered away from us, slopping water as she went. She was met halfway up the slope by a grim-faced woman, who set the pail aside, switched the weeping child unmercifully with a heavy willow switch, took a paper from her pocket, impaled it on a nail on a tree, seized the child with one hand and the bucket with the other, and plodded back to town.

I looked at the paper. "Ex. 20:12." "Well!" I let out an astonished breath. "And she had it already written!" Then I went back to Marnie. Her eyes were big and empty again, the planes of her face sharply sunken.

"Marnie," I said, touching her shoulder. There was no response, no consciousness of me as l led her back to the wagon.

Nils retrieved the bucket of water and we ate a slender, unhappy supper by the glow of our campfire. Marnie ate nothing and sat in a motionless daze until we put her to bed.

"Maybe she's subject to seizures," I suggested.

"It was more likely watching the child being beaten," said Nils. "What had she done?"

"Nothing except to talk to us and be shocked that Marnie should be in her nightgown in public."

"What was the paper the mother posted?" asked Nils.

"Exodus, 20:12," I said. "The child must have disobeyed her mother by carrying on a conversation with us."

After a fitful, restless night the first thin light of dawn looked wonderful and we broke camp almost before we had shadows separate from the night. Just before we rode away, Nils wrote large and blackly on a piece of paper and fastened it to the wall near our wagon with loud accusing hammer blows. As we drove away, I asked, "What does it say?"

"Exodus, Chapter 22, verses 21 through 24," he said. "If they want wrath, let it fall on them!"

I was too unhappy and worn out to pursue the matter. I only knew it must be another Shalt Not and was thankful that I had been led by my parents through the Rejoice and Love passages instead of into the darkness.

Half an hour later, we heard the clatter of hooves behind us and, looking back, saw someone riding toward us, waving an arm urgently. Nils pulled up and laid his hand on his rifle. We waited.

It was the anxious man who had directed us to the campsite. He had Nils's paper clutched in his hand. At first he couldn't get his words out, then he said, "Drive on! Don't stop! They might be coming after me!" He gulped and wiped his nervous forehead. Nils slapped the reins and we moved off down the road. "Y—you left this—" He jerked the paper toward us. " 'Thou shalt neither vex a stranger, nor oppress him—' " the words came in gasps. " 'Ye shalt not afflict any widow or fatherless child. If you afflict them in any wise, I will surely hear their cry and my wrath shall wax hot—' " He sagged in the saddle, struggling for breath. "This is exactly what I told them," he said finally. "I showed it to them—the very next verses—but they couldn't see past 22:18. They—they went anyway. That Archibold told them about the people. He said they did things only witches could do. I had to go along. Oh, God have mercy! And help them tie them and watch them set the shed afire!"

"Who were they?" asked Nils.

"I don't know." The man sucked air noisily. "Archibold said he saw them flying up in the trees and laughing. He said they floated rocks around and started to build a house with them. He said they—they walked on the water and didn't fall in. He said one of them held a piece of wood up in the air and it caught on fire and other wood came and made a pile on the ground and that piece went down and lighted the rest." The man wiped his face again. "They *must* have been witches! Or else how could they do such things! We caught them. They were sleeping. They fluttered up like birds. I caught that little girl you've got there, only her hair was long then. We tied them up. I didn't want to!" Tears jerked out of his eyes. "I didn't put any knots in my rope and after the roof caved in, the little girl flew out all on fire and hid in the dark! I didn't know the Graftonites were like that! I only came last year. They—they *tell* you exactly what to do to be saved. You don't have to think or worry or wonder—" He rubbed his coat sleeve across his face. "Now all my life I'll see the shed burning. What about the others?"

"We buried them," I said shortly. "The charred remains of them."

"God have mercy!" he whispered.

"Where did the people come from?" asked Nils. "Where are their wagons?"

"There weren't any," said the man. "Archibold says they came in a flash of lightning and a thunderclap out of a clear sky—not a cloud anywhere. He waited and watched them three days before he came and told us. Wouldn't *you* think they were witches?" He wiped his face again and glanced back down the road. "They might follow me. Don't tell them. Don't say I told." He gathered up the reins, his face drawn and anxious, and spurred his horse into a gallop, cutting away from the road, across the flat. But before the hurried hoofbeats were muffled by distance, he whirled around and galloped back.

"But!" he gasped, back by our wagon side. "She must be a witch! She should be dead. You are compromising with evil—"

"Shall I drag her out so you can finish burning her here and now?" snapped Nils. "So you can watch her sizzle in her sin!"

"Don't!" The man doubled across the saddle horn in an agony of indecision. " 'No man having put his hand to the plow and looking back is fit for the kingdom.' What if they're right? What if the Devil is tempting me? Lead me not into temptation! Maybe it's not too late! Maybe if I confess!" And he tore back down the road toward Grafton's Vow faster than he had come.

"Well!" I drew a deep breath. "What Scripture would you quote for that?"

"I'm wondering," said Nils. "This Archibold. I wonder if he was in his right mind—"

" 'They fluttered up like birds,' " I reminded him, "and Marnie was floating."

"But floating rocks and making fire and coming in a flash of lightning out of a clear sky!" Nils protested.

"Maybe it was some kind of a balloon," I suggested. "Maybe it exploded. Maybe Marnie *doesn't* speak English. If the balloon sailed a long way—"

"It couldn't sail too far," said Nils. "The gas cools and it would come down. But how else could they come through the air?"

I felt a movement behind me and turned. Marnie was sitting up on the pallet. But what a different Marnie! It was as though her ears had been unstopped or a window had opened into her mind. There was an eager listening look on her tilted face. There was light in her eyes and the possibility of smiles around her mouth. She looked at me. "Through the air!" she said.

"Nils!" I cried. "Did you hear that! How did you come through the air, Marnie?"

She smiled apologetically and fingered the collar of the garment she wore and said, "Gown."

"Yes, gown," I said, settling for a word when I wanted a volume. Then I thought, *Can I reach the bread box?* Marnie's bright eyes left my face and she rummaged among the boxes and bundles. With a pleased little sound, she came up with a piece of bread. "Bread," she said, "bread!" And it floated through the air into my astonished hands.

"Well!" said Nils. "Communication has begun!" Then he sobered. "And we have a child, apparently. From what that man said, there is no one left to be responsible for her. She seems to be ours."

When we stopped at noon for dinner, we were tired. More from endless speculation than from the journey. There had been no signs of pursuit and Marnie had subsided onto the pallet again, eyes closed.

We camped by a small creek and I had Nils get my trunk out before he cared for the animals. I opened the trunk with Marnie close beside me, watching my every move. I had packed an old skirt and shirtwaist on the top till so they would be ready for house cleaning and settling-in when we arrived at Margin. I held the skirt up to Marnie. It was too big and too long, but it would do with the help of a few strategic pins and by fastening the skirt up almost under her arms. Immediately, to my surprise and discomfort, Marnie skinned the nightgown off over her head in one motion and stood arrow-slim and straight, dressed only in that undergarment of hers. I glanced around quickly to see where Nils was and urged the skirt and blouse on Marnie. She glanced around too, puzzled, and slipped the clothing on, holding the skirt up on both sides. I showed her the buttons and hooks and eyes and, between the two of us and four pins, we got her put together.

When Nils came to the dinner tarp, he was confronted by Marnie, all dressed, even to my clomping slippers.

"Well!" he said, "a fine young lady we have! It's too bad we had to cut her hair."

"We can pretend she's just recovering from typhoid," I said, smiling. But the light had gone out of Marnie's face as if she knew what we were saying. She ran her fingers through her short-cropped curls, her eyes on my heavy braids I let swing free, Indian-fashion, traveling as we were, alone and unobserved.

"Don't you mind," I said, hugging her in one arm. "It'll grow again."
She lifted one of my braids and looked at me. "Hair," I said.

"Hair," she said and stretched out a curl from her own head. "Curl."

What a wonderful feeling it was to top out on the flat above Margin and to know we were almost home. Home! As I wound my braids around my head in a more seemly fashion, I looked back at the boxes and bundles in the wagon. With these and very little else we must make a home out here in the middle of nowhere. Well, with Nils, it would suffice.

The sound of our wheels down the grade into town brought out eager, curious people from the scattering of houses and scanty town buildings that made up Margin. Margin clung to the side of a hill—that is, it was in the rounded embrace of the hill on three sides. On the other side, hundreds and hundreds of miles of territory lost themselves finally in the remote blueness of distance. It was a place where you could breathe free and unhampered and yet still feel the protectiveness of the everlasting hills. We were escorted happily to our house at the other end of town by a growing crowd of people. Marnie had fallen silent and withdrawn again, her eyes wide and wondering, her hand clutching the edge of the seat with white-knuckled intensity as she tried to lose herself between Nils and me.

Well, the first few days in a new place are always uncomfortable and confused. All the settling-in and the worry about whether Marnie would go floating off like a balloon or send something floating through the air as she had the bread combined to wear me to a frazzle. Fortunately Marnie was very shy of anyone but us, so painfully so that as soon as the gown was washed and clean again and we borrowed a cot, I put Marnie into both of them, and she lay in a sort of doze all day long, gone to some far place I couldn't even guess at.

Of course we had to explain her. There had been no mention of her when we arranged to come, and she had no clothes and I didn't have enough to cover both of us decently. So I listened to myself spin the most outrageous stories to Mrs. Wardlow. Her husband was the schoolmaster–lay preacher and every other function of a learned man in a frontier settlement. She was the unofficial news spreader and guardian of public morals.

"Marnie is our niece," I said. "She's my younger sister's girl. She is just recovering from typhoid and—and brain fever."

"Oh, my!" said Mrs. Wardlow. "Both at once?"

"No," I said, warming to my task. "She was weakened by the typhoid and went into a brain fever. She lost her hair from all the fever. We thought we were going to lose her, too." It didn't take play acting to shiver, as, unbidden into my mind, came the vision of the smoke pluming slowly up—

"My sister sent her with us, hoping that the climate out here will keep Marnie from developing a consumption. She hopes, too, that I can help the child learn to talk again."

"I've heard of people having to learn to walk again after typhoid, but not to talk—"

"The technical name for the affliction is aphasia," I said glibly. "Remember the brain fever. She had just begun to make some progress in talking, but the trip has set her back."

"She—she isn't—unbalanced, is she?" whispered Mrs. Wardlow piercingly.

"Of course not!" I said indignantly. "And, please! She can hear perfectly."

"Oh," said Mrs. Wardlow, reddening, "of course. I didn't mean to offend. When she is recovered enough, Mr. Wardlow would be pleased to set her lessons for her until she can come to school."

"Thank you," I said. "That would be very kind of him." Then I changed the subject by introducing tea.

After she left, I sat down by Marnie, whose eyes brightened for my solitary presence.

"Marnie," I said, "I don't know how much you understand of what I say, but you are my niece. You must call me Aunt Gail and Nils, Uncle Nils. You have been sick. You are having to learn to speak all over again." Her eyes had been watching me attentively, but not one flick of understanding answered me. I sighed heavily and turned away. Marnie's hand caught my arm. She held me, as she lay, eyes closed. Finally I made a movement as if to free myself, and she opened her eyes and smiled.

"Aunt Gail, I have been sick. My hair is gone. I want bread!" she recited carefully.

"Oh, Marnie!" I cried, hugging her to me in delight. "Bless you! You *are* learning to talk!" I hugged my face into the top of her curls, then I let her go. "As to bread, I mixed a batch this morning. It'll be in the oven as soon as it rises again. There's nothing like the smell of baking bread to make a place seem like home."

As soon as Marnie was strong enough, I began teaching her the necessary household skills and found it most disconcerting to see her holding a broom gingerly, not knowing, literally, which end to use, or what to do with it. Anybody knows what a needle and thread are for! But Marnie looked upon them as if they were baffling wonders from another world. She watched the needle swing back and forth sliding down the thread until it fell to the floor because she didn't know enough to put a knot in the end.

She learned to talk, but very slowly at first. She had to struggle and wait for words. I asked her about it one day. Her slow answer came. "I don't know your language," she said. "I have to change the words to my language to see what they say, then change them again to be in your language." She sighed. "It's so slow! But soon I will be able to take words from your mind and not have to change them."

I blinked, not quite sure I wanted anything taken from my mind by anyone!

The people of Margin had sort of adopted Marnie and were very pleased with her progress. Even the young ones learned to wait for her slow responses. She found it more comfortable to play with the younger children because they didn't require such a high performance in the matter of words, and because their play was with fundamental things of the house and the community, translated into the simplest forms and acted out in endless repetition.

I found out, to my discomfort, a little of how Marnie was able to get along so well with the small ones—the day Merwin Wardlow came roaring to me in seven-year-old indignation.

"Marnie and that old sister of mine won't let me play!" he tattled wrathfully.

"Oh, I'm sure they will, if you play nicely," I said, shifting my crochet hook as I hurried with the edging of Marnie's new petticoat.

"They won't neither!" And he prepared to bellow again. His bellow rivaled the six o'clock closing whistle at the mine, so I sighed, and laying my work down, took him out to the children's play place under the aspens.

Marnie was playing with five-year-old Tessie Wardlow. They were engrossed in building a playhouse. They had already outlined the various rooms with rocks and were now furnishing them with sticks and stones, shingles, old cans and bottles, and remnants of broken dishes. Marnie was arranging flowers in a broken vase she had propped between two rocks. Tessie was busily bringing her flowers and sprays of leaves. And not one single word was being exchanged! Tessie watched Marnie, then trotted off to get another flower. Before she could pick the one she intended, she stopped, her hand actually on the flower, glanced at Marnie's busy back, left that flower and, picking another, trotted happily back with it.

"Marnie," I called, and blinked to feel a wisp of something say *Yes?* inside my mind. "Marnie!" I called again. Marnie jumped and turned her face to me. "Yes, Aunt Gail," she said carefully.

"Merwin says you won't let him play."

"Oh, he's telling stories!" cried Tessie indignantly. "He won't do anything Marnie says and she's the boss today."

"She don't tell me nothing to do!" yelled Merwin, betraying in his indignation his father's careful grammar.

"She does so!" Tessie stamped her foot. "She tells you just as much as she tells me! And you don't do it."

I was saved from having to arbitrate between the warring two by Mrs. Wardlow's calling them in to supper. Relieved, I sank down on the southwest corner of the parlor—a sizable moss-grown rock. Marnie sat down on the ground beside me.

"Marnie," I said. "How did Tessie know what flowers to bring you?"

"I told her," said Marnie, surprised. "They said I was boss today. Merwin just wouldn't play."

"Did you tell him things to do?" I asked.

"Oh, yes," said Marnie. "But he didn't do nothing."

"Did nothing," I corrected.

"Did nothing," she echoed.

"The last flower Tessie brought," I went on. "Did you ask for that special one?"

"Yes," said Marnie. "She started to pick the one with bad petals on one side."

"Marnie," I said patiently, "I was here and I didn't hear a word. Did you *talk* to Tessie?"

"Oh, yes," said Marnie.

"With words? Out loud?" I pursued.

"I think—" Marnie started, then she sighed and sagged against my knees, tracing a curve in the dirt with her forefinger. "I guess not. It is so much more easy—" ("Easier," I corrected) "—easier to catch her thoughts before they are words. I can tell Tessie without words. But Merwin—I guess he needs words."

"Marnie," I said, taking reluctant steps into the wilderness of my ignorance of what to do with a child who found "no words more easy," "you must always use words. It might seem easier to you—the other way, but you *must* speak. You see, most people don't understand *not* using words. When people don't understand, they get frightened. When they are frightened, they get angry. And when they get angry, they—they have to hurt."

I sat quietly watching Marnie manipulate my words, frame a reply, and make it into words for her stricken, unhappy lips.

"Then it was because they didn't understand, that they killed us," she said. "They made the fire."

"Yes," I said, "exactly.

"Marnie," I went on, feeling that I was prying, but needing to know. "You have never cried for the people who died in the fire. You were sad, but—weren't they your own people?"

"Yes," said Marnie, after an interval. "My father, my mother, and my brother—" She firmed her lips and swallowed. "And a neighbor of ours. One brother was Called in the skies when our ship broke and my little sister's life-slip didn't come with ours."

And I saw them! Vividly, I saw them all as she named them. The father, I noticed before his living, smiling image faded from my mind, had thick dark curls like Marnie's. The neighbor was a plump little woman.

"But," I blinked, "don't you grieve for them? Aren't you sad because they are dead?"

"I am sad because they aren't with me," said Marnie slowly. "But I do not grieve that the Power Called them back to the Presence. Their bodies were so hurt and broken." She swallowed again. "My days are not finished yet, but no matter how long until I am Called, my people will come to meet me. They will laugh and run to me when I arrive and I—" She leaned against my skirt, averting her face. After a moment she lifted her chin and said, "I *am* sad to be here without them, but my biggest sorrow is not knowing where my little sister is, or whether Timmy has been Called. We were two-ing, Timmy and I." Her hand closed over the hem of my skirt. "But, praise the Presence, I have you and Uncle Nils, who do not hurt just because you don't understand."

"But where on Earth—" I began.

"Is this called Earth?" Marnie looked about her. "Is Earth the place we came to?"

"The whole world is Earth," I said. "Everything—as far as you can see—as far as you can go. You came to this Territory—"

"Earth—" Marnie was musing. "So this refuge in the sky is called Earth!" She scrambled to her feet. "I'm sorry I troubled you, Aunt Gail," she said. "Here, this is to promise not to be un-Earth—" She snatched up the last flower she had put in the playhouse vase and pushed it into my hands. "I will set the table for supper," she called back to me as she hurried to the house. "This time forks at each place—not in a row down the middle."

I sighed and twirled the flower in my fingers. Then I laughed helplessly. The flower that had so prosaically grown on, and had been plucked from our hillside, was glowing with a deep radiance, its burning gold center flicking the shadows of the petals across my fingers, and all the petals tinkled softly from the dewdrop-clear bits of light that were finely pendant along the edges of them. Not un-Earth! But when I showed Nils the flower that evening as I retold our day, the flower was just a flower again, limp and withering.

"Either you or Marnie have a wonderful imagination," Nils said.

"Then it's Marnie," I replied. "I would never in a million years think up anything like the things she said. Only, Nils, how can we be sure it isn't true?"

"That what isn't true?" he asked. "What do you think she has told you?"

"Why—why—" I groped, "that she can read minds, Tessie's anyway. And that this is a strange world to her. And—and—"

"If this is the way she wants to make the loss of her family bearable, let her. It's better than hysterics or melancholia. Besides, it's more exciting, isn't it?" Nils laughed.

That reaction wasn't much help in soothing my imagination! But *he* didn't have to spend his days wrestling hand to hand with Marnie and her ways. He hadn't had to insist that Marnie learn to make the beds by hand instead of floating the covers into place—nor insist that young ladies wear shoes in preference to drifting a few inches above the sharp gravel and beds of stickers in the back yard. And he didn't have to persuade her that, no matter how dark the moonless night, one doesn't cut out paper flowers and set them to blooming like little candles around the corners of the rooms. Nils had been to the county seat *that* weekend. I don't know where she was from, but this *was* a New World to her, and whatever one she was native to, I had no memory of reading about or of seeing on a globe.

When Marnie started taking classes in Mr. Wardlow's one-room school, she finally began to make friends with the few children her age in Margin. Guessing at her age, she seemed to be somewhere in her teens. Among her friends were Kenny, the son of the mine foreman, and Loolie, the daughter of the boardinghouse cook. The three of them ranged the hills together, and Marnie picked up a large vocabulary from them and became a little wiser in the ways of behaving unexceptionally. She startled them a time or two by doing impossible things, but they reacted with anger and withdrawal which she had to wait out more or less patiently before being accepted back into their companionship. One doesn't forget again very quickly under such circumstances.

During this time, her hair grew and she grew, too, so much so that she finally had to give up the undergarment she had worn when we found her. She sighed as she laid it aside, tucking it into the bottom dresser drawer. "At Home," she said, "there would be a ceremony and a pledging. All of us girls would know that our adult responsibilities were almost upon us—" Somehow, she seemed less different, less, well, I suppose, alien, after that day.

It wasn't very long after this that Marnie began to stop suddenly in the middle of a sentence and listen intently, or clatter down the plates she was patterning on the supper table and hurry to the window. I watched her anxiously for a while, wondering if she was sickening for something, then, one night, after I blew out the lamp, I thought I heard something moving in the other room. I went in barefootedly quiet. Marnie was at the window.

"Marnie?" Her shadowy figure turned to me. "What's troubling you?" I stood close beside her and looked out at the moonlight-flooded emptiness of hills around the house.

"Something is out there," she said. "Something scared and bad— frightened and evil—" She took the more adult words from my mind. I was pleased that being conscious of her doing this didn't frighten me any more the way it did the first few times. "It goes around the house and around the house and is afraid to come."

"Perhaps an animal," I suggested.

"Perhaps," she conceded, turning away from the window. "I don't know your world. An animal who walks upright and sobs, 'God have mercy!' "

Which incident was startling in itself, but doubly so when Nils said casually next day as he helped himself to mashed potatoes at the dinner table, "Guess who I saw today. They say he's been around a week or so." He flooded his plate with brown meat gravy. "Our friend of the double mind."

"Double mind?" I blinked uncomprehendingly.

"Yes." Nils reached for a slice of bread. "To burn or not to burn, that is the question—"

"Oh!" I felt a quiver up my arms. "You mean the man at Grafton's Vow. What was his name anyway?"

"He never said, did he?" Nils's fork paused in mid-air as the thought caught him.

"Derwent," said Marnie shortly, her lips pressing to a narrow line. "Caleb Derwent, God have mercy."

"How do you know?" I asked. "Did he tell you?"

"No," she said, "I took it from him to remember him with gratitude." She pushed away from the table, her eyes widening. "That's it—that's the frightened evil that walks around the house at night! And passes by during the day! But he saved me from the fire! Why does he come now?"

"She's been feeling that something evil is lurking outside," I explained to Nils's questioning look.

"Hmm," he said, "the two minds. Marnie, if ever he—"

"May I go?" Marnie stood up. "I'm sorry. I can't eat when I think of someone repenting of good." And she was gone, the kitchen door clicking behind her.

"And she's right," said Nils, resuming his dinner. "He slithered around a stack of nail kegs at the store and muttered to me about still compromising with evil, harboring a known witch. I sort of pinned him in the corner until he told me he had finally—after all this time—confessed his sin of omission to his superiors at Grafton's Vow and they've excommunicated him until he redeems himself—" Nils stared at me, listening to his own words. "Gail! You don't suppose he has any mad idea about taking her back to Grafton's Vow, do you!"

"Or *killing* her!" I cried, clattering my chair back from the table. "Marnie!" Then I subsided with an attempt at a smile. "But she's witch enough to sense his being around," I said. "He won't be able to take her by surprise."

"Sensing or not," Nils said, eating hastily, "next time I get within reach of this Derwent person, I'm going to persuade him that he'll be healthier elsewhere."

In the days that followed, we got used to seeing half of Derwent's face peering around a building, or a pale slice of his face appearing through bushes or branches, but he seemed to take out his hostility in watching Marnie from a safe distance, and we decided to let things ride—watchfully.

Then one evening Marnie shot through the back door and, shutting it, leaned against it, panting.

"Marnie," I chided. "I didn't hear your steps on the porch. You *must* remember—"

"I—I'm sorry, Aunt Gail," she said, "but I had to hurry. Aunt Gail, I have a trouble!" She was actually shaking.

"What have you done now to upset Kenny and Loolie?" I asked, smiling.

"Not—not that," she said. "Oh, Aunt Gail! He's down in the shaft and I can't get him up. I know the inanimate lift, but he's not inanimate—"

"Marnie, sit down," I said, sobering. "Calm down and tell me what's wrong."

She sat, if that tense tentative conforming to a chair could be called sitting.

"I was out at East Shaft," she said. "My people are Identifiers, some of them are, anyway—my family is especially—I mean—" She gulped and let loose all over. I could almost see the tension drain out of her, but it came flooding back as soon as she started talking again. "Identifiers can locate metals and minerals. I felt a pretty piece of chrysocolla down in the shaft and I wanted to get it for you for your collection. I climbed through the fence—oh, I know I shouldn't have, but I did—and I was checking to see how far down in the shaft the mineral was when—when I looked up and he was there!" She clasped her hands. "He said, 'Evil must die. I can't go back because you're not dead. I let you out of a little fire in this life, so I'll burn forever. 'He who endures to the end—' ' Then he pushed me into the shaft—"

"Into the—" I gasped.

"Of course, I didn't fall," she hastened. "I just lifted to the other side of the shaft out of reach, but—but he had pushed me so hard that he—he fell!"

"He fell!" I started up in horror. "He fell? Child, that's hundreds of feet down onto rocks and water—"

"I—I caught him before he fell all the way," said Marnie, apologetically. "But I had to do it our way. I stopped his falling—only—only he's just staying there! In the air! In the shaft! I know the inanimate lift, but he's alive. And I—don't—know—how—to—get—him—up!" She burst into tears. "And if I let him go, he will fall to death. And if I leave him there, he'll bob up and down and up and—I *can't* leave him there!" She flung herself against me, wailing. It was the first time she'd ever let go like that.

Nils had come in at the tail end of her explanation and I filled him in between my muttered comforting of the top of Marnie's head. He went to the shed and came back with a coil of rope.

"With a reasonable amount of luck, no one will see us," he said. "It's a good thing that we're out here by ourselves."

Evening was all around us as we climbed the slope behind the house. The sky was high and a clear, transparent blue, shading to apricot, with a metallic orange backing the surrounding hills. One star was out, high above the evening-hazy immensity of distance beyond Margin. We panted up the hill to East Shaft. It was the one dangerous abandoned shaft among all the shallow prospect holes that dotted the hills around us. It had been fenced with barbwire and was forbidden territory to the children of Margin—including Marnie. Nils held down one strand of the barbwire with his foot and lifted the other above it. Marnie slithered through and I scrambled through, snatching the ruffle of my petticoat free from where it had caught on the lower barbs.

We lay down on the rocky ground and edged up to the brink of the shaft. It was darker than the inside of a hat.

"Derwent!" Nils's voice echoed eerily down past the tangle of vegetation clinging to the upper reaches of the shaft.

"Here I am, Lord." The voice rolled up flatly, drained of emotion. "Death caught me in the midst of my sin. Cast me into the fire—the everlasting fire I traded a piddlin' little shed fire for. Kids—dime a dozen! I sold my soul for a scared face. Here I am, Lord. Cast me into the fire."

Nils made a sound. If what I was feeling was any indication, a deep sickness was tightening his throat. "Derwent!" he called again, "I'm letting down a rope. Put the loop around your waist so we can pull you up!" He laid the rope out across a timber that slanted over the shaft. Down it went into the darkness—and hung swaying slightly.

"Derwent!" Nils shouted. "Caleb Derwent! Get hold of that rope!"

"Here I am, Lord," came the flat voice again, much closer this time. "Death caught me in the midst of my sin—"

"Marnie," Nils said over the mindless mechanical reiteration that was now receding below. "Can you do anything?"

"May I?" she asked. "May I, Uncle Nils?"

"Of course," said Nils. "There's no one here to be offended. Here, take hold of the rope and—and go down along it so we'll know where you are."

So Marnie stepped lightly into the nothingness of the shaft and, hand circling the rope, sank down into the darkness. Nils mopped the sweat from his forehead with his forearm. "No weight," he muttered, "not an ounce of weight on the rope!"

Then there was a shriek and a threshing below us. "No! No!" bellowed Derwent, "I repent! I repent! Don't shove me down into everlasting—!" His words broke off and the rope jerked.

"Marnie!" I cried. "What—what—"

"He's—his eyes turned up and his mouth went open and he doesn't talk," she called up fearfully from the blackness. "I can't find his thoughts—"

"Fainted!" said Nils. Then he called, "It's all right, Marnie. He's only unconscious from fright. Put the rope around him."

So we drew him up from the shaft. Once the rope snatched out of our hands for several inches, but he didn't fall! The rope slacked, but he didn't fall! Marnie's anxious face came into sight beside his bowed head. "I can hold him from falling," she said, "but you must do all the pulling. I can't lift him."

Then we had him out on the ground, lying flat, but in the brief interval that Nils used to straighten him out, he drifted up from the ground about four inches. Marnie pressed him back.

"He—he isn't fastened to the Earth with all the fastenings. I loosed some when I stopped his fall. The shaft helped hold him. But now I—I've got to fasten them all back again. I didn't learn that part very well at home. Everyone can do it for himself. I got so scared when he fell that I forgot all I knew. But I couldn't have done it with him still in the shaft anyway. He would have fallen." She looked around in the deepening dusk. "I need a source of light—"

Light? We looked around us. The only lights in sight were the one star and a pinprick or so in the shadows of the flat below us.

"A lantern?" asked Nils.

"No," said Marnie. "Moonlight or sunlight or enough starlight. It takes light to 'platt'—" She shrugged with her open hands.

"The moon is just past full," said Nils. "It'll be up soon—"

So we crouched there on boulders, rocks, and pebbles, holding Derwent down, waiting for the moonrise to become an ingredient in fastening him to the Earth again. I felt an inappropriate bubble of laughter shaking my frightened shoulders. What a story to tell to my grandchildren! If I live through this ever to have any!

Finally the moon came, a sudden flood through the transparency of the evening air. Marnie took a deep breath, her face very white in the moonlight. "It's—it's frightening!" she said. " 'Platting' with moonlight is an adult activity. Any child can 'platt' with sunlight, but," she shivered, "only the Old Ones dare use moonlight and sunlight together! I—I think I can handle the moonlight. I hope!"

She lifted her two cupped hands. They quickly filled with a double handful of moonlight. The light flowed and wound across her palms and between her fingers, flickering live and lovely. Then she was weaving the living light into an intricate design that moved and changed and grew until it hid her arms to the elbows and cast light up into her intent face. One curve of it touched me. It was like nothing I'd ever felt before, so I jerked away from it. But, fascinated, I reached for it again. A gasp from Marnie stopped my hand.

"It's too big," she gasped. "It's too powerful! I—I don't know enough to control—" Her fingers flicked and the intricate light enveloped Derwent from head to foot. Then there was a jarring and a shifting. The slopes around us suddenly became unstable and almost fluid. There was a grinding and a rumbling. Rocks clattered down the slopes beyond us and the lip of East Shaft crumpled. The ground dimpled in around where the shaft had been. A little puff of dust rose from the spot and drifted slowly away in the cooling night air. We sorted ourselves out from where we had tumbled, clutched in each other's arms. Marnie looked down at the completely relaxed Derwent. "It got too big, too fast," she apologized. "I'm afraid it spoiled the shaft."

Nils and I exchanged glances and we both smiled weakly. "It's all right, Marnie," I said. "It doesn't matter. Is he all right now?"

"Yes," said Marnie, "his thoughts are coming back."

"Everything's fine," muttered Nils to me. "But what do you suppose that little earth-shaking has done to the mine?"

My eyes widened and I felt my hands tighten. What, indeed, *had* it done to the mine?

Derwent's thoughts came back enough that he left us the next day, sagging in his saddle, moving only because his horse did, headed for nowhere—just away—away from Margin, from Grafton's Vow, from Marnie. We watched him go, Marnie's face troubled.

"He is so confused," she said. "If only I were a Sorter. I could help his mind—"

"He tried to *kill* you!" I burst out, impatient with her compassion.

"He thought he would never be able to come into the Presence because of me," she said quickly. "What might I have done if I had believed that of him?"

So Derwent was gone—and so was the mine, irretrievably. The shaft, laboriously drilled and blasted through solid rock, the radiating drifts, hardly needing timbering to support them because of the composition of the rock—all had splintered and collapsed. From the mine entrance, crushed to a cabin-sized cave, you could hear the murmur of waters that had broken through into, and drowned, the wreckage of the mine. The second day a trickle of water began a pool in the entrance. The third day the stream began to run down the slope toward town. It was soaked up almost immediately by the bone-dry ground, but the muddy wetness spread farther and farther and a small channel began to etch itself down the hill.

It doesn't take long for a town to die. The workmen milled around at the mine entrance for a day or two, murmuring of earthquakes and other awesome dispensations from the hand of God, hardly believing that they weren't at work. It was like a death that had chopped off things abruptly instead of letting them grow or decrease gradually. Then the first of the families left, their good-bys brief and unemotional to hide the sorrow and worry in their eyes. Then others followed, either leaving their shacks behind them to fall into eventual ruin, or else their houses moved off down the road like shingled turtles, leaving behind them only the concrete foundation blocks.

We, of course, stayed to the last, Nils paying the men off, making arrangements about what was left of the mining equipment, taking care of all the details attendant on the last rites of his career that had started so hopefully here in Margin. But, finally, we would have been packing, too, except for one thing. Marnie was missing.

She had been horrified when she found what had happened to the mine. She was too crushed to cry when Loolie and Kenny and the Wardlows came to say good-by. We didn't know what to say to her or how to comfort her. Finally, late one evening, I found her sitting, hunched on her cot, her face wet with tears.

"It's all right, Marnie," I said, "we won't go hungry. Nils will always find a way to—"

"I am not crying for the mine," said Marnie and I felt an illogical stab of resentment that she wasn't. "It is a year," she went on. "Just a year."

"A year?" Then remembrance flooded in. A year since the sullen smoke plumed up from the burning shed, since I felt the damp curling of freshly cut hair under my fingers—since Nils grimly dug the multiple grave. "But it should be a little easier now," I said.

"It's only that on the Home it would have been Festival time—time to bring our flowers and lift into the skies and sing to remember all who had been Called during the year. We kept Festival only three days before the angry ones came and killed us." She wiped her cheeks with the backs of her hands. "That was a difficult Festival because we were so separated by the Crossing. We didn't know how many of us were echoing our songs from Otherside."

"I'm not sure I understand," I said. "But go on—cry for your dead. It will ease you."

"I am not crying for those who have been Called," said Marnie. "They are in the Presence and need no tears. I am crying for the ones—if there are any—who are alive on this Earth we found. I am crying because— Oh, Aunt Gail!" She clung to me. "What if I'm the only one who was not Called? The only one!"

I patted her shaking shoulders, wishing I could comfort her.

"There was Timmy," she sniffed and accepted the handkerchief I gave her. "He—he was in our ship. Only at the last moment before Lift Off was there room for him to come with us. But when the ship melted and broke and we each had to get into our life-slips, we scattered like the baby quail Kenny showed me the other day. And only a few life-slips managed to stay together. Oh, I wish I knew!" She closed her wet eyes, her trembling chin lifting. "If only I knew whether or not Timmy is in the Presence!"

I did all that I could to comfort her. My all was just being there.

"I keep silent Festival tonight," she said finally, "trusting in the Power—"

"This is a solemn night for us, too," I said. "We will start packing tomorrow. Nils thinks he can find a job nearer the Valley—" I sighed. "This would have been such a nice place to watch grow up. All it lacked was a running stream, and now we're even getting that. Oh, well—such is life in the wild and woolly West!"

And the next morning, she was gone. On her pillow was a piece of paper that merely said, "Wait."

What could we do? Where could we look? Footprints were impossible on the rocky slopes. And for a Marnie, there could well be *no* footprints at all, even if the surroundings were pure sand. I looked helplessly at Nils.

"Three days," he said, tightly angry. "The traditional three days before a funeral. If she isn't back by then, we leave."

By the end of the second day of waiting in the echoless ghostiness of the dead town, I had tears enough dammed up in me to rival the new little stream that was cutting deeper and deeper into its channel. Nils was up at the mine entrance watching the waters gush out from where they had oozed at first. I was hunched over the stream where it made the corner by the empty foundation blocks of the mine office, when I heard—or felt—or perceived—a presence. My innards lurched and I turned cautiously. It was Marnie.

"Where have you been?" I asked flatly.

"Looking for another mine," she said matter-of-factly.

"Another mine?" My shaking hands pulled her down to me and we wordlessly hugged the breath out of each other. Then I let her go.

"I spoiled the other one," she went on as though uninterrupted. "I have found another, but I'm not sure you will want it."

"Another? Not want it?" My mind wasn't functioning on a very high level, so I stood up and screamed, "Nils!"

His figure popped out from behind a boulder and, after hesitating long enough to see there were two of us, he made it down the slope in massive leaps and stood panting, looking at Marnie. Then he was hugging the breath out of her and I was weeping over the two of them, finding my tears considerably fewer than I had thought. We finally all shared my apron to dry our faces and sat happily shaken on the edge of our front porch, our feet dangling.

"It's over on the other side of the flat," said Marnie. "In a little canyon there. It's close enough so Margin can grow again here in the same place, only now with a running stream."

"But a new mine! What do you know about mining?" asked Nils, hope, against his better judgment, lightening his face.

"Nothing," admitted Marnie. "But I can identify and I took these—" She held out her hands. "A penny for copper. Your little locket," she nodded at me apologetically, "for gold. A dollar—" she turned it on her palm, "for silver. By the identity of these I can find other metals like them. Copper—there is not as much as in the old mine, but there is *some* in the new one. There is quite a bit of gold. It feels like much more than in the old mine, and," she faltered, "I'm sorry, but mostly there is only silver. Much, much more than copper. Maybe if I looked farther—"

"But, Marnie," I cried, "silver is better! Silver is better!"

"Are you serious?" asked Nils, the planes of his face stark and bony in the sunlight. "Do you really think you have found a possible mine?"

"I don't know about mines," repeated Marnie, "but I know these metals are there. I can feel them tangling all over in the mountainside and up and down as the ground goes. Much of it is mixed with other matter, but it's like the ore they used to send out of Margin in the wagons with the high wheels. Only some of it is penny and locket and dollar feeling. I didn't know it could come that way in the ground."

"Native silver," I murmured, "native copper and gold."

"I—I could try to open the hill for you so you could see," suggested Marnie timidly to Nils's still face.

"No," I said hastily. "No, Marnie. Nils, couldn't we at least take a look?"

So we went, squeezing our way through the underbrush and through a narrow entrance into a box canyon beyond the far side of the flat. Pausing to catch my breath, almost pinned between two towering slabs of tawny orange granite, I glanced up to the segment of blue sky overhead. A white cloud edged into sight and suddenly the movement wasn't in the cloud, but in the mountain of granite. It reeled and leaned and seemed to be toppling. I snatched my eyes away from the sky with a gasp and wiggled on through, following Marnie and followed by Nils.

Nils looked around the canyon wonderingly. "Didn't even know this was here," he said. "No one's filed on this area. It's ours—if it's worth filing on. Our own mine—"

Marnie knelt at the base of the cliff that formed one side of the canyon. "Here is the most," she said, rubbing her hand over the crumbling stone. "It is all through the mountain, but there is some silver very close here." She looked up at Nils and read his skepticism.

"Well," she sighed. "Well—" And she sank down with the pool of her skirts around her on the sandy ground. She clasped her hands and stared down at them. I could see her shoulders tighten and felt something move—or change—or begin. Then, about shoulder high on the face of the rock wall, there was a coloring and a crumbling. Then a thin, bright trickle came from the rock and ran molten down to the sand, spreading flowerlike into a palm-sized disk of pure silver!

"There," said Marnie, her shoulders relaxing. "That was close to the outside—"

"Nils!" I cried. "Look!" and snatching up the still-hot metallic blossom, I dropped it again, the bright blood flowing across the ball of my thumb from the gashing of the sharp silver edge.

It doesn't take long for a town to grow. Not if there's a productive mine and an ideal flat for straight, wide business streets. And hills and trees and a running stream for residential areas. The three of us watch with delighted wonder the miracle of Margin growing and expanding. Only occasionally does Marnie stand at the window in the dark and wonder if she is the only one—the last one—of her People left upon Earth. And only occasionally do I look at her and wonder where on Earth—or off it—did this casual miracle, this angel unawares, come from.

Interlude: Mark & Meris 3

"This angel unawares," Bethie's whisper echoed the last phrase of the Assembly.

"Why, I've *been* in Margin!" cried Meris. "I was there their last Founding Day and I didn't hear a word about Marnie!"

"What did you hear?" asked Bethie, interested.

"Well, about the first mine collapsing and starting the creek and about the new mine's being found—"

"I suppose that's enough," said Bethie. "How would you have included Marnie?"

"At least mention her name!" cried Meris. "Why, even the burro a prospector hit with a piece of ore and found Tombstone or Charleston or wherever is remembered. And not word one about Marnie—"

"Maybe," suggested Bethie, "maybe because that wasn't her real name."

"It wasn't!" Meris's eyes widened.

"Do you think she was called Marnie on the Home?" teased Mark. "Look at what we did to Lala's name. At least 'Marnie' couldn't be that bad a miss."

"Who was she then?" asked Meris. "What was her real name?"

"Why, I thought you knew—" Bethie started.

"Marnie was Lytha. She used both names later on—Marnie Lytha."

"Lytha!" Meris sat down absently, almost off the chair, and scooted back slowly. "Lytha and Timmy. Oh! Of course! Then Eva-lee's promise to them must have come true—"

"She didn't promise them each other," reminded Mark. "Only love."

"Only love!" mocked Meris. "Oh, Mark! *Only* love?"

"I was just thinking," said Mark slowly. "If Marnie was Lytha, then all those people who died in the fire—"

"Oh, Mark!" Meris drew a breath of distress. "Oh, Mark! But Eve wasn't one of them. Bethie's mother escaped!"

"Others did, too," said Bethie. "The flow of Assembling about Marnie kept right on in the same general area and I didn't stop when Marnie's segment was finished. The next part—" She hesitated. "It's hard to tell what is bright and happy and what is dark and sad. I'll let you decide. The boy—well, he wasn't sure either—"

Bethie gathered up the two willing hands gently and began—

Troubling of the Water

Sometimes it's like being a castaway, being a first settler in a big land. If I were a little younger, maybe I'd play at being Robinson Crusoe, only I'd die of surprise if I found a footprint, especially a bare one, this place being where it is.

But it's not only being a castaway in a place, but in a time. I feel as though the last years of the century were ruffling up to my knees in a tide that will sweep me into the next century. If I live seven more years, I'll not only be of age but I'll see the Turn of the Century! Imagine putting 19 in front of your years instead of 18! So, instead of playing Crusoe and scanning the horizon for sails, I used to stand on a rock and measure the world full circle, thinking—the Turn of the Century! The Turn of the Century! And seeking and seeking as though Time were a tide that would come racing through the land at midnight 1899 and that I could see the front edge of the tide beginning already!

But things have happened so fast recently that I'm not sure about Time or Place or Possible or Impossible any more. One thing I am sure of is the drought. It was real enough.

It's the responsibility of the men of the house to watch out for the welfare of the women of the house, so that day I went with Father up into the hills to find out where Sometime Creek started. We climbed up and up along the winding creek bed until my lungs pulled at the hot air and felt crackly clear down to their bottoms. We stopped and leaned against a boulder to let me catch my breath and cool off a little in what shadow there was. We could see miles and miles across the country—so far that the mountains on the other side of Desolation Valley were swimmy pale against the sky. Below us, almost at our feet because of the steepness of the hill, was the thin green line of mesquites and river willows that bordered Chuckawalla River and, hidden in a clump of cottonwoods down to our left, was our cabin, where Mama, if she had finished mixing the bread, was probably standing in the doorway with Merry on her hip, looking up as I was looking down.

"What if there isn't a spring?" I asked, gulping dryly, wanting a drink. I thought Father wasn't going to answer. Sometimes he doesn't—maybe for a day or so. Then suddenly, when you aren't even thinking of the same thing, he'll answer and expect you to remember what you'd asked.

"Then we'll know why they call this Sometime Creek," he said. "If you've cooled down some, go get a drink."

"But we've always got the river," I said, as I bellied down to the edge of the plunging water. It flowed so fast that I couldn't suck it up. I had to bite at it to get a mouthful. It was cold and tasted of silt. It was shallow enough that I bumped my nose as I ducked my hot face into its coldness.

"Not always." Father waited until I finished before he cupped his hands in a small waterfall a step upstream and drank briefly. "It's dropped to less than half its flow of last week. Tanker told me yesterday when he stopped for melons that there's no snow left in the Coronas Altas, this early in the summer."

"But our orchard!" I felt dread crawl in my stomach. "All our fields!"

"Our orchard," said Father, no comfort or reassurance in his voice. "And all our fields."

We didn't find a spring. We stood at the bottom of a slope too steep to climb and watched the water sheet down it from the top we couldn't see. I watched Father as he stood there, one foot up on the steep rise, his knee bent as if he intended to climb up sheer rock, looking up at the silver falling water.

"If the river dries up," I offered, "the creek isn't enough to water everything."

Father said nothing but turned back down the hill.

We went down in half the time it took us to climb. Part way down I stumbled and fell sideways into a catclaw bush. Father had to pull me out, the tiny thorns clinging to my clothes like claws and striping the backs of my hands and one of my cheeks with smarting scratches.

"People have to drink," said Father. "And the animals."

We were leveling out on the flat by the house when I finally figured out what Father meant. He had already given our young orchard back to the wilderness and turned his back on the vegetable crops that were our mainstay and on the withering alfalfa fields. He was measuring water to keep us alive and still clinging to Fool's Acres Ranch.

Mama and Merry met us as we came down the path. I took the burden of Merry and carried her on down to the house. I wasn't supposed to know that Mama was going to have a baby in a couple of months. Boys aren't supposed to notice such things—not even boys who are past fifteen and so almost men.

That night we sat around the table as usual and read to each other. I read first. I was reading *Robinson Crusoe* for the second time since we came to the ranch, and I had just got to where he was counting his wheat seeds and figuring out the best way to plant them. I like this part better than the long, close pages where he talks philosophy about being alone and uses big, hard-to-pronounce words. But sometimes, looking out across the plains and knowing there is only Father and Mama and Merry and me as far as my eye can reach, I knew how he felt. Well, maybe the new baby would be a boy.

I read pretty well. Father didn't have to correct my pronunciation very often. Then Mama read from *Sense and Sensibility* and I listened even if it was dull and sleepy to me. You never know when Father is going to ask you what a word means and you'd better have some idea!

Then Father read from *Plutarch's Lives,* which is fun sometimes, and we ended the evening with our Bible verses and prayers.

I was half asleep before the lamp was blown out, but I came wide awake when I heard Mama's low carrying voice.

"Maybe mining would have been better. This is good mining country."

"Mining isn't for me," said Father. "I want to take living things from the earth. I can feel that I'm part of growing things, and nothing speaks to me of God more than seeing a field ripening ready for harvest. To have food where only a few months before was only a handful of seed—and faith."

"But if we finally have to give the ranch up anyway—" Mama began faintly.

"We won't give it up." Father's voice was firm.

Father and I rode in the supply wagon from Raster Creek Mine over the plank bridge across the dwindling thread of the river to our last gate. I opened the gate, wrestling with the wire loop holding the top of the post, while Father thanked Mr. Tanker again for the newspapers he had brought us. "I'm sorry there is so little for you this time," he said, glancing back at the limp gunny sacks and half-empty boxes. "And it's the last of it all."

Mr. Tanker gathered up the reins. "Reckon now you're finding out why this is called Fool's Acres Ranch. You're the third one that's tried farming here. This is mining country. Never be nothing else. No steady water. Shame you didn't try in Las Lomitas Valley across the Coronas. Artesian wells there. Every ranch got two-three wells and ponds with trees and fish. Devil of a long way to drive for fresh garden truck, though. Maybe if we ever get to be a state instead of a Territory—"

Father and I watched him drive away, the wagon hidden in dust before it fairly started. We walked back to the planks across the stream and stopped to look at the few pools tied together with a thread of water brought down by Sometime Creek that was still flowing thinly. Father finally said, "What does Las Lomitas mean in English?" And I wrestled with what little Spanish I had learned until that evening at the table. I grinned to myself as I said, "It means 'The Little Hills,' " and watched Father, for a change, sort through past conversations to understand what I was talking about.

Mama's time was nearing and we were all worried. Though as I said, politeness had it that I wasn't supposed to know what was going on. But I knew about the long gap between Merry and me—almost fourteen years. Mama had borne and buried five children in that time. I had been as healthy as a horse, but after me none of the babies seemed able to live. Oh, maybe a week or so, at first, but finally only a faint gasp or two and the perfectly formed babies died. And all this back East where there were doctors and midwives and comfort. I guess Mama gave up after the fifth baby died, because none came along until after we moved to Fool's Acres. When we knew Merry was on the way, I could feel the suspense building up. I couldn't really remember all those other babies because I had been so young. They had come each year regularly after me. But it had been ten years between the last one and Merry. So when Merry was born out in the wilderness with Father for midwife, none of us dared breathe heavily for fear she'd die. But she was like me—big lungs, big appetite, and no idea of the difference between day and night.

Mama couldn't believe it for a long time and used to turn suddenly from her work and go touch Merry, just to be sure.

And now another baby was almost due and dust and desolation had settled down on the ranch and the whole area except for our orchard. Father explained the upside-down running of the rivers in a desert area that was, so far, keeping our young trees alive.

Anyway, there came a day that I took the water bucket and went to find a new dipping place, because our usual one where the creek flowed into the river was so shallow even a tin dipper scooped up half sand at each attempt.

I had started up Sometime Creek hoping to find a deeper pool and had just stopped to lean in the thin hot shade of a boulder when it came.

Roaring! Blazing! A locomotive across the sky! A swept-back fountain of fire! A huge blazing something that flaked off flames as it roared away across Desolation Valley!

Scared half to death, I crouched against my boulder, my eyes blinking against the violence and thundering speed, my front hair fairly frizzling into beads from the impression of heat. Some of the flames that flaked off the main blaze blackened as they zigzagged down out of the sky like bits of charred paper from a bonfire. But some flakes darted away like angry hornets and one—one flame that kept its shape as it blackened and plunged like an arrow down through the roaring skies—headed straight for me! I threw my arms up to shield my face and felt something hit below me with a swishing thud that shook the hill and me.

And stillness came back to the ranch.

Only a brief stillness. I heard the crackle of flames and saw the smoke plume up! I scrambled downhill to the flat, seeing, like lightning, the flames racing across our cinder-dry fields, over our house, through our young orchard, across the crisped grass of Desolation Valley, leaving nothing but a smudge on the sky and hundreds of miles of scorched earth. It had happened other places in dry years.

I skidded to a stop in the edge of the flames, and, for lack of anything else I could do, I started stamping the small licking tongues of flame and kicking dirt over them.

"Barney!" I heard Father's shout. "Here's a shovel!"

I knuckled the smoke tears out of my eyes and stumbled to meet him as he ran toward me. "Keep it from going up the hill!" And he sped for the weed-grown edge of the alfalfa field.

Minutes later I plopped sand over the last smoking clump of grass and whacked it down with the back of my shovel. We were lucky. The fire area was pretty well contained between the rise of the hill and the foot of the field. I felt soot smudge across my face as I backhanded the sweat from my forehead. Father was out of my sight around the hill. Hefting the shovel, I started around to see if he needed my help. There was another plume of smoke! Alerted, I dropped the point of my shovel. Then I let it clatter to the ground as I fell to my knees.

A blackened hand reached up out of a charred bundle! Fingers spread convulsively, then clenched! And the bundle rolled jerkily.

"Father!" I yelled. "Father!" And grabbed for the smoldering blackness. I stripped away handsful of the scorching stuff and, by the time Father got there, my hands were scorching too.

"Careful! Careful!" Father cautioned. "Here, let me." I moved back, nursing my blistered fingers. Father fumbled with the bundle, and suddenly it ripped from one end to the other and he pulled out, like an ear of corn from its shuck, the twisting body of a person!

"He's badly burned," said Father. "Face and hands. Help me lift him." I helped Father get the body into his arms. He staggered and straightened. "Go tell your mother to brew up all the tea we have in the house—strong!"

I raced for the house, calling to Mama as soon as I saw her anxious face. "Father's all right! I'm all right! But we found someone burned! Father says to brew up all our tea—strong!"

Mama disappeared into the cabin and I heard the clatter of stove lids. I hurried back to Father and hovered anxiously as he laid his burden down on the little front porch. Carefully we peeled off the burned clothes until finally we had the body stripped down and put into an old nightshirt of Father's. The fire hadn't got to his legs nor to his body, but his left shoulder was charred—and his face! And arms! A tight cap thing that crumbled to flakes in our hands had saved most of his hair.

Father's mouth tightened. "His eyes," he said. "His eyes."

"Is he dead?" I whispered. Then I had my answer as one blackened hand lifted and wavered. I took it carefully in mine, my blisters drawing as I closed my fingers. The blackened head rolled and the mouth opened soundlessly and closed again, the face twisting with pain.

We worked over the boy—maybe some older than I—all afternoon. I brought silty half bucket after half bucket of water from the dipping place and strained it through muslin to get the silt out. We washed the boy until we located all his burns and flooded the places with strong cold tea and put tea packs across the worst ones. Mama worked along with us until the burden of the baby made her breathless and she had to stop.

She had given Merry a piece of bread and put her out in the little porch-side pen when we brought the boy in. Merry was crying now, her face dabbled with dirt, her bread rubbed in the sand. Mama gathered her up with an effort and smiled wearily at me over her head. "I'd better let her cry a little more, then her face will be wet enough for me to wash it clean!"

I guess I got enough tea on my hands working with the boy that my own burns weren't too bad. Blisters had formed and broken, but I only needed my right thumb and forefinger bandaged with strips from an old petticoat of Mama's. We left Mama with the boy, now clean and quiet on my cot, his face hidden under the wet packs, and went slowly down the path I had run so many times through the afternoon. We took our buckets on past the dipping place where a palm-sized puddle was all that was left of the water and retraced our steps to where the fire had been.

"A meteor?" I asked, looking across the ashy ground. "I always thought they came only at night."

"You haven't thought the matter over or you'd realize that night and day had nothing to do with meteors," said Father. "Is 'meteor' the correct term?"

"How funny that that fellow happened to be at the exact place at the exact time the piece of the meteor hit here," I said, putting Father's question away for future reference.

" 'Odd' is a better word," Father corrected. "Where did the boy come from?"

I let my eyes sweep the whole wide horizon before us. No one on foot and alone could ever have made it from *any* where! Where had he come from? Up out of the ground? Down out of the sky?

"I guess he rode in on the meteor," I said, and grinned at the idea. Father blinked at me, but didn't return my smile.

"There's what set the fire," he said. We plopped through feathery ashes toward a black lump of something.

"Maybe we could send it to a museum," I suggested as we neared it. "Most meteors burn up before they hit the ground."

Father pushed the chunk with his foot. Flame flared briefly from under it as it rocked, and a clump of grass charred, the tips of the blades twisting and curling as they shriveled.

"Still hot," said Father, hunkering down on his heels beside it. He thumped it with a piece of rock. It clanged. "Metal!" His eyebrows raised. "Hollow!"

Carefully we probed with sticks from the hillside and thumped with rocks to keep our hands from the heat. We sat back and looked at each other. I felt a stir of something like fear inside me.

"It's—it's been made!" I said. "It's a long metal pipe or something! And I'll bet he was inside it! But how could he have been? How could he get so high in the sky as to come down like that? And if this little thing has been made, what was the big thing it came from?"

"I'll go get water," said Father, getting up and lifting the buckets. "Don't burn yourself any more."

I prodded the blackened metal. "Out of the sky," I said aloud. "As high and as fast as a meteor to get that hot. What was he doing up there?" My stick rocked the metal hulk and it rolled again. The split ends spread as it turned and a small square metal thing fell out into the ashes. I scraped it to one side and cautiously lifted it. The soot on it blackened my bandages and my palms. It looked like a box and was of a size that my two hands could hold. I looked at it, then, suddenly overwhelmed and scared by the thought of roaring meteors and empty space and billowing grass fires, I scratched a hasty hole against a rock, shoved the box in, and stamped the earth over it. Then I went to meet Father and take one of the dripping buckets from him. We didn't look back at the crumpled metal thing behind us.

Father could hardly believe his eyes when he checked the boy's burns next morning. "They're healing already!" he said to Mama. "Look!"

I crowded closer to see, too, almost spilling the olive oil we were using on him. I looked at the boy's left wrist where I remembered a big, raw oozing place just where the cuff of his clothes had ended. The wrist was dry now and covered with the faint pink of new skin.

"But his face," said Mama. "His poor face and his eyes!" She turned away, blinking tears, and reached for a cup of water. "He must have lots of liquids," she said, matter-of-factly.

"But if he's unconscious—" I clutched at my few lessons in home care of the sick.

Father lifted the boy's head and shoulders carefully, but even his care wasn't gentle enough. The boy moaned and murmured something. Father held the cup to his blistered mouth and tipped the water to the dry lips. There was a moment's pause, then the water was gulped eagerly and the boy murmured something again.

"More?" asked Father clearly. "More?"

The face rolled to him, then away, and there was no answer.

"He'll need much care for a while," Father said to Mama as they anointed his burns and put on fresh bandages. "Do you think you can manage under the circumstances?"

Mama nodded. "With Barney to help with the lifting."

"Sure I'll help," I said. Then to Father, "Should I have said 'meteorite'?"

He nodded gravely. Then he said, "There are other planets." And left me to digest that one!

Father was spending his days digging for water in the river bottom. He had located one fair-sized pool that so far was keeping our livestock watered. We could still find drinking water for us up Sometime Creek. But the blue shimmer of the sky got more and more like heated metal. Heat was like a hand, pressing everything under the sky down into the powdery dead ground.

The boy was soon sitting up and eating a little of the little we had. But still no word from him, not a sound, even when we changed the dressings on his deeply charred left shoulder, or when the scabs across his left cheek cracked across and bled.

Then, one day, when all of us had been out of the cabin, straining our eyes prayerfully at the faint shadow of a cloud I thought I had seen over the distant Coronas, we came back, disheartened, to find the boy sitting in Mama's rocker by the window. But we had to carry him back to the cot. His feet seemed to have forgotten how to make steps.

Father looked down at him lying quietly on the cot. "If he can make it to the window, he can begin to take care of his own needs. Mother is overburdened as it is."

So I was supposed to explain to him that there would be no more basin for his use, but that the chamberpot under the cot was for him! How do you explain to someone who can't see and doesn't talk and that you're not at all sure even hears you? I told Father I felt like a mother cat training a kitten.

"Come on, fellow," I said to him, glad we had the cabin to ourselves. I tugged at his unscarred right arm and urged him until, his breath catching between clenched teeth, he sat up and swung his feet over the cot edge. His hand went out to me and touched my cheek. His bandaged face turned to me and his hand faltered. Then quickly he traced my features—my eyes, my nose, my ears, across my head, and down to my shoulders. Then he sighed a relieved sigh and both his hands went out to rest briefly on my two shoulders. His mouth distorted in a ghost of a smile, and he touched my wrist.

"What did you expect?" I laughed. "Horns?"

Then I sat back, astonished as his fingertip probed my temple just where I had visualized a horn, curled twice and with a shiny black tip.

"Well!" I said. "Mind reader!"

Just then Mama and Father came back into the cabin. The boy lay down slowly on the cot. Oh, well, the explanation could wait until the need arose.

We ate supper and I helped Mama clear up afterward. I was bringing the evening books to the pool of light on the table around the lamp when a movement from the cot drew my eyes. The boy was sitting on the edge, groping to come to his feet. I hurried to him, wondering what to do with Mama in the room, then as I reached for the boy's arm, I flicked a glance at Father. My mouth opened to wonder how I had known what the boy wanted, and how *he* knew about the Little House outside. But a hand closed on my arm and I moved toward the door, with the boy. The door closed behind us with a *chuck*. Through the starry darkness we moved down the path to the Little House. He went in. I waited by the door. He emerged and we went back up the path and into the house. He eased himself down on the cot, turned his face away from the light, and became quiet.

I wet my astonished lips and looked at Father. His lips quirked. "You're some mother cat!" he said.

But Mama wasn't smiling as I slid into my place at the table. Her eyes were wide and dark. "But he *didn't* touch the floor, James! And he didn't take one single step! He—he floated!"

Not one single step! I quickly reviewed our walk and I couldn't remember the rhythm of any steps at all—except my own. My eyes questioned Father, but he only said, "If he's to mingle with us, he must have a
name."

"Timothy," I said instantly.

"Why Timothy?" asked Father.

"Because that's his name," I said blankly. "Timothy."

So after awhile Timothy came to the table to eat, dressed in some of
my clothes. He was wonderfully at ease with knife and fork and spoon
though his eyes were still scabbed over and hidden behind bandages. Merry
babbled to him happily, whacking at him with her spoon, her few words
meaning as much to him as all our talking, which apparently was nothing. He labored at making his feet take steps again and Mama didn't have
his steplessness to worry about any more. He sat with us during our evening
readings with no more response than if we sat in silence. Except that after
the first evening he joined us, his right hand always made some sort of
sign in the air at the beginning and end of our prayer time. His left arm
wasn't working yet because of the deep burns on his shoulder.

Though Mama's worries over Timothy's steplessness were over, I had
all kinds of worries to take my mind off the baking, dust-blown fields
outside and even off the slow, heart-breaking curling of the leaves on our
small orchard trees. I was beginning to hear things. I began to know when
Timothy was thirsty or when he wanted to go to the Little House. I began to know what food he wanted more of and what he didn't care for.
And it scared me. I didn't want to know—not without words.

Then Mama's time came. When at last the pains were coming pretty
close together, Father sent me with Timothy and Merry away from the
house, away from the task the two had before them. I knew the worry
they had plaguing them besides the ordinary worry of childbirth, and I
prayed soundlessly as I lifted Merry and herded Timothy before me out
to our orchard. And when my prayers tripped over their own anxiety and
dissolved into wordlessness, I talked.

I told Timothy all about the ranch and the orchard and how Father
had found me the other night pouring one of my cups of drinking water
on the ground by my favorite smallest tree and how he'd told me it wouldn't
help because the roots were too deep for so little water to reach. And I
talked about all the little dead babies and how healthy Merry was but
how worried we were for the new baby. And—and—well, I babbled until
I ran out of words and sat under my dying favorite, shivering in the heat
and hugging Merry. I pushed my face against her tumbled hair so no one

could see my face puckering for tears. After I managed to snuff them back, I looked up and blinked.

Timothy was gone. He was streaking for the house, with not even one step! His feet were skimming above the furrows in the orchard. His arms were out in front of him like a sleepwalker but he was threading between the trees as though he could see. I started after him, fumbling with Merry, who was sliding out of my arms, leaving her crumpled clothes behind, her bare legs threshing and her cries muffling in her skirts. I snatched her up more securely and, shucking her dress down around her as I ran, dropped her into her porch-pen. Timothy was fumbling at the door latch. I opened it and we went into the house.

Father was working over a small bundle on the scrubbed kitchen table. Timothy crouched by Mama's bed, his hands holding one of hers tightly. Mama's breath was quieting down in shuddering gulps. She turned her face and pressed her eyes against her free wrist. "It hasn't cried," she whispered hopelessly. "Why doesn't it cry?"

Father turned from the table, his whole body drooping. "It never even breathed, Rachel. It's perfectly formed, but it never breathed at all."

Mama stared up at the roof of the cabin. "The clothes are in the trunk," she said quietly, "and a pink blanket."

And Father sent me out to find a burying place.

The light went out of our house. We went the weary round of things that had to be done to keep living and even Merry stood quietly, her hands on the top board of her porch-pen, her wide eyes barely overtopping it, and stared out at the hillside for long stretches of time. And Father, who had always been an unmoved mainstay no matter what happened, was broken, silent and uncommunicating.

We seldom mentioned the baby. We had buried my hoped-for little brother up on the hill under a scrub oak. When Mama was well enough, we all went up there and read the service for the dead, but no one cried as we stood around the tiny, powdery-dry, naked little grave. Timothy held Mama's hand all the way up there and all the way back. And Mama half smiled at him when we got back to the house.

Father said quietly, as he laid down the prayer book, "Why must he hang onto you?" Mama and I were startled at his tone of voice.

"But, James," Mama protested. "He's blind!"

"How many things has he bumped into since he's been up and around?" asked Father. "How often has he spilled food or groped for a chair?" He turned a bitter face toward Timothy. "And hanging onto you, he doesn't have to see—" Father broke off and turned to the window.

"James," Mama went to him quickly, "don't make Timothy a whipping boy for your sorrow. God gave him into our keeping. 'The Lord giveth—' "

"I'm sorry, Rachel." Father gathered Mama closely with one arm. "This 'taking away' period is bad. Not only the baby—"

"I know," said Mama. "But when Timothy touches me, the sorrow is lessened and I can feel the joy—"

"Joy!" Father spun Mama away from his shoulder. I shook for the seldom seen anger in his face.

"James!" said Mama. " 'Weeping may endure for a night but joy cometh in the morning.' Let Timothy touch your hand—"

Father left the house without a glance at any of us. He gathered up Merry from the porch-pen and trudged away through the dying orchard.

That night, while Mama was reading, I got up to get Timothy a drink.

"You're interrupting your mother," said Father quietly.

"I'm sorry," I said. "Timothy is thirsty."

"Sit down," said Father ominously. I sat.

When our evening was finished, I asked, "May I get him a drink now?"

Father slowly sat down again at the table. "How do you know he wants a drink?" he asked.

"I—I just know," I stumbled, watching Timmy leave the table. "It comes into my mind."

"Comes into your mind." Father seemed to lay the words out on the table in front of him and look at them. After a silence he said, "How does it come into your mind? Does it say, Timothy is thirsty—he wants a drink?"

"No," I said, unhappily, looking at Father's lamplight-flooded face, wondering if he was, for the first time in my life, ridiculing me. "There aren't any words. Only a feeling—only a *knowing* that he's thirsty."

"And you." His face shadowed as he turned it to look at Mama. "When he touches your hand, are there words—Joy, have joy?"

"No," said Mama. "Only the feeling that God is over all and that sorrow is a shadow and that—that the baby was called back into the Presence."

Father turned back to me. "If Timothy can make you know he is thirsty, he can tell you he is. You are not to give him a drink until he asks for it."

"But, Father! He can't talk!" I protested.

"He has a voice," said Father. "He hasn't talked since he became conscious after the fire, but he said some words before then. Not our words, but words. If he can be blind and still not stumble, if he can comfort a bereaved mother by the touch of the hand, if he can make you know he's thirsty, he can talk."

I didn't argue. You don't with Father. They started getting ready for bed. I went to Timothy and sat beside him on the cot. He didn't put out his hand for the cup of water he wanted. He knew I didn't have it.

"You have to ask for it," I told him. "You have to say you're thirsty." His blind face turned to me and two of his fingers touched my wrist. I suddenly realized that this was something he often did lately. Maybe being blind he could hear better by touching me. I felt the thought was foolish before I finished it. But I said again, "You have to ask for it. You must tell me, 'I'm thirsty. I want a drink, please.' You must talk."

Timothy turned from me and lay down on the cot. Mama sighed sharply. Father blew out the lamp, leaving me in the dark to spread my pallet on the floor and go to bed.

The next morning we were all up before sunrise. Father had all our good barrels loaded on the hayrack and was going to Tolliver's Wells for water. He and Mama counted out our small supply of cash with tight lips and few words. In times like these water was gold. And what would we do when we had no more money?

We prayed together before Father left, and the house felt shadowy and empty with him gone. We pushed our breakfasts around our plates and then put them away for lunch.

What is there to do on a ranch that is almost dead? I took *Pilgrim's Progress* to the corner of the front porch and sat with it on my lap and stared across the yard without seeing anything, sinking into my own Slough of Despond. I took a deep breath and roused a little as Timothy came out onto the porch. He had a cup in his hand.

"I'm thirsty," he said slowly but distinctly. "I want a drink, please."

I scrambled awkwardly to my feet and took the cup from him. Mama came to the door. "What did you say, Barney?"

"I didn't say anything," I said, my grin almost splitting my face. "Timmy did!" We went into the house and I dipped a cup of water for Timmy.

"Thank you," he said and drank it all. Then he put the cup down by the bucket and went back to the porch.

"He could have got the drink himself," Mama said wonderingly. "He can find his way around. And yet he waited, thirsty, until he could ask you for it."

"I guess he knows he has to mind Father, too!" I laughed shakily.

It was a two days' round trip to Tolliver's Wells and the first day stretched out endlessly. In the heat of noon, I slept, heavily and unrepfreshingly. I woke, drenched with sweat, my tongue swollen and dry from sleeping with my mouth open. I sat up, my head swimming and my heart thumping audibly in my ears. Merry and Mama were still sleeping on the big bed, a mosquito bar over them to keep the flies off. I wallowed my dry tongue and swallowed. Then I staggered up from my pallet. Where was Timothy?

Maybe he had gone to the Little House by himself. I looked out the window. He wasn't in sight and the door swung half open. I waited a minute but he didn't come out. Where was Timothy?

I stumbled out onto the front porch and looked around. No Timothy. I started for the barn, rounding the corner of the house, and there he was! He was sitting on the ground, half in the sun, half in the shade of the house. He had the cup in one hand and the fingers of the other hand were splashing in the water. His blind face was intent.

"Timmy!" I cried, and he looked up with a start, water slopping. "Daggone! You had me scared stiff! What are you doing with that water?" I slid to a seat beside him. His two wet fingers touched my wrist without fumbling for it. "We don't have enough water to play with it!"

He turned his face down toward the cup, then, turning, he poured the water carefully at the bottom of the last geranium left alive of all Mama had taken such tender care of.

Then, with my help, he got to his feet and because I could tell what he wanted and because he said, "Walk!" we walked. In all that sun and dust we walked. He led me. I only went along for the exercise and to steer him clear of cactus and holes in the way. Back and forth we went, back and forth. To the hill in front of the house, back to the house. To the hill again, a little farther along. Back to the yard, missing the house about ten feet. Finally, halfway through the weary monotony of the afternoon, I realized that Timmy was covering a wide area of land in ten-foot swaths, back and forth, farther and farther from the house.

By evening we were both exhausted and only one of Timmy's feet was even trying to touch the ground. The other one didn't bother to try to step. Finally Timmy said, "I'm thirsty. I want a drink, please." And we went back to the house.

Next morning I woke to see Timmy paddling in another cup of water, and all morning we covered the area on the other side of the house, back and forth, back and forth.

"What are you doing?" Mama had asked.

"I don't know," I said. "It's Timmy's idea." And Timmy said nothing.

When the shadows got short under the bushes, we went back to the porch and sat down on the steps, Merry gurgling at us from her porch-pen.

"I'm thirsty. I want a drink, please," said Timmy again, and I brought him his drink. "Thank you," he said, touching my wrist. "It's sure hot!"

"It sure is!" I answered, startled by his new phrase. He drank slowly and poured the last drop into his palm. He put the tin cup down on the porch by him and worked the fingers and thumb of his other hand in the dampness of his palm, his face intent and listening-like under his bandaged eyes.

Then his fingers were quiet and his face turned toward Merry. He got up and took the two steps to the porch-pen. He reached for Merry, his face turned to me. I moved closer and he touched my wrist. I lifted Merry out of the pen and put her on the porch. I lifted the pen, which was just a hollow square of wooden rails fastened together, and set it up on the porch, too.

Timmy sat down slowly on the spot where the pen had been. He scraped the dirt into a heap, then set it to one side and scraped again. Seeing that he was absorbed for a while, I took Merry in to be cleaned up for dinner and came back later to see what Timmy was doing. He was still scraping and had quite a hole by now, but the dirt was stacked too close so that it kept sliding back into the hole. I scraped it all away from the edge, then took his right arm and said, "Time to eat, Timmy. Come on."

He ate and went back to the hole he had started. Seeing that he meant to go on digging, I gave him a big old spoon Merry sometimes played with and a knife with a broken blade, to save his hands

All afternoon he dug with the tools and scooped the dirt out. And dug again. By evening he had enlarged the hole until he was sitting in it, shoulder deep.

Mama stood on the porch, sagging under the weight of Merry, who was astride her hip, and said, "He's ruining the front lawn." Then she laughed. "Front lawn! Ruining it!" And she laughed again, just this side of tears.

Later that evening, when what cooling-off ever came was coming over the ranch, we heard the jingle of harness and then the creak of the hayrack and the plop of horses' hooves in the dust.

Father was home! We ran to meet him at our gate, suddenly conscious of how out-of-step everything had been without him. I opened the gate and dragged the four strands wide to let the wagon through.

Father's face was dust-coated and the dust did not crease into smiles for us. His hugs were almost desperate. I looked into the back of the wagon, as he and Mama murmured together. Only half the barrels were filled.

"Didn't we have enough money?" I asked, wondering how people could insist on hard metal in exchange for life.

"They didn't have water enough," said Father. "Others were waiting, too. This is the last they can let us have."

We took care of the horses but left the water barrels on the wagon. That was as good a place as any and the shelter of the barn would keep it—well, not cool maybe, but below the boiling point.

It wasn't until we started back to the house that we thought of Timmy. We saw a head rising from the hole Timmy was digging, and Father drew back his foot to keep it from being covered with a handful of dirt.

"What's going on?" he asked, letting his tiredness and discouragement sharpen his voice.

"Timmy's digging," I said, stating the obvious, which was all I could do.

"Can't he find a better place than that?" And Father stomped into the house. I called Timmy and helped him up out of the hole. He was dirt-covered from head to heels and Father was almost through with his supper before I got Timmy cleaned up enough to come inside.

We sat around the table, not even reading, and talked. Timmy sat close to me, his fingers on my wrist.

"Maybe the ponds will fill a little while we're using up this water," said Mama, hopelessly.

Father was silent and I stared at the table, seeing the buckets of water Prince and Nig had sucked up so quickly that evening.

"We'd better be deciding where to go," said Father. "When the water's all gone—" His face shut down, bleak and still, and he opened the Bible at random, missing our marker by half the book. He looked down and read, " 'For in the wilderness shall waters break out, and streams in the desert.' " He clapped the book shut and sat, his elbows on each side of the book, his face buried in his two hands, this last rubbing of salt in the wound almost too much to bear.

I touched Timmy and we crept to bed.

I woke in the night, hearing a noise. My hand went up to the cot and I struggled upright. Timmy was gone. I scrambled to the door and looked out. Timmy was in the hole, digging. At least I guess he was. There was a scraping sound for a while, then a—a wad of dirt would sail slowly up out of the hole and fall far enough from the edge that it couldn't run down in again. I watched the dirt sail up twice more, then there was a clatter and three big rocks sailed up. They hovered a little above the mound of dirt, then thumped down—one of them on my bare foot.

I was hopping around, nursing my foot in my hands, when I looked up and saw Father standing stern and tall on the porch.

"What's going on?" He repeated his earlier question. The sound of digging below stopped. So did my breath for a moment.

"Timmy's digging," I said, as I had before.

"At night? What for?" Father asked.

"He can't see, night or light," I said, "but I don't know why he's digging."

"Get him out of there," said Father. "This is no time for nonsense."

I went to the edge of the hole. Timmy's face was a pale blur below. "He's too far down," I said. "I'll need a ladder."

"He got down there," said Father unreasonably, "let him get out!"

"Timmy!" I called down to him. "Father says come up!"

There was a hesitating scuffle, then Timmy came up! Straight up! As though something were lifting him! He came straight up out of the hole and hovered as the rocks had, then he moved through the air and landed on the porch so close to Father that he stumbled back a couple of steps.

"Father!" My voice shook with terror.

Father turned and went into the house. He lighted the lamp, the upflare of the flame before he put the chimney on showing the deep furrows down his cheeks. I prodded Timmy and we sat on the bench across the table from Father.

"Why is he digging?" Father asked again. "Since he responds to you, ask him."

I reached out, half afraid, and touched Timmy's wrist. "Why are you digging?" I asked. "Father wants to know."

Timmy's mouth moved and he seemed to be trying different words with his lips. Then he smiled, the first truly smile I'd ever seen on his face. " 'Shall waters break out and streams in the desert,' " he said happily.

"That's no answer!" Father exclaimed, stung by having those unfitting words flung back at him. "No more digging. Tell him so."

I felt Timmy's wrist throb protestingly and his face turned to me, troubled.

"Why no digging? What harm's he doing?" My voice sounded strange in my own ears and the pit of my stomach was ice. For the first time in my life I was standing up to Father! That didn't shake me as much as the fact that for the first time in my life I was seriously questioning his judgment.

"No digging because I said no digging!" said Father, anger whitening his face, his fists clenching on the table

"Father," I swallowed with difficulty, "I think Timmy's looking for water. He—he touched water before he started digging. He felt it. We—we went all over the place before he settled on where he's digging. Father, what if he's a—a dowser? What if he knows where water is? He's different—"

I was afraid to look at Father. I kept my eyes on my own hand where Timmy's fingers rested on my wrist.

"Maybe if we helped him dig—" I faltered and stopped, seeing the stones come up and hover and fall. "He has only Merry's spoon and an old knife."

"And he dug that deep!" thundered Father.

"Yes," I said. "All by himself."

"Nonsense!" Father's voice was flat. "There's no water anywhere around here. You saw me digging for water for the stock. We're not in Las Lomitas. There will be no more digging."

"Why not!" I was standing now, my own fists on the table as I leaned forward. I could feel my eyes blaze as Father's do sometimes. "What harm is he doing? What's wrong with his keeping busy while we sit around waiting to dry up and blow away? What's wrong with hoping?"

Father and I glared at each other until his eyes dropped. Then mine filled with tears and I dropped back on the bench and buried my face in my arms. I cried as if I were no older than Merry. My chest was heavy with sorrow for this first real anger I had ever felt toward Father, with the shouting and the glaring, and especially for his eyes falling before mine.

Then I felt his hand heavy on my shoulder. He had circled the table to me. "Go to bed now," he said quietly. "Tomorrow is another day."

"Oh, Father!" I turned and clung to his waist, my face tight against him, his hand on my head. Then I got up and took Timmy back to the cot and we went to bed again.

Next morning, as though it was our usual task, Father got out the shovels and rigged up a bucket on a rope and he and I and Timmy worked in the well. We called it a well now, instead of a hole, maybe to bolster our hopes.

By evening we had it down a good twelve feet, still not finding much except hard, packed-down river silt and an occasional clump of round river rocks. Our ladder was barely long enough to help us scramble up out and the edges of the hole were crumbly and sifted off under the weight of our knees.

I climbed out. Father set the bucket aside and eased his palms against his hips. Timmy was still in the well, kneeling and feeling the bottom.

"Timmy!" I called. "Come on up. Time to quit!" His face turned up to me but still he knelt there and I found myself gingerly groping for the first rung of the ladder below the rim of the well.

"Timmy wants me to look at something," I said up to Father's questioning face. I climbed down and knelt by Timmy. My hands followed his tracing hands and I looked up and said, "Father!" with such desolation in my voice that he edged over the rim and came down, too.

We traced it again and again. There was solid rock, no matter which way we brushed the dirt, no matter how far we poked into the sides of the well. We were down to bedrock. We were stopped.

We climbed soberly up out of the well. Father boosted me up over the rim and I braced myself and gave him a hand up. Timmy came up. There was no jarring of his feet on the ladder, but he came up. I didn't look at him.

The three of us stood there, ankle-deep in dust. Then Timmy put his hands out, one hand to Father's shoulder and one to mine. " 'Shall waters break out and streams in the desert,' " he said carefully and emphatically.

"Parrot!" said Father bitterly, turning away.

"If the water is *under* the stone!" I cried. "Father, we blasted out the mesquite stumps in the far pasture. Can't we blast the stone—"

Father's steps were long and swinging as he hurried to the barn. "I haven't ever done this except with stumps," he said. He sent Mama and Merry out behind the barn. He made Timmy and me stay away as he worked in the bottom of the well, then he scrambled up the ladder and I ran out to help pull it up out of the well and we all retreated behind the barn, too.

Timmy clung to my wrist and when the blast came, he cried out something I couldn't understand and wouldn't come with us back to the well. He crouched behind the barn, his face to his knees, his hands clasped over the top of his head.

We looked at the well. It was a dimple in the front yard. The sides had caved in. There was nothing to show for all our labor but the stacked-up dirt beside the dimple, our ladder, and a bucket with a rope tied to the bale. We watched as a clod broke loose at the top of the dimple and started a trickle of dirt as it rolled dustily down into the hole.

" 'And streams in the desert,' " said Father, turning away.

I picked up the bucket, dumped out a splinter of stone, and put the bucket carefully on the edge of the porch.

"Supper," said Mama quietly, sagging under Merry's weight.

I went and got Timmy. He came willingly enough. He paused by the dimple in the front yard, his hand on my wrist, then went with me into the shadowy cabin.

After supper I brought our evening books to the table, but Timmy put out seeking hands and gathered them to him. He put both hands, lapping over each other, across the top of the stack and leaned his chin on them, his face below the bandage thoughtful and still.

"I have words enough now," he said slowly. "I have been learning them as fast as I could. Maybe I will not have them always right, but I must talk now. You must not go away, because there *is* water."

Father closed his astonished mouth and said wearily, "So you have been making fools of us all this time!"

Timmy's fingers went to my wrist in the pause that followed Father's words. "I have not made fools of you," Timmy went on. "I could not speak to anyone but Barney without words, and I must touch him to tell and to understand. I had to wait to learn your words. It is a new language."

"Where are you from?" I asked eagerly, pulling the patient cork out of my curiosity. "How did you get out there in the pasture? What is in the—" Just in time I remembered that I was the only one who knew about the charred box.

"My *cahilla!*" cried Timmy—then he shook his head at me and addressed himself to Father. "I'm not sure how to tell you so you will believe. I don't know how far your knowledge—"

"Father's smarter than anyone in the whole Territory!" I cried.

"The Territory—" Timmy paused, measuring Territory. "I was thinking of your world—this world—"

"There are other planets—" I repeated Father's puzzling words.

"Then you *do* know other planets," said Timmy. "Do you—" he groped for a word. "Do you transport yourself and things in the sky?"

Father stirred. "Do we have flying machines?" he asked. "No, not yet. We have balloons—"

Timmy's fingers were on my wrist again. He sighed. "Then I must just tell and if you do not know, you must believe only because I tell. I tell only to make you know there is water and you must stay.

"My world is another planet. It *was* another planet. It is broken in space now, all to pieces, shaking and roaring and fire—and all gone." His blind face looked on desolation and his lips tightened. I felt hairs crisp along my neck. As long as he touched my wrist I could see! I couldn't tell you what all I saw because lots of it had no words I knew to put to it, but I saw!

"We had ships for going in Space," he said. I saw them, needlesharp and shining, pointing at the sky and the heavy red-lit clouds. "We went into space before our Home broke. Our Home! Our—Home." His voice broke and he leaned his cheek on the stack of books. Then he straightened again.

"We came to your world. We did not know of it before. We came far, far. At the last we came too fast. We are not Space travelers. The big ship that found your world got too hot. We had to leave it in our life-slips, each by himself. The life-slips got hot, too. I was burning! I lost control of my life-slip. I fell—" He put his hands to his bandages. "I think maybe I will never see this new world."

"Then there are others, like you, here on Earth," said Father slowly.

"Unless they all died in the landing," said Timmy. "There were many on the big ship."

"I saw little things shoot off the big thing!" I cried, excited. "I thought they were pieces breaking off, only they—they *went* instead of falling!"

"Praise to the Presence, the Name, and the Power!" said Timmy, his right hand sketching his sign in the air, then dropping to my wrist again.

"Maybe some still live. Maybe my family. Maybe Lytha—"

I stared, fascinated, as I saw Lytha, dark hair swinging, smiling back over her shoulder, her arms full of flowers whose centers glowed like little lights. Daggone, I thought, Daggone! She sure isn't his Merry!

"Your story is most interesting," said Father, "and it opens vistas we haven't begun to explore yet, but what bearing has all this on our water problem?"

"We can do things you seem not able to do," said Timmy. "You must always touch the ground to go, and lift things with tools or hands, and know only because you touch and see. We can know without touching and seeing. We can find people and metals and water—we can find almost anything that we know, if it is near us. I have not been trained to be a finder, but I have studied the feel of water and the—the—what it is made of—"

"The composition," Father supplied the word.

"The composition of water," said Timmy. "And Barney and I explored much of the farm. I found the water here by the house."

"We dug," said Father. "How far down is the water?"

"I am not trained," said Timmy humbly. "I only know it is there. It is water that you think of when you say 'Las Lomitas.' It is not a dipping place or—or a pool. It is going. It is pushing hard. It is cold." He shivered a little.

"It is probably three hundred feet down," said Father. "There has never been an artesian well this side of the Coronas."

"It is close enough for me to find," said Timmy. "Will you wait?"

"Until our water is gone," said Father. "And until we have decided where to go.

"Now it's time for bed." Father took the Bible from the stack of books. He thumbed back from our place to Psalms and read the "When I consider the heavens" one. As I listened, all at once the tight little world I knew, overtopped by the tight little Heaven I wondered about, suddenly split right down the middle and stretched and grew and filled with such a glory that I was scared and grabbed the edge of the table. If Timmy had come from another planet so far away that it wasn't even one we had a name for—! I knew that never again would my mind think it could measure the world—or my imagination, the extent of God's creation!

I was just dropping off the edge of waking after tumbling and tossing for what seemed like hours, when I heard Timmy.

"Barney," he whispered, not being able to reach my wrist. "My *cahilla*— You found my *cahilla?*"

"Your what?" I asked, sitting up in bed and meeting his groping hands. "Oh! That box thing. Yeah, I'll get it for you in the morning."

"Not tonight?" asked Timmy, wistfully. "It is all I have left of the Home. The only personal things we had room for—"

"I can't find it tonight," I said. "I buried it by a rock. I couldn't find it in the dark. Besides, Father'd hear us go, if we tried to leave now. Go to sleep. It must be near morning."

"Oh, yes," sighed Timmy, "oh, yes." And he lay back down. "Sleep well."

And I did, going out like a lamp blown out, and dreamed wild, exciting dreams about riding astride ships that went sailless across waterless oceans of nothingness and burned with white-hot fury that woke me up to full morning light and Merry bouncing happily on my stomach.

After breakfast, Mama carefully oiled Timmy's scabs again. "I'm almost out of bandages," she said.

"If you don't mind having to see," said Timmy, "don't bandage me again. Maybe the light will come through."

We went out and looked at the dimple by the porch. It had subsided farther and was a bowl-shaped place now, maybe waist-deep to me.

"Think it'll do any good to dig it out again?" I asked Father.

"I doubt it," he answered heavily. "Apparently I don't know how to set a charge to break the bedrock. How do we know we could break it anyway? It could be a mile thick right here." It seemed to me that Father was talking to me more like to a man than to a boy. Maybe I wasn't a boy any more!

"The water is there," said Timmy. "If only I could '*platt*'—" His hand groped in the sun and it streamed through his fingers for a minute like sun through a knothole in a dusty room. I absently picked up the piece of stone I had dumped from the bucket last evening. I fingered it and said, "Ouch!" I had jabbed myself on its sharp point. Sharp point!

"Look," I said, holding it out to Father. "This is broken! All the other rocks we found were round river rocks. Our blasting broke *something!*"

"Yes." Father took the splinter from me. "But where's the water?"

Timmy and I left Father looking at the well and went out to the foot of the field where the fire had been. I located the rock where I had buried the box. It was only a couple of inches down—barely covered. I scratched it out for him. "Wait," I said, "it's all black. Let me wipe it off first." I rubbed it in a sand patch and the black all rubbed off except in the deep lines of the design that covered all sides of it. I put it in his eager hands.

He flipped it around until it fitted his two hands with his thumbs touching in front. Then I guess he must have thought at it, because he didn't do anything else but all at once it opened, cleanly, from his thumbs up.

He sat there on a rock in the sun and felt the things that were in the box. I couldn't tell you what any of them were except what looked like a piece of ribbon, and a withered flower. He finally closed the box. He slid to his knees beside the rock and hid his face on his arms. He sat there a long time. When he finally lifted his face, it was dry, but his sleeves were wet. I've seen Mama's sleeves like that after she has looked at things in the little black trunk of hers.

"Will you put it back in the ground?" he asked. "There is no place for it in the house. It will be safe here."

So I buried the box again and we went back to the house.

Father had dug a little, but he said, "It's no use. The blast loosened the ground all around and it won't even hold the shape of a well any more."

We talked off and on all day about where to go from here, moneyless and perilously short of provisions. Mama wanted so much to go back to our old home that she couldn't talk about it, but Father wanted to go on, pushing West again. *I* wanted to stay where we were—with plenty of water. I wanted to see that tide of Time sweep one century away and start another across Desolation Valley! There would be a sight for you!

We began to pack that afternoon because the barrels were emptying fast and the pools were damp, curling cakes of mud in the hot sun. All we could take was what we could load on the hayrack. Father had traded the wagon we came West in for farm machinery and a set of washtubs. We'd have to leave the machinery either to rust there or for us to come back for.

Mama took Merry that evening and climbed the hill to the little grave under the scrub oak. She sat there a long time with her back to the sun, her wistful face in the shadow. She came back in silence, Merry heavily sleepy in her arms.

After we had gone to bed, Timmy groped for my wrist. "You do have a satellite to your earth, don't you?" he asked. His question was without words.

"A satellite?" Someone turned restlessly on the big bed when I hissed my question.

"Yes," he answered. "A smaller world that goes around and is bright at night."

"Oh," I breathed. "You mean the moon. Yes, we have a moon but it's not very bright now. There was only a sliver showing just after sunset." I felt Timmy sag. "Why?"

"We can do large things with sunlight and moonlight together," came his answer. "I hoped that at sunrise tomorrow—"

"At sunrise tomorrow, we'll be finishing our packing," I said. "Go to sleep."

"Then I must do without," he went on, not hearing me. "Barney, if I am Called, will you keep my *cahilla* until someone asks for it? If they ask, it is my People. Then they will know I am gone."

"Called?" I asked. "What do you mean?"

"As the baby was," he said softly. "Called back into the Presence from which we came. If I must lift with my own strength alone, I may not have enough, so will you keep my *cahilla?*"

"Yes," I promised, not knowing what he was talking about. "I'll keep it."

"Good. Sleep well," he said, and again waking went out of me like a lamp blown out.

All night long I dreamed of storms and earthquakes and floods and tornadoes all going past me—fast! Then I was lying half awake, afraid to open my eyes for fear some of my dreaming might be true. And suddenly, it was!

I clutched my pallet as the floor humped, snapping and groaning, and flopped flat again. I heard our breakfast pots and pans banging on the shelf and then falling with a clatter. Mama called, her voice heavy with sleep and fear, "James! James!"

I reached for Timmy, but the floor humped again and dust rolled in through the pale squares of the windows and I coughed as I came to my knees. There was a crash of something heavy falling on the roof and rolling off. And a sharp hissing sound. Timmy wasn't in bed. Father was trying to find his shoes. The hissing noise got louder and louder until it was a burbling roar. Then there was a rumble and something banged the front of the house so hard I heard the porch splinter. Then there was a lot of silence.

I crept on all fours across the floor. Where was Timmy? I could see the front door hanging at a crazy angle on one hinge. I crept toward it.

My hands splashed! I paused, confused, and started on again. I was crawling in water! "Father!" My voice was a croak from the dust and shock. "Father! It's water!"

And Father was suddenly there, lifting me to my feet. We stumbled together to the front door. There was a huge slab of rock poking a hole in the siding of the house, crushing the broken porch under its weight. We edged around it, ankle-deep in water, and saw in the gray light of early dawn our whole front yard awash from hill to porch. Where the well had been was a moving hump of water that worked away busily, becoming larger and larger as we watched.

"Water!" said Father. "The water has broken through!"

"Where's Timmy?" I said. *"Where's Timmy?"* I yelled and started to splash out into the yard.

"Watch out!" warned Father. "It's dangerous! All this rock came out of there!" We skirted the front yard searching the surface of the rising water, thinking every shadow might be Timmy.

We found him on the far side of the house, floating quietly, face up in a rising pool of water, his face a bleeding mass of mud and raw flesh.

I reached him first, floundering through the water to him. I lifted his shoulders and tried to see in the dawn light if he was still breathing. Father reached us and we lifted Timmy to dry land.

"He's alive!" said Father. "His face—it's just the scabs scraped off."

"Help me get him in the house," I said, beginning to lift him.

"Better be the barn," said Father. "The water's still rising." It had crept up to us already and seeped under Timmy again. We carried him to the barn and I stayed with him while Father went back for Merry and Mama.

It was lucky that most of our things had been packed on the hayrack the night before. After Mama, a shawl thrown over her nightgown and all our day clothes grabbed up in her arms, came wading out with Father, who was carrying Merry and our lamp, I gave Timmy into her care and went back with Father again and again to finish emptying the cabin of our possessions.

Already the huge rock had gone on down through the porch and disappeared into the growing pond of water in the front yard. The house was dipping to the weight of our steps as though it might float off the minute we left. Father got a rope from the wagon and tied it through the broken corner of the house and tethered it to the barn. "No use losing the lumber if we don't have to," he said.

By the time the sun was fully up, the house was floating off its foundation rocks. There was a pond filling all the house yard, back and front, extending along the hill, up to the dipping place, and turning into a narrow stream going the other way, following the hill for a while, then dividing our dying orchard and flowing down toward the dry river bed. Father and I pulled the house slowly over toward the barn until it grated solid ground again.

Mama had cleaned Timmy up. He didn't seem to be hurt except for his face and shoulder being peeled raw. She put olive oil on him again and used one of Merry's petticoats to bandage his face. He lay deeply unconscious all of that day while we watched the miracle of water growing in a dry land. The pond finally didn't grow any wider, but the stream widened and deepened, taking three of our dead trees down to the river. The water was clearing now and was deep enough over the spring that it didn't bubble any more that we could see. There was only a shivering of the surface so that circles ran out to the edge of the pond, one after another.

Father went down with a bucket and brought it back brimming over. We drank the cold, cold water and Mama made a pack to put on Timmy's head.

Timmy stirred but he didn't waken. It wasn't until evening, when we were settling down to a scratch-meal in the barn, that we began to realize what had happened.

"We have water!" Father cried suddenly. "Streams in the desert!"

"It's an artesian well, isn't it!" I asked. "Like at Las Lomitas? It'll go on flowing from here on out, won't it?"

"That remains to be seen," Father said. "But it looks like a good one. Tomorrow I must ride to Tolliver's Wells and tell them we have water. They must be almost out by now!"

"Then we don't have to move?" I asked.

"Not as long as we have water," said Father. "I wonder if we have growing time enough to put in a kitchen garden—"

I turned quickly. Timmy was moving. His hands were on the bandage, exploring it cautiously.

"Timmy." I reached for his wrist. "It's all right, Timmy. You just got peeled raw. We had to bandage you again."

"The—the water—" His voice was barely audible.

"It's all over the place!" I said. "It's floated the house off the foundations and you should see the pond! And the stream! And it's cold!"

"I'm thirsty," he said. "I want a drink, please."

He drained the cup of cold water and his lips turned upward in a ghost of a smile. "Shall waters break out!"

"Plenty of water," I laughed. Then I sobered. "What were you doing out in it, anyway?"

Mama and Father were sitting on the floor beside us now.

"I had to lift the dirt out," he said, touching my wrist. "All night I lifted. It was hard to hold back the loose dirt so it wouldn't slide back into the hole. I sat on the porch and lifted the dirt until the rock was there." He sighed and was silent for a minute. "I was not sure I had strength enough. The rock was cracked and I could feel the water pushing, hard, hard, under. I had to break the rock enough to let the water start through. It wouldn't break! I called on the Power again and tried and tried. Finally a piece came loose and flew up. The force of the water—it was like—like—blasting. I had no strength left. I went unconscious."

"You dug all that out alone!" Father took one of Timmy's hands and looked at the smooth palm.

"We do not always have to touch to lift and break," said Timmy. "But to do it for long and heavy takes much strength." His head rolled weakly.

"Thank you, Timothy," said Father. "Thank you for the well."

So that's why we didn't move. That's why Promise Pond is here to keep the ranch green. That's why this isn't Fool's Acres any more but Full Acres. That's why *Cahilla* Creek puzzles people who try to make it Spanish. Even Father doesn't know why Timmy and I named the stream *Cahilla*. The pond had almost swallowed up the little box before we remembered it.

That's why the main road across Desolation Valley goes through our ranch now for the sweetest, coldest water in the Territory. That's why our big new house is built among the young black walnut and weeping willow trees that surround the pond. That's why it has geraniums windowsill high along one wall. That's why our orchard has begun to bear enough to start being a cash crop.

And that's why, too, that one day a wagon coming from the far side of Desolation Valley made camp on the camping grounds below the pond.

We went down to see the people after supper to exchange news. Timmy's eyes were open now, but only light came into them, not enough to see by.

The lady of the wagon tried not to look at the deep scars on the side of Timmy's face as her man and we men talked together. She listened a little too openly to Timmy's part of the conversation and said softly to Mama, her whisper spraying juicily, "He your boy?"

"Yes, our boy," said Mama, "but not born to us."

"Oh," said the woman. "I thought he talked kinda foreign." Her voice was critical. "Seems like we're gettin' overrun with foreigners. Like that sassy girl in Margin."

"Oh?" Mama fished Merry out from under the wagon by her dress tail.

"Yes," said the woman. "She talks foreign too, though they say not as much as she used to. Oh, them foreigners are smart enough! Her aunt says she was sick and had to learn to talk all over again, that's why she sounds like that." The woman leaned confidingly toward Mama, lowering her voice. "But I heard in a roundabout way that there's something queer about that girl. I don't think she's really their niece. I think she came from somewhere else. I think she's really a foreigner!"

"Oh?" said Mama, quite unimpressed and a little bored.

"They say she does funny things and Heaven knows her name's funny enough. I *ask* you! Doesn't the way these foreigners push themselves in—"

"Where did your folks come from?" asked Mama, vexed by the voice the lady used for "foreigner."

The lady reddened. "*I'm* native born!" she said, tossing her head. "Just because my parents— It isn't as though England was—" She pinched her lips together. "Abigail Johnson for a name is a far cry from Marnie Lytha Something-or-other!"

"Lytha!" I heard Timmy's cry without words. *Lytha?* He stumbled toward the woman, for once his feet unsure. She put out a hasty hand to fend him off and her face drew up with distaste.

"Watch out!" she cried sharply. "Watch where you're going!"

"He's blind," Mama said softly.

"Oh," the woman reddened again. "Oh, well—"

"Did you say you knew a girl named Lytha?" asked Timmy faintly.

"Well, I never did have much to do with her," said the woman, unsure of herself. "I saw her a time or two—"

Timmy's fingers went out to touch her wrist and she jerked back as though burned. "I'm sorry," said Timmy. "Where are you coming from?"

"Margin," said the woman. "We been there a couple of months shoeing the horses and blacksmithing some."

"Margin," said Timmy, his hands shaking a little as he turned away. "Thanks."

"Well, you're welcome, I guess," snapped the woman. She turned back to Mama, who was looking after us, puzzled. "Now all the new dresses have—"

"I couldn't see," whispered Timmy to me as we moved off through the green grass and willows to the orchard. "She wouldn't let me touch her. How far is Margin?"

"Two days across Desolation Valley," I said, bubbling with excitement. "It's a mining town in the hills over there. Their main road comes from the other side."

"Two days!" Timmy stopped and clung to a small tree. "Only two days away all this time!"

"It might not be your Lytha," I warned. "It could be one of us. I've heard some of the wildest names! Pioneering seems to addle people's naming sense."

"I'll call," said Timmy, his face rapt. "I'll call and when she answers—!"

"If she hears you," I said, knowing his calling wouldn't be aloud and would take little notice of the distance to Margin. "Maybe she thinks everyone is dead like you did. Maybe she won't think of listening."

"She will think often of the Home," said Timmy firmly, "and when she does, she will hear me. I will start now." And he threaded his way expertly through the walnuts and willows by the pond.

I looked after him and sighed. I wanted him happy and if it was his Lytha, I wanted them together again. But, if he called and called again and got no answer—

I slid to a seat on a rock by the pond, thinking again of the little lake we were planning where we would have fish and maybe a boat— I dabbled my hand in the cold water and thought, this was dust before Timmy came. He was stubborn enough to make the stream break through.

"If Timmy calls," I told a little bird balancing suddenly on a twig, bobbing over the water, "*someone* will answer!"

Interlude: Mark & Meris 4

Meris leaned back with a sigh. "Well!" she said, "thank goodness! I never would have rested easy again if I hadn't found out! But after Timmy found The People, surely his eyes—"

"Never satisfied," said Mark. "The more you hear the more you want to hear—"

"I've never Assembled much beyond that," said Bethie. Then she held up a cautioning hand. "Wait—

"Oh," she said, listening. "Oh, dear! Of course." She stood up, her face a pale blur in the darkness of the patio. "That was Debbie. She's on her way here. She says Dr. Curtis needs me back at the Group. Valancy sent her because she's the one who came back from the New Home and 'Peopled all over the place,' as she says. I have to leave immediately. There isn't time for a car. Luckily it's dark enough now. Debbie has her part all Assembled already so she can—"

"I wish you didn't have to leave so soon," said Meris, following her inside and helping her scramble her few belongings into her small case.

"There is so much— There's always so much— You'll enjoy Debbie's story." Bethie was drifting steplessly out the door. "And there are others—" She was a quickening shadow rising above the patio and her whispered "Good-by" came softly down through the overarching tree branches.

"Hi!" The laughing voice startled them around from their abstraction. "Unless I've lost my interpretive ability, that's an awfully wet, hungry cry coming from in there!"

"Oh, 'Licia, honey!" Meris fled indoors, crooning abject apologies as she went.

"Well, hi to you, then." The woman stepped out of the shadows and offered a hand to Mark. "I'm Debbie. Sorry to snatch Bethie away, but Dr. Curtis had to have her stat. She's our best Sensitive and he has a puzzlesome emergency to diagnose. She's his court of last resort!"

"Dr. Curtis?" Mark returned her warm firm clasp. "That must be the doctor Johannan was trying to find to lead him to the Group."

"Is so," said Debbie. "Our Inside-Outsider. He's a fixture with us now. Not that he stays with the Group, but he functions as One of Us."

"Come on in," said Mark, holding the kitchen door open. "Come in and have some coffee."

"Thank you kindly," laughed Debbie. "It's right sightly of you to ask a stranger to 'light and set a spell.' No." She smiled at Mark's questioning eyes. "That's not the way they talk on the New Home. It's only a slight lingual hangover from the first days of my Return. That's the Assembly Valancy sent me to tell you."

She sat at the kitchen table, and Mark gathered up his battered, discolored coffee mug and Meris's handleless one and a brightly company-neat cup for Debbie. There wasn't much left of the coffee, but by squeezing hard enough, he achieved three rather scanty portions.

After the flurry of building more coffee and Meris's return with a solemnly blinking 'Licia to be exclaimed over and inspected and loved and fed and adored and bedded again, they decided to postpone Debbie's installment until after their own supper.

"This Assembling business is getting to be as much an addiction as watching TV," said Mark, mending the fire in the fireplace.

"Well, there's addiction and addiction," said Meris as Mark returned to the couch to sit on the other side of Debbie. "I prefer this one. This is for real—hard as it is to believe."

"For real," mused Debbie, clasping their hands. "I could hardly believe it was for real then, either. Here is how I felt—"

Return

I was afraid. When the swelling bulk of the Earth blotted our ports, I was afraid for the first time. Fear was a sudden throb in my throat and, almost as an echo, a sudden throb from Child Within reminded me why it was that Earth *was* swelling in our ports after such a final good-by. Drawn by my mood, Thann joined me as the slow turning of our craft slid the Earth out of sight.

"Apprehensive?" he asked, his arm firm across my shoulders.

"A little." I leaned against him. "This business of trying to go back again is a little disquieting. You can't just slip back into the old mold. Either it's changed or you've changed—or both. I realize that."

"Well, the best we can do is give it the old college try," he said. "And all for Child Within. I hope he appreciates it."

"Or she." I glanced down at my unfamiliar proportions. "As the case may be. But you do understand, don't you?" Need for reassurance lifted my voice a little. "Thann, we just had to come back. I just couldn't bear the thought of Child Within being born in that strange—tidy—" My voice trailed off and I leaned more heavily, sniffing.

"Listen, Debbie-my-dear!" Thann shook me gently and hugged me roughly. "I know, I know! While I don't share your aching necessity for Earth, I agreed, didn't I? Didn't I sweat blood in that dern Motiver school, learning to manipulate this craft? Aren't we almost there?"

"Almost there! Oh, Thann! Oh, Thann!" Our craft had completed another of its small revolutions, and Earth marched determinedly across the port again. I pressed myself against the pane, wanting to reach—to gather in the featureless mists, the blurred beauties of the world, and hold them so close—so close that even Child Within would move to their wonder.

I'm a poor hand at telling time. I couldn't tell you even to within a year how long ago it was that Shua lifted the Ship from the flat at Cougar

Canyon and started the trip from Earth to The Home. I remembered how excited I was. Even my ponytail had trembled as the great adventure began. Thann swears he was standing so close to me at Takeoff that the ponytail tickled his nose. But I don't remember him. I don't even remember seeing him at all during the long trip when the excitement of being evacuated from Earth dulled to the routine of travel and later became resurrected as anxiety about what The Home would be like.

I don't remember him at all until that desolate day on The Home when I stood at the end of the so-precise little lane that wound so consciously lovely from the efficient highway. I was counting, through the blur of my tears, the precisely twenty-six trees interspersed at suitable intervals by seven clumps of underbrush. He just happened to be passing at the moment and I looked up at him and choked, "Not even a weed! Not one!"

Astonished, he folded his legs and hovered a little above eye level. "What good's a weed?"

"At least it shows individuality!" I shut my eyes, not caring that by so doing the poised tears consolidated and fell. "I'm so sick of perfection!"

"Perfection?" He lifted a little higher above me, his eyes on some far sight. "I certainly wouldn't call The Home perfect yet. From here I can see the North Reach. We've only begun to nibble at that. The preliminary soil crew is just starting analysis." He dropped down beside me. "We can't waste time and space on weeds. It'll take long enough to make the whole of The Home habitable without using energy on nonessentials."

"They'll find out!" I stubbornly proclaimed. "Someday they'll find out that weeds *are* essentials. Man wasn't made for such—such *neatness*. He has to have unimportant clutter to relax in!"

"Why haven't you presented these fundamental doctrines to the Old Ones?" He laughed at me.

"Have I not!" I retorted. "Well, maybe not to the Old Ones, but I've already expressed myself, and furthermore, Mr.— Oh, I'm sorry, I'm Debbie—"

"I'm Thannel," he grinned.

"—Thannel, I'll have you know other wiser heads than mine have come to the same conclusion. Maybe not in my words, but they mean the same thing. This artificiality—this—this— The People aren't *meant* to live divorced from the—the—" I spread my hands. "Soil, I guess you could say. They lose something when everything gets—gets paved."

"Oh, I think we'll manage." He smiled. "Memory can sustain."

"Memory? Oh, Thann, remember the tangle of blackberry vines in back of Kroginold's house? How we used to burrow under the scratchy, cool, green twilight under those vines and hunt for berries—cool ones from the shadows, and warm ones from the sun, and always at least one thorn in the thumb as payment for trespassing. Mmmm—" Eyes closed, I lost myself in the memory.

Then my eyes flipped open. "Or are you from the other Home? Maybe you've never even seen Earth."

"Yes, I have," he said, suddenly sober. "I'm from Bendo. I haven't many happy memories of Earth. Until your Group found us, we had a pretty thin time of it."

"Oh, I'm sorry," I said. "Bendo was our God Bless for a long time when I was little."

"Thank you." He straightened briskly and grinned. "How about a race to the twenty-third despised tree, just to work off a little steam!"

And the two of us lifted and streaked away, a yard above the careful gravel of the lane, but I got the giggles so badly I that I blundered into the top of the twenty-first tree and had to be extricated gingerly from its limbs. Together we guiltily buried at its foot the precious tiny branch I had broken off in my blundering, and then, with muffled laughter and guilty back-glances, we went our separate ways.

That night I lay and waited for the pale blue moon of The Home to vault into the sky, and thought about Earth and the Other Home.

The other Home was first, of course—the beautiful prototype of this Home. But *it* had weeds! And all the tangled splendor of wooded hillsides and all the soaring upreach of naked peaks and the sweet uncaring, uncountable profusion of life, the same as Earth. But The Home died—blasted out of the heavens by a cosmic Something that shattered it and scattered the People like birds from a falling tree. Part of them found this Home— or the bare bones of it—and started to remake it into The Home. Others found refuge on Earth. We had it rough for a long time because we were separated from each other. Besides, we were Different, with a capital D, and some of us didn't survive the adjustment period. Slowly, though, we were Gathered In until there were two main Groups—Cougar Canyon and Bendo. Bendo lived in a hell of concealment and fear long after Cougar Canyon had managed to adjust to an Outsider's world.

Then that day—even now my breath caught at the wonder of that day when the huge ship from the New Home drifted down out of the skies and came to rest on the flat beyond the schoolhouse!

And everyone had to choose. Stay or go. My family chose to go. More stayed. But the Oldest, Cougar Canyon's leader, blind, crippled, dying from what the Crossing had done to him, he went. But you should see him now! You should see him *see!* And Obla came too. Sometimes I went to her house just to touch her hands. She had none, you know, on

Earth. Nor legs nor eyes, and hardly a face. An explosion had stripped her of all of them. But now, because of transgraph and regeneration, she is becoming whole again—except perhaps her heart—but that's another story.

Once the wonder of the trip and the excitement of living without concealment, without having to watch every movement so's not to shock Outsiders, had died a little, I got homesicker and homesicker. At first I fought it as a silly thing, a product of letdown, or idleness. But a dozen new interests, frenzied activities that consumed every waking moment, did nothing to assuage the aching need in me. I always thought homesickness was a childish, transitory thing. Well, most of it, but occasionally there is a person who actually sickens of it and does not recover, short of Return. And I guess I was one of those. It was as though I were breathing with one lung or trying to see with one eye. Sometimes the growing pain became an anguish so physical that I'd crouch in misery, hugging my hurt to me, trying to contain it between my knees and my chest—trying to ease it. Sometimes I could manage a tear or two that relieved a little—such as that day in the lane with Thann.

"Thann!" I turned from the port. "Isn't it about time—"

"One up on you, Debbie-my-dear," Thann called from the Motive room. "I'm just settling into the old groove. Got to get us slowed down before we scorch our little bottoms and maybe even singe Child Within."

"Don't joke about it!" I said. "Remember, the first time, the atmosphere gave us too warm a welcome to Earth. Ask the Oldest."

"The Power be with us," came Thann's quick answering thought.

"And the Name and the Presence," I echoed, bowing my head as my fingers moved to the Sign and then clasped above Child Within. I moved over to the couch and lay down, feeling the almost imperceptible slowing of our little craft.

Thann and I started two-ing not long after we met and, at *flahmen* Gathering time, we Bespoke one another and, just before Festival time, we were married.

Perhaps all this time I was hoping that starting a home of my own would erase my longing for Earth, and perhaps Thann hoped the same thing. The Home offered him almost all he wanted and he had a job he loved. He felt the pioneering thrill of making a new world and was contented. But my need didn't evaporate. Instead, it intensified. I talked it over with the Sorter for our Group (a Sorter cares for our emotional and mental problems) because I was beginning to hate—oh, not hate! That's such a poisonous thing to have festering in your mind. But my perspective was getting so twisted that I was making both myself and Thann unhappy. She Sorted me deftly and thoroughly—and I went home to Thann and he started training to develop his latent Motive ability. We both knew we could well lose our lives trying to return to Earth, but we had to try. Anyway, I had to try, especially after I found out about Child Within. I told Thann and his face lighted up as I knew it would, but—

"This ought to make a bond between you and The Home," he said. "Now you'll find unsuspected virtues in this land you've been spurning."

I felt my heart grow cold. "Oh, no, Thann!" I said. "Now more than ever we must go. Our child *can't* be born here. He must be of Earth. And I want to be able to enjoy this Child Within—"

"This is quite a Child Without," said Thann, tempering the annoyance in his voice by touching my cheek softly, "crying for a lollipop, Earth flavored. Ah, well!" He gathered me into his arms. "Hippity-hop to the candy shop!"

A high thin whistle signaled the first brush of Earth's atmosphere against our craft—as though Earth were reaching up to scrape tenuous incandescent fingers against our underside. I cleared my mind and concentrated on the effort ahead. I'm no Motiver, but Thann might need my strength before we landed.

Before we landed! Setting down on the flat again, under Old Baldy! And seeing them all again! Valancy and Karen and the Francher Kid. Oh, the song the Kid would be singing would be nothing to the song my heart would be singing! *Home! Child Within! Home again!* I pressed my hands against the swell of Child Within. *Pay attention,* I admonished. *Be ready for your first consciousness of Earth.* "I won't look," I told myself. "Until we touch down on the flat. I'll keep my eyes shut!" And I did.

So when the first splashing crash came, I couldn't believe it. My eyes opened to the sudden inrush of water and I was gasping and groping in complete bewilderment trying to find air. "Thann! Thann!" I was paddling awkwardly, trying to keep my head above water. What had happened? How could we have so missed the Canyon—even as inexperienced a Motiver as Thann was? Water? Water to *drown* in, anywhere near the Canyon?

There was a gulp and the last bubble of air belched out of our turning craft. I was belched out through a jagged hole along with the air. *Thann! Thann!* I abandoned vocal calling and spread my cry clear across the band of subspeech. No reply—no reply! I bobbed on the surface of the water, gasping. *Oh, Child, stay Within. Be Careful. Be Careful! It isn't time yet. It isn't time!*

I shook my dripping hair out of my eyes and felt a nudge against my knees. Down I went into darkness, groping, groping—and found him!

Inert, unresponsive, a dead weight in my arms. The breathless agony of struggle ended in the slippery mud of a rocky shore. I dragged him up far enough that his head was out of the water, listened breathlessly for a heart-beat, then, mouth to mouth, I breathed life back into him and lay gasping beside him in the mud, one hand feeling the struggle as his lungs labored to get back into rhythm. The other hand was soothing Child Within. *Not now, not now! Wait—wait!*

When my own breathing steadied, I tore strips off my tattered travel suit and bound up his head, staunching the blood that persistently threaded down from the gash above his left ear. Endlessly, endlessly, I lay there listening to his heart—to my heart—too weak to move him, too weak to move myself. Then the rhythm of his breathing changed and I felt his uncertain thoughts, questioning, asking. My thoughts answered his until he knew all I knew about what had happened. He laughed a ghost of a laugh.

"Is this untidy enough for you?" And I broke down and cried.

We lay there in mud and misery, gathering our strength. I started once to a slithering splash across the water from us and felt a lapping of water over my feet. I pulled myself up on one elbow and peered across at the barren hillside. A huge chunk of it had broken off and slithered down into the water. The scar was raw and ragged in the late evening sunshine.

"Where did it come from?" I asked, wonderingly. "All this water! And there *is* Baldy, with his feet all awash. What happened?"

"The rain is raining," said Thann, his voice choked with laughter, his head rolling on the sharp shale of the bank. "The rain is raining—and don't go near the water!" His nonsense ended with a small moan that tore my heart.

"Thann! Thann! Let's get out of this mess. Come on. Can you lift? Help me—"

He lifted his head and let it fall back with a *thunk* against the rocks. His utter stillness panicked me. I sobbed as I reached into my memory for the inanimate lift. It seemed a lifetime before I finally got him up out of the mud and hovered him hand high above the bank. Cautiously I pushed him along, carefully guiding him between the bushes and trees until I found a flat place that crunched with fallen oak leaves. I *"platted"* him softly to the ground and for a long time I lay there by him, my hand on his sleeve, not even able to think coherently about what had happened.

The sun was gone when I shivered and roused myself. I was cold and Thann was shaken at intervals by an icy shuddering. I scrambled around in the fading light and gathered wood together and laid a fire. I knelt by the neat stack and gathered myself together for the necessary

concentration. Finally, after sweat had gathered on my forehead and trick-
led into my eyes, I managed to produce a tiny spark that sputtered and
hesitated and then took a shining bite out of a dry leaf. I rubbed my hands
above the tiny flame and waited for it to grow. Then I lifted Thann's head
to my lap and started the warmth circulating about us.

When our shivering stopped, I suddenly caught my breath and grimaced wryly. How quickly we forget! I was getting as bad as an Outsider!
And I clicked my personal shield on, extending it to include Thann. In
the ensuing warmth, I looked down at Thann, touching his mud-stained
cheek softly, letting my love flow to him like a river of strength. I heard
his breathing change and he stirred under my hands.

"Are we Home?" he asked.

"We're on Earth," I said.

"We left Earth years ago," he chided. "Why do I hurt so much?"

"We came back." I kept my voice steady with an effort. "Because of
me—and Child Within."

"Child Within—" His voice strengthened. "Hippity-hop to the
candy shop," he remembered. "What happened?"

"The Canyon isn't here any more," I said, raising his shoulders carefully into my arms. "We crashed into water. Everything's gone. We lost
everything." My heart squeezed for the tiny gowns Child Within would
never wear.

"Where are our People?" he asked.

"I don't know," I said. "I don't know."

"When you find them, you'll be all right," he said drowsily.

"*We'll* be all right," I said sharply, my arms tightening around him.
"In the morning, we'll find them and Bethie will find out what's wrong
with you and we'll mend you."

He sat up slowly, haggard and dirty in the upflare of firelight, his
hand going to his bandaged head. "I'm broken," he said. "A lot of places.
Bones have gone where bones should never go. I will be Called."

"Don't say it!" I gathered him desperately into my arms. "Don't say
it, Thann! We'll find the People!" He crumpled down against me, his cheek
pressed to the curve of Child Within.

I screamed then, partly because my heart was being torn shred by
shred into an aching mass—partly because my neglected little fire was
happily crackling away from me, munching the dry leaves, sampling the
brush, roaring softly into the lower branches of the scrub oak. I had set
the hillside afire! And the old terror was upon me, the remembered terror
of a manzanita slope blazing on Baldy those many forgotten years ago.

I cradled Thann to me. So far the fire was moving away from us,
but soon, soon—

"No! No!" I cried. "Let's go home. Thann! I'm sorry! I'm sorry! Let's go home! I didn't mean to bring you to death! I hate this world! I hate it! Thann, Thann!"

I've tried to forget it. It comes back sometimes. Sometimes again I'm so shaken that I can't even protect myself any more and I'm gulping smoke and screaming over Thann. Other times I hear again the rough, disgusted words, "Gol-dinged tenderfoots! Setting fire to the whole gol-dinged mountain. There's a law!"

Those were the first words I ever heard from Seth. My first sight of him was of a looming giant, twisted by flaring flames and drifting smoke and my own blurring tears.

It was another day before I thought again. I woke to find myself on a camp cot, a rough khaki blanket itching my chin. My bare arms were clean but scratched. Child Within was rounding the blanket smoothly. I closed my eyes and lay lapped in peace for a moment. Then my eyes flew open and I called, "Thann! Thann!" and struggled with the blanket.

"Take it easy! Take it easy!" Strong hands pushed me back against the thin musty pillow. "You're stark, jay-nekkid under that blanket. You can't go tearing around that way." And those were the first words I heard from Glory.

She brought me a faded, crumpled cotton robe and helped me into it. "Them outlandish duds you had on'll take a fair-sized swatch of fixing 'fore they're fit t' wear." Her hands were clumsy but careful. She chuckled. "Not sure there's room for both of yens in this here wrapper."

I knelt by the cot in the other room. There were only three rooms in the house. Thann lay, thin and unmoving as paper, under the lumpy comforter.

"He wants awful bad to go home." Glory's voice tried to moderate to a sickroom tone. "He won't make it," she said bluntly.

"Yes, he will. Yes, he will! All we have to do is find The People—"

"Which people?" asked Glory.

"*The* People!" I cried. "The People who live in the Canyon."

'The Canyon? You mean Cougar Canyon? Been no people there for three-four years. Ever since the dam got finished and the lake started rising."

"Where—where did they go?" I whimpered, my hands tightening on the edge of the cot.

"Dunno." Glory snapped a match head with her thumbnail and lighted a makin's cigarette.

"But if we don't find them, Thann will die!"

"He will anyway less'n them folks is magic," said Glory.

"They are!" I cried. "They're magic!"

"Oh?" said Glory, squinting her eyes against the eddy of smoke. "Oh?"

Thann's head moved and his eyes opened. I bent my head to catch any whisper from him, but his voice came loud and clear.

"All we have to do is fix the craft and we can go back Home."

"Yes, Thann." I hid my eyes against my crossed wrists on the cot. "We'll leave right away. Child Within will wait till we get Home." I felt Child Within move to the sound of my words.

"He shouldn't oughta talk," said Glory. "He's all smashed inside. He'll be bleeding again in a minute."

"Shut up!" I spun on my knees and flared at her. "You don't know anything about it! You're nothing but a stupid Outsider. He won't die! He won't!"

Glory dragged on her cigarette. "I hollered some, too, when my son Davy got caught in a cave-in. He was smashed. He died." She flicked ashes onto the bare plank floor. "God calls them. They go—"

"I'm Called!" Thann caught the familiar word. "I'm Called! What will you do, Debbie-my-dear? What about Child—" A sudden bright froth touched the corner of his mouth and he clutched my wrist. "Home is so far away," he sighed. "Why did we have to leave? Why did we leave?"

"Thann, Thann!" I buried my face against his quiet side. The pain in my chest got worse and worse and I wished someone would stop that awful babbling and screaming. How could I say good-by to my whole life with that ghastly noise going on? Then my fingers were pried open and I lost the touch of Thann. The black noisy chaos took me completely.

"He's dead." I slumped in the creaky rocker. Where was I? How long had I been here? My words came so easily, so accustomedly, they must be a repetition of a repetition. "He's dead and I hate you. I hate Seth. I hate Earth. You're all Outsiders. I hate Child Within. I hate myself."

"There," said Glory as she snipped a thread with her teeth and stuck the needle in the front of her plaid shirt. My words had no impact on her, though they almost shocked me as I listened to them. Why didn't she notice what I said? Too familiar? "There's at least one nightgown for Child Within." She grinned. "When I was your age, folks woulda died of shock to think of calling a baby unborn a name like that. I thought maybe these sugar sacks might come in handy sometime. Didn't know it'd be for baby clothes."

"I hate you," I said, hurdling past any lingering shock. "No lady wears Levi's and plaid shirts with buttons that don't match. Nor cuts her hair like a man and lets her face go all wrinkledy. Oh, well, what does it matter? You're only a stupid Outsider. You're not of The People, that's for sure. You're not on our level."

"For that, thanks be to the Lord." Glory smoothed the clumsy little gown across her knee. "I was taught people are people, no matter their clothes or hair. I don't know nothing about your folks or what level they're on, but I'm glad my arthritis won't let me stoop as low as—" She shrugged and laid the gown aside. She reached over to the battered dresser and retrieved something she held out to me. "Speaking of looks, take a squint at what Child Inside's got to put up with."

I slapped the mirror out of her hands—and the mad glimpse of rumpled hair, swollen eyes, raddled face, and a particularly horrible half sneer on lax lips—slapped it out of her hands, stopped its flight in mid-air, spun it up to the sagging plasterboard ceiling, swooped it out with a crash through one of the few remaining whole windowpanes, and let it smash against a pine tree outside the house.

"Do *that!*" I cried triumphantly. "Even child's play like that, you can't do. You're stupid!"

"Could be." Glory picked up a piece of the shattered window glass. "But today I fed my man and the stranger within my gates. I made a gown for a naked baby. What have you done that's been so smart? You've busted, you've ruined, you've whined and hated. If that's being smart, I'll stay stupid." She pitched the glass out of the broken window. "And I'll slap you silly, like I would any spoiled brat, if you break anything else."

"Oh, Glory, oh, Glory!" I squeezed my eyes shut. "I killed him! I killed him! I made him come. If we'd stayed Home. If I hadn't insisted. If—"

"If," said Glory heavily, lifting the baby gown. "If Davy hadn'ta died, this'd be for my grandkid, most likely. If-ing is the quickest way I know to get the blue mullygrubs."

She folded the gown and put it away in the dresser drawer. "You haven't told me yet when Child Within is s'posed to come Without." She reached for the makin's and started to build a cigarette.

"I don't know," I said, staring down at my tight hands. "I don't care." What was Child Within compared to the pain within?

"You'll care plenty," snapped Glory around the smooth curve of the cigarette paper, "if'n you have a hard time and no doctor. You can go ahead and die if you want to, but I'm thinking of Child Within."

"It'd be better if he died, too," I cried. "Better than having to grow up in this stupid, benighted world, among savages—"

"What'd you want to come back so bad for then?" asked Glory. "You admit it was you wanted to come."

"Yes," I moaned, twisting my hands. "I killed him, If we'd only stayed Home. If I hadn't—"

I lay in the dusk, my head pillowed on Thann's grave. Thann's grave— The words had a horrible bitterness on my tongue. "How can I bear it, Thann?" I whimpered. "I'm lost. I can't go Home. The People are gone. What'll I do with Child Within? How can we ever bear it, living with Outsiders? Oh, Call me too, Call me too!" I let the rough gravel of the grave scratch against my cheek as I cried.

And yet I couldn't feel that Thann was there. Thann was a part of another life—a life that didn't end in the mud and misery of a lakeside. He was part of a happy adventure, a glad welcome back to the Earth we had thought was a thing of the past, a tumultuous reunion with all the dear friends we had left behind—the endless hours of vocal and subvocal news exchange—Thann was a part of that. Not a part of this haggard me, this squalid shack teetering on the edge of a dry creek, this bulging, unlovely, ungainly creature muddying her face in the coarse gravel of a barren hillside.

I roused to the sound of footsteps in the dark, and voices. "—nuttier than a fruitcake," said Glory. "It takes some girls like that, just getting pregnant, and then this here other shock—"

"What's she off on now?" It was Seth's heavy voice.

"Oh, more of the same. Being magic. Making things fly. She broke that lookin' glass Davy gave me the Christmas before the cave-in." She cleared her throat. "I picked up the pieces. They're in the drawer."

"She oughta have a good hiding!" Anger was thick in Seth's voice.

"She'll get one if'n she does anything like that again! Oh, and some more about the Home and flying through space and wanting them people again."

"You know," said Seth thoughtfully, "I heard stuff about some folks used to live around here. Funny stuff."

"All people are funny." Glory's voice was nearer. "Better get her back into the house before she catches her death of live-forevers."

I stared up at the ceiling in the dark. Time was again a word without validity. I had no idea how long I had huddled myself in my sodden misery. How long had I been here with Glory and Seth? Faintly in my consciousness, I felt a slight stirring of wonder about Seth and Glory. What did they live on? What were they doing out here in the unfruitful hills? This shack was some forgotten remnant of an old ghost town—no electricity, no water, four crazy walls held together by, and holding up, a shattered roof. For food—beans, cornbread, potatoes, prunes, coffee.

I clasped my throbbing temples with both hands, my head rolling from side to side. But what did it matter? What did anything matter any more? Wild grief surged up in my throat and I cried out, "Mother! Mother!" and felt myself drowning in the icy immensity of the lonely space I had drifted across—

Then there were warm arms around me and a shoulder under my cheek, the soft scratch of hair against my face, a rough hand gently pressing my head to warmth and aliveness.

"There, there!" Glory's voice rumbled gruffly soft through her chest to my ear. "It'll pass. Time and mercy of God will make it bearable. There, there!" She held me and let me blot my tears against her. I didn't know when she left me and I slept dreamlessly.

Next morning at breakfast—before which I had washed my face and combed most of the tangles out of my hair—I paused over my oatmeal and canned milk, spoon poised. "What do you do for a living, Seth?" I asked.

"Living?" Seth stirred another spoonful of sugar into the mush. "We scratch our beans and bacon outa the Skagmore. It's a played-out mine, but there's a few two-bittin' seams left. We work it hard enough, we get by—but it takes both of us. Glory's as good as a man—better'n some."

"How come you aren't working at the Golden Turkey or the Iron Duke?" I wondered where I had got those names even as I asked.

"Can't," said Glory. "He's got silicosis and arthritis. Can't work steady. Times are you'd think he was coughing up his lungs. Hasn't had a bad time though since you came."

"If I were a Healer," I said, "I could cure your lungs and joints. But I'm not. I'm really not much of anything." I blinked down at my dish. *I'm nothing. I'm nothing without Thann.* I gulped. "I'm sorry I broke your window and your mirror, Glory. I shouldn't have. You can't help being an Outsider."

"Apology accepted." Glory grinned dourly. "But it's still kinda drafty."

"There's a whole window in that shack down-creek a ways," said Seth. "When I get the time, I'll go get it. Begins to look like the Skagmore might last right up into winter, though."

"Wish we could get some of that good siding—what's left of it—and fill in a few of our holes," said Glory, tipping up the scarred blue and white coffee pot for the last drop of coffee.

"I'll get the stuff soon's this seam pinches out," promised Seth.

I walked down-creek after breakfast, feeling for the first time the sun on my face, seeing for the first time the untidy tangle and thoughtless profusion of life around me, the dream that had drawn me back to this tragedy. I sat down against a boulder, clasping my knees. My feet had known the path to this rock. My back was familiar with its sun-warmed firmness, but I had no memory of it. I had no idea how long I had been eased of my homesickness.

Now that that particular need was filled and that ache soothed, it was hard to remember how vital and how urgent the whole thing had been. It was like the memory of pain—a purely intellectual thing. But once it had been acute—so acute that Thann had come to his death for it.

I looked down at myself and for the first time I noticed I was wearing jeans and a plaid shirt—Glory's, indubitably. The jeans were precariously held together, bulging under the plaid shirt, by a huge blanket pin. I smiled a little. Outsider makeshift—well, let it stay. They don't know any better.

Soon I aroused and went on down-creek until I found the shack Seth had mentioned. It had two good windows left. I stood in front of the first one, reaching into my memory for my informal training. Then I settled to the job at hand.

Slowly, steadily, nails began to withdraw from around the windows. With toil and sweat and a few frustrated tears, I got the two windows out intact, though the walls around them would never be the same again. I had had no idea how windows were put into a house. After the windows, it was fairly simple to detach the few good lengths of siding left. I stacked them neatly, one by one, drifting them into place. I jumped convulsively at a sudden crunching crash, then laughed shakily to see that the poor old shack had disintegrated completely, having been deprived of its few solid members. Lifting the whole stack of my salvage to carrying height, I started back up-creek, panting and sweating, stumbling and pushing the load ahead of me until I got smart and, lifting, perched on the pile of planks, I directed my airborne caravan up-creek.

Glory and Seth were up at the mine. I set the things down by the house and then, suddenly conscious of weariness, made my way to Thann's grave. I patted the gravelly soil softly and whispered, "They'll like it, won't they, Thann? They're so like children. Now Glory will forget about the mirror. Poor little Outsider!"

Glory and Seth were stupefied when they saw my loot leaning against the corner of the shack. I told them where I'd got the stuff and how I had brought it back.

Seth spat reflectively and looked sideways at Glory. "Who's nuts now?" he asked.

"Okay, okay," said Glory. "You go tell that Jick Bennett how this stuff got here. Maybe he'll believe you."

"Did I do something wrong?" I asked. "Did this belong to Mr. Bennett?"

"No, no," said Glory. "Not to him nor nobody. He's just a friend of ours. Him and Seth're always shooting the breeze together. No, it's just—

just—" She gestured hopelessly, then turned on Seth. "Well? Get the hammer. You want her to do the hammering too?"

We three labored until the sun was gone and a lopsided moon had pushed itself up over the shoulder of Baldy. The light glittered on the smug wholeness of the two windows of the shack and Glory sighed with tired satisfaction. Balling up the rag she had taken from the other broken window, she got it ready to throw away. "First time my windows've been wind-tight since we got here. Come winter that's nothing to sneeze at!"

"Sneeze at!" Seth shook with silent gargantuan laughter. "Nothing to sneeze at!"

"Glory!" I cried. "What have you there? Don't throw it away!"

"What?" Glory retrieved the wad from the woodpile. "It's only the rags we peeled off'n both of yens before we put you in bed. And another hunk we picked up to beat out the fire. Ripped to tatters. Heavy old canvassy stuff, anyway."

"Give it to me, Glory," I said. And took the bundle from her wondering hands. "It's *tekla*," I said. "It's never useless. Look." I spread out several of the rags on a flat stone near the creek. In the unreal blend of sunset and moonrise, I smoothed a fingernail along two overlapping edges. They merged perfectly into a complete whole. Quickly I sealed the other rips and snags and, lifting the sheet of *tekla,* shook off the dirt and wrinkles. "See, it's as good as new. Bring the rest in the house. We can have some decent clothes again." I smiled at Glory's pained withdrawal. "After all, Glory, you must admit this pin isn't going to hold Child Within much longer!"

Seth lighted the oil lamp above the table and I spread *tekla* all over it, mending a few rips I'd missed.

"Here's some more," said Glory. "I stuck it in that other stovepipe hole. It's the hunk we used to beat the fire out with. It's pretty holey."

"It doesn't matter," I said, pinching out the charred spots. "What's left is still good." And she and Seth hung fascinated around the table, watching me. I couldn't let myself think of Thann, flushed with excitement, trying to be so casual as he tried on his travel suit to show me, so long—so long ago—so yesterday, really.

"Here's a little bitty piece you dropped," said Seth, retrieving it.

"It's too little for any good use," said Glory.

"Oh, no!" I said, a little intoxicated by their wonder and by a sudden upsurge of consciousness that I was able to work so many—to them—miracles. "Nothing's too small. See. That's one reason we had it made so thick. To spread it thin when we used it." I took the tiny swatch of *tekla* and began to stretch and shape it, smoother and farther. Farther and farther until it flowed over the edges of the table and the worn design on the oilcloth began to be visible through it.

"What color do you like, Glory?" I asked.

"Blue," breathed Glory, wonderingly. "Blue."

I stroked blue into the *tekla,* quickly evened the edges, and, lifting the fragile, floating chiffony material, draped it over Glory's head. For a half moment I saw my own mother looking with shining eyes at me through the lovely melt of color. Then I was hugging Glory and saying, "That's for the borrow of your jeans and shirt!" And she was fingering unbelievingly the delicate fabric. *There,* I thought, *I even hugged her. It really doesn't matter to me that she's just an Outsider.*

"Magic!" said Glory. "Don't touch it!" she cried, as Seth reached a curious hand toward it.

"He can't hurt it," I laughed. "It's strong enough to use for a parachute—or a trampoline!"

"How did you do it?" asked Seth, lifting another small patch of *tekla,* his fingers tugging at it.

"Well, first you have to—" I groped for an explanation. "You see, first— Well, then, after that— Oh, I don't know!" I cried. "I just know you do it." I took the piece from him and snatched it into scarf length, stroking it red and woolly, and wound it around his neck and bewildered face.

I slept that night in a gown of *tekla,* but Glory stuck to her high-necked crinkle-crepe gown and Seth scorned nightclothes. But after Glory blew out the light and before she disappeared behind the denim curtain that gave me part of the front room for a bedroom of my own, she leaned over, laughing in the moonlight, to whisper, "He's got that red thing under his pillow. I seen it sticking out from under!"

Next morning I busied myself with the precious *tekla,* thinning it, brushing up a soft nap, fashioning the tiny things Child Within would be needing some day. Glory stayed home from the mine and tried to help. After the first gown was finished, I sat looking at it, dreaming child-dreams any mother does with a first gown. I was roused by the sound of a drawer softly closing and saw Glory disappear into the kitchen. I went over and opened the drawer. The awkward little sugar-sack gown was gone. I smiled pityingly. *She realized,* I said to myself. *She realized how inappropriate a gown like that would be for a child of The People.*

That night Seth dropped the lamp chimney and it smashed to smithereens.

"Well, early to bed," sighed Glory. "But I did want to get on with this shirt for Seth." She smoothed the soft, woolly *tekla* across her lap. We had figured it down pretty close, but it came out a dress for each of us and a shirt for Seth as well as a few necessities for Child Within. I blessed again the generousness of our travel clothes and the one small part of a blanket that had survived.

"If you've got a dime," I said, returning to the problem of light, "I haven't a cent—but if you've got a dime, I can make a light—"

Seth chuckled. "If we've got a dime, I'd like to see it. We're 'bout due for a trip into town to sell our ore. Got any change, Glory?"

Glory dumped her battered purse out on the bed and stirred the contents vigorously. "One dollar bill," she said. "Coffee and sugar for next week. A nickel and three pennies. No dime—"

"Maybe a nickel will work," I said dubiously. "We always used dimes or disks of *argen*. I never tried a nickel." I picked up the coin and fingered it. Boy! Would this ever widen their eyes! If I could remember Dita's instructions. I spun the coin and concentrated. I spun the coin and frowningly concentrated. I spun the coin. I blushed. I sweated. "It'll work," I reassured the skeptical side glances of Seth and Glory. I closed my eyes and whispered silently, "We need it. Bless me. Bless me."

I spun the coin.

I saw the flare behind my eyelids and opened them to the soft, slightly blue handful of light the nickel had become. Seth and Glory said nothing, but their eyes blinked and were big and wondering enough to please anyone, as they looked into my cupped hand.

"A dime is brighter," I said, "but this is enough for here, I guess. Only thing is, you can't blow it out."

The two exchanged glances and Seth smiled weakly. "Nutty as a fruitcake," he said. "But don't it shine pretty!"

The whole room was flooded with the gentle light. I put it down in the middle of the table, but it was too direct for our eyes, so Seth balanced it on the top of a windowsill and Glory picked up the half-finished shirt from the floor where it had fallen and asked in a voice that only slightly trembled, "Could you do this seam right here, Debbie? That'll finish this sleeve."

That night we had to put the light in a baking powder can with the lid on tight when we went to bed. The cupboard had leaked too much light and so had the dresser. I was afraid to damp the glow for fear I might not be able to do it again the next night. A Lady Bountiful has to be careful of her reputation.

I sat on the bank above the imperceptibly growing lake and watched another chunk of the base of Baldy slide down into the water. Around me was the scorched hillside and the little flat where I had started the fire. Somewhere under all that placid brown water was our craft and everything we had of The Home. I felt my face harden and tighten with sorrow. I got up awkwardly and made my way down the steep slant of the bank. I leaned against a boulder and stirred the muddy water with one sneaker-clad toe. That block of *tekla,* the seed box, the pictures, the letters. I let the tears wash downward unchecked. All the dreams and plans. The pain caught me so that I nearly doubled up. My lips stretched thinly. How physical mental pain can be! If only it could be amputated like— Pain caught me again. I gasped and clutched the boulder behind me. *This is pain,* I cried to myself. *Not Child Within! Not out here in the wilds all alone!* I made my way back to the shack in irregular, staggering stages and put myself to bed. When Glory and Seth got back, I propped up wearily on one elbow and looked at them groggily, the pain having perversely quitted me just before they arrived.

"Do you suppose it *is* almost time? I have no way of knowing. Time is—is different here. I can't put the two times together and come out with anything. I'm afraid, Glory! I'm afraid!"

"We shoulda taken you into Kerry to the doctor a long time ago. He'd be able to tell you, less'n—" she hesitated "—less'n you are different, so'st he'd notice—"

I smiled weakly. "Don't tiptoe so, Glory. I won't be insulted. No, he'd notice nothing different except when birth begins. We can bypass the awfullest of the hurting time—" I gulped and pressed my hands to the sudden emptiness that almost caved me in. "That's what I was supposed to learn from our People here!" I wailed. "I only know about it. Our first child is our learning child. You can't learn it ahead."

"Don't worry," said Glory dryly. "Child Within will manage to get outside whether you hurt or not. If you're a woman, you can bear the burden women have since Eve."

So we planned to go into town the next day and just tell the doctor I hadn't been to a doctor yet—lots of people don't, even today. But it started to rain in the night. I roused first to the soft sound of rain on the old tin roof of the kitchen—the soft sound that increased and increased until it became a drumming roar. Even that sound was music. And the vision of rain falling everywhere, everywhere, patting the dusty ground, dimpling the lake, flipping the edges of curled leaves, soothed me into sleep. I was wakened later by the sound of Seth's coughing. *That* wasn't a soothing sound. And it got worse and worse. It began to sound as though he actually were coughing up his lungs as Glory had said. He could hardly draw a breath between coughing spasms. I lay there awake in the dark, hearing Glory's murmurs and the shuff-shuff of her feet as she padded out to the kitchen and back to the bedroom. But the coughing went on and on and I began to get a little impatient. I tossed in bed, suddenly angrily restless. I had Child Within to think of. They knew I needed my rest. They weren't

making any effort to be quiet— Finally I couldn't stand it any longer. I
padded in my turn to their bedroom and peered in. Seth was leaning back
against the head of the iron bedstead, gasping for breath. Glory was sitting beside him, tearing up an old pillowcase to make handkerchiefs for
him. She looked up at me in the half light of the uncovered baking powder can, her face drawn and worn.

"It's bad, this time," she said. "Makin' up for lost time, I guess."

"Can't you do something to stop his coughing?" I asked. I really
hadn't meant it to sound so abrupt and flat. But it did, and Glory let her
hands fall slowly to her lap as her eyes fixed on me.

"Oh," she said. "Oh." Then her eyes fairly blazed and she said, "Can't
you?"

"I'm not a Healer," I said, feeling almost on the defensive. "If I were,
I could give—"

"You wouldn't give anybody anything," said Glory, her face closed
and cold. "Less'n you wanted to show off or make yourself comfortable.
Go back to bed."

I went, my cheeks burning in the dark. How dare she talk to me
like this! An Outsider to one of The People! She had no right— My anger
broke into tears and I cried and cried on my narrow Outsider bed in that
falling-down Outsider house, but under all my anger and outrage, so
closely hidden that I'd hardly admit it to myself even, was a kernel of
sorrow. I'd thought Glory liked me.

Morning was gray and clammy. The rain fell steadily and the bluish
light from the baking powder can was cold and uncheerful. The day
dragged itself to a watery end, nothing except a slight waning and waxing
of the light outdoors to distinguish one hour from the next. Seth's coughing eased a little and by the second rain-loud morning it had finally
stopped.

Seth prowled around the cramped rooms, his shoulders hunched
forward, his chest caved in as though he had truly coughed out his lungs.
His coughing had left him, but his breath still caught in ragged chunks.

"Seth," said Glory, tugging at his sleeve. "You'll wear yourself and
me out too, to-ing and fro-ing like that."

"Don't ease me none to set," said Seth hoarsely. "Leave me be. Let
me move while I can. Got a hunch there won't be much moving for me
after the next spell."

"Now, Seth." Glory's voice was calm and a little reprimanding, but
I caught her terror and grief. With a jolt I realized how exactly her feelings were mine when I had crouched beside Thann, watching him die.
But they're old and ugly and through with life! I protested. *But they love,*
came the answer, *and love can never be old nor ugly nor through with life.*

" 'Sides, I'm worried," said Seth, wiping the haze of his breath off the newly installed window. "Rain like this'll fill every creek around here. Then watch the dam fill up. They told us we'd be living on an island before spring. When the lake's full, we'll be six foot under. All this rain—" He swiped at the window again, and turning away, resumed his restless pacing. "That slope between here and the highway's getting mighty touchy. Wash it out a little at the bottom and it'll all come down like a ton of bricks. Dam it up there, we'd get the full flow right across us and I ain't feeling much like a swim!" He grinned weakly and leaned against the table.

"Glory." His breathing was heavy and ragged. "Glory, I'm tired."

Glory put him to bed. I could hear the murmur of her voice punctuated at intervals by a heavy monosyllable from him.

I shivered and went to the little bandy-legged cast-iron stove. Lifting one of its four lids, I peered at the smoldering pine knot inside. The heaviness outside pushed a thin acrid cloud of smoke out at me and I clattered the lid back, feeling an up-gush of exasperation at the inefficiency of Outsiders. I heated the stove up until the top glowed dull red, and reveled in the warmth.

Glory came back into the kitchen and hunched near the stove, rubbing her hands together.

"How'd you get the wood to burn?" she finally asked. "It was wet. 'S'all there is left."

"I didn't," I said. "I heated the stove."

"Thanks," said Glory shortly (not even being surprised that I could do a thing like that!).

We both listened to the murmur of the rain on the roof and the pop and creak of the expanding metal of the stovepipe as the warmth reached upward.

"I'm sorry," said Glory. "I shouldn'ta spoken so short the other night, but I was worried."

"It's all right," I said magnanimously. "And when my People come—"

"Look, Debbie." Glory turned her back to the stove and clasped her hands behind her. "I'm not saying you don't have folks and that they won't come some day and set everything right, but they aren't here *now*. They can't help *now*, and we got troubles—plenty of troubles. Seth's worrying about that bank coming down and shifting the water. Well, he don't know, but it came down in the night last night and we're already almost an island. Look out the window."

I did, cold apprehension clutching at my insides. The creek had water in it. Not a trickle, but a wide, stainless-steel roadbed of water that was heavy with red silt where it escaped the color of the down-pressing clouds. I ran to the other window. A narrow hogback led through the interlacing of a thousand converging streams, off into the soggy grayness of the mountain beyond us. It was the trail—the hilltop trail Glory and Seth took to Skagmore.

"I hate to ask it of you," said Glory. "Especially after telling you off like I did, but we gotta get outa here. We gotta save what we can and hole up at the mine. You better start praying now that it'll be a few days more before the water gets that high. Meanwhile, grab your bedroll and git goin'."

I gaped at her and then at the water outside and, running to my cot, grabbed up the limp worn bedding and started for the door.

"Hold it! Hold it!" she called. "Fold the stuff so you can manage it. Put on this old hat of Seth's. It'll keep the rain outa your eyes for a while, maybe. Wait'll I get my load made up. I'll take the lead."

Oh, no! Oh, no! I cried to myself as panic trembled my hands and hampered my folding the bedclothes. *Why is this happening to me? Wasn't it enough to take Thann away? Why should I have to suffer any more?*

"Ready?" Glory's intent eyes peered across her load. "Hope you've been praying. If you haven't, you better get started. We gotta make it there and back. Seth's gotta rest some before he tackles it."

"But I can lift!" I cried. "I don't have to walk! I have my shield. I don't have to get wet! I can go—"

"Go then," said Glory, her voice hard and unfriendly. "Git goin'!"

I caught at my panic and bit my lips—I needed Glory. "I only mean I could take your load and mine, too," I said, which wasn't what I had originally meant at all. "Then you could take something else. I can transport all this stuff and keep it dry."

I lifted my own burden and hovered it while I took hers from her reluctant arms. I lifted the two together and maneuvered the load out the door, extending my personal shield to cover it all. "How—how do I get there?" My voice was little and scared.

"Follow the hogback," said Glory, her voice still unwarmed, as though she had been able to catch my hidden emotion, as the People do. "You'll see the entrance up the hill a ways soon as you top out on the ridge. Don't go too far inside. The shoring's rotted out in lots of places."

"Okay," I said. "I'll come back."

"Stay there," said Glory. "Git goin'. I gotta get Seth up." My eyes followed hers and recoiled from the little brown snake of water that had welled up in one corner of the room. I got going.

Even inside my shield, I winced away from the sudden increased roar of descending rain. I couldn't see a yard ahead and had to navigate from boulder to boulder along the hogback. It was a horrible eternity before I saw the dark gap of the mine entrance and managed to get myself and my burden inside. For several feet around the low irregular arch of the entrance, the powdery ground was soggy mud, but farther back it was dry and the roof vaulted up until it was fairly spacious.

I put the bedding down and looked around me. Two narrow strips of rail disappeared back into the mine and an ore car tilted drunkenly off one side, two wheels off and half covered with dirt on the floor beside it. I unearthed one wheel and, tugging it upright, rolled it, wobbling and uncooperative, over to the stack of bedding. I started heating the wheel, making slow work of so large a task because I had done so little with the basic Signs and Persuasions—the practices of my People.

Suddenly it seemed to me a long time since I'd left the shack. I ran to the entrance and peered out. No Glory or Seth! Where could they be! I couldn't be all alone here with no one around to help me! I swished out into the storm so fast my face was splattered with rain before my shielding was complete. Time and again I almost lost the hogback. It was an irregular chain of rocky little islands back toward the shack. I groped through the downpour, panting to Child Within, *Oh, wait! Oh, wait! You can't come now!* And tried to ignore a vague, growing discomfort.

Then the miracle happened! High above me I heard the egg-beater whirr of a helicopter! Rescue! Now all this mad rush and terror and discomfort would be over. All I had to do was signal the craft and make them take me aboard and take me somewhere away—I turned to locate it and signal it to me when I suddenly realized that I couldn't lift to it—I *couldn't* lift around Outsiders who would matter. This basic rule of The People was too deeply engrained in me. Hastily I dipped down until I perched precariously on one of the still-exposed boulders of the trail. I waved wildly up at the slow swinging 'copter. They had to see me! "Here I am! Here I am!" I cried, my voice too choked even to carry a yard. "Help me! Help me!" And, in despair as the 'copter slanted away into the gray falling rain, I slid past vocal calling into subvocal and spread my call over the whole band, praying that a receptor somewhere would pick up my message. "There's need!" I sobbed out the old childish distress cry of the Group. "There's need!"

And an answer came!

"One of us?" The thought came startled. "Who are you? Where are you?"

"I'm down here in the rain!" I sobbed, aloud as well as silently. "I'm Debbie! I used to live in the Canyon! We went to the Home. Come and get me! Oh, come and get me!"

"I'm coming," came the answer. "What on Earth are you doing on Earth, Debbie? No one was supposed to return so lightly—"

"So lightly!" Shattered laughter jabbed at my throat. All the time I'd spent on Earth already had erased itself, and I was caught up by the poignancy of this moment of meeting with Thann not here—this watery welcome to Earth with no welcome for Thann. "Who are you?" I asked. I had forgotten individual thought patterns so soon.

"I'm Jemmy," came the reply. "I'm with an Outsider Disaster Unit. We've got our hands full fishing people out of this dammed lake!" He chuckled. "Serves them right for damming Cougar Creek and spoiling the Canyon. But tell me, what's the deal? You shouldn't be here. You went back to the Home, didn't you?"

"The Home—" I burst into tears and all the rest of the time that the 'copter circled back and found a settling-down space on a flat already awash with two inches of water, Jemmy and I talked. Mostly I did the talking. We shifted out of verbalization and our thoughts speeded up until I had told Jemmy everything that had happened to me since that awful crashing day. It was telling of someone else—some other far, sad story of tragedy and graceless destitution—Outsider makeshifts. I had just finished when the 'copter door swung open and Jemmy stepped out to hover above the water that was sucking my sneakers off the slant of the boulder I was crouched on.

"Oh, thanks be to The Power," I cried, grabbing for Jemmy's hands, but stubbing my own on my personal shield. "Oh take me out of this, Jemmy! Take me back to The People! I'm so sick of living like an Outsider! And Child Within doesn't want to be born on a dirt floor in a mine! Oh, Jemmy! How horrible to be an Outsider! You came just in time!" Tears of thankfulness wet my face as I tried to smile at him.

"Debbie!"

Surely that couldn't be my name! That cold, hard, accusing word! That epithet—that—

"Jemmy!" I collapsed my shield and reached for him. Unbelievably, he would not receive me. "Jemmy!" I cried, the rain wetting my lips. "What's the matter? What's wrong?"

He floated back so I couldn't reach him. "Where are Glory and Seth?" he asked sternly.

"Glory and Seth?" I had to think before I could remember them. They were another life ago. "Why, back at the cabin, I guess." I was bewildered. "Why?"

"You have no concern for them?" he asked. "You ask for rescue and forget them? What did The Home do to you? You're apparently not one of Us any more. If you've been infected with some sort of virus, we want no spreading of it."

"You don't want me?" I was dazed. "You're going to leave me here! But—but you can't! You've got to take me!"

"You're not drowning," he said coldly. "Go back to the cave. I have a couple of blankets in the 'copter I can spare. Be comfortable. I have other people who need rescue worse."

"But, Jemmy! I don't understand. What's wrong? What have I done?" My heart was shattering and cutting me to pieces with its razor-sharp edges.

He looked at me coldly and speculatively. "If you have to ask, it'd take too long to explain," he said. He turned away and took the blankets from the 'copter. He aimed them at the mine entrance and, hovering them, gave them a shove to carry them through into the mine.

"There," he said, "curl up in your comfort. Don't get your feet wet."

"Oh, Jemmy, don't leave me! Help me!" I was in a state of almost complete collapse, darkness roaring over me.

"While you're curled up, all nice and safe," Jemmy's voice came back to me from the 'copter, "you might try thinking a little on 'Just who on Earth do you think you are!' And if you think you have the answer to that, try, 'I was hungry—' "

I didn't hear him go. I sat hunched in my sodden misery, too far gone even to try to puzzle it all out. All my hopes had been built on when my People would find me. They'd set everything right. I would be freed from all my worry and hardships—and now—and now—

A wave of discomfort that had been building up slowly for some time suddenly surged over me and my fingers whitened as I clutched the rock. How could I have mistaken that other pain for this? "Glory!" I whimpered. "It's Child Within!" *Now* I could remember Glory and Seth. I was back in the miserable half-life of waiting for my People. I scrambled to my feet and closed my shield, setting it to warmth to counteract the chill that stuck to my bones. "I can't face it alone! Anything, anything is better than being alone!"

I streaked back along the hogback that had almost disappeared under the creeping muddy tide. The cabin was in a lake. The back door was ajar. The whole thing tilted slightly off true as though it were thinking of taking off into the roar of the incredible river that swept the creek bed from bank to bank. I staggered against the door as another hard surge of pain tightened my hands and wrung an involuntary cry from me.

When it subsided, I wiped the sweat from my upper lip and pushed the door further open. I stepped into the magnified roaring of the rain on the roof. Blue light was flooding serenely from the baking powder can on the table in the empty kitchen. I snatched it up and ran to the bedroom.

Seth lay white and unmoving on his bed, his eyes sunken, his chest still. I pressed the back of my clenched hand hard against my mouth, feeling the bruise of my teeth. "Oh, no!" I whispered, and gasped with relief as a quick shallow breath lifted the one thin quilt Glory had left him from the bundle of bedding.

"You came back."

My eyes flew to Glory. She sat on the other side of the bed, a shoe box in her lap, one hand clutching a corner of the battered old quilt.

"You didn't come," I whispered. "I waited."

"No need to whisper." Her voice was quite as usual except for a betraying catch on the last word. "He can't hear you."

"But you must come!" I cried. "The house will go in a minute. The creek's already—"

"Why should I come," she asked without emphasis. "He can't come."

We both watched another of the shaken breaths come and go.

"But you'll be washed away—"

"So'll you if you don't git goin'." She turned her face away from me.

"But, Glory—" Her name came, but twisted—a muffled cry of pain. I clenched both hands on the doorjamb and clung until the pain subsided.

"Child Within," said Glory—her eyes intent on me.

"Yes," I gasped. "I guess so."

Glory stood up and laid the shoe box on the corner of the sagging dresser. She leaned over and smoothed the covers under Seth's chin. "I'll be back," she told him. She waded through the ruffle of water that covered the floor ankle-deep and rounded the bed.

"We better go," she said. "You'll have to point me the way. The trail's gone—"

"You mean you'd leave him here alone!" I was stunned. "Your own husband!"

She looked back at Seth and her lips tightened. "We all die alone, anyway," she said. "He'd tell me to go, if'n he could."

Then I was still as I caught the passionate outpouring of her grief and love—her last, unspoken farewell to Seth. With an effort she turned her eyes back to me. "Our duty's to the living," she said. "And Child Within won't wait."

"Oh, Glory!" Anguish of sorrow filled my chest till I could only gasp again. "Oh, Glory! We can't, we can't!" My throat ached and I blinked against tears of quite a different sort than those I'd been shedding since Thann died.

I snatched the glowing nickel out of the baking powder can and shoved it into my pocket. "Tuck him in good," I said, nodding at Seth. "Bring whatever you need."

Glory looked at me briefly, hope flaring in her eyes, then, with hasty shaken hands, she tucked the covers tight around Seth and, grabbing up her shoe box, she pushed it under the covers next to him. There was a grating grind and the whole shack swung a quarter circle around.

"Can we get the bed through the doors?" I asked shrilly.

"Not unless we take it apart," said Glory, the quietness of her voice steadying me, "and there isn't time."

"Then—then—"

"The mattress will bend," she said. "If both of us—"

With all my faith and power I withdrew into the Quiet within me. *Help me now,* I prayed. *I can do nothing of myself. Strengthen me, guide me, help me—*

The last words came audibly as I clutched the foot of the bed, waiting until the wave subsided. Then, slowly, deliberately, quietly and unhurried, I lifted the mattress Seth lay on and bent its edges enough to get it out of the bedroom. I hovered it in the kitchen. Glory and I both staggered as the house swayed underfoot—swayed and steadied.

"Have you something to put over him to keep the rain off?" I asked. "I can't extend my shield that far and lift that much at the same time."

"Our slickers," said Glory, her eyes intent on me with that different look in them. "They'll help a little."

"Get them then," I said, "and you'll have to get on the mattress, too, to keep him covered."

"But can you—" Glory began.

"I will," I said, holding my Quietness carefully in my mind. "Hurry—the house is going."

Hastily, Glory snatched the two yellow slickers from the nails behind the front door. She scrambled into one and spread the other over Seth. "His head, too," I said, "or he'll nearly drown. You'd better cover your head, too. It'll be easier to take. Hurry! Hurry!"

Glory gave one look at the hovering mattress and, setting her lips grimly, crawled on and lay beside Seth, one arm protectively across his chest. She'd hardly closed her eyes before I started the mattress out the door. The house began spinning at the same time. By the time we got outside, it had turned completely around and, as we left it, it toppled slowly into the creek and was lost in the tumult of the waters.

It's no more than the windows and siding, I whispered to myself. *In fact, it's less because there's no glass to break.* But all my frantic reassurances didn't help much. There were still two lives hanging on my ability to do the inanimate lift and transport them. Doggedly I pushed on, hardly able to see beyond the cascade of rain that arched down my shield. Below me the waters were quieting because they were getting so deep that they no longer quarreled with the boulders and ridges. They smothered them to silence. Ahead and a little below me, rain ran from Glory and Seth's slickers, and the bed, other than where they lay, was a sodden mess.

Finally I could see the entrance of the mine, a darker blot in the pervading grayness. "There it is, Glory!" I cried. "We're almost there. Just a little—" And the pain seized me. Gasping, I felt myself begin to fall. All my power was draining out thinly—my mind had only room for the all-enveloping anguish. I felt the soggy end of the mattress under one arm, and then two strong hands grabbed me and began to tug me onto the bed.

"Try—" Glory's voice was almost too far away. "Help yourself! Onto the bed! Help yourself!"

Deliberately I pushed all thought of pain aside. As though in slow motion I felt myself lift slightly and slide onto the end of the bed. I lay half on, half off and tried to catch my breath.

"Debbie," Glory's voice came calmly and deliberately. "We're almost in the water. Can you lift us up a little?"

Oh, no, I thought. *It's too much to ask! Let me rest.*

Then for no reason at all I heard Jemmy's voice again. "Where's Glory and Seth?" as though in some way I were responsible. *I am!* I cried to myself. *I am responsible for them. I took their lives in my hands when we left the bedroom. Even before that! I made myself responsible for them when they took me in—*

With infinite effort I pushed myself into the background and reached out again to lay hold on The Power and, slowly, the bed rose from the lapping of the waters and, slowly, it started again toward the mine entrance and I held Glory's hand in such a bruising grasp you would have thought I was birthing something or someone out there in the pelting rain.

The events of the next few minutes ran hurriedly and clear, but as far removed from me as though I were watching everything through the wrong end of binoculars. I settled the mattress near the glowing wheel. Glory was off in unflurried haste. She spread my bedclothes and got me undressed by the light of the nickel she had propped up on a ledge on the wall. I cried out when I felt the warmth of my *tekla* nightgown gliding over my head. I'd forgotten the clothes for Child Within! The muddy waters were tumbling all their softness and smallness now.

Another pain came and when it subsided, Glory had brought a coffee pot from somewhere—one of those huge enameled camp pots—and had filled it from somewhere and put it on the wheel-stove to heat. The cases were gone from our pillows and they lay beside my bed torn into neat squares in a little heap, topped by a battered old jackknife with one sharp blade open. One of the thin blankets had been ripped in four.

Glory's face appeared over me, rugged, comforting. "We're doin' fine," she said. "Me and Seth had a few things stashed here in the mine. Seth's breathing better. You got nothing to worry about now 'ceptin' Child Within. Nothing to worry about there neither 'ceptin' what you'll name him now that he won't be within any more."

"Oh, Glory!" I whispered and turned my cheek to press against her hand.

From there on, I was three people—one who cried out and gasped and struggled with the pain and against the pain and was bound up in the blindness of complete concentration on the task at hand, and an accusing one—one sitting in judgment. And the third me was standing before the bar of that judgment, defenseless and guilty.

The indictment was read from the big Book.

"I was hungry," came the accusation, "and they fed me."

"I ate their food," I admitted. "Unearned—"

"I was naked and they clothed me—"

" 'Now we can have decent clothes,' " I heard myself saying again.

"I was a stranger and they took me in—"

"I condescended to let them care for me," I admitted.

"I was in the prison of my grief and they visited me."

"And I accepted their concern and care of me as an unquestioned right. I took and took and took and gave nothing—" Remorse was sharper than the pain that made the other cry out and struggle on the thin bedclothes.

Think no more highly of yourself than you should. The voice had stopped. Now the words ran in ribbons of flames, wavering before my closed eyes, searing the tears dry.

To whom much is given, much is expected. Who would be first must be last. Who would be greatest must be the servant of all.

Whatsoever you do unto the least of these—

Then suddenly the separation was over and the three of me coalesced in a quick blind rush and I listened blissfully to the lusty, outraged cry of My Child.

"Oh, Thann!" I whispered as I slid into a cloud of comfort and relaxation. "Oh, Thann, he's here. Our child—our Thann-too."

"You're mighty sure, aren't you?" Glory's voice was amused. "But you're right. He's a boy."

I pushed sleep away from me a little to fret, "Let me see my poor naked baby. All his little clothes—"

"Not so naked," said Glory. "Here, hold him while I get things squared around." She laid the blanket-wrapped bundle beside me and I lifted up on one elbow to look down into the miracle of the face of my child. I brushed my forefinger across the dark featherdown of his damp hair and lost myself in the realization that here was Child Within. This was what had been Becoming, serenely untouched, within me during all the tumultuous things that had happened. I protested from my half sleep when Glory came back for my child.

"Just going to dress him," said Glory. "You can have him back."

"Dress him?" I asked fuzzily.

"Yes," said Glory, unwrapping the blanket. "I had that sugar-sack gown in my shoe box and them old pillowcases make pretty soft diapers. Not very wetproof though, I'm afraid."

"A boy?" It was Seth's voice, shaken but clear—his first words since the cabin.

"A boy!" Glory's voice was a hymn of thankfulness. "Want to see him?"

"Sure. Us men gotta stick together!"

I lay and smiled to keep from crying as I heard their murmuring over my child.

"Dark like Davy," Glory finally said softly. "Well, better give him back, I guess." She laid him beside me.

"Glory," I said, "the gown could have been for Davy's child. So you and Seth must be grandparents for my Thann-too."

"I—" Glory bit her lips and smoothed his blanket with a trembling hand. "We—" She swallowed hard. "Sure. It's a pleasure."

"Hey, Grandma," called Seth, hardly above a whisper. "I could do with some coffee!"

"Okay, Grampa, keep your shirt on," said Glory. "One coffee coming up!"

That night after Glory had got us all settled and the nickel light was tucked under a rusty tin can and sleep was flowing warmly around us all, I roused a little and leaned up on one elbow, instinctively curving myself around the precious bundle of my child. The wheel-stove glowed on, taking a little of the raw chill off the rocky room. Glory and Seth were sleeping on the other side of the wheel, their bedding augmented by one of the blankets Jemmy had left. When I told Glory where they were, but not where they came from, she got them and, looking at me over the folded bulk of them, opened her mouth, closed it again, and silently spread one blanket for me and one for them. Now they were both asleep and I was awake listening to the "voice of many waters, praising—" and added my praise to theirs. Outside, the sky was clearing, but the murmuring lap of the waters reminded that the numberless creeks in the hills had not yet emptied themselves and the tide was rising higher.

I turned over in my mind the odd duality of events of the night. I heard and saw again all the accusations, all the admonitions. They must have all been waiting for just such a chance when the Distorted Me wasn't watching, to break through and confront me with myself. I had known all the words before. Their pertinent wisdom had been familiar to The People before they ever arrived on Earth and it was one of the endearing things of Earth that we had there found such beautifully rhythmic paraphrases of them.

As I had laid down the burden of Child Within only to assume the greater burden of Thann-too, so also must I lay down the burden of my spoiled-brat self and take up the greater burden of my responsibility as one of The People toward Glory and Seth and whatever the Power sent into my life. Jemmy had been right. I *wasn't* of The People. I had made myself more of an Outsider than an Outsider, even. Well, remorse is useless except insofar as it changes your way of doing things. And change I would—the Power being my helper.

Then I closed my eyes and felt them begin to dampen a little, as I wondered wistfully how long it would be before Jemmy would come again. Thann-too stirred in the curve of my arm. I looked down into the shadow that held him. "But I do think Jemmy was unnecessarily hard on Child Within!" I whispered as I gathered the warm little life closer.

"I do, too," came a voice—subvocally.

Startled, I glanced up. There were two of them standing in the cave entrance.

"And I told him so, too." The figures moved in, quiet inches above the crunch of the mine floor "Remember me Debbie? It's Valancy. Maybe you've forgotten—"

"Forgotten? Oh, Valancy!" And we were hugging each other tightly. There was a lovely, warm intermingling of thoughts among the three of us, and all sorts of explanations—Jemmy had had no idea Child Within was so nearly ready to be born—and apologies—"If I'd had *any* idea, but when you—" and acceptances and reasons why and such things as Necessary Patterns—" "Since you had the situation in hand I went to see if someone else—" until finally, chastened and relaxed, I watched Valancy cuddling my child.

How could I ever have forgotten Jemmy and Valancy—the glamorous Grown-ups—the Old Ones of the Group of my People in Cougar Canyon, when the Canyon was still habitable. We had all waved them good-by when our ship left for the Home so long ago.

"You can look," said Valancy to Jemmy. "But don't touch." Then she contradicted herself by putting the sleeping bundle into his arms. She snapped her fingers and a small bundle floated in from the mine entrance.

"I brought some clothes," she said. "Though it looks as if Glory has things well in hand. But here are some of Our Child's clothes. She grew so fast that she hardly got to use some of them. If we don't tell him, Thann-too will never know he had to wear girl-type clothes." She unfolded the torn blanket square from around the baby. "And there's the gown," she said, smiling, fingering the hem of it, now regrettably damp.

"There's the gown," I said. "Oh, Valancy, wasn't I the luckiest person in the whole world to have Glory with me? I didn't deserve it a bit! What a mess I was!"

"The Glorys of this world have to put up with a lot of messes," said Valancy, deftly changing my child from the skin out, and returning him, still blissfully sleeping, to my arms. She folded the wet clothes and bundled them up.

"We're taking you and the child back with us," said Jemmy. "We'd better wake Glory and tell her."

"Glory!" I called softly and audibly.

Instantly she was awake and out of bed, blinking in the dimness. "Glory, my People have come," I said. "They want to take me and Thann-too back with them. But I'll be back, just as soon as I can."

Valancy surrendered the baby into Glory's waiting arms. She held him close. "I reckon you do have to go," she said, her voice muffled against his blanket. "He's going to be needing diapers by the dozen pretty darn soon. It'd keep us hopping, washing out what we have."

"We brought some supplies for you," said Jemmy. "They're from the disaster unit. We're working all around this area helping people who got flooded out."

"Is Jicker all right?" Seth's voice came huskily.

"Jicker?" Jemmy did some fast scanning— "Oh, yes," chuckled Jemmy. "I remember him. We fished him off the roof of his cabin. Never heard such cussing in all my life. Ten minutes solid without repeating himself once!"

"That's Jicker," grinned Seth and settled back down. "I'm glad the old cuss is okay."

Jemmy was looking around the shadowy room. "This is the Skagmore, isn't it?" he said. "I thought she was played out a long time ago."

"She was—a couple of times," said Seth. "But we managed to find a few more pockets. Enough to keep us going for a while, but I reckon she's about done for now, with all this water and stuff."

"We had a mine on the other side of Baldy," said Jemmy. "When we moved on up into the hills we didn't think there was enough left to make it worthwhile to leave a crew behind. I think there's pretty good pickin's there for a couple of willing workers. A sort of shack's there, too, where the fellows bunked when it was their shift. I think we piped the spring into the kitchen the last summer. It's not bad. As soon as we get Debbie settled at home, we'll come back and take you there. You can look the setup over and see if you'd like to take a whack at it."

"Thanks," said Glory huskily. "We'll give her a look. We're kinda wiped out here. This is it." She gestured at the few possessions huddled around the glowing wheel.

"And only the clothes they stand in," I added. "And Glory's treasure box." I lifted the shoe box from the edge of Seth's bed and floated it to Glory's hands. "Glory," I said on sudden impulse, "do you have your mirror in there?"

"The pieces." Glory's face reddened slightly. "Silly, keeping useless things."

"Show it to them," I asked. "They know I broke it."

Slowly Glory took the lid off the box and carefully lifted out the mirror. She had fitted all the broken pieces together and they caught and cut into pieces what little light there was in the cave. I took the mirror from her and looked into it at my shattered, shamed face. "Jemmy," I said, holding it out to him. "I broke it. I ruined something I can't make right. Can you help me?"

Jemmy took the mirror and stared down into it, his face tight with concentration. After long seconds, there was a sudden liquid flow of light and the broken pieces of glass melted into one another and glazed across. He gave the mirror back to me and I saw myself mended and whole again.

"Here, Glory," I said, putting it into her hands. "It's only a part of all the apologies and makings-up for what I owe you."

She ran her finger across the mended glass, her face tender with memories.

"Thanks," she said. "I appreciate it."

Jemmy was bringing in a carrycase for me so I wouldn't have to exert myself at all on the return trip. Glory held Thann-too while Valancy and Jemmy got me settled. She fingered the soft warmth of the baby blanket and burrowed in to uncover one of the tiny pink hands. She tucked it back gently, folding the cuff of the gown around it first.

"Where's the other stuff?" she asked. "No sense taking makeshifts back with you."

"No," I said. "You can't have the gown back, even if you *do* want to keep it. That's Thann-too's very first gown, and might have been his only gown if things hadn't worked out as they did. It's staying in our family, every thoughtful stitch of it, and Thann-too's first child will wear it—" I broke off, overwhelmed by a sudden thought. "Oh, Valancy! I'm a *mother!* And when Thann-too grows up, I'll be a *grandmother!*"

They all laughed at my shocked astonishment. And the emotional temperature of our parting eased.

When Jemmy and Valancy were ready to transport me out into a sky aglow with moonlight and puffy leftover clouds, Glory knelt to surrender my baby into my arms. I reached up and hugged her fiercely to me. "You're Thann-too's grandma, and don't you forget it," I whispered. "I'll be back. We'll both be back, and make everything as right as we can after such a horrible beginning. Honestly, all the People aren't as bad as I make them seem. Don't judge them by me."

"Your folks seem to be mighty nice." Glory was ignoring the tears that stood in her eyes. "I—I never minded you too much. Kids will be kids and then there was Child Within—" Her finger touched his sleeping cheek and she stood up abruptly. "Lordee! Here I am in my nightclothes in front of ever'body!" And she retreated into the shadows to find her slicker to use for a robe.

I waved good-by once as we launched out over the waters. Glory's arm went up in brief salute and she turned back into the darkness without waiting to see us gone.

"You certainly lucked out there, didn't you?" said Jemmy from behind me.

"Didn't I?" I murmured drowsily. "I didn't expect an angel in jeans and plaid shirt. That's not an excuse. It's an explanation."

Jemmy chuckled and in silence we streaked across the sky. I closed my eyes against the brightness of the moon. Swallowing sorrow and hugging my child close against me, I whispered, "Oh, Thann—oh, Thann—oh, Thann!"

And felt him very near.

Interlude: Mark & Meris 5

"Chee!" Meris's breath came out in a long sigh.

"Hmm," said Mark, unfolding his long legs to attend again to the fire. "Not exactly—" He broke off, absorbed in poking the coals.

Debbie laughed. "Not exactly the behavior you would expect from one of the People?" she said.

"Well, I guess that's it." He reached for another length of wood.

"Don't think it wasn't a big blow to me, too, when I finally stepped back for a good look." Debbie sobered, the flaring fire lighting her face. "Of course the People are far from perfect, but it was terribly humbling to me to realize that I was a big, fat part of the clay on the feet thereof and an excellent object lesson to the rising generation. Believe me, I've learned to check myself often against a standard more reliable than my own ego-centric two-foot yardstick."

"Thann-too," mused Meris. "Eva-lee's husband was named Thann."

"Yes," said Debbie. "He was one of my-Thann's Befores. Thann is a fairly common name among us."

"Speaking of names," said Meris casually, "do you know a Timmy and—"

"And a Lytha?" Debbie laughed. "I passed Bethie on my way in! She said you were wondering— Maybe someday you can hear their story from them in person. I don't have it well enough to pass it on."

"Well, I just thought..." Meris smiled.

"Bed." Mark stood and stretched. "Bed for our guest along with our many thanks. How long can you stay?"

"Only tonight and tomorrow night," said Debbie. "I have involvements back with the Group, but Bethie wants me to stay long enough to tell you about Shadow."

"Shadow?" Meris laughed.

Mark laughed. "Look at her ears prick up!"

"Yes, Shadow," said Debbie. "She's a Too, too. In fact she is Bethie-too. She and—you know her brother—Remy had quite an experience not so long ago. In the light of recent developments, Bethie thought you might like to hear of it. Also, it all started pretty close to your summer cabin. You see, from where you live, you go northeast about—" She broke off. "Bed," she said firmly. "Bed, right now. Talking is almost as addictive as listening."

The next evening—school keeps, guest or no guest, and Mark had daily duties—Debbie settling down on the couch between Mark and Meris said, "I suppose that Bethie was relieved to be called away before she could tell you this segment of our story. It concerns mostly her own family and she's so shy about talking of herself or those close to her." Debbie laughed. "It is to smile a little ruefully for me to realize how parallel my actions and thinking were with Remy's, only he's really a Teener and I was supposed to be a responsible married woman.

"Well, anyway, give me your hands and listen to Shadow—"

Shadow on the Moon

"No, we can't even consider it." Father smoothed his hand along the board he was planing. It was to be a small table for Mother's birthday. I curled one of the good-smelling shavings around my finger as I listened.

"But, Father—" I could see Remy's hands clenching themselves as he tried to control his voice and keep it low and reasonable—a real job for the volatile person he was. "If you'd only—"

Father put the plane down and looked at Remy. I mean really looked at him, giving him his full attention. "Has anything changed materially since last we discussed the matter?" he asked.

"Apparently not." Remy laughed shortly. "I hoped *you* might have— If you'd only consider it—"

"You know I'm not the only one that thinks this way," said Father. "Though I concur heartily with the thinking of the rest of the Old Ones. No good would be served. Can't you see that, Remy?"

"I can't see any flat statement like that!" cried Remy, his control of his impatience beginning to slip. "Every step of progress anyone makes is some good. Why don't you let us—"

"Look, Remy." Father sat on one hip on the edge of the workbench. "Shall we A B C it again? A—we couldn't possibly let anyone else know we had gone to the moon in a spacecraft. B—to the best of our knowledge, there is no immediate need for anything to be found on the moon. C"—he smiled—" 'We bin there already.' At least on our way in. And that was enough for most of us. It looked as good to us as the Statue of Liberty did to the flood of immigrants that used to come over from Europe, but we're most of us content to stay where we are now—looking at it from this side, not that." He grinned at Remy. "Unless you have any information that would materially alter any of these three checkpoints, I'm afraid the discussion is closed—"

"Why *couldn't* we tell?" cried Remy desperately, feeling the whole situation going down the drain. "Why do we have to keep it a secret? Isn't everyone risking their lives and spending fortunes trying to get into Space? Why can't we help?" He broke off because his throat got so tight with anger and frustrated tears that he couldn't talk any more.

Father sighed patiently. "So we go to the moon and back and announce it. So they all swarm around. Can't you hear them screaming?— What propellant? What engine? Escape velocity—air pressure—radiation—landing—return launching—reentry! What would you tell them? Go on, boy-type, answer the nice people. Show them the engines. What? No engines! Show them the fuel tank. *¿Que?* No fuel tank! Show them our protection against radiation. *Quoi?* No protection?

"No, Remy. I wish, because you want it so much, that we could make this expedition for you. Your grandfather's memories of Space can hardly be much comfort to you at your age. But it's out of the question. We cannot deliver ourselves over to the Outsiders for the whim of just one of us. If only you'd reconcile yourself to it—"

"What's the use then?" Remy flung at Father. "What's the use of being able to if we don't?"

"Being able to is not always the standard to go by," said Father. He flicked his fingers at the ceiling and we three watched the snowflakes drift down starrily to cover the workbench. "Your mother loves to watch the snow," he said, "but she doesn't go around snowing all the time." He stopped the snow with a snap of his fingers and it dampened the wood shavings with its melting. "No, just being able to is not a valid reason. And reason there must be before action."

Remy kicked a block of wood out of the workshop and all the way up the slope to our walnut tree on the hill above the twisted, glittering string that was Cayuse Creek. I followed along. I always follow along— Remy's shadow, they call me—and he usually pays about that much attention to me. What can I expect else, being a girl and his sister besides. But I like it because Remy does things—lots of things—and he can usually use a listening ear. I am the willing ear. I'm Bethie-too, because Mother is Bethie.

"Then we'll do it by ourselves!" he muttered as he dug a rock out of the ground where it was poking his shoulder when he tried to relax against the hillside. "We'll build our own craft and we'll go by ourselves!" He was so used to me that he automatically said "we"—though it usually meant *he* had decided *he'd* do something—a sort of royal "we." He lay back under the tree, his hands under his head, his eyes rebelliously on the leaves above. I sat by him, trying to snow like Father had, but all I got was cold fingertips and one big drop of rain that I flicked at Remy. He wiped it off and glared up at the canopy of leaves. "Derned old birds!"

I laughed.

"Go on! Laugh!" he said, jerking upright. "Fine deal when my own sister laughs!"

"Remy." I looked at him, smiling. "You're acting about ten years below yourself, and a seven-year-old isn't very attractive in a frame the size of yours!"

He sank back and grinned. "Well, I bet I could. A craft wouldn't be so hard to build. I could use scrap metal—though why does it have to be metal? And we could check in the newspaper for when Canaveral says is the best time—"

"Remy"—the light in his eyes quenched at the tone of my voice—"how far is it to the moon?"

"Well, uh—I'm not so sure. I think it's about 250,000 miles, give or take a couple of blocks."

"How far have you ever lifted a vehicle?" I asked.

"Well, at least five miles—with your help! With your help!" he hastened as I looked at him.

"And how far out of the atmosphere?" I asked.

"Why none at all, of course! Father won't let me—"

"And in free fall? And landing in no air? And coming back?"

"All right! All right! Don't rub it in," he said sulkily. "But you wait!" he promised. "I'll get into Space yet!"

That evening, Father quirked an eyebrow when Remy said he wanted to start training to become a Motiver. Oh, he could learn it—most any of The People could—but it's a mighty uphill job of it if you aren't especially gifted for it. A gifted Motiver hardly needs any training except in how to concentrate on a given project for the time necessary. But Remy would have to start from scratch, which is only a notch or two above Outsider performance—which is mostly nil. Father and Remy both knew Remy was just being stubborn because he so wanted to go out into Space, but Father let him go to Ron for study and I got pretty lonely in the hours he spent away from camp. After all, what is there for a shadow to do when there's no one to follow around?

For a day or two I ranged above the near slopes and hills, astonishing the circling buzzards by peering over their thin, wide wings, or catching a tingly downward slide on the last slants of the evening sun through the Chimneys. The Chimneys are spare, angular fingers of granite that thrust themselves nakedly up among the wooded hills along one bank of the Cayuse. But exploring on your own stops being fun after a while, and I was pretty lonesome the evening I brought Mother a little cottontail rabbit I'd taken away from a coyote on the edge of night.

"I can tell he's hurt," I said, holding the soft, furry thing gently in my hands and securely in my Concern. It lay unwinking on my palms, its quick nose its only movement. "But I can't decide whether it's a break or a strain. Tell me again how to tell the difference."

Mother laid her hand softly on the creature after reassuring it with her Concern. "It's a strain," she said softly. "Don't you sense—" And the rest of it was thinking that has no separate words for it so I can't write it down. And I did finally Sense the strain in the rabbit's muscles and the difference between it and how a break in a bone would feel.

"Oh, yes," I said. "I won't forget again. Shall I let him go, then?"

"Better put him in the patient-pen," said Mother. "At least for the night. Nothing will fright him there and we can let him go tomorrow."

So we slipped him into the pen and Mother and I leaned over to watch him hide himself in the green tangle of growing things at the far end. Then I carefully did as Mother did. We reached inside ourselves to channel away the pain we had Sensed. That's one of the most important things to be learned if you're a Sensitive—which we both are. When Mother was a girl, she lived among Outsiders and she was almost destroyed before she found our Group and was taught how to Channel.

Still full of the warm, prayerlike feeling that follows the Channeling, we walked back toward the house in the half dark.

"You've been missing Remy," said Mother.

"Yes," I sighed. "It wouldn't be so bad if we were back with the Group, but being up here till Father's shift is over makes it kinda lonesome. Even with Remy coming back here to sleep, it's not the same. There's nothing to do—"

Mother laughed. "I'd like a dime for every time a child has said that to a parent! Why not use this so empty time to develop a new Gift or Persuasion?"

"Like what?" I wasn't very enthusiastic.

"Well." Mother considered. "Why not something that would go along with being a Sensitive? You're Gifted with that already. Choose something that has to do with Sensing things. Take metal or water or some Awareness like that. It might come in handy sometime, and you could map the springs or ore deposits for the Group. Your father has the forestry maps for this area, but the People haven't mapped it yet."

Well, the idea was better than nothing, so that evening Mother helped me review the Awareness of water and metal and I set my mind to Group Memory that night so by morning I had a pretty good idea of the Basics of the job. It'd take years really to be an expert, but I could play around with it for the rest of the summer.

Water wasn't scarce enough in Cayuse Canyon to make looking for it much fun, though I loved the little blind stream I found in a cave above the creek, so I tried the metal Awareness and got pretty adept by the evening of the first day. Adept, that is, at finding campers' dumps and beer cans—which isn't much to brag about. It's like finding a telephone pole when you're really looking for a toothpick.

By the end of the week, I had fined down my Sensing. Hovering a hundred feet or so over the surface, I had found an old, two-tined fork buried under two and a half feet of silt at the base of one of the Chimneys, and an ox shoe caught in in a cleft of rock six feet above the creek on another of the Chimneys. Don't ask me how it got there.

"Big deal!" Remy shoved the shoe with his finger when I showed the family my spoils after supper that night. "Both of them iron—both manufactured. Big deal!"

I flushed and talked right back at him as I practically never do. "How far did you move the world today, wise guy? Was that the house I heard roaring past me this afternoon or a matchbox you managed to tilt off the table?"

Which was hardly fair of me, because he was having a lot of trouble with his Motiving and had got his reactions so messed up that he could hardly lift anything now. Sort of a centipede trying to watch his feet when he walks. The trouble would clear up, of course, with further training, but Remy's not the patient type.

"Who's a wise guy?" Before I knew it, I was pressed against the ceiling, the light fixture too hot near the back of my neck.

"Remy!" Mother cried out. "Not at the table!"

"Put her down." Father didn't raise his voice, but I was tumbled back so fast that the hem of my skirt caught the flower bowl and nearly pulled it off the table.

"I'm sorry." Remy glared at his clenched hands on the table and shut us all out so completely that we all blinked, and he kept us out all the rest of the evening.

He hardly said good-by when he left next morning, kicking petulantly at the top of the piñon tree by the gate as he went by. Mother and Father looked at each other and shook their heads like parents and Father folded his mouth like a father and I was sorry I had started the whole thing—though I'm not sure I did.

I had fun all day. I was so absorbed in sorting out the different junk I Sensed that I lost track of time and missed lunch completely. When I checked the shadows for the time, it was long past the hour and I was too far to bother with going home. I wanted to finish this part of the Chimneys before going home anyway. So I sighed and filled my empty stomach with fresh cold spring water and took off again, enjoying the sweep of wind that brushed my hair back from my neck and dried the perspiration.

Well, concentration paid off! Around about four o'clock I sensed a metal deep inside the last of the towering Chimneys. Or the first one, depending on which mountain you started counting from. Anyway, I sensed a metal near the base of the last one—and not iron and not manufactured! Excitedly I landed on the flank of the mountain and searched out the exact spot. I tore my shirt and scratched my cheek and broke two fingernails before I found the spot in the middle of a brush pile. I traced with my finger the short, narrow course. Wire gold. Six feet inside the solid rock beneath me. Almost four inches of it, as thick as a light bulb filament! I laughed at my own matchbox I'd tilted off the table, but I was pleased anyway. It was small, for sure, but I'd found it, hadn't I? From over a hundred feet up?

It was getting late and I was two-meal hungry, so I lifted up to the top of the last Chimney and teetered on its crumbling granite capstone to check my directions. I could short-cut home in a fraction of the time I'd taken to get here. The panorama laid out at my feet was so breathtakingly lovely that I could hardly leave it, but I finally launched myself in the direction of home. I cut diagonally away from the Chimneys, headed for the notch in the hills just beyond the old Selkirk mine. Half unconsciously I checked off metal as I passed above it. It was all ABC easily detected stuff like *barbwire fence, tin can, roofing, barrel hoop*—all with the grating feeling that meant rust.

Then suddenly there it was in my Awareness—slender and shiny and smooth and complicated! I checked in mid-air and circled. *Beer can, wire fence, horseshoe—slender and shiny and smooth and not iron!* I slid to a landing on the side of the mountain. What could it be? A water tank? Some mining equipment? But it was unrusted, sleek and shiny and slender. But how tall? If only I knew a little about sizes and contents. I could tell sizes of things I was familiar with, but not of this thing. I lifted and circled till I caught it again and narrowed my circle smaller and smaller until I was hovering. Over the old Selkirk mine. I grimaced, disappointed, and Sensed, a little annoyed, the tangly feeling of all the odds and ends of silver left in the fifty-years-abandoned old mine, and the traces of a lot of other metals I didn't know yet. Then I sighed. Must have misinterpreted, but big and shiny, smooth and complicated—that's what it still felt like to me. Nasty break! Back to the Differentiations again, girl!

My hunger hurried my lifting for home so much that I had to activate my personal shield to cut the wind.

Before I even got in sight of the ranger station where we were spending our summer in our yearly required shift for the Group, I felt Remy calling for me. Well, maybe not me by name, but he was needing comfort in large quantities and who better than his shadow to give it to him. So I zeroed in on our walnut tree and stumbled to a stop just behind him as he sat hunched morosely over himself.

"I'm grounded," he said. "Ron says not to come back until I'm Purged. Father says I can start clearing brush out of the campsites tomorrow."

"Oh, Remy!" I cried, dismayed for his unhappiness. "Why?"

He grinned unhappily. "Ron says I can't learn as long as I'm trying to learn for the wrong reason."

"Wrong reason?" I asked.

"Yeah. He said I don't want to be a Motiver just to be a Motiver. I want to learn to be one so I can show people up, like Father and you and the Old Ones. He says I don't want to get into Space because of any real interest in Space, but because I'm mad at The People for not telling the world they can do it right now if they want to. He says—" Remy pulled a double handful of grass with sharp, unhappy yanks "—he says he has no intention of teaching me anything as long as I only want to learn it for such childish reasons. What does he think I'm going to do, drop another Hiroshima bomb?"

I checked firmly the surge of remembered sorrow at his words. "One of us *was* there in that plane," I said. "Remember?"

"But he didn't use any of the Designs or Persuasions in the dropping of the Bomb—"

"No. If he had, we probably never would have been able to help him out of the Darkness afterward. Maybe Ron's afraid you might do something as bad as that if you learn to be a Motiver and then get mad."

"That's silly!" cried Remy. "I wasn't even born when the Bomb fell! And as if I'd ever do a thing like that anyway!"

"Maybe you wouldn't, but if you don't know how to be a Motiver, you can't. Remember, every person who ever did anything bad was seventeen once, and anger starts awfully early. Some kids start to crook their trigger fingers in their cradles—"

"I still think it's a lot of foolish fuss over nothing—"

"If it's nothing," I said, "give it up."

"Why should I?" he flared. "I want—"

"What's the matter with you this summer, Remy?" I asked. "Why are you so prickly?"

"I'm not—!" he began. Then he flushed and lay back against the hillside, covering his eyes with his arm. "Sorry, Shadow," he said gently after a while. "I don't know what it is. I just feel restless and irritable. Growing pains, I guess. And I guess it bothers me that I don't have any special outstanding Gift like you do. I guess I'm groping to find out what I'm supposed to do. Do you think it's because we're part Outsider? Remember, Mother's a Blend."

"I know," I said, "but Mother managed to work out all her difficulties. You will too. You wait and see. Besides, a lot of kids that aren't Blends don't develop their Gifts until later. Just be patient." Then I sighed without sound, thinking that to tell Remy to be patient was like telling the Cayuse to flow uphill.

It wasn't until we were at the supper table that I remembered my find of the day. "I found gold today!" I said, feeling a flush of pleasure warming my face. "Real unmanufactured gold!"

"Well!" Father's fork paused in mid-air. "That's pretty good for a second week. When do we start carting it away? Will a bucket do, or shall I get a wheelbarrow?"

"Oh, Father, don't tease," I said. "You know this isn't gold-like-that country! It was just a short wire of it, six feet inside a granite slope. But now I know what gold feels like—and silver and—and something slender and shiny—"

I broke off, suddenly not wanting to detail all my findings. Fortunately my last words were swallowed up in activity as Remy cleared the table so Mother could bring in the dessert. It was his table week and my dishes week.

Remy put in the next morning hacking and grubbing to clear the underbrush out of some of the campsites along Cayuse Creek. Very few people ever come this far into the wilderness, but the Forestry Service has set up several camp places for them just in case, and Father had this area this summer. Any other year he'd be spending his time in his physics lab back with The Group, trying to find gadgets to help Outsiders do what The People do without gadgets.

Anyway, Father released Remy after lunch and I talked him into going metal Sensing with me.

"Shall I bring Father's bucket?" he teased. "It might be diamonds this time!"

"Diamonds!" I wrinkled my nose at him. "I'm *metal* Sensing, goonchild. Even you know diamonds aren't metal!"

I didn't do much Sensing on the way out, what with his chasing me over the ridge for my impertinence to my elders—he's a year older—and my chasing him up-creek for chasing me across the ridge. We were both laughing and panting by the time we got to the Chimneys.

The Chimneys? "Wait—" I held out my hand and we stopped in mid-flight. "I just remembered. Remy, what's slender and shiny and not iron and complicated?"

"What do you mean, slender? How slender? How complicated?" Remy sat cross-legged in the air beside me. "Is it a riddle?"

"It's a riddle, all right, but I don't know the answer." And told him all about it.

"Well, let's go over and see," he said, his eyes shining, his ears fairly quivering with interest. "If it's something at the Selkirk, at least we know *where* it is." We started off again. "Can't you remember anything that'd give you any idea of its size?"

"No-o-o," I said thoughtfully. "It could be most any size from a needle up to—up to—" I was measuring myself alongside my memory. "Gee, Remy! It could be higher than my head!"

"And shiny?" he asked. "Not rusted?"

"Shiny and not rusted."

We were soon hovering over the old Selkirk mine, looking down on the tailings dump, the scant clutter of falling-apart shacks at the mine opening.

"Somewhere there—" I started, when suddenly Remy caught me by the arm and we plummeted down like falling stars. I barely had time to straighten myself for landing before we were both staggering into the shelter of the aspens at the foot of the dump.

"What on earth!" I began.

"Hush!" Remy gestured violently. "Someone came out of the shack up there. An Outsider! You know we can't let Outsiders see us lifting! And we were right overhead!"

"I didn't even know there was anyone in the area," I said. "No one has checked in since we got here this spring. Can you see them from here?"

Remy threaded his way through the clump of aspen and was peering out dramatically, twining himself around the trunk of a tree that wasn't nearly big enough to hide him. "No," he said. "The hill hides him. Or them. I wonder how many there are."

"Well, let's stop lurking like criminals and go up and see," I said. "It's only neighborly—"

The trail up to the Selkirk was steep, rocky, and overgrown with brush and we were both panting when we got to the top.

"Hi!" yelled Remy. "Anybody home?" There was no answer except the squawk of a startled jay. "Hey!" he yelled again. "Anyone here?"

"Are you sure you saw someone?" I asked, "or is this another—"

"Sure I saw someone!" Remy was headed for the sagging shack that drooped against the slope of the hill.

It was too quick for me even to say a word to Remy. It would have been forever too late to try to reach him, so I just lifted his feet out from under him and sent him sprawling to the ground under the crazy paneless window of the shack. His yell of surprise and anger was wiped out by an explosive roar. The muzzle of a shotgun stabbed through the window, where smoke was eddying.

"Git!" came a tight, cold voice, "Git going back down that trail. There's plenty more buckshot where that came from."

"Hey, wait a minute." Remy hugged the wall under the window. "We just came to see—"

"That's what I thought." The gun barrel moved farther out. "Sneaking around. Prying—"

"No," I said. "You don't yell 'hi' when you're sneaking. We just wondered who our neighbors were. We don't want to pry. If you'd rather, we'll go away. But we'd like to visit with you—" I could feel the tension lessening and saw the gun waver.

"Doesn't seem like they'd send kids," the voice muttered, and a pale, old face wavered just inside the window. "You from the FBI?" the old man asked.

"FBI?" Remy knelt under the window, his eyes topping the sill. "Heck, no. What would the FBI be wanting up here?"

"Allen says the government—" He stopped and blinked. I caught a stab of sorrow from him that made me catch my breath. "Allen's my son," he said, struggling with some emotion or combination of emotions I hadn't learned to read yet. "Allen says nobody can come around, especially G-men—" He ran one hand through his heavy white hair. "You don't look like G-men."

"We're not," I laughed. "You just ask your son."

"My son?" The gun disappeared and I could hear the thump of the butt on the splintered old floor of the shack. "My son—" It was a carefully controlled phrase, but I could hear behind it a great soaring wail. "My son's busy," he said briskly. "And don't ask what's he doing. I won't tell you. Go on away and play. We got no time for kids."

"We just wanted to say 'hi,' " I hastened before Remy could cloud up at being told to go play. "And to see if you need anything—"

"Why should we need anything?" The voice was cold again and the muzzle of the gun came back up on the sill, not four inches from Remy's startled eyes. "I have the plans. Practically everything was ready—" Again the hurting stab of sorrow came from him and another wave of that mixture of emotions, so heavy a wave that it almost blinded me, and the next thing I knew, Remy was helping me back down the trail. As soon as we were out of sight of the shack, we lifted back to the aspen thicket. There

I lay down on the wiry grass and, closing my eyes, I Channeled whatever the discomfort was, while Remy sat by sympathetically silent.

"I wonder what he's so tender of up there," he finally said after I had sighed and sat up.

"I don't know, but he's suffering from something. His thoughts don't pattern as they should. It's as though they were circling around and around a hard something he can't accept nor deny."

"Something slender and shiny and complicated?" said Remy idly.

"Well, yes," I said, casting back into my mind. "Maybe it does have something to do with that, but there's something really bad that's bothering him."

"Well, then, let's figure out what that slender, shiny thing is, then maybe we can help him figure out that much— By the way, thanks for getting me out of range. I could have got perforated, but good—"

"Oh, I don't know," I said. "I don't think he was really aiming at you."

"Aiming or not, I sure felt drafty there when I saw what he was holding."

I smiled and went on with the original topic. "If only we could get up closer," I said. "I'm not an expert at this Sensing stuff yet."

"Well, try it anyway," said Remy. "Read it to me and I'll draw it and then we'll see what it is." He cleared a little space, shoving the aspen litter aside, and taking up a twig, held it poised.

"I've studied hardly a thing about shapes yet," I said, lying back against the curve of the slope, "but I'll try." So I cleared my mind of everything and began to coax back the awareness of whatever the metal was at the Selkirk. I read it to Remy—all that metal so closely surrounded by the granite of the mountain and yet no intermingling! If you took away the metal there'd be nothing left but a tall, slender hole—

My eyes flipped open. "The mine shaft!" I cried. "Whatever it is, it's filling the mine shaft—the one that goes straight down. All the drifts take off from there!"

"So now we have a hole," said Remy. "Fill it up. And I'll bet it's just the old workings—the hoist—the cage—"

"No, it isn't." I closed my eyes and concentrated again, Sensing diagonally up through the hill and into the Selkirk. Carefully I detailed it to Remy contour by contour.

"Hey!" I sat up, startled at Remy's cry. "Look what we've made!" I leaned over his sketch, puzzling over the lines in the crumbly soil.

"It looks a little like a shell," I said. "A rifle shell. Oh, my gosh! Do you suppose that's what it is? That we've spent all of this time over a rifle shell?"

"If only we had some idea of relative size." Remy deepened one of the lines.

"Well, it fills the hole it's in," I said. "The hole felt like a mine shaft and that thing fills it."

"A rifle shell that big?" Remy flicked a leaf away with his twig. "Why, that'd be big enough to climb into—"

Remy stiffened as though he had been jabbed. Rising to his knees, he grabbed my arm, his mouth opening wordlessly. He jabbed his twig repeatedly at the tailings dump, yanking my arm at the same time.

"Remy!" I cried, alarmed at his antics. "What on earth's the matter?"

"It's—" he gasped. "It's a rocket! A rocket! A spaceship! That guy's building a spaceship and he's got it down in the shaft of the Selkirk!"

Remy babbled in my ear all the way home, telling again and again why it *had* to be a spaceship and, by the time we got home, I began to believe him. The sight of the house acted as an effective silencer for Remy.

"This is a secret," he hissed as we paused on the porch before going into the house. "Don't you dare say a word to anyone!"

I promised and kept my promise but I was afraid for Remy all evening. He's as transparent as a baby when he gets excited and I was afraid he'd give it away any minute. Both Mother and Father watched him and exchanged worried looks—he acted feverish. But somehow we made it through the evening.

His arguments weren't nearly so logical by the cold light of early morning, and his own conviction and enthusiasms were thinned by the hard work he had to put in before noon at the campsites.

Armed with half a cake and a half-dozen oranges, we cautiously approached the Selkirk that afternoon. My shoulders felt rigid as we approached the old shack and I Sensed apprehensively around for the shotgun barrel—I knew *that* shape! But nothing happened. No one was home.

"Well, dern!" Remy sat down by me on a boulder near the door. "Where d'you suppose he went?"

"Fishing, maybe," I suggested. "Or to town."

"We would have seen him if he were fishing on the Cayuse. And he's an Outsider—he'd have to use the road to go to town, and that goes by our place."

"He could have hiked across the hills instead,"

"That'd be silly. He'd just parallel the road that way."

"Well, since he isn't here—" I paused, lifting an inquiring eyebrow.

"Yeah! Let's go. Let's go take a look in the shaft!" Remy's eyes were bright with excitement. "Put this stuff somewhere where the ants won't get into the cake. We'll eat it later, if he doesn't turn up."

We scrambled across the jumble of broken rock that was the top of the dump, but when we arrived where the mouth of the shaft should be, there was nothing but more broken rock. We stumbled and slipped back and forth a couple of times before I perched up on a boulder and, closing my eyes, Sensed for metal.

It was like being in a shiny, smooth flood. No matter on which side of me I turned, the metal was there and, with that odd illusion that happens visually sometimes, the metal under me suddenly seemed to cup upward and contain me instead of my perching over it. It was frightening and I opened my eyes.

"Well?" asked Remy, impatiently.

"It's there," I said. "It's covered over, but it's there. We're too close, now, though. I can't get any idea of shape at all. It could be a barn door or a sheet of foil or a solid cube. All I know is that it's metal, it's under us, and there's lots of it."

"That's not much help." Remy sagged with disappointment.

"No, it's not," I said.

"Let's lift," said Remy. "You did better from the air."

"Lift? With him around?"

"He's not around now," said Remy.

"He might be and we just don't Sense him."

"How could we keep from it?" asked Remy. "We can always Sense Outsiders. He has no way to shield—"

"But if that thing *is* a rocket and he's in it, that means he'd be shielded—and that means there's some way to get in it—"

We looked at each other and then scrambled down the dump. It was pretty steep and rugged and we lifted part of the way. Otherwise we might have ended up at the bottom of a good-sized rockslide—us under. We searched the base of the hill, trying to find an entrance. We searched all afternoon, stopping only a few minutes to shake the ants off of and out of the cake and eat it and the oranges, burying the peels carefully before we went back to work. We finally gave up, just before sunset, and sprawled in the aspen thicket at the base of the dump, catching our breath before heading home.

I raised up on one elbow, peering upward to the heights I couldn't see. "He's there now," I said, exasperated. "He's back. How'd he get past us?"

"I'm too tired to care," said Remy, rubbing the elbow he'd banged against a rock—and that's pretty tired for Remy.

"He's crying," I said softly. "He's crying like a child."

"Is he hurt?" Remy asked, straightening.

"No-o-o, I don't think so," I said, trying to reach him more fully. "It's sorrow and loneliness—that's why he's crying."

We went back the next day. This time I took a deep-dish apple pie along. Most men have a sweet tooth and miss desserts the most when they're camping. It was a juicy pie and, after I had dribbled juice down the front of me and down onto Remy where he lifted below, I put it into a nice, level inanimate lift and let it trail behind me.

I don't know exactly what we expected, but it was rather an anticlimax to be welcomed casually at the Selkirk—no surprise, no shotgun, no questions, but plenty of thanks for the pie. Between gulps and through muffling mouthfuls, we learned that the old man's name was Thomas.

"Should have been Doubting Thomas," he told us unhappily. "Didn't believe a word my son said. And when he used up all our money buying—" He swallowed hard and blinked and changed the subject.

We never did find out much about him and, of course, ignored completely whatever it was in the shaft of the Selkirk. At least we did that trip and for many more that followed. Remy was learning patience the hard way, but I must admit he was doing wonderfully well for Remy. One thing we didn't find out was the whereabouts of his son. Most of the time for Thomas his son had no other name except My Son. Sometimes he talked as though his son were just over the hill. Other times he was so long gone that he was half forgotten.

Not long after we got on visiting terms with Tom, I felt I'd better alert Remy. "He's not completely sane," I told him. "Sometimes he's as clear as can be. Other times his thoughts are as tangled as baling wire."

"Old age," suggested Remy. "He's almost eighty."

"It might be," I said. "But he's carrying a burden of some kind. If I were a Sorter, I could Go-In to him and tell what it it is, but every time he thinks of whatever is troubling him, his thoughts hurt him and get all tangled up."

"Harmless, though," said Remy.

"Yes?" I brought back to his mind the shotgun blast we had been greeted with. Remy moved uneasily. "We startled him then," he said.

"No telling what will startle him. Remember, he's not always tracking logically. We'd better tread lightly for a while."

One day about a week later, a most impatient week for Remy, we were visiting with Tom again—or rather watching him devour half a lemon pie at one sitting—when we got off onto mines and mining towns.

"Father said the Selkirk was quite a mine when it was new. They took over a million dollars' worth of silver out of her. Are you working her any?" Remy held his breath as he waited Tom's response to this obvious fishing.

"No," said Tom. "I'm not a miner. Don't know anything about mines and ores and stuff. I was a sheet metal man before I retired." He frowned and stirred uneasily. "I can't remember much of what I used to do. My memory isn't so good any more. Not since my son filled me up with this idea of getting to the moon." I felt Remy freeze beside me. "He's talked it so much and worked at it so hard and sunk everything we ever owned into it that I can't think of anything else any more either. It's like a horn blaring in my ears all the time. Gets so bad sometimes—" He pressed his hands to his ears and shook his head.

"How soon will you be blasting off?" Remy asked carefully casually.

"My son says there's only a little left to do. I ought to be able to figure it out from the plans."

"Where is your son?" asked Remy softly.

"My son's—" Tom stopped and frowned. "My son's—" His eyes clouded over and his face set woodenly. "My son said no one was to come around. My son said everyone had to stay away." His voice was rising and he came to his feet. "My son said they'd come and try to stop us!" The voice went up another notch. "He said they'd come snooping and take the ship away!" He was yelling now. "He said to keep them away! Keep them away until he—until he—" His voice broke and he grabbed for the nearest chunk of rock. I reached out quickly with my mind and opened his hand so it dropped the rock and, while he was groping for another, Remy and I took off down the hill, wordless and shaken. We clutched each other at the foot of the slope.

"It *is* a rocket!" stuttered Remy, shaken with delight. "I told you so! A real rocket! A moon rocket!"

"He kept saying 'my son said,'" I shivered. "Something's wrong about that son of his."

"Why worry about that?" exulted Remy. "He's got a spacecraft of some kind and it's supposed to go to the moon."

"I worry about that," I said, "because every time he says 'my son' his mind tangles more. That's what triggered this madness."

Well, when we got back home, almost bursting with the news we couldn't share, Mother was brisking around gathering up some essential things. "It's an emergency," she said. "Word came from the Group. Dr. Curtis is bringing a patient out to us and he needs me. Shadow, you're to come with me. This will be a good chance for you to begin on real diagnosis. You're old enough now. Remy, you be good and take care of your father. You'd better be the cook, and no more than two meals a day of fried eggs!"

"But, Mother—" Remy looked at me and frowned. "Shadow—"

"Yes?" Mother turned from the case she was packing.

"Oh, nothing," he said, his bottom lip pushing forward in his disappointment.

"Well, this'll have to be your exclusive little red wagon, now," I murmured as he reached down a case for me from the top shelf of the closet. "But drag it mighty carefully. If in doubt—lift!"

"I'll wave to you as we go by, headed for the moon!" he teased.

"Remy." I paused with a handful of nightgown poised above the case. "It might still be all a mad dream of Tom's. We've never seen the rocket. We've never seen the son. I could be misreading the metal completely. It'll be fun if you can find out for sure, but don't get your heart set on it too much. And be careful!"

Mother and I decided to take the pickup truck because Father had the forestry jeep and we might need transportation if we went among Outsiders. So we loaded in our cases. Mother got in touch with Father and told him good-by. As the pickup lifted out of the yard and drifted upward and away over the treetops, I leaned out and waved at Remy, who was standing forlornly on the front porch.

It was a wonderful two weeks—in a solemn sort of way. We have a very small hospital. The People are pretty healthy, but Dr. Curtis, who is an Outsider friend of ours, brings patients out every so often for Mother to help him diagnose. That's her Gift—to put her hands on the suffering and read what the trouble is. So when he's completely puzzled with a case, he brings it out to Mother. She's too shy to go Outside. Besides, the People function more efficiently when they are among their own.

It wasn't an easy two weeks, because a Sensitive must experience whatever the patient is experiencing. Even if it is vicarious, it's still very real and very uncomfortable, especially for a beginner such as I am. One evening I thought I was going to die when I got so caught up in the smothering agony of a seizure that I forgot to Channel and lost my way in the suffering. Mother had to rescue me and give me back my breath.

When we finally finished at the hospital, we headed home again. I felt as though I were ten years older—as though I had left home as a child and returned as an adult. I had forgotten completely about Tom and the rocket and had to grope for memory when Remy hissed to me, "It's real!" Then memory went off like a veritable rocket of its own and I nearly burst with excitement.

There was no opportunity that night to find out any details, but it made pleasant speculation before I fell asleep. Next morning we left right after breakfast, lifting into the shivery morning chill, above the small mists that curled up from the *cienega* where antelope grazed, ankle-deep in the pooling water or belly-deep in dew-heavy wild flowers.

"No campsites?" I asked, as we left the flats behind us.

"I finished them last week," said Remy. "Father said I could have some time off. Which is a real deal because Tom needs so much help now."

Remy frowned down at me as he lifted above me. "I'm worried, Shadow. He's sick. I mean more than a wandery mind. I'm afraid he'll be Called before—"

"Before the ship is done?" I asked with a squeeze in my heart that he should be still so preoccupied with his own dream.

"Exactly!" flashed Remy. "But I'm not thinking of myself alone. Sure I want the ship finished, and I want in it and out into Space. But I know Tom now and I know he's only living for this flight and it's bigger to him than his hope of Heaven or fear of Hell. You see, I've met his son—"

"You have!" I reached for his arm. "Oh, Remy! Really! Is he as— uh—eccentric as Tom? Do you like him? Is he—" I stopped. Remy was close to me. I should have been able to read his "yes" or "no" from the plainest outer edges of his thinking, but he was closed to me.

"What's wrong, Remy?" I asked in a subdued voice. "Is he worse than Tom? Won't he let you—"

"Wait and ask Tom," said Remy. "He tells me every day. He's like a child and he's decided he can trust me so he talks and talks and talks and always the same thing." Remy swallowed visibly. "It takes some getting used to—at least for me. Maybe for you—"

"Remy!" I interrupted. "We're almost there and we're still airborne. We'd better—"

"Not necessary," he said. "Tom's seen me lift lots of times and use lots of our Signs and Persuasions." Remy laughed at my astonishment. "Don't worry. It's no betrayal. He just thinks I've gone to a newfangled school. He marvels at what they teach nowadays and is quite sure I can't spell for sour apples or tell which is the longest river in South America. I told you he's like a child. He'll accept anything except the fact—" We were slanting down to the Selkirk.

"The fact—" I prompted. Then instinctively looked for a hiding place. Tom was waiting for us.

"Hi!" His husky, unsurprised voice greeted us as we landed. "So the sister got back? She's almost as good in the air as you are, isn't she? You two must have got an early start this morning. I haven't had breakfast yet."

I was shocked by his haggard face and the slow weakness of his movements. I could read illness in his eyes, but I winced away from the idea of touching his fragile shoulders or cramped chest to read the illness that was filling him to exhaustion. We sat quietly on the doorstep and smelled the coffee he brewed for breakfast and waited while he worried down a crumbly slice of bread. And that was his breakfast.

"I told my sister about the ship," Remy said gently.

"The ship—" His eyes brightened. "Don't trust many people to show them the ship, but if she's your sister, I trust her. But first—" His eyes

closed under the weight of sorrow that flowed almost visibly down over
his face. "First I want her to meet my son. Come on in." He stepped back
and Remy followed him into the shack. I bundled up my astonishment
and followed them.

"Remember how we looked for an entrance?" grinned Remy. "Tom's
not so stupid!"

I don't know what all Tom did with things that clanked and pulleys
that whined and boards that parted in half, but the end result was a big
black square in the middle of the floor of the shack. It led down into a
dark nothingness.

"He goes down a ladder," whispered Remy as Tom's tousled head
disappeared. "But I've been having to help him hold on. He's getting
awfully weak."

So, as we dropped down through the trapdoor, I lent my help along
with Remy's and held the trembling old hands around the ladder rungs
and steadied the feeble old knees as Tom descended. At the bottom of the
ladder, Tom threw a switch and the subdued glow of a string of lights led
off along a drift.

"My son rigged up the lights," Tom said. "The generator's over by
the ship." There was a series of thuds and clanks and a shower of dust
sprinkled us liberally as the door above swung shut again.

We walked without talking along the drift behind Tom as he scurried along the floor that had been worn smooth in spots by countless
comings and goings.

The drift angled off to one side and when I rounded the corner I
cried out softly. The roof had collapsed and the jaggedy tumble of fallen
rock almost blocked the drift. There was just about edging-through space
between the wall and the heaped-up debris.

"You'd better Channel," whispered Remy.

"You mean when we have to scrape past—" I began.

"Not that kind of Channeling," said Remy.

The rest of his words were blotted out in the sudden wave of agony
and sorrow that swept from Tom and engulfed me—not physical agony,
but mental agony. I gasped and Channeled as fast as I could, but the wet
beads from that agony formed across my forehead before I could get myself
guarded against it.

Tom was kneeling by the heaped-up stones, his eyes intent upon
the floor beside them. I moved closer. There was a small heap of soil beside a huge jagged boulder. There was a tiny American flag standing in
the soil, and above it on the boulder was painted a white cross, inexpertly,
so that the excess paint wept down like tears.

"This," mourned Tom almost inaudibly, "is my son—"

"Your son!" I gasped. "Your son!"

"I can't take it again," whispered Remy. "I'm going on to the ship and get busy. He'll tell it whether anyone's listening or not. But each time it gets a little shorter. It took all morning the first time." And Remy went on down the drift, a refugee from a sorrow he couldn't ease.

"—so I said I'd come out and help him." Tom's voice became audible and I sank down on the floor beside him.

"His friends had died—Jug, of pneumonia, Buck, from speeding in his car to tell my son he'd figured out some angle that had them stopped. And there my son was—no one to help him finish—no one to go out to Space with—so I said I'd come out and help him. We could live on my pension. We had to, because all our money was spent on the ship. All our money and a lot more has gone into the ship. I don't know how they got started or who got the idea or who drew the plans or which one of them figured out how to make it go, but they were in the service together and I think they must have pirated a lot of the stuff. That's maybe why they were so afraid the government would find them. I don't hold with dishonesty and mostly my son don't either, but he was in on it along with the other two and I think he wanted to go more than any of them. It was like a fever in his blood. He used to say, 'If I can't make it alive, I want to make it dead. What a burial! Blackness of Outer Space for my shroud— a hundred million stars for my candles and the music of the spheres for my requiem!' And here he lies—all in the dark—" Tom's whole body drooped and he nearly collapsed beside me.

"I heard the crack and crumble," he whispered urgently. "I heard the roof give away. I heard him yell, 'No! Not down here!' and I saw him race for the ship and I saw the rocks come down and I saw the dust billow out—" His voice was hardly audible, his face buried in his hands. "The lights didn't go. They're strung along the other wall. After the dust settled, I saw—I saw my son. Only his hand—only his hand reaching— reaching for Space and a hundred million stars. Reaching—asking— wanting." He turned to me, his face awash with tears. "I couldn't move the rock. I couldn't push life back into him. I couldn't save my son, but I swore that I'd take his ship into Space—that I'd take something of his to say he made it, too. So I gave him the flag to hold. The one he meant to put where the other moon-shot landed. 'Litterbugs!' he called them for messing up the moon. He was going to put this flag there instead—so small it wouldn't clutter up the landscape. So he's been holding it—all this time—and as soon as Remy and I get the ship to going, we'll take the flag and—and—"

His eyes brightened and I helped him—shielding strongly from him—to his feet. "You can come, too, if you bring one of those lemon pies!" He had paid his admission ticket of sorrow and was edging past the heap of fallen rock.

"We'll save that to celebrate with when we get back," I said.

"Get back?" He smiled over his shoulder. "We're only going. We have a capsule to send back with all the information, and a radio to keep in touch as long as we can, but we never said anything about coming back. Why should we ever come back?"

Stunned, I watched him edge out of sight off down the drift, his sorrow for the moment behind him. I leaned against the wall, waiting for my Channeling to be complete. I looked down at the small mound of earth and the quietly drooping flag and cried in a sudden panic—"We can't handle this alone! Not a one-way trip."

I clasped my hands over my mouth, but Tom was gone. I hurried after him, the echo of my feet slipping on the jagged rocks canceling out the frightened echo of my voice.

As I followed Tom down the drift I was trying frantically to find some way out of this horrible situation. Finally I smiled, relieved. "We just won't go," I said aloud. "We just won't go—"

And then I saw the ship, curving gently up into the darkness of the covered shaft. It was almost with a feeling of recognition that I saw and sensed the quiet, efficient beauty of her, small, compact, lovely, and I saw inside where everything flowed naturally into everything else, where one installation merged so logically and beautifully into another. I stood and felt the wonderful wholeness of the ship. It wasn't something thrown together of tags and leftovers. It had grown, taking into itself each component part and assimilating it. It was a beautiful, functional whole, except for—

I followed the unfinished feeling and found Tom and Remy where they were working together. Tom's working consisted of holding a corner of a long sheet of diagrams while he dozed the facile doze of age and weariness. Remy had wound himself around behind some sort of panel and was making mysterious noises.

"Finally get here?" His voice came hollowly. "Take a look at the plans, will you? Tom left his reading specs in the shack. See where—" and his speech went off into visualization of something that was lovely to look at but completely incomprehensible to me. I gently took the sheet from Tom. He snorted and his eyes opened. He half grinned and closed his eyes again. I looked at the sheet. Lines went all over it. There were wiggly lines bisecting other lines and symbols all over it, but I couldn't find anywhere the thing Remy had showed me.

"He must have the wrong paper," I said. "There's nothing here like you want. There's only—" and I visualized back at him.

"Why, it's right there!" And he showed me a wiggly sign and equated it to the picture he had given me.

"Well, how am I to tell what's what when it's put down in such a mysterious way!" I was annoyed. Remy's feet wiggled and he emerged backward.

"Ha!" he said, taking the sheet from me. "Anybody knows what a schematic diagram is. Anybody can see that this"—he waved it at me—"is *this*." And he showed me mentally a panel full of complications that I never could have conceived of.

"Well, maybe anyone can, but I can't," I said. "When did you learn to read this? In school?"

" 'Course not in school," said Remy. "Tom showed me all the plans of the stuff that was left to do. He couldn't figure them out, so I'm doing it. No sweat."

"Remy," I said, pointing to a cluster of symbols on the page. "What's that?"

"Why, this, of course." And he visualized back the things that were symbolized.

"Had you ever seen any of those parts before?" I asked seriously.

"No." Remy put down his tools and his own seriousness matched mine. "What use would they be around The People? They're things Tom's son brought."

"But you looked at all this—this—" I waved the page at him. "And you knew what went where?"

"Why, of course," said Remy. "How could I help it when there the thing is before me, big as life and twice as natural. Anybody—"

"Stop saying 'of course' and 'anybody,' " I said. "Remy, don't you realize that to most people these marks are nonsense until they put in hours and even years of study? Don't you realize that most people can't see three-dimensionally from something two-dimensioned? Don't you know even with study it takes a special knack to *see* the thing complete when you're working with blueprints and diagrams? A special knack—" My voice slowed. "A special Gift? Oh, Remy!"

"Special Gift?" Remy took the plan from my hand and looked at it. "You mean you can't see this solid enough that you could almost pick it up off the paper?"

"No," I said. "It's just lines and odd marks."

"And when we looked at the plans for the addition to the cabin the other night, couldn't you see that funny little room sitting on the paper?"

"No," I said, smiling at the memory. "Is that why you pinched at the paper?"

"Yes," Remy grinned. "I was trying to pick it up, to show Father that it wasn't quite right along the back wall, but he found the mistake in the plans and changed it. That straightened the back wall out okay."

"Remy." I caught his eyes with mine. "Maybe you *do* have a special Gift. Maybe this is what you've been looking for! Oh, Remy!"

"Special Gift—" Remy's eyes were clouded with speculation. "Special Gift?"

I looked around the compartment where we were. "You changed some things, didn't you?"

"Not much," he said absently, still busy with his thoughts. "A few minor shapings that didn't look right—didn't fit exactly."

"That's why it all goes together so wonderfully, now. Oh, Remy, I'll bet you've found your Gift!"

Remy looked down at the paper. "My Gift!" His eyes glowed. "And it's to take me into Space!"

"But not back!" Tom's shaken voice startled us. "Strictly a one-way trip. We've got a capsule—"

"Yeah, Tom, yeah," said Remy, rolling his eyes at me. "Strictly a one-way trip."

I felt an awful cave-in inside me and my lips were stiff with fear. "Remy, you can't mean that! To go into Space and never come back!"

"It'd be worth it, wouldn't it?" he asked, beginning to crawl back behind the panel again. "Tom, will you go get my yellow-handled screwdriver? I left it in the drift by the tool chest."

"Sure, sure!" Tom scrambled to his feet and shuffled away.

"For Pete's sake," hissed Remy, his eyes glaring around the end of the panel, "go along with the gag! Don't get into an argument with Tom. I tried it once and he nearly died of it—and so did I. He got his shotgun again. He's going out to Space, like making a trip to the cemetery. He knows he'll never make it back and he wouldn't want it any other way. All he wants is that little flag on the moon and his body somewhere out there. But he wants it so much we've *got* to give it to him. I'm not fool enough to want to leave my bones out there. Give me credit for a little brains!"

"Then it's okay? There is a way to bring the ship back?"

"It's okay! It's okay!" Remy's voice came muffled from behind the panel. "Hand me back the screwdriver when Tom gets here with it."

So the days went, much too fast for us. We were working against the deadline of summer's ending and the fatal moment when Father and Mother would finally question our so-long absence from the cabin. So far we'd skipped the explanations. So it was that I felt a great release of tension on the day when Remy put down a tool, wiped his hands slowly on his jeans, and said quietly, "It's finished."

Tom's face went waxen and I was afraid he'd faint. I felt my face go scarlet and I was afraid I'd explode.

"Finished," whispered Tom. "Now my son can go into Space. I'll go tell him." And he shuffled off.

"How are we ever going to talk Mother and Father into letting us go?" I asked. "I doubt that even with the ship all ready—"

"We can't tell them," said Remy. "They don't have to know."

"Not tell them?" I was aghast. "Go on an expedition like this and not tell them? We can't!"

"We must." Remy had put on a measure of maturity he had never showed before. "I know very well they'd never let us go if they knew. So you've got to keep the secret—even after we're gone."

"Keep the secret! You're not going without me. Where did you get such a fool idea! If you think for one minute—" I was shrieking now. Remy took hold of my arm.

"Be quiet!" he said, shaking me lightly. "I couldn't possibly let you go along under the circumstances. You've got to stay—"

"Under the circumstances," I repeated, my eyes intent on his face. "Remy, *is* there a way to bring the ship back?"

"I said there was, didn't I?" Remy returned my look steadily.

"To bring the ship back under its own power?"

Remy's hand dropped from my arm. "It'll get back all right. Stop worrying."

"Remy." It was my turn to take his arm. "Have you the instructions for a return flight? Tom said—"

"No," said Remy. His voice was hard and impersonal. "There are no instructions for a return flight—nor for the flight out. But I'll make it—there and back. If not with the ship, then by myself."

"Remy! You can't!" My protest crowded out of the horrified tumult of my thoughts. "Even the Old Ones wouldn't try it without a ship, and they have *all* the Signs and Persuasions among them. You can't Motive the whole craft by yourself. You're not strong enough. You can't break it out of orbit— Oh, Remy!" I was almost sobbing. "You don't even know all the things—inertia—trajectory—gravitational pull— it's too complicated. No one could do it by himself! Not even the two of us together!"

Remy moved away from my hand. "There's no question of your going," he said. "You told me—this is my own little red wagon and I'll find some way of dragging it, even if a wheel comes off along the way." He smiled a little and then sobered.

"Look, Shadow, it's for Tom. He's so wrapped up in this whole project that there's literally nothing for him in this life but the ship and the trip. He'd have died long ago if this hope hadn't kept him alive. You haven't touched him unshielded or you'd know in a second that he was Called months ago and is stubbornly refusing to go. I doubt if he'll live through blast-off, even with all the shielding I can give him. But I've *got* to take him, Shadow. I've just got to. It—it—I can't explain it so it makes sense, but it's as necessary for me to do this for Tom as it is for Tom to do it. Why, he's even forgotten God except as a spy who might catch us in the act and stop us. I think even the actual blast-off or one look at the Earth from Space will Purge him and he will submit to being Called and go to where his son is waiting, just the Otherside.

"I've got to give him his dream." Remy's voice faltered. "Young people have time to dream and change their dreams, but old people like Tom have time for only one dream, and if that fails them—"

"But, Remy," I whispered forlornly. "You might never make it back."

"It is in the hands of The Power," he said soberly. "If I'm to be Called, I'm to be Called."

"I don't think you're right," I said thickly, finding it difficult after all these years to contradict Remy in anything of importance. "You're trying to catch the sun in a sieve—and you'll die of it!" Tears were wet on my face. "I can't let you—I can't—"

"It isn't for you to say 'no' or 'go,' " said Remy, flatly. "If you won't help, don't hinder—"

Tom was back, holding out his hands, bloodstained across the palms.

"Come help me," he panted. "I can't get the rocks off my son—"

Remy and I exchanged astonished glances.

"But, Tom—" I took one of his hands in mine to examine the cut flesh—and was immediately caught up in Death! Death rolled over me like a smothery cloud. Death shrieked at me from every corner of my mind. Death! Death! Rebellious, struggling Death! Nothing of the solemn Calling. Nothing of preparation for returning to the Presence. I forced my stiff fingers to open and dropped his hand. Remy had my other hand, pulling me away from Tom, his eyes anxiously on me.

"But, Tom," he said into the silence my dry mouth couldn't fill, "we're going to take the little flag. Remember? That's to be the memorial for your son—"

"I promised my son I'd go into Space with him," said Tom serenely. "It cuts both ways. He's going into Space with me. Only there are so many rocks. Come help me, you kids. We don't want to be late." He wiped his palms on the seat of his pants and started back down the drift.

"Wait," called Remy. "You help us first. We can't go anywhere until we fuel up. You've got to show me the fuel dump. You promised you would when the ship was finished. Well, it's finished now—all but pumping the fuel in."

Tom stopped. "That's right," nodded his head. "That's right." He laughed. The sound of it crinkled my spine. "I'm nobody's fool. Always keep an ace in the hole."

We followed him down another drift. "Wonder what fuel they have," said Remy. "Tom either wouldn't say, or didn't know. Never could get a word out of him about it except it would be there when we were ready for it. The fuel compartment was finished before we ever found him. He wouldn't let me go in there. He has the key to it."

"It's awfully far from the ship," I worried. "How're we going to get it back there?"

"Don't know," Remy frowned. "They must have had something figured out. But if it's liquid—"

Tom had stopped at a padlocked door. He fumbled for a key and, after several abortive attempts, found the right one and opened the lock. He flung the door wide. There was a solid wall of metal blocking the door, a spigot protruding from it the only thing that broke its blank expanse.

"Liquid, then," whispered Remy. "Now, how on earth—"

Tom giggled at our expressions. "Used to keep water in here. 'S'all gone now. Nothing but the fuel—" He pushed a section of the metal. It swung inward. It had been cut into a rude door.

"There 'tis," cried Tom. "There 'tis."

At first we could see nothing because our crowding into the door shut out all the light that came from behind us; then Tom shuffled forward and the shaft of light followed him. He stopped and fumbled, then turned to us, lifting his burden triumphantly. "Here 'tis," he repeated. "You gotta put it in the ship. Here's the key to the compartment. I'll go get my son."

Remy grasped and almost dropped the thing Tom had given him. It was a box or something like a box. A little more rectangular than square, but completely featureless except for a carrying handle on each end and a smooth, almost mirrorlike surface on the top.

"What is it?" I asked. "How does it work?"

"I don't know." Remy was hunkered down by it on the floor, prodding at it with curious fingers.

"Maybe it's a solid fuel of some kind. It must be. Tom says it's the fuel."

"But why such a big fuel compartment if this is all that goes in it?" I had sensed the big empty chamber several times—padlock and all.

"Well, the only answer I have to that is let's go put it where it belongs and maybe we'll see."

We carried the object between us, back to the ship and into the fuel compartment—at least what was so labeled on the plans. We put it down on the spot indicated for it and fastened it down with the metal clamps that were situated in just the right places to hold the object. Then we stepped back and looked the situation over. The object sat there in the middle of the floor—plenty of room all around it and above it. The almost mirror surface reflected cloudily the ceiling above. There were no leads, no wires, no connections, nothing but the hold-clamps, and they went no farther into the structure of the floor than was necessary to hold them secure.

"Remy?" I looked at his mystified face. "How does it work? Do the plans say?"

"There aren't any plans about this room," he said blankly, searching back in his memory of the plans that were available. "Only a label that says 'fuel room.' There's one notation. I couldn't figure it out before. It says, 'After clamps are secure, coordinate and lift off!!!!' With four exclamation points. That's all. You see, Tom had only the plans for finishing the ship. Nothing for the actual trip."

"And you thought you could—" I was horrified.

"Oh, relax, Shadow," said Remy. "Of course I could see how everything fitted into everything and what the dial readings meant *after* we got started, but—" His voice stopped and his thoughts concentrated on the plans again. "Nowhere a starter button or lever—" He bit his lip and frowned down at the object. In the silence we heard a clatter of rock and Tom's voice echoing eerily, "Come on out, Son. It's time to go! Rise and shine!"

Both of us listened to Tom's happy chant and we just looked at each other.

"What'll we do, Shadow?" asked Remy helplessly. "What'll we do?"

"Maybe Tom knows more about this," I suggested. "Maybe we can get him to talk." I shuddered away from the memory of his hand in mine.

So we went to Tom where he was clawing at the broken rock, trying to free his son, the tiny flag still standing upright in the little mound of earth. Tom was prying at a rock that, if he freed it, would bring half the slide roaring down upon him.

"Tom!" Remy called. "Tom!" And finally got his attention. "Come down here. I need help."

Tom scrambled awkwardly down the slope, half falling the last little way. And I let him stumble because I couldn't bear to touch him again.

"'Tom, how does that fuel work?" Remy asked.

"Work? Why, just like you'd think a fuel would work," said Tom wonderingly. "You just install it and take off."

"What connects it to the engines?" asked Remy. "You didn't give me that part of the plans."

"What engines?" grinned Tom.

"Whatever makes the ship go!" Remy's patience was running out rapidly.

"My son makes the ship go," said Tom, chuckling.

"Tom!" Remy took him by his frail shoulders and held him until the wander-eyes focused on his face. "Tom, the ship's all ready to go, but I don't know how to start it. Unless you can tell me, *we—can't—go!*"

"Can't go?" Tom's eyes blinked with shock. "Can't go? We have to go! We have to! I promised!" The contours of his face softened and sagged to a blur under the force of his emotion. "We gotta go!" He took Remy's hands roughly off his shoulders and pushed him staggering away. "Stupid brat! 'Course you can't make it go! My son's the only one that knows how!" He turned back to the heap of stone. "Son!" His voice was that of a stern parent. "Get outa there. There's work to be done and you lie there lazing!" He began tearing again at the jagged boulders.

We moved away from him—away from the whirlwind of his emotions and the sobbing, half vocal panting of his breath. We retreated to the ladder that led up to the cabin, and, leaning against it, looked at each other.

"His son's been under there for months—maybe a year," Remy said dully. "If he uncovers him now—" He gulped miserably. "And I can't make the ship go. After all your fussing about making the trip, and here I am stuck. But there *are* engines—at least there are mechanisms that work from one another after the flight begins. I don't think that little box is all the fuel. I'll bet there was liquid fuel somewhere and it's all evaporated or run off or something." He gulped again and leaned against the foot of the ladder.

"Oh, Shadow," he mourned. "At first this was going to be my big deal. I was going to help Tom find his dream—and all on my own. It was my declaration of independence to show Father and Ron that I could do something besides show off—and I guess that was showing off, too. But, Shadow, I gave that all up—I mean showing them. All I wanted was for Tom—" His voice broke and he blinked fast. "And his son—" He turned away from me and my throat ached with his unshed tears.

"We're not finished yet," I said. "Come on back."

There was a silence in the drift that sounded sudden. Nowhere could we hear Tom. Not a stone grated against another stone. Not a cry nor a mumbled word. Remy and I exchanged troubled looks as we neared the jagged heap of broken rock.

"Do you suppose he had a heart attack?" Remy hurried ahead of me, edging past the rockfall.

"Remy!" I gasped. "Oh, Remy, come back!" I had Sensed ahead of him and gulped danger like a massive swallow of fire. "Remy!" But it was too late. I heard him cry out and the sudden triumphant roar of Tom's voice. "Gotcha!"

I pressed myself against the far side of the drift away from the narrow passageway and listened.

"Hey, Tom!" Remy's voice was carefully unworried. "What you got that cannon for? Looks big enough from this end for me to crawl in."

" 'Tain't a cannon," said Tom. "It's a shotgun my son gave me to guard the ship so'st you couldn't kill him and keep the ship from taking off. Now you've killed him anyway, but that's not going to stop us."

"I didn't kill—"

"Don't lie to me!" The snarling fury in Tom's voice scared me limp-legged. "He's dead. I uncovered his hand—my son's dead! And you did it! You pushed all that stuff down on him to try to hide your crime, but murder will out. You killed my son!"

"Tom, Tom," Remy's voice was coaxing. "I'm Remy, remember? You showed me where your son lay. Remember the little flag—"

"The little flag—" Tom's voice was triumphant. "Sure, the little flag. He was going to put it on the moon. So you killed him. But now *you're* going to put it on the moon—or die in the attempt." He laughed. It sounded like two stones being rapped together. "Or die in the attempt! Get going!"

"But, Tom—there's no fuel!" protested Remy.

"You got what was in the tank room, didn't you?" demanded Tom. "Well, then, get to flying. My son said it would go. It'll go!"

And I heard their footsteps die off down the drift and Remy's distress came back to me like a scarlet banner. "Shadow! Shadow!"

I don't remember racing back to the ladder or opening the trapdoor or leaving the shack. My first consciousness of where I was came as I streaked over the ridge, headed for home. The stars—when had night come?—the treetops, the curves of the hills all lengthened themselves into flat ribbons of speed behind me. I didn't remember to activate my shield until my eyes were blinded with tears.

I hit the front porch so fast that I stumbled and fell and was brought up sharp with a rolling crash against the front door. Before I could get myself untangled, Mother and Father were there and Mother was checking me to see if I was hurt.

"I'm all right," I gasped. "But Remy—Remy!"

"Shadow, Shadow—" Father gathered me up, big as I am, and carried me into the house and put me down on the couch. "Shadow, clear yourself before you try to begin. It'll save time." And I forced myself to lie back quietly, though my tears ran hotly down into both my ears—and let all the wild urgency and fear and distress drain out of my mind. Then, as we held each other's hands, our three minds met in the wordless communication of The People.

Thoughts are so much faster than words and I poured out all the details in a wild rush—now and then feeling the guidance of my father leading me back to amplify or make clear some point I'd skidded by too fast.

"And now he's there with a madman pointing a shotgun at him and he can't do a thing—or maybe he's already dead—"

"Can we handle him?" Father had turned to Mother.

"Yes," she whispered whitely. "If we can get there in time."

Again the meteoric streaking across the dark hills. And Mother's reaching out ahead, trying to find Tom—reaching, reaching. After an eternity, we swung around the shoulder of a hill and there was the Selkirk—but different! Oh, different!

A shiny, needle-sharp nose was towering above the shack; the broken rock and shale had been shed off on all sides like silt around an ant hole. And the ship! The ship was straining toward the stars! Even as we watched, the nose wavered and circled a wobbly little circle and settled back again, out of sight in the shadows.

"Remy's trying to lift it!" I cried. "A thing that size! He'll never make it— And then Tom—"

We watched the feeble struggle as the nose of the ship emerged again from the shaft—not so far this time—much more briefly. It settled back with an audible crash and Mother caught her breath. "There!" she breathed, clasping her hands. "There!" Slowly she drifted down toward the shack, holding firmly whatever it was that she had caught. Father and I streaked to the shack and down the ladder. We rushed along the drift, past the huddle of rocks, and into the shaft. It took Father a fumbling eternity to find how to get into the ship. And there we found them both—Tom sprawled across his gun, his closed eyes sunken, his face a death mask of itself. And Remy—Remy was struggling to a sitting position, his hand pushing against the useless box from the tank room. He smiled a wavery smile and said in a dazed voice, "I have a little Shadow—That goes in and out with me—And what can be the use of her—I see, I see, I see—"

Then he was held tight in Father's arms and I turned my tears away only to be gathered into Mother's arms. And Tom slept peacefully the quiet sleep Mother had given him as we had a family-type wallow in tears and sobs and murmurs and exasperated shakings and all sorts of excited explanations and regrets.

It was a much more solemn conclave back at the house later on. Tom was still sleeping, but in our back bedroom now. I think Mother was afraid to waken him for fear the shock of opening his eyes on Earth might kill him. She had experienced his gigantic, not-to-be-denied surge toward Space before she had Slept him, and knew it for the unquenchable fire it was.

Of course by the time we were finally reduced to vocal words, most of the explanations had been made—the incredulity expressed, the reprimands given, and the repentance completed—but the problem of Tom was still unanswered.

"The simplest way, of course," said Remy, "is just to write 'finis' to the whole thing, wake Tom up, and then hold his funeral."

"Yes," said Father. "That would be the simplest."

"Of course, Mother and Shadow will have to be ready to Channel instantly to bypass that agonized moment when Tom realizes he has been betrayed." Remy was inspecting his jagged thumbnail and didn't meet Father's eyes.

"Bethie, what do you think?" Father turned to Mother.

She blushed pinkly—that's where I get my too-ready coloring up—and murmured, "I think we ought to look at the ship at least," she said. "Maybe that would help us decide, especially if we have Ron look it over, too."

"Okay, tomorrow." Father parted the curtain at the big window. "Today," he amended as he blinked at the steely gray light of dawn. "Today we'll get in touch with him and take a look. After all, the ship *is* finished." And he turned away with a sigh, only a faint quirk at the corner of his mouth to betray the fact that he knew Remy and I were having a hard time containing our jubilation.

After lunch—even our frantic impatience couldn't pry Mother and Father away from what seemed such minor matters—Ron finally arrived and we all went out to look the ship over. Remy and I streaked on ahead of the others, and I laughed as I caught myself visualizing me dusting the ship frantically from end to end so it'd look its best for our visitors.

There it was! The shaft at least, with the concealing shale and rock shed away on all sides. When we arrived above it, we could see the gleam of the nose of the ship. In all the excitement the night before, we had forgotten to conceal it. But it didn't matter now. Soon that bright nose would be lifting! Remy and I turned joyous somersaults as we shot down to the old shack.

The men—I include Remy in that—were like a bunch of kids with a new toy. They toured the ship, their eyes eager and seeking, their manner carefully casual, their hands touching and drinking in the wonder of it. A spacecraft! Remy's replies to their questions were clipped and practically monosyllabic. His containment surprised me and I wondered if this was a foretaste of what he'd be like as an adult. Of course, Ron's being there—the head Motiver of the Group—may have awed him a little, but it wasn't awe in his eyes, it was assurance. He *knew* the ship.

Mother took advantage of the preoccupation of the men to get in touch with Valancy and, through her, with Dr. Curtis, who hadn't gone back Outside yet. I suppose they discussed Tom's condition and what—if anything—could be done for him. Mother was sitting near a wall of the fuel room, to all appearances daydreaming.

So again I was a Shadow. Not a part of the inspection team—not meshed with Mother. I sighed and wandered over to the fuel box where it sat lonesomely in the middle of the floor. I lay down on my stomach beside it and looked at the shining upper surface. It reflected softly the light in the room, but the reflection seemed to come from deeper into the box than just the upper surface. It had depth to it. It was like looking at the moon. I have never quite believed that the light of the moon is just a reflection of the sun, especially a full moon when the light seems to have such depth, such dimension. And now—and now—if the ship were found spaceworthy, we'd be able to see firsthand if the moon had any glowing of its own.

I caught my own eyes shadowed in the surface and thought, *We'll be going up and up and more up than anyone has ever been before—lifting, soaring, rising—*

Mother cried out. Everything shook and moved and there was a grinding, grating sound. I heard the men shout from somewhere in the ship. Frightened, I rolled away from the fuel box and cried, "Mother!"

There was another scraping sound that shook the ship, and then a crunching thud. For a half second there was silence and then a clatter of feet as the men rushed into the fuel room, and Father, seeing us unhurt, was demanding, "Who lifted the ship!"

"Lifted the ship?" Remy's jaw was ajar. Father's eyes stabbed him. "Did you, Remy?"

"I was with you!" Remy protested.

"Bethie?"

Mother colored deeply and her eyes drifted shyly away from the sternness of Father's face. "No," she said, "I'm not a Motiver. I was talking with Valancy."

I scrambled to my feet, my eyes wide, my color rising as Mother's had. "Father, I'll bet I did it!"

"You *bet* you did it?" Father was annoyed. "Don't you know?"

"I'm—I'm not sure," I said. "You know I'm not even as much a Motiver as Mother is. I still have to struggle to lift the pickup, but—but I was looking at the fuel box and thinking. Father, I'll try it again. You and Ron had better stand by, just in case."

I lay down beside the box again, my eyes intent on the surface, and consciously lifted with all my might.

There was no grinding, grating this time. There was a shriek of metal on stone, a gasp from Mother as her knees buckled under the sudden upthrust, and Father's voice came clear and commanding, "Let go, Shadow. I've got it."

Light was streaming into the ship from windows we'd hardly noticed before. We all exchanged astonished looks, then rushed to look out. We were hovering above the Selkirk—hundreds of feet above the gaping shaft visible off to one side. The scraping on its walls had thrown us sideways.

Father turned to Ron and said, "Take over and maintain, will you?" Then he knelt beside the little box, prodding it with his fingers, smoothing it with his palm. Then he said, "Release to me," and, kneeling there, he brought the nose of the ship down so we lay horizontal to the ground. We all started sliding down as the floor slanted, but we lifted and waited until a wall became a floor, then Father moved the ship to an open flat below the Selkirk and brought it down gently on its side.

We all gathered around him as he stood looking at the box that was now head-high on the wall. We all looked at it and then Father's voice came slow and wonderingly, "It's an amplifier! Why, with that, it wouldn't even take a Motiver to make it to the moon. Three or four people lifting, coordinating in this, this amplifier, could do it, if they didn't tire."

" 'Coordinate and lift off!!!!' " cried Remy. "*Four* exclamation points!"

Father had laid the ship on its side so we could find what damage had been done by Remy and me when we churned the poor thing up and down in the shaft. Mother and I went back home to check on Tom and to ready things for the voyage. No one needed to say we'd go. We all knew we'd go. The men were busy repairing the beat-up undercarriage or whatever you'd call that part of the ship, and we brought a picnic supper out to them a little while before sunset.

We all sat around on the flat. I sat on an anthill first and moved in a hurry. We ate and feasted our eyes on the ship. Remy had come out the other side of ecstasy and was serenely happy. Father and Ron were more visibly excited than he. But then they hadn't lived with the ship and the idea as long as Remy had.

Finally a silence fell and we just sat and watched the night come in from the east, fold by fold of deepening darkness. In the half light came Ron's astonished voice.

"Why, that's what it is! That's what it is!"

"That's what what is?" came Father's voice, dreamily from where he lay looking up at the darkening sky.

"The ship," said Ron. "I've been trying all afternoon to remember what it reminds me of. Now I know. It's almost the same pattern as our life-slips."

"Our life-slips?" Father sat up slowly. "You mean the ones the People escaped in when their ships were disabled entering Earth's atmosphere?"

"Exactly!" Ron's voice quickened. "It's bigger and it's cluttered with a lot of gadgets we didn't have, but basically, it's almost identical! Where did those fellows get the design of our life-slips? We didn't keep any. We don't need to with our Group memory—"

"And its motive power." Father's voice was thoughtful. "It's the power the People use. And Tom's son was supposed to know how to make it go. Do you suppose Tom—"

"No." Mother's voice came softly in the darkness. "I Sorted him after we took him to the house. He's not one of Us."

"His wife then, maybe," I said. "So many of us were scattered after the Crossing. And their son could have inherited—" My voice trailed off as I remembered what his son had inherited—the darkness, the heap of stones, and no chance ever for the stars, not even a reflection of them.

"We could rouse Tom and ask?" offered Remy questioningly.

"Tom is past remembering," said Mother. "He's long since been Called, and as soon as we waken him, he will be gone."

"Well," Ron sighed, "we don't *need* to know."

"No," I admitted. "But it would be fun to know if Our Own built the ship."

"Whoever did," said Father, "is Our Own whether he ever knew the Home or not."

So we went, the next day.

But first, Ron and Father spent a quiet hour or so in the drift and emerged bearing between them a slender pine box with a small flag fluttering atop it. By now the ship was upright again and Remy, Mother, and I had provisioned it. When we were ready to go, we all went back to the house and got Tom, still and lifeless except for the flutter of a pulse faintly in his throat and a breathing that seemed to stop forever after each outflowing sigh. We brought him, cot and all, and put him in the ship.

And then, our Voyage Prayer and the lift-off—not blast-off. No noise pushed us on our way nor stayed behind to shout of our going.

Slowly, at first, the Earth dropped behind us, alternately convex and concave, changing sometimes from one to the other at a blink of the eyes. I won't tell you in detail how it all looked. I'll let you find it all new when you make your first trip. But I will say my breath caught in a sob and I almost wept when first the whole of Earth outlined itself against the star-blazing blackness of space. At that point, Ron and Father put the ship on maintain while they came and looked. We had very little to say. There are no word patterns yet for such an experience. We just stood and worshiped. I could feel unsaid words crowding up against my wonder-filled heart.

But even a wonder like that can't hold the restlessness of a boy for long, and Remy soon was drifting to all parts of the ship, clucking along with the different machines that were now clucking back at him as they activated to keep the ship habitable for us. He was loving every bolt and rivet, every revolution and flutter of dial, because they were his, at least by right of operation.

Mother and I lasted longer at the windows than Remy. We were still there when Ron and Father finally could leave the ship on maintain and rejoin us.

I'm the wrong one to be telling this story if you want technical data. I'm an illiterate for anything like that. I can't even give you the time it took. Time is the turning of the Earth and we were free of that tyranny for the first time in our lives.

I know that finally Father and Ron took the ship off maintain and swung it around to the growing lunar wonder in our windows and I watched again that odd curve and collapse sequence as we plunged downward.

Then we were there, poised above the stripped unmovingness of the lunar landscape. We landed with barely a thud and Father was out, testing his personal shield to see if that would be sufficient protection for the time needed to do what we had to do. It was. We all activated our shields and stepped out, closing the door carefully behind us to safeguard the spaced gasping of Tom.

We stood there looking up at the full Earth, losing ourselves in its flooding light, and I found myself wondering if perhaps it wasn't only the reflection of the sun, if Earth had its own luminousness.

After a while we went back in and warmed ourselves a little, and then the men brought out the slender pine box and laid it on the pumicey crunch of the ground. I stirred the little flag with my fingers so that it might flutter its last flutter.

Then inside the ship they lifted Tom to a window. Mother Went-in to him before she woke him completely and told him where we were and where his son was. Then she awakened him gently. For a moment his eyes were clouded. His lips trembled and he blinked slowly—or closed his eyes, waiting for strength. He opened them again and looked for a long moment at the bright curve of the plain and the spangled darkness of the sky.

"The moon," he murmured, his thin hand clenching on the rim of the window. "We made it, Son, we made it! Let me out. Let me touch it."

Father's eyebrows questioned Mother and her eyes answered him. We lifted him from the cot and, enveloping him in our own shields, moved him out the door. We sustained him for the few staggering steps he took. He half fell across the box, one hand trailing on the ground. He took up a handful of the rough gravel and let it funnel from his hand to the top of the box.

"Son," he said, his voice surprisingly strong. "Son, dust thou art, go back to dust. Look out of wherever you are up there and see where your body is. We're close enough that you ought to be able to see real good." He slid to his knees, his face resting against the undressed pine. "I told you I'd do it for you, Son."

We straightened him and covered him with Mother's double wedding ring patchwork quilt, tucking him gently in against the long, long night. And I know at least four spots on the moon where water has fallen in historical time—four salty, wet drops, my own tears. Then we said the Parting Prayers and returned to the ship.

We went looking for the littering that had annoyed Tom's son so much. I found it, Sensing its metal from miles farther than I could have among the distractions of Earth. Remy wanted to lift it right back out into Space, but Father wouldn't let him. "It wouldn't change things," he said. "It did get here first. Let it stay."

"Okay, then," said Remy, "but with this on it." He pulled a flag out of his pocket and unfolded it. He spread it carefully as far as it would go over the metal and laid a chunk of stone on each corner. "To keep the wind from blowing it away," he grinned, stepping back to look it over. "There, that takes the cuss off it!"

So we took off again. We made a swoop around behind the moon, just to see what it was like, and we were well on our way home before it dawned on me that I hadn't even got one pebble for a souvenir.

"Don't mind," said Mother, smiling as she remembered other rock-collecting trips of mine. "You know they never look as pretty when you get them home."

Now we're back. The ship is stashed away in the shaft. We may never use it again. The fire of Remy's enthusiasm has turned to plans and blueprints and all things pertaining to his Gift, his own personal Gift, apparently the first evidence of a new Gift developing among us. He's gone in so much for signs and symbols and schematic diagrams that he'd talk in them if he could. Personally I think he went a trifle too far when he drew a schematic diagram of me and called it a portrait. After all! Mother and Father laughed at the resultant horror, but Remy thinks if he keyed colors in he might have a new art form. Talk about things changing!

But what will never, never change is the wonder, the indescribable wonder to me of seeing Earth lying in space in the hollow of God's hand. Every time I return to it, I return to the words of the Psalmist—the words that welled up in me unspoken out there half way to the moon.

When I consider thy heavens, the work of thy fingers, the moon and the stars which thou hast ordained; What is man that thou art mindful of him—

Tell Us a Story

"Tell us a story, Nathan." Lucas' voice was hardly more than a whisper at Nathan's elbow in the darkness of the loft. "Tell about the plow again."

"Oh, yes!" Adina's voice came on a long, indrawn breath from the far corner. "And the cradle. The cradle in the tree."

The loft wasn't very big and it was crowded with things waiting for use again when the seasons swung. So there was hardly room on the floor for the quilts laid over heaps of straw that had long ago lost their crinkle and resilience. Lucas and Nathan were side by side, and Adina, behind bundles, was out of sight against the far wall where she had to roll off the bed before she tried to sit up—because of the pitch of the roof.

"Again?" Nathan mock-protested, pleased. "I've already told it a dozen times."

"It's better'n a story," said Adina. " 'Cause it's true, isn't it, Nathan?"

"Sometimes I get to thinking and I kinda wonder." Lucas' voice came, hoarsely cautious. He coughed tentatively a couple of times, but it wasn't very winter yet and a couple of times was enough.

"Wonder!" Adina's voice came indignantly, followed by a *whack* as she forgot to roll before sitting up.

"Shhh! Shhhh!" The cabin was so quiet that breathing was too loud, but there was no sound of grown-ups turning to wake, and so the children breathed again.

"Oh," Lucas' voice came a little louder. "They don't ever wake up. They're too tired."

"No matter," Adina's voice snapped. "You don't believe—"

"I didn't say that!" protested Lucas. "I only wonder sometimes!" There was a scrabble as Lucas sat up and leaned forward in the darkness. "Don't *you?*"

"But it's true, isn't it, Nathan?" Adina's half-whispering voice wanted comfort.

"It's true," said Nathan. "But sometimes I wonder, too—"

"Yeah!" said Lucas. "What if he told Father—"

"I had to go after Kelly Cow." Nathan's voice slid smoothly into the silence, into the well-worn grooves of the story. "Now we know where she goes when she runs away, but last spring I had to hunt for her and got all tore up in the thicket by the river. Course, I know now to go around the thicket instead of through. I found her footprints in the mud on our side of the thicket and followed them through. And Kelly Cow was browsing right along the edge of the field."

Nathan drew a deep breath of mingled pleasure and wonder. "And the plow was plowing—straight as a string, all the length of the field and back again. With no horse pulling! And nobody following! I—I wondered what made it work. I was kinda scared, but I followed it clear down the field, and it just went along with a kind of crunching, sussing sound coming from it. I don't mean it was making any noise by itself. The sound was just the furrow opening up as the plow cut through. I stood in front of it and watched it come. I was watching it so hard that I mighty near got Plowed my own self."

"Plowed your own self!" Lucas echoed, with a giggle.

"And then the baby cried," said Adina. The rustle of her pleased settling down under her covers filled the little pause.

"Made me jump," said Nathan. "To hear a baby crying out there. I hadn't seen anyone around and I couldn't figure where it was—the baby. I looked and looked along the field and under the trees—not moving much, just looking. I didn't know—but I was looking too low. It was up in a tree! There was a cradle hanging from a limb by a couple of ropes. Just like *Rockaby baby up in a tree top*—and a baby was crying in it. It was clear across the field from me, but I could see its little fists waving while it cried. And then the cradle began to rock."

Adina sang softly, *"When the wind blows, the cradle will rock—"*

"Only there wasn't any wind," said Nathan. "It just started to rock. And not a leaf moving except when the cradle touched it. But the baby kept crying. So—so a lady came out of another tree and went over and got the baby from the cradle, and *then*—and *then* she walked on the ground! She just slid through the air and stopped by the cradle to take the baby out—on her way down to the ground."

"And a father came," Lucas prompted.

"A father came and threw the baby up in the air and laughed. And the baby laughed, too, waving its hands and kind of bouncing around up there. And it didn't come down! Its father went up and got it. Then he hugged the mother with one arm and carried the baby with the other. They went away through the trees. I waited to be sure they were gone.

Then, all at once, a little brown basket came down out of the other tree and went away after them."

Nathan's voice died; then he said, "It was a black walnut tree, and the basket was full of green leaves. That seemed crazy to me until Adina reminded me later."

"For the dye pot," said Adina, complacently, in the dark. "To dye brown."

There was a sudden rustle as Nathan sat up on his pallet. "I just remembered," he said. "The baby's dress was pink—real pink—like—like the little wild roses on the edge of the thicket—when they're only part open."

"Like a rose?" Adina was unbelieving. "Like a rose!" She was wistful. "I wish we could make pretty colors."

"Well," said Nathan, "Kelly Cow was going back toward the river. So I went after her. The plow was still going back and forth and back and forth. A lot of birds would fly up from the furrows at the far end, when it came; then, after the plow turned back, they all settled down again. I watched the plow go down the last row and run off the field and make a kind of curlicue at the end of the field, as if—as if it'd been writing something all over the field and was just finishing it. Then it got up in the air and went off through the trees after the people." Nathan sighed.

"It was a good field. No stumps. No stones. There was a pile of stumps near the thicket. The roots were all long and spidery looking. None of them were cut off. They reminded me a little bit of a bunch of radishes pulled up and dropped in a pile.

"And that's all." There was an empty feeling after Nathan's voice stopped. There had to be more—

"But you've gone back a lot of times," said Lucas. "Kelly Cow keeps running away."

"Yes," said Nathan. "They have a real good stand of corn. That's all I ever see any more—the corn."

The silence lengthened and lengthened until it became slow breathing sleep.

Nathan was hunting for Kelly Cow again. He shivered and groped in the ankle-deep snow for a more secure footing. No matter what they did to keep her home, short of locking her in the barn, she always managed to get away. And always headed for the farm beyond the thicket. Nathan started on, miserable with the cold and wanting supper. He bumped carelessly against a snow-laden bush, which immediately flipped and slapped him with a handful of snow. He sank down to sit on the ground—and sat where a hollow under the snow sprawled him sideways.

He lay there, twisted, with difficult tears forcing themselves out of his eyes. Then he scrambled to his knees, alert and startled.

Someone was standing, half-concealed, behind a screen of bare bushes.

"Oh, hello," said Nathan, backhanding his eyes. "I didn't hear you coming."

"Hello." The voice was soft and friendly—with just a hint of accent about it. "Are you hurt?"

"No," said Nathan, getting slowly to his feet, stiff with cold and shyness. "I'm just cold. That Kelly Cow—"

"Here." The figure moved into plain sight. "Here is warmness." Ungloved girl hands offered something to Nathan.

Automatically, he took the thing, his hand sagging a bit under the slight weight, and warmness flowed from it into his hands and began to creep slowly into his coldness.

"What is it?" he asked, looking more closely at the dark, irregular chunk in his hands.

"It is warmness. We use it in the time of cold when we do not want to shield. It is small. It will last small."

"Thank you," said Nathan. "It feels good." He pressed the warmness against his cold cheek and felt the hurting warmth of returning circulation in his ear. "I'm going to die of that Kelly Cow yet," he said, wishing he had a warmness for each cold foot. "I can't figure why she keeps coming over here anyway."

The person's face turned pink. "I think that perhaps we—we call her to our loneliness. And we pet her. And give her things to eat, though—" thoughtfully—"she didn't care for the rabbit bone."

"Cows don't eat meat," Nathan scoffed. "Well, I hafta be getting home or the dark will catch me." He looked around for the cow.

"She is over on the other side of the small trees," said the person. "Why do you always come for Kelly Cow? If she doesn't want to stay, why do you want her to?"

Nathan was startled. "Don't you know anything about cows?" he asked. "Who are you anyway?"

"I'm Eliada," said the girl. "But what about Kelly Cow?"

"We need her milk," said Nathan patiently. How could anyone not know about *cows?* "We drink her milk and use it for bread-and-milk and mush, and, if she's giving enough, we can make butter and cheese—a little, anyway. Sometimes it's the only food we have, between crops."

"Oh." Eliada was thoughtful. Then she smiled. "Like our multi-beasts. I had a multiyouny, but—" Her face tightened and she struggled with something in her throat until she could add: "We had to leave it, when we left. It liked to have its ears rubbed. It was Mahco." Her eyes were very bright and her voice broke.

Nathan was embarrassed before her emotion. "Yeah, I know," he said, tossing the warmness from one hand to the other. "I had to leave my dog. He was too old to travel all that way afoot and Papa said he couldn't ride. Jimmy said he'd take good care of him." His face stilled for a breath-length. "I had to leave Jimmy, too—my best friend."

"Now," said Eliada, her face serene again. "Here is Kelly Cow. May I taste the—the milk of Kelly Cow?"

Nathan had jumped at the nudge of Kelly Cow's nose against his back. He whirled and gathered up the raggedy old rope end as though the cow were going to take off at a dead run. Then he dropped it and half grinned at Eliada. "But how?" he asked. "What'll you drink out of?"

"Oh, yes, a container." Eliada looked around as though containers grew magically on trees; then she squatted down and, drawing a double handful of snow toward her, molded it rapidly into a bowl shape. A piece of the rim crumbled out as the two looked at it. With an embarrassed glance at Nathan, Eliada cupped her hands around the container and closed her eyes in concentration. The bowl melted immediately into a puddle of clear water that began to dull into ice.

"Oops!" she said, smiling up at Nathan. "That was for metal."

She quickly formed another bowl from the snow. Again she cupped it. Again she concentrated. And the surface of the bowl flowed upon itself, then solidified into ice. Eliada grasped it with both hands and lifted firmly. The bowl came away with an audible snap at its base.

"There. A container. If milk isn't too warm and we don't use a slow time."

Nathan closed his mouth and shrugged. He didn't know everything about everything. And the two of them waded through the loose snow to Kelly Cow, who, perversely, was wandering slowly homeward again.

"Here," said Nathan, holding out the warmness. "I need both hands."

"Do you have a place in your clothes to put it?" she asked.

"Sure, I've got a pocket," said Nathan, half smiling at her odd way of talking. You meet all kinds of strangers in a wilderness. He slipped the small chunk into his shirt pocket. "Now give me that snow thing."

Squatting awkwardly without a milking stool, he managed to half fill the snow cup. He handed it to Eliada. She took it and lifted it to her mouth. She hesitated and smiled at him apologetically. "There have been so many things lately that—" she shuddered a little, then tilted her head and the bowl and drank.

"It's good!" Eliada lowered the cup, a little mustache of milk foam at the corners of her mouth.

"Kelly Cow gives good milk," said Nathan. "But I gotta go now. It's settin' in to snow all night." He wound the short frazzled end of the old rope around his hand, but something about Eliada kept him from starting. She was standing, staring down at the snow cup. Without moving her head, her eyes lifted to Nathan. The tip of her tongue wiped away the milk smudges on her lip. "We are hungry," she said. "We are very hungry."

"Hungry?" Nathan asked. "How come? You had a good corn crop—"

"If that is all you have to eat, it does not last until the year turns." Eliada's finger tightened on the bowl. "We are trying different barks now. But they are bitter!" Her voice broke. "And we are hungry!"

"Well, my golly! I don't have—" Nathan fumbled for words.

"You have Kelly Cow." Eliada's eyes were shut as she forced the words out. "And it has milk—"

"Yeah, but we have to eat, too!" Nathan defended.

Eliada drooped from crown to snow, the bowl slipping from her hand and plopping wetly at her feet.

"All right! All right!" he said gruffly. "I'll give you some of the milk." Visions of milkless cornmeal mush streaked through his mind and, even milkless, made him hungry. "I guess a cup of cold—milk—"

Eliada was suddenly close to him, pinching a fold of his coat between her finger and thumb.

"You know, too!" She cried softly. "Who feeds the hungry feeds two."

Nathan twisted away and thumped the heel of his hand against Kelly Cow's shoulder. "What you going to put it in?" he asked. "But not all of it! Papa would tan my hide if I brought Kelly Cow home dry!"

"I will go," said Eliada eagerly. "I will go quickly. We have a container." She whirled and fled over the snow, swiftly, lightly, as though the snow were no hindrance to her feet—as though she flew through the deepening snowfall.

She was back, panting, with her container, its odd misshapenness bending her wrists downward.

Nathan looked at it dubiously. "Where'd you get that thing?" he asked. "If it's that heavy empty, how you going to carry it full?"

"I will carry it," she said, her eyes shining. "It is made of—of what was left after—after—" She hugged it to her with both arms. "It is not beautiful. We have not had much time for beauty yet. Besides, there is no metaller among us now. But it is loved. It is from Home."

"Yeah—well—home," said Nathan, reaching for the container. "Mama has her little trunk. We couldn't bring much, either."

He took the container and squatted again by Kelly Cow and began milking. White foam backed away from the far edge and the stream of milk rang musically against the metal.

"Almost a song," said Eliada. "Can you hear it?" She paced her words to the rhythm of the milking. "Praise—praise—food—food—Sing—sing. Oh, let us sing our praise for food!"

Her words caught Nathan's fancy and he tried it. "Praise—God—from—whom—all—blessings—" Then he slipped sideways and almost spilled the milk, righted himself, and ended up triumphantly, though the rhythm was a little muffled because of the level of the milk rising. "Praise Father, Son, and Holy Ghost!" Then he looked a little dismayed at the amount of the milk in the container—and a little dubiously at depleted Kelly Cow. Eliada caught his uncertainty.

"You have given us too much?" she asked.

"Naw, guess not. Can't put it back anyway. If I'm gonna catch it, another cup or two won't change things. Think you can carry it?" He lifted the awkward, slopping basin up to her hands.

"Oh, yes!" Her eyes were shining. "I will make it less heavy. This good gift of food you have given us. But the best gift is—well, I knew it was the same everywhere, but to hear you sing to Them—" softly she echoed, "Praise Father, Son, and Holy Ghost— Though you named them other—that is the best gift you have given. Thank you."

Nathan wound the tattered rope around his hand again, shy to hear her speak so freely of such things. "You're welcome. Now you got something to go on your mush."

"Mush?"

"Well, porridge."

"Porridge?"

"Gollee! You *must* be foreigners! Look, have you got any corn left?"

"Yes." She shuddered a little. "But, now, our stomachs—"

"Well, grind some up to make meal, but not as fine as flour—here—" he said to her not-knowing look—"about this coarse." He held out his hand and the grainy snow began settling on his old green mitten. "See? About that big. And cook it with water and a little salt." He watched her comprehending nods at each step of the directions. "Stir it good or you'll get lumps. Then put it in a dish and pour milk on it. If you've got any sweetening, put that on, too." His stomach suddenly spoke to him out of its hunger.

"Gotta go." He dragged at Kelly Cow. "I'm late now, and the snow—"

He looked back from the far side of the thicket and saw only the flick of Eliada's skirt disappearing among the trees. He became conscious of the warmness against his chest and caught his breath to call out. But, eying the distance, he turned and trudged off with Kelly Cow, the warmness in his cold, free hand.

"You're late." Mama was brisk about the table and didn't look at Nathan. "Strain the milk into the crock. Supper's almost ready. Adina, you help him."

Adina stretched the strainer cloth tight across the top of the heavy crock and watched carefully as Nathan poured the milk, to make sure that the cheese cloth didn't slip.

"Is that all?" she asked, her clear voice loud in the evening silence.

"Shush!" Nathan elbowed her sharply.

"Mama!" came her outraged squawk.

"Nathan." Papa's voice was heavy with weariness.

"Yes, sir," said Nathan.

"Is something wrong with the milk tonight?"

"No, sir," said Nathan. "There's nothing wrong with it."

"Is so!" said Adina.

"Is not!" retorted Nathan. "There's nothing *wrong* with the milk. There just isn't as much as usual."

"Oh, dear!" Mama came over to see. "You didn't throw rocks at her again, and scare her so that—"

"Rocks scare Kelly Cow—ha!" Adina said pertly, then wilted at Papa's glance.

"Wolves might!" Lucas' eyes were big. "Was it wolves, Nathan?"

"No," said Nathan, shortly. "I gave some of the milk away."

"Give it away? Who on earth could you meet way out here—?" Mama was anxious to know. Who out here in all this loneliness—?

"The people on the place where Kelly Cow always goes. You know, the other side of the thicket. That old man that won't ever talk—only this was a girl from there. We talked." Nathan was getting more and more uncomfortable. "She said they were hungry."

"This was a good year," said Papa slowly.

"But I guess they had only corn—and maybe rabbits. She said they were trying different barks to find something they could eat."

"Bark?" cried Lucas. "Like the deer do?"

"They must be very slack, not to have laid in provisions for the winter," said Papa.

"I don't know," said Nathan, holding the snow bowl tightly in his mind. "Only she tasted the milk and told me they were hungry. I didn't mean to milk so much for them, but—"

"Well," Papa said ponderously. "No matter, for one time. But remember, family must come first."

"Yes, sir," said Nathan. He had a sudden notion. "She—she gave me something—" He reached into his pocket for the warmness and, with a pang, held it out to Papa on the palm of his hand.

"A rock," said Papa, not taking it. "Not much good for supper. Maybe that's why she gave it to you."

Nathan smiled and put the warmness back into his pocket. "Yes, sir," he said, and the room swept back happily into supper activity. Papa was in a good mood.

"*We* called them other?" Adina was shocked. "How could they be anything but Father-Son-and-Holy-Ghost? Maybe they're bad people!"

"Adina!" Nathan's voice came sternly through the dark of the loft. "If you don't shut up, I won't *ever* tell you about the baby again."

A rustling plop signified Adina's lying down again.

"People don't all talk the same language. All the languages have a different name for God."

"But," Adina was shaken, "I thought God was always God!"

"He is!" said Nathan. "But—"

"If you keep fighting about God," said Lucas, "you won't never get to finish what happened."

Silence came in the loft. Then there was a sound of turning on the rustling, unsoft pallets. Nathan's voice came again.

"Then I told her how to make corn-meal mush—"

"Mush! She didn't even know that!" Adina was horrified.

"No," said Nathan shortly, resenting the criticism. "They're foreigners. So I told her how and she went away. I forgot to give her back the warmness, and that's why we've still got it."

"It isn't very warm now," said Lucas, coughing as he squeezed it in his hands. "Bet Adina wore it out before I ever got it."

"Did not," said Adina, too tired to get mad.

"Eliada said it wouldn't stay warm very long. It's little." Silence grew again in the loft and became very drowsy. Nathan's voice came sleepily.

"She said she'd make that bowl thing less heavy to carry it home." Silence and heavy breathing were his only answer. Then, sharply awake, Nathan's voice came again. "But she didn't leave any tracks! Not even in the snow!"

The weather closed in that night and snow fell on snow and storm followed storm, seemingly endlessly. During those days in the dusky one room that flickered with firelight, the children worked at the lessons set for them by their mother. Lucas struggled with his alphabet and numbers and his name—and the cough that shook his thin body.

Adina sounded out the stories in Mama's old Primary reading book that had to be read at the table because it was so fragile and so apart—and so precious. Nathan rather guiltily used part of his time to re-read David and Goliath in the Old Testament part of the Bible. He could have read it with his eyes shut, but he read it again, because it belonged to a time and place like this—shut in, sheltered. The shadowy room swirling with warmth and cold as the fire leaped and sank and the drafts billowed the clothes hanging on pegs against the wall.

Finally, he set aside the Bible and the pleasant containment of the old story, and got out the box of carefully hoarded pieces of newspapers they had salvaged from wherever they happened to be found. Some made no sense at all when you tried to read what there was of them, but some were exciting and engrossing—and seldom complete. But something to read, words to learn.

It was a warm, contained sort of time, with no world except the house. Its outside corners shrieked in the wind, but its inside corners were sheltering, though chilly. Outside was lightless tumult. Inside at one or two places beneath the roof, there was the companionable sound of dripping water—the hurried *plik, plik, plik* intermingling with the deeper, slower *plunk-a, plunk-a*.

Papa rocked in his big chair that he had made after they got here. He looked long into the fire or at the dark ceiling, thinking whatever thoughts came to a wilderness farmer in off season. Or he worked on the horses' harness. Or sat with the Bible on his knees, drowsing, his chair slowing—rousing, his chair picking up tempo.

Mama never lacked for something to do, but even she arrived at a time when she could sit for long, resting moments, her current task on her lap, with no urgency about it.

There were no days or nights. Time was kept only by the checking of the stock in the small barn behind the house, and the coming of bedtime and rising and the diminishing of the woodpile beside the fireplace.

At some point in this timelessness, Nathan glanced up from his reading—*bride wore white mousseline de soie*—as if someone had called him. No one in the room was even looking at him, and so he bent to his work again. Again the call came, sharply, urgently, with not a sound—not a word. He got up uneasily and went to the fireplace. The woodbox had been refilled recently. The fire was about its secret munching and crunching of the old wood from clearing the land. Even the *plunk-a, plunk-a* was the same.

"I think I'll go check the stock," he said, trying to sound like Papa.

"Little early for that," said Papa, glancing up.

"I need to stretch my legs," Nathan said, reaching for his coat. He lighted the small lantern with a splinter blazed from the fire, and turned to the door. Lucas was ahead of him, coughing in his hurry, hacking at the frozen lumps at the bottom of the door with the crowbar.

"Don't let go of the rope," said Mama, anxious because of the wilderness out of doors.

The call caught Nathan as he opened the door, and he stumbled a little on the uneven floor. What was it? What was urging him? Not *out*, he realized, just—just *listen*. No—he wrestled with the problem as he wrestled with closing the door. No—not *listen*. It was *there's need!* Who called?

He got the door shut and clung firmly to the rope stretched from house to barn, while he caught his balance against the howling fury of the wind and the knifing of the snow against the exposed parts of his face. He hugged the lantern to him, under his coat, to keep it from being blown out—and away.

It seemed like a hundred miles and a hundred years before he half stumbled, half fell into the barn. The animals swung drowsy faces to look at him, their eyes catching, with unexpected brightness, what little light came from the lantern that flared smokily, then settled to its small glow.

The snow had housed the animals completely against the wind. Their own bodies had warmed the place and melted some of the snow that had sifted in at the top of the rough walls. The moisture had run down the logs to freeze smoothly again near the floor. The water trough was partly frozen, and Nathan hacked at the thin ice with his heel.

There's need! It was words now, that came so shocking loud inside his head that Nathan whirled, his elbow going up defensively. No one was in the half-light of the chilly stillness except the huddled animals who rippled across with small movement. Then they swung about to stare at the wall opposite the door. Nathan went to the wall and rested his hands against it, his eyes fanning a scared look over the rough logs.

There's need! There's need! The soundless words sobbed into the silence.

"El—" His voice wouldn't work. He tried again. "Eliada?"

Nathan! Nathan! Relief cried in every syllable.

"You can't get in that way," Nathan called foolishly to the rough wall and the quiet stock. "The door is around two corners from you."

The animals blinked their eyes and came apart from their concerted staring, and swung slowly away from each other, unpatterned. There was a thud on the door, and Nathan moved to it quickly, pushing out against the frantic pushing in, and Eliada fell into the barn.

"Nathan! Nathan!" she cried from the floor, reaching blindly.

Nathan knelt and reached a hand to help her up. His fingertips rapped and his fingers bent and slid away with no touch of Eliada.

"Oh!" She drew a sobbing breath. "I'm shielding." Then she reached out for Nathan's hand and clung. "Oh, Nathan," she cried as he pulled her, shivering, to her feet. She sagged and almost fell before he caught and held her. "We're dying! There is nothing to eat! Not anything! And no small creatures in the forest because of the—the falling whiteness."

"Snow," said Nathan, wondering that his face was slowly warming to a tingle and that water on the walls was sliding liquidly down to the floor.

"You don't have a coat," he said blankly.

"A—a coat?" Eliada sank down on a hump of hay near the wall. "Oh—oh. No—no coat. I can warm without, and my— Oh, but, Nathan! You don't understand? We are being Called. We are—dying of—of hunger! There is *nothing*. Oh, Nathan, to have nothing! To put out your hand and there is nothing to fill it. To swallow nothing and hurt and hurt—!" She curled herself down on the hay and cried.

Nathan looked around at the dim animals, their eyes taking turns at catching the light as their jaws crunched, wondering what on earth he could do.

"Come on," he said. "Come to the house. We'll tell Mama and Papa. How—how many people? I mean, how big a family do you have?" He helped Eliada up from the hay.

"We are only six—now," she said, a great sorrow filling the room. "All the others—all those I could see from my slip—went in flicks of brightness—back to the Presence. But what was left—we finally found each other, and we are six. But soon our bodies will not be able to contain us—unless we can find food—" She sagged down against his holding hand.

"We can share," said Nathan. "But for how long—" He used two hands trying to hold the weight.

"Only until the—the snow goes," she said. "We found roots to eat and food even inside the hard round black things under the trees—"

"Walnuts," said Nathan. "Why didn't you gather them last fall? Not much meat for a lot of work but—"

"But we didn't know!" cried Eliada. "We don't know this new world. We came so far— And now to die—" Her eyes closed and she floated, slowly down—not quite to the floor—and hovered there in a small unconscious heap. Nathan grabbed clumsily for her, rapping his knuckles against her shoulder. And she slid slowly—inches above the barn floor—away from him to bump softly against Kelly Cow's winter shaggy legs.

Kelly Cow backed up a step, and went on chewing her cud, her eyes large and luminous in the half dark.

Nathan snatched the lantern and turned to the door. He felt cold flooding back all round him. Then he turned from the door and reached for Eliada. Then turned back—panic squeezed his breath. He crouched on the floor beside Eliada and closed his eyes as tightly as he could, fighting against running and screaming and—

A sudden blast of cold air on his back whirled him around. Papa was leaning back against the push of the door, getting it shut.

"What's keeping you?" Papa asked, thumping snow off his boots. "Your mother—" He broke off as Nathan's shift to hide Eliada pushed her out between them. She straightened out as she floated, and her hair spilled darkly bright, longer than the distance to the floor.

"It's—it's Eliada," Nathan said, his eyes intent on Papa's face as he gathered the inert body into his arms. "The girl I gave the milk to. She came for help. They're starving in this storm."

"She'll freeze in this storm if you stay out here," said Papa. "Give her to me."

Nathan stood up, lifting Eliada with him. He looked at his father, his eyes wide with wonder. "She is less heavy—like she said she'd make the milk."

"You're wasting time," said Papa and took Eliada. His arms jerked upward at the lack of expected weight. Nathan caught the limpness of a trailing hand and kept Eliada from leaving Papa's grasp. Papa took a firmer hold, one arm over and one under, turning Eliada so her face pressed against his shoulder.

"The door," he said, and Nathan slipped around him and opened the door to the blast of the storm.

After endlessly struggling with wind and the stinging slap of driven snow, Nathan, clinging to the stretched rope with one hand and the darkened lantern with the other, stopped to gasp for breath. Papa stopped close behind him, pushing Eliada against him to provide some small, brief shelter. Nathan felt a movement against his back and felt Eliada say something. He turned and groped to touch her to—to warn her?

"Cold," said Eliada, stirring. "Cold."

And the howl and shove of the storm slowly muted. The sting and slap of the snow-laden wind swirled, hesitated, and was stilled. And slowly, slowly warmth wrapped them about. Slowly? It was all in the space of a started in-breathing and an astonished out-breathing.

Nathan clung to the rope, trying to see Papa. It was too dark. Papa muttered something and pushed Eliada against Nathan's back. Nathan stumbled on toward the house, his troubled face seeking for the wind and snow that should be punishing him.

Then he saw the lighted doorway ahead, with Mama anxiously peering out, a quilt clutched around her for warmth. As they moved into the lightened darkness of the doorway, Nathan glanced up. He saw the snow driving, swirling down, but it never reached them. It curved and slid away as if—as if there were something between them and the night. Then Eliada stirred again, lifting her pale face to look up. And, with a doubled roar and chill, the storm smote them again.

Then they were in and the door was shut and the unbelievable warmth and comfort of the house enveloped them.

"It is so good." Eliada looked up from the bowl of bread-and-milk— hard crusts of bread broken into a bowl of milk—hot milk, this time, because of the cold.

"Best not eat anything else now," said Mama, who glowed with having a guest to feed. "What with being hungry so long—"

"Else?" said Eliada, her eyes widening. "More to eat than this?" She lifted a white spoonful. "At the same eating? In *this* world?"

"Eggs," said Mama, her worried look sliding to Papa.

"From our hens. Before the storm began, they were laying pretty good—"

"Eggs?" Eliada slid back into some place in her head that she seemed to have to go to often, for some reason.

"Oh, eggs!" Her eyes shone again. "The bird ones were so small. But they all went away when the cold came. Did your birds not go away?" she asked Lucas, who had followed her like a clumsy, quilt-wrapped shadow ever since she had come in. He leaned on the table opposite her, his eyes feeding even more hungrily than her mouth did.

"Yes," he said hoarsely. "The birds went away, but our hens—" He wrapped his arms tightly around himself and coughed until he gagged. He sat swiping at the cough-driven tears with the worn quilt over his arm, and sniffed and shook with the cold that shook anyone if they left the reach of the fireplace. Everyone except Eliada.

Eliada looked around at the rest of the family, her cheeks becoming faintly pink. "You are all cold," she said. "I'm sorry. I forgot you are not my People." She broke off, then turned to Papa. "I am not strong enough or skilled enough in that Persuasion, since it is not my gift, but if you have a metal—something—I can make it give heat for you for a while."

Papa looked at her, his eyes too deep in shadows to show any glint. Nathan rushed into the moment of silence. "Like the little one she gave me. You know, you thought it was a rock, but it was metal and it was warm."

Before Papa could say anything, Lucas darted for the door, shedding his outer layer as he went, and got there at the same moment as Adina, and both snatched up the heavy metal crowbar that, at this season, was the tool for breaking the ice from the door when the drifts froze too hard to kick aside. It was a short, stout metal bar, bent into a hook at one end and flattened to a stubbly blade at the other.

Together, the two children wrestled the bar back to Eliada.

"Yes," she smiled. "Put it with the fire."

"Aw, heating it in the fire's no good. The pots get cold right away when you take them off." Lucas was disappointed.

"Do what she says," said Adina, tugging at the bar. "Give it to me and I'll—"

The two, tugging against each other, managed to plop the bar into the front of the ashes. It raised a small grimy snow from the feathery ashes.

"It is better in front," said Eliada. "In the fire, the warmness would go up the opening to outside. It is odd—" Her cheeks pinked-up and she moved to the fireplace.

Eliada knelt in front of the bar, little puffs of ashes stirring around her as she knelt. She made a quick sign with one hand; then she reached a finger to touch the end of the bar. She glanced back at the absorbed faces. "I'm not practiced," she said. "I must touch first."

There was a brief silence during which the sound of the wind filled the house as completely as though it were empty of life. Then Eliada lifted her finger from the bar and sat back sideways, but still looking at the bar. She lifted herself a little to pull her dress free from where it had twisted under her, and sat again.

Slowly, wonderfully, warmth began. And flowed into the chilly room like a warming stream, loosening muscles that were unconsciously tightened against the cold, making cheeks and ears start to tingle.

Eliada came to her feet. "I cannot make it more than warm," she said. "Some can make it glow dull red, but—"

"Gollee!" Adina's eyes were wide. "That's magic! Where did you learn that?"

"At Home," said Eliada. She seemed suddenly unsteady and held tightly to the edge of the table with white fingertips. "Before our Crossing. Before we fell here—" Then she straightened and managed a smile. "But we learn here also," she said. "We have learned to make mush from corn—"

"Mush!" Lucas' scorn was large again. "How to make mush!"

"It fed us," said Eliada. "And the bar—it warms you. Why is one more wonderful than the other?"

Nathan shook his head. Maybe so. But to compare something like making mush to this miracle—and yet—he shook his head again.

"Feeding," said Papa suddenly. "Your people. They're still hungry?"

"Yes." Eliada's face sobered. "They were so hungered that I was the only one who could come. The others are in protective sleep until I come with food. And, if I could not find food, or if I should be Called while I am away, they will sleep until their Calling."

"Oh," said Mama, clutching the side of her apron. "We'll have to—" Her eyes went to Papa, but he was going back to his rocking chair, hitching it to an angle to put the fireplace out of his sight. "Well," said Mama, hesitantly. Then she smiled and turned to Eliada, her face alight with the pleasure of being able to share.

"And these?" Eliada touched one finger to the rosy brown curve of an egg.

"Eggs," said Lucas, torn between scorn for her ignorance and his fascination with her.

"So big!" said Eliada. "The bird one, so small! So small to hold all that feathers and singing! Do your—do your hens sing, too?"

"They might call it singing," said Nathan smiling. "On warm summer days, all lazy in the sun—" Tears bit suddenly at the back of his eyes at the remote memory.

"We can let you have these," said Mother. "When they are gone, there will be others." She gathered them, with a practiced outspreading of her fingers, lifting them from the bowl. "But how—they'll break—"

"I can carry them," assured Eliada. And Mama, hesitating for a moment, put them down on the table. One egg began a slow, flopping roll to the edge, but Eliada looked at it, and it reversed itself and hid itself in the middle of the small cluster.

"And to eat them?" Eliada's cheeks were less white now, and her eyes were losing their hooded look of suffering.

"If you were hungry enough, raw would do," said Nathan with a grimace. "But, cooked—? You have fire to cook with?"

"We have to cook with," said Eliada, her eyes going to the bar on the hearth.

"But how can you carry all this by yourself?" Nathan shivered. Even Eliada's magic didn't operate very well on the far side of the room. Eliada's eyes were on the little heaps of food, as if her eyes were still hungry. Then her smile, fed and comfortable, said, "I can carry it. We—we can carry much. I will show you."

She folded the rough piece of canvas Nathan had found up in the loft up around the food; then, stepping back a little from the table, she looked at the lumpy package. It suddenly quivered through, then lifted a little from the table and slid toward Eliada. She took hold of one loose corner of the canvas and moved over to the door. The bundle followed her, obedient to the tug of her fingertips.

Eliada smiled, her eyes touching each person, like a warm hand. "And, see? One whole hand left to carry the container of milk!" The lard can, with its tightly fitted cover, lifted up at a gesture of her hand and hung itself on her fingers.

"How are you going to get home?" asked Adina, anxiously. "It's so cold and dark."

"I can always find home," said Eliada, smiling at her. "And I can shield against the storm." Her glance gathered them together again, her eyes glowing in the twilight of the room. "Truly the Presence, the Name, and the Power are here with you. From your little, you have given us abundance. Even here—so far from Home. So the Old Ones assured us, but—but—" Nathan felt her spasm of grief and sorrow, and then she smiled a little. "It is so much easier to doubt than to believe."

She glanced at the fireplace, where the heavy length of the crowbar sent out almost visible waves of warmth. "It will cool," she reminded. "A day or two days. Or, if gratitude counts, maybe many more days." She made a farewell sign with her hand. "Dwell comforted in the Presence." And then she was gone, the door stubbing back on the chunks of ice and snow that had fallen against the threshold.

There was a silence, broken only by the vast rush of the wind. Surely not so loudly now that warmth was in the room.

Then Papa moved to the fireplace and kicked thoughtfully at the crowbar. "I'm not sure I want to be warmed by this warmth," he said, his voice rolling deep through the unaccustomed length of his sentence. "It may be of evil. This will take some thinking out."

"Papa," Nathan's voice was urgent. "It can't be evil. She knew Father, Son, and Holy Ghost, only she said they called them something else. Other languages—"

"And yet," said Papa, "the Devil can quote Scriptures for his purposes. This will take some thinking out." And he sat again in his chair, the Bible on his lap again, his eyes deep-shadowed by his heavy brows, and stared into the almost visible warmth of the bar.

"Too easy," he muttered. "By the sweat of thy brow—"

The storm cleared from the skies and the crackling cold came. It lay heavily on the land, so heavily that it crushed every vestige of color from everything so that, in a black and white world, Nathan's red cap was like a sudden shout.

He had walked over the crispness of the frozen world to the thicket where even Kelly Cow had sense enough not to venture this day. He stood on the other side of the thicket, his hands in his pockets, his shoulders hunched against the cold, and looked across the smooth, stumpless, sunless field beyond, wondering how those people were doing.

Then he heard a clear call and the sound of laughter, and shrank back, startled, into the shadow of the thicket.

A streak of color shot across the smoothness of the field, dark hair streaming free, bright blue clothes an exclamation point against the white. Eliada? It seemed of a size.

Then came the others, staying in a little cluster, a small child piggy-back on one of them. Brightly, laughingly, they followed Eliada, skimming the snow as if—

Nathan clutched a limb for something solid to hang on to. Eliada swung by him, close enough for him almost to touch. And was gone before he could blink. But she couldn't have! No one— Then the cluster swirled past, the laughing child clinging to the hair of the laughing man. Then they were all at the far side of the field again.

"They can't!" Nathan whispered indignantly. "They can't skate with no skates on. And without moving their feet! They can't."

And a thin, sweet memory stabbed back to him from Back Home. A red sled, and a very high hill, and the delightful terror of letting go at the top—and collecting your breath again at the bottom. But you had to have a hill—and a sled—

He looked across the flatness of the field. The people had stopped now and were clustered together. Then one slid away from the others, and Eliada was skimming the snow, back across the field. Toward him? He shrank farther back in the thicket, suddenly afraid.

Eliada came slower and slower and stopped. "Nathan?" she called. "Nathan?"

Nathan crunched snow to face her. "Yeah," he said.

"Oh, Nathan!" Eliada took his two hands and pulled him out of the thicket. "I sensed you as we went by! But I wasn't sure, so I came— Isn't it a beautiful day?" She whirled lightly around Nathan, making him feel heavy-footed and as awkward as a hub. Then she shot away from him—not even *touching*—but, yes, because, as she turned, a skiff of snow sprayed briefly—and again when she returned to him and stopped, laughing and panting.

"You're all right now?" he asked. "You have plenty to eat?" Her glowing face told him how unnecessary was the question.

"Oh, Nathan!" she laughed. "It would be all funny, if we hadn't so nearly been Called because of hunger."

"What happened?" Nathan hunched and shivered. Standing still, the cold flowed into you fast.

"Oh, I forgot," said Eliada. "Here, I'll extend."

And a motion came between Nathan and the cold, a motion that circled him completely and closed him into warmth with Eliada.

"How do you do that!" he asked, unhappily.

Eliada's face sobered. "Does it offend you?" she asked. "It is more comfortable, merely."

Nathan rubbed his nose, which had started to tingle.

"What was funny?" he asked.

Eliada's face brightened. "After we ate your food—and, Nathan, nothing, not even the festival foods we had to leave behind on The Home, ever tasted so good. We cried for its goodness as we ate. And laughed because we cried. But the food didn't last very long. And we thought to sleep again to our Calling rather than to take food again from your family. But one morning I received a directive to go dig in the little hill behind the house. Such a silly thing to do! But a directive! So two of us went. I could hardly lift the digging thing, but Roth was stronger. He has no sight because of the Crossing, but he is strong. So we tried to dig— and blocks fell away and there was a door! And we opened it—and food! Food!"

"The root cellar," said Nathan. "The people before you put the food by for the winter. How come they didn't tell you before they left?"

Eliada's face saddened. "There was only one, and he did not leave. He was Called the day we arrived. One of the life slips shattered and his body was too broken to hold him more. So he was Called. With my brother. It was his slip that shattered." She tightened her lips and a tear slid from the corner of one eye. "How joyfully he went Otherside, but how lonely for us who are still this side."

"Your brother—" Nathan swallowed with an effort that didn't get rid of the heavy lump choking him. "My—my—" He watched his toe kick against a skeletal bush until he could stop his lips.

"It's too bad you didn't get the directive before you got that hungry," he said, still not looking at her. "Whatever a directive is."

"A directive?" asked Eliada. "But surely—I mean, maybe you have another name for it. For when the Power says to you, *Do,* unless you are too far separated from the Presence, you *do* for that is what must be done, when it must be done."

"No," said Nathan. "At least, I don't know. Still think it could have passed the word—"

"We sometimes wonder," said Eliada, "but we never question. If the directive had come sooner, I would not have gone to you. And I would not now be saying, how can I help loose you from the burden you bear of sorrow and—and evil, Nathan? Evil?"

Nathan turned his face away, biting his lip to hold his face straight. Eliada moved to where she could see his face again. "And evil? Oh, Nathan!"

"My father killed my brother!" Nathan's voice grated his throat with its suppressed intensity. "I hate him!"

"Killed?" Eliada touched Nathan's arm. "You mean, sent him ahead of his time, back into the Presence? Oh, surely not! Not really so?"

"The same as—" Nathan raked a violent fist across his face because of the wetness.

"But—but his own son—" Eliada's face was troubled. "Oh, Nathan, tell me!"

"My father." The words were bitter in his tight mouth. "He decided it was an evil power you used to heat up the crowbar. He raked it out of the fireplace with a stick and shoved it out the door into the dark. He said you had no right to warm us better than he could, and that at least we know why wood makes us warm. Lucas—" his voice died and he gulped. "Lucas cried and grabbed my father's arm, trying to keep him from throwing the warm away, but my father back-handed him clear across the room and did anyway. And Lucas coughed and coughed and wouldn't put the quilt around him again. He sort of settled down, only crying and coughing and shivering, and he wouldn't go over by the fire.

"Then all at once he had the door open and was out in all that wind and storm, trying to find the crowbar in the puddle of water it had melted in the snow. By the time we got him back inside, he was sopping wet, with ice sliding out of his hair when I lifted him.

"And he died. He only lasted a day. My father killed him."

And Nathan cried into the crook of his elbow and into the vast warm comfortingness that flowed from Eliada.

"Nathan," Eliada said finally. "We cannot know if Lucas was truly Called or if he was sent ahead, but you must not hate. It is an evil you must not take for a burden. It will eat your heart and cloud your mind and, worst of all, it will separate you from the Presence."

"But Lucas is dead." Nathan's voice was dull.

"He is back in the Presence," said Eliada. "He is healed of the body that was so frail and so often with pain."

Nathan shook his heavy hanging head. "Words—all kinds of words. But Lucas is dead and my father killed him."

He surged away from Eliada and felt a sudden tightness against his forehead. It released suddenly, flooding him with the crisp, cold air. He blinked at the sun as he ran clumsily. The sun? The sun was still shining?

Spring came slowly. Then, one day, it seemed as if every drop of water tied up in every snowflake let go all at once. For days the house perched on a rise that was usually hardly noticeable but that held it above the rising waters. Then the waters began to move, coursing down to the river. The river came up to meet the house and nibbled away at the rise, slowly, slowly, with the whole world a-swim.

Then the torrents began. They ripped across the field Nathan and his father had worked so hard to clear, gouging out gullies and wiping out almost every trace of last year's furrows.

Then the barn went, hardly splashing, as it slid into the greedy waters, just after Nathan and his father had led Kelly Cow and the other stock up the hill behind the barn and left them there with three raggedly wet chickens. The rest of the flock was gone.

Water gathered around the house closer and lapped at the bottom course of logs. The whole family watched from the small window and the door—watched the waters quiver and lift towards the house. Once, the sun came out suddenly and they were in the middle of a glittering sea of brightness. They had to squint their eyes against the glory. Then it was gray and miserable again.

Adina's breath was a warm tickle on Nathan's ear. "It's gone, Nathan! It's gone!" And hot tears started down her scalded-looking cheeks.

"What's gone?" Nathan whispered.

"Where," she gulped. "Where we buried Lucas. Under the little tree. The tree's gone. The grave's gone. Lucas is gone!" Nathan held her while she shook with crying. He lifted his head as Mama came heavily across the floor. She sat down on the bed, then lay back, her feet still on the floor. One bent arm covered her eyes and she said, in a tight, small voice, "Lucas is gone. And I have to carry this other one to be born and be killed—"

Father turned from the window, but he didn't go to Mama.

"I didn't kill him," he said, his voice tired of making the same words over and over. "I didn't kill him. Before that evil creature—"

"She isn't evil." Nathan's voice was loud and defiant in the room. "She wanted to warm us—"

"With evil," said Father. "With evil."

"Is everything you don't understand evil?" asked Nathan. "Do you know what makes the sun shine? But you let it warm you anyway."

"God—" said Father.

"God," said Nathan. "God made her, too. And taught her how to warm the crowbar."

"The devil," said Father. He turned back to the window, hunched inside the body that suddenly looked too big for him, that skunched down on Father, bending and stooping, trying to fit.

Then suddenly, briefly, the whole cabin lifted a little and settled again. There was a dark wetness along the long cracks of the rough floor.

"Good," said Mama into the startled silence. "Take it all. Take it all." And she turned her face away from all of them.

But the waters had taken all they were to take, and they shrank away from every rise, compressing down into all the low places. There was one spot in the front yard that held a puddle of water for a long time, and it glittered like a watching eye until long after everything else had dried up.

Nathan and his father now faced the task of clearing more land to replace that scoured-out, washed-away, deeply gullied part of the farm. Everything around shouted and hummed and smelled of spring and new life and abundant blossoming, but Nathan had no part in the singing, springing upsurge of delight that was on the land. He was a dark, plodding figure, bowed and unresponsive in the sunlight.

The tree shuddered under every blow of Father's ax. The brightness of the sky hurt Nathan's eyes, and his neck ached from looking up at the shaken branches. Every move that he made was awkward and aching because of the tight hampering of the darkness inside him. He squatted down against a bank of earth and pulled his knees up to his chest, trying to ease the endless aching.

A sharp *crack* from the tree snatched his eyes upward. The tree was twisting—turning unnaturally—splitting!

Something in Nathan cried out, rejoicing—*Now he'll die, too! Now he'll die, too!* But even before the thought formed itself in his mind, he was surging forward on his hands and knees, scrambling to get to his feet.

"Papa!" he yelled. "Papa!"

Papa looked up, dropped his ax, and stood for one long, stunned moment before turning to run—to run in exactly the wrong direction. The splintering tree twisted again and seemed to explode. Papa's cry and Nathan's cry were drowned in the crash.

"Papa!" Nathan groped frantically among the branches. "Papa! Papa!"

Then he found Papa's face. And his hands groped to slide under Papa's shoulders. He cried out as he fell forward over Papa's chest. There was nothing under Papa's shoulders! His head and neck and part of his shoulders were pushed out across the bank of the ragged gully. The weight of the splintery heaping of the tree across his legs and body was all that kept him from slithering backwards down into the rock-jumbled gully behind and below him.

"Papa!" Nathan whispered urgently. He touched the quiet face, his hand wincing away, almost immediately, from the intimacy of the touch.

The face twisted to pain, and the eyes opened, unfocusing beyond Nathan's left shoulder. Then the eyes focused with a vast effort.

"Get it off!" The whisper jerked with the painful effort. "Get it off!" The eyes rolled shut and the head rolled to press against Nathan's startled hand.

"But, Papa!" The words were so loud they splintered the silence. "But, Papa!" he whispered. Then he turned to the twisted mountain of limbs behind him. He scrambled over and grabbed one piece of the splintered trunk. But it was shredded to another piece that peeled from another piece that rocked the edge of the gully, spilling more dirt and rocks from under Papa's shoulder.

Nathan let go hurriedly and could see even that little movement of release flow jerkily through the whole scrambled length of the trunk. And it pushed two more pebbles from under Papa's shoulders.

Nathan slumped down to his knees and slid sideways, his hands grabbing each other and his arms going up to hide his scared face.

"What can I do? What can I do? Oh, God, help me—!"

He jerked around, lifting himself on his knees. *Nathan! Nathan!* Calling him? Not Mama—not Adina!

"Eliada!" he called. "Eliada! Come help! I need—"

There's need? Eliada's call came clearly to him.

"Yes!" he called. "There's need! Come help! I can't—!"

For a long, tight pause Nathan listened to all the busy small sounds of the world of growth. Then a rustle in the trees just back of the jagged half-stump snatched his attention. The branches shuddered and parted, and an anxious-looking Eliada threw herself over the fallen tree to Nathan.

"Oh, Nathan!" She caught her eyes checking Nathan rapidly. "There was a directive—so strong! So strong! You have need?"

"Papa," gulped Nathan. "The tree fell on him. I can't move him—"

"Tree?" Eliada's eyes widened. "The broken one? But your papa—"

"Can you help?" Nathan scrambled back to the branches. "Papa is caught under the tree. I can't lift it. Can you help?"

Eliada crouched beside him. "Let me—let me—" She took a deep breath and sat back on her heels, her hand on Papa's arm, her hair swaying forward over her intent face.

"I cannot lift the tree from him," she said from behind the curtain of her hair. "He would fall to the rocks. I cannot lift him and the tree at one time. It is two different Persuasions—animate and inanimate. If he would not waken—but he would—"

"You gotta help!" cried Nathan. "We can't let him—"

"So you must take from under him the rocks and dirt—" as though Nathan hadn't spoken. "And I will hold him until you have freed him—" She backed away and huddled herself over the edge of the slope down in the gully. "You have digging things?"

"Yes, but—" he turned hopelessly to Papa and then to Eliada.

"He will hurt when he wakens." Eliada sighed without opening her eyes. "While he is not awake—"

Nathan stumbled over to the clutter of tools under the near tree. He brought back the shovel and the crowbar. Sweat streaked his face, and dust streaked the sweat as Nathan labored. He hacked away at the bank under Papa with the bar, scrabbled at it with his bare hands, and whacked with the edge of the shovel.

Slowly, slowly, the bank crumbled. And Nathan stubbornly refused to look up at Papa, wondering why he believed Eliada could "hold" Papa, but believing desperately.

He had stopped to drag his muddy sleeve across his face again, when Papa cried out and moved, sending dirt cascading down on Nathan.

"Don't move!" Nathan cried. "Papa, don't move! I'm getting you out. Stay still!"

Desperately, he pried at the rounded rock that stuck out of the bank. With a sudden jolt, the rock came loose—and Nathan barely stumbled out of the way of the smothery cascade of the dissolving bank.

The dust cleared slowly and Nathan looked up. There, above him, pressed still up against the splintered tree, lay Papa. Up there! In the air! With nothing between him and Nathan except—nothing! And Papa's terrified face peered down at Nathan.

Then Papa screamed hoarsely and, with one hand, groped blindly at the emptiness under and around him. Then both hands waved frantically. They found the splintery tree above him and clung to it with desperate strength.

"I cannot move him," said Eliada past the still circling of her arms. "He is holding so strong. If I move him, the tree will go with him."

"Papa!" yelled Nathan. "Let go! Let go!"

But Papa paid no attention, only fumbled with one foot, trying to find a holding place with it.

"I cannot sleep him," said Eliada, her voice unsteady. "I am not strong enough to do it all at the same time. And, until his hands open—"

Nathan stood, fists clenched at his ribs, staring up at Papa. Then he wet his lips with his tongue. "When I holler," he said, "let him fall—a little ways. Can you do that?"

"Yes," said Eliada. "When you holler—a little fall—"

"Papa!" yelled Nathan. "The tree's going! You're falling! You're falling!"

And Papa fell about a foot. He screamed once before his eyes rolled and his hands relaxed to let his arms dangle below him.

There was an ominous splinter above him and the tree began to sag. Eliada cried out, "Back, Nathan! Quick!" And Nathan, stumbling backward, caught his feet on the rough ground and fell heavily, feeling the scrunching under his doubled knees. He heard a cry from Eliada and twisted, to see Papa jerking away from the falling tree. For a moment Papa hovered in the dusty air above the up-puff from the broken wood landing. Then, as Nathan watched, Papa drifted over Nathan's head. A something hit Nathan's hand, and his other hand smeared it to a wet, red streak as Papa slanted slowly down to the uneven floor of the gully.

Nathan scrambled on hands and knees over to him. "He's bleeding somewhere," he said, glancing up at Eliada.

And she wasn't there.

Nathan never could remember how he got up out of the gully and to Eliada. She was lying quietly, her face turned to the sky, her eyes closed, her mouth a little open, and blood running darkly down from her forehead where a flying stub of a branch had hit her.

Nathan afterwards remembered that day as something that had no meaning in his ordinary life. And yet, in itself, that day was a whole lifetime that fitted together like a jeweled watch. All those impossibilities fitting so neatly together to make the only possible possibility.

Eliada was unconscious only briefly. Then she cried out, her hand going to her head. She lifted dizzily on her elbow and peered about in the bright sunlight. "Lytha? 'Chell? Oh, Simon, look again! Did we come this far to be Called?" The desolation in her voice called Nathan from halfway back down the gully back up to her in a hurried scramble.

"I had to go see. It's a big cut on Papa's leg," he said. "I tore his shirt and wrapped it up, but something white—" He reached out a startled hand and touched Eliada's forehead. "Oh, Eliada!"

Her wide, blind-looking eyes turned to him, then she surged across the space between them. She clung to him so tightly that he had no breath. "Oh, David, David! I thought you crashed! Oh, David!"

"I'm Nathan," he said, prying her fingers gently loose so she could lie down again. "You're hurt—your head—" He touched it again, his eyes anxious on her face.

Eliada's eyes slowly cleared and focused on Nathan. The patient sorrow that resolutely came back over her face made Nathan want to cry.

"Yes," said Eliada, touching her head, then looking at her fingers. She closed her eyes for a moment, then she sat up, leaned forward, and wiped her forehead with the under part of the hem of her skirt. "But it is not bleeding now. Your Papa—"

Weakly, as though from far off, he heard Papa's voice.

"Nathan! You all right? Nathan!"

Nathan turned from Eliada and scrambled down the unsure footing of the slope of the gully.

"Papa! You all right?" and dropped to his knees by him.

"Don't know," said Papa. "Help me up."

And Nathan sagged under the weight of Papa's hands as he pulled himself to a sitting position. Papa got his arm around Nathan's shoulder and the two of them strained to lift him to his feet. They had only started upward when Papa cried out and slid down Nathan to the ground again. Nathan straightened him out, moving the rocks that kept him from lying flat, then he looked up at Eliada, who was drifting down the slope.

"What are we going to do?" he asked hopelessly. "Papa's hurt."

"I have a need for water," said Eliada. "And perhaps your Papa has, too. Is there water?"

Nathan hurried over to where they had put their water pail and the tools. He lifted the lard bucket that sloshed heavily with water and looked back toward where Papa and Eliada were.

Maybe he ought to go get Mama. Maybe somebody else could help them better. Maybe if he just left—he grinned unhappily. With Mama in the family way? And who else to help? Just to walk off from Papa and Eliada? That was kid thinking. *I can't ever be a kid again!* Nathan swung the pail and hurried back.

"It is good." Eliada's eyes were large and luminous on Nathan. Then she smiled a small smile. "Always you are feeding the hungry and giving the cup of water." The smile faded and the eyes closed. "And always, I receive. It is hard always to receive."

"You saved Papa," said Nathan, uneasily looking up the slope.

"For you to hate—" Eliada's eyes opened again.

"I don't hate him," said Nathan, startled that it was so. "Not any more. He is—is Papa." He moved over to look at his father. Papa opened his eyes briefly to dull slits and closed them again as if forever. "Papa?"

"We must move him," said Eliada, wearily, drifting up to her feet, leaning for a moment on some unseen support. "I cannot lift him. I am not now strong enough. But I can make him less heavy for you. Lift him."

Nathan knelt on one knee and slid his hands under Papa, lifting him at knees and shoulders. For a moment, the sheer size of Papa made it awkward; then he had stumbled to his feet and was walking slowly toward the house, leaning back from the less-heavy load. It suddenly seemed as if he were carrying Lucas, for under the whiskered, grown-up face, he could trace in the features—as of Lucas—the other long-ago boy who became Papa. Who maybe was as unhappy and hurting now as Lucas had been—a tenderness welled up inside him and he felt his eyes get wet.

"Na—than! Din—ner!" Nathan's head jerked up at the far, thin cry. "Na—than!" Adina's voice came across the scarred wreckage of the field in the long, familiar calling chant. "Din—ner!"

"It's Adina," said Nathan. "Time to eat. Are you coming? Can you come?"

"Yes," said Eliada. "I can come. If I may hold—" She reached out and took Papa's hand where it drooped down, and Nathan started on, carrying the too-light Papa. Feeling a tug, he looked back to see Eliada, trailing like a limp scarf after him, holding fast to Papa's hand.

Adina came running to meet them.

"Is that Eliada? Oh, Eliada!" Then they got close enough for her to see, and her happy call fell silent and her two hands clasped over her open mouth. Her eyes looked again at Nathan, sagging to a stop under the bulk of Papa. And Papa, white and dead-looking, with blood dripping down over one shoe. And Eliada, a pool of limpness at Nathan's feet. And her eyes filled with frightened tears.

"Oh, Nathan! What's the matter with Papa? And Eliada? There's just us kids, because Mama can't— Oh, Nathan! What are we going to do? What are we going to do?"

Papa was lying on the bed, damply clean, his cream-colored night shirt pulled smoothly and decently down to the folded-back quilt covering him to the waist. His eyes were open and wary, watching as Eliada's hair shook itself in a swirly cloud until it was dry and smoothed itself decorously down against her head, only to lift again into exuberant curls and waves.

"Oh, it is good to be clean again," she said. "Pain is twice as much when there is dirt and confusion—and blood!" Her finger touched her head where the flesh had closed itself to a thin, red line.

"You sure get well fast," said Adina, engrossed in curling a strand of Eliada's hair around her hand and letting it spring free.

"It was small," said Eliada, smiling at her. Then she went over to the bed and melted down upon herself until she was eye to level eye with Papa, straight across.

"But yours is not small," she said. "Your bone is broken. And there is a—a—the flesh is torn to show the bone. It will be long for it to get well after it is put right again. Do you have those whose gift is to put right?"

Papa looked at her for a long moment, then he said, "Doctors. None closer than the county seat. Six days' horseback."

"Then—" Eliada's face pinked a little. "Then will you let us help you? My People? We can make your leg more right so it will get well and be straight, but I cannot do it alone. Will you let us?"

"Evil," said Papa, but slowly, not so quickly sure any more.

"Evil," said Eliada, thoughtfully, twisting her hand in her hair. "I am not sure I know this evil you know so well—"

"Badness," said Nathan. "Disobeying God. Sometimes it seems good, but only to lead you astray. Thou shalt not—"

"Oh," said Eliada after searching somewhere inside herself. "Separation. Oh, but we would do nothing to separate anyone from the Presence!" She was astonished. "We want to help you, but not if you feel it would separate—"

Papa looked at Eliada for a sharp, short moment. Then he turned his face away. "No," he said. "Get thee behind me, Satan."

Eliada toiled to her feet wearily, her face drawn and unhappy, one foot caught in her skirt. Adina, with a sharp little cry, rushed to hinder by trying to help. Nathan lifted Eliada free of her skirts' tangle and of Adina.

"I'm sorry," he said. "Papa sees so much evil—"

"It's because Lucas is dead," said Mama. "That's why he won't let you help. He was so sure that Lucas died because of—of you, that he can't let you help him now, because, if he gets well— And Lucas is dead."

Eliada's head turned alertly. "Roth is here," she said, moving to the door. "We had hoped—"

The tall man who had skated so happily with the small child on his shoulders—so long, oh, so long ago—moved into sight at the door.

"But you said he was blind," said Nathan.

"Yes," said Eliada. "But he has learned to move freely in many places. And there is Moorma—"

A shy, smiling face peered from behind Roth's right leg. Then dodged away, only to peek again from behind his left leg. Nathan felt a smile crack through his tired face, and looked at Eliada. She was smiling, too, as Moorma disappeared again. Adina's giggle was smothered behind quick hands and even Mama's face lightened.

"Moorma is like that," said Eliada. "Smiles come with her always, but she is shy with new people. She sees for Roth, when Roth requires it." She went to the door and put her hand into Roth's reaching hand.

"We will help—when you will accept it," she said. "Take comfort in the Presence." And the three of them were gone.

Adina ran out of the door after them crying, "Goodbye! Goodbye!"

She came back into the cabin with a happy little skip. "They're flying," she said. "I knew they would! And Moorma—Moorma's doing it best—holding onto Roth!"

Nathan straightened his weary back by the bed, which had been pulled to the middle of the room, and looked across it at Mama. Mama, her hand holding the wet, folded cloth on Papa's briefly quiet forehead, looked across it at Nathan. Adina wept quietly in the far corner in her shadowy refuge behind hanging clothes.

"He isn't getting better," said Nathan.

"No," said Mama. "He is getting worse. The poultice isn't doing any good at all. The infection is spreading. And we can't keep the splint straight, the way he tosses—"

Papa jerked away from Mama's hand. "Hell's fires! Hot! Warm warm warm warm—Lucas—!"

Then his eyes opened to look into Nathan's, too close for comfort at the edge of the bed. "It hurts!" His voice was thin and young and painfully surprised. The shadowy little boy again looked through the thicket of pain and whiskers and age. Then his eyes closed and his body twisted as he cried out in a ragged shaken voice.

And Adina wailed from her corner.

Mama straightened up, her hand pressing the swell of her side. She smoothed her hair back with both hands, her eyes shut, her chin tightly lifted. Then she shrugged herself wearily, twisting to ease her own aching.

"Go get them," she said. "He can die if he wants to, but not like this. Not to kill us all with him. Go get Eliada and that man—"

"And Moorma!" Adina was prancing at Mama's elbow. "Get Moorma!"

"Get them all," said Mama. "He can talk about evil, but by their fruits ye shall know them—"

Nathan heard the last words fade as he pounded across the front yard. *Why, it's daylight,* he thought, astonished. *The sun is shining!*

Halfway across the ruined field, he faltered and stumbled. They were coming! All of them! Fast! Don't ask how they come. Don't think of how they come! A *band of angels, coming*—

Three grown-ups and Eliada and the little girl and a cradle—the cradle—tell me a story—

"We have waited," said Eliada, taking Nathan's hand to hurry him back to the cabin. "Each day we have been renewing our strength through

the Power, and we have waited. We can help! Oh, truly, Nathan, we can
help!"

Mama and Nathan hunched under the tree across the flat from the
cabin. Adina had slipped sideways across Mama's lap, and slept, her hands
still tightly interlaced under her chin.

Eliada had told them when they were banished from the cabin: "If
you have a way of coming into the Presence—to speak the Name—"

"We can pray," he told her.

"Pray," she said. "Help us with your prayers."

And the family had prayed—aloud and silently—until the words blurred
and Adina could only remember *Now I lay me*. Now Mama's head was leaning back against the tree trunk, her eyes closed, her breath coming quietly.

Nathan looked around. *It is a good country,* he thought. *Everything
about it is good—now. If only we could—could be more like the country.
Open—busy—growing—* His head drooped with his heavy eyes. *With singing and wings and how big the snowflakes are—the stars—*and he slept.

He woke, too warm in the late afternoon sun, his neck aching, his
mouth dry. He straightened his neck cautiously with the pressure of one
hand—and his whole body throbbed with alarm before he knew it was
Eliada. She was sitting quietly in the pool of her skirts, her hands loosely
clasped in her lap.

She smiled and said quietly, "He is sleeping."

Mama woke to the strange voice.

"We have done what we could—the Power helping," said Eliada.
"His leg—" she faltered. "It was bad. We got it straight again, and se-
cured, and have started it back from the—the—"

"Infection," supplied Mama. "The infection—" She was getting
awkwardly to her feet, leaving Adina fisting weary eyes.

"Yes, the infection." Eliada drifted up to her feet. "It will be long,
but it will get well. Already we are planning a Rejoice for when he walks
again—our first Rejoice since—"

"Moorma—where's Moorma?" Adina grabbed at Mama's skirt and
hugged a handful of it tightly to her face before Mama broke away to
hurry stiffly toward the cabin.

"She is waiting for you," Eliada said, smiling. "She found a—a play-
people of yours. It looks like a little girl—"

"My doll!" cried Adina. "Where did she find it? I lost it—"

"It's in the green growth by the animals' house. She would not touch
it until you came—but she is singing to it."

"Moorma!" called Adina. "Moorma!" as she ran toward the lean-to,
makeshift barn.

Eliada and Nathan went toward the cabin to meet Mama. Her face was smoother and younger. "He's sleeping," she said. And the breath she took seemed to push away all the burdens she had been carrying.

"Before he slept," said Eliada, "he was much troubled because of—of the fields. That, we think we know. And the—the crops. That we do not know. We must know to put it right so that his rest will not be broken by worry."

Mama turned to Nathan. He felt suddenly grown up.

"Our field was practically ruined by the floods," he said. "We were trying to clear another field to get ready to plant. The crops are what we grow—" he half smiled at Eliada. "And we grow things besides corn, too. If we are too late with the planting, we'll have nothing to eat when winter comes."

"Oh! We know crops!" said Eliada happily. "We know growing and harvesting! At Home—at Home!—"

"Roth—" she called. "Marilla—Dor—"

They came sedately, quickly across the yard to meet Mama and Nathan halfway. Marilla held the baby with the wild-rose-pink dress against her shoulder, and Dor's arm across her back steadied her in case of roughness.

The two groups looked at each other. Then smiled. Then they were strangers no more.

"Roth," said Eliada eagerly. "The crops are the things—" She and the men—Nathan grew up some more—huddled under the tree to plan.

Marilla and Mama—who was now holding the baby and smiling—went back toward the cabin, talking supper and baths for a weary, hungry family.

There was never a happier made field in all the world, Nathan thought in the days that followed. Laughter and foolishness and fun—except when Papa came to watch the world, helped by Roth and Dor. Slowly out into the thin shadows near the field he would come, not knowing that even his one good leg never took all his weight. Then, settled cautiously in his big chair, sometimes with Mama sitting near him, he watched the effort and the sweating, the blister-raising labor that went with clearing and leveling the field.

Papa was satisfied when the men individually came to the shade to drink great, dribbling drinks of the spring water and to splash their sweating faces and heads with coolness, then pause briefly to catch their breaths. Papa could accept this, Nathan knew, because—by the sweat of your brows thou shalt—whatever you had to do to get things to eat. Papa distrusted anything that was too easy. But he could accept the neighborly help in time of need. He felt bound to do the same for those who had a need.

The making of the field was a long, hot, hard job—when Papa was watching. But, oh! when Papa had been helped back into the cabin! It was still hard and hot and heavy—but not blister-making. And Nathan had learned to laugh and he laughed often—with surprise and pleasure and astonishment—and just sheer enjoyment. And his ribs never quite broke—it only felt that way. They weren't used to laughter movements.

He saw, one day, the reason why the roots around Eliada's field looked like radishes. They had been pulled up, bodily, like radishes.

"Together like that, at the Home," said Eliada as they watched Marilla, Dor, and Roth, hovering in a handholding circle above the last big tree to be uprooted. "Making the Circle. Remembering, 'We are gathered in Thy Name,' then the Power arrives to be used. That's the way they sealed the ships, on the Home, before we left—"

Nathan turned, thoughtfully, away from her struggle with tears, to watch the tree. It lurched and creaked and lifted, rocks and dirt jolting off in chunks from its roots as it rose. It shook the roots free and drifted over to the edge of the field. And the three workers drifted down to a far shade, thinly, wearily still against the ground.

"But you didn't pull up the ships," said Nathan, wondering if he was just helping Eliada make up a story. But the stories she told—

"No," said Eliada. "But I watched while the Old Ones finished our craft. The outside of it was made in pieces, you know, as the cabin is made of individual logs. So, to finish it, they made the Circle and—and the whole outside of the craft wrinkled and flowed and stilled and became one, a shell for all the craft." Eliada was sadly-happy, back on the Home.

A shout across the field brought them to their feet.

"The last one!" shouted Roth. "Oh, rejoice—rejoice!" And the three grown-ups shot across the field, tumbling and soaring, diving and twisting like young wild things set free, up and up!

And Eliada was gone, romping in the air over the field, joining in the song that lifted brightly, clearly. Nathan heard the high, thin piping of Moorma's voice, as she lifted jerkily, uncertainly, up from the edge of the field, to be gathered in by the others and tossed, with laughter and delighted shrieking, from one to another of the laughing, singing group.

Adina came through the underbrush and stood by Nathan, watching with longing, as Nathan was.

"I wish I could," she said, lifting her arms and rising on her tiptoes. Then she sighed and lowered her arms. "Well, anyway, the baby can't yet. I'll go play with her."

When she was safely gone on her way back to the shade where the baby lay in the cradle, Nathan lifted his arms and came, clumsily, to tip-toe. He gave a longing little hop. Then hunkered down on a fallen log, hunched over his soundless, welling cry—*Oh, if only I could! If only I could!*

Then the plows came! Theirs and Papa's, snicking past the idle, astonished horses, slicing through the field, each with one of the workers hovering as an attendant, who at the first click of a rock, whisked it out of the way, arching through the air, to the rock pile filling in one of the gashes across the land.

Then, the first plowing done, came the rippling of the land as though it were a quilt on a bed, shaking across, filling hollows and smoothing humps, until the whole field lay smooth and dark and ready.

Papa watched some of the furrowing. And some of the planting. And said, heavily pleased, to Mama one evening, "Many hands make light work."

And Mama's eyes crinkled at Nathan as she snipped off her sewing thread with her front teeth and snapped another knot in her sewing thread and bent again to a wild-rosebud-pink ruffle for Adina's new Sunday dress.

"Tell us a story, Eliada," said Adina, softly, in the darkness of the loft. Because, in and out of the hours and days and the long evenings, Eliada had told Adina and Nathan much of the Home. She sighed for the lostness of the Home. They sighed for the wonder of her stories.

"Story!" Moorma's voice was high and clear. "Story!"

"Shh!" said Adina. "Don't wake Papa and Mama!"

"Don't wake Papa and Mama." Moorma's voice was as light as a breath.

Eliada and Moorma were staying the night at the cabin because their folks had gone somewhere, at sunset, their eyes excited and hopeful, their attention long gone ahead of their last goodbyes.

"Tell us a story, Eliada," Nathan repeated from his far, alone corner. "About the Crossing again." *If only Lucas could hear her! Oh, if only!*

"—so when we found the Home would be destroyed, we made ships to take us away. There were three in our valley and we were assigned to one of them. And my cousin was filled with sorrow—"

"Because her love had to go in another ship—" Adina's voice mourned for them.

"Yes," said Eliada. "And then, at the last moment, Eva-lee was Called, so she left the ship—"

"Called?" asked Adina, knowing the answer—

"Called back to the Presence," said Eliada. "Her days totaled. Always, at Home, we were Called before we went back into the Presence.

So we had time for our farewells and to put things in order and to give our families and friends the personal things we wanted them to have. And, most important, time to cleanse ourselves of anything that might make it hard to return to the Presence that sent us forth." Eliada sighed deeply. "At Home—at Home—there was time. We could go quietly Otherside, loving hands holding ours, back into the Presence, and have our cast-asides put in some shadowy place among the growing things, in the cool, growing soil—but—but here—we were so snatched—"

"So snatched—" Moorma parroted in her light, now-yawning voice.

"Tell about the moon," said Nathan, to turn Eliada's thoughts.

"The moon—" Eliada's voice crinkled a little in the darkness. "When we first saw the moon, we hoped it was our new Home, because we knew we could not go as far as another sun. But when we skimmed just above its surface for all those miles and saw it all dead and dry and pocked with holes and not a blade of green and with only a thin slice of shadow far on the horizon, we were *afraid* it would be our new Home!

"Then we swept to the other side, and saw—"

"Our world!" cried Adina, softly. "Our world!"

"Our world," said Eliada. "All clouds and blue and wonderful! We sang! Oh, how we sang for journey's end and the loveliness offered us—" Her voice broke abruptly.

"But you had forgotten—" reminded Nathan.

"We had forgotten," sighed Eliada. "For so many years there had been no need to know how to move the ships, or take them into other atmospheres; so we had forgotten. During all the journey, the Motivers had sought back through all of us and our memories of our Befores, to find the skills they needed, but they were not wise enough. They knew too little. They could do so few of the things that should have been done. Our ship was alone now. All the others had other parts of the sky to search. They were too far for us to work together to get the knowledge we needed before—"

"Before the air—" prompted Adina.

"Before the air," said Eliada. "Like a finger of flame pulled along our ship. By then we were all in our life slips—each all alone—to leave the craft before we died of the heating. Then we moved our slips—or our parents moved us, if we were not of an age to have the skill. And, out there all alone in the empty dark, I saw the ship glow brighter and brighter and—and flow apart and drip down and down—" A sob broke the story.

"Don't tell any more," said Nathan, groping through the multitude of new pictures tonight's story fanned out in his mind. "We shouldn't ask you. It makes you—"

"But telling it helps to end the pain," said Eliada. "I cannot change what happened, but I can change the way I remember it.

"I saw the life slips around me dart down through the air like needles of light, and I got caught up in trying to remember how to move mine—how to bring mine down safely—"

Silence filled the loft, and the wind spoke softly to one corner of the cabin.

"It was so wonderful to find we could breathe unshielded right from the beginning. And that there was land and trees, and the food and water were friendly to us. And some of us had landed close together—"

"We put into the new soil the cast-asides of those who were Called by the time we landed. My brother. Moorma's parents. Roth's wife and little boy. But not—" hope glowed. "Not my parents. Not Roth's daughter. Not Moorma's older brother. So perhaps somewhere, they are still alive—maybe half the world away—wondering if we are still alive. But maybe—"

In the silence, the even breathing from Adina's corner told that she and Moorma were sleeping.

Eliada lifted onto one elbow and spoke to the darkness where Nathan was. "That's where they have gone, Roth, Marilla, and Dor. Roth thinks he has been hearing the Questing of the People. Somewhere, not too far away. If they can find—maybe it will be—"

She lay back with a sigh. "It is hard to wait. But—weeping endureth for a night, but joy cometh in the morning. That was in the book we read to comfort the one who lived in our cabin before he was Called from his broken body. To find a book that has the thoughts—the words—and even—" her voice was hardly a whisper—"even our Brother— Truly, though I take the wings of the morning—"

The wind spoke softly again. Moorma murmured in her corner. And the quiet breathing of sleep was the only sound in the loft.

"Tell us a story, Daddy," said Little Lucas. "Tell about those People and the happy field."

"Isn't very happy now," said Nat, roughly, pretending disinterest. " 's where the lumber yard is."

"Lumber yards are happy!" Dena protested. "They smell of forest and they build houses—"

"When it was the happy field," said Nathan, leaning back in Papa's big old chair, about the only thing left from the old cabin. "Ours was the only cabin for ten miles or so, except where—those People lived."

"That's where the school is now!" cried Dena, perching on one of the rockers, clinging to Nathan's arm. "At the end of Koomatka road."

"Koomatka!" scoffed Nat. "Crazy Indian names!"

"It isn't Indian," said Nathan automatically, his eyes far and seeking. "On their Home, the People had a fruit called *koomatka*. It tasted like music sounds and was for special holidays— They sang—they had songs for every—"

"Tasted like music—" The children snuggled down into themselves on the floor with quick, happy looks at each other. It had worked! Daddy was started on a People story!

"—and they came back the next day, so happy they could hardly land in our front yard. And they had brought three more of the People with them—starving—broken—raggedy. They had never found a settling place since their Landing. And Mama cried while she helped Marilla bathe and care for them. They had come to our place because two of the new People were Eliada's parents. They had to let her know—and Mama could help. Eliada couldn't help. All she could do was hover—*half the time* above *the bed*—so close they had to keep pushing her out of the way. Finally they told me to take her out under the big tree across the yard. So I did. And I held onto her there until she suddenly—like fainting—was asleep across my lap.

"The other one they found was Moorma's brother—Perez. He had cared for the others and defended them and starved so they could eat and was strong until they got him to our place, and then he collapsed—"

"But they got well!" Little Lucas was anxious—as always—clambering up to lean hard against Nathan's arm.

"They got well." Nathan nodded, his arm tight about Little Lucas' fragile shoulders, wondering that Lucas was in the face of his child as he had been in Papa's face—Papa—

"Papa was pleased at how well the field did," said Nathan. "He even thanked the People for helping him." The children settled back around him, used to sudden changes in Daddy's stories, after Daddy thought.

"Besides the field, we had our kitchen garden, and it grew more than enough to feed us—and them too, if they had needed it. But—"

The long, old sorrow was as piercing as when it was new. No, it couldn't be—or how could you live?

"But they went away," prompted Dena.

"They went away," said Nathan. "Perez—his gift was communications—had spent an hour every day, sending out their Questing call. He changed the hour every day in case someone was listening at a different time. And he finally got an answer.

" 'A Group!' Perez could hardly speak. 'A lot of families! So many! So many of our old Group! And they're coming! They have a craft!' he laughed, half crying. 'A little cobbled-together, busted-up thing!' they said. 'But they're coming as soon as the dark of the moon, so no one—' "

"And they went away—" Little Lucas' voice was sad.

"In an airship!" cried Nat, his eyes big with his crowding dreams.

"And left the cradle for when Gramma's little baby came." Dena looked at the cradle by the fireplace, with Adina's play-person, tattered and fragile, still in it. "And the baby was *my* Uncle Luke!" she said triumphantly.

"And mine, too!" hastened Little Lucas. "And I'm named after him!"

"Daddy." Dena leaned against his knees, her eyes intent on his face. "Were you sorry when they went?"

"Sorry—" Even this long after, he hadn't been able to change much the way he "remembered it." He could never forget the quick smother of Eliada's embrace. And his stiffness that could not relax quickly enough to close his arms around her. There had been a quick, smooth swirl of her hair across his face. And she was gone. Up into the dark yawning of that door that waited, treetop high above the yard. Then the whisperings came—but not through his ears. All the thankings and rememberings and then the final—*Rest secure in the Presence through the Name and the Power.*

And they were gone—somewhere far. Somewhere west. But—scant comfort—still in this world.

"Don't cry, Daddy," said Dena, patting his cheek.

"Men don't cry!" scoffed Nat.

No, men don't cry—but boys do. Face-down in the darkness in the grass behind the big tree, wetting huddling sleeves through with hot tears—crying for a magic that was gone and could never come again.

"Yes, I was very sorry," said Nathan. But—

Nathan looked around the good room, felt the blessed warmth of Miriam, busy in the kitchen, and the wholeness of his life. The tightness inside him began to loosen, as it always finally did.

"We'll hug you happy," said Dena. And the three children clustered and climbed on the chair and on his lap—even Nat, who sometimes now was too old to hug people happy.

So—life widens. All kinds of loves come. Others come into the circle to complete it. And someday—maybe Otherside—but someday Eliada would be there again, sitting in the pool of her skirts, her hands lightly folded in her lap, her luminous eyes smiling, and her soft voice saying:

"Tell us a story, Nathan. Tell us all the wonderful story of after we left—"

That Boy

There was an evil in the land. Maybe we should have known it, but at first it was sort of like an iceberg, just points and ripples. There was nothing big—nothing to put a name to or to struggle against. Just things like ten-year-old Jareb, rising from baptismal waters with a lie on his tongue. The very first words he spoke, even as he spluttered the creek water from his mouth and nose and shook it off his hair, were a lie. Instead of saying "Hallelujah, amen!" as he had been instructed, he gasped, "There's a boy down there! He smiled at me!"

Well, Sister Gail, his mother, just plain cried, right there in front of everyone. She had wrestled so long and so hard with the stubborn spirit of untruth that seemed to possess Jareb, and he had promised solemnly that after he was cleansed of his sins in the waters, he'd never lie again, plain or fancy. Jareb sloshed up out of the water and ran to her, all dripping as he was, with the hem of his holy garment trailing in the sand and dust so that it wiped mud against his ankles as he went. "Honest, Mamma! It's true! There's a boy down there!"

"Oh, Jareb, Jareb!" Sister Gail hugged him to her, paying no mind to how wet he got her Sunday clothes. She hid her face against his hair so no one could see her tears.

Brother Helon waded out of the pool in the creek. He took hold of Jareb's shoulders and turned him away from Sister Gail. "Those who mock the Lord shall feel the weight of his mighty wrath!" His voice was like an organ rolling heavy darkness against the granite boulders that backed the pool.

"I'm not mocking the Lord!" Jareb's eyes were big and shocked. "It's true! Just think! A boy down there! I didn't know you could smile under water! Where did—"

"Jareb." Sister Gail gathered his hand into hers. Her eyes were dry again and her emotions decently tucked away. "Come change your clothes." They started toward the wagons. She looked back over her shoulder. "I'm sorry, Brother Helon. I thought we had prayed the spirit of un-truth from him."

When they were gone, the rest of us looked uneasily at each other, the solemn joy of Baptism Day sullied by Jareb's behavior. Then Sister Ruth started the hymn *Bringing in the Sheaves,* and by the time we got to "—home we come rejoicing—" we *were* rejoicing and looking forward to the big noontime feed that waited in bulging baskets in the back of the wagons. We were plenty ready for food. We fast on Baptism Day until after the services.

Jareb looked so little and lonesome sitting on a log all by himself, clutching the chunk of corn bread that was all Sister Gail would let him have in the midst of fried chicken and cake, that I stopped by him on my way down to the creek to get the watermelons that had been cooling in the shallows of the creek since the night before.

"Want to come help?" I asked him. He looked up, resigned. "Mamma said to stay here," he said. I caught Sister Gail's eye and jerked my thumb over my shoulder. She hesitated, then nodded. She thinks I'm good for the boy, his dad being dead. She doesn't want him to get too miss-ish.

"She says it's all right," I told him. He put the corn bread down carefully on his log and followed me out of the shadows of the huge cottonwood trees into the blaze of sun.

"Do *you* think I'm lying, Mr. Lambert?" asked Jareb as he trotted along with me. For some reason, everyone Misters me while they Brother and Sister everyone else in the Conclave.

"Well," I said, "if there's a boy down there, he sure goes a long time without breathing."

"Yeah," said Jareb thoughtfully. "Maybe he doesn't have to come up—like a frog. Or maybe he went back the other way."

"Back where?" I asked, scanning the bare hills and the clustered river willows and cottonwoods along the creek.

"To wherever he came from," said Jareb. "We didn't see him get in—"

"*We* didn't see him at all," I reminded him.

Silently we went on down the slope to the creek edge. I fished the watermelons out of the water, spanking them with satisfaction as I handled them. Fine melons! As soon as we got settled down, we'd raise just as good or better. Then there'd be no need to cart all our kitchen truck fifteen miles over the hills from Everly, our closest neighboring settlement.

Jareb spanked the melons too, his head bent to hear the hollow, ripe echoes.

"Listen, Jareb," I said. "Folks are going to expect you to be different, now that you've been baptized. I don't think you'd better go on with this story about a boy. It just makes your mother feel bad and gets you corn bread instead of fried chicken." He opened his mouth to protest. "Wait," I said. "If you think you'll bust if you don't finish talking it out of you, come to the shop and talk to me. I've got big ears." I grinned at him. After a frowning moment, he grinned too.

We both started back, a melon under each arm. Halfway up the slope, I paused to get a better grip on one of the melons and looked back. "—Four, five, and two's seven," I counted to myself. "Hmm. Someone got hungry. I brought eight." Then I shrugged and followed Jareb up the slope.

That shrieking kid, Jobie, met us halfway, skidding excitedly down the gravel slope. "Hurry up!" he yelled. "Ever-body's waiting."

"Don't yell," I told him automatically. "We're coming. You go on down and get a couple more. Save us a trip."

"Mom dint tell me to work!" yelled Jobie. "She owny told me to tell you—"

"I'm telling you," I said. "Stop yelling and go get a couple more melons. There are a couple about your size down there."

He glared at me and opened his mouth. I looked at him. He shut his mouth and skidded on down toward the creek. Jareb juggled his melons for a minute and followed me back to the flat. Jobie was as fast as he was loud, and as we laid the melons in the middle of the crowd, Jobie elbowed importantly through with his load. Jareb watched me cut the first one—so crisply ripe that it split ahead of the knife all the way across. The insides glowed as red as campfire coals, and that smell of watermelon—like nothing else on earth!—made us all breathe deeper. Jareb, gulping down his mouth-water, resolutely turned away.

"I'll go get the other one," he said. He didn't whine, not even with his eyes. Punishment was punishment and he accepted it.

A while later he came back, a melon under each arm. "Two?" I asked. "I thought there was only one left." His mouth opened but he reddened and closed it again. He went back to his log and his chunk of corn bread that by this time was swarming with ants. I glanced at him several times while the rest of us ate the melons, but he seemed absorbed in watching what was going on with his bread.

It was time to pack up for home after we finished the melons; so while the women were clearing the tarps we had eaten on and the men were getting the horses, I strolled over to Jareb and his log.

"What happened down at the creek?" I asked.

"Nothing," he said, reddening again.

"Come on. Out with it." I sat down far enough from the corn bread not to get me any ants. "There was just one melon left."

"There's *still* a melon left," he said.

"Can't be," I said, tallying again in my head. "I only got eight from Everly."

"There's still one," he persisted. "The—" he paused, gulped, and went on. "That boy just brought back two because last night he took one of ours and he figgered that wasn't very fair so he brought one back and an extra one to make up for it." Jareb's eyes were pleading. "You *said*—" He gulped again. "You *said* talk to you—" His eyes dropped and he clasped his hands between his pressing knees. "You said—" His shoulders sagged.

My besetting sin flared up in me, shaking my insides. I can be patient without end with dumb brutes that you can't reason with. I handle plenty in my smithy, but human beings who are given the power of reasoning and won't use it— When I felt that I could control my voice, I said, "You're right. I told you to talk to me, but that doesn't mean I intend to countenance your lying—"

"I'm not lying." Tears welled up in his eyes. "I thought you believed me." He flipped the ant-crowded corn bread to the ground and left me sitting alone.

I looked after him—wondering, with one corner of my mind, how long it'd be before I got over wanting to reach for my pipe at times like this. I gave it up along with strong drink when I joined the Conclave. I shook my head and stood up. Then, feeling foolish, instead of going to help with the hitching-up, I went back down to the creek.

There *was* another watermelon, wavering wet-green under the quiet waters of the creek. The ninth melon.

As our short line of wagons curled around the foothills back to the settlement, I wondered again about the wisdom of our choosing this place. It was just another of those points of uneasiness that plagued me. True, there was the year 'round creek. Maybe that was it. There was the creek. After the endless dusty miles with the sun glaring in our eyes and heavy on our laps until the days spun around us in a never-ending glare of weight and heat, the sight of the flowing waters had been like sighting the gates of the Eternal City. So we chose to accept this second of the three places recommended by the scouts the Conclave sent out when we all voted to move West to free ourselves of a world that grinned or frowned or sneered when the Conclavers were mentioned. You can't serve God with one eye on the world and a shoulder always hunched against the next attack. At least so most of the Conclavers thought.

The first place was out in the middle of the prairies and fair to see for all its wide miles and farmable land. We could have pastures aplenty for the herds we hoped to build to begin us on our cheese-making, which was to be our special ministry to the world. But there were no hills—or trees—or flowing water, except during rainstorms. And because of where we came from, we all felt we'd rather lift up our eyes unto the hills—

We were all fixed to call this green and wet and tall country Gates Ajar. Or Edenside. Or Maketh Glad. Then we found in the land office that it was already named Hellesgate, and no matter what we chose to call it, the red tape was too tangled for them ever to change it. Even finding that it was named for Omer Hellesgate, because he mapped it first, didn't cleanse it in our minds. Some wanted to move on, but already we had started putting down roots. And besides, we were so tired—so absolutely worn out. So we stayed. And now I half wondered if the name of the place had anything to do with Jareb's rising from baptism with a lie on his lips—and his persisting in his error. But then—there was the ninth melon. Even a half lie couldn't account for a melon.

My smithy was the first thing finished in the settlement. It wasn't much more than a lean-to. I had the big idea of digging out a room in the hillside and then having a shed out front, but after I saw how the point of the pick merely whitened a pockmark on the hard surface and scaled off only a pinch of a dust, I gave up. Four notched tree trunks help up my roof of branches and brushwood. The open-faced lean-to that protected the forge was made of the branches lopped from the four trees, the chinks mud-filled. Before I became a Conclaver, I wouldn't have been caught dead in such a shop, but I left my worldly pride behind—far behind—on the other side of my baptismal waters. If only I had been cleansed also of my besetting sin! But hearing the ring of the anvil again and having the echo of my hammering coming back to me multiplied from the red and grey mountain walls of Hellesgate, made the thin-with-strangeness country around me begin to fatten up into familiarity. Home was beginning.

Well, the other kids wouldn't let Jareb forget his baptismal day. When there weren't any adults close enough to interfere, they called him Ananias. He mostly shrugged and took it. But one day I had to pull him out from under a whole pile of flailing younguns. I set them skittering with a backhand whack or two and set about sorting Jareb out. He was intact, though considerably roughed up.

"What happened?" I asked him.

"They called her Sapphira," he explained. "They can call me Ananias all they want to, but they can't get away with calling Mamma Sapphira. Why'd you chase them off? I was beating up on them!"

"Are you sure they knew that?" I asked, whacking the seat of his overalls to jar the dirt off. "I think they thought they were beating up on you!"

"Jobie knows!" said Jareb, spitting blood from a split lip. "He started it. I knocked his teeth out for him!" He caught my skeptical eye. "Well, one tooth. It was loose already."

I took him back to the smithy to wash off the worst of his battle.

"Hey!" he said past his shirttail he was using for a towel. "That boy—"

"What boy?" I asked, setting to work shearing nails from the slender rod of iron.

"That watermelon boy," he offered.

"I thought we'd decided you'd give up your lying—" I paused in my work.

"I'm not lying!" he protested.

"Well, making up tales, then," I said. "If that suits you better."

"I'm not making it up neither! I went back there that night to see about that watermelon, and so did he. And we decided since my mamma told me not to eat any, he wouldn't either. So we buried it under a tree."

I searched his troubled face for a moment. It was plainly real to him, whatever it was. I sighed. Well, so long as it did no evil—

"That boy—" I left the sentence open for him.

"He doesn't have to stay in the water." Jareb's words poured out happily. " 'Member, I thought maybe he was like a fish, but he ain't—isn't. N'en I thought maybe he was like a frog—you know, living in the water and out, but he ai—isn't. He's just a boy."

"Just a boy!" I said. "Down in a pond and never coming up for air—or have you changed that?"

"Oh, but he does come up," protested Jareb. "I asked him. Every half hour, he says, but when he gets big, it will be only every hour. It takes time to learn. Like lifting does. He sure likes to lift."

"Mountains, of course!" I grinned, hard-pressed to keep my patience with his fancy tales. "Or maybe he lifts the pond like a pitcher and pours the water on his garden. Wonderful! Saves ditch-digging."

"No," said Jareb thoughtfully. "Not mountains. I asked him, on account of faith doing it, you know. But that's for grownups and they haven't done any of that since they got here. They're scared to. No, he lifts himself."

"Himself? Well, well!" my voice jeered. "Like a bird, I suppose. Flip-flap she flied, huh?"

"No," said Jareb. "He doesn't have to flap to fly. He just—" he waved his hand, "lifts off the ground and goes along. It sure looks fun." He was wistful. "I wish I could."

"Now, listen, Jareb," I said, waiting to catch his eye to make sure I had his whole attention. "You can't go on making things up like this. The more you do, the more likely you are to forget and start one of your tales around some of the others. You've got enough to live down now. Better you and your mother concentrate on truth a little more and grammar a little less. Better pray out this spirit of untruth before it becomes a devouring monster in you."

"A devouring monster!" Jareb was visibly savoring the phrase. "But there's nothing to pray out!" he protested. "You can't pray out the truth, can you?" His eyes were very wide and blue as he looked at me.

"Well," I said slowly. "It *has* been done—so they tell me."

"And you know," Jareb went on, shrugging off all my earnest words, "that boy talks twice."

"Talks twice?" I let myself be drawn back into his story again.

"Yes," said Jareb. "Not as much now as he did at first. He talks something I don't know, then he looks at me and waits, then he talks what I know." He stopped and frowned. "I mean he talks words I know, but he doesn't always make sense."

"Like attracts like," I muttered into his cascade of words.

"Like he said this is an ungood place."

"Ungood?" I glanced up. "You mean evil?"

"No, I asked him if he meant bad. He waited a long time, then he said no, not bad, but good isn't here." Jareb frowned. "Does that make sense?"

"Not to me," I admitted, but the sun wasn't quite so bright on the dirt floor at my feet and my shoulders wanted to shiver.

"He said they tried it first but went away. Then other people came, they went away, too, because good wasn't here."

"Couple of groups have camped here a spell," I mused. "And some fields were cleared once—the creek—"

"Oh, that boy's people make the creek. I mean, make it to run all the time. Before, it only had water once in a while."

"Make the—!" I swallowed hard at my anger. "What about his folks? He has folks, I suppose."

"Sure. He's got lots of them." Jareb smiled. "At the other end of the water."

"Where's that?" I asked.

"I don't know," Jareb admitted. "But that's where they live—the other end of the water. That's where they found a place with good. He showed me some—like dusty salt."

"Now, Jareb," I said, "that's enough. Now you've overreached yourself. You'd better scoot on. I've got work to do. My listener is fresh worn out. Scoot!"

He scooted, heading not home, but toward Benson's. He'd taken quite a shine to their little girl, Tally, a tiny mite about three or four. He

"Our hens are laying like molting season," said Darius. "C'n put a thumb through the egg shells too. 'S a wonder the hens get them laid whole."

"Benson's youngun's going into a decline," I said, staggering off-balance because my pick hit hard rock where we'd planned another post-hole. "She didn't even have a smile for me this morning when they brought Blinky in to be shod. Looks like you could *blow* through her without puckering up, even."

"Maybe we should move on—" Dab straightened his back in sections, his hand pressing the hurt. "There was another place—"

"Pull up stakes again?" Darius shifted his thin shoulders under his overall straps. "The wife had her heart half pulled out her, leaving the home place. She'd never pack up again, even for the Conclave. Awful hard on her, this whole thing. Aged something awful of late. Starting to lose her teeth— 'Sides, all the crops are in again. This year's gotta be better. Dunno though. Creek's been pretty much come and go lately—slacking off, then coming again. If it doesn't come back some time—"

The sound of hooves shifted our attention to the trail that was slowly becoming a road. "There's a horse that's not failing." Dab's voice was unduly sharp.

"Hi yuh!" called Jareb as he trotted up on Prince. His legs were hardly long enough to curve the horse's fat sides. He had a basket clutched in front of him. "Mamma wonders can you come up, Mr. Lambert. She's kinda wincy about being alone there with Bessie having her calf. She's big enough it might be twins."

"All right, Jareb," I said, dropping my pick and reaching for my coat. "Didn't realize her time was close. You go on back. I'll be there."

"Gotta take these eggs to Mrs. Benson first," he said. "They're for Tally." He trotted off.

I shrugged and headed for my shop.

"Eggs to spare." Dab's voice followed me. "That kid's not wasting away neither!" Venom tipped his tongue. I turned and walked back slowly. I stood and looked at Dab a moment.

"You make it sound like it's wrong for a kid and his horse to be healthy. And for a neighbor to oblige another neighbor with foodstuff."

Dab colored, but he looked me right back. "You're naming it wrong," he said. "But so're some others. Abigail Curtis is a woman alone. There are them that say she shouldn'ta come along with us—especially after she wouldn't take—" He stopped and wet his dry lips with a slow tongue.

"Wouldn't take you," I said

"Wouldn't take a husband," said Dab. "Like she doesn't need a man around. And that farm of hers, up there on that flat by itself, looking like—

like *ours* oughta look. She hasn't had any more help from us than any
other of us—but look! Hand of righteousness isn't the only hand that can
help this world. And *she* ain't losing no teeth. *She* ain't got a child going
into a decline. *She* ain't got stock wasting away. *She* ain't got hens not laying!"

"One thing she has got," Darius interrupted. "She's got a son that
rises from the waters of baptism with lies on his tongue and deceit in his
mouth—"

"The wicked flourish like a green bay tree," said Dab solemnly.

"If you think evil is among us," I reminded him, "it is your duty to
go to Brother Helon and warn him so he can warn the Conclave and
prepare us to be purged of all unrighteousness!"

Dab stepped back from me though I had kept my voice soft to hold
bound the leaping demon within me.

"If I don't, someone else will," he said stoutly. "The sinner shall not
sit in the congregation—"

"Let's get this straight," I said, squaring my sagging shoulders with
an effort. "You're saying Sister Gail is flourishing because she is evil? And
she's evil because she keeps herself to herself—"

"As far as we know," said Dab stubbornly. "How do we *know* she's
keeping herself to herself?" His arm flew up defensively when he caught
sight of my face. "It's been known!" he cried, his voice shriller and shriller.
"Women giving themselves to the Devil! All I know is she is prospering
and the rest of us are failing. Why? Are we evil? Have we sinned in the
sight of God? And she hasn't? Are we evil or is she?"

I swallowed a wild shout of laughter at the idea of Abigail Curtis
giving herself to the Devil for the gift of eggs and productive cows! Then
as quickly, I remembered how very small the mess of pottage is that lots
of people sell their birthrights for. I swallowed hard, groping for grace to
make a right answer.

"Is it necessary for either to be evil?" I asked. "Couldn't it be—"

"Couldn't it be what?" asked Darius heavily.

"I don't know," I said helplessly. "I don't know. Maybe that this is
an ungood place—"

Jareb came back just then, shifting easily with Prince's long, slow
stride. Jareb was frowning. "Tally sure looks bad. Her mother says she
won't eat nothin'—anything—any more. What's wrong with her, Mr.
Lambert?"

"Don't know," I said shortly. "Come on. Prince'll carry double as
far as my place." I bellied across Prince behind Jareb and straightened up,
straddling the horse, steadying Jareb and me as Prince danced sideways
under my added weight.

"I'm going to tell mamma about Tally," Jareb said. "She looks real bad."

It was twins. Two wobbly-legged heifer calves. I leaned on the rail fence and looked at Bessie, who had serenely and competently gone about the business of birthing the young as though twins were commonplace. Sister Gail came to the corral and leaned her arms on the top rail with me.

"Twins!" she was pleased. "And both heifers! Surely Providence has smiled on us!"

"Truly," I said solemnly. "In the last two months, three cows have aborted and two newborn calves barely breathed before they died."

Her smile died slowly. "So I heard," she said. "A heavy loss to the settlement. Then surely this is a blessing to be shared. Praise to our Father."

"Amen," I said, suddenly startled as I realized how separate Sister Gail had become of late. Was the Conclave shouldering her out? Or was she withdrawing because of—of what? I watched a wisp of her hair blow across her cheek as she looked again at the livestock. Not evil! I swore to myself. Not evil!

I was so sick from thinking about what Dab had said about Sister Gail and with my own physical coming-apart that I wasn't fit to be lived with for the next couple of weeks. I went to Brother Helon about Dab. He looked at me with a half smile, hampered by his strained breathing.

"Brother Jonadab came to me about the matter also," he said. "We all have our burdens to be borne patiently. Yours is Brother Jonadab. Brother Jonadab's is his unbridled imagination. In all forbearance—" His words were broken by the strangling tightening of his breath. When he could speak again he said, "Would God felt me worthy of the gift of health such as he has given to Sister Gail—"

I hadn't seen Jareb for quite a while, and it had to be the day my demon took possession of me and led me to shout and curse at Jonadab over some trifle connected with a saddle—I couldn't even remember what I was yelling about after I cooled down—that Jareb chose to arrive again. I was in the smithy pumping the bellows, watching the iron bar I held in the heat of the forge turning slowly from red to white-hot, wondering if it was any hotter than the rage that had sucked and torn shapelessly at my insides—and still threatened to blaze again. I grunted when Jareb came in and, carrying the bar to the anvil, began shaping it, the white heat shimmering up against my face. But the shaping was more work than pleasure, as all effort was of late. My muscles were protesting the effort already.

Jareb sat down on Dab's saddle he'd dropped by the door when he fled my wrath.

"That boy," he said casually. "He still comes down there."

"What boy?" I said, pacing my hammer to my words. "Down where?"

"You know. The watermelon pond," he said. "I saw him again yesterday. He gave me some more salt with the dusty stuff on it—that good."

"*That* boy!" My demon flared up explosively. I hit the bar so hard and awkwardly that I lost hold of it completely. It shot off the anvil and sizzled against my leather apron before it dropped to the cindery dirt floor,. My wrist, banging against the apron, sizzled too. Rage roared up in every aching bone in me like a black fountain. "Take your lies somewhere else!" I roared so loud that Jareb flattened his eyelids like in a high wind.

"I told him about Tally," Jareb went on stubbornly. "He says it's 'cause she doesn't get any good and for me to give her some. It keeps us from getting sick—Mamma and me. I could put it in a cup of water. It isn't nasty. If her mother—"

"Listen, Jareb," I said, sagging against the anvil, waiting for my sight to clear and my heart to stop jerking my breath. I nursed my burned wrist in my other hand. "Leave Tally alone. Get over there and get those bellows to going. I've got this whole job to start over. Git!"

And he got. Pumping the bellows, working up the heat again on the forge, I lifted the bar with my pincers and jabbed it down into the glowing, fluctuating center of the coals.

"Long time ago," grunted Jareb as he pumped, "he gave me this funny salt."

"Salt for a dickeybird's tail!" I jeered sourly.

"No, to put in the water pail." Jareb flicked sweat from his nose. "He said the dust was the good that isn't here."

"Jareb," I said slowly from between clenched teeth. "Go—away!"

"But you said pump—" He was bewildered.

"And now I say go away. Go away with your frog boy and your dickeybird's tail!"

"But I—" he began, wide-eyed.

"Go!" I roared.

He went.

I pulled down viciously on the bellows handle. Above the creak of the leather, I heard him call, "And in the water for the stock—and in the irrigation head gate, too!"

The nightmare began closing in tighter and tighter after that. Nobody died, but they either stayed inside with their sufferings or were creeping, bent shadows in the sun, slowly moving. Sister Gail stayed up on the flat. How can you come down among the people when they look through you and don't hear you and let the foodstuff you bring wither on the front step?

Finally came the day I sat outside my smithy, too sick and worn even to pretend to work. I caught Jareb as he cut through the field on his way to the Bensons'. I sat on a tree stump in front of the smithy, flexing a dry pine twig in my two shaking hands.

"Jareb," I said, "remember you said that boy said good wasn't here?"

"Yeah." Jareb was a bit cautious. This was the first time I'd ever started a "boy" conversation.

"Did—I mean—" I snapped the twig sharply. "Why is it you and your mother aren't ailing like the rest of us? Did that boy—I mean—"

"You told me not to talk about it any more." Jareb's face reddened.

"Talk now," I said, tasting the subtle salt of my own bleeding gums. "Has he told you why we are all dying?"

"Dying?" Jareb's eyes widened. "Are we dying?"

"Look," I said. I held out my right hand—a smith's hand with big knuckles and thick calluses and heavy tendons—made to grip and lift and use. And we both watched the increasing tremor that shook it harder and harder until I finally hid it between my knees.

"Like I told you," said Jareb. "He brought me some of that salt-looking stuff. That's what it is—dusty salt. But he says the dust is the good."

"The dust is the good." I sighed heavily. But then, had Jareb ever told me a lie that I could prove was a lie? "Go on."

"He said his Daddy said he could bring it to me. He said some was salty to use instead of salt when we eat, but some is just to put in drinking water for us and the stock and in the irrigation water."

"And then—?"

"That's all." He spread his hands. "That's all."

"Jareb," I ran my tongue around my tender mouth, "have you got any of that salt with you?"

"Sure," said Jareb promptly. He fished in his pants pocket. "Here's some." He handed me a rag tied into a tight little bundle. "It's what I wanted to give to Tally but nobody would let me. So I carry it around in case I find something to eat somewhere. You can have it."

"Your mother won't care?" I asked, suddenly bitterly ashamed.

"Naw!" scoffed Jareb. "She doesn't care—we got plenty. I'da offered sooner but—"

"Thanks," I said. "I'm sorry I've been so mean to you, Jareb. And not just because you gave me this. I was sorry already—before."

"Aw!" Jareb reddened. "Never mind. I'm going to see Tally. She worries me. Last time Sister Ruth wouldn't let me talk to her. She was sleeping."

I untied the packet after he left. I touched my finger to my tongue, to the salt, to my tongue again. It was just dusty salt. But two days later, after using it with my meals and in my drinking water, my eyes opened without my having to pry the gummy lids apart in the morning. The next afternoon my gums stopped oozing blood under the pressure of my fingertip, and the burn on my wrist, left from my tantrum with Jareb, had visibly begun to heal. A week later, back in my smithy in the clear sharpness of a sunrise, I let my hammer fall on the anvil with a joyous *chank* that splintered to echoes against the mountains beyond.

Darius and Dab came down to the smithy that evening to find out what was happening. They had heard me off and on all that day. I told them about the dusty salt. I showed them my healed scars. I beat a tattoo on my anvil with my second-heaviest hammer. I showed them some of the salt—a small box Jareb had brought me last night.

"I'll share with you," I said, as a Christian brother should. "I think I can get us some more."

"Evil—" Darius shook his head, his lips sucking in where his teeth used to be. "Lead us not into—"

"Dope," said Dab through his cracked lips. "Makes you feel good for a spell, then kills you."

I felt a sudden flare inside me. I closed the box slowly. "By their fruits—" I reminded them. "A good tree can't bear bad fruit."

But they wouldn't even touch it. I watched them shamble gingerly off. They had to rest twice before they were out of sight.

An hour later I met Sister Ruth coming out of the meeting house. She had been crying, and her hand, clutching her shawl under her chin, was like a claw. One wild strand of grey hair scraped her ravaged cheek. She had been twenty-five her last birthday. She was a shattered forty in the fading evening light.

"Sister Ruth!" I said. "How is Tally?"

"Dying," she said hoarsely, "I hope. I bin in there to dedicate her to Death. A quick, merciful death." She turned her face away.

"Let me help—" I said, touching her sagging shoulder.

"I heard," she whispered hastily, slipping like a shadow from under my hand. "I heard about the salt but the mister won't let me listen. That's why I'm giving her willingly to Death. He won't let me try to help. Why should I keep her suffering?" and she was gone.

Jareb was waiting for me at my shop—a restless shadow in the deepening darkness.

"What are you doing here this time of night?" I asked him. "You should be home. Your mother—"

"Mr. Lambert," he burst into my reprimand, "is Tally really dying? They wouldn't even let me in the house. They chased me away. Is she *dying?*"

"I don't know," I admitted. "Sister Ruth thinks so."

"I tried to give Sister Ruth some good for her, but she's scared of Brother Rual. Mr. Lambert, do they really think I want to give something bad to Tally? To hurt her?"

"They're hurting so bad themselves that they can't think straight about anything," I said. "You better scoot on home. Your mother will be worried."

"But they *can't* just let her die!" cried Jareb. "How can they not—"

"Do you think they want her to die?" I asked heavily. "You'd better go on home."

Jareb hesitated a moment, then faded soundlessly into the dark. I sat there on the edge of my anvil for a long time, letting the darkness flood me inside and out. I was finally roused by the sound of voices and the soft thudding of feet along the trail.

"Hello, there!" I called.

The voices cut off. I moved toward the dark huddle in the shadow of the path. "Who's there? Where you headed?"

"Don't tell *him* nothing!" Dab's slurred voice was venomous. "Consorting—"

"Dab," I snapped. "Don't be any more of a fool than you have to be. What's going on? Wait. Let me get some light on the subject."

I stirred the banked coals in the forge with a pitchy pine stick and laid a couple of others across when flame leaped up. Pale ovals of faces came out of the dark.

"Sister Ruth!" I reached out a hand to her faltering, stricken face. Brother Rual struck my hand down feebly. "Don't touch my woman!" he snarled. "Evil—!"

"*What's* going on?" I demanded. "Sister Ruth, is Tally—worse?"

"Tally's gone." Her flat voice was choked with grief.

"Dead?" I cried. "But—"

"We don't know if she's dead or not!" Sister Ruth cried. "She's gone! She's gone! She's gone!" Her tautly clasped hands swung up to hide her anguished face in the crook of one elbow.

"Gone?" My mind whirled blankly. "But where—"

"We got a good idea where!" It was Dab's snarl. "And we know who! Leave us be, you devil-lover!"

It was no trick for me to outdistance them in the dark. Nor to tell where they were headed. The only house above was Sister Gail's. I knew my way through the wood lot as well as I did by road, and I lost the group behind me before they could get started again. I was across the front porch of the house with one stride, the flat of my hand heavy on the door. It was unlatched and swung open to the shove of my shoulder.

Jareb and Sister Gail looked up, frightened, as I plunged in. Sister Gail held Tally on her lap, a Tally so wasted and limp in the flicker of that candle that she looked dead to me. Her chin was wet and Jareb was holding a dripping cup.

"Jareb! What in the name of—" I began.

With one quick swoop, Jareb dropped the cup and swept Tally up into his arms. "I won't let them take her back to die!" he cried. "But she won't drink! Mr. Lambert, what'll we do!"

"You'd better think of something fast," I said. "Dab and Darius and Rual and I don't know who all else are coming! Jareb, you can't pull a fool thing like this. You've got to—" I stopped trying to push words into unopened ears and turned to Sister Gail.

"Sister Gail! They're ready to kill—"

"But Jareb says this powder will save her. It has kept us healthy—at least he says so—"

"He *stole* the child, Sister Gail! Don't you realize what your son—*Jareb!*" I caught just the flicker of his heels as he slipped out the back door into the dark—with Tally.

"I'll get him!" I cried. "Fasten that door, Sister Gail! Don't let them in—"

I stumbled to a halt beyond the house, searching in the darkness. Where had that fool kid gone? Then I heard the snap of a branch on the hill above me. He was cutting across to the creek. The creek! The watermelon pond.

I took out after him. I should have been able to catch him—burdened as he was—but he had the same advantage of me as I had had of the others—he knew every step of the way, even in the dark. Before I could plunge down to the pond, he was there, wading out, slipping and stumbling with Tally clutched tightly to him.

"Jareb!" I called. "Jareb! Wait!"

"Don't stop me, Mr. Lambert!" he cried. "Don't try to stop me. Tally will die unless—"

"Are you sure she's not dead already?" I panted, moving slowly down to the water's edge. Jareb's head bent sharply to his burden.

"She's still breathing," he said in relief. "Oh, Mr. Lambert! What if it *is* too late to save her—"

"Jareb, you must be crazy," I said. "You can't steal a child like this! Bring her back before her dad gets hold of you. If anything happens to her, they'll call it murder—"

Jareb backed away from me, deeper into the pond. "I gotta do something!" he said. "I'm going to take her to that boy's people."

"That boy!" I sagged with despair. "Jareb, there *isn't* any boy! You can't take her to someone who doesn't exist—"

"If there isn't any boy, where did I get the good I gave you!" cried Jareb. "How come you aren't sick any more like the rest of them? There is so that boy!"

"Then where are his people?" I asked, inching forward. "And what makes you think they can do anything—"

"If they know where to get the good, then they ought to know how come it works and maybe they know some way to make Tally take it. And they live at the other end of the water! I told you already!"

"Fine," I said, moving ankle-deep into the water. "Now all you have to do is turn fish and get there."

"I'll get there," said Jareb, backing away. "That boy told me how. You only have to be underwater right here, and you don't have to hold your breath very long. N'en you get in a tunnel and it goes to the end of the water. And he said it isn't far in the tunnel, but you have to use roads and horses outside and go up and down; so it's lots longer."

We looked at each other across the shimmer of the dark water. Then Jareb said, "Mr. Lambert, I know that boy's people can make Tally well. Tell Mamma I'll be back as soon as I can. Tell Sister Ruth I'll take good care of Tally, and I'll bring her back as soon as I get her well. Please don't be mad, Mr. Lambert. I gotta take her! I'll bring her back well."

"Jareb!" I caught him with my voice. "If you're going to take Tally underwater, hold your hand tight over her nose and mouth until you come up."

He fumbled for Tally's face, turned with her clasped close, and plunged down into the dark waters. I stood and watched the waters churn and roll. I watched them quiet and smooth to a dull mirror of the sky. I wondered as I sloshed out of the water and started up the hill—had he disappeared into the waters as he had risen from them—with a lie on his lips?

I got back to Jareb's house as fast as I could, my heart torn for Sister Gail. What if that scraggly mob had been able to give each other strength enough to do her some harm? The place was dark and silent. I stumbled across the porch.

"Sister Gail!" I called. "Gail!" She wasn't there. I groped for the candle on the mantel. It was gone. I bent to stir the fire. In its flicker I found the broken candle lying on the braided hearth rug. I hunched to the heat of the coals and lifted the lighted candle to look at the room. It told me nothing I didn't already know. Gail was gone. Willingly? Had she gone willingly? Or had she been dragged by the scrawny, feverish bite of sick fingers?

I pelted back downhill to my smithy. Where now? I paused, groping in the dark with my eyes. Where could she be? I gulped for breath and started down the path. A shadow slid out of the dark.

"That's far enough." Dab's voice was a scared loudness. "Don't come no farther!"

"Where's Sister Gail?" I demanded. "Dab, if you've done her harm—" I started forward.

"No farther!" screeched Dab. "I got my shotgun on you!" There was a breathless pause, then Dab snickered. "Gotta shaky trigger finger, too. Might squeeze anytime. Can't control my fingers like I usta."

"Where is she?" I demanded and started forward.

"Far enough," he snarled. "Don't make me kill you. Back it up."

I did, but I persisted. "Where is she?"

"Where's Tally?" he retorted

"I don't know," I said truthfully. "I didn't catch Jareb."

"We caught Sister Gail." Dab's snicker was old and tired. "Gonna trade you straight across."

"Trade?" I asked.

"Trade," said Dab. "Her for Tally."

"But I haven't got Tally!" I said.

"Jareb has," said Dab.

"But I don't know where he is!" My voice was rising.

"We know where Sister Gail is," said Dab softly. "And we're keeping her there till Tally gets back. You want her, bring us Tally. Straight-across trade—dead or alive."

"What're you doing to her?" I demanded.

"Nothing." Dab's voice was moving away. "Just nothin'. Oh, 'ceptin' water to drink, of course. We're still disputin' about bread. Some say yes and some say no. She could live off her fat for a month, *some* say. Some say let her eat our bread and be like us!"

"Dab!" I called. "You're crazy, every one of you!"

"We feel crazy," he said. "Some say yes and some say no. I say why bother to feed her? Tally's dead. We're dead. Make her dead, too!"

"Dab, you've gotta—" Then I realized there was no one in the shadows anymore.

I stumbled wearily back to my bed in the smithy lean-to, my years and the past months catching up with me. I huddled into myself on the edge of my cot. "God—" I started to tell him about it. "God—" My face crumpled behind my hands. "Gail!" I suddenly admitted that she wasn't sister to me anymore. Despair surged up in me like a gushing freshet.

Driven by a sort of delirium, I started for the pond. Then I staggered back toward the huddle of the settlement. Then veered towards the Curtis place. When rational thinking came back, I was huddled in my smithy again, trying to warm my chilled soul through hands held over the banked, crinkling coals of my forge. I groped my way to the back of the lean-to, to my cot that had served me except in the very coldest weather of last winter. Whatever I had to do—find Gail—find Jareb—find Tally—alive—I had to have light to do it by. Gail could be hidden anywhere, in anyone's house, in any of the shacks or lean-tos or sheds. Or in the meeting house—a thousand places. Search would have to wait for light. And Jareb and Tally. Soon enough when light came to grope for their floating drowned bodies—or to drown myself trying to follow where they went.

I lay back with a sigh that was mostly a weary groan, blinked my hot, staring eyes—and opened them, hot and staring, to full daylight and a cold dawn breeze stiffening my cramped, hanging knees.

The pool was still in shadow when I got there. The red bluff in back of it shouldered out the early morning sun. I felt the chill of the waters bite up to my thighs as I waded in, almost to the bluff. I leaned and groped in the water. I felt the slacked flow of a current against my hands. I don't know what happened then, but I felt the despair in me die, cooled perhaps in the flow of the water, the clean blueness of the early sky, and the first shaft of sun past the shoulder of the bluff.

I waded back to shore with a last look in case there was a floating body—or two. This, after all, was the creek that gave us our drinking water—if it didn't forget to flow again after one of the more-frequent stoppages we had had recently. I climbed back up the hill and went to the Curtis place and methodically did the morning chores. Livestock has to be taken care of. I carried the two brimming buckets of milk back to the settlement with me. I put them on the steps of the meeting house and went into the chill shadow inside. I looked around me. There was no hiding place—quite literally. I spanned the one bare, barn-like room and went back out. I left the milk where it was, hoping someone would find it, and started through the settlement.

I knocked at every door—and not one opened to me. I searched every place I could, and saw not a soul, living or dead. I doubled back past the meeting house on my way to the Curtis place. The two milk buckets lay on their sides, the milky mud around them hardening in the sun. A scrap of ragged kitten fur crouched at the corner of one splotch and bumped a hopeful, searching nose against the stiffening dust.

Night came. From my vantage point on Curtis' front porch I had seen movement in the settlement. The flip of a skirt in a chicken yard—

the slow movement of cows to their milking places, but no sound came to me except from behind the house where I sat.

I had made my decision. If I didn't find Gail by morning, I was going to Everly and get help. Then we'd come back and turn this God-forsaken settlement inside out until we found her. Oh, God! Help me find her! I scratched my head painfully. Then I looked at my hand. Scratching again? I was suddenly conscious that I had been trying to reach an itch for some time. But I wasn't getting to it. My hand went up involuntarily again—but my skull was between me and the itch.

I snorted a half laugh at myself as I tried to go back to my prayer. Talk about minds wandering! In the midst of the worst worry I'd had since I joined the Conclave, I got an itch I couldn't scratch! And it kept me from prayer—well, prayer's a lot of things besides words. I got up and started back toward the pond. I'd try again. Maybe someone would be going to take her bread—or water—

I pulled up abruptly. If I was looking for Gail, what was I doing hiking over the hill in the half darkness to the pond? I hesitated, my hand reaching up again to that odd itch, stubbing my fingers on skull again. I plunged down the darkening hillside.

"Mr. Lambert—"

I swear I learned in one split second what they mean by jumping out of your skin!

"Jareb—!" I gritted toward his vague shadow, gulping my jagged breath. "If you ever again—!"

"I didn't mean to scare you," said Jareb. "I just wanted to tell you to tell Mamma that Tally drank a whole cup of milk this morning, and—"

"Where is she?" I snapped. "Even overnight isn't long enough for you to get anywhere and back. There's nothing and no one for fifteen miles—"

"We didn't go all the way." His voice was apologetic. "That boy was going to take us to his home so he lifted us—"

"Did what?" I rasped.

"He—he was going to take us to his home, and it would be faster with no feet—"

"Jareb! Jareb!" He caught the exasperated anger in my voice.

"It's true," he cried. "That boy can—"

"That boy can take a running jump—"

"He called you!" shrilled Jareb. "He called you with no words and you came!"

"He called—" My hand tried to reach that feeling again—

"Over here, Mr. Lambert." That boy's voice was just a boy voice, but being convulsed by shock twice in one evening was almost the end of me.

I was glad for the rough support of the jack pine behind my shaken back. That boy was just a boy to look at, too, and he dug the same sort of hole in the sand with the twisting toe of his shoe that any embarrassed boy does. Then he went out! Like a snuffed candle! And I realized that somehow he had quite literally been lighted up so I could see him. I felt numb.

"So if you'll tell Mamma—"

"She's gone," I said flatly.

"Where to?" asked Jareb, startled. "Did she go to look for me?"

"She didn't go," I said. "They took her. They've got her locked up somewhere. They want to trade her for Tally."

"But you can't," cried Jareb. "Tally's gotta stay—"

"You tell them," I suggested. "They don't hear me."

"Well then, when Tally's better, we can trade," said Jareb.

"They aren't going to feed your mother," I said. "I think maybe they'll give her water, though."

"Not going to feed—!" Jareb's eyes flashed white at me in the heavy dusk. "They can't—"

"You tell them," I repeated.

"All right, then," said Jareb. "If they're going to be mean, I'll take Mamma back with me—to Tally."

"First catch your mother!" I smiled mirthlessly over the old receipt. We were in a bad enough stew, heaven knows.

"That boy can," said Jareb. "That boy can sure do a lot of things. His name's Theo. Hey! You know where they live? You know where it is? I mean it's the other end of the water, but do you know where it really is? And Theo says the pump works backwards so's they can—"

"Your mother," I broke in on his senseless babble, weariness dissolving my knees and elbows.

"Let's go get her," said that boy—I mean Theo.

"You go," I said. "I'll follow."

And he did go. And I did follow—a crazy path that wound around every structure in the settlement, same as I had already. But this path was always semivisible for one more step ahead of me—and one more step and one more— And at each structure, Theo would pause a moment, then shuffle his feet and say "Nope" and we'd go on. Finally we finished the last—the meeting house, and Theo said the final "Nope."

Wordlessly we went back up to Jareb's house. We didn't go in. We didn't even go up on the porch. We huddled in the dark in the tangled grass under the salt cedar trees. Even the path light was gone. I heard Jareb gulp and sniff. Then Theo squatted down.

"Tell me your mamma again," he said. "Tell me her worried and sorry."

"But I can't *tell* worried and sorry," protested Jareb, squatting down too.

"No words," said Theo. "Just think worried and sorry for your mamma."

I presume that's what Jareb did for the next few minutes. Anyway, in the silence that's what I did—thought worried. Then Theo grunted.

"Now," he said, "think *you* the scaredest you've ever been in all your life. Think scared to death!" It only took half a minute of silence to send Jareb tight up against my shins, shaking and whimpering, and to hear Theo whisper in awe, *"Adonday veeah!"* or some such sound.

"All right!" said Theo, a little shaken in his breath. "Now I think I'm patterned—"

"What's going on?" I asked. "What are you—"

"I'm not very good at it." Theo's voice was apologetic. "I guess I haven't paid attention when I should've. He told me his mamma so I'll know her when I find her—she'll be sorry and worried—and I got him so I can make her find us because she'll think harder if she thinks he's scared—"

"But that doesn't—" I began.

"Words!" Theo's voice was shrill as he shot to his feet. "Why do all of you have to have words all the time! No wonder Tally's almost untimely Called! No wonder his mamma's lost—" His voice cut off sharply. Then he said quietly, "I'm sorry. I have no right to add hurting to your hurting. Let's start. Give me your hands."

I groped my hand towards him and clutched Jareb's with the other. We made a tight little triangle in the darkness, and I heard his voice, serene and soft, "We are gathered together in Thy Name—"

"Amen," I whispered.

"Amen," whispered Jareb. "Why?"

Then Theo squatted down again and for a long time we listened to the stirring of the needles above us and the blades about us. Then Theo's breath caught and he said, "There! There! Jareb, think to her hard! Where is she?"

"Mamma!" Jareb clutched my arm, his voice hoarse and terrified. "Mamma! Where are you! Mamma!" And he began to sob the hard, ugly sobs of someone unused to crying.

"Where is she?" I asked tensely.

"Under—under the ground!" said Theo.

My whole soul collapsed and the blackness around me began to waver.

"Under the ground!" wailed Jareb. "She's dead! She's dead!"

"Don't be a silly *toolah!*" snapped Theo. "How could she think under the ground if she was dead? Be still!" There was another tense silence and then he murmured, "Shut in like a beast. Dirt falls down. Too hard to dig. It fell. It all fell. He'll come. When morning comes, he'll come. My—my boy, my boy, my—" He turned to me. "Where is she?" he asked, his face a pale oval. "Every time she thinks of where she is, she thinks of you, only not your name. But it's you—and warm—and strong—"

"Thinks of me!" I felt my face flush in the dark. Then I put aside my personal astonishment and set my mind to our problem. "Where is she? Under the ground—under the ground—*in* the ground—" That picture was different. My voice quickened. "Jareb, it could be *in* the ground! In a root cellar or—or—"

"We went to them all," reminded Jareb tearfully. "Even the one Dab—I mean Brother Jonadab—started by the meeting house."

"Yeah." I slumped again. "Theo, can't you give me anything else to go on? Anything?"

"It's kinda hard," said Theo hesitatingly. "I don't know what will help. I have to take your thinking and get words from Jareb and make talking for you before—"

"Dirt falls down," I recounted. "Too hard to dig—and me—something to do with me—anything else, Theo! *Anything?*"

"Well—uh—" Theo fumbled. "Oh, now she's—she's—no, it's not singing—'look in at the open door. They love to see the something, something and hear the bellows roar—' "

"Look in at the open door—" I stood slowly. "Come on," I said. "Come on!" I shouted. "Get going!" I skidded down the slope of the hill, half on my heels, half sitting. A bush whacked me across the eyes stingingly, making the dim outlines around us swim in protective tears. Behind me clattered the boys.

"Where—where—?" I heard Theo gasp.

"Dunno," jerked Jareb. "Dunno!"

"Mist-er Lam-bert," gasped Theo. "They will hear. They will come!"

I stopped. The two boys slid into the backs of my outstretched arms. We listened until the last of the pebbles rattled to rest below us. Until the last tentative echo dissolved against the far hillside. Then we moved on silently, silently. The path light was with us again, barely bright enough to be visible. Sometimes it flicked around erratically; then Theo would mutter and it would steady again. I lowered myself down the face of the drop-off at the bottom of the hill and lifted my arms to help the boys. Jareb grunted and lurched against me down to the level. And Theo came down at the same time, disturbing no rock, because he touched not one— nor me. "It could be fun," I thought. "Just to lift up and go along—"

"Where we going?" whispered Jareb. "Where we going, Mr. Lambert?"

"To the smithy," I said. "Don't you remember the poem your mother made you learn last winter out of your reader—'Under the spreading—'"

"Yeah—yeah—I guess so—" Jareb wasn't much of a poetry lover.

I stumbled into my smithy and peered around. "But I slept here last night!" I remembered deflatingly.

"*In* the ground, Mr. Lambert," reminded Jareb.

I yanked my cot away from the hillside. "It was too hard to dig—" I found myself echoing Theo's words. "But where? Theo, can you find her again?" I asked.

"Wait." I slumped on the edge of my cot as I felt Theo wiggle and slump down to his squat again. "Jareb, call your mamma. No—no! Not words! Call to her hard inside your head." I heard the rustle of Jareb squatting down, too. After an endless silence, I heard Jareb's sniff and unhappy gulp, and felt him collapse sideways into a huddle against my legs. Then, without warning, I felt myself snatched up into a shining stream of something that pulled me out of me and shot me away from me like a spark struck from an anvil, and I knew—there was no sight or hearing or feeling, only knowing—I knew Gail was sobbing Jareb's name and mine. She was huddled over her dried-mud-caked shoes and dabbled skirts, sobbing and clutching the bent little lard pail that hadn't been refilled since she had been shoved roughly into—into—

"Thank you, God," I gulped aloud. "Thank you, God."

"Amen," said Jareb. "What for?"

And Theo echoed, "Amen."

"The water hole," I said. "They've shut her up in the cave above the water hole."

"But there's no way to shut it up," protested Jareb.

"She's shut up there anyway," I said.

We had to go the long way around. My smithy was actually built on the edge of the creek, but you'd never know it. The bank and the rise behind my cot dropped off sheerly down to the creek, which was in a wash nearly a hundred feet below my shop. When we first arrived in the settlement, we had pastured all our livestock together and had used the pool below my shop as a watering place. The swirling action of the sometimes heavy flood waters down the creek had scoured out a big pothole that made a natural water hole. A cave had been worn out of the hillside, too, but it was never under water except, I suppose, in the highest of the floods. We had stabled our livestock there for a while behind a quick fence of cottonwood and salt cedar branches.

But why, I wondered as we rounded the hill and started our rattling, scrambling slide down the creek path, the eerie light showing us our way, why was Gail staying there? Why didn't she get out or holler or something? Unless they had tied her—in a blind flare of helpless rage, I jumped the last drop-off and staggered back against the bank, my feet squishing in mud.

I looked around me. I checked the creek. And the trees. And the hills beyond. I was in the right place, but where was the pond? The cave? Gail!

"It's not there!" cried Jareb. "The cave's gone! Mr. Lambert, where's—Mamma! Mamma!" He threw himself against me and I staggered back, holding him and me up by the clutch of my hand across his shoulders.

"So that's why," I thought dully. "Be quiet, Jareb," I said. "Bawling won't help any. The hill's caved in and covered up the cave." The tinkling fall of a pebble and a small funneling of a thin line of silt underlined the silence.

"Mamma!" cried Jareb. "She's dead!"

"She's not either!" cried Theo. "I couldn't have found her if she was dead! We can't find the Called Ones. They're in the Presence! She isn't either dead!"

Dead or not dead—what did a day or so matter? My thoughts slumped. She had no water now and even the three of us couldn't hope to move a hillside in time—*Move a hillside! Lift a mountain!*

"Theo!" I clutched his shoulder, and with his startled gasp the light went out. Darkness flooded in around us and suddenly the stars were very bright and very close. "Theo, Jareb said you could lift mountains. Can you? Can you really do that?"

"No." Theo's voice was very small. "Someday I'll be able to, but I'm too young now. Mountains—no, no, I can't. Not yet!"

"Your father—" I pursued desperately. "Could he—"

"Sure," said Theo, unhappily. "Only he doesn't even know where—"

"Theo!" I thought it was a voice, but a voice doesn't start inside you and shake its way out past your bones. "Theo!"

"Father!" Theo's startled eyes were white glints in the starshine—and his arms went up. "Oh, Father! You can—"

Words stopped and Theo leaped into the air and he didn't come down! Jareb and I clutched each other and stared up into the night. Theo hurled himself into a clustered shadow above us, and for a long, unbroken moment, all the world waited and listened with us—to silence.

Then the clustered shadow dissolved and became Theo and a man and a woman and another man. They slanted down to us out of the night sky, but they didn't muddy their feet in the muck at the base of the slide. They didn't have to. They didn't touch the ground. Not quite.

"Your love is behind the slide?" the man asked me quickly.

I recoiled at the bluntness of his words. "No!" I protested. "Yes!" I gasped, giving up my evasions. "Behind the slide!"

"Your pardon," said the man, and Jareb and I were whisked out of the way like children. I don't know how we got to the other side of the creek and up on the shelf halfway up the other side, but we crouched there and watched the loose scree on the slope begin to funnel up like a slow tornado, pebbles grating softly against pebbles as they rose. Light came on the slope, and we could see a hole starting and deepening into the slide. And no dirt caved from above it and no rocks rattled down into it—only the lengthening dark streak rose up from the hillside and up. Then there was a *thunk* and a satisfied murmur from the clustered people over there. The funnel of displaced dirt relaxed itself out of existence against the creek bank farther downstream. I watched the mouth of the hole with my life crushed in my unbreathing chest. *Lazarus!* my thoughts babbled. *Come forth!*

And there she was! There was Gail! Stooping out of the hole, dazed and bewildered, her hair tumbled down over her shoulders and half obscuring her mud-streaked face. One hand steadied her against the edge of the hole—the other was still clutching that bent old lard pail.

I heard the woman cry out something shocked and sorry and saw her draw Gail up into her arms. Then Gail was in *my* arms and Jareb was clutching her skirts and sobbing into them. Gail's shaking hands were clamped onto my arm and she looked back over her shoulder.

"Are they angels?" she asked. "Are they angels?" Then she was warm and heavy against me, clinging and sobbing, and my life started again with a shaken breath.

"Your pardon." The man was back by us. "We must go." And the three clustered, tightly but untouching, about us. I had one look of the earth scurrying back, far beneath us, and, helpless to react any more, hid my face against Gail's hair. I clutched her to me with one aching arm and held Jareb desperately against my side with the other. Then the thought came out of panic. *We would have fallen long ago if we were going to fall.* But the thought brought no comfort.

"Step," said Theo's father. "Step." And I did—staggering across the front porch of Gail's house.

Quickly we were inside and a dim light filled the fireplace. Gail murmured, and she and the woman disappeared into the other room.

The man drew Theo to him. "Tell me," he said.

In the scurrying silence, I backed toward the fireplace, my hands spreading to gather warmth. There was no warmth, only light. Jareb shivered against me, and I gathered him into the crook of my arm.

Theo began to cry and his father left him to turn to us. He opened his mouth and then closed it. Perhaps he had to talk twice, too, as Jareb had told me Theo had to. Jareb shivered and I shivered, too. The light in the fireplace brightened and warmth began to creep out into the room.

"Theo tells me that he and Jareb took a little girl from her mother—"
The voice rang some bell for me. Where had I—?

"Yes," I said, "they took Tally. But didn't you—"

"We knew nothing of it," said Theo's father. "We thought Theo was
on one of his—his finding-out journeys. The boys have the child con-
cealed in the waterway between here and the end of the water. Theo says
she is suffering from the lack of—good."

"She's dying," I said flatly.

"Dying?" The man's startled face leaned into the light.

"But you—" I groped. "I've seen you—"

"Another time." He cut my stuttering with a motion of his hand.
"Shan—" The other man drifted to the door, paused briefly, looking back
at Theo's father, then he was gone soundlessly, out into the dark.

The man drew Theo to him again and held him comfortingly as he
went on.

"Children—" he began. Theo squirmed.

"Children—" I nodded, and Jareb stirred in the circle of my arm.

The man smiled. "So you know, too, Mr. Lambert," he said. Then
he sobered. "But that doesn't excuse what they have done. Tally's mother
must be—"

"She is," I said. "The whole Conclave is. And they're sick, too. That's
why they're acting like this—"

"I can't understand." The man frowned, puzzled. "Theo says you
offered them—"

"I did," I said. "*They* couldn't understand. That's why—"

"And they'd rather die—" He shook his head.

"That's the way people are," I said. "Surely you've heard of people
dying because of misunderstanding."

His face was bleak in the warm light, and I felt such a pang of sorrow from him that my eyes blurred. Then they cleared in a hurry as Gail
and the woman came back, Gail, clean and decently dressed, braiding the
second of the two long braids of her heavy hair.

"The boys have Tally," she began.

The woman interrupted. "Shan's gone to get her."

"It isn't very far," said Jareb. "We didn't take her very far. Theo said—"
His eyes flicked to the man. "Theo said his daddy and mamma didn't
know and if they found out, they wouldn't let him—" He broke off, conscious as I was of the cold feeling of unacceptance that filled the room.
For a minute his shoulder pushed against me, then he got mad.

"She was dying!" he shouted. "She was dying!" He lowered his voice,
his eyes apprehensively turned toward the door. "Did you want me to
just let her die? Her daddy wouldn't let her mamma give her any of the

good, and when Mamma and I tried to, they were coming to get her. So I went and got Theo and we took her—we went—" his voice faltered. "Maybe she's dead now!" he wailed. "And Sister Ruth feels so bad! We didn't have any dry clothes for her—" There was a movement at the door and Shan came in. I felt a relaxation all around me, and Theo ventured a quick half-smile at Jareb.

In a flurry of movement, Shan gave up the muddy bundle of rags into the hands of Theo's mother. She and Gail disappeared again into the other room. The indignant cry of a wakened child made us all smile. It was like the ending of a birth-wait.

"She couldn't even cry, before," said Jareb. "She'd open her mouth, but no crying would come out! The good's working already!"

I looked at Shan. He wasn't even wet! How had he managed to go get her without going down into the pond?

"He shielded." Theo was answering me, shamefaced. "I forgot. I could have kept Jareb and me dry if I'd thought, but it was so fast—" He thought he had explained!

Dawn was steel-grey at the window. Tally, full of warm milk spiked with good, was sleeping in Gail's arms. The rest of us were resting our voices and our minds. Only our minds wouldn't rest. We had no solution yet. What were we to do about Tally? If we gave her back to her folks with them feeling as they did about the good, she'd die. If we kept her, her parents' agony would be something we couldn't bear. If we told them that we had her and wouldn't give her back—no telling what the half-crazed batch would do.

Finally Theo's father said, "Your Conclave came here to separate itself from the world to worship the Presence—your God—in the way they felt right."

"Yes," I said, not liking the sound of "separate," though it was true.

"Then you feel a nearness to the Presence."

"We hope for it," I answered.

"And when we released Gail from the cave, she asked if we were related to the Presence—"

"Related?" I frowned, trying to think. Gail stirred and lowered her head so that her cheek was pressed to the spiky dampness of Tally's hair.

"I thought they were angels," she said softly. "And they are!"

"Angels?" asked Theo's father.

"Messengers of God," I explained. "They carry out His will in the world."

"Intermediaries?" suggested Theo's father. "Coming between you and the Presence?"

"Not coming between!" I was a little annoyed. It didn't sound right. "Going between!"

"Oh." The man fell silent, then he said, "If an angel of God appeared to Tally's parents and told them to give her the good, would they obey?"

"I—I think so," I said. "If they believed—"

"This is such a roundabout way," said the man, impatiently. "Just because there's not good in the soil here—if only you had chosen a place like Everly—"

"Everly—" I straightened my weary back with astonishment. "So *that's* where I've seen you—at Everly when I went for the garden truck—"

"That's what I tried to tell you," cried Jareb, suddenly rousing. "That's the other end of the water! They came here first, then went away because there wasn't any good here, and they came here in wagons without any wheels. Theo didn't know the words; so he showed them to me inside my head. I want to go there and see some of them wagons. How can wagons go without wheels? Or horses either? In the sky! I want to see—"

"Wagons without wheels!" I turned my eyes up in exasperation. Even in this troubled moment, Jareb had to go on with his foolish fantasies.

"I'm sorry, Jareb," said Mr. Jensus—that's who he was in Everly!—matter-of-factly. "They were all burned, long ago."

"Aw!" Jareb was disappointed.

"Some of us were burned—" began Theo, but his voice stopped in midword. He colored to his eyebrows, and his eyes crept away from his father's face.

"The angel," suggested Mr. Jensus.

"It's Tally's father that needs convincing," said Gail. "But I think he would accept an angel. You don't argue with angels."

"Good," said Mr. Jensus, standing up briskly. "Then I'll go to him and tell him I'm an angel—"

"But," Gail lowered her head again and then lifted it resolutely, "you don't look like an angel."

"Oh?" Mr. Jensus looked down at himself. "I am the same as when you saw me and thought—"

"Yes," said Gail, "because of what you were doing. But if you are going to convince Sister Ruth and Brother Rual, you'll have to look like a real angel—"

"And that is—?" asked Mr. Jensus.

"A long white robe—" Mr. Jensus nodded. "And wings—" "Wings!" Mr. Jensus was startled. "Feathered wings," Gail went on.

"Feathers!" Mr. Jensus' jaw dropped.

"Aven," said Mrs. Jensus chidingly, "you must look through other eyes."

"And a halo," said Gail. "A ring of brightness above your head."

Mr. Jensus turned despairing eyes to his wife. She smiled at him and touched his arm. "I'll do it," she said. "I don't mind."

Well, Gail, handing me the sleeping Tally, blushingly took a white nightgown from the trunk by the fireplace, and Mrs. Jensus put it on in the other room. She came back to us, letting down the shining length of her light hair all around her shoulders and her back. She and her husband in some way devised wings, like feathered curves of light, and set a halo glowing above her head. She truly looked like an angel!

"Except," said Gail.

"Except?" asked Mrs. Jensus. Her eyes twinkled. "Not a tail, too!"

"No," Gail smiled. "That's for devils. The shoes." She pointed to the sturdy shoes showing beneath the hem of the gown.

"No shoes?" Mrs. Jensus asked. "What do they wear?"

Well, no one knew, except that they wouldn't wear sturdy shoes.

"Well," said Mrs. Jensus, and the shoes dissolved into light.

She took the sleeping Tally, and a measure of good tied up in a handkerchief. We all moved out onto the front porch and watched her lift herself and Tally into the cool chill of the predawn morning and move off towards Benson's. I stood there, silent. What could you say in the face of all the impossible things that were happening? Then a niggling little thought crept through the awed wonder. Shouldn't she be flapping the wings? Or did angels flap—

"Mamma, I'm hungry," Jareb's voice broke the moment. "I bet Theo is, too."

"Of course," said Gail. "It's almost breakfast time. You men go do the chores while I get breakfast."

I was just coming back into the cabin with the first bucket of milk and Gail had started cracking the second dozen eggs into the skillet when I heard it—I heard Tally crying, "Mamma! Mamma!"

My chest tightened and apprehension ran through my blood like icy water. I yanked the door open. There was Mrs. Jensus, her eyes wide and shocked, clutching a struggling Tally to her crumpled gown.

"They wouldn't take her!" She could hardly make the words. "They said she was—was—dead! She was a—a—ghost. What's a ghost? How could a child be something so evil that she'd frighten her own parents?"

Gail deftly took the screaming Tally, hushed her into sobs, and gave her a crust of bread. Tally considered it for a moment as she clutched it in her tear-wet hand. Then she drew a shuddering breath and greedily stuffed all the crust she could into her mouth.

"A ghost is a dead person who—who stays on earth and haunts—" I began.

"But the Dead are received into the Presence!" cried Mrs. Jensus. "Why would they ever want to—"

"Tell us." Mr. Jensus was there, his hands touching hers gently. "Aloud," he added. "For our friends."

"I went," said Mrs. Jensus, her face smoothing out from its uncomprehending shock. "I went to the meeting house. They were all there because one had been Called. They were to commit his cast-aside to earth."

Gail and I exchanged startled looks. The first death in the Conclave. "Who?" I asked.

Mrs. Jensus hesitated. "Their—their Man of God."

"Brother Helon!" I felt a dissolving. Now that the keystone was gone, what would happen—

"I went in—like an angel," said Mrs. Jensus. "I went to the mother and held out Tally. The father knocked away her reaching hands because a—a person—Dab?" I shut my eyes and nodded dumbly. Of course, Dab! "Cried 'Ghost, ghost!' and everyone—they—it was—" Mrs. Jensus hid her face against Mr. Jensus.

Theo and Jareb came in with another bucket of milk, and Gail gave me Tally and turned back to the eggs. She knelt to the fireplace and steadied the skillet on the grate as though every day she cooked on red-hot iron with no fire under it. We were all watching her. The smell of cooking eggs had snared our attention, and suddenly starved us all.

"Dab or no Dab," said Gail, "Sister Ruth wouldn't turn from her baby. Brother Rual or no Brother Rual—"

We heard the voice call, breathlessly. We heard the stagger of steps on the porch.

"I want my baby!" Sister Ruth slid slowly to her knees, the door frame supporting her back. "I want Tally!"

Tally surged in my arms toward her mother, her face and hands liberally smeared with wet bread crumbs. Crooning inarticulately, Sister Ruth took the child from me, but had to sag her weight immediately to the floor. "I—I want some of that salt stuff too!" she gasped. "Look at Tally! *Look at Tally!*" The child was standing alone on shaky little legs. She lurched toward the fireplace and the savory-smelling eggs. "Sumpin a-yeat!" she said, collapsing on hands and knees against Gail. "Sumpin a-yeat!"

Then, as if that wasn't enough, the door was darkened again. There stood Brother Rual, wavering on spread legs, his black scowl on his pallid face.

"I want my woman!" he said, trying to moisten his dry lips. "And my child! And to hell with that damn Dab!"

I choked back a massive shout of laughter as the whole insane affair climaxed in Jareb's shrill, shocked, "Ah—M-m-m! Mamma! He cussed! He cussed!"

We all went to Everly—Shan and the two boys going back by the waterway—the rest of us openly in the light wagon, with only the fewest possessions possible. With no need for discussion, our doors had closed unopenably on the Conclave. We drove slowly by the meeting house, and Gail clutched my arm as we saw the bare rectangle of grassless soil marking where Brother Helon's body lay. The flat scar on the land was waiting for the grass to heal it and to erase Brother Helon from this world.

As we pulled up the rise to the Everly road, I saw the roadside brush jerk and shake and be still suddenly. I leaned back and reached down into the wagon, lifting my eyebrows at Mr. Jensus. He nodded and put into my hand the bundle of good Mrs. Jensus had carried. I tossed it into the grass by the road. As our wheels ground gravel turning the corner above Hellesgate, I looked back. Dab was crouched in the road looking after us, the good clutched his hand. He was fumbling at the string as we rounded the corner. I wondered. Was he going to taste it—or dump it out on the ground?

Arriving at Everly was like coming home. We weren't among strangers—only friends too considerate to gather around in droves, but we could feel their warmth and support all around us. I don't know why I knew we couldn't stay, but I did. But stay or not, it was wonderful just to relax for a while—only that Dab-worry was still nagging me.

The day after our arrival, Theo was showing us around their place. It was new to everyone but me—and most of it was new to me, too. I had only seen the part where I picked up the garden truck for Hellesgate.

"The pump's over here," said Jareb. "Only it's—it's—" He paused a moment, then grinned. "It's busted!"

"Pump trouble?" I asked Mr. Jensus.

"Yes," he said. "It works for a while and then it stops. It's a type we don't know. We're trying to analyze the difficulty—"

"I've worked on pumps." I said. "Want me to take a look?"

"Take a look?" He paused and then smiled. "If you would, please, take a look."

It was a simple matter to fix. It made me wonder that they couldn't have told right off what was the matter. I didn't say anything and went ahead and fixed it. I put it in gear and watched the blades of the windmill bite the wind. I watched with satisfaction the gush of the water—then I blinked and looked again. The water was being pumped *into* the hill! It leaped out of the well pipe, twisted in the sun, and disappeared into a crack in the hill!

Mr. Jensus caught my questioning. "It's the creek," he nodded. "It hasn't rained for a long time. We can't let the creek run dry."

"The creek?" I blinked, my mind churning. "Yeah, Jareb said you made—"

Mr. Jensus' face saddened. "I'll have to speak to Theo again about talking unwisely outside the Group," he said. "That is strictly Group business."

"You keep the creek flowing?" Then I frowned a little. "Bur why? None of you live down there—"

"But you do," he smiled. "You need water. We can provide it; so of course, we do."

"Oh, of course," I repeated. It sounded too simple. Why should— Then another thought caught me. "Then this *is* the other end of the water!"

"Well, yes," said Mr. Jensus after the usual pause. "You could say that."

"Theo told Jareb," I said. "He said that's where you lived."

"Theo enjoys flowing with the water on warm days. He's forbidden to go farther than the pool."

"But if he hadn't—" I said.

"If he hadn't," nodded Mr. Jensus. "But he disobeyed."

From the tone of his voice I decided maybe Theo wasn't getting away with very much with his dad.

"Then the broken pump is why the creek has been drying up lately?"

"Yes," said Mr. Jensus. "We try to have someone here to keep the water flowing, but sometimes—"

"Keep the water flowing without the pump?" I asked. Mr. Jensus nodded.

"Look here," I said, a kind of dizziness roaring in my ears. "I'm going to ask you something flat-out. I want a flat-out answer. Who *are* you people, anyway?"

"We?" Mr. Jensus' eyebrows rose. "We're The People." His hand went out at my sudden scowl. "No, please. I'm not trying to—to mock you. We have no name for ourselves except The People. We, like you, seek a new home. We can never go back—"

"Back where?" I asked flatly.

"Back Home." His lips lifted in a half smile. "We had no other name for it either."

"Then you're from across the sea—"

"The sea?" His voice was a sigh.

"The sea," I said, remembering it as last I had seen it so long ago.

"Oh, the sea!" His face brightened. "Then you do have wide waters in this world too—"

"This world?" I felt a clenching in my chest.

"Yes." It was more a sigh than a word. "We had a crossing—but not of the sea—"

And for the second time I was snatched into that bright stream. The hills and flats were gone for me. The pump and the glittering water faded into dark. I watched a world die in the sky, flame licking like tongues as far as across a whole hemisphere. I saw vehicles rise before the flames and lose themselves in the darkness of space. I felt madness crisp the edges of my mind as I tried to find a solid something in a dissolving nothing. Then the pump coughed and caught and again spewed the steady stream into the hillside.

Mr. Jensus' eyes were warily on mine.

"Another world," I said. "Wagons without wheels—"

Mr. Jensus nodded. "And some burned up in the atmosphere when we came to this world. And some of us died here because of un-understanding—" His voice wavered and, for a minute, I looked at Everly through his eyes—the eyes of a refugee who knew the gates of Eden were forever slammed behind him and that the turning sword of flame of burning craft forever stood guard. I blinked myself back to myself.

"I don't understand," I said. "Not only what you have told me, but why you go on helping—"

He frowned a little. "Surely none of the facts cancel any others. It wasn't Hellesgate that—that killed. Hellesgate needs water, so—"

"Of course," I said. "I guess—" Then all at once I wanted to hold my hand out to him and as quickly knew I didn't have to. I knew we were touching for a small moment somewhere where it mattered most. I cleared my throat and kicked at the base of the hill. The dust sifted across my toe—

"Say!" I said, turning with relief to the dust again. "The good—where do you get it?"

"From this hill," said Mr. Jensus. "There is more of it here than elsewhere. It takes many buckets of the hill to yield a very small amount of good. But it takes a very, very small amount of good to—to set right the un-goodness."

"I wonder what happened that Hellesgate doesn't have it," I said.

"I do not know your world well," said Mr. Jensus. "But I think good must be almost everywhere. There must be very few places where good is not. Otherwise you would know of it and how to put good where it is not."

"Put good—" I stared at the water. I swallowed. "If good could get into the soil—"

"Then it would feed into the water and into the plants, and there would be no need to add—" His words died. "Yes," he said slowly. "Of course!" he cried. "As you think! As you think!"

And before nightfall the pump was repositioned so that the gush of water cut through the edge of the hill before plunging out of sight. The creek ran good and muddy down to Hellesgate! And good soaked into the soil along every irrigation ditch and in every field and swirled roily in every cup of drinking water—and I hope it gritted between Dab's teeth every time he drank! I could hear him cuss! But try throwing *that* good out!

Well, that was all long ago and far away. We left Everly, as we knew we had to. We never saw Hellesgate again. But we heard of it—of the demons that possessed it at first and of the brave, holy war waged against them until they were banished. And how the evil spells were lifted then, and the Gates of Hell did not prevail against the Second Conclave. That's why the town is called Hellesgate. Brother Jonadab says so and he should know! Only one as strong and holy as the leader of the Second Conclave could have cast out the demons and removed the evil from the land, and he, Brother Jonadab, was the only one who dared pursue the demons as they finally fled!

And the other people—The People. I know they are sometimes around. I know it when, in a rare, wonderful moment, I have a feeling that I am touching someone somewhere where it matters, and I know what that boy meant when he said words aren't always necessary, and for a blessed moment, my heart just—lifts up and goes along.

Michal Without

As I accomplished the last tortured inch of the turning of my body, I saw the child. My first reaction was annoyance. My face had been showing more of the agony I felt than I customarily let be evident. I had thought myself alone except for the other—sleeping—patient.

"Hello," I said, deciding absently that the blue-jeaned child was a girl.

"Hello." Her voice was quiet and unusually rich. With a quick, fluid movement, she was by my bedside. "It hurts you."

I was startled by the nearness of the deep eyes, with a blue light running the length of the dark lashes and splintering on the tips of them.

"Yes, it does." My own voice was breathless. Pain is a burden that takes the breath. "It hurts a lot right now, but it comes and goes. I'll be better—tomorrow."

"I'm Michal," she said. "Without an *e*."

"Where's David?" I asked with a feeble grin at my feeble pleasantry.

There was a moment of searching silence, then a quick smile. "Most people don't know," she said. "I get tired of explaining." She put out a finger and touched my knotted, swollen hand. "Arthritis," she said.

"Yes."

"Aunt Lydie had some other arthritics here before. Mostly, though, she takes only senile, bedridden men. You aren't senile."

"Not quite yet." I did better with the smile. "But I am incontestably bed-ridden. Isn't your vocabulary a little above your age level?"

"Yes," she nodded. "I get words from other people."

"Like stamps for a collection," I suggested.

She had left the door ajar and I heard the warm depth of her voice as she talked to someone across the hall.

"Hey!" the hail came from the other bed. "When'd you get here?"

"Last night," I said to, I presumed, Mr. Apfel. "You've had a good long sleep."

"Yeah." His face was troubled. "I been doing that since they pilled me when Jake died. You know," Mr. Apfel hunched up in bed, "he just died. He said, 'Mr. Apfel,' and he died. It scared me. I tried to go home but they caught me on the back stairs and made me come back." He settled back on his pillows and chuckled. "In my hospital gown. Kinda drafty. Those stairs go right down to the back yard with nothing around them. I mean, they're outside." He nodded at the door near his bed.

"Aren't they afraid you'll leave sometime?" I asked. "The door isn't locked, is it?"

"No, it isn't," he said. "It'd be against the law. But I'm bedfast. They don't take the other kind. Not since Old Mr. Ames got away from the house. It took them seven hours to track him down. He was behind the biggest tombstone in the cemetery—two miles away. He was playing games of naughts-and-crosses on the back of the stone—and winning all of them. He cheated."

"Well, if you're bedfast," I objected, "how could you have started to go home?"

"Scared," he grinned. "Scared stiff. Mostly I'm so limp-legged I can't walk a step,"

"That child," I said. "Michal."

"Without an *e*," he nodded.

"Odd child," I said. "Who is she?"

"She gives me rememberies," he said with a soft smile. "Bless the child."

"Rememberies?" I asked, talking to keep at bay the blazing ache that was munching down my shin bones to meet the scorching pain munching up my shin bones from my ankles.

"And you can't have any!" Mr. Apfel's eyes blazed. The pitch of his voice raised about three tones. "She hasn't got any time for you! You have no business coming here anyway! Jake might be back and want his bed. *He* didn't want any rememberies. Go away!" He flounced over in bed with his back turned to me. "Buttinski!"

"Oh, Lord!" I thought, half exasperation, half prayer. "What has this miserable carcass of mine got me into now?" I shut my eyes as tightly as I could, thinking ruefully, "At least my eyelids aren't involved—yet!"

"Good morning!" Mrs. Norwich, Michal's "Aunt Lydie," came in, pushing her nurse's cart before her, her steps as firm and purposeful as her skinned-back hairdo. "Sleep well?" Her eyes were kindly and interested behind her glitteringly clean bifocals.

"Fine, thanks," I said through set teeth.

"You lie well," she said, rattling various objects on the cart. "I'll take Mr. Apfel first so's we won't have to hurry you."

"Thanks," I said again, feeling the pain beginning to subside a little. If I lucked out, I should have a fairly comfortable day.

"Good morning, Mr. Apfel," she said cheerfully.

"Go away!" He dragged the covers up over his head, leaving his bony old feet uncovered.

"Oh, come on," said Mrs. Norwich. "Breakfast pretty soon. Coffee cake with pecans."

One eye appeared between the clutch of sheet and flare of white hair. "With frosting?"

"Slathers of gooey white frosting *and* pecans," she said.

Mr. Apfel emerged smiling and rosy, eager as a child.

Michal came back about 10:30, bearing juice and cookies. Afterwards, she wiped Mr. Apfel's chin skillfully and de-crumbed his spread and murmured and tucked him into a quick nap. Then she came to my bed and eyed the foot of it. "It would flex too much," she said, "and start the munching again."

Startled at her choice of words, I almost slopped orange juice from my tumbler.

She sat on a straight chair by my bed, her legs folded Turk style. Her eyes glinted at me mirthfully. "I get words from people."

"Oh?" I remarked, a little less than gleefully.

"Would you prefer to talk or to listen?" she asked.

"I have nothing to say," I said shortly. "Children should be seen, not heard."

"About Deega," she said. "You haven't come for me, so I'd better explain about Deega. You might find it interesting. Aunt Lydie doesn't like to hear it. It makes her uncomfortable."

"Do you customarily go around telling your life history to strangers?" I jerked.

"Being rude is a dry way of crying," she said, lacing her fingers together around her shins as she rearranged her legs. "It's too bad men do not customarily cry.

"No, I don't tell everyone my life history," she went on. "But I need to—to communicate." She nodded a small nod and said the word I had been thinking. "Aunt Lydie gets uncomfortable. Mr. Apfel laughs. I'm—I'm troubled."

"A twelve-year-old," I scoffed, interested without wanting to be.

"Your equating age with trouble makes my trouble seem even odder," she said. "You see, I'm troubled because I—I have no past—none that I can remember. I—started—when I was five."

"You customarily should have memories dating previous to that," I said.

"I know." She frowned a little and laid her cheek on her doubled-up knees. "And I do have them. I can feel them pushing and tugging at me inside, but they can't get through to me. They'd answer a lot of questions I'd like to ask, but—something is keeping them back."

"Maybe if you tell me—" After all, my swollen hands couldn't hold even a magazine for long, and children can be amusing, especially such a precocious one as Michal.

"It'll have to be piecemeal," she said. "Aunt Lydie likes me to keep busy.

"I don't know who Deega is—or was. I slept on her kitchen floor. If I kept under the table, hardly anyone ever stepped on me, not until break-fast time, anyway. She had wall-to-wall kids, and no one ever bothered trying to sort out whose kids they all were. Some were hers. She hit them the most, but fed them the most. I went hungry a lot.

"We lived in the city, I'm not sure which one, but it was big and noisy and tall and dirty. I remember once I was awfully cold. I was sitting on my feet on the steep front step of our building, wondering why the light from the street lamp wasn't hot like the sun used to be. I got up off the step, so stiff with cold that I stumbled and nearly fell. I staggered out under the lamp and gathered the light up by the handsful, but I couldn't hold very much—it flows so—so I clutched the hem of my skirt and made a lap. I filled it with the cool yellow light and went up to show Deega. I asked her why it wasn't hot. I can still see her eyes and mouth getting wider and wider with the yellow light flickering on them, then she screamed and slapped my hands down and gave me a licking for showing my underpants. A girl six years old is supposed to know not to show her underpants. I remember that my tears were hot, rolling down my cheeks, and I caught one on my tongue. It tasted of dirt and salt and I was so interested in the salty taste that I forgot to cry."

"Michal!" Mrs. Norwich was calling from across the hall. "Don't you go wearing Mr. Evans out with your chattering nonsense. Come help me."

Michal slipped from the chair, her eyes large upon my face. "I'll tell you some more when I get a chance," she said. "I think you have consid-erable food for thought from this much."

"Where did you read this story?" I asked.

"I didn't." Her voice floated back from the closing door. "I lived it."

"Well!" I reached for my magazine and saw that Mr. Apfel was awake again. "What an imagination that child has," I said, tentatively, wonder-ing if it was Mr. Apfel or Child Apfel this time.

"Yes." It was Mr. Apfel. "And helpful, too. She even talked with Jake."

"That's special?" I asked.

"Well, sort of," Mr. Apfel grinned cheerfully. "Up to the night he died, he hadn't said a single word to anyone in two-three years. Having him call me by name scared me more than his dying, I guess. His voice was all rusty—"

"But she talked to him—"

Mr. Apfel's look was tolerant of a new-comer. "She doesn't need words to talk—you'll see. She was the only one who knew what Jake thought or how he felt. It was funny, listening to their conversations. You could usually hear everything Michal said, but there'd be long pauses while Jake had his say. And half the time he'd even have his back turned."

"It could have been a play-act of Michal's," I suggested.

"No." Mr. Apfel considered for a moment. "She said he really wanted to talk, but his body had ganged up on him and wouldn't let him say a word. The tyranny of the flesh—" He leaned back against the pillows, his eyes desolately on his relaxed, vein-ropy hands.

"This," I gritted to myself as I shifted over enough to put my magazine down on the bedside table, "is without doubt the most stupid—" The magazine slithered to the floor. My involuntary snatch for it was a major mistake. I prefer to forget the rest of the day.

Night came and brought little relief except from the hard light that had raked across me all day from the window. I could tell I was in for a waking night again—the kind of night that wrings you and squeezes out everything from the world except pain, discomfort, and rebellion. Even prayer gets tissue-thin and crumply. Then, along about two hours before waking time, sleep comes and irons out a little of the fatigue so that when you wake you're left wide open to the "Have a nice sleep?" gambit.

But this time, somewhere in the unmetered endlessness of the night, Michal was there. I didn't hear her coming, but I wasn't startled to find her there. She seeped into my consciousness so gently that there was no one moment of realization. She hunched on the chair again, her feet drawn up under the voluminous flow of her nightgown that defined nothing of her except her shoulders. Her hair was unwound and shifted as shadows around the blur of her face.

"If you would try to lengthen out your breaths," she suggested softly, "it might ease you."

"I'm having trouble enough," I gasped, "breathing. Please omit," I gulped, "helpful suggestions."

"Try," she said.

Anything—anything. I snatched the extra little gulp of air that was necessary before I could empty my lungs. After two or three deliberately slow, long expirations and inspirations, I actually felt a little eased, a little less tense, and the pain ebbed a little.

"Speaking of breathing," Michal's voice wasn't much more than a breath itself, "once at Deega's it was so hot that I felt as though I'd just melt and run down the steps all red and sticky like strawberry ice cream. It got so hot that I stopped breathing for a little while, but I found out it was cooler to breathe, so I did."

"Well, that's one way to start a bedtime story," I said. "A trifle above 'Once upon a time.' "

"Please listen to me with something besides logic," she said. "I'm hoping so that you'll be able to help me find—"

"Find what?" I asked into her silence.

"Myself, I guess." Her voice was thoughtful. "I'm here, but I can't fit myself into any category—"

"I can," I grinned. "Human, female, pre-adolescent—"

"That's the whole thing!" she cried. "I have only while I am pre-adolescent to find myself—to find where I belong. That's the memory that keeps coming into everything I do. I've *got* to find out! I *have* to get there before—before I mature—"

"Get where?" I needled her.

"Get there," she said with such a desolation in her voice that even in the shadowy darkness the smile slipped from my face. No matter what this was to me, to her it was real and important.

She spoke into our growing silence, her voice taking on its narrative cadence.

"That hot evening, Deega and I leaned out of our window on the fifth floor. We could see way down into the airshaft—down to the bottom, where there was all kinds of garbage and junk and one thing that was green and moved a little.

" 'What's that?' I asked Deega.

" 'Bless me, if it don't look like a little tree!'

" 'A tree?' I asked. 'What's that?'

" 'Why, a tree, like at the park,' said Deega.

" 'What's a park?' I asked.

" 'With grass and flowers,' said Deega. 'Yes, I know," she sounded tired. 'What's grass and flowers?' She wiped the sweat off her forehead with the back of her hand and said, 'And to think I thought when you finally learned to talk instead of chattering a lot of no-words, that you'd be as smart as the next one. Well—' And she went away.

"That's how I got to be a Fresh-Air Kid. Miz Teeman's little girl was supposed to go but she got run over by a truck, so Deega went down and over and told Miz Teeman there wasn't no use wasting a free vacation, so they gave me two of Miz Teeman's little girl's dresses—they almost fit—and pushed me forward when Miz Teeman's little girl's name was called and that's how I got out to Aunt Lydie's."

"When I finally got out into the country, it was like coming home. I knew what everything was—except I didn't know the right names. I recognized—almost—every bird and beast. I had no names for them either. The first thing I did when we got home from the depot was to kick off my raggedy old sneakers and scuff my feet through the soft silty *clean* dust by the gate. I squatted down and poured the dirt over my feet and said, 'Eat, feet, eat!' I knew then about roots."

Michal paused and was silent for a while. Then she said, "I'm almost sure that wherever I came from, it wasn't from a big, paved city. I needed the earth."

"The introduction to your story is overly long," I said crossly. "When does the plot begin to develop?"

She was standing by my bed. I was beginning to get used to her no-motion moving. "I had hoped you might help it," she said. "But I guess I have more waiting yet to do." She was at the door, then back at my bedside. "You know!" she said, leaning close to me, her eyes shining, "I've just remembered something new. The most surprising thing to me was sunrise and sunset. I had no memory of the sun in the sky. I thought when it was morning, someone rolled up a big, big green blind from a big, big window. Deega did at her windows. And at night they just pulled the blind down like Deega. I was so fascinated by the sky that I had a stiff neck for a long time. The sun made my eyes water and I wanted to taste the moon. But—" she paused a moment, "I *knew* when I saw the clouds, that they were for walking through and rolling under and for hide-and-seek before the thunder."

She was gone, easing the door shut, before I had a reply for her. Indeed, I had droned myself into an unusually early sleep with *For hide-and-seek before the thunder* before I even had a reply for myself.

I'll admit that in the days that followed, I became more and more interested in Michal's story. Mostly, I think, because I was idle and she was an unusual child, though if you had tried to pin me down, I couldn't have detailed to you the unusualness. Several days later when I was enjoying a brief remission of the pain, I even jotted down, in my own personal shorthand, the highlights of what she had told me. Of course I came to a full stop just beyond the "eat, feet, eat," and the "hide-and-seek before the thunder."

School started for Michal and we didn't see so much of her. Mr. Apfel missed her and reverted more and more often to his childish patterns of behavior. One day he had been shouting ever since he wakened after his after-breakfast nap. He was a fretful, uncomfortable child and nothing would please him. He threw his pillows on the floor and himself with them and had to be lifted, protesting and kicking, back into bed. Aunt Lydie gathered up his matchstick bundle of arms and legs with practiced ease and reinserted them deftly into the bed, snapped up the side bars, and smiled down at his rage-reddened face. "Be a good boy," she said, and left him.

"Damn crib!" he muttered, using bad words as if in defiance of a possible mouth-washing with soap. "Damn crib."

It was then that Michal arrived.

"You've been misbehaving again," she said. He yanked the covers up over his head, uncovering, as usual, his skinny old feet. "How about a remembery, just to smooth things over?"

"No!" The muffled answer came explosively through feathers and linen.

"About Hochberg?" she coaxed.

"Well—" One eye reappeared, then the whole shamefaced countenance. "I'm sorry, Michal." Mr. Apfel was back. "It's just—it's just—"

"I know." Michal touched his hand briefly. "Hochberg is always nice. Remember, you were getting ready to climb it and you found you had forgotten—"

Mr. Apfel, leaning against his pillows, closed his eyes and smiled softly. "I had forgotten—" and silence came into the room.

Michal patted the edge of Mr. Apfel's bed and then was at my bedside. "He'll be happy and quiet for a while now," she said. "It doesn't take much to start him on a remembery, then it only takes a nudge or two to keep him going. He usually falls asleep. I don't think he's ever stayed awake until he remembers getting to the top of Hochberg."

Her voice was small and tentative. "Maybe you'd like to hear some more about me," she said. "I find it a very absorbing question, myself, as though I were talking about someone else—not myself. Do you suppose that by going over and over what I do remember, I might eventually remember some more? I did the clouds!"

"I'm no authority," I replied, easing myself back among my pillows. "But even if you don't, you might be happier with the memories you do have." I customarily use the reflective method when logic makes no impression. Michal was woman enough to be thoroughly illogical. I don't subscribe to the female super-logic theory.

"Well, after the two weeks were up," she went on as though the interruption had been minutes ago, "I didn't want to go back to the city. I was as rigid as a board and refused to get ready. Aunt Lydie tried to dress me. She shook me impatiently as she tried to bend my arm to put it through my sleeve.

" 'Child! Child! You have to get dressed. You have to go back.'

" 'Why?' I let my arm go so limp it wouldn't poke through the sleeve. 'I don't want to. I don't want to.' I didn't yell. I just melted down through Aunt Lydie's hands. She sighed sharply down at me, huddled on the floor. Then she gathered me up in her arms and sat down in the rocking chair. She rocked me and I felt her warmth wrap me around like a soft blanket.

" 'You have to go back to your family,' she said calmly and with an unemphatic finality that I recognized and acknowledged. 'We all have to do things in this world that we don't want to. And we owe it to folks around us not to bother them with our fussing. Maybe next year we can have you back again.'

"Next year? An eighth of my lifetime. I didn't do the math then, but I felt the endlessness of the time to next year.

" 'What if they don't want me back?' I asked, my cheek tight against her shoulder.

" 'Of course they want you back.' Aunt Lydie sat me up and poked my arms into my dress sleeves. 'You'll see. When you get home, you'll be glad.'

" 'Maybe Deega's letting someone else sleep under the table now,' I said. 'Can I come back if she is?'

"Aunt Lydie laughed. 'Just push them over,' she said. 'There's room for two.'

"I knew she didn't believe me. She thought I was joking. Kids don't sleep under tables.

"An hour later I pressed my whole crying face against the train window, my eyes squeezed shut as the train gathered speed. I felt Aunt Lydie's distress follow the train until a curve in the tracks swung us out of sight. I pulled my feet up on the seat and buried my face on my knees, my brown paper bag luggage bumping softly against my shins. I wouldn't talk with the excited kids and I couldn't let them see me cry. After a while I slept.

"I thought it was a bad dream when we were herded out of the train and into the huge echoing train station. I forgot to use the little steps the man put by the door, but drifted down to the cold concrete floor without stepping. One of the big girls from our block—her name was Velia— grabbed me and yanked me down to my feet.

" 'Hurry up!' she cried. 'We're almost home!'

"My toes were curling away from the cold concrete that bit through my sneakers and shriveled my new roots, so I just lifted my feet off the floor and let Velia tow me along in the air until she swatted me and said, 'You're too heavy to drag—walk!'

"They herded us around some more and separated us and put us together again. We rode some more and the noise around us was so big that I could hardly see anything. And then we were being checked off one by one in front of the building and Velia's mother was crying all down her rippling chins and hugging Velia almost out of sight in her doughy arms. I watched them with my eyes wide. I wondered who decided who got mothers and who didn't, and, absorbed in the question, found my way back to my own building. I peered up past the grimy ugly old walls. No sky up there. No more sun or moon. Only the old green blind rolling up and pulling down. I went in and looked up in the bad-smelling darkness. I held my breath. How quickly my nose had forgotten. As I looked up into the darkness, a sudden empty feeling caught my breath. Something was wrong—was gone. Deega? No Deega? No Deega?

"Suddenly I was stumbling down to the floor on the fifth-floor landing with no memory whatsoever of any steps leading up. All I had was a blurred impression of myself shooting up past the landings, curving narrowly to thread from one flight to another until my staggering arrival.

"I hammered on the door. 'Deega!' I yelled. 'Deega! Deega!'

"The door was flung open with a familiar yelp of hinges.

" 'Stop yer yellin, I ain't deef.' A huge, strange woman filled the door, except for the spot over her right hip where a small dirty boy face was peering out, making faces at me.

" 'Where's Deega?' I asked, my mouth cottony with foreknowledge.

" 'Dunno,' said the woman. 'Don' know nobody round here. On-y been here a week. Git back in there, Chuck,' and she yanked the boy in and shut the door.

"It's hard to remember what happened next. I remember being at Miz Teeman's place. I heard Velia's happy chatter next door as Miz Teeman edged her door shut, glaring at me resentfully. 'Guv'er my own little girl's two dresses and my own little girl's vacation and what she want? More! More! Why ain't *she* dead? Who wants *her?*'

"Who wants her? Who wants her? Who wants her?

"The frightening, unanswered words pushed me back again to my building, shot me up the stairwell past the fifth landing and out onto the roof. I ran to the edge of the roof and clutched the parapet with cold shaking hands, straining towards my last memory of warmth. I closed my eyes against the smudged, lightless sky and leaned outwards into emptiness.

" 'Aunt Lydie! Aunt Lydie! Where are you?' I couldn't even cry because of the terror that was over-flooding me. I quested around me in a tight circle, like a blind dog, inside my head. Then, all at once, I found the right direction and scrambled up over and stepped out into the nothingness beyond the edge of the roof. Someone behind me screamed, then the wind was roaring past my ears. My hair was snapping in an icy slipstream and my eyes were held shut by the pressure of speed. I was cold. I was shaken. I was going to Aunt Lydie!"

"Michal!" It was Mrs. Norwich's voice cutting through the enchantment of Michal's story. I drew a deep breath and stepped mentally down out of my voluntary suspension of disbelief, a little ashamed to have been so caught up into this wand-less fairytale.

"Yes, Aunt Lydie." Michal's voice had no hint of impatience in it. She was down from her chair and to the door with her smooth movement. "I'm in here."

"I couldn't have guessed." Aunt Lydie's voice was amused under its brusqueness. "Would you go out and tell Arn I'll need the car this afternoon to go to East Medbury? Tell him to clean out that back seat. Fishing equipment I have no use for, and it's been in there for three weeks."

"Okay."

Michal was gone—she was gone down the stairs and out of the house, *but her voice was telling me the rest of the story!* Her words were speaking inside my head and I had to fight to keep myself from trying to wrench nonexistent earphones off my astonished ears, as I heard,

"Time started again when I stumbled across Aunt Lydie's porch and fell against the door with a clatter that brought her and Unc Arn out to see what was the matter.

" 'They weren't there!' I wailed into Aunt Lydie's arms. 'Deega's gone! Chuck's sleeping under the table! I'm not Miz Teeman's little girl! I'm Michal—without an *e!* Let me stay! Let me stay!'

"And they did! They took me in! They didn't have to. There was no reason why they should. They only did because they—they love. They love clear down to the middle of their hearts. And it's the kind of love that doesn't *have* to do anything. It does it because that's what love does."

That evening Michal put her head in at the door. "I'm sorry," she said, her eyes glowing. "I didn't mean to without asking you, but I've got so used to it with the patients that I forgot you were different. *You* can tell whether I'm vocalizing or not. Most of them can't."

"Come in," I said sternly.

She slipped in, very slender, very quiet, her hands tightly clasped behind her, her eyes very shining. "I admit nothing," I said. "I ignore the whole incident. But finish the episode. I do not enjoy loose ends."

"Yes, Mr. Evans." She was perched on the chair again. "I heard Unc and Aunt talking once about how I came back. It sounded as if they were going over an old, smooth-worn argument.

" 'Then how *did* she get back?' asked Unc Arn.

" 'Came back,' said Aunt Lydie shortly.

" 'She didn't have any money,' he persisted. 'Nobody I talked to in town gave her any. And anyway, how could a kid her age figure out how to get all the way back here, money or no money? That far? So fast?'

" 'Look here, Arn,' said Aunt Lydie crisply. 'She came back. We tried to find her Deega and couldn't. Everyone said Miz Teeman's little girl was dead. We said we'd keep her. She'll be a help when she gets older. You can rack your brains trying to figure out how-come, but I don't ever expect to find out and I'm not so sure I *want* to find out. You can ask her if she flew back if you want to. I won't.'

"But he never did, though I could read the question in his face for a long time after that."

Michal leaned forward from the chair. "You see? They have question marks and I have question marks and you have question marks, and, so far, no one has the answers. I've been hoping that you might—"

"I've got questions, too," piped up Mr. Apfel from his bed. "When's supper?"

"Pretty soon," laughed Michal. "I'll go down and see if I can hurry it up a little."

With her gone, I eyed Mr. Apfel, and Mr. Apfel eyed me.

"Half the time," he said matter-of-factly, "no one will listen to a word I say. That is because this body of mine is running down and half the time it talks nonsense. But you're still young enough to have your mind more or less in one piece. If *I* were even sixty again, I'd do something for Michal. I think that Deega person found her someplace. If she was lost, she must have been lost from someone or somewhere. And if anyone ever had Michal and lost her, they're still looking for her."

"I'm nowhere near sixty yet," I said crossly. "And, one mind or a dozen, I can't take her story at face value. You don't know how many people liven up their drab existences with fanciful tales like this."

Mr. Apfel blinked at me a couple of times. "What color is Michal's hair?" he asked and went to sleep, bolt upright against his pillows.

I turned his question over in my mind. Light running along—light splintering—light— What color *was* Michal's hair?

After supper was over and the calmness of night was pouring in through the windows, darkening the rooms, Michal came back, wistfully.

"Do you believe me a little?" she asked.

"Believe you!" I exploded. "That you can mind-read? That you can teleport? That you can home in on a geographical point like a pigeon? That you can gather up light as if it were daisies? That you can stop breathing, except that it's cooler not to! Oh, I'll enjoy your story and listen to each new development you dream up, but don't ask me to believe!"

"Your mind," she said scathingly, quite un-Michalish, "is about as flexible and receptive as your two hands right now!" I resisted the impulse to try to flex my swollen joints. "Supposing I told you I didn't believe you hurt anywhere! I can't see your pain!"

I was jolted. I found myself snapping back at her as if I were on her age level. "Anyone knows arthritis—"

"Of course," she cried. "Lots of people have it. It's—it's customary!" she flung my word back at me. She leaned towards me, her eyes blazing. "What if *I'm* customary somewhere?" We glared at each other a moment, then her face cleared and blanked of all emotion. She stepped back from the bed and walked slowly up to the ceiling, then, leaning forward, she hovered over me like a blue-jeaned angel, her hair—Michal-colored—spreading out fan-wise behind each shoulder, spilling light off its edges.

"I'm sorry," she said down into my stupefaction, "I shouldn't have got mad. It's only that I am disappointed—"

"Hey!" Child Apfel was sitting up in bed, wide-eyed. "Can I do that, too? It looks fun!"

Michal drifted over to his bed and perched on the edge of it. I heard her hair whispering softly back down behind her shoulders.

"In your hospital gown?" she teased gently. "Besides, where'd you go? A remembery is much more fun and lots less work!"

"Yes! Yes!" It was the eager child. "Give me a remembery!" He burrowed down under his covers, leaned against his pillows, and smiled his soft, wet smile. "This time about when there were bonfires on every hilltop across the Scandinavian peninsula—"

Silence came into the room and I closed my gaping mouth.

Then she was back by my bed—feet safely at floor level. "I've told you true, Mr. Evans," she said softly. "Will you please think about it—my past, I mean."

"But—but—" The pleading eyes were too much to face. I turned stiffly away. "Yes, I'll think." A twinge twisted my hip joint and I snapped, "But I won't believe!"

I thought about her, that's true, but what could she expect from me? Professionally, I arrived at no answers. Could I conjure up a "past" for a twelve-year-old? And even if I could, she would probably be off on another interest tangent before I could formulate a story completely. I milled around in the dead-end of believing and disbelieving, ridiculing and wondering. Unhappily restless, I began to mutter to myself.

This undesirable state of affairs was sidetracked by Mrs. Norwich. She came in one afternoon and announced to me and Mr. Apfel in a half-questioning tone that implied permission to object, that another patient was to arrive the next day and have a bed in the corner of our room.

"Usually we have only two to a room," she said, peering over her glasses at me. Mr. Apfel was busy breaking the teeth out of a new comb. "But this one is different." She waited for comment. I lifted an eyebrow and waited silently for pain to slither down my leg again. "He won't bother you any. He won't do anything. He was injured in a car crash four months ago—a head injury that left him in a coma. Two cars had a head-on collision. There were seven dead altogether and one survivor in each car. And this man. No one knows him. No one ever saw him before. No one knows how he got involved in the accident. There was nothing to identify him by and he never wakens. They've kept him at the hospital trying everything in the book to waken him, but they need his bed now, and time is the only thing they haven't tried."

"After all," said Mr. Apfel, lucidly, brushing the broken teeth of the comb to the floor, "you can't bury a body as long as it keeps breathing, can you?"

They brought the new patient to our room and transferred him to his bed, newly installed in the corner. From my position I could see the cold clarity of his profile, the statue-like stillness of his body under the white sheet and spread. It reminded me of—I suppose it's a crusader—who lies on his tomb in Salisbury Cathedral in England with just that same marble patience. The only difference was the slow rise and fall of the spread over his chest and the accompanying slight flaring of his nostrils. I wondered where he was—I mean where *he* was. His body was there on the crisp-cornered bed, but where was he? I was pursuing this line of thought, trying to pin down what I meant by "he." I knew exactly what I meant, but when I tried to reduce it to a simple declarative sentence, it eluded me. All kinds of modifiers crowded around to be tried and discarded and I spent an absorbing few minutes before Mr. Apfel flipped his eyes open from one of his numerous cat-naps and spoke as though he hadn't been asleep at all.

"Do you suppose he's dead and just forgot to turn his body off?"

"I don't know," I said, caught by the aptness of the suggestion. "I've been wondering about that myself. I wonder where he is?"

"I don't suppose they'll let him through the Gates until his body stops, will they?" he asked, troubled.

"Sorry, I'm no authority," I said.

"I'm worried," he said. "What if he's in there and wants to get out and can't? Like Jake. He wanted to talk and he couldn't. Not until he died.

Maybe this one wants to open his eyes and move and talk." Mr. Apfel's voice was rising in dismay. "What if he doesn't know what happened to him! What if he's scared! Somewhere in the dark! And no one will find him!" And Child Apfel wept great unwiped tears down his sorrowing face.

"There, there," I said clumsily, trying to find words appropriate to the Child Apfel. "He's just sleeping. Don't worry." But he turned his face to his pillow and sobbed.

Michal was in the doorway and then by Mr. Apfel's bed. He turned and, clutching her hands, wailed, "Find him, Michal! Find out if he's there!"

Michal looked back over her shoulder at me. "Is that the man-in-a-coma?"

"Yes," I said. "And Mr. Apfel's all upset because he thinks the man is like Jake—wanting to communicate and not being able to."

Michal loosened her hands from Mr. Apfel's grasp and slowly approached the new bed. She knelt down by it. It was so high that her eyes just overtopped the mattress. She turned the man's head gently so they were face to face.

"Are you there?" she whispered. "Please, are you there?"

There was no response, of course. There was a silence that lengthened and lengthened as Michal knelt there. I was about to summon Mrs. Norwich when finally Michal moved. She got up slowly from her knees and turned the man's head back straight on the pillow.

She walked—most unlike her usual moving—over to my bed.

"I went in," she said, slowly and thoughtfully. "I squirmed and elbowed my mind into his. It's as dark in there as if God had blotted up all the light He ever made. It was like trying to move around in corridors that were flexible and that pushed me from every side. I heard nothing, nothing at all from him, not even so much as the creep-and-eat that's in a caterpillar's mind."

"Couldn't—couldn't you rouse him?" I asked, believing for a split second.

"No." She settled down on the chair, her troubled look still on the man. "I screamed as loud as a mind can scream. I thought light so bright, so dazzling, that I wonder you didn't see the outline of his face bones like holding your hand up to a light globe. Nothing I did even changed his breathing." Her mouth drooped and her slender shoulders slumped.

"Michal!" I said sharply. "Don't sound so—so involved. A child your age shouldn't concern herself with such morbid matters. The man's simply in a coma. He's nothing to you—"

"There's nobody who's nothing to me," said Michal, her eyes turned in my direction but seeing nothing of me. "But there's something else—something special." I was startled to see the tears start to slide down her cheeks. "When I touched him, I felt as though I were folding the hands of my own dead. I've never folded the hands of my own dead and he isn't dead—is he? Is he?"

"Mr. Apfel thinks he is. He thinks he just forget to turn his body off," I offered.

"Michal!" Mrs. Norwich called from the hall. Michal turned her face away from me and when she looked back, the tears were gone, the trouble was gone from her face, and she answered, "Here, Aunt Lydie!" without a quaver in her voice.

Mrs. Norwich stood in the doorway, looking sharply at Michal. "You are *not* to start worrying about this man," she stated flatly. "If you make yourself unhappy over him, I will forbid your coming up here among the patients."

"Yes, Aunt Lydie," said Michal meekly, and was gone without another word.

"What makes you think—" I began.

"I don't have to think," she said shortly. "She was just getting home from school when they brought him. I could *feel* her getting all worked up." Mrs. Norwich reddened and brushed a brisk hand back over her hair. "It's catching," she defended. "Michal's always 'feeling' things about the patients. I'm getting so I 'feel' things about her."

"Is there any reason why this particular one should upset her more than any of the others?" I asked.

"Only that he has a mystery about him," she said. "If he'd open his eyes and say, 'I'm Joe Doakes,' she'd be satisfied. She's the flighty kind that puts herself in others' shoes too much. She's probably worrying about where he is, during this long unconsciousness."

Mr. Apfel and I exchanged glances and then we both said, simultaneously, "Well, where *is* he?"

Mrs. Norwich plumped her two hands on her hips and let out an exasperated breath. "Not you two, too! It's worse than measles!"

I was lying awake that night with my customary insomnia, watching the moonlight squeeze through the maple by the window to make little wavering gold coins on the bedroom walls, when Michal came in, in her voluminous gown and robe. She drifted over to the man's bed and, gathering up a double handful of the light, she tipped it carefully over the man's face. She studied his features closely until the light all drained away and the room was dim in the shivery semi-light again. "What is your name?" she whispered, and again and again, "What is your name, what is your name?"

"Sometimes," she said, her hand gently on my pillow, though I had not seen her move, "sometimes you can reach them by their names, but I don't even have a name to call him by—"

"Must you?" I whispered.

"I must," she said. "May I use you?"

"Use me?" I gaped.

"Yes," she said. "If I can think with me and with you, it'll be stronger and maybe I can reach him. Maybe he's waiting now—waiting just on the edge of the shock that blanked him out—"

"But I—but I—" I stammered, not wanting to compound a childish illusion, and yet—

"I think you're first cousin to the cat anyway," she said with a glint of amusement. "So if not because that's what love does, then do it for the sake of your curiosity."

I must have consented because suddenly Michal and I were pouring a thought out together, *What is your name? What is your name?* until the words lost their identity and meaning, at least for me. Then suddenly, it was as though there were three voices, Michal's, mine, and another one, echoing.

What is your name? we reiterated and heard our thought split and double and come back a repetition, *What is your name?*

Michal! we thought back sharply.

Michal, came the reply. I clenched my fists and then clenched my teeth against the resulting pain. Michal was kneeling by his bedside.

What is your name?

And this time, perceptibly behind our question, came the echo, *What is your name?*

Michal! we returned quickly.

Michael! came the echo, *with an* e!

"Michael?" Michal verbalized silently, with me.

"Michael," came the reply, verbalized this time.

"What is your other name?" we asked quickly. We were answered only by silence, but this time there was a difference in the silence. It was a not-answering, surely, but not the not-there-ness it had been before.

"Your other name?" we insisted.

The thought of laughter came, warm and light, into our minds.

"Must there be two?" came the amused answer. "I've only just now found out that there are words and that either a word is me or I am a word. Don't be greedy!"

And after that, no matter what we thought, there was no reply.

Michal drifted back to my bed. "Thank you," she said. "I knew you could help me if you would."

"Do you customarily hook up sending stations like this?" I asked, feeling a little giddy with the recent developments.

"Never before," she said. "I didn't know I could. *I* couldn't. We did." She began to drift towards the door. "I knew I had to—I just had to. I suppose you think we were communicating in English." And she was gone.

Stung, I glared after her in the dark. "It was English to me!" I shouted in a whisper, and was answered by the thought of her laughter.

With no one in the room to gather up the light, it trembled and wavered through the cooling air and showed me only the white hump of the man's bed—and the glare from Mr. Apfel's blazing eyes.

"First you—then him!" he gritted harshly. "Everybody comes to take Michal away from me. You go away! Jake went away! You go away the same way! Michal is for me. She's to give me rememberies and—and—she hasn't got any time for anybody else. You go away!" His glare was as though he had spit at me, and he shoved himself vigorously down into the bed, hauling up the bedclothes with such vigor that his bony old feet were left out—coldly uncomfortable and hotly defiant.

Michal and I teamed up several nights following our initial venture, but nothing happened, except that we started calling him Mike.

"Mike?" asked Mrs. Norwich when she first heard the name. "Why Mike?"

"Well, we can't go on calling him the-man-in-a-coma," said Michal. "And Mike is easy to remember."

"And very like Michal," said Mrs. Norwich, narrowing a little. "I don't particularly care for your twinning yourself with him."

"We could call him Merihildo Esteven," I offered.

Mrs. Norwich's mouth-corners betrayed what she thought of my levity. "I suppose it is handier to have a name to call him by, and if you've set on Mike already, Mike it will be."

"I call him a—" Vindictive Apfel, who was so often in evidence now, went on extremely explicitly with an amazingly comprehensive vocabulary. Mrs. Norwich shooed Michal out of the door and advanced on him with a bar of soap in one hand. Vindictive Apfel choked over some wild-sounding foreign word and became suddenly Child Apfel and burrowed down under his covers to escape the threatened mouth-washing.

A day or two later, he said suddenly as though continuing a conversation, "I'm mad at Michal."

"Are you really?" I asked idly.

"Yes," he persisted. "She's spending all her time with that—" He looked what he was afraid to say.

"It hasn't done any good," I said. "Since that first night, we haven't heard a word."

"We?" Vindictive Apfel laughed shortly. "What makes you think she'd bother with you, once she got through to him? Ask her about last night. Yap, yap, yap! Kept me awake to all hours!"

"She wasn't even in here last night," I said patiently. "She's coming tonight. We're going to try again."

"Try again!" he sneered. "Since when does Michal have to be here to talk to anyone? Ask her—go on—ask her tonight!"

I felt a sharp pang that I diagnosed, at first, as a shoulder joint. But, after careful consideration, decided might be jealousy. Jealousy! Of a child and a man-in-a-coma! Of Michal and Michael—with an *e!* I didn't want to believe it, but I held my reaction up against Vindictive Apfel's reaction and decided that they were practically the same jealousy. Still, I had only the word of a change-with-the-wind old man. I'd ask her, as soon as she came in again. I felt very little of the patience I had developed of necessity over the last few afflicted years, but the hours finally seeped out to evening.

It seemed to me that I could sense Michal's coming, though this may have been hindsight, but finally she was there, her cheeks theatrically reddened by the brisk outdoor wind before which she had fled home from the store. I barely had time to wonder what I could know about anything brisk and out-of-doors since I was almost hermetically sealed in this room, in this bed, in this body, when Michal exclaimed,

"How odd! That's almost the exact way he went—almost exactly!"

I surveyed her coolly, still conscious of what Apfel had said. "I presume you plan to explain that remark," I said. "It lacks intelligibility in its present form."

She smiled at me, slowly and warmly. I felt heat surge up into my face and tried to turn away from her eyes. "No," she said, her hand going out to me. "Don't mind. I suppose Mr. Apfel Told All. Last night—" she moved closer to me, eagerly. "Last night he came looking for me. Michael, I mean. He wanted to know where he was. That's what I meant by my unintelligible remark. I told him he was in a nursing home, but that didn't satisfy him. Then in a bed. In a room. But he wanted it closer. So I told him he was in a body. That's when the anguish came."

Then I suddenly knew she was no longer speaking. She was thinking to me and I was so busy listening to her that I had no time to protest the impossibility of such a thing. *Words went. Her story was reenacted somewhere in my perceiving.*

"A body?" Mike said slowly. "And just always dark? Just always night? Just always no any other thing!" He was in anguish.

"Mike," Michal spoke to him comfortingly. "You've been hurt. It won't—it wasn't always just dark. Remember, Mike. Do you remember before?"

"Remember before—?"

There was a long blank wait and then she fairly staggered under his outcry. *So did I!*

"I remember to fall!" he cried wildly. "I remember to hurt! I remember to blind!"

"Mike, Mike," she murmured, and comfort seemed to flow warmly. "Mike, listen, don't try to remember that any more. Try to remember who you are and what your name is."

"Mike?" he asked, with an obvious effort. "Is that my name? I thought it was Michael, with an *e*."

"Mike is another way to say it," she said. "Isn't it odd that our names are so nearly alike?"

"That's the only name I know." Mike was surprised.

"Oh." She was taken aback. "You mean you just called yourself Michael because my name is Michal?"

"That's the only name I know," he repeated.

I was looking at Michal again, and she was smiling at me. "You see," she said aloud, "I wasn't trying to leave you out." I felt the warm surge to my face again.

"Mr. Apfel—" I stumbled.

She leaned close to me. "Shhhh!" she said, her eyes dancing. "The only reason he knows anything about it, is that Mike used his mind to come to me. The one in the body is running down and it won't work very long at a time."

"Michal," I said, wanting to give her something as a sort of apology. "If Mike knows no other name than yours, how does he know the masculine spelling customarily is with an *e*?"

For a moment she was as still as if not even breathing was left to her, then hope flared up in her face in a way that I couldn't possibly describe in physical terms.

"Then he could really be a Michael," she said softly. "And remembering, not mimicking. And I *keep* feeling that he belongs to—to—before Deega!"

Mr. Apfel became more and more Child Apfel in the days that followed. He waited eagerly for Michal to come up after school and sometimes cried when she was late. He made her a Kleenex rose and grinned all evening after she thanked him and put it in her hair. It glowed there and pulsated with any number of colors for which I had no name, and gave off a subtle, delicate fragrance.

"That's the way it seems to him," she said to me. "I'm only making it obvious so he can see I enjoy it too."

He presented her another night with his toothless comb. His fluff of white hair looked the same combed and uncombed, so the lack of teeth didn't affect his grooming—nor did the loss of the comb.

"I'm going to make you something pretty," he said to her, hanging onto her hand. "I'll give it to you when I get it all together."

"Why, thank you!" she said. "Shall I guess?"

"Oh, you couldn't guess!" he giggled. "Not in a million million years. It's prettier than—"

"Ah-ah!" she laughed. "Don't tell until it's all ready!"

"I won't! I won't!" He clasped his hands over his laughing mouth. "I can keep a secret!" His voice was muffled and gleeful.

I had turned away uncomfortably from his elephantine playfulness, and opened my eyes only when Michal touched the back of my hand with one of her cool fingers.

"How can you put up with it?" I asked, needlessly whispering since he had gone off into one of his sudden naps. "That senile old man talking and acting like a child—"

"I'm not talking to a senile old man," said Michal. "I'm talking with Mr. Apfel. He can't help it if his mind is wrinkled a little along with his body."

My hand was trying to reach my forehead to massage away some of my mental discomfort, but my shoulder-joint wouldn't let it. Michal's hand suddenly closed upon my hand and her eyes closed tightly. She drew a sharp breath. "He's there," she said. "He put Mr. Apfel to sleep so he could come through him, but you're stronger. When I touched you it made the necessary contact."

Then she was sitting on the chair by Mike's bed. "If Aunt Lydie comes," she said, "we're discussing my geography test." She clasped her hands loosely and I felt the odd motion inside my mind that told me she was setting up our network again and Mike suddenly came in clearly, in mid-sentence.

"...so you must remember before Deega. Any child has memories before six."

"I don't." The thought came stronger through the tandem of our minds. "The very most firstest thing I can remember is the underside of Deega's table. I woke up in the dark and I watched the table grow over me when the light came in the window."

"And yet, this happened before," said Mike. *And the picture shimmered and resolved into clarity.*

The wind was cool, The clouds were puffy and softly blue-white. The little girls, dressed in bright-colored dresses, their arms full of flowers, were tumbling, laughing, through the clouds. Then a small boy popped out of a cloud and let a brilliant winged lizard slither into the middle of the group of girls. They shrieked and scattered, their flowers falling like pastel rain.

"Whose memory is that?" Mike's voice broke the picture.

"Mine!" whispered Michal. "I went back to make sure the lizard's wings weren't so crumpled that it couldn't fly! But Mike, Mike! I haven't a single other memory to go with it. It's all alone—"

"Bless the Presence," came Mike's voice reverently prompting.

"And the Name and the Power," we continued automatically.

"For the gift of Life, for The Home—" the three of us chanted on, I, in my vast astonishment, trying to separate myself from them far enough to examine this unexpected development. I looked quickly at Michal. Tears were slipping down her cheeks. "What is it, Mike? What is it?" she cried. "Whose prayer am I praying?"

"So it is you!" cried Mike. "And to think that I—" Then he broke off to answer her. "That is your own prayer," he said. "The one that all the children—"

Communication shut off, flatly, unechoingly. Michal flung herself down by his bedside. "Mike!" she cried. "Who am I? By the Presence—"

"Nobody brings me presents any more," mourned Child Apfel. "Not even on my birthday." He was propped up on one elbow, peering over at Michal.

She got up heavily and angularly. "I do, Mr. Apfel," she said. "I brought you a present just last week. Remember the peanuts?"

"Peanuts!" he beamed. "I like peanuts. Especially with shells on. Did I ever show you that smart trick? The one where I do something nobody ever did before and can never do again? You see, I break a peanut shell, and of course nobody ever broke that shell before and nobody can ever do it again—isn't that smart!"

"I think you're very clever, Mr. Apfel," said Michal, smiling at him. "Did you hear Mike talking a while ago?"

"Sure, I did. You don't think I sleep all the time, do you?" He was indignant.

"Of course you don't," soothed Michal. "You hear a lot I don't even hear. For instance, I didn't hear the first part of what Mike said. Did you?"

"I don't like Mike," he sulked.

"I never gave Mike any peanuts," she reminded.

"That's right!" His face brightened. "Well, he only said he thought you might be the one they had been looking for and if you were, you must be able to remember before Deega—"

Michal's face flushed and then paled until the whiteness glowed. "Who were they looking for?" she whispered. "*Who* is looking?"

"Oh, for whoever got lost when the ship went off course," he said airily. "Such a silly-looking ship! Anybody knows ships go on the water. They don't crash into the water from the sky. Ooo! Splash! Way up! Like a big fountain! So big a splash that it caught two of the bees that flew out just before the crash. But there was one bee that got away, rolling over and over in the sky before it straightened up and flew into the clouds!" He waved his arms excitedly, then folded against his pillows in sudden exhaustion. "Anyway, these People thought there was nobody left alive at all until about five years ago. Some one of them was in Town and one night they heard a Cry, but they couldn't ever find where it came from. So they've been looking whenever anyone comes into Town. Mike was flying along the road when the cars hit. I'm having a hard time getting what I need for your present," he said drowsily. "It'll be awful pretty. The Presence, the Name, the Power—" and he had gone to sleep again.

"Oh, Mike! Oh, Mike!" Michal was kneeling by his bed, her trembling hands closing over the hem of his spread, her eyes shining.

"Stop bothering Mike." Aunt Lydie's voice from the doorway was harsh, but not enough to conceal her concern. "Michal, I told you that if you got too involved—"

"I'm not," said Michal, turning a serene face to her. "I was just seeing if calling his name would rouse him."

"It would be a wonder if it did," snapped Aunt Lydie, "seeing as how you named him out-of-hand. His name might well be Merihildo Esteven! Calling him Mike wouldn't mean anything to him. Besides, Mr. Osanti won't eat his supper. Will you go see what you can do?"

Michal's thoughts floated back to me as she disappeared out the door. "Oh, Mr. Evans! What if Mike's body dies before he gets up enough strength to finish telling me who I am! What if I stay lost this close to being found?"

I was unusually restless that night, and there's nothing quite so laborious as being restless and unable to toss and turn. Mike was his usual crusader-on-a-tombstone, and Mr. Apfel had burrowed himself down under his covers. The silence was broken at intervals only by his muttering and the sudden upheaval of the spread at one corner or the other.

I watched the moonlight crawl slowly up the wall. I so concentrated on its movement that I almost groaned aloud when it did not reveal the next half-pattern in the wallpaper, but was prevented by the shadow of the geraniums on the window sill. "This sort of thinking is the utter end of nothing!" I thought. So, to swing the pendulum its limit, I tried to send my thoughts out to Mike. If I could find out something for Michal— I concentrated—which seemed to require holding my breath—and concentrated, but felt no vestige of stir in my mind that could mean contact.

Mr. Apfel had subsided into stillness. I had inched my way up so I was propped a little against my pillows. Sleep slid across my eyes and cracked into a dozen uncomfortable segments that I felt, with a terrible sense of urgency, I had to put back together again with masking tape and bent pins with little minnows on them. One quivering, shaken piece was of Mr. Apfel creeping on hands and knees, bare-shanked, to the door of our room and disappearing into the hall. The shock of this little byplay was such that I snapped awake and glanced over to where the moonlight trembled on the hump of Mr. Apfel, burrowed out of sight down under his covers. The light was moving on Mike's face, too, with one fragile coin of it fluttering on his mouth so that it seemed as if his lips were moving.

I grinned feebly and closed my eyes. Hallucinations, asleep and awake! Well, at least it wasn't dull. The shattered pieces of sleep scraped back over me.

A crunching sound wakened me again later. Mr. Apfel was still hunched in bed, but now he was methodically crumpling page after page of a writing tablet and tucking each page down into his bed. Everything normal, go to sleep, I told myself. I heard Mr. Apfel's childish giggle, then a series of scratching sounds, spaced by mutters. I turned slowly, wearily, away from the humped-up white shadow of Mr. Apfel. Maybe sleep would come anyway. Surely by now I was used to the sounds of Apfel.

I drowsed—I don't know how long. Then there was a sudden cry of triumph that twisted me incautiously around. My anguish was answered by a protesting cry from Mr. Apfel as his bed erupted in a flare of flames. "No!" he screamed. "Not yet! Not all at once! It's for Michal!" He beat feebly at the flames that were spreading erratically across the bed, smoke billowing as the spread caught and flared. Mr. Apfel coughed and choked and his bewildered child-wail, "Michal! Michal!" rose and lifted into a scream that cut off with a gasp.

I shouted, "Mrs. Norwich! Michal! Hey!" Time got lost somewhere in the confusion. I remember smoke rolling across Mike's bed and his still, unseeing face. I heard cries from the patients across the hall and a pounding of feet on the stairs. I remember how the smoke swirled when the door was flung open and how the curtains became a bright reversed Niagara of flame up the wall. I was caught up—it felt actually physically so—

Suddenly I knew Michal was there—a tortured Michal who spun away from the flames of Mr. Apfel's bed, and then was by my bed, her quick hands tucking the covers about me as she sobbed, "Mike! Mike!"

Then I felt myself lifted into the air and a corner of the shattered window bruised my shoulder, a shard of broken glass ripped one side of the bedspread from my shoulder level to my ankle level. Around me was the night. Above me, the sky, still innocent of smoke, and below me—below me, nothing! The agonizing wrench of my whole body against the old, old fear of falling shot me right out of the conscious world.

Michal was kneeling by me where I lay on the grass in the shadows of the little maple grove. Her hand, cool but insistent on my cheek, had wakened me.

"Mr. Evans! Help me! Help me!"

"Mike!" I muttered dizzily.

"Help me find him," she said tensely. "The fire—maybe it hasn't got to his bed yet. We've got to find him or I'll never find—"

I felt the movement that signaled our mental hookup, and together we cried, "Mike! Mike! Mike!"

The leaping flames from the tinder-dry house were flicking the shadows of the tree trunks back and forth across us. Michal crouched close to me. Her gown was grimed and singed, her hair was swinging brightly, darkly free about her bent shoulders. I could smell the fire in her hair and I saw tight charred beads on her brows and lashes.

"Mr. Evans!" she whispered hoarsely. "Pray! Pray!" And our pulsating repetition of *Mike, Mike, Mike* was both a prayer and a seeking.

After an eternity I heard it—Mike's voice—faintly far away.

"Michal! Michal!"

"He's there!" I cried. "Talk to him, Michal!"

"I can't hear him!" Michal's eyes were anguished. "Are you sure—"

"Listen!" I cried. "He's calling you!"

"I'll have to read it from you," she said despairingly. "Listen, oh, listen!"

I heard the roar of flames in the silence as I waited. Then his voice came again, impossibly faint and remote. And he was talking to *me* for the first time.

"I'll have to talk fast," he said. "I've been Called. You'll have to tell Michal good-by for me."

"Mr. Apfel set the fire. It was a gift for Michal. He wanted to give her a midsummer bonfire. He was only going to try one match to see if it would look as pretty as he thought it would. He sneaked across the hall and stole a book of matches from Mr. Osanti. No one else has died of the fire. The others are safe. Aunt Lydie will be over here in a couple of minutes. I made her know you and Michal were all right.

"They're coming for her—people of her own kind—of my kind. They should be here by now. I was gone after them—that's why I wasn't here—"

The voice faded and I struggled upright, straining to find it again. It came loud and clear and triumphant, "By the Presence, the Name, and the Power—"

Michal's hands tightened on my arm and relaxed as she slumped beside me.

"Why didn't you bring Mike out first?" I fretted, aching for this grieving child.

"There was time for only one," she said simply. "Mr. Apfel was already gone. Mike would never awaken to this life again. You—" Her deep, dark eyes were intent on me. "You are alive and conscious—and your days haven't been totaled yet. No, if I'm to be found, I will be found—someday, maybe in time. Mike—" Her composure broke and she sobbed against my shoulder that forgot to ache under the shaken pressure of her sorrow. "Mike said they'd come. He *said!*"

My arm circled her slender shoulders and my eyes blurred. I blinked—and blinked again, past her shoulder. I caught my breath and held it.

Down from the sky, parting the luridly lit leaves of the trees, they came, two people, dropping down, hand in hand, as casually as if they were on a sidewalk. The man held back a branch until the woman ducked under, and then they were both standing, smiling in the flickering shadows just beyond my feet.

"Michal!" I gasped. "They're here—already! Look!"

Michal spun in my arms, the firelight glinting on the swinging fan of her hair, and knelt, looking up blindly.

"Michal—" The woman's voice was gentle and warm. "Michal, Mike told us he'd found you—"

I felt an incredulous, wildly hopeful exclamation flick past my mind and knew communication had been established. I closed my eyes to shut myself in with my sense of inevitable loss. I heard Michal cry out softly.

"Karen! Jemmy! I know you! I knew you before! Before Deega—"

There was a crash and a roar as a wall of the house collapsed. The clustered three moved deeper into the shadows, and I turned to watch the new upsurge of fire.

"Michal! Mr. Evans!" It was Aunt Lydie, hurrying, an angular, black cartoon of herself, away from the glare. "Are you all right? Are you all right?"

Michal was back beside me, her hand warmly insistent on my arm. "Here, Aunt Lydie!" Her voice was joyously shaken. "We're all right! We're both all right!"

I blinked up at the arch of leaves above me. On one side of me, Aunt Lydie was gathering Michal into an unaccustomed warm embrace. On the other side of me, the two strangers—Jemmy and Karen—were waiting patiently in the shadows. I felt the stiff bristle of grass under my cheek and grimaced.

This was *not* a situation in which I customarily found myself!

The Indelible Kind

I've always been a down-to-earth sort of person. On re-reading that sentence, my mouth corners lift. It reads differently now. Anyway, matter-of-fact and just a trifle sceptical—that's a further description of me. I've enjoyed—perhaps a little wistfully—other people's ghosts, and breathtaking coincidences, and flying saucer sightings, and table tiltings and prophetic dreams, but I've never had any of my own. I suppose it takes a very determined, or very childlike—not childish—person to keep illusion and wonder alive in a lifetime of teaching. "Lifetime" sounds awfully elderly-making, doesn't it? But more and more I feel that I fit the role of observer more than that of participant. Perhaps that explains a little of my unexcitement when I did participate. It was mostly in the role of spectator. But what a participation! What a spectacular!

But, back to the schoolroom. Faces and names have a habit of repeating and repeating in your classes over the years. Once in a while, though, along comes one of the indelible kind—and they mark you, happily or unhappily beyond erasing. But, true to my nature, I didn't even have a twinge or premonition.

The new boy came alone. He was small, slight, and had a smooth cap of dark hair. He had the assurance of a child who had registered many times by himself, not particularly comfortable or uncomfortable at being in a new school. He had brought a say-nothing report card, which, I noted in passing, gave him a low grade in Group Activity Participation and a high one in Adjustment to Redirective Counseling—by which I gathered that he was a loner but minded when spoken to, which didn't help much in placing him academically.

"What book were you reading?" I asked, fishing on the shelf behind me for various readers in case he didn't know a specific name. Sometimes we get those whose faces overspread with astonishment and they say, "Reading?"

"In which of those series?" he asked. "Look-and-say, ITA, or phonics?" He frowned a little. "We've moved so much and it seems as though every place we go is different. It does confuse me sometimes." He caught my surprised eye and flushed. "I'm really not very good by any method, even if I do know their names," he admitted. "I'm functioning only on about a second-grade level."

"Your vocabulary certainly isn't second grade," I said, pausing over the enrollment form.

"No, but my reading is," he admitted. "I'm afraid—"

"According to your age, you should be third grade." I traced over his birthdate. This carbon wasn't the best in the world.

"Yes, and I suppose that counting everything, I'd average out about third grade, but my reading is poor."

"Why?" Maybe knowing as much as he did about his academic standing, he'd know the answer to this question.

"I have a block," he said. "I'm afraid—"

"Do you know what your block is?" I pursued, automatically probing for the point where communication would end.

"I—" his eyes dropped. "I'm not very good in reading," he said. I felt him folding himself away from me. End of communication.

"Well, here at Rinconcillo, you'll be on a number of levels. We have only one room and fifteen students, so we all begin our subjects at the level where we function best—" I looked at him sharply. "And work like mad!"

"Yes, ma'am." We exchanged one understanding glance; then his eyes became eight-year-old eyes and mine, I knew, teacher eyes. I dismissed him to the playground and turned to the paper work.

Kroginold, Vincent Lorma, I penciled into my notebook. A lumpy sort of name, I thought, to match a lumpy sort of student—scholastically speaking.

Let me explain Rinconcillo. Here in the mountainous West, small towns, exploding into large cities, gulp down all sorts of odd terrain in expanding their city limits. Here at Winter Wells, city growth has followed the three intersecting highways for miles out, forming a spidery, six-legged sort of city. The city limits have followed the growth in swatches about four blocks wide, which leaves long ridges, and truly ridges—mountainous ones—of non-city projecting into the city. Consequently, here is Rinconcillo, a one-roomed school with only 15 students, and only about half a mile from a school system with eight schools and 4800 students. The only reason this school exists is the cluster of family units around the MEL (Mathematics Experimental Laboratory) facilities, and a half dozen fiercely independent ranchers who stubbornly refuse to be urbanized and cut up into real estate developments or be city-limited and absorbed into the Winter Wells school system.

As for me—this was my fourth year at Rinconcillo, and I don't know whether it's being fiercely independent or just stubborn, but I come back each year to my "little inside corner" tucked quite literally under the curve of a towering sandstone cliff at the end of a box canyon. The violently pursuing and pursued traffic, on the two highways sandwiching us, never even suspects we exist. When I look out into the silence of an early school morning, I still can't believe that civilization could be anywhere within a hundred miles. Long shadows under the twisted, ragged oak trees mark the orangy gold of the sand in the wash that flows—dryly mostly, wetly tumultuous seldomly—down the middle of our canyon. Manzanitas tangle the hillside until the walls become too steep and sterile to support them. And yet, a twenty-minute drive—ten minutes out of here and ten minutes into there—parks you right in front of the MONSTER MERCANTILE, EVERYTHING CHEAPER. I seldom drive that way.

Back to Kroginold, Vincent Lorma—I was used to unusual children at my school. The lab attracted brilliant and erratic personnel. The majority of the men there were good, solid citizens and no more eccentric than a like number of any professionals, but we do get our share of kooks, and their sometimes twisted children. Besides the size and situation being an ideal set-up for ungraded teaching, the uneven development for some of the children made it almost mandatory. As, for instance, Vincent, almost nine, reading, so he said, on second-grade level, averaging out to third grade, which implied above-age excellence in something. Where to put him? Why, second grade (or maybe first) and fourth (or maybe fifth) and third—of course! Perhaps a conference with his mother would throw some light on his "block." Well, difficult. According to the enrollment blank, both parents worked at MEL.

By any method we tried, Vincent *was* second grade—or less—in reading.

"I'm sorry." He stacked his hands on the middle page of *Through Happy Hours,* through which he had stumbled most woefully. "And reading is so basic, isn't it?"

"It is," I said, fingering his math paper—above age-level. And the vocabulary check test—"If it's just words, I'll define them," he had said. And he had. Third year of high school worth. "I suppose your math ability comes from your parents," I suggested.

"Oh, no!" he said, "I have nothing like their gift for math. It's—it's—I like it. You can always get out. You're never caught—"

"Caught?" I frowned.

"Yes—look!" Eagerly he seized a pencil. "See! One plus one equals two. Of course it does, but it doesn't stop there. If you want to, you can back right out. Two equals one plus one. And there you are—out! The doors swing both ways!"

"Well, yes," I said, teased by an almost grasping of what he meant. "But math traps me. One plus one equals two whether I want it to or not. Sometimes I want it to be one and a half or two and three-fourths and it won't—ever!"

"No, it won't." His face was troubled. "Does it bother you all the time?"

"Heavens, no, child!" I laughed. "It hasn't warped my life!"

"No," he said, his eyes widely on mine. "But that's why—" His voice died as he looked longingly out the window at the recess-roaring playground, and I released him to go stand against the wall of the school, wistfully watching our eight other boys manage to be sixteen or even twenty-four in their wild gyrations.

So that's why? I doodled absently on the workbook cover. I didn't like a big school system because its one-plus-one was my one and one-half—or two and three-fourths? Could be—could be. Honestly! What kids don't come up with! I turned to the work sheet I was preparing for consonant blends for my this-year's beginners—all both of them—and one for Vincent.

My records on Vincent over the next month or so were an odd patchwork. I found that he could read some of the articles in the encyclopedia, but couldn't read *Billy Goats Gruff*. That he could read *What Is So Rare as a Day in June*, but couldn't read *Peter, Peter, Pumpkin Eater*. It was beginning to look as though he could read what he wanted to and that was all. I don't mean a capricious wanting-to, but that he shied away from certain readings and actually *couldn't* read them. As yet I could find no pattern to his un-readings; so I let him choose the things he wanted and he read—oh, how he read! He gulped down the material so avidly that it worried me. But he did his gulping silently. Orally, he wore us both out with his stumbling struggles.

He seemed to like school, but seldom mingled. He was shyly pleasant when the other children invited him to join them, and played quite competently—which isn't the kind of play you expect from an eight-year-old.

And there matters stood until the day that Kipper—our eighth grade—dragged Vincent in, bloody and battered.

"This guy's nearly killed Gene," Kipper said. "Ruth's out there trying to bring him to. First aid says don't move him until we know."

"Wait here," I snapped at Vincent as I headed for the door. "Get tissues for your face!" And I rushed out after Kipper.

We found Gene crumpled in the middle of a horrified group gathered at the base of the canyon wall. Ruth was crying as she mopped his muddy forehead with a soggy tissue. I checked him over quickly. No obvious bleeding. I breathed a little easier as he moaned, moved, and opened his eyes. He struggled to a sitting position and tenderly explored the side of his head.

"Ow! That dang rock!" He blinked tears as I parted his hair to see if he had any damage besides the egg-sized lump. He hadn't. "He hit me with that big rock!"

"My!" I giggled, foolish with relief. "He must have addled your brains at the same time. Look at the size of that rock!" The group separated to let Gene look, and Pete scrambled down from where he had perched on the rock for a better look at the excitement.

"Well." Gene rubbed his head tenderly. "Anyway, he did!"

"Come on inside," I said, helping him up. "Do you want Kipper to carry you?"

"Heck no!" Gene pulled away from my hands. "I ain't hurt. G'wan— noseys!" He turned his back on the staring children.

"You children stay out here." I herded Gene ahead of me. "We have things to settle inside."

Vincent was waiting quietly in his seat. He had mopped himself fairly clean, though he still dabbled with a tissue at a cut over his left eye. Two long scratches oozed redly down his cheek. I spent the next few minutes rendering first aid. Vincent was certainly the more damaged of the two, and I could feel the drumming leap of his still-racing heart against me as I turned his docile body around, tucking in his shirt during the final tidying up.

"Now." I sat, sternly teacher, at my desk and surveyed the two before me. "Gene, you first."

"Well." He ruffed his hair up and paused to finger, half proudly, the knot under his hair. "He said let my ground squirrel go and I said no. What the heck! It was mine. And he said let it go and I said no and he took the cage and busted it and—" Indignation in his eyes faded into defensiveness. "—and I busted him one and—and— Well, then he hit me with that rock! Gosh! I was knocked out, wasn't I?"

"You were," I said, grimly. "Vincent?"

"He's right." His voice was husky, his eyes on the tape on the back of one hand. Then he looked up with a tentative lift of his mouth corners. "Except that I hit the rock with him."

"Hit the rock with him?" I asked. "You mean like judo or something? You pushed him against the rock hard enough to knock him out?"

"If you like," he shrugged.

"It's not what I like," I said. "It's—what happened?"

"I hit the rock with him," Vincent repeated.

"And why?" I asked, ignoring his foolish insistence.

"We were having a fight. He told you."

"You busted my cage!" Gene flushed indignantly.

"Gene," I reminded. "You had your turn. Vincent?"

"I had to let it go," he said, his eyes hopefully on mine. "He wouldn't, and it—it wanted to get out—the ground squirrel." His eyes lost their hopefulness before mine.

"It wasn't yours," I reminded.

"It wasn't *his* either!" His eyes blazed. "It belonged to itself! He had no right—!"

"I caught it!" Gene blazed back.

"Gene! Be still or I'll send you outside!"

Gene subsided, muttering.

"You didn't object to Ruth's hamster being in a cage." "Cage" and "math" seemed trying to equate in my mind.

"That's because it was a cage beast!" he said, fingering the taped hand again. "It didn't know any better. It didn't care." His voice tightened. "The ground squirrel did. It would have killed itself to get out. I—I just *had* to—"

To my astonishment, I saw tears slide down his cheek as he turned his face away from me. Wordlessly I handed him a tissue from the box on my desk. He wiped his face, his fingers trembling.

"Gene?" I turned to him. "Anything more?"

"Well, gollee! It was mine! And I liked it! It—it was *mine!*"

"I'll trade you," said Vincent. "I'll trade you a white rat in a real neat aluminum cage. A pregnant one, if you like. It'll have four or five babies in about a week."

"Gollee! Honest?" Gene's eyes were shining.

"Vincent?" I questioned him.

"We have some at home," he said. "Mr. Wellerk at MEL gave me some when we came. They were surplus. Mother says I may trade if his mother says okay."

"She won't care!" cried Gene. "Us kids have part of the barn for our pets, and if we take care of them, she doesn't care what we have. She don't even ever come out there! Dad checks once in a while to be sure we're doing a decent job. They won't care."

"Well, you have your mother write a note saying you may have the rat, and Vincent, if you're sure you want to trade, bring the rat tomorrow and we'll consider the affair ended." I reached for my hand bell. "Well, scoot, you two. Drinks and rest room, if necessary. It's past bell time now."

Gene scooted and I could hear him yelling, "Hey! I getta white rat—"

Vincent was at the door when I stopped him with a question. "Vincent, did your mother know before you came to school that you were going to let the ground squirrel go?"

"No, ma'am. I didn't even know Gene had it."

"Then she *didn't* suggest you trade with Gene."

"Yes, ma'am, she did," he said reluctantly.

"When?" I asked, wondering if he was going to turn out to be a twisted child after all.

"When you were out getting Gene. I called her and told her." He smiled his tentative lip-smile. "She gave me fits for fighting and suggested Gene might like the rat. I like it, too, but I have to make up for the ground squirrel." He hesitated. I said nothing. He left.

"Well!" I exploded my held breath out. "Ananias K. Munchausen! Called his mother, did he? And no phone closer than MONSTER MERCANTILE! But still—" I was puzzled. "It didn't *feel* like a lie!"

Next afternoon after dismissal time I sighed silently. I was staring moodily out the window where the lonely creaking of one swing signified that Vincent, as well as I, was waiting for his mother to appear. Well, inevitable, I guess. Send a taped-up child home, you're almost sure to get an irate parent back. And Vincent had been taped up! Still was, for that matter.

I hadn't heard the car. The creaking of the swing stopped abruptly, and I heard Vincent's happy calling voice. I watched the two of them come up onto the porch, Vincent happily clinging.

"My mother, Teacher," he said. "Mrs. Kroginold."

"Good afternoon, Miss Murcer." Mrs. Kroginold was small, dark haired, and bright eyed. "You wait outside, erring man-child!" She dismissed him with a spat on his bottom. "This is adult talk." He left, his small smile slanting back over his shoulder a little anxiously.

Mrs. Kroginold settled comfortably in the visitor's chair I had already pulled up beside my desk.

"Prepared, I see," she sighed. "I suppose I should have come sooner and explained Vincent."

"He is a little unusual," I offered cautiously. "But he didn't impress me as the fighting kind."

"He isn't," said Mrs. Kroginold. "No, he's—um—unusual in plenty of other ways, but he comes by it naturally. It runs in the family. We've moved around so much since Vincent's been in school that this is the first time I've really felt I should explain him. Of course, this is also the first time he ever knocked anyone out. His father could hardly believe him.

Well, anyway, he's so happy here and making such progress in school that I don't want anything to tarnish it for him, so—" she sighed and smiled. "He says you asked him about his trading the rat—"

"The pregnant rat," I nodded.

"He *did* ask me," she said. "Our family uses a sort of telepathy in emergencies."

"A *sort* of telepathy—!" My jaw sagged, then tightened. Well, I could play the game, too. "How interesting!"

Her eyes gleamed. "Interesting aberration, isn't it?" I flushed and she added hastily, "I'm sorry. I didn't mean to—to put interpretations into your mouth. But Vincent did hear—well, maybe 'feel' is a better word—the ground squirrel crying out against being caged. It caught him right where he lives. I think the block he has in reading is against anything that implies unwilling compulsion—you know, being held against your will—or prevented—"

Put her in a pumpkin shell, my memory chanted. *The three Billy Goats Gruff were afraid to cross the bridge because—*

"The other schools," she went on, "have restricted him to the reading materials provided for his grade level, and you'd be surprised how many of the stories—

"And he *did* hit the rock with Gene." She smiled ruefully. "Lifted him bodily and threw him. A rather liberal interpretation of our family rules. He's been forbidden to lift any large objects in anger. He considered Gene the lesser of the two objects.

"You see, Miss Murcer, we do have family characteristics that aren't exactly—mmm—usual, but Vincent is still just a school child, and we're just parents, and he likes you much and we do, too. Accept us?"

"I—" I said, trying to blink away my confusion. "I—I—"

"Ay! Ay!" Mrs. Kroginold sighed and, smiling, stood up. "Thank you for not being loudly insulted by what I've told you. Once a neighbor of ours that I talked a little too freely to, threatened to sue—so I appreciate. You are so good for Vincent. Thanks."

She was gone before I could get my wits collected. It had been a little like being caught in a dustless dust-devil. I hadn't heard the car leave, but when I looked out, there was one swing still stirring lazily between the motionless ones, and no one at all in sight on the school grounds.

I closed up the schoolroom and went into the tiny two-roomed teacherage extension on the back of the school to get my coat and purse. I had lived in those two tiny rooms for the first two years of my stay at Rinconcillo before I began to feel the need of more space and more freedom from school. Occasionally, even now, when I felt too tired to plunge out into the roar of Winter Wells, I would spend a night on my old narrow bed in the quiet of the canyon.

I wondered again about not hearing the car when I dipped down into the last sand wash before the highway. I steered carefully back across the packed narrowness of my morning tracks. Mine were the only ones, coming or going. I laid the odd discovery aside because I was immediately gulped up by the highway traffic. After I had been honked at and muttered at by two Coast drivers and had muttered at (I don't like to honk) and swerved around two Midwest tourist types roaring along at twenty-five miles an hour in the center lane admiring the scenery, I suddenly laughed. After all, there was nothing mysterious about my lonely tire tracks. I was just slightly disoriented. MEL was less than a mile away from the school, up over the ridge, though it was a good half hour by road. Mrs. Kroginold had hiked over for the conference and the two of them had hiked back together. My imagination boggled a little at the memory of Mrs. Kroginold's strap'n'heel sandals and the hillsides, but then, not everyone insists on flats to walk in.

Well, the white rat achieved six offspring, which cemented the friendship between Gene and Vincent forever, and school rocked along more or less serenely.

Then suddenly, as though at a signal, the pace of space exploration was stepped up in every country that had ever tried launching anything; so the school started a space unit. We went through our regular systematic lessons at a dizzying pace, and each child, after he had finished his assignment, plunged into his own chosen activity—all unrealizing of the fact that he was immediately putting into practice what he had been studying so reluctantly.

My primary group was busy working out a moonscape in the sand table. It was to be complete with clay moon-people—"They don't *have* to have any noses!" That was Ginny, tender to critical comment. "They're different! They don't breathe. No air!" And moon-dogs and cats and cars and flowers; and even a moon-bird. "It can't fly in the sky 'cause there ain't—isn't any air so it flies in the dirt!" That was Justin. "It likes bottoms of craters 'cause there's more dirt there!"

I caught Vincent's amused eyes as he listened to the small ones. "Little kids are funny!" he murmured. "Animals on the moon! My dad, when he was there, all he saw—" His eyes widened and he became very busy choosing the right-sized nails from the rusty coffee can.

"Middle-sized kids are funny, too," I said. "Moon, indeed! There aren't any dads on the moon, either!"

"I guess not." He picked up the hammer and, as he moved away, I heard him whisper, "Not now!"

My intermediates were in the midst of a huge argument. I umpired for a while. If you use a BB shot to represent the Earth, would there be room in the schoolroom to make a scale mobile of the planetary system? I extinguished some of the fire bred of ignorance, by suggesting an encyclopedia and some math, and moved on through the room.

Gene and Vincent, not caring for such intellectual pursuits, were working on our model space capsule, which was patterned after the very latest in U.S. spacecraft, modified to include different aspects of the latest in flying saucers. I was watching Vincent leaning through a window, fitting a tin can altitude gauge—or some such—into the control panel. Gene was painting purple a row of cans around the middle of the craft. Purple was currently popular for flying saucer lights.

"I wonder if astronauts ever develop claustrophobia?" I said idly. "I get a twinge sometimes in elevators or mines."

"I suppose susceptible ones would be eliminated long before they ever got to be astronauts," grunted Vincent as he pushed on the tin can. "They go through all sorts of tests."

"I know," I said. "But people change. Just supposing—"

"Gollee!" said Gene, his poised paint brush dribbling purple down his arm and off his elbow. "Imagine! Way up there! No way out! Can't get down! And claustrophobia!" He brought out the five syllables proudly. The school had defined and discussed the word when we first started the unit.

The tin can slipped and Vincent staggered sideways, falling against me.

"Oh!" said Vincent, his shaking hands lifting, his right arm curling up over his head. "I—"

I took one look at his twisted face, the cold sweat beading his hairline, and, circling his shoulders, steered him over to the reading bench near my desk. "Sit," I said.

"Whatsa matter with him?" Now the paint was dripping on one leg of Gene's Levi's.

"Just slightly wampsy," I said. "Watch that paint. You're making a mess of your clothes."

"Gollee!" He smeared his hand down his pants from hip to knee. "Mom'll kill me!"

I lifted my voice. "It's put-away time. Kipper, will you monitor today?"

The children were swept into organized confusion. I turned back to Vincent. "Better?"

"I'm sorry." Color hadn't come back to his face yet, but it was plumping up from its stricken drawnness. "Sometimes it gets through too sharply—"

"Don't worry about it," I said, pushing his front hair up out of his eyes. "You could drive yourself crazy—"

"Mom says my imagination is a little too vivid—" His mouth corners lifted.

"So 'tis," I smiled at him, "if it must seize upon my imaginary astronaut. There's no point to your harrowing up your soul with what might happen. Problems we have always with us. No need to borrow any."

"I'm not exactly borrowing," he whispered, his shoulder hunching up towards his wincing head. "He never did want to, anyway, and now that they're orbiting, he's still scared. What if—" He straightened resolutely. "I'll help Gene." He slid away before I could stop him.

"Vincent," I called. "*Who's* orbiting—" And just then Justin dumped over the whole stack of jigsaw puzzles, upside down. That ended any further questions I might have had.

That evening I pushed the newspaper aside and thoughtfully lifted my coffee cup. I stared past its rim and out into the gathering darkness. This was the local newspaper, which was still struggling to become a big metropolitan daily after half a century of being a four-page county weekly. Sometimes its reach exceeded its grasp, and it had to bolster short columns with little folksy-type squibs. I re-read the one that had caught my eye. Morris was usually good for an item or two. I watched for them since he had had a conversation with a friend of mine I'd lost track of.

Local ham operator, Morris Staviski, says the Russians have a new manned sputnik in orbit. He says he has monitored radio signals from the capsule. He can't tell what they're saying, but he says they're talking Russian. He knows what Russian sounds like because his grandmother was Russian.

"Hmm," I thought. "I wonder. Maybe Vincent knows Morris. Maybe that's where he got this orbiting bit."

So the next day I asked him.

"Staviski?" He frowned a little. "No, ma'am, I don't know anyone named Staviski. At least I don't remember the name. Should I?"

"Not necessarily," I said. "I just wondered. He's a ham radio operator—"

"Oh!" His face flushed happily. "I'm working on the code now so I can take the test next time it's given in Winter Wells! Maybe I'll get to talk to him sometimes!"

"Me, too!" said Gene. "I'm learning the code, too!"

"He's a little handicapped, though," Vincent smiled. "He can't tell a *dit* from a *dah* yet!"

The next morning Vincent crept into school with all the sun gone out. He moved like someone in a dream and got farther and farther away. Before morning recess came, I took his temperature. It was normal. But he certainly wasn't. At recess the rapid outflow of children left him stranded in his seat, his pinched face turned to the window, his unfinished work in front of him, his idle pencil in the hand that curved up over the side of his head.

"Vincent!" I called, but there was no sign he even heard me. "Vincent!"

He drew a sobbing breath and focused his eyes on me slowly. "Yes, ma'am?" He wet his dry lips.

"What *is* the matter?" I asked. "Where do you feel bad?"

"Bad?" His eyes unfocused again and his face slowly distorted into a crying mask. With an effort he smoothed it out again. "I'm not the one. It's—it's—" He leaned his shaking chin in the palm of his hand and steadied his elbow on the top of his desk. His knuckles whitened as he clenched his fingers against his mouth.

"Vincent!" I went to him and touched his head lightly. With a little shudder and a sob, he turned and buried his face against me.

"Oh, Teacher! Teacher!"

A quick look out the window showed me that all the students were down in the creek bed building sand forts. Eight-year-old pride is easily bruised. I led Vincent up to my desk and took him onto my lap. For a while we sat there, my cheek pressed to his head as I rocked silently. His hair was spiky against my face and smelled a little like a baby chick's feathers.

"He's afraid! He's afraid!" he finally whispered, his eyes tight shut. "The other one is dead. It's broken so it can't come back. He's afraid! And the dead one keeps looking at him with blood on his mouth! And he can't come down! His hands are bleeding! He hit the walls wanting to get out. But there's no air outside!"

"Vincent," I went on rocking, "have you been telling yourself stories until you believe them?"

"No!" He buried his face against my shoulder, his body tense. "I know! I know! I can hear him! He screamed at first, but now he's too scared. Now he—" Vincent stilled on my lap. He lifted his face—listening. The anguish slowly smoothed away. "It's gone again! He must go to sleep. Or unconscious. I don't hear him all the time."

"What was he saying?" I asked, caught up in his—well, whatever it was.

"I don't know." Vincent slid from my lap, his face still wary. "I don't know his language."

"But you said—" I protested. "How do you know what he's feeling if you don't even know—"

He smiled his little lip-lift. "When you look at one of us kids without a word and your left eyebrow goes up—what do you mean?"

"Well, that depends on what who's doing," I flushed.

"If it's for me, I *know* what you mean. And I stop it. So do the other kids about themselves. That's the way I know this." He started back to his desk. "I'd better get my spelling done."

"Is that the one that's orbiting?" I asked hopefully, wanting to tie something to something.

"Orbiting?" Vincent was busily writing. "That's the sixth word. I'm only on the fourth."

That afternoon I finally put aside the unit tests I'd been checking and looked at the clock. Five o'clock. And at my hands. Filthy. And assessed the ache across my shoulders, the hollow in my stomach, and decided to spend the night right where I was. I didn't even straighten my desk, but turned my weary back on it and unlocked the door to the teacherage.

I kicked off my shoes, flipped on the floor lamp, and turned up the thermostat to take the dank chill out of the small apartment. The cupboards yielded enough supplies to make an entirely satisfying meal. Afterwards, I turned the lights low and sat curled up at one end of the couch listening to one of my Acker Bilke records while I drank my coffee. I flexed my toes in blissful comfort as I let the clear, concise, tidy notes of the clarinet clear away my cobwebs of fatigue. Instead of purring, I composed another strophe to my Praise Song:

Praise God for Fedness—and Warmness—and Shelteredness—and Darkness—and Lightness—and Cleanness—and Quietness—and Unharriedness—

I dozed then for a while and woke to stillness. The stereo had turned itself off, and it was so still I could hear the wind in the oak trees and the far, unmusical blat of a diesel train. And I also could hear a repetition of the sound that had wakened me.

Someone was in the schoolroom.

I felt a throb of fright and wondered if I had locked the teacherage door. But I *knew* I had locked the school door just after four o'clock. Of course, a bent bobby pin and your tongue in the correct corner of your mouth and you could open the old lock. But what—who would want to? What was in there? The stealthy noises went on. I heard the creak of the loose board in the back of the room. I heard the *yaaaawn* of the double front door hinges and a thud and clatter on the front porch.

Half paralyzed with fright, I crept to the little window that looked out onto the porch. Cautiously I separated two of the slats of the blind and peered out into the thin slice of moonlight. I gasped and let the slats fall.

A flying saucer! With purple lights! On the porch!

Then I gave a half grunt of laughter. Flying saucers, indeed! There was something familiar about that row of purple lights—unglowing—around its middle. I knew they were purple—even by the dim light—because that was *our* space capsule! Who was trying to steal our cardboard-tincan-poster-painted capsule?

Then I hastily shoved the blind aside and pressed my nose to the dusty screen. The blind retaliated by swinging back and whacking me heavily on the ear, but that wasn't what was dizzying me.

Our capsule was taking off!

"It can't!" I gasped as it slid up past the edge of the porch roof. "Not that storage barrel and all those tin cans! It can't!" And, sure enough, it couldn't. It crash-landed just beyond the flagpole. But it staggered up again, spilling several cans noisily, and skimmed over the swings, only to smash against the boulder at the base of the wall.

I was out of the teacherage, through the dark schoolroom, and down the porch steps before the echo of the smash stopped bouncing from surface to surface around the canyon. I was halfway to the capsule before my toes curled and made me conscious of the fact that I was barefooted. Rather delicately I walked the rest of the way to the crumpled wreckage. What on earth had possessed it—?

In the shadows I found what had possessed it. It was Vincent, his arms wrapped tightly over his ears and across his head. He was writhing silently, his face distorted and gasping.

"Good Lord!" I gasped and fell to my knees beside him. "Vincent! What on earth!" I gathered him up as best I could with his body twisting and his legs flailing, and moved him out into the moonlight.

"I have to! I have to! I have to!" he moaned, struggling away from me. "I hear him! I hear him!"

"Hear whom?" I asked. "Vincent!" I shook him. "Make sense! What are you doing here?"

Vincent stilled in my arms for a frozen second. Then his eyes opened and he blinked in astonishment. "Teacher! What are *you* doing here?"

"I asked first," I said. "What *are* you doing here, and what is this capsule bit?"

"The capsule?" He peered at the pile of wreckage and tears flooded down his cheeks. "Now I can't go and I have to! I have to!"

"Come on inside," I said. "Let's get this thing straightened out once and for all." He dragged behind me, his feet scuffling, his sobs and sniffles jerking to the jolting movement of his steps. But he dug in at the porch and pulled me to a halt.

"Not inside!" he said. "Oh, not inside!"

"Well, okay," I said. "We'll sit here for now."

He sat on the step below me and looked up, his face wet and shining in the moonlight. I fished in the pocket of my robe for a tissue and swabbed his eyes. Then I gave him another. "Blow," I said. He did. "Now, from the beginning."

"I—" He had recourse to the tissue again. "I came to get the capsule. It was the only way I could think of to get the man."

Silence crept around his flat statement until I said, "*That's* the beginning?"

Tears started again. I handed him another tissue. "Now look, Vincent, something's been bothering you for several days. Have you talked it over with your parents?"

"No," he hiccoughed. "I'm not supp-upposed to listen in on people. It isn't fair. But I didn't really. He came in first and I can't shut him out now because I know he's in trouble, and you can't *not* help if you know about someone's need—"

Maybe, I thought hopefully, maybe this is still my nap that I'll soon wake from—but I sighed. "Who is this man? The one that's orbiting?"

"Yes," he said, and cut the last hope for good solid sense from under my feet. "He's up in a capsule and its retro-rockets won't fire. Even if he could live until the orbital decay dropped him back into the atmosphere, the re-entry would burn him up. And he's so afraid! He's trapped! He can't get out!"

I took hold of both of his shaking shoulders. "Calm down," I said. "You can't help him like this." He buried his face against the skirt of my robe. I slid one of my hands over to his neck and patted him for a moment.

"How did you make the capsule move?" I asked. "It *did* move, didn't it?"

"Yes," he said. "I lifted it. We can, you know—lift things. My People can. But I'm not big enough. I'm not supposed to anyway, and I can't sustain the lift. And if I can't even get it out of this canyon, how can I lift clear out of the atmosphere? And he'll die—scared!"

"You can make things fly?" I asked.

"Yes, all of us can. And ourselves, too. See?"

And there he was, floating! His knees level with my head! His shoe laces drooped forlornly down, and one used tissue tumbled to the steps below him.

"Come down," I said, swallowing a vast lump of some kind. He did. "But you know there's no air in space, and our capsule—*Good Lord! Our* capsule? In *space?*—wasn't airtight. How did you expect to breathe?"

"We have a shield," he said. "See?" And there he sat, a glint of something about him. I reached out a hand and drew back my stubbed fingers. The glint was gone. "It keeps out the cold and keeps in the air," he said.

"Let's—let's analyze this a little," I suggested weakly, nursing my fingers unnecessarily. "You say there's a man orbiting in a disabled capsule, and you planned to go up in our capsule with only the air you could take with you and rescue him?" He nodded wordlessly. "Oh, child! Child!" I cried. "You couldn't possibly!"

"Then he'll die." Desolation flattened his voice and he sagged forlornly.

Well, what comfort could I offer him? I sagged, too. Lucky, I thought then, that it's moonlight tonight. People traditionally believe all kinds of arrant nonsense by moonlight. So. I straightened. Let's believe a little— or at least act as if.

"Vincent?"

"Yes, ma'am." His face was shadowed by his hunched shoulders.

"If you can lift our capsule this far, how far could your daddy lift it?"

"Oh, *lots* farther!" he cried. "My daddy was studying to be a regular Motiver when he went to the New Home, but he stopped when he came back across space to Earth again because Outsiders don't accept—oh!" His eyes rounded and he pressed his hands to his mouth. "Oh, I forgot!" His voice came muffled. "I forgot! You're an Outsider! We're forbidden to tell—to show—Outsiders don't—"

"Nonsense," I said. "I'm not an Outsider. I'm a teacher. Can you call your mother tonight the way you did the day you and Gene had that fight?"

"A fight? Me and Gene?" The fight was obviously an event of the neolithic period for Vincent. "Oh, yes, I remember. Yes, I guess I could, but she'll be mad because I left—and I told—and—and—" Weeping was close again.

"You'll have to choose," I pointed out, glad to the bones that it wasn't my choice to make, "between letting the man die or having her mad at you. You should have told them when you first knew about him."

"I didn't want to tell that I'd listened to the man—"

"Is he Russian?" I asked, just for curiosity's sake.

"I don't know," he said. "His words are strange. Now he keeps saying something like *Hospodi pomelui*. I think he's talking to God."

"Call your mother," I said, no linguist I. "She's probably worried to death by now."

Obediently, he closed his eyes and sat silent for a while on the step below me. Then he opened his eyes. "She'd just found out I wasn't in bed," he said. "They're coming." He shivered a little. "Daddy gets so mad sometimes. He hasn't the most equitable of temperaments?"

"Oh, Vincent!" I laughed. "What an odd mixture you are!"

"No, I'm not," he said. "Both my mother and daddy are of the People. Remy is a mixture 'cause his grampa was of the Earth, but mine came from the Home. You know—when it was destroyed. I wish I could have seen the ship our People came to Earth in. Daddy says when he was little, they used to dig up pieces of it from the walls and floors of the canyon where it crashed. But they still had a life ship in a shed behind their house and they'd play they were escaping again from the big ship." Vincent shivered. "But some didn't escape. Some died in the sky and some died because Earth people were scared of them."

I shivered too and rubbed my cold ankles with both hands. I wondered wistfully if this wasn't asking just a trifle too much of my ability to believe, even in the name of moonlight.

Vincent brought me back abruptly to my particular Earth. "Look! Here they are already! Gollee! That was fast. They sure must be mad!" And he trailed out onto the playground.

I looked expectantly toward the road and only whirled the other way when I heard the thud of feet. And there they stood, both Mr. and Mrs. Kroginold. And he *did* look mad! His—well—rough-hewn is about the kindest description—face frowning in the moonlight. Mrs. Kroginold surged toward Vincent and Mr. Kroginold swelled preliminary to a vocal blast—or so I feared—so I stepped quickly into the silence.

"There's our school capsule," I said, motioning towards the crushed clutter at the base of the boulder. "That's what he was planning to go up in to rescue a man in a disabled sputnik. He thought the air inside that shiny whatever he put around himself would suffice for the trip. He says a man is dying up there, and he's been carrying that agony around with him, all alone, because he was afraid to tell you."

I stopped for a breath and Mr. Kroginold deflated and—amazingly—grinned a wide, attractive grin, half silver, half shadow.

"Why the gutsy little devil!" he said admiringly. "And I've been fearing the stock was running out! When I was a boy in the canyon—" But he sobered suddenly and turned to Vincent. "Vince! If there's need, let's get with it. What's the deal?" He gathered Vincent into the curve of his arm, and we all went back to the porch. "Now. Details." We all sat.

Vincent, his eyes intent on his father's face and his hand firmly holding his mother's, detailed.

"There are two men orbiting up there. The capsule won't function properly. One man is dead. I never did hear him. The other one is crying for help." Vincent's face tightened anxiously. "He—he feels so bad that it nearly kills me. Only sometimes I guess he passes out because the feeling goes away—like now. Then it comes back worse—"

"He's orbiting," said Mr. Kroginold, his eyes intent on Vincent's face.

"Oh," said Vincent weakly, "of course! I didn't think of that! Oh, Dad! I'm so stupid!" And he flung himself on Mr. Kroginold.

"No," said Mr. Kroginold, wrapping him around with the dark strength of his arms. "Just young. You'll learn. But first learn to bring your problems to your mother and me. That's what we're for!"

"But," said Vincent, "I'm not supposed to listen in—"

"Did you seek him out?" asked Mr. Kroginold. "Did you know about the capsule?"

"No," said Vincent. "He just came in to me—"

"See?" Mr. Kroginold set Vincent back on the step. "You weren't listening in. You were invaded. You just happened to be the right receptivity. Now, what were your plans?"

"They were probably stupid, too," admitted Vincent. "But I was going to lift our capsule—I had to have something to put him in—and try to intercept the orbit of the other one. Then I was going to get the man out—I don't know how—and bring him back to Earth and put him down at the FBI building in Washington. They'd know how to get him home again."

"Well." Mr. Kroginold smiled faintly. "Your plan has the virtue of simplicity, anyway. Just nit-picking, though, I can see one slight problem. How would the FBI ever convince the authorities in his country that we hadn't impounded the capsule for our own nefarious purposes?" Then he became very business-like.

"Lizbeth, will you get in touch with Ron? I think he's in Kerry tonight. Lucky our best Motiver is This End right now. I'll see if Jemmy is up-canyon. We'll get his okay on Remy's craft at the Selkirk. If this has been going on for very long, time is what we've got little of."

It was rather anti-climactic after all those efficient rattlings-out of directions to see the three of them just sit quietly there on the step, hands clasped, their faces lifted a little in the moonlight, their eyes closed. My left foot was beginning to go to sleep when Vincent's chin finally dropped, and he pulled one hand free from his mother's grasp to curl his arm up over his head. Mrs. Kroginold's eyes flipped open. "Vincent?" Her voice was anxious.

"It's coming again," I said. "That distress—whatever it is."

"Ron's heading for the Selkirk now," she said, gathering Vincent to her. "Jake, Vincent's receiving again."

Mr. Kroginold said hastily to the eaves of the porch, "—as soon as possible. Hang on. Vincent's got him again. Wait, I'll relay. Vince, where can I reach him? Show me."

And damned if they didn't all sit there again—with Vincent's face shining with sweat and his mother trying to cradle his twisting body. Then Mr. Kroginold gave a grunt, and Vincent relaxed with a sob. His father took him from his mother.

"Already?" I asked. "That was a short one."

Mrs. Kroginold fished for a tissue in her pocket and wiped Vincent's face. "It isn't over yet," she said. "It won't be until the capsule swings behind the Earth again, but he's channeling the distress to his father, and he's relaying it to Jemmy up-canyon. Jemmy is our Old One. He'll help us handle it from here on out. But Vincent will have to be our receptor—"

" 'A sort of telepathy,' " I quoted, dizzy with trying to follow a road I couldn't even imagine.

"A sort of telepathy." Mrs. Kroginold laughed and sighed, her finger tracing Vincent's cheek lovingly. "You've had quite a mish-mash dumped in your lap, haven't you? And no time for us to be subtle."

"It *is* bewildering," I said. "I've been adding two and two and getting the oddest fours!"

"Like?" she asked.

"Like maybe Vincent's forefathers didn't come over in the *Mayflower,* but maybe a spaceship?"

"But not quite *Mayflower* years ago," she smiled. "And?"

"And maybe Vincent's Dad *has* seen no life on the moon?"

"Not so very long ago," she said. "And?"

"And maybe there *is* a man in distress up there and you *are* going to try to rescue him?"

"Well," said Mrs. Kroginold. "Those fours look all right to me."

"They *do?*" I goggled. Then I sighed, "Ah well, this modern math! I knew it would be the end of me!"

Mr. Kroginold brought his eyes back to us. "Well, it's all set in motion. Ron's gone for the craft. He'll be here to pick us up as soon as he can make it. Jemmy's taking readings on the capsule so we'll be able to attempt rendezvous. Then, the Power being willing, we'll be able to bring the fellow back."

"I—I—" I stood up. This was suddenly too much. "I think maybe I'd better go back in the house." I brushed the sand off the back of my robe. "One thing bothers me still, though."

"Yes?" Mrs. Kroginold smiled.

"How *is* the FBI going to convince the authorities of the other country?"

"Ay!" she said, sobering. "Jake—"

And I gathered my skirts up and left the family there on the school porch. As I closed the teacherage door behind me, I leaned against it. It was so dark—in here. And there was such light out there! Why, they had jumped into helping without asking one single question! Then I wondered what questions I had expected— Was the man a nice man? Was he worth saving? Was he an important personage? What kind of reward? *Is there a need?* That's all they needed to know!

I looked at the sleepcoat I hadn't worn yet, but I felt too morning to undress and go to bed properly, so I slid out of my robe and put my dress back on. And my shoes. And a sweater. And stood irresolutely in the middle of the floor. After all! What is the etiquette for when your guests are about to go into orbit from your front porch?

Then there was a thud at the door and the knob rattled. I heard Mrs. Kroginold call softly, "But Vincent! An Outsider?"

"But she isn't!" said Vincent, fumbling again at the door. "She said she isn't—she's a teacher. And I know she'd like—" The door swung open suddenly and tumbled Vincent to the schoolroom floor. Mrs. Kroginold was just outside the outer door on the porch.

"Sorry," she said. "Vincent thinks maybe you'd like to see the craft arrive—but—"

"You're afraid I might tell," I said for her. "And it should be kept in the family. I've been repository for odd family stories before. Well, maybe not *quite*—"

Vincent scrambled for the porch. "Here it comes!" he cried.

I was beside Mrs. Kroginold in a split second and, grasping hands, we raced after Vincent. Mr. Kroginold had been standing in the middle of the playground, but he drifted back to us as a huge—well, a huge *nothing* came down through the moonlight.

"It—where is it?" I wondered if some dimension I didn't know was involved.

"Oh," said Mrs. Kroginold. "It has the unlight over it. Jake! Ask Ron—"

Mr. Kroginold turned his face to the huge nothing. And there it was! A slender silver something, its nose arcing down from a rocket position to rest on the tawny sands of the playground.

"The unlight's so no one will see us," said Mrs. Kroginold, "and we flow it so it won't bother radar and things like that." She laughed. "We're not the right shape for this year's flying saucers, anyway. I'm glad we're not. Who wants to look like a frosted cupcake on a purple lighted plate? That's what's so In now."

"Is it really a spaceship?" I asked, struck by how clean the lovely gleaming craft was that had come so silently to dent our playground.

"Sure it is!" cried Vincent. "The Old Man had it and they took him to the moon in it to bury him and Bethie-too and Remy went with their Dad and Mom and—"

"A little reticence, Son," said Mr. Kroginold, catching Vincent's hand. "It isn't necessary to go into all that history."

"She—she realizes," said Mrs. Kroginold. "It's not as if she were a stranger."

"We shouldn't be gone too long," said Mr. Kroginold. "I'll pick you up here as soon—"

"Pick us up! I'm going with you!" cried Mrs. Kroginold. "Jake Kroginold! If you think you're going to do me out of a thing as wild and wonderful as this—"

"Let her go with us, Dad," begged Vincent.

"With *us?*" Mr. Kroginold raked his fingers back through his hair. "You, too?"

"Of course!" Vincent's eyes were wide with astonishment. "It's *my* man!"

"Well, *adonday veeah* in cards and spades!" said Mr. Kroginold. He grinned over at me. "Family!" he said.

I studiously didn't meet his eyes. I felt a deep wave of color move up my face as I kept my mouth clamped shut. I *wouldn't* say anything! I couldn't ask! I had no right to expect—

"And Teacher, too!" cried Vincent. "Teacher, too!"

Mr. Kroginold considered me for a long moment. My wanting must have been a flaring thing because he finally shrugged an eyebrow and echoed, "And Teacher, too."

Then I nearly died! It *was* so wild and wonderful and impossible and I'm scared to death of heights! We scurried about getting me a jacket. Getting Kipper's forgotten jacket out of the cloak room for Vincent, who had come off without his. Taking one of my blankets, just in case. I paused a moment in the mad scramble, hand poised over my Russian-English, English-Russian pocket dictionary. Then left it. The man might not be Russian at all. And even if he was, people like Vincent's seemed to have little need for such aids to communication.

A door opened in the craft. I looked at it, thinking blankly, *Ohmy! Ohmy!* We had started across the yard toward the craft when I gasped, "The—the door! I have to lock the door!"

I dashed back to the schoolhouse and into the darkness of the teacherage. And foolishly, childishly, there in the dark, I got awfully hungry! I yanked a cupboard door open and scrabbled briefly. Peanut butter—slippery, glassy cylinder—crackers—square-cornered, waxy carton. I slammed the cupboard shut, snatched up my purse as though I were on the way to the MONSTER MERCANTILE, staggered out of the door, and juggled my burdens until I could manipulate the key. Then I hesitated on the porch, one foot lifting, all ready to go to the craft, and silently gasped my travel prayer. "Dear God, go with me to my destination. Don't let me imperil anyone or be imperiled by anyone. Amen." I started down the steps, paused, and cried softly, "To my destination *and back!* Oh, please! And back!"

Have you, oh, have you ever watched space reach down to surround you as your hands would reach down to surround a minnow? Have you ever seen Earth, a separate thing, apart from you, and see-almost-all-able? Have you ever watched color deepen and run until it blared into blaze and blackness? Have you ever stepped out of the context in which your identity is established and floated un-anyone beyond the steady pulse of night and day and accustomed being? Have you ever, for even a fleeting second, shared God's eyes? I have! *I have!*

And Mrs. Kroginold and Vincent were with me in all the awesome wonder of our going. You couldn't have seen us go even if you had known where to look. We were wrapped in unlight again, and the craft was flowed again to make it a nothing to any detection device.

"I wish I could space walk!" said Vincent, finally, turning his shoulders but not his eyes away from the window. "Daddy—"

"No." Mr. Kroginold's tone left no loophole for further argument.

"Well, it would be fun," Vincent sighed. Then he said in a very small voice, "Mother, I'm hungry."

"So sorry!" Mrs. Kroginold hugged him to her briefly. "Nearest hamburger joint's a far piece down the road!"

"Here—" I found, after two abortive attempts, that I still had a voice. I slithered cautiously to my knees on the bare floor—no luxury liner, this—and sat back. "Peanut butter." The jar clicked down. "And crackers." The carton thumped—and my elbow creaked almost audibly as I straightened it out from its spasmed clutch.

"Gollee! Real deal!" Vincent plumped down beside me and began working on the lid of the jar. "What'll we spread it with?"

"Oh!" I blankly considered the problem. "Oh, I have a nail file here in my purse." I was fishing for it amid the usual clutter when I caught Mrs. Kroginold's surprised look. I grinned sheepishly. "I thought I was hungry. But I guess that wasn't what was wrong with my stomach!"

Shortly after the jar was opened and the roasty smell of peanuts spread, Mr. Kroginold and another fellow drifted casually over to us. I preferred to ignore the fact that they actually drifted—no steps on the floor. The other fellow was introduced as Jemmy. The Old One? Not so old, it seemed to me. But then "old" might mean "wise" to these people. And on that score he could qualify. He had none of the loose ends that I can often sense in people. He was—whole.

"Ron is lifting," said Mr. Kroginold through a mouthful of peanut butter and crackers. He nodded at the center of the room, where another fellow sat looking intently at a square, boxy-looking thing.

"That's the amplifier," Jemmy said, as though that explained anything. "It makes it possible for one man to manage the craft."

Something buzzed on a panel across the room. "There!" Mr. Kroginold was at the window, staring intently. "There it is! Good work, Ron!"

At that moment Vincent cried out, his arms going up in their protesting posture. Mrs. Kroginold pushed him over to his father, who drew him in the curve of his shoulder to the window, coaxing down the tense arms. "See? There's the craft! It looks odd. Something's not right about it."

"Can—can we take off the unlight now?" asked Vincent, jerkily. "So he can see us? Then maybe he won't feel so bad—"

"Jemmy?" Mr. Kroginold called across the craft. "What do you think? Would the shock of our appearance be too much?"

"It could hardly be worse than the hell he's in now," said Jemmy. "So—"

"Oh!" cried Vincent. "He thinks he just now died. He thinks we're the Golden Gates!"

"Rather a loose translation." Jemmy flung a smiling glance at us. "But he is wondering if we are the entrance to the afterworld. Ron, can we dock?"

Moments later, there was a faint metallic click and a slight vibration through our craft. Then we three extras stood pressed to the window and watched Mr. Kroginold and Jemmy leave our craft. They were surrounded, it's true, by their shields that caught light and slid it rapidly around, but they did look so unguarded—no, they didn't! They looked right at home and intent on their rescue mission. They disappeared from the sight of our windows. We waited and waited, not saying anything—not aloud, anyway. I could feel a clanking through the floor under me. And a scraping. Then a long nothing again.

Finally they came back in sight, the light from our window glinting across a mutual protective bubble that enclosed the two of them and a third inert figure between them.

"He still thinks he's dead," said Vincent soberly. "He's wondering if he ought to try to pray. He wasn't expecting people after he died. But mostly he's trying not to think."

They brought him in and laid him on the floor. They eased him out of his suit and wrapped him in my blanket. We three gathered around him looking at his quiet, tight face. *So young!* I thought. *So young!* Unexpectedly his eyes opened, and he took us in, one by one. At the sight of Vincent, his mouth dropped open and his eyes fled shut again.

"What'd he do that for?" asked Vincent, a trifle hurt.

"Angels," said his mother firmly, "are not supposed to have peanut butter around the mouth!"

The three men consulted briefly. Then Mr. Kroginold prepared to leave our craft again. This time he took a blanket from the Rescue Pack they had brought in the craft.

"He can manage the body alone," said Jemmy, being our intercom. A little later— "He has the body out, but he's gone back—" His forehead creased, then cleared. "Oh, the tapes and instrument packets," he explained to our questioning glances. "He thinks maybe they can study them and prevent this happening again."

He turned to Mrs. Kroginold. "Well, Lizbeth, back when all of you were in school together in the canyon, I wouldn't have given a sandwiched quarter for the chances of any Kroginold ever turning out well. I sprinkle repentant ashes on my bowed head. Some good *can* come from Kroginolds!"

And Vincent screamed!

Before we could look his way, there was a blinding flash that exploded through every window as though we had suddenly been stabbed through and through. Then we were all tumbled in blinded confusion from one wall of our craft to another until, almost as suddenly, we floated in a soundless blackness. "Jake! Oh, Jake!" I heard Mrs. Kroginold's whispering gasp. Then she cried out, "Jemmy! Jemmy! What happened? Where's Jake?"

Light came back. From where, I never did know. I hadn't known its source even before.

"The retro-rockets—" I felt more of his answer than I heard. "Maybe they finally fired. Or maybe the whole capsule just blew up. Ron?"

"Might have holed us." A voice I hadn't heard before answered. "Didn't. Capsule's gone."

"But—but—" The enormity of what had happened slowed our thoughts. "Jake!" Mrs. Kroginold screamed. "Jemmy! Ron! Jake's out there!"

And, as suddenly as the outcry came, it was cut off. In terror I crouched on the floor, my arms up defensively, not to my ears as Vincent's had gone—there was nothing to hear—but against the soundless, aimless tumbling of bodies above me. Jemmy and Vincent and Mrs. Kroginold were like corpses afloat in some invisible sea. And Vincent, burrowed into a corner, was a small, silent, humped-up bundle.

I think I would have gone mad in the incomprehensible silence if a hand hadn't clutched mine. Startled, I snatched my hand away, but gave it back, with a sob, to our shipwrecked stranger. He accepted it with both of his. We huddled together, taking comfort in having someone to cling to.

Then I shook with hysterical laughter as I suddenly realized. " 'A sort of telepathy'!" I giggled. "They are not dead, but speak. Words are slow, you know." I caught the young man's puzzled eyes. "And of very little use in a situation like this."

I called to Ron where he crouched near the amplifier box, "They are all right, aren't they?"

"They?" His head jerked upward. "Of course. Communicating."

"Where's Mr. Kroginold?" I asked. "How can we ever hope to find him out there?"

"Trying to reach him," said Ron, his chin flipping upward again. "Don't feel him dead. Probably knocked out. Can't find him unconscious."

"Oh." The stranger's fingers tightened on mine. I looked at him. He was struggling to get up. I let go of him and shakily, on hands and knees, we crawled to the window, his knees catching on the blanket. For a long moment, the two of us stared out into the darkness. I watched the lights wheel slowly past until I reoriented, and we were the ones wheeling. But as soon as I relaxed, again it was the lights wheeling slowly past. I didn't know what we were looking for. I couldn't get any kind of perspective on anything outside our craft. Any given point of light could have been a dozen light-years away—or could have been a glint inside the glass—or was it glass?—against which I had my nose pressed.

But the stranger seemed to know what he was looking for. Suddenly I cried out and twisted my crushed fingers to free them. He let go and gestured toward the darkness, saying something tentative and hopeful.

"Ron!" I called, trying to see what the man was seeing. "Maybe—maybe he sees something." There was a stir above me and Jemmy slid down to the floor beside me.

"A visual sighting?" he whispered tensely.

"I don't know," I whispered back. "Maybe he—"

Jemmy laid his hand on the man's wrist, and then concentrated on whatever it was out in the void that had caught the stranger's attention.

"Ron—" Jemmy gestured out the window and—well, I guess Ron gestured with our craft—because things outside swam a different way until I caught a flick or a gleam or a movement.

"There, there, there," crooned Jemmy, almost as though soothing an anxious child. "There, there, there. Lizbeth!"

And all of us except Ron were crowded against the window, watching a bundle of some sort tumbling toward us. "Shield intact," whispered Jenny. "Praise the Power!"

"Oh, Daddy, Daddy!" choked Vincent against his whitened knuckles. Mrs. Kroginold clung to him wordlessly.

Then Jemmy was gone, streaking through our craft, away outside from us. I saw the glint of his shield as he rounded our craft. I saw him gather the tumbling bundle up and disappear with it. Then he was back in the craft again, kneeling—unglinted—beside Mr. Kroginold as he lay on the floor. Mrs. Kroginold and Vincent launched themselves toward them.

Our stranger tugged at his half-shed blanket. I shuffled my knees off it and he shivered himself back into it.

They had to peel Mr. Kroginold's arms from around the instrument packet before they could work on him—in their odd, undoing way of working. And the stranger and I exchanged wavery smiles of congratulations when Mr. Kroginold finally opened his eyes.

So that was it. After it was all over, I got the deep, breath-drawing feeling I get when I have finished a most engrossing book, and a sort of last-page-flipping feeling, wistfully wishing there were more—just a little more!

Oh, the loose ends? I guess there were a few. They tied themselves quite casually and briskly in the next few days.

It was only a matter of moments after Mr. Kroginold had sat up and smiled a craggy smile of satisfaction at the packet he had brought back with him that Ron said, "Convenient." And we spiraled down—or so it felt to me—to the Earth beneath while Jemmy, fingers to our stranger's wrist, communicated to him in such a way that the stranger's eyes got very large and astonished and he looked at me—at *me!*—questioningly. I nodded. Well, what else could I do? He was asking something, and, so far, every question around these People seemed to have a positive answer!

So it was that we delivered him, not to the FBI in Washington, but to his own doorstep at a launching base somewhere deep in his own country. We waited, hovering under our unlight and well flowed, until the door swung open and gulped him in, instrument packet, my blanket, and all.

Imagination boggles at the reception there must have been for him! They surely knew the capsule had been destroyed in orbit. And to have him walk in—!

And Mr. Kroginold struggled for a couple of days with "Virus X" without benefit of the company doctor, then went back to work.

A couple of weeks later they moved away to another lab, half across the country, where Mr. Kroginold could go on pursuing whatever it is he is pursuing.

And a couple of days before they left, I quite unexpectedly gave Vincent a going-away gift.

That morning Vincent firmed his lips, his cheeks coloring, and shook his head. "I can't read it," he said, and began to close the book.

"*That* I don't believe," I said firmly, my flare of exasperation igniting into sudden inspiration. Vincent looked at me, startled. He was so used to my acceptance of his reading block that he was shaken a bit.

"But I *can't*," he said patiently.

"Why not?" I asked bluntly.

"I have a block," he said as flatly.

"What triggers it?" I probed.

"Why—why, Mother says anything that suggests unhappy compulsion—"

"How do you know this story has any such thing in it?" I asked. "All it says in the title is a name—*Stickeen*."

"But I *know*," he said miserably, his head bent as he flicked the pages of the story with his thumb.

"I'll tell you how you know," I said. "You know because you've read the story already."

"But I haven't!" Vincent's face puckered. "You only brought this book today!"

"That's true," I said. "And you turned the pages to see how long the story was. Only then did you decide you *wouldn't* read it—again!"

"I don't understand—" Wonder was stirring in his eyes.

"Vincent," I said, "you read this whole story in the time it took you to turn the pages. You gulped it page by page and that's how you know there's unhappy compulsion in it. So, you refuse to read it—again."

"Do—do you really think so?" asked Vincent in a hopeful half whisper. "Oh, Teacher, can I really read after all? I've been so ashamed! One of the People, and not able to read!"

"Let's check," I said, excited, too. "Give me the book. I'll ask you questions—" And I did. And he answered every single one of them!

"I can read!" He snatched the book from me and hugged it to him with both arms. "Hey! Gene! I can read!"

"Big deal!" said Gene, glancing up from his labor on the butcher paper spread on the floor. He was executing a fanciful rendition, in tempera, of the Indians greeting Columbus in a chartreuse, magenta, and shriek-pink jungle. "I learned to read in the first grade. Which way do a crocodile's knees bend?"

"All you have to remember," I said to a slightly dashed Vincent, "is to slow down a bit and be a little less empathetic." I was as pleased as he was. "And to think of the time I wasted for both of us, making you sound out your words—"

"But I need it," he said. "I still can't spell for sour apples!"

Vincent gave me a going-away present the Friday night that the Kroginolds came to say good-by. We were sitting in the twilight on the school porch. Vincent, shaken by having to leave Rinconcillo and Gene, and still thrilling to knowing he could read, gave me one of his treasures. It was a small rock, an odd crystalline formation that contrived at the same time to be betryoidal. In the curve of my palm it even had a strange feeling of resilience, though there was no yielding in it when I pressed my thumb to it.

"Daddy brought it to me from the moon," he told me, and deftly fielded it as my astonishment let it fall. "I'll probably get another one, someday," he said as he gave it back to me. "But even if I don't, I want you to have it."

Mr. and Mrs. Kroginold and I talked quietly for a while with no reference to parting. I shook them a little with, "Why do you suppose that stranger could send his thoughts to Vincent? I mean, he doesn't pick up distress from everyone, very apparently. Do you suppose that man might be from People like you? *Are* there People like you in that part of the world?"

They looked at each other, startled. "We really don't know!" said Mr. Kroginold. "Many of our People were unaccounted for when we arrived on Earth, but we just assumed that all of them were dead except for the groups around here—"

"I wonder if it ever occurred to Jemmy," said Mrs. Kroginold thoughtfully.

After they left, disappearing into the shadows of the hillside toward MEL, I sat for a while longer, turning the moon-pebble in my hands. What an odd episode! In a month or so it would probably seem like a distant dream, melting into my teaching years along with all the other things past. But it still didn't seem quite finished to me. Meeting people like the Kroginolds and the others, makes an indelible impression on a person. Look what it did for that stranger—

What *about* that stranger? How was he explaining? Were they giving him a hard time? Then I gulped. I had just remembered. My name and address were on a tape on the corner of that blanket of mine he had been wrapped in. If he had discovered it—! And if things got too thick for him—

Oh, gollee! What if some day there comes a knock on my door and there—!

Katie-Mary's Trip

See—we've got this pad, like—you know?—an old farmhouse with a broad porch all around it. The local yokels call it the hippy-joint, and when the local fuzz need something to fill out a shift, they cruise up and down in front of the place and make like busy.

Now, I know it's not for real—this hippy bit. Not here. Lots of dudes and chicks stop here on their way to the Coast where the Real is. But they never stay here—not the McCoy. They all drift on in a day or two except the ones that can't or won't conform. They can't buy the whole bit and so they drop out—too individual. Listen, if you think conforming is for squares or the establishment—think twice. You conform to the hippy thing or, brother, you're out!

Take the language, for one. I've had drop-ins wrinkle foreheads at me, trying to understand me. So once I listened to myself for a while and found that I'm pretty much of a polyglot. Any form of language that pleases me, I adopt it. *Warum nicht?* But if you don't have the vocabulary of a movement—you aren't with it. You know?

No, the ones that stay on here for any time at all are the individualists—the loners who have no pack to run with, who are looking for something and think maybe if they stay in one place long enough, like here where the stream of transients flows, whatever they're looking for will come by.

And me? I've been waiting here the longest. It hasn't come by yet. Or maybe that's what passed me by.

I started this joint. Unintentionally. When I first found this place—way back there when I was still struggling, thinking maybe that was the way—I walked through its empty, echoing, dust-cloud-spawning rooms. Nothing—lovely nothing—all around, bracketed by walls and floor and roof to italicize this particular bit of nothing. I looked out the windows. On three sides—nothing, to the edge of the sky. No hills or mountains to hold up the sky, and so the peak of the roof was all that kept the sky from being flat to the ground. On the other side, the barnyards and beyond—the beginning of town. I wouldn't need to look that way.

So I square-pointed the silt out of the rooms, swept the dust out, then mopped down to the bare boards. I straightened the stove pipe and lighted a fire in the potbelly. Then, for a long, satisfying evening, I sat on my bedroll on the floor and watched the fire flicker and glow behind the splintery isinglass in the cast-iron door.

I don't know who or what started it, but a couple of months later, people began drifting in to doss down on my floor. I never bothered with furniture. There were a few empty apple boxes around to put our lights on, or if someone had to sit high. I finally put up a couple more potbellied stoves and got the kitchen range—*Kalamazoo Direct to You*—in working order, the water reservoir and all, and nailed a slotted box inside by the front door. If someone wanted to drop a bit of bread in it as they drifted in or out—okay. If not, *Ça ne fait rien.*

After an initial period of revulsion, I began not to mind having strangers—none of my responsibility—around me. And, finally, I rather enjoyed it.

The other regulars?

Well, there's this chick, Katie-Mary. She's weird. Always spouting about Doing Her Thing. And keeping her area of floor on the chick side clean—bone clean—clear down to the grain of the shreddy old boards. Even to pushing and scraping out the long gray plugs of dirt and fuzz that took years to petrify between the planks. So when it's windy, the draft comes up through all those emptinesses from the crawl space under the joint and sets the edges of her blankets rippling all around her. She nearly froze last winter. The rippling scared another steady chick, Doos, into screaming half of one night because she could see the Serpent undulating around Katie-Mary—The Rosy Serpent of Contemplation who is unique among serpents in that he has a navel. But Katie-Mary'd get up each morning, stiff with the cold, and work up a sweat scrubbing her bit of floor again.

She had to carry the water from outside—no plumbing. There's a handpump standing up on a bare pipe in the back yard. We wrap it with burlap when freezing time comes—if we remember. And there's two outhouses—male and female, created we them.

Sometimes we're crowded—but Katie-Mary's not. We shove over and make room, but no one wants to step into that tawny white rectangle of Katie-Mary's. Which brings up another bit that bugs the transients. We operate dormwise—segregated. No cohabiting. *Weird, man, weird!*

Well, to get on, some night last spring, this dude came roaring in on his chopper. Young kid—the whole cycle bit—black leather, spaceman helmet, the kind that reflects so you can't see through it. Kinda filled the joint that first night, you know? There you'd be, rapping with someone, and there he'd be, listening like—like—well, like a thirsty guy drinks. But some of the congregation began to get real uptight, and he nearly got clobbered a couple of times—just for listening. But remember, his listening was like the sucking of a vacuum. Finally I decided I'd better point out to him the error of his ways, not wanting open warfare. I stopped at his shoulder—and for a minute there I thought I was having a delayed replay of a bad trip. It was like—like, well, like a drift of Something curling around the cerebellum, poking in long question marks and raking at the roots of me, trying to find—to know—

Then he grinned at me lazylike over his shoulder and said, "Yeah, I'll cool it, Frederic—no open warfare."

And he went looking for a place to doss down, while I stood blinking, wondering, my unused words drying my mouth out, hearing my right name for the first time since—

He ended up in what used to be a pantry, barely large enough to lie down in, and you'd rap your knuckles on two walls if you stretched too quickly.

"Central," he answered—before I asked. "Easy reaching."

I thought he'd be long gone come morning, but he wasn't. He stayed—a dropout.

He never had much to say, but there seemed always to be someone rapping with him. His thing was listening, except it seemed to me that his listening was asking. He was a Hunter, too, a Waiter. But sometimes he'd break in and start asking questions, out loud. But, then, he wasn't the Listener any more. So the other dude—or chick, maybe—'d split, and the Listener would roar off on that Pollution Producer (Noise) and manage to come back sometime after the last candle or lamp—no electricity—was doused, without waking me. And I'm a light sleeper.

Don't know the rationale, but there for a while several months ago, we were bulging. Must have been a wholesale migration to the Coast—maybe the lemming syndrome?

The pump in the yard squeaked at all hours. There were lines forming to the two-holer outhouses. Matches flared fitfully from every corner.

Candles, sure! But this lamp bit! Lookit the damn thing smoke! Yiy! That glass thing's hot! Hey, it does give light! What they won't think of next!

Separate? Man, I can't sleep without my old lady! I mean, like the eyes won't close—

Happy insomnia. My thing is running this joint—the way I want to. You're free to split.

Yeah. Free. The next pad eighty miles down the pike!

So, for a while there, the joint filled and emptied like it was breathing, and the slotted box by the front door filled and emptied too. Bread stacked up until I thought maybe of electricity—but unthought it in a hurry. First thing I knew about Katie-Mary's trip was in the lovely lull after all the crowdedness. Guesky, another stayer—ostensibly, his thing is contemplating, which looks on him about the same as sleeping, if you ask me. I think his real thing is seeing how little activity he can get along with, this side of dying. So it was a real departure for him to climb all the way up to my pad in the unfinished attic that spread blankly across the top of the whole house, dust undisturbed except immediately around me. He nudged me awake with his foot. *He* sleeps on a bench. Can't get up and down good enough for the floor. His meat's in his way.

"Hey, man—shake it!" he said. "Katie-Mary's back. Got back's evening. Man, she had a bad trip. Still freakin' out. She's down there shrieking and hammering the floor. Doos don't wanta touch her. Says she sees alienation all around her—"

"Nothing I can do," I yawned, scratching me where the blankets had been scratching too long.

"Stop her mouth or something," said Guesky, "till she shakes the trip."

"What she on?" I asked. "I thought her thing was the next-to-godliness bit—"

"No, man, you ain't with it!" Guesky's voice squeaked. "She split. She traveled. She went off with some dude after he ran her down in town with his wheels. She split, man. *She—was—gone!* Now she's back, shrieking and hammering the floor."

"Better the Listener than me," I said, sliding back under my blanket, cradling the back of my head on my bent elbow. "Katie-Mary and I, we don't jibe. She's always expecting me to expect her to expect me to make a pass at her. Better the Listener."

So Guesky went away and I shut my eyes. But they didn't stay shut. What was bugging Katie-Mary? She was usually fairly unflappable.

Finally I rolled over until my ear felt the chill of the metal grating set in my floor. It was above one in the ceiling of the chicks' dorm. No, you can't see down through it. Dirt, dust, cobwebs, and a four-inch offset between gratings, that's why. But if Guesky had brought the Listener instead of taking Katie-Mary— He had.

Katie-Mary's voice was the only one I heard. The Listener was The Compleat Listener.

"...wasn't hurt but it shook him so bad that I took him to Harmon Park until he got his cool back. He said he wasn't used to driving. 'Not on streets,' he said!" Katie-Mary's voice was rising and thinning. " 'And you don't meet many pedestrians above the trees!'

"That started it," said Katie-Mary. "That hooked me. I hung around wondering how long he could keep up a line like that. He asked me again if I was hurt, and I told him again he'd only nudged me, not even to push me off my feet. He was so relieved, he began to talk—like, man! *talk!* Sometimes he'd pull up and look sorry for something he'd told, but off he'd go again.

"Seems like he'd left his People. No, not a runaway. They gave him the car and what I suppose was the local equivalent of their blessing. Old. The car was old. But it ran brand new. He liked my talk about doing your thing and letting others do theirs.

" 'I told them,' he said, so pleased! 'I told them no one minded any-more. Nobody'd care if I forgot and—and lifted instead of walking—or—other—little—things—like—that.' " Katie-Mary was having trouble with her articulation and voice modulation. There was a gasping silence; then her voice squealed hysterically.

"You think he was putting me on? Man, are you ever wrong! Did you know he didn't buy drop one of gas for that weird set of wheels of his the whole time he was in town. He laughed when I asked him about it. 'Oh, I don't need gas. I just lift the car so there's just enough pressure to make the wheels turn. Of course, I do have to let the motor make enough noise to be convincing.' " Katie-Mary sobbed noisily, then gulped and went on.

"He was so pleased to hear anyone could do anything any more and not—not—oh, I said that! But he *was*. Seems like his People—it sounds like a commune, but it isn't. I saw—anyway, they've always been out of step with everyone—all of them. And uptight about letting anyone know. He—what? Oh, his name's Degal—no, just Degal. I never asked.

" 'It's a good joke on the People,' he told me once, like as if his People were the only people around. 'They think they're so different, and all along—wait until I tell them! You *do* have Sensitives, don't you?'

" 'What's that?' I asked.

" 'Oh, you know. Maybe you call them something else. You know—to touch the suffering—to read the reason for pain and illness. To go in. To heal.'

" 'Man, you've flipped!' I told him. 'This faith-healing bit. Well, sure, if you go for that kind—' But he looked at me—" Katie-Mary's voice faltered. I barely could hear her when she spoke again, small and soft and wondering. "Then I felt him in my mind—asking—asking—hoping. Then he was gone—disappointed—still wanting to hope. Some way—some way I'd failed.

" 'Some of our People,' he said in a hurry, I guess, to comfort me, 'have been so closed for so long that they find it hard to open to anyone, too. I'm sorry.'

"No," Katie-Mary said to a murmur. "Not all at one time. Oh, a month or six weeks. Little bits and pieces at different times. He's so young—oh, older than I am, but so young—so *new*—" Tears were gone from her voice but not the wonder.

"I asked him once where he came from. 'From the Home,' he said. 'Orphan's home?' I asked. He laughed. 'No! From the Home! Of course, *I* didn't. I was born on Earth, in the Canyon, but my grandfather—' Get this, man '—my grandfather was one who came to Earth from the Home.' 'How?' I asked. He said, like wondering why I'd ask something so plain, 'Why, in the ship, of course. At the Crossing!'

"That did it," said Katie-Mary. "Flying saucers yet. 'What you on?' I asked him. 'On?' he asked, then waited a minute and laughed. 'I don't need to be *on* anything to get high. Watch this!' "

Katie-Mary's voice faltered. "I didn't want to watch after the first little bit. I—I was afraid. I couldn't understand. I thought maybe I *was* out of my skull. But I kept looking—

"We were down by the river, at the bend, one night. A bright night. He told me the moon was poured out on the water, and it looked like it. Well, he shot up into the air over the river like a rocket. Then up there above the shining water, above the shadowy trees, he—he—you know? like those gymnasts at the Olympics—on TV—only not held down. No danger of falling. No sweat. Easy—fast—like a wingless bird. Like a jet gone mad. When he came down with a swoosh, laughing and panting and saying, 'That's the kind of high—' he found me huddled and scared under the trees, and he stopped smiling. He—he patted my shoulder. He said he was sorry. That he shoulda known I didn't mean a physical high—

"No!" Katie-Mary's voice lifted. "No—not anything! You *know* I wasn't! I don't, ever! He did! He—he flew—he did! He did!"

"Then what? Then he asked me to split with him. To go meet his People. To prove to them that they didn't need to keep being isolated any more. That it was time for them to move out into society and share all their Gifts and Persuasions—"

I heard Katie-Mary squeal, "Don't—don't! You're hurting me!"

And the Listener with rough anger in a voice I hadn't heard enough really to know: "You're—putting—me—on!" He grated. "Who clued you? Who told—!"

"No!" Katie-Mary squealed again. "Nobody—!"

"Sorry." The Listener's voice really was. "Forget it. Just forget it—"

I heard Katie-Mary's wail cut off in the middle of a word. I was about to scramble out of the sack when I heard her ask blankly, "Where was I?"

"He asked you to split—" prompted the Listener.

"*Yeah,* he did," said Katie-Mary. She sighed a long sigh as though she'd never breathe in again. "I can't," she said. "I can't."

"Yes," said the Listener. "Tell and it'll be gone."

"It was at night." Her voice was very quick and tiptoey, as though she was afraid she'd break through into something. "It was at night or I'd have flipped completely. We—we never touched a tire to a road. We never *saw* a road after we left town. I pried my eyes open once and saw mountains streaming by under us—way, *way* under us—like a jaggedy river streaked with white foam. And all the time he jabbered on and on with that space opera of his about the Home and the—the Crossing and— well, I stopped listening. I wanted out. I wanted out bad. I shivered and he—he smiled and said, 'Oh, sorry.' *And the car got warm!* All around. Softly, gently—lovingly—"

Katie-Mary's voice slowed and faltered. "Oh, can't you see?" she cried passionately. "Can't you understand? I haven't told you everything! I haven't told you all the bits and pieces Degal told me that kept fitting together and getting clearer and clearer until that night, when he finally shouted, 'There!' and the car tilted and swooshed down like—like an eagle—and I saw his People coming up for him, pale faces way down there, streaming up to meet him in the air. And the car door opening to let him shoot out into all kinds of happy surroundings like Arms, and Love and Returning and—and the car drifted down, tilting back and forth like a dry leaf, the left door flapping open and shut, open and shut. And me tick-tocking back and forth inside the car, hanging on for dear life, while outside—

"I was outside that beautiful world—Degal's Home—that he thought wasn't so much different from the way the world is now. Oh, *brother!*

"I reached over and flipped on the car lights. As the car swung, the lights swept back and forth across treetops and the happy chattering group darting around like big hummingbirds, clustering around Degal.

"You know what those car lights looked like to me all at once? Do you know?" She was crying again, her voice choked.

"'*And he placed at the east of the Garden,*'" the Listener said slowly, "'*a flaming sword which turned every way to keep—*'"

"To keep me out," said Katie-Mary. "Oh, I walked in, all right. I met them all. I met Valancy and Jemmy—they're the Wheels. And Robelyn—that girl with the big eyes, all for Degal—and all those cunning little kids learning to fly across the creek. One of them fell in when she forgot how halfway across. They pulled her out and hugged her and teased her and gave her a goodie to stop her tears. The goodie was a fruit that made music when she took a bit of it. Her teeth were crimson from the juice when she giggled.

"I was there for—well, I can't tell you how long. One night I didn't sleep for wondering what I'd got into. Another night I leaned on the windowsill and watched Degal and that Robelyn up against the moon and the treetops doing a sort of wild, wonderful dance, or something, all in the sky. And it seemed like it was to music—music that moved them like light moves—oh, there aren't words! But there wasn't any music either, when they disappeared. I guess their moving made the music. I listened with all my eyes—

"And below my window someone said, 'Skying? Already? Valancy'd better hurry the spinning.' And happy laughter moving away.

"But all the time I felt under—way down—as if I had to look up—

"No! No way! They never put me down—not ever. They wouldn't! They—they couldn't! Together. One. Loving. Helping. Oh, you know! So many people talk it—they *do* it!"

The Listener murmured into her tired silence.

"No, no lockstep at all," Katie-Mary said. "Everyone's his own self. No one does something just because others do—except maybe the children."

Again a murmur.

"No different from any town in the hills," said Katie-Mary. "Campers stop for directions. They don't notice anything, except they go away smiling and comfortable. Not many come. The Canyon is out of the way—

"Yes, there's a road—but it's not much of one. They—because, of course, they don't use it much."

Katie-Mary's voice was tired now—no longer twanging like a too-tight string. "I still remember the soft sound of footsteps back and forth, back and forth. They have a big room for a meeting place, and I heard the footsteps upstairs—back and forth, back and forth. It kinda bugged me, and Karen laughed and took me up there. Valancy was there spinning thread on a huge spinning wheel like in old pictures. Not sitting—pacing back and forth across the floor, in and out of the splash of sun that came through a little window, pulling the thread out fine and letting it wind on a spindle.

"That finished me—again," Katie-Mary whispered painfully. "She was spinning the sunlight into thread! Sun! Maybe something else with it," she answered the Listener. "But all I saw was the sun. 'It's special,' Karen told me. 'For weddings and christenings. We weave it—' She held up a piece of light and smoothed her hand across it. It changed colors as she stroked it. 'We don't decide what color to hold it until we're ready to use it.' I wish now I had touched it. I was afraid to. Did you ever stroke the sun?

"Imagine! Cloth of the sun and a guy out back chopping wood for the fireplaces. No roads 'cause they don't need them—and the kids picking peas in the garden for supper—"

There was a long silence, and I wondered if Katie-Mary had gone to sleep. She sounded tired enough. But the silence sounded busy—awfully busy. Then the Listener said something brief and broken.

"*Take* you there!" Katie-Mary's voice squealed into life. "No way, man! No way! I'm not bleeding again for *no* dude! No way!" Then her voice changed and pleaded. "I can't. Honest, I can't. Not even if you are lost. Not even if you've been looking all your life. I can't! I don't know the way—*remember?* How do you expect me to remember a road we never touched? You think maybe there are signposts on *clouds?* I don't even know which direction—except—" her voice was thoughtful. "Except just before we started to walk down into the Canyon, the sun came up behind us and pointed our shadows into the Canyon."

Silence again.

Then Katie-Mary: "Oh, no! Not another kook! What's with me that every—" Her surrendering sigh was long and wavery, clearly audible to me. "Okay, then, okay. Maybe this *is* my thing I've been waiting here all this time to do. Okay, you do that." She was resigned. "If you think you can make me have total recall, okay, we'll give it a try. I don't think my total will be very, but I'm too tired to fight with you. One kook more—"

I scrambled down the ladder.

They were waiting for me just outside the door, already on the bike, helmets in hand. Katie-Mary looked at me helplessly. "I'll be back," she said. "He says I will." She nodded against the back of the Listener and pulled the helmet down and busied herself with the fastenings.

The Listener smiled at me—like an eager child bursting with anticipation—maybe for Christmas. "Thanks, Frederic," he said. "Thank you."

"You're welcome," I said, "I think. But what for?"

"Your floor was comfortable. The water was cool." He grinned at me. "And Katie-Mary was here." He pulled on his face-covering helmet. Light ran across the dark blankness where his face had been. I caught myself looking down at his hands to see if they were green—a little green man from—where? But he had gloves on.

I didn't see them after they left the rectangle of lamplight by the open door. I stood there a long time in the cold slant of light until the stuttering roar of their going was long gone.

Sometimes I think it was a century—other times it was maybe ten minutes before Katie-Mary was standing there again in the lamplight, her face quiet and unsmiling. Actually, it was about a week. I think.

"Hi, chick!" I said. "Come on in." If I hadn't stepped back, she would have walked right into me. She was like a dream walker.

"I took him," she said. "On that chopper of his. We split all that lovely, horrible silence. It was like sharp splinters all around us when we finally stopped at the Canyon. Degal was there at the entrance to the Canyon, waiting. And the Old Ones, Jemmy and Valancy. And the girl with big eyes. How could they have known?

"The Listener sat there waiting—even after I got down. Then Degal said, 'Hi, Katie-Mary. Hi, Listener!' " Something rippled across Katie-Mary's face. "He never even met the Listener before, but he knew him.

"Then the Listener got down. Just left his bike standing there, and it didn't fall. He looked at those People from the Canyon. Then he— he—the Listener, all black in his biking outfit, lifted up in the air and stumbled toward them, as awkward as those little kids just learning to fly. They lifted up to him and they all touched hands and he didn't stumble any more.

" 'Home?' asked the Listener as they settled slowly back down on the hillside.

" 'Home,' said Jemmy. 'I'm Jemmy and this is—'

" 'Valancy and Robelyn,' said the Listener. He smiled. He was another person. You—you'd hardly recognize him. All at once he was way too big for how small I remembered him." Katie-Mary suddenly sagged to the floor and sat, her empty hands palm up on the floor on each side of her, her hair falling forward and hiding her turned-down face. After a while her voice woke again.

"It was so—so warm that I nearly froze to death outside. Forever outside. Waiting. They were talking. All of them. So fast—so fast! And all at the same time. And—not—one—sound!

"When they finally stopped and looked at me, I had to look twice before I could tell which was the Listener and which was Degal. They had the same shiningness. The same—you know?—they'd put it all together.

" 'Thank you, Katie-Mary,' said the Listener. 'All my life I've been looking, not even knowing if I'd ever find. Thank you. We'll send you home again—' " She peered up through her hair at me. " '*We*, not 'they' or 'I,' but *we'll* send you home again,' he said. 'And give you forgetfulness after you tell Frederic. You'll be happier so. Frederic needs to know the ending. Loose ends distress him.'

"They sent me back." Katie-Mary's face was tilted up, eyes closed, her hand tangled in her hair. "They closed my eyes and sent me back all by myself—no chopper, no car. A little while ago they sent me back. The wind was cold on my cheeks and nose. There was a feeling of farness below me and above me. And speed. How fast! How fast!" She almost sang it, drowsily, softly, fading to silence.

"Where is this Canyon?" I asked roughly, suddenly homesick for—something.

Katie-Mary's eyes opened. "What Canyon?"

"The one where you took the Listener," I insisted. "Where he flew to his People."

"Flew!" Katie-Mary grimaced. "Man, what you on?" She came up from the floor in that one smooth surging motion she has.

We will give you forgetfulness after—

"Doos spilled soup on your floor," I told her, giving it up.

"That Doos!" said Katie-Mary but made no motion toward getting cleaning things. "You know, Frederic," she said thoughtfully. "I'm being a zero sort of creature, but a zero on the other side of a number can change it into tens or hundreds or thousands. And maybe counting counts—you know?" She lingered at the hall door, looking back at me. "I'm thinking maybe I'll move around to the other side—you know? I better get started looking for a side I'd like to get counting on. Not that it hasn't been nice here, but after all, I can't scrub a floor forever."

Well—

Katie-Mary's pale rectangle of floor isn't so pale any more, since she left. Anyone walks on it or sleeps on it, but no one scrubs it now. And the restless and rootless still surge in and out, in and out, like feverish breathing.

I don't know why I'm staying. The juice has gone out of the whole deal. But if I went—where would I go? None of this can kid me into thinking that there's a warm, loving home waiting anywhere on this earth for *me*—

But then, maybe, like Katie-Mary, I'll just move over to the other side. *Two* zeros on the other side of that numeral—

The People Series

Zenna Henderson wrote this summary of the People series and of her life in 1980 for the anthology The Great Science Fiction Series *edited by Frederik Pohl, Martin H. Greenberg, and Joseph Olander.*

By profession, I am a school teacher. My avocation is writing. I have just about taught myself into retirement. Almost all my teaching has been in the first grade, though I have, at one time or another, taught all elementary grades and a little high school.

I am a native Arizonian and have lived most of my life in this state. However, I taught for two years in France. During this time, my first book, *Pilgrimage,* was put together. And I taught a year in Connecticut, with my feet almost in Long Island Sound. In Arizona, I've taught at a Japanese relocation camp during World War II and, much later, at a military post—Fort Huachuca. I've taught at a semi-ghost mining town where the kids brought jars of water to school when the water pressure was too low to make it up to the hill-top school house, and we had to unlock the Little Houses left over from a much earlier era. That's where I taught high school typing and journalism. We had either four or five high school graduates that year.

The first story of the People, "Ararat," was published in *The Magazine of Fantasy & Science Fiction* in October 1952. It was the second science fiction story of mine that they had published and the second science fiction story I ever had published.

"Ararat" in 1952 was followed by "Gilead" in 1954 (the first time I had my name on the magazine cover), and "Pottage" in 1955. "Wilderness" was published in 1957, "Captivity" in 1958, and "Jordan" in 1959. These six stories, tied together by the narrative of Lea, were published by Doubleday as *Pilgrimage: The Book of the People,* in 1961.

The reason there was a fairly wide gap between the two books of the People is it took that long to accumulate enough stories to make another book-length narrative.

"Return" was published in 1961, "Shadow on the Moon" in 1962, "Angels Unawares" in March 1966, and "Troubling of the Water" in September 1966. These stories were tied together with the Assembling idea after being rearranged into the People chronological order, titled *The People: No Different Flesh,* and published by Doubleday in 1967.

Both of the People books were later brought out in Avon paperbacks and are still in print.

The interval between the People stories usually indicated other science fiction or fantasy stories—non-People stories—but usually only one or maybe two. The interval between the publishing of the two People books was occupied by compiling these miscellaneous stories into a short story collection, *The Anything Box.*

After the second People book, another collection of miscellaneous stories titled *Holding Wonder* was published. Both of these volumes also were brought out as Avon paperbacks and *Holding Wonder* is still in print. A second edition of *The Anything Box* is currently being arranged.

All four of the books were published in England by Gollancz, and the People books in Germany also.

When I first started writing "Ararat," the People were supposed to be a weird group crossing, by magic, the Atlantic Ocean as refugees from a Transylvania-type country. However, I have difficulty writing about unpleasant people, so my characters got People-er and People-er until I discarded the original idea and developed, instead, the refugees from another world idea.

I had trouble naming the first story. I forget whether it was J. Francis McComas or Anthony Boucher—they were co-editors of the magazine at that time—who suggested "Ararat." That was the beginning of a train of thought that resulted in all the People stories. Both Boucher and McComas were very helpful and friendly. I never got a printed rejection slip from them. When I sent something that bombed completely, they let me know, firmly, but were always most encouraging to me. When the first book was just beginning to be an idea, they helped me find an agent to take care of the complicated business. They were both midwives to my career as a writer.

Readers not familiar with the Bible miss many nuances to the People stories. Many of my titles come from there, and most of my character names. "Deluge" was the Flood after which the ark finally came to rest on Mount Ararat. All the stories in *Pilgrimage* plus "Deluge" have themes from the Old Testament and applied to individuals or small groups: selling a birthright for a mess of "Pottage"; wandering hopeless years in the "Wilderness"; seeking healing in the balm of "Gilead"; being carried off into an alien "Captivity"; crossing the river "Jordan" into the Promised Land.

I enjoyed writing the People stories because I often started with only a first sentence and surprised and engrossed myself in the new characters that emerged and the new Gifts, Signs, and Persuasions that developed.

I think one of the appeals of the People is that they are a possible forgotten side of the coin that seems always to flip to evil, violence, and cruelty.

I have received a vast—to me—amount of fan mail since I started writing about the People. Some letters were wild and far-out. One said only, "What do you do and what do you know." I was saddened by others who insisted that the People were real and that, if I wanted to, I could tell them where the People were. They *had* to know because they were one of the un-found-yet People.

In the last few years, I have begun to receive fan letters from teenagers whose parents were former teenage fans—

Well, it's nice to get fan letters, anyway.

The People Chronology

by Mark & Priscilla Olson

Zenna Henderson never published a chronology of the People stories, nor was she in the habit of putting explicit references to dates in
them. Nonetheless, the People stories happen to real people in our real
world and are embedded in our world. Between that evidence and the
characters and events which link the stories, a clear chronology emerges.

1875 Lytha, Timmy born
> They are early teens in "Deluge".

1880 Simon born
> He is about ten years old in "Deluge".

1885 Eve born
> In "Deluge" she is a small girl at the time of the destruc-
> tion of the Home.

1890 **Deluge, Angels Unawares, Troubling of the Waters**
> Stories take place at destruction of the Home or immedi-
> ately upon landing on Earth.

1890 The Home is destroyed; the People's ship crashes in Arizona
> While narrating "Troubling of the Water", which seems to
> have occured a few years after the events themselves, the
> boy thinks about how it will be only seven years to the
> new century. There is no evidence that the trip from the
> Home to Earth took a very long time. The lack of mention
> of supplies for a long trip and the lack of comment on the
> length of the trip suggest that it was not long.

1890 David, 'Chelle, Simon, and many other characters from "Del-
> uge" die as ship crashes or in the aftermath.
> "In Angels Unawares", Lytha says that David, 'Chelle and
> her brothers died in crash or at hands of fundamentalists.

1891 **Tell Us a Story**

Story takes place mostly in the first winter and spring after the ship crashes. The People have been on Earth long enough to have grown a crop of corn. Eliada is Lytha's cousin.

1902 **That Boy**

The evidence is ambigious: Cars are still unknown, at least in Arizona. Theo was probably born on Earth. Theo is around 12.

1912 **Tell Us a Story** (ending frame)

Ending frame of story takes place when Nathan is grown with young children of his own.

1916 Peter born

Peter was Eve's first child. He is nine years older than Bethie. This means that Eve had her first child at 30 which isn't unbelievable, particularly considering that she probably was reluctant to take a chance with an Earth-human father.

1916 Jemmy born

Jemmy was 24 during "Ararat".

1918 Valancy Carmody born

In "Ararat", we learn that Valancy's parents were babies or very small children when the People's ship crashed. They were adopted by an elderly couple of the People (who also survived the crash), grew up, and married.

1921 Karen born

Karen was 19 during "Ararat".

1925 Bethie born

Bethie was Eve's second child and in "Gilead" she is stated as being nine years younger than Peter. It appears that she was in her late teens in Gilead.

1931 Jake Kroginold and Lizbeth born

They are ten or eleven in "Ararat" and at least in their thirties in "The Indeliable Kind".

1938 Bram born

Bram is a late teen in "Jordan".

1939 Francher Kid born

He was a mid-teen in "Captivity".

1940 Karen's father becomes an Old One

It happened a year before "Ararat".

1941 Valancy comes to Cougar Canyon
   Valancy was 23 when she came to Cougar Canyon in
   "Ararat".

1941 **Ararat**
   Jake Kroginold is about 10 years old.

1942 Explosion maims Obla and kills Bram's parents
   The explosion happened at such a young age that Bram
   doesn't remember it in "Jordan" where he is a mid-teen.

1942 Karen spends a year in teacher's college and befriends Melodye
   Amerson.
   She was ready to go to college when Valancy arrived in
   Cougar Canyon. Melodye's remembrance in "Pottage" says
   that she was many years out of school, so Karen's schooling
   needs to be as early as possible.

1943 Valancy and Jemmy marry

1943 **Gilead**
   Bethie was about 18 in "Gilead". Valancy already was part
   of the Cougar Canyon Group, and Karen is obviously an
   adult, though still quite young, so it has to be at least a
   couple of years after "Ararat".

1945 Remy born
   Remy is Bethie's first child, and he was 17 in "Shadow on
   the Moon" which takes place in 1962.

1947 Shadow (Bethie-too) born
   She's about two years younger than Remy, and is Bethie's
   second child.

1950 **Wilderness**
   Fairly arbitrary date based on it happening before "Jordan"
   (Dita and Low participate in remembering) and after
   "Ararat" (Valancy is part of the Cougar Canyon Group.)
   Saddle shoes also date story to 40s or 50s.

1951 **Pottage**
   Karen has adult responsibilities. Melodye Amerson had
   heard of the People from Karen quite a few years previ-
   ously when Karen was in teacher's college with her. It is
   remembered in "Jordan".

1954 **Captivity**
   Fairly arbitrary date based on it happening before "Jordan"
   and a few years after "Pottage". (Dr. Curtis has been
   working with the People for some time.) Jeeps are in
   common use, and rock 'n' roll is preferred teen music.

1955 Jordan

Ship from new Home arrives

Lea is succored by Karen

Lea framing story

> The ship from New Home has just arrived and is the reason for the remembering. Jemmy and Valancy have their first child which seems a matter for inordinate rejoicing. This fits their having been trying to have a child for thirteen years. Jemmy is also an Old One.

1956 Michal Without

> Very hard to assign, but general flavor suggests definitely post-WW II. Jemmy and Karen are adults.

1958 Cougar Canyon abandoned

> The Group moves out of Cougar Canyon because it will be flooded by rising waters from dam. (There's not a whole lot of reason for this specific date—it could be any time between about 1955 and 1962 or '63. We picked this date to keep Jemmy from being too old in "Return", see below.)

1961 Return

> Happens about three years after Cougar Canyon is abandoned. The fact that Jemmy—who would be 46 in 1961—is still active in rescue work suggests that this date may still be a bit too late. Helicopters are in fairly common use in rescue work. We also know that trips between Earth and New Home are still uncommon.

1962 Shadow on the Moon

> We know that Remy is 17 and Shadow is about 15. We also know that a very small number of probes have crashed on the Moon, but that no moon landings have taken place. More People have made the trip between Earth and New Home.

1966 The Indelible Kind

> They use the spaceship from "Shadow on the Moon" to rescue a stranded Russian cosmonaut. Jake Kroginold has an 8-year-old son and has travelled to New Home and back.

1967 No Different Flesh

Mark & Meris framing story

> Occurs post–"Shadow on the Moon" and post–"Return" since characters tell both stories in the course of the story and the framing. Also, Debbie's child is old enough to be

away from his mother for multiple days. Dr. Hilf, an old doctor, "has been around since Territorial days," which ended in 1912.

1970 **Katie–Mary's Trip**

Set sometime in the vaguely hippy era. From references to gymnastics, it is probably not more than a year or two following the 1968 Olympics.

Acknowledgments

As with all NESFA Press publications, *Ingathering* is the product of many people's volunteer efforts: It was edited by Mark and Priscilla Olson. We thank George Flynn, Master Proofreader, without whom the textual and typographic quality of this book would have been diminished. The dustjacket was designed by Elizabeth Rhys Finney. Merle Insinga scanned much of the material. Preliminary proofreading of the text, a necessary but tedious task, was done by Merle Insinga, Pat Vandenberg, Ann Crimmins, Ann Broomhead, Claire Anderson, Deb Geisler, Lois Mangan, Paula Lieberman, Sue Kahn, Elisabeth Carey, and Rick Katze. George Flynn provided useful comments on the chronology. We thank you all!

Inagthering was printed by Bookcrafters of Fredericksburg, Va. It is printed on acid-free 60# Booktext natural. The text is set in Adobe Garamond, and the display font is (naturally) New Century Schoolbook.

— Mark and Priscilla Olson
January 1995